determined to make an appearance at dinner—so they don't susp␣

"Marianna."

But Marianna refused to be dissuaded by the warning. "You must tell them."

"They've suffered enough. I won't ruin Christmas by placing that burden on them."

"You aren't a burden. You are part of the family. They deserve to know. They'd *want* to know."

"And I want a hot dinner—which I won't get if you continue to quarrel with me."

Stubborn, annoying woman. Or. . .afraid? Grief tightened around Marianna's heart. "If—"

A gentle knock interrupted Marianna's response. She opened the door to a maid and gestured toward the water that ran across the table. "As you can see, we had a mishap."

But the young woman wasn't looking at the spill. "Miss Granville?"

Marianna peered more closely at the wide green eyes under the maid's lace cap. "Anna?"

"Oh, miss, it is you!" Anna's smile split wide then faltered.

An awkward silence ensued as Marianna realized she and her former maid were now closer to colleagues than their prior employer-employee relationship. "Yes, well, it is good to see you again."

"Marianna, if you are ready?" Miss Nowell tapped her fingers against the dressing table. "I should hate to be responsible for delaying dinner."

"Of course." Marianna followed the older woman into the corridor—a space already occupied by Lucinda Collingwood, née Nowell.

"Aunt Dorothea!" Despite last year's adversity, Lucinda's dark eyes had lost none of their merriment. "I'm so pleased you came to Hollyford for Christmas this year."

"Yes, I could tell by the enthusiasm you displayed for my arrival."

Rather than take offense at her aunt's acerbic response, Lucinda laughed. "I assure you, I meant no insult. I only wanted to rescue Tristram from the commotion."

Marianna hung back in the shadows while Lucinda continued chattering. "A pity you were unable to come to our wedding, Aunt Dorothea. Mama and I both missed you."

"You were probably the only ones." The invitation had arrived when Miss Nowell had first become aware of the illness that would soon claim her life. Marianna herself had penned Miss Nowell's regrets.

Lucinda patted the arm of the tall man by her side. "John, this is my aunt, Miss Nowell, and her companion." She glanced Marianna's direction and let out a squeal loud enough to reach Yorkshire. "Marianna!"

"Mr. and Mrs. Collingwood." Marianna curtsied as a proper subordinate should. Next to her one-time friend's vivaciousness, Marianna had always felt rather dull. Tonight, with Lucinda's exquisite gown of painted silk in such stark contrast to her own of plain black wool, she added drab to the unflattering comparison.

Lucinda gestured her husband to assist Miss Nowell on the stairs. "Shame on you, Marianna, leaving like that without a word. Where have you been? I tried to find you after. . . but you had just vanished."

By design. Even now, embarrassment at her father's disgrace made her long for the remoteness of the Yorkshire moors. Lacking a means to escape, she changed the subject instead. "How are you enjoying life as Mrs. Collingwood? You look happy."

"I am the most fortunate of women—except for the worry you caused. Have you been with Aunt Dorothea all this time?" Lucinda wouldn't be easily dissuaded from prying into

Marianna's affairs. "She never said a word."

"She offered me a position, so I accepted."

"I didn't realize you even knew her."

"You introduced us." Marianna steadied herself on the banister. The glossy varnish brought to mind the day an eleven-year-old Tristram had dared the girls to ride it down to the entrance hall. Lucinda had wisely refrained, but ever desirous of pleasing her idol, Marianna had succumbed to the challenge. That episode of their past hadn't ended well for her either.

"Me? Oh. Oh yes! I remember. At the Christmas party. You made her laugh. That's a great feat. Tristram is the only other person I know who can amuse her." Lucinda glanced at the couple ahead of them and leant as close to Marianna as her wide skirt allowed. "To tell the truth, she rather intimidates me."

They followed the others to the gathering in the yellow salon—the five members of the Nowell family and Marianna. Lucinda grabbed her by the arm and hauled her along when she greeted her mother. The dowager baroness smiled at her daughter and offered Marianna a polite, if noticeably cooler, greeting.

As for Tristram, he nodded with a formality that matched his dinner apparel of dark tail coat and white cravat. "Miss Granville."

Marianna dropped into a curtsy, and as soon as Lucinda relaxed her grip, she escaped to Miss Nowell's side where she resolved to spend the evening keeping her head down, her mouth closed, and her presence inconspicuous.

"Shall we?" Tristram proffered his elbow and led his aunt to the dining room.

Mr. Collingwood followed with Lady Lyddlebury, but the male-female imbalance relegated Lucinda and Marianna to making their own way.

"Put me next to your mother," Miss Nowell was ordering her nephew when the young women reached the room.

"You don't wish to sit beside me?" Tristram did as commanded and escorted her to the end of the table. "I thought you liked me."

"I like you so much, I'm going to spare you the tedious conversation of a couple of old ladies."

He chuckled as he held the seat for her. Marianna waited until he retreated before she slipped onto the chair next to her employer. And then she felt his presence on her other side.

Only then did she realize Miss Nowell had craftily arranged the seating to place Marianna next to her erstwhile suitor.

# Chapter 5

Tristram waited until all the ladies had taken their seats before lowering himself onto his chair—the one at the head of the table. Another first. An expectant silence hung in the air as five pairs of eyes watched him and waited.

His mother folded her hands. "Tristram?"

Too late, he realized that as the man of the family, the blessing now fell to him. He bowed his head and stumbled through appropriate words of thanks.

The staff brought the first course, and he turned to his left—away from *her*—to speak to his sister. Alas, with his mother and aunt engaged in conversation, Lucinda's husband had no one to talk to but his wife. The two of them whispered like disobedient children, lost in a world that excluded everyone else. Tristram stared at his soup. Didn't seating a married couple adjacent to each other violate some unwritten dinner table protocol?

Though he tried to focus on his meal, he found his gaze drawn to the woman on his other side, like a compass needle inexorably pulled north. Unconcealed by a bonnet, Marianna's ebony hair shimmered in the candlelight, its reddish highlights creating tiny flames of their own. She'd arranged it into a practical knot at the back of her head, and yet, its simplicity became her, as did the unpretentious gown. His gaze followed the line of her arm—along the white cuffs of her undersleeves which provided the only splash of contrast in her otherwise uniformly dark attire—to her slender hands and the bare, ringless fingers that gripped her spoon.

Reminded anew of the object in the desk, he wrenched his gaze upward again. She centered her attention on his aunt, leaving him to study her face in profile. The soup's warmth infused her cheek with faint color—

Aunt Dorothea hunched forward and coughed—gently at first, then more urgently. The butler stepped forward, but Marianna waved him away and patted her employer's back until the fit subsided. A look of silent communication passed between the two women.

"Would you like us to send for the doctor?" his mother inquired.

"No, no." Aunt Dorothea steadied herself with a sip from her goblet. "Just a bit of soup that went the wrong direction."

Mother looked doubtful. "If you're certain. . ."

"Of course. If I have any further difficulties, I'll mention it to my physician in Yorkshire when we return. He calls regularly. . .although, come to think of it, perhaps he doesn't come to check on me. He spends an inordinate amount of time with Miss Granville."

The flush on Marianna's face deepened. "I don't think—"

"He's sweet on her."

Though Aunt Dorothea said the words to his mother, Tristram got the distinct impression they were aimed at him. Because Marianna had confided in her about his unsuccessful proposal? Did his aunt really think he cared about the romantic interests of the woman who'd so adamantly dismissed his suit five years ago? The very idea amused him. Annoyed him.

Angered him.

"Perhaps you could make time on your return to consult with a physician in London." John Collingwood interjected himself into the conversation. "One who is more up to date on the latest discoveries than a simple country doctor."

A spark of umbrage on the far-off man's behalf smoldered in Marianna's eye. "I've always found Dr. Ellis more than competent."

"I'm sure John meant no disrespect to your Dr. Ellis, only that a London physician would have better access to the latest research and devices." As a politician's daughter, his mother could always be counted on for a diplomatic response.

"Alas, to my knowledge, not even the best London doctors have discovered a cure for getting old." Aunt Dorothea set down her spoon with a clink. "But it's better than the alternative."

Mother responded with an appreciative chuckle and steered the conversation to Aunt Dorothea's property in Yorkshire, an unentailed estate Tristram's grandfather had bequeathed to her many decades past.

Tristram addressed Lucinda while the footman served the next course. "And how shall you be filling your time now that you are feeling better?"

"Mama has put me in charge of the decorating."

He admired the boughs of holly and boxwood entwined with red ribbon that garnished the fireplace mantel and windowsills. A fir decorated in red and white filled the room's corner. "I like it."

"I thought you would." Lucinda looked across the table. "Marianna, you'll join me, won't you? We have so much to catch up on, and your input would be so helpful. You were always so creative."

Creative? How ironic. When she'd jilted Tristram, she'd used the most predictable of excuses—her sudden discovery that they wouldn't suit. He'd heard rumors she'd succumbed to her father's preferences for another, better endowed and connected, suitor, but if so, the mystery man had disappeared at the same time as the Granville family fortune.

Marianna paused, salmon-laden fork raised halfway. "I, ah, well, I'm not certain Miss Nowell can spare me."

"I need Miss Granville's assistance in the morning, but she has tomorrow afternoon free."

"Thank you, Aunt Dorothea. Tomorrow afternoon it is. I'll meet you in the ballroom at two, Marianna. Bring your best ideas."

Marianna's complexion blanched, as if her dinner suddenly disagreed with her constitution. "Well then, I guess it's settled."

At precisely two the next afternoon, Marianna clutched her sketchpad to her chest and made her way down the staircase, her stomach in more knots than the ribbons securing the greenery to the banister. Of all the rooms in Hollyford Hall...

In the silence of the empty corridor, her heart beat a thundering tattoo as she hesitated before the closed door. Obviously Lucinda hadn't grown more punctual over the years.

Perhaps it was just as well. Marianna could face the specters of her past alone. Unseen.

With a deep breath for courage and a quick twist of the knob, Marianna let herself into the ballroom and closed the door behind her. She slumped against its heavy wood and waited for her pulse to steady as she surveyed the once-familiar room.

Giant crystal chandeliers still hung from a high ceiling embellished with plaster medallions, their prisms muted under their dark, unlit candles. Sunlight stole through the french doors, glistening across a parquet floor devoid of dancers. A tall, unadorned evergreen stood against the far wall, lonely but for a crate that waited beside it.

The staff had recently cleaned, and the twin scents of beeswax and polish hung heavy in the room, so unlike the holiday blend of cinnamon delicacies, citrusy pomanders, and evergreen branches that had sweetened the air that Christmas five years ago.

Waves of emotion washed over her and drained the strength from her knees. Marianna lowered herself onto a gilt chair and allowed the memories to flood through her.

# Chapter 6

*Hollyford Hall, Devonshire, England*
*Five years earlier—December 21, 1850*

H elp me, Lucinda!" Too upset to concern herself with proper protocol, Marianna rushed to her best friend's side and interrupted her conversation with a disapproving dowager.

"Marianna? Whatever is the matter?"

"Lord Bourke." Marianna positioned herself behind her friend so as to minimize the sight of her wide skirt. "He's engaged me for two dances already and now seeks a third."

"That is excessive." Lucinda flicked her fan. "Like your very own odious. . .what was the name of that cad in your book?"

"Wickham."

"I yield to your superior knowledge of *Pride and Prejudice*."

The tiny woman at Lucinda's side, despite her diminutive stature, somehow managed to look down at them over her spectacles. "Only because you can seldom be bothered to read."

Lucinda laughed. "True enough. Aunt Dorothea, do you know our neighbor, Miss Granville?"

Marianna tried to execute a polite greeting as Lucinda finished the introduction, but her gaze kept reverting to the man whose beady eyes searched for her. Or rather, her future fortune.

"What's the matter with Bourke?" Miss Dorothea Nowell demanded. "You realize he'll inherit his father's earldom?"

"Yes, but that won't compensate for the fact that he already possesses his father's rotten teeth, wandering eye, and bad disposition."

The older woman's hoot of laughter caught Marianna by surprise. "Do be fair, Miss Granville. His father is a charming scoundrel. Bourke cultivated the bad disposition all on his own."

Lucinda's brother swept to their side, the gold braid on his hussar's jacket resplendent in the chandeliers' glow. His striking features and breezy cheer had sent feminine hearts in the district aflutter—Marianna's included—even before his commissioning had added the irresistible appeal of a cavalry uniform. "You signaled to me, dear sister?"

"Yes, but I'm not the damsel in distress. Be a hero and ask Marianna to dance."

"Of course." Captain Tristram Nowell extended his hand and aimed a smile teeming with reckless charm at her. "Miss Granville, may I have this dance?"

Giddiness and terror warred in her belly. "O–of course." She placed a gloved palm against his.

He wrapped his arm around her and swung her into the midst of the dancers. Strength radiated against the hand she settled on his shoulder. "I can't believe you and Lucinda are all grown up."

He might have noticed 'ere now if he'd visited his family in Devonshire with more regularity. Or if he'd at least glanced toward the Granville pew on Sunday mornings during those infrequent occasions when he had. "Time marches on, even if you aren't around to mark its passing."

"So serious a response! I never envisioned you as a philosopher. You were such a hoyden as a child."

"I could push you into the pond again if it would feel more familiar to you."

He tossed his head back and let out a whoop. "Please don't. The men will never respect me should they catch wind of it. My disgrace was difficult enough to keep secret the first time."

"You did deserve it, you know."

"I was rather insufferable as a youth, wasn't I? But you'll be pleased to know that you and Lucinda aren't the only ones who have matured over the years."

"So you don't pull girls' hair anymore?"

"Boys only do that to girls they like. These days, when I wish to annoy a young lady, I ask her to dance." His grip tightened, pulling her closer to avoid a collision with another couple. "Are you enjoying your evening, Miss Granville?"

"Yes, yes, I am." Especially now, with his hand warming her back through the white brocade of her first ball gown.

"I can see why. You haven't lacked for partners. I fear my poor skills on the dance floor will fail to impress."

"It is true your approach to waltzing is more akin to a military march than an elegant dance."

"A march! That is a grave offense to a cavalry man."

"A gallop?"

"You would compare me to my horse? I haven't once trod on your toe. Yet." His roguish grin flashed, and his dark eyes smoldered with laughter and. . .

Awareness rippled along her spine. "True. And unlike my most recent partner, you have managed to look at my face."

He focused on her for several moments past propriety. "The bright and shining beauty of your countenance is like the sun."

"Oh, good heavens. I take back my commendation. Your inflated and insincere words are as empty as the moor."

His feigned look of distress was comical to behold. "My dear Miss Granville, you misunderstand. I only meant to suggest that perhaps Bourke fears too long a look will blind him."

Marianna's heart beat faster than the music's quick tempo. He knew the identity of her unwelcome suitor. . .he had been observing her! "Ha! More likely he can't stop staring at my bright and shining diamonds—which is probably the reason his managing mama compelled him to stand with me in the first place."

"Ah, the sad lot of an heiress. You could always push him into the pond." Tristram's gaze flickered to the gems at the base of her neck, then his stare returned to hers, dubiousness wrinkling the bridge of his nose. "Did you say diamonds?"

"Yes, purple diamonds. It is one of the rarest of diamond colors."

"How fitting for an exceptional jewel such as you. But while they do gleam brightly, they cannot compare to your smile, Miss Granville."

"Flattery again?"

"And risk another dunking? Truth. Were they your mother's?"

"Her mother's, actually. My grandparents had little more than deep love and big dreams when Grandfather proposed. He owned a struggling tin mine, but he discovered some amethysts there. He had one set in my grandmother's wedding ring. Years later, after he had significantly increased his holdings and investments, he bought her purple diamonds to match."

"A very romantic story."

"Isn't it? After my grandfather died, Grandmother bestowed the jewels on me with explicit instructions I was never to sell the ring. It was special to her."

His gaze slid along her bare arm to the gloved hand clasped in his. Her skin tingled beneath the intensity of his perusal. "I should like to see this cherished ring. Perhaps we could take a turn about the garden."

She glanced at the french doors that opened onto the terrace. "It's December, Captain Nowell. Don't you think it's a little cold to be outside?"

"Then a quiet alcove?" He nodded toward a shadowy corner, and an unruly lock of dark hair dipped across his brow. "You could show me your ring. . .and I could show you our mistletoe."

Marianna's breath caught in her throat as she inspected the ribbon-entwined boughs of holly and ivy that festooned Hollyford Hall's ballroom. "Lucinda said she hid it. Are you sure it's there?"

"She's not as devious as she believes."

"No, Lucinda is honest and sincere."

"Whereas I'm a wicked reprobate trying to tempt you along some murky path to your doom."

"My doom? You would be the one tendering a proposal should you succeed."

He bent closer, until his lips were inches from her ear, until his breath stirred the loose tendrils along her cheek. "That could be part of my sinister plot—to compromise an heiress into marriage."

"I have half a mind to go with you, if only to see you try to charm your way out of that situation."

"Only half?"

"My intelligence is equal to my curiosity, and it urges caution."

"How very unlike the Marianna I remember."

"You did say I'd grown up. I'm not so easily provoked into intemperate behavior."

"Like a ride down the banister? Very well. If you insist on being all conventional these days, then let me escort you to supper."

She tilted her head and stared into his eyes. A new intensity had replaced the teasing in those dark depths. Her mouth felt dry, parched even. "I—I should enjoy that."

"And a ride tomorrow afternoon?"

Excitement tightened around her chest and trapped the air in her lungs. For the past few years, she'd harbored a secret *tendre* for her best friend's brother, the dashing Captain Tristram Nowell. Could it be. . . ?

# Chapter 7

*Present day*

M arianna?" A soft hand clasped her shoulder. "Marianna!"
Marianna opened her eyes to the sight of Lucinda's amused smile. "My apologies. I didn't hear you enter." She pushed the lingering memories aside and jumped to her feet.

"I'll have you know, I'm not so late that you should have fallen into such a deep slumber."

"I had to get up during the ni—" Marianna stopped, lest she divulge too much about Miss Nowell's condition. But it did remind her of the decision she had reached during the early hours of the morning, to ask Lucinda—

"You too? I wake at least once every night. And then I find myself dozing at all hours of the day. Helen tells me the sleep problems will only worsen as the baby grows."

"Baby?" Diverted from her problems, Marianna considered her friend's beaming countenance. "Lucinda, are you saying. . ."

"This spring, probably early May."

"Oh, I'm so happy for you! And what does Mr. Collingwood think?"

"He's overjoyed, and so solicitous, even in my most irrational moods—as a good husband should be of course."

"Of course." Marianna's glance shifted away from Lucinda's radiance to the empty fireplace. "I'm afraid I owe him an apology for my outburst at dinner."

"I'm sure he's forgotten it already, if he even noticed. Have I mentioned my own disposition has been somewhat irrational of late? But if it truly bothers you, I'll pass your words along." Lucinda threaded an arm through Marianna's and pulled her into the center of the room. "Now then, the housekeeper will be arriving presently. What spectacular ideas can you come up with for this place?"

Marianna passed her the sketchpad and debated how to approach the other woman with her delicate question.

Lucinda flipped through the rudimentary drawings once then perused them more slowly, pausing at Marianna's favorite. "I begin to see why you failed to get adequate sleep last night. What is this one?"

"If I remember correctly, you usually have swags of holly and ivy hanging from the ceilings and around the windows. I thought we could ornament them with white flowers and bows made from paper, ribbon, and tulle. The tree would have similar white flowers and bows, circled with paper angel chains, also in white."

"Just white?" Lucinda wandered a few steps away as she studied the chandeliers. "You don't think we need something more. . .interesting or traditional? Some red perhaps?"

"I noticed the other rooms had many red decorations. With simple white on the greenery here, the guests will feel as though they are dancing in a snowy winter's night. Besides, the ladies' dresses will be a virtual kaleidoscope of colors."

"Yes, and they would appreciate not being outshined by our decorations. After being swathed in black last year, the Nowells need something bright. Victoria will love this—that's my niece, Benedick's daughter."

"Yes, I know."

"Of course you do. You've lived with Aunt Dorothea all this time. How unnerving to think of you knowing all our secrets while your life has been a mystery to me for these past five years."

"I lived in Yorkshire with your aunt. A detailed accounting of my time would put you to sleep."

"Marianna, everything puts me to sleep these days." Lucinda laughed. "Now then, how complicated are the flowers to make?"

"Not so much as you might think. Lu—"

"Mrs. Collingwood?"

Lucinda turned as the housekeeper entered the room. "Ah, Mrs. Willings, we have decided on white decorations for this room. We will need white paper, white ribbon, and white tulle."

The housekeeper's dubious frown had Marianna rethinking the idea that had seemed so marvelous during the night. "Only white, Mrs. Collingwood?"

"Yes, we are going with a simple design of flowers and bows. About how many do you think, Marianna?"

"At least two hundred of each. Five hundred total would be better. Plus paper for the angel chains."

"There you go, Mrs. Willings. Lots and lots of paper, ribbon, and tulle. Send to London if the local merchants are unable to meet our demands."

"I'll see to it right away, Mrs. Collingwood."

"Good. Have some of the maids come with what supplies we have, and they can begin. Oh, and have a footman bring a ladder." Lucinda laughed again as the housekeeper departed. "I hope you can teach the maids how to make those decorations quickly, Marianna. I'd like to get this room finished before Helen returns with Victoria on Friday."

"If we don't get as many made as we hope, we'll add more bows." Marianna hesitated then plunged into her petition before more staff came. "I have a personal favor to ask of you."

"Anything."

"Would you provide me with a reference I could present to future employers? I'd need it before I return to Yorkshire."

Lucinda looked at her quizzically. "Surely such a letter would be better from my aunt."

Yes, Marianna thought so too, but she hated to bother Miss Nowell again when the woman was already dealing with so much. A reference from Lucinda would protect Marianna's future without reminding Miss Nowell of her approaching mortality. "Well, one doesn't know what the future will bring, and a woman in my position can never have too many recommendations. You are very respected in these parts. Such a letter would carry much weight."

"I'm surprised you seek other employment. My aunt enjoys your company, and I can tell you are fond of her."

"Yes, well—" At that moment, two maids arrived with paper and scissors. While Lucinda directed them to set up at a table, Marianna silently thanked them for their impeccable timing.

"Marianna, why don't you show them what to do with—ah, perfect." A footman entered bearing a ladder. "Put it by the tree. Then see if the gardeners have finished with the greenery for this room."

He settled the ladder in place and left.

Lucinda marched to the crate and began rummaging through its contents. "I'll arrange the candleholders on the tree." She grabbed hold of the ladder and put her foot on the lowest rung.

"You should let me do that."

"No, you get the maids working on the decorations. My talents are best put to use here. You know I make a sore hash of anything creative."

"You're not as bad as that."

"Obviously you've forgotten the quality of my work. Remember that time Mrs. Rallison complimented my sketch of a mouse? It was supposed to be a horse."

"Yes, but. . ."

"I'm not an invalid. And you have work to do."

Marianna watched as Lucinda climbed to the top and began stationing the holders in position. She then reluctantly crossed the room to join the maids at the table. They eyed her warily, as uncertain as to her status as she. Such was the lot of a companion—not quite family, not quite servant, but rather, some nebulous region between the two.

Marianna spent the next hour teaching them how to create camellias and roses with paper, scissors, and paste. The chambermaid's inventions would need to be high on the swags to disguise their idiosyncrasies, but the parlor maid's creations were a work of art, and Marianna made a mental note to recommend her to Lucinda as a future lady's maid.

"What do you think, Marianna?" Lucinda gestured to the tree.

"About two rows down. . ."

She descended a rung and pointed. "This one?"

"Yes, they need to shift slightly to the right."

Lucinda adjusted a couple of the holders. "Like so?"

"Yes. The one—"

"Lucinda! What are you doing?" The masculine bellow reverberated through the room.

Lucinda jerked and turned so sharply she nearly toppled from her perch.

Lady Lyddlebury, who'd accompanied her son, let out a shriek.

Fortunately, Tristram was beside the ladder in two large steps to steady her.

"Oh, Tristram. You startled me." Lucinda smiled as she climbed down.

He ignored her gentle words and whirled to focus his fury on Marianna. "How could you let her endanger not only her own life, but the baby's too?"

Marianna recoiled, barely registering Lucinda's protestations or Lady Lyddlebury's uncomfortable silence as the older woman settled a restraining hand on his sleeve. Frantically, Marianna searched for an avenue of escape and gave copious thanks for Anna's opportune appearance in the doorway. And then guilt and fear rushed in. She hurried to meet the maid. "Is Miss Nowell. . . ?"

"She's awake and asking for you."

"I'll go to her at once." But before she left, Marianna glanced over her shoulder.

Tristram's conflicted features betrayed the same agitated jumble of emotions that churned within her.

Tristram beat a hasty retreat—as quick as a man with a limp could manage—to the study. Alas, his thoughts moved faster than his feet, condemning him with each step. He dropped down into the chair behind the desk, dragged open the drawer, and extracted the ring. He'd hoped the anger that drove him to procure it had mitigated over the years. Today's eruption suggested otherwise.

The door flew open with such force it crashed against the wall. "That was badly done of you, Tristram." Lucinda marched into the room with all the determination of a general going to war.

He dropped the ring into the drawer and slammed it shut before she identified the piece. "I realize that."

She checked her advance, as if she hadn't expected him to concede so quickly. "Well then, what are you going to do?"

"Apologize, of course. What kind of man do you take me for?"

"Sorry." Lucinda dropped onto one of the fireside chairs. "Your outburst caught me by surprise."

"Me too. I thought. . .I thought I'd forgiven her."

His little sister rested her chin on her folded hands, her gaze intent upon him. "Tristram, I don't pretend to know what offense you attribute to Marianna—although I have my suspicions. However, in addition to apologizing for your rant, you need to tell her you've forgiven her, to her face. If you can't, then perhaps you haven't really let go of your grudge."

Words of wisdom, so easy to say but so very, very difficult to practice. He glanced at the portrait above Lucinda's head, realizing for the first time how much she resembled Father, though she'd been but a child at the time of his passing.

"I didn't come here to berate you."

"But I'm such a deserving target."

"Rarely, though it happens sometimes. Fortunately, you have me to hold you accountable when it does."

"God certainly blessed me with a wonderful family."

"Speaking of family. . .Tristram, did you notice anything unusual about Aunt Dorothea last night?"

"Aunt Dorothea?" The question caught him by surprise. He mentally skipped back to dinner. He'd been so intent on ignoring Marianna—unsuccessfully, at that—he'd observed little else. "Why do you ask?"

"I think she's ill."

"She's old, Lucinda—older than Father would have been—and she traveled the length of England. Undoubtedly she was tired."

"Of course, but I think there's more. Marianna asked me for a letter of reference she could present to potential employers."

"Perhaps she's considering leaving Aunt Dorothea." After all, it wouldn't be the first time she'd deserted someone close to her.

"Or perhaps she knows Aunt Dorothea will be leaving her. You've seen them together.

Under that cantankerous exterior, Aunt Dorothea adores her. Marianna wouldn't be thinking of another position unless she thought this one was ending and feared Aunt Dorothea wouldn't be able to write a reference herself. Marianna is nothing if not loyal."

They would have to disagree on that point. "I yield to your greater knowledge of the lady."

Lucinda's green eyes stared levelly at him as if reading his thoughts. "You weren't always so cynical, dear brother. I don't know if the war or Marianna's presence brought it about, but it's not a quality you wear well."

# Chapter 8

The moor's slight rise and open spaces offered a panoramic vision of Hollyford Hall below. A pity that the sun, which had beckoned in vain to Marianna this morning, had disappeared now that she had a few minutes free this afternoon. Guilt niggled that she had so readily abandoned Lucinda, but given Tristram's reaction yesterday, perhaps it was best for all if she disappeared.

Marianna added a few more strokes to her drawing. The wind swept across the lonely land, stirring the dead grass and riffling her papers. December wasn't the best time to sketch, but this might be her last visit. The gathering clouds—which were quickly turning the landscape to something dark, gloomy, and cold—amplified the grim sense of foreboding. Every day brought closer the end of her time with Miss Nowell.

Relief and gratitude had been Marianna's primary emotions when she first arrived in Yorkshire. But over the years, her feelings toward her employer had deepened to fondness and eventually to love.

The soft thud of hooves on the sod ripped her attention from the looming heartache to her current problem. A man approached astride a dark bay roan. Though his hat hid the details of his face, that familiar form revealed his identity. Trepidation coiled inside her until nausea burned at her throat. Surely it could be no accident—given the wide, empty moor—he should find himself riding so near her place of respite.

Tristram's continued advance confirmed her suspicions. The tension visible in his broad shoulders suggested the sky wasn't the only thing portending a storm. He halted the horse some ten or so feet away, and for several moments they watched each other, like wary combatants in a ring.

"It's December, Miss Granville. Don't you think it's a little cold to be outside?"

Her pulse accelerated at his allusion to a happier time. "I'm better prepared for such a venture today." She scrambled to her feet, her picture braced in front of her like a shield. Even then, his perch on the horse still gave him an intimidating advantage.

"You are a difficult woman to find. I looked for you at dinner last night." He dismounted and ambled the last few feet to her. Bereft of his walking cane, he shuffled with a pronounced limp.

"Miss Nowell wished to eat in her room. Did you need something from me?"

He stood there through interminable minutes of awkward silence, as if battling a decision between making peace or war. "Forgiveness. I came to apologize for my rude attack yesterday."

An apology? Marianna drew in a steadying breath. His outburst paled in comparison to the wrong she had done him. Not for the first time, the desire to explain—to seek absolution—rose within her, but to what end? Rather than restore his opinion of her, he would likely suspect she had designs on his recently acquired title. "Lucinda told me about the baby. It was an understandable reaction."

"To blame you for her impetuousness? No, it was hasty, ill-considered, and unfair. I've known my sister long enough to know who was at fault."

"Lucinda is spirited, but she is not careless. I doubt she was in any great danger."

"It is at her behest I've come."

"I'm sorry. I shouldn't have taken off like that when she's so busy with—"

"Marianna, you are my aunt's companion, not one of Lucinda's employees to order about." He circled around to her side and studied the drawing in her hands. "You were always talented, but this is beyond anything I remember. My compliments on your increased skills."

"I've had more time to practice. There aren't many distractions in Yorkshire." Unlike here. Now.

"Knowing Aunt Dorothea as I do, I'm amazed you have any time to call your own. I would have thought working for her to be. . .more demanding."

Did he question Marianna's commitment, her care? "She regularly sees to personal matters in the afternoons and has encouraged me to pursue my own interests during those hours."

He raised a hand as if to ward off an attack. "I'm not accusing you of negligence. It's only that I have never known my aunt to be a particularly compliant or considerate woman."

"She is more bluster than bite."

"Strangely, she seems uncharacteristically lacking in both categories during this visit."

Marianna swallowed, as if to tamp down the truth. "It is a long way from Yorkshire to Hollyford Hall. The trip is fatiguing."

"But it's more than that, isn't it?" He leveled a probing stare. But unlike their previous interactions, this one lacked censure and animosity.

Marianna weighed the competing loyalties of an employer's confidences versus the family's concerns—so great, it seemed, even Tristram had sought her out. "Miss Nowell's affairs are not mine to divulge. You must go directly to her with your questions." Her eyes burned with pent-up emotion, and she shifted her gaze from Tristram's conflicted features to the moor.

"Fair enough."

She opened her mouth to say. . .something when a tear spattered against her hand. Dismayed at her inability to contain her sorrow, she wiped her eyes with her sleeve when another drop of water plopped onto the sketch and smudged the charcoal. She tilted her head to study the ever-darkening clouds, and rain splashed against her cheeks. Wonderful. Her day wanted only this.

"Grab your supplies!" Tristram wrenched the unfinished drawing from her fingers and tucked it inside his dark coat.

Marianna shoved her charcoal pencils and sketches willy-nilly into the writing box, but the accelerating rainfall warned it was probably too late to save her last efforts to preserve Devonshire on paper.

Perhaps 'twas just as well. Some images, like some dreams, were best consigned to the past.

"We must hurry if we intend to reach the hall without a dousing." Even as Tristram said the words, the sprinkle intensified to a shower. He retrieved Marianna's discarded gloves and passed them to her.

She tugged them over her fingers, folded the easel, and grabbed the writing box by its handle. "I'm sure we're already too late."

He collected the blanket where she had been sitting. A gust of wind whipped him, blowing rain against his face and tossing the ends of the blanket toward the horse, which snorted and shied. "Whoa!" He dropped the wayward fabric and used both hands to steady the animal.

"Here. I'll take that." Marianna retrieved the blanket.

"Give me your writing box and ride the horse. I'll follow." He reached for the case, but she backed away.

"You need the horse more than I."

For the second time in two days, a woman in his life questioned his honor as a gentleman. That both had reason only increased his pique. "I'm not an invalid."

Opposition tightened along Marianna's jaw. "This is no time to take umbrage at an unintentional insult to your pride. The fact is, I can run and you can't." With a toss of her head, made somewhat lacking in the desired condescension by the water scuttling down her pert nose, she set off along the path.

"In those skirts?" He tugged on the horse's reins and fell into step behind her. "They'll soon be so heavy with water, you'll be fortunate to drag them down the hill."

"That's not the way gravity works, you know."

Tristram had half a mind to do precisely as she suggested—ride off and leave her, as she'd abandoned him five years earlier. If only she'd shown that much obstinacy under her father's pressure to marry someone with more prospects than a younger son. How different their lives would have been!

She glanced at him over her shoulder and shook her head. "Still here? I don't know why— Ahhh!" With a cry, she stumbled and plummeted, her writing box and easel skittering in two different directions across the rocky ground.

Tristram's heart tumbled with equal speed. "Marianna!" He dropped to the ground beside her.

She pushed herself to her knees. "I stepped in a hole." Devonshire mud plastered the front of her skirt, and rain ran down her cheeks under the askew bonnet.

"Are you hurt?"

She met his concern with a self-deprecating grimace. "My pride."

"I suppose we're even on that account then." He glanced at the indentation marring the path. Probably a rabbit's burrow. "Can you walk?"

"Perhaps."

He threaded his arm under hers and around her back. The familiar scent of lavender tickled his senses, evoking memories of their courtship—twirling her around the dance floor at the Nowell Christmas party, lifting her onto a horse for a Sunday afternoon ride, sitting across the chessboard from her on a cold January evening.

She clung to his shoulder as he helped her rise. But when she placed her weight on the injured foot, she sagged to the ground again with another cry. "Or perhaps not."

How humiliating. Marianna had spent five years hiking the moors of Yorkshire alone without mishap, only to tumble on this particular day and in front of this particular person.

Tristram knelt beside her. Again. "Is it your foot?"

"My ankle."

"Let me see it."

Marianna hesitated, but discomfort and desperation triumphed over decorum. She stretched out her left foot.

He fumbled with the row of buttons and pulled off the shoe. Marianna gave an involuntary yelp when he manipulated her ankle.

"Well, doctor?"

"I think it's just sprained, but we should have a real doctor come when we return to the hall. I can't promise Dr. Clarke will be as enthralled by your eyes as your Yorkshire man, but he is competent."

At this reminder of her dinnertime defense of Miss Nowell's physician, Marianna shook her head. "I know Dr. Clarke—I used to live here, remember?"

"Of course. Didn't he set your arm when you had the mishap on our banister?"

"These things only seem to happen to me when I'm with you."

Tristram's teeth flashed in an I-told-you-so grin. "Now you'll have to take the horse."

Five years' separation hadn't lessened the impact of his smile on her senses. Her heart pounded harder in her chest than the rain upon the rocks. "You needn't look so pleased about it."

His mouth sobered, but a glint continued to lurk in those dark eyes. "Would you rather I point out that this is exactly how gravity works?"

A giggle bubbled in her throat. Then another. And another—until she could no longer contain the laughter.

Tristram joined in, and for several moments, the downpour pelted them while they sat on the cold ground, lost in their amusement.

"Do you remember that time we went for a ride and got caught in the rain?"

"Your father was furious with me when we returned soaking wet."

"He might not have been so angry if you'd told him it was my idea to ride so far."

"I'm not sure it would have mattered. He never did think much of me."

As it turned out, he'd had his reasons for wanting Marianna to seek a man of wealth and rank. Primarily selfish, though not wholly so. "Well, I thought it was very gallant of you to take the blame." A poignant sense of loss replaced her earlier mirth.

"Come, I'll help you onto the horse." Tristram lifted her to her feet. While she balanced on her uninjured foot, he circled her waist with his hands.

Marianna braced her palms on his shoulders, on either side of his face in a position hauntingly like an embrace. For the past five years, she'd lived a life devoid of human touch but for her ministrations to Miss Nowell, and her loneliness craved a connection. Especially with this man. She glanced at his face—a mistake. In the dark abyss of his gaze, the shadows of what-might-have-beens were reflected back to her. His jaw worked, as if he intended to speak but could find no words.

With a single motion, he lifted her into the saddle and stepped back. The spell broken, she became uncomfortably aware of the cold soaking through the wool of her coat. He retrieved her writing box and easel and walked beside the horse the entire, rain-drenched way back, past the stables to Hollyford Hall's front entrance.

When a groom ran up to them, Tristram passed the reins and assisted her dismount himself. "I'll help you into the house."

"Please don't." A tremble escaped with the hoarse words.

He ignored her request and swung her up into his arms. "How else are you going to get there? Crawl up the steps?"

She'd rather crawl into a hole.

He hefted her to the door then set her down in the entrance hall before the butler, who managed to maintain an impressively impassive mien.

Lady Lyddlebury's inscrutable gaze oscillated between Tristram and Marianna. "Tristram?"

"Miss Granville has suffered an injury to her ankle."

The dark eyes, so like Tristram's, widened with concern. "Are you in much pain?"

"A little."

Immediately, Lady Lyddlebury ordered the butler to send for a doctor and assign maids to care for Miss Nowell while Miss Granville rested.

"Very good, my lady." The butler signaled, and two young women appeared.

"And Marianna." Tristram passed the writing box and easel to one of the women flanking her. Water dripped from his coat onto the parquet floor like a deluge of tears. His smile had retreated, leaving his face stern and unapproachable again. "I'm sorry about your sketches. I'm afraid they are ruined."

Ruined, like the dreams of her youth, washed away by the storms of life.

# Chapter 9

*Granville House, Devonshire, England*
*Four years earlier—May 14, 1851*

M arianna stowed the last of her mourning gowns in the valise. The remaining personal items she would pack in the morning, before she left for the train station. As for her hopes and dreams, she'd already locked those away. Forever.

Even though she'd known this day was coming, she couldn't quash the dread churning inside. Perhaps one could never adequately prepare for eviction from one's lifelong home.

"Miss Granville?" The housekeeper loomed in the doorway. "The staff have gathered in the salon."

"Very well, Mrs. Babington." Marianna lingered several moments to take in the spring sunlight shining on her bedchamber's ice-blue walls.

In twenty-four hours, she would depart Granville House, never to see it again. A train ticket waited in her purse, ready to sprint her far away to Yorkshire. What if she hated her new home? Her new position? Her new life?

"Allow me to walk you to the salon, Miss Granville."

A refusal sprang to Marianna's tongue, but she held it back. Never again would Mrs. Babington perform such a service for her. After today, Marianna would serve others, at the mercy of her employer. "Thank you." Slowly and silently, the two women descended the grand staircase.

In the salon, somber eyes stared at her from solemn faces. April's rumors had transformed into May's facts, and they knew the conclusion. Her father's imprudent investments—rash, some in the village whispered—had exhausted the once-bountiful family coffers.

"The creditors will be arriving Monday to assume ownership. I don't know how many of you, if any, they will retain, so I have assembled some provisions." One by one, she called them forth, offering each in turn a profusion of praise, an extra week's pay, a letter of reference, and prayers for their future endeavors.

She forced a smile through the acknowledgments, well wishes, and even a few tears. They filed out, until only Mrs. Babington and Marianna remained.

"I'm not certain the creditors will approve of my generosity to the staff."

"There, there, you did the right thing." Mrs. Babington patted her hand. "I'll see about some tea."

"Let's retire to the kitchen and save you the effort of carrying—"

Several sharp raps reverberated through the cavernous house. The two of them looked at each other. Neighborly calls had ended with her father's internment.

"I'll handle this." Marianna marched to the entrance hall, Mrs. Babington following in her wake, and pulled open the door.

A motley group of men stood on the other side.

"Can I help you?"

"Andrew Granville 'ere?" The most forward—and frightening—of the bunch pushed his way into the house.

Marianna gathered as much dignity as she could muster under the circumstances. "Mr. Granville passed away three days ago."

"And 'oo do you be?"

"His daughter, Marianna Granville."

"We 'ave an order forfeiting the property of an Andrew Granville to 'is creditors. We've come to claim the 'ouse and furnishings."

Marianna retreated a step. Her pulse started to escalate. "I wasn't planning to leave until tomorrow."

He gestured to his men, and they followed him into the entrance hall. "Sorry, but you 'ave to go now."

"Now?" Her voice rose. She swallowed and tried to modulate her tones and increasing hysteria. "But I was informed you wouldn't take possession of the house until Monday."

A second, thinner man wandered over to the Hepplewhite pier table and lifted the porcelain Ming vase, examining it with a critical eye. "And allow you time to carry off the valuables?"

Mrs. Babington moved protectively close. "How dare you impugn Miss Granville's character!"

Marianna placed a placating hand on her sleeve. "I'll fetch my clothes, then I'll leave."

The obnoxious man followed them up the stairs, all the way to Marianna's bedchamber. Before she could retrieve her valise, he stepped in front of her.

"Let me look at it." He snapped open the case and riffled through Marianna's belongings—hair accessories, gowns, shoes, and. . .other things.

Anger and mortification warred for prominence. "As I said, just clothes. Now if you'll excuse me—"

"Ye can't take 'em."

"But of course I can. They are mine."

"My orders are to see that the 'ouse and all personal property of Andrew Granville pass to 'is creditors. These items are in 'is 'ouse, so they must stay to cover 'is debts."

"I. . .see." The room spun as realization set in. They were going to cast her out of her home with nothing.

She reached for her reticule—

"The bag 'as to stay too." He gestured toward her beaded purse with its sterling silver clasp.

Marianna extracted an envelope and waved it in front of his unshaven face. "Can I at least keep the letter? As you can see, it's addressed to me, not my father, so it's not part of his personal property."

He verified it was indeed addressed to Marianna Granville before acquiescing. "Very well. But the ring stays."

"Ring?" With growing horror, she realized he was staring at her grandmother's amethyst with its simple gold setting.

Tears ran down Marianna's cheeks as she twisted the ring from her finger. He seized it from her grasp, severing her last connection to her past.

# Chapter 10

*Present day*

Marianna jerked awake. She blinked and peered through the dark at the unfamiliar room. Where. . . ? As the grogginess cleared, awareness set in. She flopped back on the bed and closed her eyes—

Only to have her attempt to return to sleep interrupted by a moan. Miss Nowell!

The cold floor stung Marianna's feet. She snatched the nearby robe, wrapped it around herself, and crept to the door that led to a larger, more opulent room. Raspy breaths grated against the night, sporadically punctuated by groans of pain.

"Miss Nowell?" Marianna let herself into the room and padded across the carpet to the bed.

The glowing embers of the fire reflected in the old woman's eyes. "Laudanum."

Marianna lit the bedside lantern. The hands on the mantel clock pointed to a few minutes before midnight. The woman's last dose had been only three hours before. A chill owing nothing to the winter's night crept under Marianna's robe and swirled around her heart as she fetched the bottle. Miss Nowell's time was drawing ever nearer.

"Don't be miserly." Miss Nowell imbued the weak words with command. "It's not as if I have to worry about developing a dependency on the stuff."

"The pain is getting worse, isn't it?" The medicine's sickly sweet odor set Marianna's stomach churning as she measured a generous dose and held it to Miss Nowell's lips. "You have to tell them."

"You nag more than a cranky old lady. At least I have the excuse of being one." Miss Nowell swallowed the medicine with a grimace. "Vile stuff."

"Tri—Lord Lyddlebury knows something is wrong." She poured the last of the water from the bedside pitcher into a glass and helped Miss Nowell wash down the laudanum's bitter taste.

"Fine. After Christmas."

By then everyone else might have guessed, so the news wouldn't come as a surprise. "Would you like me to read to you?" At Miss Nowell's nod, Marianna retrieved the Bible and flipped through the pages to the place where they'd left off earlier in the evening.

She hadn't finished the chapter when Miss Nowell's eyes drifted shut and her even breathing murmured through the quiet. At least the laudanum still brought her a modicum of relief.

Marianna closed the book and carried the lantern to the adjoining room. Despite her exhaustion, she found herself too restless to readily return to sleep. Perhaps a walk would clear her mind. She quickly changed into one of her drab dresses and added a knit shawl, heavy socks, and serviceable shoes for warmth.

Her lantern cast shadows on the walls as she trekked through the ancient building.

Long ago she had played with Lucinda in these hallways, running their length and hiding in the many rooms whenever they heard her friend's nanny approach. For years, fear of pain had caused Marianna to avoid recollections of her past. Now, surrounded by so many familiar sights and sounds, the memories flooded back, bringing not only sadness but surprising joy.

She had decided to investigate the library for some suitably slumber-inducing tome when she spied a shaft of light beaming through the study doorway.

Curiosity trumped caution. She stole closer and peeked in. Tristram relaxed in a fireside chair, his left foot propped on a stool. The blaze in the hearth ignited copper sparks in the inky darkness of his tousled hair. After their awkward encounter the day before, she had avoided any chance meetings—an easy enough feat with her ankle as an excuse—and now she carefully backed away—

Onto a squeaky floorboard.

His head jerked up. "Marianna?" Was it her exhaustion that heard wistful notes in that solitary word?

Guiltily she poked her head around the door. "I saw the light. I didn't mean to disturb you."

"My apologies. I didn't wake you, did I?"

"I was already up."

"And walking, I see."

"I'm much better." She hesitated then stepped into the room. When he started to rise, she lifted her hand to forestall him. "Please. Don't stand on my account."

He accepted her admonition with surprisingly good grace for a man who abhorred his weakness. "Then at least take the other chair. The doctor told you to rest that ankle."

"I was...restless." She placed the lantern on a table and perched on the edge of the seat. There was something disturbingly intimate about sharing the still of the night with him.

"You won't be able to dance at the party if you don't obey the doctor's orders."

"That won't be a problem." Not when she would be spending the evening sitting with Miss Nowell. Unlike her last Christmas party here, she wouldn't need rescue from any over-eager fortune hunters. Dowerless, on-the-shelf companions didn't have full dance cards.

"I heard Bourke fled to the continent several years back after a string of irrecoverable losses." Strange, and a little frightening, how easily Tristram read her thoughts.

"He won't be missed."

"Except by the money-lenders still awaiting payment."

Not unlike her own situation when her father's creditors had appeared. In the awkward silence that descended, Tristram absently rubbed his elevated leg. Was that what kept him awake in the wee hours of the night? "Is it your injury?"

Other than the tic of annoyance pulsing in his jaw, he became very still. "You heard about it from Aunt Dorothea, of course. I'd rather nobody talk about it."

"Which is precisely why I have leave to bring it up. I am a nobody these days, my lord."

A whoosh of exasperation escaped him, and his face cracked into a smile. "How like a woman to insist we talk about the very subject a man doesn't wish to discuss."

"It's a gift—and it would be a shame not to utilize the gifts God provides."

He was silent for several moments before beginning again with a shrug. "I retain shell fragments from Balaclava. Fortunately, the pain is rarely this bad. Most times, it's a dull ache that has become so much a background to my life, I forget about it."

She didn't believe it to be that simple. Not when he relied on a cane to assist him from place to place. No doubt yesterday's adventure—lifting her onto a horse and leading it down from the moor—had aggravated the wound. At the time, when she'd selfishly relished the sensation of being in his embrace once more, she'd given little thought to how his exertions would affect him.

"You know, I had intended to fix myself a cup of tea. I, ah, I'll bring some back for you, if you like, and we can continue our conversation."

At his nod, she excused herself and fled down the hallway to regain her composure.

Tristram's heart gave a leap when the familiar footsteps clicked in the hallway. Marianna's skirts swished as she crossed the study and set the tea tray on the desk. "We have servants who do that sort of thing."

"I am one of the servants who does this sort of thing. Besides, I hope the others are having a better night than I."

"Little will be accomplished tomorrow if they aren't." He admired her quick, efficient movements as she poured the steaming brew into two cups. What would she say if she knew how close her hands were to her grandmother's ring? He nearly blurted out the truth, but at the last moment, he held off. Surely there was a better time than. . .he glanced at the clock that someone, Lucinda probably, had decorated with a big red Christmas bow. Almost three. "I'd begun to worry you'd decided to seek sleep instead of returning."

"I'm not so fickle as that." In the silence that followed, her face darkened, but Tristram refrained from a sarcastic retort. "I had to revive the fire."

"And find provisions and utensils in an unfamiliar kitchen. I'm sure it seemed longer to me than to you."

Tension eased from her shoulders. She picked up the sugar tongs. "The same way?"

"Yes." Had it really only been days since their return to Hollyford Hall? How quickly they fell into the old, familiar patterns.

Marianna added the requisite sugar and milk and paused before him with the cup. She leaned forward, and her shawl—a confection of white lace that provided a cheerful contrast to her oppressively dark clothes—slipped from her shoulder to the crook of her elbow.

Unthinkingly, Tristram smoothed it back into place. It was a simple gesture, intended as a kindness to someone hampered by a cup of hot liquid. And yet. . . As his thumb hovered near her face, he fought a consuming urge to caress her cheek, to ease the anguish that had pervaded the brilliant blue of her eyes when he'd so unwittingly spoken of bankruptcies and creditors.

"Thank you." He fitted his hands around the saucer to take it from her. Their fingers—devoid of gloves this night—brushed during the transfer, intensifying the porcelain's warmth. "The heat feels good. Last winter, it was so cold in Crimea, so very, very cold."

"I—I didn't know." She retreated to the desk, retrieved her own drink, and settled into the chair across from him.

"There weren't enough blankets or warm clothes. Some of the men took to growing beards for an extra bit of warmth."

Her gaze dropped to his mouth. "Is that why you no longer wear a moustache?"

"And keep the fire burning so fiercely. I vowed I would never be that cold again."

"Miss Nowell has difficulty focusing sometimes. I read the letters your mother sent to her."

Their shared look conveyed more than words that she understood how close to death he'd truly been. "Unpleasant reading, I'm sure. I didn't think I would live to see England again, and neither did the doctors."

"Fortunately, you were all wrong." She studied him over the edge of her raised cup. "Can they do nothing for the pain?"

He held her gaze for several long moments until he dropped his stare to the amber liquid in his cup. "They tell me I will probably have it for the rest of my life."

"I'm sorry."

He shook his head. "When you've seen as many of your friends die as I did. . ."

"We read the newspaper accounts, but I suspect they didn't do justice to the horrors."

"I doubt any description could." The fire on the hearth popped, like the echo of a pistol shot. The noise, the smoke, the confusion, and especially the fear rushed back. His gut roiled at the memory. "The enmity between two of our officers cost us the most. I feared the order to charge was a mistake, but what choice did I have? What was I, a lowly captain, to do? Disobeying a direct order is a capital offense. And so we rode down into the valley, into a veritable death trap with guns waiting on either side of us. Brave men died because the officers refused to communicate with each other."

"It's a horrid situation to be in, when you must choose between two terrible alternatives. While it does not compare, my father's imprudent behavior also left me with no good options."

Tristram glanced at the portrait above the mantel, the reminder of how fortunate he'd been to have two loving parents. With great effort, he refrained from asking the question that had haunted him for nearly five years. What had happened to the other man, the one her father preferred over him? The man whose attentions waned faster than her father's assets when the collapse came? For the first time since she'd spurned him, Tristram felt sorrow, rather than satisfaction, at the thought. "When you. . .suggested we would not suit, I was very angry."

"Understandably so. I'm sorry I hurt you Tristram. I didn't. . ." She pursed her lips and tilted her head to stare at the ceiling.

"I thought I'd let go of the bitterness when I was close to death last year."

"It's in moments like those we learn what is truly important."

"One would think so, and yet this week, I discovered grudges can be stubborn things. Lucinda says I need to tell you I've forgiven you—that if I can't, I'm still clinging to my resentment."

"Have you?"

"Forgiven you? Yes." Even as he said the words, warmth radiated through him, as if someone had settled another shovelful of coal on the fire.

Marianna's face softened into a serene smile. She gathered the cups and stacked them on the tray. "I doubt I'll ever be in Devon again. I'm glad we had this last chance to reconcile."

Sunshine reflected on the desktop's oak finish when Tristram returned to the study the following morning. He slid the chair out and dropped into it. Other than the miscellaneous papers now arranged in neat piles, the room looked much the same as when he'd arrived. And yet, he felt as though his world had shifted.

"My lord?"

Tristram glanced to the open door where the butler waited. "Yes?"

"A message has arrived for you." He passed the missive to Tristram and disappeared as quietly as he'd arrived.

Tristram unfolded the note. As he read the words, relief welled in him. His lawyer had located Pentreath residing in London and had forwarded Tristram's message.

*Pentreath.*

Tristram opened the drawer and retrieved the ring the lieutenant had obtained for him. With his finger, he traced—

"Am I interrupting?" His mother paused in the doorway.

"Never." He struggled to rise as she strolled into the room.

"I seem to find you in here frequently of late."

"I don't mean to shut you out. I feel closer to Father here."

A wistful smile curved her mouth. "He— What's that?"

Tristram followed her gaze to his hand. He extended his palm with the ring in the center.

"Isn't that one of the Granville diamonds?"

"Not exactly." He gave her a brief explanation of the jewel, and then hesitantly confessed his ignoble means of procuring it.

"What will you do with it now?"

"Return it to Marianna." Perhaps his inexplicable discovery of the ring all those years ago hadn't been an incredible coincidence but part of a Providential plan.

"Do you still have feelings for her? I couldn't fail to notice your reaction the other day was rather more vehement than the situation warranted."

Unwilling to give voice to something so personal, Tristram prevaricated. "I've already apologized."

"I thought you were going to propose years ago—then the mess with her father happened and Marianna disappeared." Mother braced her hand against the desk. "She'll leave again if you don't intervene."

Tristram dropped his gaze to study the ring, and his mind replayed the previous night's conversation—every detail of Marianna's appearance, every nuance of her expression, every inflection of her voice. As for himself, he'd never shared so much about his experiences. She'd even understood the horrible dilemma—

He froze, staring at the amethyst as if it were purple ice. What had she said? Something about choosing between two terrible alternatives. He'd been so focused on the rest of her statement, about her father's intemperance, that he'd missed the implications.

What two terrible choices had she faced related to her father's bankruptcy?

Aunt Dorothea had sought out Marianna five years ago. She knew what had transpired.

He dropped the ring in his coat pocket and snatched his walking stick. "Excuse me, Mother. I have an urgent errand."

A smile curved the corners of her mouth. "Of course."

Tristram kissed her cheek and left to seek his aunt. But the housekeeper hadn't seen Miss Nowell yet that morning. Nor had the butler. At last a maid suggested he seek her in her chamber. At this time of day? Tristram frowned, recalling Lucinda's concerns and Marianna's evasions.

He climbed the stairs past greenery that suddenly didn't seem so festive and knocked on Aunt Dorothea's door.

It opened several inches to reveal Marianna's blue eyes growing large at the sight of him. "Tristram?"

"I'd like to speak to my aunt. Is she available?"

"She'll go downstairs later."

"Marianna?" The breathy voice wafted to them. "Who is it?"

"Your favorite nephew," he called before Marianna had a chance to answer.

"Send him in."

"Are you certain, Miss Nowell?" Marianna's brows drew together. "You need—"

"After a week of nagging me to tell everyone my personal affairs, you question me now?"

"Very well." Marianna's lips twisted into a frown, but she let him in. Still, she followed him across the room to the bed where his aunt yet reclined.

"Shouldn't you be helping with the decorations?" Aunt Dorothea gave her companion a pointed stare.

Doubt and concern tightened along Marianna's jaw, but her five years' employment had evidently taught her no one won an argument with Dorothea Nowell. Instead, she aimed her misgivings at Tristram. "Don't tire her." She swept out, skirts swaying with her steps.

"Yes." Aunt Dorothea's voice drew Tristram's attention from Marianna's departing back.

"I beg your pardon?"

"The answer to your question—yes, I'm ill." The worrisome pallor of her complexion matched the whiteness of the sheets, but her dark eyes snapped with lively intelligence. "Unless you invaded my privacy to ogle my companion, in which case I suspect you'll be making a hasty excuse to depart."

"No, I came to see you."

"A good thing, since you won't have that pleasure much longer. My physician says this will be my last venture to Devon."

Heavy seconds ticked by as he swallowed. "I suspected as much. Did he estimate. . . ?"

"Only God knows for certain. Months. Maybe weeks."

"Not long then."

"Death comes for each of us eventually. All we can do is be prepared."

Tristram drew in a deep breath. He hadn't been particularly close to Aunt Dorothea— the separation of distance and time ensured that—but she'd been a tangible link to his father, his past. Emotion clogged his throat and blurred his vision. "Are you?"

"I am, but I suspect Marianna will grieve for a while."

Tristram was silent, trying to reconcile this week's observations of Aunt Dorothea's companion with his longstanding belief in Marianna's avarice. Because if she wasn't materialistic, if she wasn't the kind of woman who jilted a suitor for a better option, where did that leave him?

The man she didn't love enough to marry?

"Are you going to tell the rest of the family about my condition?"

"Do you want me to? Lucinda already suspects."

"I'd rather wait until after Christmas. Or at least until after the party tomorrow."

"Very well." He drew near and gently squeezed a frail hand with his own. "Helen and her daughter return today. My niece should provide more than enough distraction for the immediate future."

"Now, did I answer your questions satisfactorily?"

"All but the one I came to ask—about Marianna. What happened five years ago?"

# Chapter 11

Aunt Dorothea folded her arms across her chest and stared at Tristram under drawn brows. "Do you mean to tell me you still haven't figured it out? I thought you were smarter than that."

"Her father made no secret of his dissatisfaction with me as a suitor. And she mentioned him when. . ." He tried to remember back to her sudden and unexpected rejection.

"Of course she mentioned him. She knew about her father's looming insolvency."

Had she ended their romance in order to ensnare a man with better prospects before Andrew Granville's true financial situation became known? If so, she'd badly miscalculated. "If she'd but given me the word, I would have married her immediately."

"And then what? How would you have supported a wife and family?"

"I had my officer pay. We would have had to practice economies, but many have subsisted on less."

"You overlook the ramifications of the associated scandal. Some speculate her father did not die of a heart attack brought on by the news of his ruin, but by something more sinister. There were rumors of illegalities and improprieties—never proven and dropped after Granville's death—but their stench would have sullied you. Especially since your commander's family members numbered among those who suffered as a result of the fall of Andrew Granville's empire. Marianna knew this."

Tristram settled into a chair and stared out at the cloudless sky. What consequences would have ensued to an officer with a father-in-law embroiled in such a financial and legal disaster? None good.

"She set you free."

"I wish she would have let me determine for myself if I wished to be free."

"Marianna knew you would feel obligated to marry her at that point. Perhaps she wronged you by not letting you decide for yourself if she was worth the cost. But she did it to spare you from being trapped into marriage by your honor."

Honor? He didn't feel particularly honorable at the moment. Not when he'd thought so badly of her character. "How did she come to be in your employ in Yorkshire, so far from Devon?"

"I have contacts in the financial world. I guessed what was happening and sent her an offer for a position as my companion. A shame she didn't get the letter sooner so she could have left before the creditors arrived. They claimed possession of everything in the house and left her with literally nothing but the clothes she was wearing."

"Very generous of you."

"Generosity isn't a quality many accuse me of."

"Only because you hide it so well."

"Very well. Since you think so much of me, I might as well let you know I've made provisions for Marianna when I'm gone. She will be an independent woman. You might want to give the implications of that some consideration before we return to Yorkshire. And my attentive physician."

Aunt Dorothea closed her eyes and rested her head against the pillow, as if her speech had tired her out. Tristram rose. But before departing, he bent over and placed a kiss on her cheek. Although her eyes remained shut, a smile curved her lips.

Thoughts raced through Tristram's mind as he strode to his bedchamber. Everything around him, the people, the furnishings, the very walls, reminded him of everything he held dear. What would he have done when faced with the loss of the entirety of his world?

He turned a corner and almost crashed into a woman hurrying toward him. Marianna's eyes widened as she scrambled to avoid a collision. Some kind of white frippery fabric thing filled her arms, almost disguising her standard dark dress.

Memories overwhelmed him—a young, carefree Marianna in a snow-white ball gown, the sparkle in her eyes outshining the purple diamonds around her throat. He'd held her in his arms that night while the orchestra played a waltz.

"Excuse me, my lord." Her reticence-laced voice drew him back to the present.

"I . . ." Inundated with details provided by his aunt, Tristram's tangled thoughts formed no coherent words. Yes, Marianna had once loved him—five years ago. But now? She'd created a new life for herself—one without him in it. He nodded and continued on his way to mull over what he'd learned about her. About himself.

He opened the bedchamber door, still feeling that sense of loss whenever he entered the suite of rooms reserved for the master and mistress of Hollyford Hall. He'd hated displacing Helen, but she'd insisted she knew the house was hers only so long as Benedick lived. The same would happen to Tristram's wife, should she outlive him.

Wife.

Tristram crossed the plush blue carpet to an armoire and extracted a rolled-up page. Wrinkled, curled, even torn, the paper should have been thrown away. And yet, he'd saved it. He straightened it out and stared at the depiction of Devonshire. Though smudged by rain, the bold strokes captured the wild sweep of the moor surrounding Hollyford Hall. A solitary horse and rider galloped along a road.

Him?

Tristram wanted to think so, needed to think so. His future depended on the answer. And in that moment, he realized he'd made a decision about Marianna before his aunt's revelations, even before their late night tête-à-tête.

Was he too late, or could he convince her before she returned to Yorkshire forever?

Marianna's hands still trembled from her chance encounter with Tristram. The intimacy of night had given way to the glaring light of day, and already she regretted her imprudent confidences. She'd never shared so much about that terrible time five years ago, and even the knowledge that Tristram's pain exceeded her own did little to mitigate her chagrin.

She poked the needle through the fabric—and into her skin. A red droplet beaded on her thumb, and she tossed the unfinished handkerchief aside before a bloodstain added to the poor item's disgrace. She hated sewing, embroidery, and pretty much any endeavor that required a needle, and her work—in this case, several wilted roses surrounded by drooping leaves—attested to her apathy.

Of course, her inattention today no doubt contributed to this latest injury. Last night's conversation had brought healing—but also an undeniable recognition that her heart still belonged to Tristram. Only he was now a lord with expectations for his future. None of which included a penniless spinster.

"That's all, Anna." Miss Nowell dismissed the maid.

"Yes, madam." Anna gave the snow-white hair one final adjustment, offered the lady a curtsy, and let herself out the door.

Miss Nowell picked up Marianna's discarded work and shook her head. "How someone so talented can botch simple stitchery has never failed to amaze me."

"Pencils and pens don't attack back. Did you wish to join the ladies downstairs? I understand Lady Lyddlebury and her daughter return today."

"Presently. There is a matter I wish to discuss with you first." The old woman pointed toward the clothespress. "Look in there."

Marianna tugged open the inlaid door to reveal a gown of indigo silk. "But what. . ."

"You can't go to a Christmas party in black. We're celebrating a joyous occasion."

"I—I don't know what to say."

"You start by thanking your benefactress."

Marianna ripped her stare from the dress and joined Miss Nowell at her chair. "Thank you, but it's too much."

"Arguing with your employer demonstrates a lack of good business sense. Besides, it's already made to your size, so it won't do me any good."

"Very well. Since you insist."

"Now then, you've asked me for a letter of reference." Miss Nowell reached for her retinue and pulled out a surprisingly thick sheaf of papers which she passed to Marianna. "I thought I would offer you this instead."

Marianna unfolded the pages. The words at the top jumped out at her—Last Will and Testament of Dorothea Nowell. "But this isn't. . ."

Miss Nowell tapped the top sheet. "The first few pages are my final chance to get in the last word to my relatives and tender the customary legacies to my friends and staff. Look on the last page."

Marianna riffled through the pages to the final one and skimmed the words—words that made her an independent woman. She swallowed once, twice, trying to dislodge the lump that swelled in her throat and prevented any sound from escaping. "Me?"

"It's a modest estate, so you won't be able to spend extravagantly."

"But—"

"I wish you wouldn't keep saying that word. It's my property. I can do with it as I wish."

"B—" At Miss Nowell's narrowed look, Marianna settled for shaking her head. "Surely the Nowells—"

"Don't need another estate. And though we share no blood, we both know you are my closest family member."

The knot in Marianna's stomach intensified to queasiness as she donned the lustrous blue gown then strengthened to full-fledged nausea by the time she exited her chamber. Even the orchestra's cheerful tune wafting from the ballroom below couldn't alleviate her apprehension.

"The dress is lovely on you." Miss Nowell eyed Marianna's attire critically. "But you've worn so much black these past five years, I wish I'd chosen a lighter shade of blue."

"It feels rather. . .odd." And not only the color. Marianna placed her hand against her bare throat. Five years in clothes that covered all but her face made even the modest cut of this ball gown a disconcerting experience. How strange to realize she'd once worn such necklines regularly. "I think I would prefer one like yours."

"And when you are my age, you should wear one like this, but for now, enjoy your youth, Marianna." A shadow crossed over Miss Nowell's face. "It will pass quickly enough."

In many ways, it already had. Marianna walked beside Miss Nowell as the woman descended the stairs carefully, one hand gripping the banister and the other clutching the silver head of her cane.

Miss Nowell paused at the ballroom's entrance and stared at the tall evergreen, glowing with candles and frosted with bows. "White?"

Once again, Marianna pondered the wisdom of her suggestion. "I rather thought it would remind the guests of a snowy evening. . ."

"Stop worrying, Marianna." Miss Nowell let out one of her throaty cackles. "I like it. Only see that I do not sit next to the tree or right below a chandelier. So much brightness will emphasize my age."

With the rest of the family engaged in greeting their guests, Marianna set about procuring a chair that afforded Miss Nowell maximum visibility with a minimum of exertion. Then she took her place in the shadows behind it.

Miss Nowell was forthwith besieged by friends old and new come to pay their respects. None appeared to notice Marianna lurking nearby, and gradually she relaxed enough for her queasiness to ease. Under the cloak of anonymity, she monitored her employer, determined to compel her to her chamber at the first sign of fatigue.

Besides, none would miss Marianna when she took an early exit. Her gaze strayed to Tristram, occupied as he was with his newfound duties of host and lord of the manor. A bevy of young women hovered around him—as one would expect for a man suddenly endowed with title and lands.

"Marianna!" Lucinda bounced over wearing a smile stuffed with more holiday cheer than a plum pudding. "Oh my goodness, the dress is beautiful! The color is a perfect match to your eyes."

"A gift from your aunt, of course."

"Gift? I have no doubt you earned it through diligent work." A smirk teased the corner of Lucinda's mouth. "And I notice it contrasts so nicely with the colors in the room—almost as if you designed it that way."

"I didn't know Miss—"

Lucinda's laugh cut off Marianna's protest. "I'm teasing."

"You've always enjoyed that a bit too much."

"Never more than now. You've become so serious. You need more levity in your life. Look at you, standing in the shadows rather than enjoying yourself."

"I have responsibilities. Your aunt—"

"—will be fine. I'll see to her if she needs to leave."

"Go on, Marianna." Miss Nowell interrupted her conversation with a contemporary to interject.

Go where? One could hardly execute a dance alone, and it wasn't as if men queued for the honor of leading her out.

And then a form appeared at her side.

"Miss Granville, may I have this dance?" Her pulse accelerated faster than the music when the deep voice penetrated her consciousness.

# Chapter 12

For several interminable moments, Tristram feared Marianna would reject his invitation. He waited, hand extended, while caution warred with confusion in the luminous blue eyes. "Miss Granville?" he repeated.

"O–of course." She settled her gloved hand in his with the lightest of touches.

He clasped his fingers around hers, afraid she might change her mind and attempt an escape. The orchestra launched into a waltz, and he positioned his hand against her back. How different from the first time he'd led her onto the floor accompanied by this same song.

Even in his prime, she'd accused him of dancing with all the grace of his horse. Tonight, what with a four-year dancing hiatus and an injury that would never fully heal, he moved around the floor with downright ungainliness.

Her downcast head left only her hair to his perusal, its scent tantalizing his senses. "Are my buttons truly so fascinating?"

She tilted her chin up enough for her troubled gaze to meet his. "I . . ."

He tried to gather her closer, and she stiffened. Fear pressed cold along his spine. "Is it Ellis?"

"What?" Furrows creased her brow.

"Your Yorkshire doctor. I won't intrude where I'm not wanted."

"Oh. Oh no. I don't know what your aunt implied, but he is merely a friend."

So his presence generated her obvious discomfort. Was that bad. . .or good? "I didn't intend this to be a punishment, Marianna. If you don't wish to dance with me, just tell me."

"I'm sorry. It's. . .the awkwardness of the situation."

"Well, if that's all. I thought it was the awkwardness of my dancing. Who would have guessed I'd be even worse now than that first time?"

"I wouldn't say that. You haven't trod on my toes."

"Give me time. The dance has only begun." With relief, he felt her relax in his arms. "You did an excellent job decorating."

"Your staff did most of the work. I simply made suggestions." She glanced about the room. "Do you feel as though everyone is watching us?"

"No doubt they think I am most fortunate to secure such a beautiful partner."

"I see the years haven't diminished your propensity for flattery."

"Nor have they reduced your tendency to read guile into my perfectly accurate compliments."

"How could I not when you exaggerate so? Given how no other man has asked me to dance, it would seem my beauty is lacking without diamonds to embellish it, and my lineage is not so great it can overcome my lack of fortune."

A status that would change once Aunt Dorothea's will was read. Tristram dropped his gaze to the pale column of her neck where her pulse softly quivered. "A virtuous woman's price is far above diamonds."

"Rubies." The blue eyes regarded him below arched brows. "The verse says a virtuous woman's price is far above rubies."

"I have it on good authority that purple diamonds are among the most valuable gems on earth, so the sentiment is the same."

"Fair enough, I concede the point." A smile at last cracked her solemnity.

His heart began to soar with the music. "No jewel will ever outshine your smile, Marianna. You should display it more often."

"I didn't have one for the longest time. I shudder to think of what might have happened to me had your aunt not written to me and offered me a position as her companion."

"I'm so thankful she provided you a safe refuge—but I wish you'd entrusted me with your problems."

"She told you?"

"She confirmed what I should have been smart enough to figure out on my own, if I hadn't let my wounded pride cloud my judgment. I nourished my anger until I became addicted to my sense of self-righteousness." The ache in his heart matched the throbbing in his leg for sheer intensity. "How lowering to discover my sanctimony was totally without merit."

"You weren't the only one with misplaced pride. When I realized my father stood to lose everything, I couldn't face admitting the humiliating truth to you."

"Your father's debts were neither your fault nor your responsibility."

"No, but just the same, the entire family pays the price in such a situation. And I did. I lost my reputation, my future, my belongings down to the clothes I wasn't wearing. You would have gone down with my family. Martyrdom may seem a small compensation, but at least I could feel noble when I told myself you would grow to resent me for costing you so much."

"I'd like to believe I was more mature than that. . .but you may have been correct."

"We've both grown since then. Looking back, I can now see how spoiled I was as a child of privilege. I expected everyone to wait on me while I seldom served others. I didn't always treat those in my employ with the respect they deserved. I'm a better person for having to make my own way."

"In my case, it took an encounter with death. It certainly focuses one's faith."

"Speaking of your injury. . .it's troubling you, isn't it? You've winced several times in the past few minutes."

Tristram let out a sigh. "My pride begs me to deny the suggestion, but having just admitted to the danger of allowing that vice to guide me, I must confess that dancing strains the muscles."

"We could sit for a while."

"Or perhaps we could take a turn about the garden." He glanced meaningfully at the french doors that led to the terrace.

"It's December, Lord Lyddlebury." She stared at him impertinently down the length of her nose with all the hauteur of a dowager duchess. "Don't you think it's a little cold to be outside?"

"Then perhaps a quiet alcove. I never did show you our mistletoe."

"You aren't afraid I will compromise the lord of the manor into marriage?"

"I rather hope you will."

The blue eyes widened as a delightful pink crept over her cheeks. She lifted her gaze from her perusal of his face to study the swags of holly and ivy that draped from the ceiling to the chandeliers. "Lucinda hid the mistletoe again."

"And just like last time, she told me where it is."

"Truly, she told you where she put it five years ago? Rather presumptuous of her, given we'd rarely seen or spoken to each other in the three years prior."

"Not presumptuous. Hopeful. Did you think I never noticed you during my visits home?"

"I thought you were teasing with all your flirtatious banter."

"Mostly I was. The timing was not right then. But it is now. Shall we?"

Her lips curved into winsome acquiescence. "I–I think I would enjoy that."

He halted her in the center of the room. The instrumentalists played the last few bars and concluded their tune. While all the assembled guests watched, Tristram eased himself down on one knee. "Marianna Granville, would you do me the singular honor of becoming my wife?"

"Yes. Oh yes!"

Tristram pushed himself to his feet and leant closer, until their faces were mere inches apart and the scent of her filled his senses. "Look up."

Marianna tilted her head back. "Oh, Lucinda put the mistletoe in the center of—"

But Tristram cut off the rest of her sentence when he captured her perfectly positioned lips in a kiss.

# Epilogue

*Hollyford Chapel, Devonshire, England*
*Saturday, December 29, 1855*

The sunlight streaming through the stained glass bathed the chapel's stone floor in a kaleidoscope of colors on this Fifth Day of Christmas. As she stood before the vicar, giddiness bubbled inside Marianna. Not even Elizabeth Bennet had enjoyed so fine a day for her wedding nor acquired so fine a groom for her husband.

Tristram's niece looked adorable. His mother and Miss Nowell dabbed their eyes but nonetheless appeared pleased. Lucinda smiled and held the bridal bouquet while an army comrade of Tristram's stood on his other side. He'd brought this Kenver Pentreath to Hollyford Hall last night when he'd returned from Canterbury with a special license to marry immediately. She and Tristram wanted the wedding before Aunt Dorothea's health deteriorated further.

Marianna repeated the words, the promise to love and cherish no matter what trials and triumphs they faced in the future, without a single tremor of hesitation in her voice.

Then the vicar signaled to Tristram, and he slipped the cool metal of a wedding band over her fourth finger, maintaining his hold while he promised to endow her with all his worldly goods.

He whispered, "Our fortunes have reversed yet again. I just gave you all my money."

Marianna stifled a giggle while the clergyman gestured to them to kneel for the prayer. Tristram released her hand, and she glanced at the ring around her finger. Purple facets flashed in the light, winking from their gold filigree setting. "Tristram! Oh, Tristram, where did you—"

He held a finger to her lips. "Shh. It's a long story, but I'll be happy to tell you everything. . .as soon as the vicar has pronounced us man and wife."

Award-winning author **C.J. Chase** left the corporate world to stay home with her children and quickly learned she did not possess the housekeeping gene. She decided to make writing her excuse for letting the dust bunnies accumulate under the furniture. When she is not writing, you will find C.J. gardening, watching old movies, playing classical piano (badly), teaching a special-needs Sunday school class, or pretty much anything else that will excuse her from cleaning house. Visit her dirt-free home-on-the-web at www.cjchasebooks.com.

# Star of Wonder

by Susanne Dietze

# Dedication

For Karl. Merry Christmas, love!

# Acknowledgments

Thank you to the other authors in this collection, but especially Carrie, who invited me in. Hugs, my friend.

*To whom then will ye liken me, or shall I be equal? saith the Holy One. Lift up your eyes on high, and behold who hath created these things, that bringeth out their host by number: he calleth them all by names by the greatness of his might, for that he is strong in power; not one faileth.*
ISAIAH 40:25–26

*Star of wonder, star of night,*
*Star with royal beauty bright,*
*Westward leading, still proceeding,*
*Guide us to thy Perfect Light.*

JOHN HENRY HOPKINS JR., 1857

# Chapter 1

T hey say it's larger than a hen's egg—the Star of Wonder, that is. Is that true? Where's Celeste? She doesn't usually take so long dressing for dinner."

"I am here, Grandmama." Lady Celeste Sidwell slipped into the sitting room where Grandmama waited with Celeste's blond, pert-nosed sister-in-law, Maud. Celeste kissed their cheeks and took her seat, wishing they'd been discussing something else. Anything else. The Star of Wonder was not her favorite subject, but one her family had been agog about for months.

"I don't know what the Star of Wonder looks like, Grandmama, although by its name, it does indeed sound grand."

Since her arrival early this afternoon, everything Celeste had seen at the elegant stone estate, Cheltham Hall, was grand, including this sitting room allotted by Lord Cheltham for her family's private use during their stay. The comfortable chamber was cozy, decorated in rich shades of blue and gold. Celeste, Grandmama, and Maud agreed to wait here for Papa, the Marquess of Willsden, and Celeste's elder brother, Eldon, to come for them at the appointed hour when they would all join their hosts in the Hall before dinner…and to view the Star of Wonder.

Despite the fire blazing in the hearth, Celeste shivered.

Maud patted Grandmama's gloved hand. "If the Star of Wonder is as large as an egg, it would be too heavy for Celeste to wear."

"Perhaps it's a small star then." Grandmama sighed, as if disappointed by the idea. "Nevertheless, Celeste, you must be excited to come into possession of such a fine diamond."

"No, Grandmama." The words were out of Celeste's mouth with a little too much force. "What I meant to say is—not tonight."

Maud's eyes twinkled. "Celeste won't *receive* it until Christmas Eve when she accepts Lord Harwood's proposal in the Green Parlor. What a romantic tradition, for the heir to propose to his future wife on Christmas Eve and present her with the Star of Wonder necklace."

Celeste was numb to the story of the Star of Wonder. Papa had repeated the tale numerous times the past three months, since first conceiving the notion of an arranged marriage between Celeste and Bennet Hett, Lord Harwood, the son of their host.

Regardless of whether or not Celeste wanted the marriage. Or if Bennet did. Duty and dynasty were everything among their rank in society, as Papa often said, and she was almost on the shelf at her "advanced" age of five and twenty.

Celeste glanced out the window, but could see little. Flurries fluttered down as they arrived this afternoon, and the snow had thickened as darkness set in. The moon was hidden behind a blanket of clouds. She'd like to hide too, but there was no escaping duty. In a few minutes, she'd be downstairs in the Hall.

Papa already knew how she felt about being here at Cheltham Hall for Christmas instead of in London where she was needed. He also knew how she felt about being pressed into marriage, but he seemed to think she would change her mind this week. If he only knew it wasn't *her* mind that was fixed as firmly as a star in the heavens, but Bennet's too. Not five minutes ago, she and Bennet had been together in the Green Parlor across the landing, discussing their plan to end this charade without hurting or embarrassing their fathers. Their greatest hope for the week was to change their fathers' minds. . .

"Good evening." Papa, a fit, salt-and-pepper-haired gentleman in his fifties, appeared in the threshold, a smile tugging at his smooth cheeks. Eldon followed, walking straight to greet his wife. Papa eyed Celeste with eagerness. "Everyone awaits us in the Hall. Are you ready?"

Celeste wore a gown of pine-green silk, outwardly prepared, but inside? She was not ready at all. She nodded anyway.

Grandmama took Papa's elbow, and Eldon offered an arm each to Maud and Celeste.

"You look lovely," Maud assured her as they left the room. "Lord Harwood will be blinded by your radiance."

The only radiance of interest to Bennet pertained to the stars, passionate as he was about astronomy. Still, Maud was kind to encourage her. "You are lovely to say so, dear—"

Her left side hit something. Someone. A slender, fair-haired maidservant stood tucked against the hallway wall, camouflaged in the shadows. Since Celeste had been looking at Maud, she'd walked right into the young woman. It was more of a nudge than anything, but she might have caused the maid injury. "Forgive me. Have I hurt you?"

"No, milady." The blue-eyed maid met her gaze before she dipped her capped head.

"All's well, then. Come on. Is that roast beef I detect?" Eldon sniffed the air and tugged Celeste forward.

Celeste turned back to ensure the maid was well, but the hall was now empty. The maidservant had scurried away, silent as a mouse.

"So clumsy of me." *Take a deep breath.*

"No need to be nervous, Celeste." Eldon glanced at her as they descended the stairs.

Maud glared at her husband. "Were you not nervous when you asked for my hand in marriage last year?"

Eldon shrugged. "Not particularly. I knew you'd say yes."

"Because we were a love match. But Celeste scarcely knows Lord Harwood."

Celeste shrugged. "I know Lord Harwood—Bennet—well enough." Enough to know they were of the same mind.

They crossed the grand marble foyer and stepped into a wide hallway that had clearly been constructed in an earlier age, with its beamed ceilings and worn stone floors. At the end of the hallway, light and chatter spilled from open double doors. It seemed they were the last to arrive then. Breaching the threshold, Celeste sent up a short prayer for calm—and for everything she'd left in London to go well in her absence.

Guilt at leaving London panged in her stomach, but now that they'd entered the impressive hall, two stories high and paneled in dark wood, her mind cleared of everything but how the chatter ceased and every eye seemed fixed on her. Including Bennet's pale blue gaze.

"Welcome!" The balding Earl of Cheltham, Bennet's father, strode toward them, Bennet following. Bennet was taller than his father, trimmer, with reddish-blond curls, one of which flopped unfashionably over his brow. She rather liked that particular, disobedient curl.

In fact, she liked Bennet, but that wasn't the point.

They'd formed an understanding these past few months. While they desired to be obedient to their fathers and fulfill their duties, they did not wish to marry, or in Bennet's case, not yet. He knew what was required of him as a future earl, but his astronomy work at the Royal Observatory was too important to him to set aside to marry now and return to Cheltham Hall, as his father wished. As Celeste's work in Lisson Grove was important to her.

But perhaps their greatest hesitation against marriage was their own upbringing by parents whose marriages had been arranged, unhappily so. Why would their fathers now burden their children by yoking them to veritable strangers?

They'd tried speaking to their fathers back in London, but those stubborn men hadn't wished to hear reason. Then Lord Cheltham invited her family to a Christmas house party so tradition could be fulfilled and Bennet could propose on Christmas Eve with the Star of Wonder in hand. She and Bennet were in agreement, however. They had four days to persuade their fathers they would not suit. They would not become betrothed on Christmas Eve. He would not give her the Star of Wonder.

His blue eyes twinkled at her and, after meeting Grandmama, Eldon, and Maud, he bowed over Celeste's hand and gave it a reassuring squeeze. "I hope you enjoy a merry week with us."

"I am certain I shall, thank you." It was easy to offer him a genuine smile, as if she was meeting an old friend again.

Perhaps that feeling of familiarity was because he was indubitably thinking the same thing she was. Come the New Year, he would return to the life he preferred, and this time next month, she would be living out her calling, up to her elbows in porridge in a West London slum.

Bennet Hett, Viscount Harwood, preferred to be at the Royal Observatory in Greenwich. Or at least outdoors, although with the snow clouds obscuring the sky, he couldn't view the moon, much less the stars, through his telescope.

Instead he was here, at Cheltham Hall, fulfilling his duty. Although, after avoiding Father last year, Bennet would have probably come for Christmas this year, even if he hadn't been summoned.

Even though he was still angry at his father about Jane, and he expected this to be the worst Christmas of his life.

Bennet forced himself to focus on the present. Celeste smiled up at him, her large brown eyes crinkling into half-moons. It was impossible not to smile back.

He introduced her to his family, or at least the family Father hadn't driven away: his fashionable maternal aunt, Lady Marsh, and her husband, Lord Marsh; their plump, blond daughter Rose and her mustachioed husband, Sir Philip; and Peregrine Pitt, of course. Bennet required at least one ally here, and Perry had nothing else to do for Christmas anyway. Brown whiskers curved down Perry's cheeks, hiding the first signs of jowls. Nothing could obscure his smile, however, as he met Celeste and bowed from his thick waist.

"Lady Celeste, an honor."

"The honor is mine, Mr. Pitt. You and Lord Harwood are colleagues at the Astronomy Society?"

"We are indeed, friends since our Cambridge days."

Feeling someone's gaze on his neck, Bennet turned. Aunt Marsh nodded in approval, jiggling her large earrings, and Uncle Marsh waggled his brows. Cousin Rose beamed, and Sir Philip winked. Father, of course, looked about to burst with joy. Lady Celeste was perfect—well-mannered and lovely, with her dark hair curling over one slim shoulder. Little wonder Father thought her the ideal bride for Bennet.

Lord Willsden, Celeste's father, drew Bennet's attention. "Nothing more splendid than a quiet Christmas with family. Twelve of us?"

"Fifteen, with Rose and Philip's children."

"I should like to meet them." Celeste's gaze turned to Rose, whose chest expanded with maternal pride.

Fifteen was not a huge party, especially compared to other noble families' celebrations. But at the moment, it seemed overwhelming.

*God, I ask for softened hearts to accept Your will this week. May our fathers see You have called me and Celeste to other things.*

Father held up his hand and all conversations stilled. He pulled a black velvet pouch from the inner breast pocket of his coat.

"Before we adjourn to dinner, I wish to share something with you. Inside this humble bag is a treasure that has been in the family for over a hundred years." Father held the pouch out to Bennet. "And now it is time to pass it to my son."

Bennet didn't want to take it, but this wasn't the time for a spectacle. Celeste knew it too, and she'd agreed the two of them must endure this particular ceremony. They'd decided they would wait for far more private opportunities with their fathers to press their cases. Nevertheless, Bennet's neck was hot and his hands cold.

The pouch's gentle weight rested in his palm. It was time for the traditional speech. He cleared his throat before meeting Celeste's encouraging gaze.

Her tiny smile set him at ease, and he held up the pouch. "Decades ago, the second Lord Harwood, heir to the Earl of Cheltham, proposed marriage to his future wife on Christmas Eve, bestowing upon her this gift. Because of the night on which it was given, she named it the Star of Wonder in honor of the star that led the magi to the Christ Child. In the generations since, when the time has come for the heir of Cheltham to wed, he has proposed on Christmas Eve and gifted his future bride with the Star of Wonder. Father and I would like to share it with you now."

Bennet tugged the silken ribbon cinching the pouch and spilled the contents into his hand.

"What's this?" Father's brows bunched as he stared at Bennet's palm.

Instead of the Star of Wonder diamond set amongst smaller diamonds on a thick silver rope, Bennet held a rock the size of a boiled egg yolk and a few pebbles—which would simulate the sensation of the necklace within the pouch.

"The Star of Wonder." Bennet met his father's horrified gaze. "It's gone."

# Chapter 2

**W**hat *did that mean, gone?*

Celeste inched forward, enough to see the rock in Bennet's hand.

"Is this your doing, Bennet? To postpone the inevitable?" Lord Cheltham's whispered accusation met Celeste's ears.

"Certainly not." Bennet glanced at Celeste then shook his head just a fraction, assuring her he hadn't removed the necklace to cause such a scene. Good. Creating a spectacle was not part of their agreement. Rather, they'd determined to convince their fathers in private, without causing embarrassment or ruining the holiday. Hiding the Star of Wonder achieved the opposite. The atmosphere in the room had changed from celebratory to agitated, and the hairs on Celeste's nape stood at attention.

"What's this?" Papa peered at the rocks.

Lord Cheltham blanched. "It appears the Star of Wonder has been stolen."

Grandmama gasped. Lady Rose glanced at her husband, whose lips pressed into a grim line. Lady Marsh covered her mouth with ring-laden fingers, Mr. Pitt frowned, and Eldon's dark brows lowered.

"Who would do such a thing?" Lord Marsh's booming voice filled the hall.

"Celeste." Papa's voice was too low for the room at large to hear, but Celeste understood the accusation his tone.

"I had nothing to do with this."

His shoulders sagged in relief. "Forgive me, but after the incident with the pearls—"

"When did you last see the piece, Father?" Bennet's question drew every ear.

Lord Cheltham rubbed his forehead. "I ordered the Star of Wonder brought to me in the Green Parlor, maybe two hours ago? I was admiring the necklace when my estate manager arrived. I replaced the necklace in its pouch and left it on the table whilst I met him in the library. 'Twas only for—well, now that I think on it, it might have been an hour because reviewing the document took longer than I expected, and afterward I dressed for dinner. Then I returned, directly before we gathered here, and found the pouch where I'd left it, never suspecting someone had replaced it with rubbish."

"Who would have gone into the Green Parlor? Not I." Lady Marsh's hand fluttered, setting her many bracelets to clinking.

*I,* Celeste almost said. With Bennet, to confirm their plan to quietly convince their fathers. They'd told no one they would meet, but since they were unchaperoned, the door was left open. They'd seen no one enter or exit, or even pass by.

"An intruder?" Maud wondered.

Sir Philip began to pace. "It must be the servants. They sneak from room to room like mice."

As he spoke, footmen entered the hall bearing cups on a tray and a large steaming bowl. They must have overheard Sir Philip's accusation, but their expressions remained impassive.

Lord Cheltham cleared his throat loudly. "Pray do not concern yourselves with this slight mishap. I've ordered lamb's wool punch—a festive drink, perfect for the season."

"It is indeed, Father." Bennet smiled. "And our traditional way to begin our celebration of Christmas. Everyone, gather round for a cup."

"Not going to let anything spoil Christmas," Lord Marsh insisted to Papa.

Celeste took a silver cup of the spiced beverage topped with clouds of mashed apple. She had yet to taste it when Bennet drew alongside. He was so much taller than she that he had to dip his head to whisper. "I'm sorry about this."

"Your poor father, violated like this." Her heart ached for Lord Cheltham. "I confess, I didn't notice the pouch when we were in the Green Parlor. Did you?"

"No. I was focused on you." He stared at her hair then blinked. "I mean, on our conversation."

"Of course." Celeste well knew he wasn't interested in her like *that*. "What do you think happened?"

"I haven't the foggiest, but since the necklace was replaced with rocks, I think this was not a crime of opportunity. This was planned."

Perhaps she should be afraid at the prospect of a thief in the house, but she wasn't. "I am angry on your behalf, Bennet."

"Angry? Not frightened?"

"I am not prone to swooning." She pulled a face.

"No, I imagine not." He eyed her, as if impressed.

She took a sip from her cup. The ginger and nutmeg spicing the drink brought to mind a memory of trimming the tree with Mama on Christmas Eve four years ago, right before she died. It was the last time Celeste, Papa, and Eldon had celebrated the holiday with anything festive beyond church and a roast goose for dinner.

She'd almost forgotten what it was like to be among company like this at Christmas, amid chatter and the clink of silver, hands warmed by cups of hot punch—which was especially welcome to her in this cold room. A shiver coursed through her.

"You're chilled. Shall I summon a maid to fetch you a shawl?" While Bennet spoke, his fingers alighted above her elbow at the spot where her long white glove met bare skin.

Her arm erupted in gooseflesh, and not because she was cold.

Papa chose that moment to look at them, and his gaze caught Bennet's lingering touch.

In fact, almost every eye was on them—no, not quite. They gazed past to look at the window behind Celeste and Bennet. Celeste turned to peer outside the large windows overlooking the drive. Fat snowflakes fell thick and fast.

Bennet's brow furrowed as his hand fell from her arm. "With the snow like this, 'tis doubtful an intruder could depart from the house without leaving prints behind. I see no footsteps on the drive, but I'll look around back for signs of an outsider departing the estate."

"If there are no footprints, perhaps Sir Philip is correct about a servant taking the necklace."

"Few servants could justify being caught in the Green Parlor, but it is possible, I suppose." His gaze hardened a fraction. "Of course, any of the members of our party could have found an excuse to be in the room and could easily have stolen it."

The gravity of his statement settled in her stomach. *Our party.*

Celeste couldn't help but glance at each member, family and friends, all. Would one of them do such a vile thing? What a horrible thought.

She spun back to face Bennet. "Intruder, servant, or guest, it appears the thief is still here at Cheltham Hall. And so, therefore, must be the Star of Wonder. It can still be recovered. Let us look for it."

Bennet's head dipped. "Us?"

"I shall help you." She owed him that much, as kind as he'd been to her these past few months.

"I imagine the thief would not care for us to retrieve it from him. Or her." He lifted his cup as if to take a sip, but lowered it again. "I would not wish to see you hurt if the matter turns dangerous."

*Pah.* "I once thwarted a thief with a ladle in the meal house kitchen. Foolish fellow. If he'd have but asked for coin, I would have seen him fed, but I did not take kindly to being robbed."

His eyes went wide. Oh dear. Papa was right—her stories had a way of shocking people.

But Bennet's lips quirked into a charming smile. "Then you'd best bring your ladle to protect us as we search."

A laugh bubbled out of her. "A heavy candlestick will do. Do we start now?"

"No." He spoke in a teasing tone. "Dinner is in five minutes. But, oh, did you wish for a shawl? I'll send someone to fetch it." Bennet tipped his head to the threshold, where a maidservant lingered outside the door. It was the same young woman Celeste had almost bowled over in the hallway, reed-thin, a cap on her fair hair. . .but she was gone in an instant, mortified to have been caught peeking, no doubt.

No matter. "I am warm enough now, with this punch."

Bennet's eyes smiled as he took another sip.

Bennet caught sight of Father's discreet summons and smiled at Celeste. "Excuse me a moment."

He joined his father near the blazing hearth, where Father lounged in a casual pose. But there was nothing casual about his grip on his cup. "This is a disaster, Son."

"The Star of Wonder might yet be in the house. I should like to conduct a search, with your permission, Father."

"I'm glad to see you show an interest in the necklace for your bride-to-be."

Bennet swallowed punch rather than respond to Father's insinuation that Bennet had changed his mind about marrying Celeste. Despite all that the Star of Wonder symbolized in the way of marriage—something Bennet was not at all ready for—the necklace was an important part of his family's legacy. Not to mention it was of great value. It rankled that a thief dared steal within these walls. "So may I take the matter in hand then? Time is of the essence."

"Yes. Discreetly, please. I wouldn't wish our guests to question our family's suitability."

"They find us suitable, Father." *Otherwise they wouldn't be here, but that isn't the issue now.* "Footmen must search the house for intruders at once because there are as yet no signs of anyone having left in the snow. I shall also have the butler question the staff."

"Servants are not always loyal. We learned this the hard way—"

Father couldn't finish. He gulped against his collar.

"I shall take the matter in hand." Bennet nodded, glancing at Celeste before he quit the hall to speak to the butler. The matter took only a few moments, and Bennet returned to the hall confident that the house would be thoroughly searched while he and their guests enjoyed dinner.

No one spoke of the Star of Wonder during the meal, but instead of Christmases past. At first, Bennet recalled the happy memories of his childhood, but then he remembered the last Christmas he spent here, two years ago. A happy day.

But soon after, his family had disintegrated.

Their guests wouldn't guess their family had any fractures or pain in it, the way Father smiled and presided over the dinner table. Everyone was engaged as the conversations splintered: the gentlemen spoke of hunting grouse, Aunt Marsh chatted with Celeste's grandmother, and Rose occupied Maud and Celeste with stories of Bennet building a snow fort for her when they were twelve.

She didn't mention Jane at all.

He wanted to say something. The words pushed up his throat in a painful charge, but he swallowed them back. This wasn't the time or place to give them voice.

When he looked up across the mahogany table, Celeste watched him, her dark brows drawn down in concern.

What must she think of this disaster of an evening? Or his family, for that matter? He'd come to respect her opinions as they'd grown more acquainted, and she'd impressed him with her intelligence as well as her passions. Pity his passions didn't impress his family. Aunt Marsh had started to describe Bennet's astronomical pursuits to Celeste's grandmother. "There is something about Mars. . .and the temperature of stars."

Perry winked at Bennet before turning his smile on Aunt Marsh. "Your nephew is well-esteemed among his fellow astronomers."

"That is good to hear." Celeste's grandmother nodded. "Isn't it, Celeste?"

"It is." Celeste met Bennet's amused expression.

"And you, Lady Celeste?" Perry spooned his pudding. "I'm told you are involved in a meal house in London."

"I work alongside a married couple by the name of Brewer. We provide a hot meal and milk for the young ones who live in Lisson Grove."

"Lisson Grove?" Peregrine's spoon stalled halfway to his mouth.

Rose blinked. "I do not know of this place."

Philip shook his head. "It is a dastardly pocket of town. The police will only patrol it in pairs, it's so dangerous."

Celeste nodded. "Precisely, and full of hungry, poor children."

Lord Willsden waved his hand. "It is an occupation my daughter will give up with her marriage, I assure you."

"Why?" Bennet's question drew every eye. "Are her actions not in response to a calling from the Lord?"

Father forced a laugh. "Many things change with marriage, Son. Now, I suggest we gentlemen forsake our coffee and accompany the ladies to the drawing room."

"Capital idea, Cheltham," Willsden said.

Bennet rose with everyone else, lingering to escort Celeste from the dining room to the drawing room across the vestibule. "I'm sorry, Celeste."

"No, *I'm* sorry. Papa warned me not to talk about the meal house."

"I daresay you amazed us all by your strength and resolve." He swallowed hard. "I wonder if Jane lives somewhere like that."

Celeste laid her hand on his forearm. "I pray your sister is somewhere safe."

"Thank you. And thank you for your sympathy in her regard, rather than judging her. It is a shocking scandal for the earl's daughter to elope with the footman. I don't care though. I miss her."

"I imagine she misses you too."

"Then why doesn't she come home?"

"Pride, perhaps?" Her gaze caught on something above. "Well, hello there."

Bennet followed her gaze up the grand staircase to the landing, where three brunette children dressed in nightclothes crouched between the balusters of the railing. "Rose and Philip's," he whispered.

"I gathered as much." She smiled up at them. "You must have the best vantage in the house."

"We do, ma'am." Harriet, the middle child, waved. The eldest, Gilbert, scooted closer to the balusters to better see them, and the youngest, Jeffrey, darted off and returned holding a gray cat with white paws.

Ah, so that was where the cat had gone. Bennet chortled. "How is Mittens?"

"Soft," Harriet answered. "Is she your cat?"

"She was my sister Jane's." One of many things she'd left behind.

"She likes us." Jeffrey set Mittens down.

"Children!" A female voice, probably a nursemaid, loudly whispered. "Come back to bed at once!"

In a swirl of white nightclothes, the cat at their heels, they were gone.

Celeste squeezed Bennet's arm. "They're charming."

"They are. And—oh, before we reach the drawing room, I must not neglect to tell you the butler is interviewing the staff and searching their rooms for the Star of Wonder, should one of them be the thief. Footmen currently search the house for sign of an intruder, but to my knowledge, have found nothing yet. I've ordered men to keep watch all night should anyone try to slip out, but if no one is discovered, and the thief is not a servant or an intruder, I'm not sure where to start looking."

"I can think of a good place." Celeste grinned. "With the children."

# Chapter 3

Celeste was already awake the next morning when childish giggles sounded out in the hallway, followed by an even louder shush.

"But it's almost Christmas!" came the high-pitched response, fading away. Celeste rose with a smile. When she was young, the excitement of those last days before that most wondrous day of the year was almost too much to be borne.

The decorations. The sweets. Church on Christmas morn, when the most profound and marvelous message of God sending His Son into the world was shared.

And then, of course, there was the anticipation of presents.

No wonder Gilbert, Harriet, and Jeffrey were giddy.

*Lord, are the children of Lisson Grove eager this morning too?* Celeste prayed for the two dozen or so young ones who regularly came to the meal house. Before she left London, she'd done her best to ensure they would have a happy Christmas, buying presents and ensuring they had sufficient food for a feast. Nevertheless, the guilt of being away ached at her.

*I tried not to come here, Father, but to stay in London—*

Perhaps she'd had it backward. Being at Cheltham Hall might be a gift from the Lord, one that might help restore her family after Mama's passing. Celeste's parents had not gotten along well, true, but since Mama's death, Papa had grieved and ignored Christmas, as if it was too painful a reminder of her. This year, however, Papa could not escape Christmas—not the trappings of it, and hopefully not the meaning of it. God offered hope and healing. She should pray for her family to experience Him to the fullest.

After breakfast, the entire party gathered in the drawing room for tea and conversation. As with dinner last night, no one mentioned the awkward topic of the Star of Wonder, speaking instead of the amount of snow that had fallen during the night.

"A white Christmas." Lady Marsh's eyes went as wide as the stones on her large earrings and matching necklace. Several rings and bracelets added additional sparkle to her ensemble. Clearly, Lady Marsh enjoyed wearing jewelry. Lots of it.

Lord Marsh twisted back from the window, revealing a strange lump under his coat, as if a handkerchief in his breast pocket wasn't folded properly. "Two feet deep out there, at least."

Peregrine made a humming noise. "Six to eight inches, by my reckoning."

"Enough to make us snowbound, at any rate," Lord Cheltham insisted.

Snowbound. Celeste wandered toward the windows. Outside, a cloud-heavy sky hung over the white landscape. Snow shrouded shrubs and tree limbs. It was impossible to tell where the drive met the park, or even where the porch steps were. Not a single footstep marred the snowfall.

Bennet sidled beside her, smelling of shaving soap. "I've spoken to the butler. The Star of Wonder is not among any of the staff's possessions, nor have the servants encountered anyone strange in the house. The only thing of note below stairs is a domestic trifle. One of the maids is missing a frock, although the housekeeper is certain she scorched it and fibs to avoid punishment. At any rate, the necklace is probably still hidden in the house. Would you still like to help me search for it?"

"I would. Are you ready to visit the nursery?"

"Do you think the children are awake?"

"Oh yes. This close to Christmas? They've been up for hours." A laugh bubbled out of her.

"Very well. Let's go then."

When she and Bennet made their excuses to the group, no one batted an eye—although Sir Philip might have winked. How embarrassing. They all thought she and Bennet were infatuated with one another and sneaking off for time alone.

There was no time to blush like a schoolgirl over their assumptions, however. She and Bennet had a jewel to find.

The round-faced nursemaid dipped into a curtsy when they entered the nursery, a bright, airy room with yellow-papered walls. The children sprawled beside Mittens, the cat, on the blue rug, playing with painted blocks, but they scrambled to their feet to welcome the visitors.

Celeste smiled at the nursemaid. "I do not wish to interrupt, but Lord Harwood and I wished to visit the children."

"You may enjoy a quiet tea downstairs, if you like," Bennet offered.

What a thoughtful idea, and it would give Celeste and Bennet time alone with the children.

"Thank you, m'lord." The nursemaid curtsied and disappeared into the hallway.

Celeste turned back to Bennet, expecting him to speak first. Instead, he gently nudged the carved head of a well-used rocking horse, setting it in motion. His concentrated expression was a puzzle. Was he thinking of his sister, Jane, and their childhood?

Her heart aching for him, Celeste turned her full attention to the young ones eyeing her with curiosity. "We did not have time for proper introductions last night. I am Lady Celeste."

"Gilbert Olney," the oldest boy said, executing a bow that made his dark hair flop over his freckled brow. Judging by the gaps in his teeth, he looked to be about eight or nine.

The girl of perhaps seven curtsied. "I am Harriet Olney, and this is Jeffrey, our baby brother."

Jeffrey scowled. "I'm five, not a baby."

"I see that none of you are babies," Celeste said quickly. "That is why Lord Harwood and I have come to you for help."

Jeffrey's scowl melted. "I'm a good helper."

"We can only help if we stay inside." Gilbert looked wary. "Our nurse says we cannot go out until the snow is cleared."

Harriet nodded. "Tomorrow is the gathering of the greens. I hope the paths are cleared by then."

"I am certain they shall be." Celeste glanced at Bennet, who'd shoved his hands in his pockets and wandered to the far side of the room. Meanwhile, the trio of children awaited her words. She'd expected Bennet to choose how much to tell the children, but he seemed preoccupied. She'd tell them the truth then. Children could always sniff out a fib. "We are searching for something of Lord Cheltham's. It went missing from the Green Parlor, down the hall, last evening. Do you know where that room is?"

Harriet nodded. "We are not allowed inside."

Which made the room all the more tempting. Celeste would have yearned to sneak into a forbidden sanctuary. "Do any of you collect stones?"

"Gilbert does." Harriet pointed. "They're always about the house."

"Why?" Gilbert's eyes widened. "Do you have rocks for us?"

"Alas, no, but someone replaced a diamond necklace with some pebbles and a stone this big." She made a small circle with her forefinger.

"You mean the Star of Wonder." Harriet nodded. "Mama says it is astondish–astond. . ."

"Astonishing," Gilbert finished for her.

Jeffrey jumped. "Astond-ishing."

"Mama wants one like it," Harriet added, bending to pet the cat. "Papa says diamonds like that don't grow on trees, which is silly because everyone knows diamonds come from the ground."

So Lady Rose wanted a necklace like the Star of Wonder? Interesting. Celeste tucked away the information. "Lord Harwood and I hope to get the necklace back so Lord Cheltham will not be sad anymore. We will not be angry if someone borrowed it, so long as it is returned now. Do any of you have an idea of the necklace's whereabouts?"

"I want to see a di-mond." Jeffrey frowned, looking envious. So he hadn't taken it. What about the older two? Harriet's brow furrowed and Gilbert shook his head.

"No," they both said at once.

Celeste believed them.

Gilbert's countenance changed. "Cousin Bennet. What are you doing?"

Bennet had been quiet all of this time. Now she knew why. His arm was deep into a pile of toys.

While she questioned the children, he'd been searching the room.

"Do you wish to play?" Harriet was at Bennet's side within the span of a breath, pulling dolls from the heap. "These old toys were here when we arrived."

Bennet laughed. The "old" toys had belonged to him and Jane, and he was but eight-and-twenty. "I was looking for the Star of Wonder, in case it was in here by mistake."

Jeffrey hopped, making his fine hair bounce. "I like finding things."

"Like when we play Hide the Bean," Harriet said.

Bennet hadn't planned to play with them. It wasn't that he disliked children. He just didn't know what to do with them. Telescopes and spectroscopes were far more comfortable than small human beings.

Besides, they were here to look for the Star of Wonder. The children hadn't taken it, but he hadn't known that when he started searching the room. "I'm not sure—"

Jeffrey gripped Bennet's pant leg. "Please? I want to play."

"Oh yes!" Harriet cried, followed by Gilbert.

It was on his tongue to wonder when the nursemaid would finish her tea when Celeste pulled a lacy square from her pocket. "As I have no beans, we must use a handkerchief instead."

Harriet fingered the lace. "Pretty."

"My mother gave it to me." Celeste smiled. "Now, shall I hide it first?"

Bennet's fingers clenched. They would not get any searching done while hiding lace hankies. "Perhaps you all could play whilst I—"

"We have time for each of us to take a turn," Celeste told him. "Children, go into the hallway while I tell Cousin Bennet how to play."

"We can tell him."

"I wish to." She shooed them out, shut the door, and turned to Bennet. "The children didn't take the necklace, but your searching the nursery inspired me. I intend to use the opportunity to continue searching here. If the thief was not an intruder or a servant, the culprit must be one of our party, as you said last night. And if I were the thief, I would not hide the necklace in my chamber. It would seem foolish to pack it with one's stockings when all the servants know it has been stolen, wouldn't it? So perhaps the gem is hidden somewhere in the house, in a potted plant or tucked in a nook, waiting to be retrieved by the thief once suspicion has passed."

It made sense. "Then you search here. I'll rummage through the other public rooms."

"I won't have time to search the entire nursery. I'll examine the bookcase and cupboard. You do the rest during your turn to hide the 'bean.'" She smiled. "Now go entertain your cousins. Make a memory. I shall fetch you when I am ready."

She opened the door and almost pushed him out.

The children started talking at the same time.

"I want to play in the snow," Jeffrey insisted.

Gilbert's round cheeks pinked. "I shall build a fort."

"I shall make snow angels." Harriet craned to look up at Bennet. "Is Lady Celeste your fiancée?"

"Er..."

The nursery door swung open, sparing him from replying. Celeste's bright face shone with excitement. "The bean is hidden!"

"It's not a bean; it's a handkerchief," Jeffrey corrected as he darted into the room.

"So it is." Celeste grinned.

She was quite good with the children. No surprise, since she spent so much of her time with them in Lisson Grove. She would make a wonderful mother someday. If she ever married, that is.

Bennet wanted to be a father, but a much different one than his own. Bennet's love would not be conditional. But that was a long time off. He would not be marrying any time soon—

"Clever, Lady Celeste!"

Gilbert pointed at the coverlet atop a tiny bed in the dollhouse—no scrap of fabric, but Celeste's handkerchief: the bean. Harriet and Jeffrey squealed. Gilbert shooed them out into the hallway so he could hide it again. Jeffrey found it, and then Harriet the next round.

Would he never find the thing so he could search the nursery?

Once Harriet had hidden it and they searched the nursery, Celeste cleared her throat. Twice. And looked pointedly at a doll wearing a familiar "apron."

"I found the bean," he announced. Once everyone adjourned to the hall, he hid it atop a book and poked around the children's cots. There was nothing to be found but a few rocks tucked under Gilbert's mattress.

Leaving the nursery, his gaze caught on the narrow door cut into the wall. A passage led to the kitchen from here—the Hall too, but no one ever used that. The passage used to make a more convenient route for the servants to tend the children. A few years ago, something had collapsed within the space and Father had ordered the passage sealed. Pity; he and Jane had enjoyed hiding in there. *Lord, is Jane warm this winter? Please provide for her.*

He summoned everyone inside to find the handkerchief, just as the nursemaid returned. Once Harriet found the handkerchief and Celeste returned it to her pocket, she and Bennet bid the children farewell.

"The children at the meal house adore games like this," she said as they ambled down the hallway. "I hope they're well."

"You miss them."

"Yes, and I feel guilty for not being there."

"Your Mr. and Mrs. Brewer sound capable."

"Indeed, and they love the children as though they were their own—they could not have any. I left funds and food, and there is nothing I could add to the children's Christmas except for my presence. Which, Papa reminded me, is not truly needed. They will be fed without me."

"There is more to your meal house than bread, Celeste."

Her damp gaze bored into his. "Thank you, Bennet."

He wanted to embrace her, enfold her in a comforting hug, but he held back. It would not be appropriate between friends, would it? What if someone saw them and misinterpreted the gesture?

Instead he smiled. "Shall we skulk about for the Star of Wonder as you suggested, searching the potted palms and flower arrangements? I should like to hear more about the meal house while we do."

"Would you truly?"

He nodded, reaching inside an empty porcelain vase on a lacquered credenza. "Alas, nothing here."

Smiling, she poked into an arrangement of hothouse flowers on the table on the landing. "We should explore the library. Everyone has access to it. And the Green Parlor. Perhaps the thief slipped it somewhere close to where he found it."

"Brilliant. Let's go, and you may tell me about the meal house."

She did as they rummaged through the Green Parlor, library, and music room. "No diamond, but it has been time well spent," Bennet said. "We've been gone near on an hour now. Perhaps we should return downstairs."

She sighed. "Shall we resume our search tomorrow?"

Bennet offered her his arm. "Tomorrow we gather the greens so we may decorate on the twenty-third. It's tradition. All hands are needed. I hope you do not mind being put to work."

"It sounds delightful." By the look on her face, it truly did.

He used to enjoy the work, but this year, with everything that had happened with Father and Jane, the thought of gathering pine and mistletoe seemed burdensome, and Papa's enthusiasm feigned for their visitors' benefits, to put on a happy show for them. Bennet hadn't felt festive at all.

Until this minute, thanks to Celeste.

They returned to the drawing room arm in arm, and no one said a word about their long absence, although Father looked rather smug.

"Son," he called. "Word has come. A section of the bridge to Cheltham Hall has collapsed. No one can cross in or out until it is repaired. We are well and truly snowbound."

Bennet looked around at the others in the room, one of whom, it seemed likely, had stolen the Star of Wonder.

And none of them were going anywhere.

# Chapter 4

After breakfast the next morning, Celeste donned her cherry-red wool cape, sturdiest boots, and thick muffler to gather greenery—and gather information, perhaps too. She and Bennet could not hunt indoors for the Star of Wonder today, but they could glean insight into who might have taken the necklace.

She stepped out the front door into a crisp, fresh-smelling world of white. While the staff had cleared the porch and created several paths, a thick blanket of snow still shrouded the lawn and drive.

Something whizzed past Celeste's ear.

"Sorry, Lady Celeste!" Snow speckled Gilbert's mittens. "I meant to hit Cousin Bennet."

"Did you now?" Bennet scooped up a fistful of snow and sent it flying to splatter on Gilbert's coat.

Jeffrey ran past, bundled so tightly Celeste could barely make out his nose above his red muffler. Harriet shrieked as Sir Philip tossed her in the air, and Papa, Peregrine, Eldon, Maud, and Rose looked to the west, nodding and pointing.

"Mistletoe thataway, if you and Bennet are interested," Lord Marsh told Celeste, wiggling his brows as he came up beside her.

Even though it was so cold her breath was dense as fog, her cheeks went warm at his suggestion. "I think I shall gather pine instead."

Lord Marsh guffawed.

The front door opened behind them, and Grandmama and Lady Marsh stepped onto the porch. Neither was dressed for the weather. "We shall leave the work to you young people," Lady Marsh announced.

"Coward," Lord Marsh called good-naturedly.

He was a tease, this fellow, and Celeste couldn't hold his mistletoe remark against him. He thought her in love with his nephew, and he wouldn't tease her if he wasn't pleased by the idea.

Her gaze flitted to Bennet. He smacked snow into Peregrine's back. "Come on, Perry."

"And have snow down my neck? I prefer it outside of my coat, Ben, thank you."

Grandmama and Lady Marsh laughed from the porch, and Lord Marsh stomped up the steps to meet them. Maud took his place at Celeste's side. "What a different holiday than last year, is it not?"

"Indeed." But Maud wasn't her usual smiling self. "Is something amiss?"

"I shouldn't tell you, but, oh, Celeste. Eldon placed a wager at White's and. . .lost."

Celeste's gasp pulled stinging cold air into her throat. "Eldon?"

"It was a foolish impulse, one he's sworn never to repeat, but we are in debt."

More than they could afford, it seemed. "How may I help?"

"Do not give it a second thought, please. I needed to unburden myself to you, that's all. We shall sell some artwork." Her voice broke off as Peregrine strode toward them. There was no finishing the conversation now. They greeted Peregrine and then Maud wandered off to join Eldon.

Peregrine smiled. "You're doing quite admirably, if I may say so."

"I beg your pardon?"

"With your plan. Ben told me the two of you are working in tandem to break your fathers' marriage scheme."

Celeste blinked. With the Star of Wonder stolen, she'd all but forgotten to find time with Papa. Not that there had been many opportunities. Yesterday, the group had played parlor games and sung carols until tea. Then she and Bennet had slipped away to poke through the conservatory and other public rooms, but had not found the Star of Wonder hidden anywhere.

"Lady Celeste?" Peregrine dipped his head to study her face. "Are you upset I know the truth?"

"No. We all need someone to confide in."

"Have you such a confidant?"

"Maud is my oldest friend, but I haven't told her. I don't wish to put her in a difficult position. It is best that she finds out with everyone else that Bennet and I will not become engaged on Christmas Eve." She glanced at Maud, who held Harriet's hands and smiled down at her. "You are kind to support Bennet, and at Christmas too."

"My pleasure. Besides, my Christmas in London would not have been jolly like this."

Hers either. "Not like this."

"Pity about the Star of Wonder. Sounds as if a gem like that could set a fellow up for life. Bennet does not know how fortunate he is to have so many comfortable trappings. I am a younger son of a younger son. You know how that goes."

Celeste did indeed. Peregrine was by no means poor, but he was probably living at the edge of his means among the upper class.

Lord Cheltham waved his arms. "Let us get to work. There is still ivy near the greenhouse. Let's leave it for those who do not wish to walk as far. A half mile or so into the wood, there's mistletoe and a promising candidate for a Yule log."

He assigned a sled to Eldon, Sir Philip, and the children to fetch the Yule log, and the others discussed their preferences. Servants distributed saws, hatchets, empty sacks, and baskets. Papa took up a hatchet, weighing the tool in his hand. She'd follow him and perhaps, God willing, find an opportunity to tell him quietly she and Bennet were not marrying.

"You two." Lord Cheltham nodded at Celeste and Bennet in turn. "Bring us the perfect Christmas tree."

"I'll lend a hand," Peregrine offered.

Lord Cheltham stayed him with a hand. "Your strapping arms are needed to gather boughs. This way."

It was on Celeste's tongue to protest that she was no help cutting down a tree, and surely she would do better collecting pine, but clearly, this had nothing to do with her skills. This was about sending her and Bennet off, unchaperoned, with no one to look on if he stole a kiss.

He wouldn't, of course. But he could, if things were different.

For some reason, the thought of kissing Bennet made her lips warm.

Saw in hand and apologetic smile on his face, Bennet directed her toward a cleared path. "Our fathers are formidable."

"I'd hoped to speak to Papa now and persuade him to release us from this arrangement. He must be made to understand that I will not exit the Green Parlor on Christmas Eve a betrothed woman, wearing the Star of Wonder."

"You couldn't wear it anyway, with it lost," he teased.

She rolled her eyes. "You know what I mean."

"I do." He smiled down at her, but then they both looked up. His father was watching them, smiling.

Perhaps they should get to the matter at hand. She glanced down at the saw. "I don't suppose you know how to cut down a tree."

"Of course. Don't you?"

"We haven't had a tree since Mama died. Before that, the groundskeepers brought in a tree with all of the greenery."

"Do you mind helping?"

They were walking at a smart pace now into the fresh-smelling woods, their boots crunching the snow-packed path underfoot. Invigorated, she shook her head. "Not at all."

"I did not think you would."

The groundskeepers' path led them deeper into the woods, where the snow was not as deep, but it narrowed so they were forced to walk closer together if they continued on side by side. It could have been awkward, but Celeste didn't feel strange. Bennet's companionship was welcome.

And there was no one here to observe them. Perhaps that lessened the pressure.

"So how do we find a tree, O Wise Woodsman?"

"Lesson one: look in an area thick with trees for one of a nice shape about this high." He gestured to the second button of his dark gray coat. "The tree will sit atop a table in the drawing room, right in front of the window, so when the carolers arrive Christmas Eve—if they arrive, with the bridge in need of repair—they may see the candlelight from the outside."

"It sounds lovely."

"It is. And we place figures of Mary, Joseph, and Jesus beneath the tree."

"Those are traditions I'd be happy to incorporate into my Christmases." Someday. "What about that one?"

Peering at the short pine, his brow scrunched. "Hmm."

"What's wrong with it?"

"It's, well, terrible." He was smiling, his tone light.

"It is not." She was smiling too.

"There's a gap on the side."

Indeed there was, now that they were closer. "Turn that side to the wall."

"There is no wall. It's going in front of the window, recall."

"It's not that bad. It's—very well, it's terrible."

"It's not our perfect tree." His eyes twinkled with mirth. "What of this one?"

Hands fisted on her hips, she pretended to scrutinize the squat pine he indicated. "Too thick. It will be difficult to hang ornaments on it."

He fingered the pine needles, releasing the crisp pine scent into the air. "I could thin the branches."

"Or we could find a new one. Your father said the *perfect* Christmas tree."

She blinked, unaware until that moment how close they stood to one another. The hems of their coats touched. His blue eyes sparked, and all around was silence and the intoxicating scent of pine.

Off in the not-too-far-distance, one of the children screeched, breaking the intensity of the moment. Celeste lowered her gaze, embarrassed to have been staring at him like that. But when she looked up again, he was still looking at her.

"Shall—" Her mouth was dry. Licking her lips, she looked away. "Shall we try another?"

"I think that would be an excellent idea." He puffed out a breath and they continued along the path.

Within moments, a decent-looking candidate appeared to the left. "I like that one."

"I do too, but we should make sure there is no hole on the other side," he teased.

"And that it is acceptable for hanging ornaments."

Bennet circled it, wearing the same expression Papa wore when he examined horseflesh. "It's perfect."

Green and bright. As tall as his second coat button. "It is indeed perfect."

He dropped to his haunches, setting to work with the saw. Clearly, he'd done this before. His expression was almost pleased, as if he enjoyed the labor. Every motion was efficient, and it didn't take long for him to look up at her. "Stand behind me."

She obeyed. With a soft snap, the tree fell over into the snow. The odor of piney sap filled the air.

"Bravo!" She clapped, her gloved hands making muffled sounds.

He rose and bowed, grinning. "You chose an excellent tree."

"*We* chose."

He bent to grip the sawed-off base, but before his face was hidden from her, she glimpsed a change to his smile. It didn't diminish, but shifted, like he wasn't just enjoying himself. Like he was happy, and maybe a little embarrassed about it.

"I think you are content here at Cheltham Hall, Bennet."

"Perhaps it is not Cheltham Hall. Perhaps you bring out the best of me."

Their gazes held. Something had changed between them, or maybe this sense of connection had always been there, but they'd not recognized it. . .because they didn't want it. A trickle of fear snaked up her spine. This feeling had no place in their relationship. They were friends, no more, since neither one wanted marriage.

Which meant it made no sense that being near him made her heart thump hard and quick in her chest. And he too did not seem to be immune to her. Compared to their encounters in London, Bennet now smiled more. He laughed more. And he certainly stared at her more.

They walked back along the narrow path in companionable silence, single file, since he carried the tree. When they reached the broader path, she waited for him to come alongside her. They were no longer alone, and members of their families carried boughs and baskets. Maud's laughter carried over the yard, and Rose began to sing one of the old carols. Eldon and Gilbert strode alongside Philip, who tugged a sled bearing a large chunk of tree trunk atop it—the Yule log—and Jeffrey riding on top, his little face bright. Harriet ran up from behind, said something, and Philip stopped the sled. Jeffrey got down, and she took her turn riding the log.

Celeste's chest grew warm, surprised by her instant affection for Bennet's little cousins. She'd always liked children—the children's meal house testified to that—but until this moment, she'd never felt quite like this. Like she wanted a family of her own.

Bennet grinned at her and she smiled back. Was this what life could be like if she married? Companionable walks in the woods, homey pursuits, fun?

She shoved away her sudden yearning. Perhaps it was because it was Christmas, a season of faith but also one her culture had filled with a sentimentality and romance that couldn't help but make one. . .susceptible to yearning for more. More material things, in some cases, but also a desire to feel more. To be less lonely.

And Celeste, happy though she was with the meal house, had not spent time in familial fellowship like this since Mama died. There were times when she definitely felt lonely. She did not feel lonely when she was with Bennet.

However, Christmas would end. So would her relationship with Bennet, beyond the greeting of friends if they ever crossed paths in London. And one of these years, Celeste would probably see him and his wife.

Her mouth filled with the bitter taste of something she'd never experienced before. Envy? When she and Bennet were both getting what they wanted this Christmas?

This time, she had to force a smile when she looked back up at Bennet.

The sense of festivity Bennet had experienced gathering greenery continued into the evening. After dinner, the adults gathered in the drawing room. Rose sat at the piano and played carols, and though Perry nodded at Bennet and slipped out, everyone else began to sing along.

Bennet had never thought himself a talented singer, but he sang with enthusiasm anyway. Lack of ability didn't matter at times like these, when voices rose in joy. Willsden sang as softly as Father sang loud and flat. Celeste's grandmother wandered off key, Aunt Marsh was a half-beat behind, and Uncle Marsh's bass was passionate, if not precise.

All of a sudden, Bennet missed Jane's clear, lilting soprano, and his spirits flagged. No matter how fun the day had been with Celeste, bringing in a Christmas tree and enjoying his time with her, the shadow of Jane fell over him. She should be here.

At the end of "God Rest Ye Merry, Gentlemen," Father strode to Rose's side, reaching for the sheets of music. "Well as we sound, the carolers who come Christmas Eve are excellent. There is no more talented group in Durham."

Willsden's brows rose. "High praise, indeed."

Celeste smiled. "Are they members of a church choir?"

"No, they are villagers, male and female, old and young. We offer them wassail in the Hall and they entertain us for half an hour."

"If the bridge is repaired by then," Bennet said, adding a smile so others wouldn't guess how sad he was at remembering Jane's banishment.

Celeste was beside him then, a balm to his pain. "What happened just now? I see you are preoccupied. Pray tell me what concerns you."

She was so kind. "Nothing."

"My singing? Come now, it is not that bad, is it?"

He laughed. He hadn't realized his shoulders were knotted until this moment, when they relaxed. She truly was the most perceptive, kind person he'd ever met, and he couldn't help enjoying their time together. She even made being here with Father tolerable.

Ah, there was Perry again at the door, eyes wide. "Bennet?"

Father scowled. "What's all this?"

Bennet smiled an apology to the group. "Mars. The sky has cleared, and Perry set up my telescope on the balcony."

To Bennet's surprise, Father's frown disappeared. "Take Lady Celeste out then."

Father, encouraging Bennet's interest in astronomy? More like encouraging Bennet to be alone with Celeste, without chaperone, although they would be visible to anyone who peeked outside the window.

Celeste's expression was eager. "I have always wondered what it would be like to look through a telescope."

Her interest pleased him. "Would you like a heavier cloak?"

"My shawl should suffice."

While she wrapped it tighter about her narrow shoulders, Perry sighed just loud enough for Bennet to hear. "I know where I'm not wanted by your father. I'll wait my turn."

Bennet clasped his friend's shoulder. "Five minutes."

"She'll be bored by then," Perry murmured. Bennet hoped not.

Out on the balcony, frigid air nipped his hands and face, but overhead, the cloudless conditions were perfect for viewing the heavens. He led her to the telescope set up on the balcony's far corner, away from the light glowing through the windows.

"Perry will have focused it, but allow me to make certain." Bennet rubbed his thumb over the cold eyepiece to warm it and bent at the waist to peer into the telescope. Ah, perfect. He stepped back, gesturing her forward. "Mars awaits."

Casting him a shy glance, she crouched over the eyepiece and gasped. "It *is* red, isn't it? And it appears so close, I feel I could touch it." Her hand twitched, as if she'd try.

His gaze lingered on her, the way her hair fell over her slim shoulder and the natural curve of her smile. The sweet fragrance of her perfume surrounded her, a reminder of summer on a winter night. She glanced up at him then, grinning. "It's marvelous."

Shoving away the odd sense of pleasure filling his chest at the thought of her enjoying something he loved, he chided himself. Such thoughts were dangerous. So was thinking about how pretty she was in the moonlight or how she smelled like a garden in July. They had an arrangement. But that didn't mean they couldn't be friends.

And he did not want to lose that. Lose her.

When she bent back to the telescope, he forced his thoughts to remain academic. "See any dark patches or lines?"

"I think so. Patches."

"We've known about those areas for two hundred years, but don't know what they are. Neither do we know much about the two grooves, or *canali*, recently discovered on the planet's surface by an Italian priest. I wonder what future discoveries will reveal."

"It's another world." She rose, eyes liquid in the moonlight. "I thought astronomers followed the courses of the stars, did equations and such, but there's so much more, isn't there?"

"Much more." He took a turn at the eyepiece and gazed up at the red planet. "We who study the stars take pains to be accurate and careful with our observations about the stars and the laws that govern them."

"Do you know about stars of long ago?"

Something in her tone made him look up. "Some."

"What about the star that led the magi to the Christ Child?"

An intriguing question. "No one knows precisely what the Star of Bethlehem was. Some say a comet, or two stars joining in the sky to create a light so bright it could not be ignored. But I think not."

"What do you think then?"

"I've no proof, but I think the star which marked the birth of our Savior was no comet, no conjunction of planets, but something altogether unique. Whatever it was though, it was set in the heavens by God for a singular and amazing purpose."

Perhaps she'd expected a different answer, something that had to do with mathematics and constellation charts, because her lips quirked. "It is not like a man of science to accept a lack of explanation."

"I am not bothered by a little mystery where God is concerned. Are you?"

"Sometimes," she admitted, looking up at the sky. "I do not understand the world. Poverty. Suffering. Why He allows such."

"Like your children in Lisson Grove. I do not know why the world suffers so, Celeste, but Jesus came into such a world. He has not forgotten it."

She nodded, but her lips pressed tight together.

"God created these stars above us. He holds the universe in His hand. I must trust Him to hold the things that concern me too."

Like his relationship with Father. Like Jane, wherever she was. Bennet had been remiss in trusting God with his concerns—a misstep he intended to change at once.

Celeste smiled and tipped her head at the telescope. "He created a far bigger world than I'd imagined. Thank you for reminding me He is at work in the universe. And even in me."

"I needed the reminder myself."

"About that. God at work in me, I mean," she said, her voice strained. She cleared her throat and smiled at him. "I should tell you, Papa suspected I stole the Star of Wonder necklace."

"You? Never."

She shook her head. "That's just it, Bennet. I took a necklace once before and sold it to start the meal house. It was mine, from my mother, but Papa forbade me to take it and I did so anyway. I have changed since I did that. God has challenged me. I still believe it was mine to do with as I wished, but I didn't go about it the right way. I hurt Papa. I would never hurt you the same way, taking the Star of Wonder—well, I won't be receiving it anyway, but I wanted you to know what I'd done."

"I'm glad we are honest with one another."

"I am too. This is a most unexpected. . .friendship."

"I am glad we're friends, Celeste."

"Friends," she echoed.

They stood close to each other, still on either side of the eyepiece, their shoulders touching. Her faint perfume encircled him. Whatever he was thinking of her right now, it was not precisely friendship.

So it was absolutely a good thing that half the party chose that moment to join them on the balcony to see Mars. But Bennet couldn't ignore a flash of disappointment over their arrival.

# Chapter 5

C eleste did not sleep well that night, her thoughts overrun with the stars and the moon. Or, to be more precise, the gentleman who'd taken her onto the balcony and showed them to her. Bennet had been all kindness, sharing his favorite thing with her, and to her surprise, she'd found it more interesting than she imagined.

And challenging, especially what he'd said about God holding the universe in His hands. She'd struggled leaving London, feeling as if the meal house would fall apart in her absence. She hadn't trusted Mr. and Mrs. Brewer to see to things in her stead, despite their competence, nor had she trusted God to see the children fed.

She had some praying to do about it.

But that part of her conversation with Bennet wasn't what had kept her awake much of the night or occupied her thoughts all morning and into the afternoon. She must admit she was beginning to feel something for Bennet. Whatever that something was. Affection, perhaps.

Not the sort of affection she had for Grandmama, or Eldon or Maud. Even now, the sound of Bennet laughing from the hallway made her stomach flip over and her fingers tremble.

Enough of that. She required steady fingers this afternoon, making ornaments with the children—and their constant companion, Mittens—in the drawing room. She selected a fresh page of white paper and took the scissors to it, rounding one edge to create a paper cone ornament for the tree. The little cornucopias she and the children fashioned would be filled with walnuts and sweetmeats.

The other adults were busy too—the gentlemen wired pine branches together, and the ladies crafted satin bows or, in Rose and Maud's case, fashioned a kissing bough for the foyer.

She must take care to avoid passing through the foyer. Papa and Lord Cheltham would probably contrive an excuse to set her and Bennet beneath it at some point.

The idea of Bennet's lips on hers, even for a half-second of customary under-the-mistletoe tradition, made her fingers fumble all over again. Was this room overwarm? Perhaps she should open a window and admit some icy air.

"Lady Celeste." Harriet's high voice dragged Celeste back to her surroundings.

"Yes?" Celeste smeared too much glue on her paper, making her forefinger tacky. Where was her handkerchief?

"You're pink."

Celeste wore green plaid today, without a speck of red-tone on her. "Pink?"

"Right here." Harriet patted her own cheeks.

Celeste must be blushing fiercely, and my, here came Bennet striding into the drawing room with a swag of pine. Grinning, he lifted it for their approval. "For the mantel.

What do you think?"

"Lovely." Willing her cheeks to pale, Celeste started to gesture her approval, but her gluey finger stuck to the page. Then she felt hot all over again.

"Don't pet Mittens," Jeffrey warned. "You'll be glued to her."

"Or covered with fur," Gilbert noted.

Harriet pulled a face. "I don't like fur stuck to me."

Lowering the pine to the floor, Bennet offered Celeste his handkerchief. "I hate when that happens."

"You glue your fingers to paper?" Hiding from his laughing gaze, Celeste busied herself with rubbing her hand.

"No. But I suppose I shall once I help you with ornaments. After I hang the garland, that is." He turned, scooped up the fragrant pine, and lifted it above the marble mantelpiece. "Gilbert, why are there rocks on the mantelpiece?"

"Sorry. They were in my pocket."

Which explained nothing, except that Gilbert indeed had a habit of leaving his pebble collection about the house as Harriet had said. Celeste bit back a smile as Gilbert scooped them and Bennet draped the garland. "How's this?"

Gilbert turned his head this way and that. "It's too long on the right."

Jeffrey held up his hands, both of which were stuck to paper. "I'm glued, Lady Celeste." She took the handkerchief to his small fingers and glanced at Harriet. "How are your cones, Harriet?"

"Quite well." She gestured to the paper funnels, half of them glued off center. "I want to make something else though."

Jeffrey seen to, Celeste took up a fresh sheet of paper. "Let's make stars."

She hadn't done this in years, but she recalled the simple process easily. She taught Harriet how to cut the paper into strips, glue two into a cross, weave in additional strips, and then glue the ends of the strips together to form a star.

"Look!" Harriet held it up to Bennet and her brothers.

Bennet made a show of examining it. " 'Tis perfect."

"I want to make one." Gilbert reached for the scissors.

"Me too." Jeffrey sidled against Celeste, warm and smelling of glue.

"As would I." Bennet dropped to the floor.

Celeste showed them all what to do, and while they worked, Jeffrey paused to pat Bennet's shoulder. "I want to look through the tely-scup, but Mama says it's too 'spensive."

Harriet nodded. "You'll break it."

"You seem a careful bunch to me." Bennet's brow furrowed. "If conditions are clear and your parents allow, you may look through it sometime. Lady Celeste looked through it last night and seemed to enjoy herself."

She met his lazy smile. "I did. I learned some things too."

"Like what?" Gilbert pinched his paper together.

"Like. . ." *Like the fact that Bennet smelled of shaving soap. And in the moonlight, his hair shone like silver.* "Like. . .Mars has mysterious canals and patches on it."

"What are they?" Jeffrey wiped a gluey finger on his sleeve.

"No one knows," Bennet began. Using terms the children could understand, he described the variety of planets and objects in the heavens.

While he spoke, inspiration struck. Celeste took up one of the spools of stiff red ribbon awaiting the arrival of the Christmas tree and began to cut. The glue didn't dry as quickly on it as it had with the paper, and everyone had completed two star ornaments before hers was finished.

She handed it to Bennet. "Mars."

His lips parted in surprise. "Truly? I thought you were making a Christmas rose."

It did have that look, red ribbon in looped petals. Hardly a planet. "Perhaps a red ball with *canali* would be more realistic."

"No, 'tis perfect. May I keep this, after it's hung on the Christmas tree?"

He wanted to keep her red-ribbon ornament? "Of course."

"I want one," Jeffrey intruded, his face close to hers.

"Me too." Harriet dropped her paper star.

Bennet grinned. "A galaxy. Mercury, Venus, Saturn."

"A big yellow one for the sun." Jeffrey scrambled for the pastels.

"I want ribbon," Harriet said. "Argh, Mittens is sleeping on it."

Sure enough, the ribbon was no longer on the chair where Celeste left it. Apparently Mittens had undone the spool while they weren't looking and fallen asleep with the end of the red ribbon snuggled under her front paws.

"She looks charming, but we must share the ribbon." Celeste snipped the trimming a few feet from Mittens. The cat opened one eye, patted the ribbon under her paws, and settled down again.

Harriet giggled. "Silly cat."

"We shall have to watch her when the tree comes in." Bennet dabbed a neat splotch of glue on his paper strips. "Mittens has been known to be somewhat destructive with the Christmas tree. Once, she went mad for the shiny foil icicles my sister Jane fashioned—"

His jaw set. He'd not spoken much about Jane, but clearly the remembrance of her caused him great pain. Celeste glanced at the children. Their curious eyes indicated they'd be asking for more of the story, but it didn't appear Bennet wanted to continue it. Or perhaps he couldn't. She'd best change the topic.

"Foil icicles certainly make a shiny temptation for cats." Celeste reached to help Jeffrey with his gluing.

Gilbert scrutinized his handiwork with the pastels. "Maybe Mittens took the Star of Wonder."

Bennet grinned at Celeste. "Alas, Mittens couldn't have replaced the necklace with rocks."

"Oy, that's right."

"Unless she was smart," Harriet insisted. Jeffrey nodded.

"Her paws aren't quite that nimble." Celeste snipped more ribbon.

"Aunt Marsh likes shiny things," Harriet said.

Indeed she did. The woman owned more jewelry than the queen, it seemed, but that didn't mean she'd stolen the Star of Wonder. Celeste sighed. She'd hoped to help recover the necklace, but all she'd accomplished was excluding the children as suspects—and the cat.

"The Star will turn up." Her tone was bright for the children, but her gaze was on Bennet. She wanted to help him. Liked helping him. Liked him.

No, maybe *more* than liked him.

But she had a calling to the children at her meal house. Besides, Bennet had made clear he had no interest in marriage at this time. Even if she was tempted to turn from her calling at Lisson Grove and stay with him, to have a life here with him, he did not wish it.

*Lord, help me to follow Your will. To want Your will.*

Bennet leaned close. "Is something wrong?"

"Bennet?" His father's deep voice called from the door. "The tree is coming. But first, might I have a word in the library?"

Bennet stared at Celeste. "Actually, Father—"

"Go. We are almost finished." And his father had already gone anyway. He hadn't waited for Bennet to reply.

"Very well." He rose.

Watching him go, Celeste's heart thumped in her chest. He'd asked her if something was wrong, and it most undoubtedly was. It was suddenly quite hard for her to be content with her ministry and the life God had given her because she might be starting to love Bennet too.

"Ho!" Bennet ducked under the swinging pine garland Eldon and Perry held by either end. Dodging the festoon, he almost smacked into Rose, walking backward and issuing instructions over the swag's placement.

She laughed. "My apologies."

"None necessary." He passed Aunt Marsh, Maud, and Celeste's grandmother while they admired the hanging of the kissing bough in the foyer, and Uncle Marsh, Eldon, and Willsden congratulated one another over the garland they'd tied out of pine boughs. Every face looked cheery, and the scent of pine and sounds of banter followed him to the library. It smelled and sounded like Christmas, which made him both happy and sad.

Jane should be here too. With William Thewlis, her husband, awkward though it would have been, considering he'd been one of the footmen. They could have worked past the difficulties of it all, however, had Father been willing.

Bennet caught up to Father at the library door, and Father progressed to the window. At Bennet's entrance, Father indicated with a tilt of his head that Bennet should shut the door. "Did you find the Star of Wonder?"

No preamble. No warmth. Bennet's shoulders stiffened.

"Not yet. No intruder has been found, and the servants' rooms are clear. I've looked in every hidey hole in the house, on the chance the thief hid it to retrieve later, rather than in his chambers. The only things I've left alone are our guests' belongings."

"Don't dare search our guests. It would be better to lose the Star forever than sink to delving through our guests' chambers. Can you imagine the insult?" Father stared out the window. "It's probably long gone by now."

"But one of our guests must have taken it, Father—"

"Don't suggest such a ludicrous thing."

" 'Tis the only remaining possibility. Perhaps we should discuss who—"

"Forget the necklace, Bennet. Propose without it."

"Despite tradition?" The words popped out before Bennet could argue that he didn't even want to propose.

"We've no choice."

This was the chance Bennet had prayed for. "We do, Father. Celeste and I are in agreement—"

"Good." Father didn't sound happy as much as he sounded relieved.

"We agree that neither of us wish to wed. Celeste is most clear about it. There will be no proposal tomorrow."

Father's countenance purpled, but instead of shouting in anger, he turned to the window. "We need their money, Bennet."

He spoke so quietly, Bennet thought he must have misheard. "That cannot be true."

"My recent investments did not play out as I had hoped. We will recover in a few years, but Lady Celeste's dowry would prove most beneficial to us."

Bennet did not trust himself to speak until he'd counted to ten. Then fifteen. Anger surged hot through his veins. "I thought it mercenary enough when this arrangement was about joining dynasties, but Celeste is worth nothing more to you than her settlement?"

Father sighed, fogging the window. "You will be earl, and you require an heir. You can still be involved in your amateur astronomy efforts while you run the estate. And Celeste is both wealthy and, how shall I say, difficult to marry off. Willsden despairs of her finding a spouse when she is so engrossed in her charity."

"A noble cause. Feeding children."

"That doesn't matter, Son. Not to the *bon ton* of society. Besides, she can fund her project when she's married to you."

Not if she thought it was her calling. Not if she lived here, so far from London.

"I cannot force her to say yes."

"Her father can." Father's stern expression eased a fraction. "I'm sorry it's not what either of you want, but marrying well is your duty."

A duty Jane shirked, and paid the price for it. "When Jane left, I'd hoped—"

"I will not hear that name again." Father's face colored again. "You will propose tomorrow and wed in the spring or you'll inherit nothing when I'm dead except for the entailed properties and the burden to care for them. Just marry the girl, Son. You and Lady Celeste will survive. Make the best of it."

"Like you and Mother did?"

Bennet regretted the barb the instant it left his tongue, but he was too angry to take it back. Instead, he stormed from the room before he said anything worse.

The landing was deserted, except for a dainty maid who ducked her head and scurried away the moment he appeared. Perhaps his scowl had frightened her.

Much as Bennet wanted to disappear to his chambers at the moment or go for a bracing walk in the snow, he had a duty to his guests gathered in the drawing room. To Celeste. He hurried to rejoin her.

Jovial voices spilled from the drawing room. Forcing his jaw to relax, he entered the room, where everyone buzzed about like bees at work. In his absence, the tree had been brought in and placed in a tub of sand atop the table before the window. An open box of old decorations rested on the table alongside the new ornaments he and Celeste made with the children. Philip lifted Jeffrey so the boy could hang a paper star on a high limb, while Gilbert and Harriet placed paper cornucopias among the branches. Maud and Rose tucked golden apples into the boughs, and Aunt Marsh and Celeste's grandmother placed wooden figures from the nativity story beneath the tree. Uncle Marsh and Willsden sat and admired the others' work, and Perry and Eldon fixed slender white candles in brass clips to the branch tips.

"It looks splendid, everyone." Unlike his attitude.

Smiling, Celeste held out a tinsel star. "We saved this for you."

"Because you like stars," Gilbert explained.

It was impossible not to laugh.

Bennet took the star from Celeste's hand, but she did not let go of it. "Are you well?"

"Just reminded of what happens when one of our station does not do what our fathers tell us to do."

Her brow furrowed. "We should speak in private."

"Agreed. An hour from now in the portrait gallery?"

She nodded and gave him the star. He took it to the tree and hooked it at the top. Two years ago, the last Christmas Bennet had spent at Cheltham Hall, Jane had hung it. She'd had to reach so high she'd lost her balance, and the closest person to catch her fall was William, the footman. Jane had flushed scarlet. At the time, Bennet had thought it was due to embarrassment.

He hadn't known then Jane and William were already in love.

*Lord, may they be happy. And forgive me. I spoke to Celeste of Your power and ability to do the impossible, but I have forgotten my words already. Forgotten Your ability to hold the stars in the heavens and hold our lives in Your hands. Please help me to trust You in all things.*

A sense of peace nudged his anger to the side, not diminishing it altogether, but reminding it that it had no business taking residence within him.

Perhaps God had something in mind far different than what Bennet thought was best. Perhaps that plan had to do with Celeste.

She appeared at his elbow, "Mars" dangling from her fingers.

"Thank you." He took it and found a less-crowded branch from which to hang it. When he looked up to admire it with her, however, she was gone.

# Chapter 6

Celeste needed time alone to think, a prospect immediately made impossible when Papa followed her from the drawing room. "Celeste? Is something amiss?"

"No, Papa. I—" That was a lie. "Yes, Papa. May we speak?"

His brows knit in concern. "Come. That Green Parlor is probably unoccupied."

She took his arm, and they traversed to the elegant room. "The scene of the crime."

Papa frowned as they took seats on velvet-covered chairs. "I confess I am more than a little bewildered by its robbery, but it is best we all move past it. Cheltham assures me he will offer you another of the family's finest gems to replace the Star of Wonder tomorrow evening."

"Papa, Bennet will not give me any jewelry tomorrow. He will not be proposing."

"The rotter." Papa stood. "He thinks to jilt you? I must speak to Cheltham at once."

"No, Papa." She hurried to him and took his cold hands. "It is not a question of Bennet rejecting me. It's a matter of our suitability."

"You seem to suit well enough. Better than I expected. I've seen you two."

She couldn't deny it. "I enjoy his company. But my greatest concern is the meal house."

"You can marry *and* fund it. Don't you think you'll ever be in London again?"

Celeste's hands fell. "You told me I had to forget Lisson Grove. No longer go there."

Papa shrugged. "If Harwood is willing for you to do what you wish, so be it."

Could she truly have both? If so. . .

No, it didn't matter. "Bennet does not wish to wed, Papa. Not now. Not someone of his father's choosing. His parents' marriage was arranged, with sad results. And much as it grieves me to say this, I do not think you and Mama were happy either."

"I was." Papa went still. "She was the one who. . .who loved another. She always resented not being able to marry him."

Oh. "I'm sorry, Papa. I did not know."

He shrugged, as if embarrassed. "When I looked for potential husbands for you, I ensured the man I found did not harbor affection for another. You will not be hurt that way."

As he had been. "Thank you for that, but still. There will be no proposal tomorrow."

"I am not so sure of that." He kissed her forehead and left her.

This was not going as she and Bennet had planned. Weeks ago, they'd tried to convince their fathers they would not suit. When that did not work, they intended to spend this week speaking reason to their fathers, so there would be no embarrassment on Christmas Eve.

Instead they were right where they began. When Bennet did not propose, he and Celeste would humiliate their fathers. Regretting the unavoidable grief that would rise from the scene it would cause, Celeste made her way to the portrait gallery. The long, unheated room was papered in red silk, a vibrant setting to the numerous portraits of ancestors hung on the walls.

Dust rag in hand, a small-boned maid in a black gown and white cap paused before a woman's portrait. If the style of the blue gown of the woman in the painting was any indication, the portrait was perhaps thirty years old. The subject's hair was blond rather than gingery, but she was clearly Bennet's mother. "Hello."

"Oh! Pardon me, miss." The maid turned and bobbed, hiding her face, but not before Celeste caught a glimpse of her pale blue eyes and a lock of blond hair escaping at her temple. It was the same maid Celeste had almost collided with the night of her arrival.

"Don't allow me to interrupt—" Celeste began, but the maid scurried out of the room.

Celeste took the maid's spot in front of the portrait. Bennet's mother looked down on Celeste, a slight smile to her lips. About her neck she wore a thick silver chain, and at the end was a large round diamond. It could only be the Star of Wonder. "So that is what you look like," she murmured.

"Lady Celeste?" A female voice drew Celeste around.

"Good afternoon, Lady Marsh."

"I see you are visiting my sister Agatha. I thought to do the same." A smile curved Lady Marsh's lips. "She and I looked nothing alike. Perhaps that is why Cheltham chose her."

"Pardon?"

Lady Marsh burst into laughter. "It isn't really true. The Christmas I was seventeen, my family came here for a house party something like this one, and I saw the Star of Wonder hanging about the neck of Cheltham's mother. So aptly named, that diamond. I was transfixed by its clarity, its brilliance." Her ringed fingers fondled the hefty sapphire resting against her breastbone. "I wanted it terribly. I didn't mind that Cheltham came with it either. He was a handsome fellow. But little did I know, arrangements were in the works for a union between him and Agatha. The next Christmas Eve, Cheltham proposed and gave her the Star of Wonder. I was jealous."

Jealous enough to steal it this year? Could Lady Marsh have wandered into the Green Parlor that day, found the velvet pouch and, unable to stop herself, taken the Star of Wonder? "That must have been. . .difficult."

"I was an idiot." Lady Marsh let go of her necklace and patted Celeste's arm. "Their marriage was miserable. Arranged marriages may be done, but they can produce nothing but heartache. Oh—I did not mean you and Bennet. You two seem quite a pair, well-chosen and fond of one another."

If she only knew. "Thank you."

"Darling," Lord Marsh called from the threshold. "There you are. Why, hello, Lady Celeste. Visiting Agatha, I see?"

Lady Marsh nodded, her eyes suddenly bright with unshed tears.

"Now, now, dearest, none of that." Lord Marsh reached into his coat, tugging a handkerchief from an inner pocket near his breast, pulling something else out at the same time. He disentangled the handkerchief from the paper-wrapped pouch with hasty fingers, shoving the packet back into his pocket. So that explained the lump Celeste had noticed the past few days—something she'd dismissed as a wadded-up handkerchief. Lord Marsh glanced at her before pressing the handkerchief into his wife's hand. "Let's adjourn to our chamber, shall we?"

Lady Marsh nodded, and with a brief farewell, they made their retreat. Celeste scarcely had time to consider what transpired before the sounds of Bennet greeting his aunt and uncle reached her from the hallway. When he entered, he wore a look of surprise.

"Busier in here than I thought, but it should be quiet now."

"I hope so. I would not wish to be overheard." Celeste licked her lips. "I think someone in your family stole the Star of Wonder."

Bennet flinched, as if he'd been slapped. "I thought we were to speak of our fathers—*this* is what you wanted to discuss?"

"I hadn't. . .that is, no, but I promised to help you find the necklace."

"And you suspect my family?" He'd been hoping to talk about his changing feelings, to tell her he was not so against marrying anymore. Something about being around her—growing fond of her—had eaten away at his defenses.

But clearly she did not want to discuss their relationship. "Go on then. Who?"

"I don't know, but—" She swallowed. "Lady Marsh admitted she has long admired the Star of Wonder. Coveted it. It's a motive. Perhaps a weak one, but you must admit she collects gems like children collect pebbles."

"She's drawn by shiny trinkets, but that doesn't mean my aunt would steal from us. From me. Have you proof?"

"No, only observations. Take Lord Marsh. He's kept something in his breast pocket for days, but it just spilled out, a packet large enough to hold a necklace. What better place to hide it than on his person?"

"It could be anything."

True. "Rose also desires the Star of Wonder, remember? The children overheard Philip say he couldn't afford such a piece."

"Few can."

"Which brings me to Peregrine. He has financial constraints."

"He told you that?"

"Not in so many words."

"He wouldn't." The idea was ridiculous. "I suppose you suspect my father then too?"

Her head shook. "He is one of the only people who wouldn't have taken it, the other being my father."

"Who else do you suspect then? Why not your family?"

Her lips parted. "We deemed it a crime of planning, if you recall. The necklace was replaced with rocks, which I doubt my grandmother had at the ready."

"Pebbles that Gilbert could have left anywhere. Inspiration might have struck. What of Eldon? Your brother has gambling debts. Did you know this?"

She flushed and looked down. "Maud mentioned it."

"Selling a diamond would pay the debt, I imagine."

"You do not know Eldon as I do."

"And you do not know Perry, or Rose, or any of my family as I do." He stepped back, filling with shame. "I suppose we have just proven ourselves right. We suspect one another's relations, we think the worst, and we have hurt one another. Arranged marriages do not work."

She laughed then, but it was a cold sound. "Indeed. I tried speaking to Papa minutes ago, and while he would not listen to reason, he verified my suspicions. You weren't chosen for me because Papa thought we had anything in common. You were chosen because you were available and your heart was not attached to another."

"And you were chosen because we need your dowry."

Her wide eyes met his gaze. "Oh."

He was sorry at once, but couldn't form the words.

"I suppose tomorrow we will be forced to adjourn to the Green Parlor, where you will not propose, and we will embarrass our fathers by not becoming betrothed."

"Right." The word came out strangled. He bowed formally. "Good day then, Lady Celeste."

"Bennet."

He paused at the door. "Yes?"

Much as he felt as if a hole had been shot into his gut, he didn't want to leave her. But he didn't know how to make things right.

She shook her head. "Never mind."

She didn't know how to make things right either.

He'd been correct when he'd first returned home a few days ago. This Christmas would live in memory as the worst of his life.

# Chapter 7

The cold, dark morning of Christmas Eve, Celeste awoke with an ache in her chest. She hadn't celebrated a festive Christmas since Mama died, but after the frivolity of the past few days, she'd anticipated today's fun and joy more than she'd expected. Now, Christmas seemed something to be endured, not enjoyed. Making polite conversation with everyone—people she'd told Bennet she suspected of robbery—held little appeal. Tonight they would feast and receive carolers, and then she and Bennet would dash everyone's hopes and announce their refusal to marry.

It would not go well. Lord Cheltham and Papa would be disappointed, if not furious. Few would be cheerful Christmas morning when they attended church, and they'd all feast again, making a pretense of civility, but Lord Cheltham would probably not protest at Papa's indubitable decision to return home on Boxing Day.

*Lord, I'm sorry. I'd hoped to persuade Papa of my wishes. . .my wishes. . .*

A hot tear snaked down her cheek. *I thought they were Your wishes too, but perhaps I was wrong. Can I be married and support Lisson Grove at the same time? In my desire to have things my own way, have I been closed to Your will?*

It was too late now. Bennet didn't want her anyway, especially not after she'd suspected his family members.

Donning a warm wrapper over her linen nightgown, Celeste walked bare-footed to the window and pulled back the draperies. Not a single star was visible in the still-dark sky. Perhaps they were shrouded by clouds, but they were still there. Bennet had reminded her of that. Just like the God who created the stars, they were constant, still shining, although she could not currently see their light.

*I know You are with me, God. Forgive me. I pray Bennet will forgive me too.*

She rang for the maid, determined to dress and be available at the first opportunity to apologize to Bennet. He may not want her as his wife, but she could not leave things as they were between them. She could not bear to lose his friendship.

Breakfast did not provide an opportunity to see Bennet, however, much less speak to him.

"He's inspecting the bridge repairs," Lord Cheltham announced as the group gathered in the drawing room midmorning.

"Celeste?" Maud sat close to her on the settee across the room from everyone else. "Is something wrong?"

"I was thinking of the Star of Wonder." It wasn't a lie. Everything she and Bennet had discussed and done together were wound together in her thoughts. "I think. . .someone in this room stole it. There is no other explanation."

"How dreadful." Maud clutched her throat. "Are you certain?"

She nodded. "I offended Bennet by suggesting one of his family took it. I must apologize for how I spoke when he returns."

"You will. Don't fret."

Eldon dropped to Maud's feet. "Fret about what?"

"You, in part." Celeste smiled at her brother. "Maud told me of your wager."

Eldon rolled his eyes. "It will be well, Celeste. I've learned my lesson. No more gaming tables for me, and Papa will loan me the funds. I'm to repay him within three months."

"So you don't need to sell anything to repay your loss?" Like a stolen necklace?

"Not a thing." Eldon kissed Maud's hand.

Relief filled Celeste's chest, but a sense of urgency still coursed through her veins. Shouldn't Bennet have returned by now?

Luncheon came and went, and the younger members of the group joined the children playing in the snow. Peregrine and Rose helped Harriet scoop snow for a snowman, and Eldon and Philip helped the boys build a snow fort.

Gilbert waved at Celeste. "Where is Cousin Bennet?"

"I do not think he has returned from inspecting the bridge."

Peregrine looked up from the snowman. "He's been back and gone again. Something about seeing to a tenant."

Avoiding her, more like. Celeste plastered a smile on her face and joined the others at the snow fort.

They played until their feet were numb and their noses and cheeks turned pink, but every face was bright with excitement when they re-entered the house at three o'clock for a treat.

"Chestnuts!" Jeffrey cried, squirming with delight. Sure enough, the rich, earthy aroma of roasting chestnuts filled the house. They divested their damp outer garments and adjourned to the cozy drawing room where a cheery fire crackled in the hearth. Servants tended the chestnuts while footmen carried in urns of tea and warm chocolate. While Rose helped Jeffrey with his chestnuts and chocolate, Celeste assisted Harriet. To her surprise, Maud, who'd never been one to notice children, offered Gilbert assistance and then grinned as the children bustled to admire the unlit tree.

"The little ones are fun to watch, aren't they?" For a fleeting moment, Maud's hand fluttered to land on her stomach.

"Maud?" Celeste stepped closer. "Are you—?"

Maud nodded, grinning and tearing up at once. "I am waiting until tomorrow to tell Eldon. We came here happy with our life in London, but being here, celebrating Christmas, seeing the life you will have with Bennet, has rekindled a desire in Eldon and me to settle into a house in the country and focus on family. I am sure you think it silly of us, since you prefer your life in London."

"I don't think it silly at all. In fact, I envy you. A life in the country is not to be mine, Maud. Bennet and I are not marrying. I'm sorry I didn't tell you, but I didn't wish you to be burdened. He and I hoped to convince our fathers quietly, but it hasn't worked. Then I realized I have grown to love Bennet, but he does not return my feelings. . . ."

She couldn't finish.

Maud gripped Celeste's hand. "How dreadful. I'm so sorry, darling."

"I—I am getting what I wanted, after all. But Papa will be so disappointed in me."

"He will get past it, I am sure. And until he does, you will stay with us. As long as you like. And every Christmas. I know your papa loves you, but his Christmases are dour affairs."

Celeste laughed, as Maud intended. "This is a merrier way to pass the holiday."

Maud's arm went around her. "Next year, we shall have chestnuts and singing."

"And a baby." Her niece or nephew.

"And a baby."

Gilbert ran toward them, his eyes almost frantic. "Tonight we get to light the tree. Then carolers and punch. And St. Nick will visit."

"First a rest." Rose eyed the mantel clock.

The children protested, but their thundering footsteps hurried upstairs to the nursery. Celeste followed them up the stairs, tired, but with no time to rest before dinner. She changed into a silk gown of holly berry red, and her maid twisted her hair into an elaborate coiffure, topped with a delicate wreath of ivy and tiny Christmas roses.

"Beautiful, my lady," her maid said.

"Thank you. Enjoy your evening. I hear tell there will be a celebration in the kitchen."

The maid nodded her thanks, and Celeste hurried downstairs. Bennet could not miss dinner. *Lord, grant me the chance to speak to him. But no matter the outcome, I thank You for the reminder You've shown me to trust You. I want to do that, Lord.*

As if in response to her prayer, Bennet was the first one she saw in the drawing room, resplendent in evening finery, conversing with Peregrine. He was the picture of ease except for the muscle clenching in his jaw. He was still angry then. Justifiably so. Nevertheless, she must tell him she wished an audience with him later. She took a step.

"Lady Celeste, don't you look festive." Rose stopped her progress.

Maud, elegant in a gold gown, nodded. "Quite, dear. Come sit with us."

*Trust. God will provide another opportunity.* Celeste joined them until they adjourned to the dining room. The smells of roast beef, onion, and spices met them before they reached the door.

"What a feast!" Grandmama proclaimed.

"Tomorrow we shall sup on roast goose," Lord Cheltham replied. "Traditional Christmas dinner here. Bennet's favorite meal."

Bennet did not meet Celeste's gaze, but focused on his food. Celeste picked at hers, certain it was tasty, the way others went on about it through to the dessert course.

"I shouldn't have another bite. I am full to bursting," Lord Marsh said as he scooped another spoonful of treacle tart slathered in cream.

"Yet stop we must, for the carolers will be here shortly." Lord Cheltham dabbed his lips with a napkin. "Bennet informed me the bridge repairs should be complete by now." He waited for Lord Marsh to finish his dessert and then smiled. "Summon the children to light the tree," he instructed a footman.

Excellent. Celeste could catch Bennet alone, or at least, alone enough to request his company on the balcony. Once in the drawing room, however, the children arrived. "Without Mittens," Jeffrey lamented, "because she will play in the tree, so she's closed in the nursery."

Lord Cheltham took a taper to one candle on the tree. Then two footmen took the task from him, lighting each candle in slow, silent progression, whilst another footman stood to the side with a pail of water, if necessary. The gentle, flickering candlelight glittered off the tinsel star and each little ornament they'd made.

Celeste inched toward Bennet. " 'Tis beautiful."

"It is." His gaze didn't leave the tree, but the muscle worked in his cheek again. "You might wish naught to do with me, but we should speak. In private. One last time."

*One last time.* Her swallow pained her throat. "When?"

He couldn't answer, with the loud knocking from downstairs. "The carolers—"

"Come!" Harriet grabbed Bennet's hand. Jeffrey imitated her and took Celeste's fingers, and they were drawn into the joyous progression to the Hall to welcome the carolers.

The singers numbered a dozen, equal parts men and women, dressed in capes and warm hats and mufflers. Lord Cheltham had been right: their voices were glorious as they sang one carol after another in rich harmony.

At length, an ancient-looking silver kettle arrived, carried in by two sturdy footmen, accompanied by the aromas of apple and cinnamon, clove and lemon. Lord Cheltham took up the ladle and spooned generous portions of the wassail into silver cups, passing them among the carolers and the party.

Taking her cup, a flutter of nerves skittered up Celeste's torso. Once the carolers left, everyone would expect her and Bennet to withdraw to the Green Parlor. *That* would be when they could speak in private—much as she'd hoped to avoid even going to that room, because once she and Bennet went there and came out without being betrothed, well, it wouldn't be pleasant. Panic welled in her chest, but she determined to trust God. There was no other way.

She glanced up at Bennet. To her surprise, he smiled at her. "Try the wassail."

Her throat was clogged with anxiety, but she lifted the cup to her lips and tasted the sweet beverage.

"Lord Harwood?" Papa pulled Bennet away, leaving Celeste alone for a brief moment before Peregrine joined her. The groups conversed until the cups were drained and Lord Cheltham clapped his hands.

"One more song, I pray, carolers?"

"It would be our pleasure, m'lord." The carolers' leader, a large grizzled man, bowed. " 'The First Nowell.' "

It was one of Celeste's favorites. At the mention of the star, however, she bit her lip. She would never think of this song, or stars, the same way again. For this Christmas, her life had changed. No matter what happened, she would endeavor from here forward to seek God first, trust Him, and yearn for His path—

One of the carolers wasn't signing. Her head tilted down as she inched behind the others, but there—a quick flash of her face as she scanned the room before she bent down to scratch Mittens behind the neck. Mittens? Wasn't she shut in the nursery?

Celeste had seen the woman before. Her cheeks weren't rosy from cold, and she wore no muffler around her neck, although she wore a cap and a serviceable gray cape. The cape cut away in the back to accommodate a bustle that wasn't there, revealing instead a plain black skirt—the dress of a servant.

It was the maid she'd seen over and over the past few days, always quick to dart away.

She was no caroler. No true servant of Cheltham Hall either, to sneak out like this, hiding among the carolers.

And around her neck, just above the collar of her cape, she wore a thick silver rope. Celeste couldn't be positive it was the Star of Wonder, but she couldn't let this woman leave. The carolers finished on a flourish and she reached for Bennet, but his gaze fixed on the woman too.

He hurried to the woman and took gentle hold of her elbow, forestalling her exit with the carolers. "Wait."

She ducked her head. He swiveled around to better see her face. "Jane?"

"You're here." Bennet did the only thing he could think to do. The one thing he'd wanted to do for more than a year.

He pulled her into an embrace. "Welcome home, Jane."

She was stiff in his arms, unresponsive, but Bennet didn't care. She was healthy. Home. *Thank You, God.*

"What is this? Jane?" Father's voice was strangled.

Bennet loosened his hold on her, but kept one arm steady about her shoulders. "Yes, Father."

Jane's chin tilted to a proud angle, but tears began streaking down her cheeks. "Fret not, I shall be leaving."

Father stared at her, his face leached of color, his lips working but no sound coming out. Before Father could work up the words to send Jane away, Bennet had to know: "Are you well? Are you—"

Bennet saw it then, shining silver. "No, Jane."

Biting her lip, she unfastened the button of her cape, revealing the Star of Wonder glittering against the plain gown of a maidservant.

"Oh, dear," Aunt Marsh muttered.

"Who is that person?" Celeste's grandmother asked.

"His sister. The one who married the footman." Maud tried to whisper.

Rose clapped. "Time for bed, children. Papa and I will see you upstairs."

"Aw." Gilbert pouted. "I don't wish to go to bed."

"Saint Nicholas cannot come if children are not in bed," Philip warned.

That was good enough for the children to bustle toward the door. Jeffrey scooped up Mittens. "How did you get here, silly kitty?"

Willsden moved to follow them, beckoning his family. "Perhaps we too should retire."

"I'm fatigued as well." Perry offered Celeste his arm. Both of their gazes landed on Bennet as they passed, as if communicating their prayers for him. Then Celeste paused and withdrew her hand from Perry's arm. Everyone, including her family, froze in place, watching as she crossed to stand before Jane.

She held out her lace handkerchief. "I am glad you are well, Mrs. Thewlis."

Chin trembling, Jane took the handkerchief. "You've heard of me? Yet you speak kindly?"

"You're Bennet's sister. He has been anxious for you. Now he knows you are well, and I'm most grateful to you for coming home."

Bennet knew then. He would never admire a woman the way he did Celeste. Never feel he deserved her.

Jane's tears renewed. With trembling fingers, she swiped her face with Celeste's handkerchief and then unclasped the Star of Wonder, letting it drop into Bennet's palm.

He took her fingers before she could pull them back. "I know you wish to go, but first, tell me why you came." Bennet didn't need to ask why she took the necklace. She and William needed money, no doubt.

She stared at the ceiling, blinking back additional tears. "I missed you. Father said never to return, but I—I thought no one would see me. But when I came five days ago, there was so much commotion, I couldn't satisfy my curiosity with a quick peek so I—took a maid's dress so I could wander about a bit. I only planned to be here an hour or thereabouts."

Ah yes, there had been something about a missing maid's frock, hadn't there? "You came a few days ago and have been stuck here ever since because of the snow. And you took the Star of Wonder."

She nodded, crying again. "I saw the velvet pouch in the Green Parlor. I knew what was inside it. I thought of Mother. And how much I missed her. . .and home. I found some rocks in the hallway and tucked them inside the pouch. I'm sorry, Bennet. I shouldn't have taken *that*, but I wanted something of hers to recall her by. It was wrong."

"You did not take it for the money?" Bennet's throat felt full.

"William earns a good wage in a bookshop. We aren't well off, but we're happy." She looked up at Father, her jaw set. "He's worried sick, I'm certain. I was to meet him at the coaching inn in the village that first night, but the snow started and I couldn't leave. Then there were men watching the house, and I heard you say the bridge was out."

"So where have you been? The footmen searched the house."

"They didn't search the passage." She glanced at the panel in the wall, the one that hid a door leading to the kitchens and the nursery.

"It was sealed."

"Not well, and the cat followed me out." Her lips twitched. Then they quivered as tears started afresh. "Now that I've answered your questions and returned the Star of Wonder, I must go. I don't mean to interrupt your *tradition*." She tilted her head at the necklace.

"Tradition is important." Father found his voice at last. "But perhaps this is the year to start a new one."

"Father?" Bennet had never seen him like this, hesitant, blinking back moisture.

He stood before Jane, hands at his sides. "When you left, my heart broke. I cannot bear to endure such again. Seeing you tonight—I do not want to part like that again. I did not give you my blessing, but I should not have denied you my love. You are welcome here. You and. . .William. Will you forgive me?"

Every eye went wide, but Jane's the widest of all. Then she threw herself into his arms.

Bennet shut his eyes. He'd prayed for this, hoped for it. God had answered this prayer in an unexpected, wonderful way. God had a way of accomplishing the unexpected, didn't He? Bennet turned to Celeste.

Before he could speak, a tall man burst into the hall, followed by the flustered butler. The newcomer looked a little different without his footman's livery, but there was no mistaking the man's identity. He was William Thewlis, Jane's husband.

"My lord," the butler called. "Forgive me. William would not be put off."

Jane slipped from Father's embrace and took his hands. "It is well, William. We are welcome here."

"We are?" He faced Father. "My lord?"

It seemed no one in the room breathed. Bennet took a step forward. "Hello, William." William's slight bow was polite, but his gaze flitted to Father's.

Society might never accept a footman as the husband of an earl's daughter, but could Father accept it? At last Father moved, stepping toward the wassail bowl. His chin quavered, proving this was no easy task, but he lifted a cup toward his daughter and son-in-law. "Welcome, William. And Happy Christmas. Wassail?"

# Chapter 8

Celeste's spare handkerchief was a soggy mess of happy tears. Jane had come home. Lord Cheltham had reconciled to her and welcomed her husband. The future might be difficult, but there was hope, and tonight, celebration.

The camaraderie was palpable, warm and vibrant as everyone greeted Jane and William. Rose and Philip returned, and it was impossible not to cry a little more when Rose and Jane embraced.

When Bennet drew alongside Celeste, she looked up at him, memorizing the look of wonder and amazement on his face. "What a Christmas gift."

He smiled down at her. "Having Jane back is all I wanted this year. Well, almost."

"Almost?"

"Did someone say gifts?" Lord Cheltham raised his voice. "I have one of my own to give. Bennet, may I have a moment of your time?"

Bennet glanced at Celeste before leaving the Hall with his father.

"It seems we are giving presents early." Lord Marsh retrieved the paper packet from his breast pocket—the lump she'd seen in his pocket—and handed it to his wife. "This is for you, my dear."

She opened it, revealing a diamond necklace. " 'Tis gorgeous! My own Star of Wonder! I shall call it The Christmas Star." Lady Marsh fluttered her lashes at him.

"I received a star too." Rose smiled up at Philip and adjusted a deep blue silk shawl shot with silver stars around her shoulders. She hadn't worn it before adjourning upstairs. It seemed Philip had given his wife an early gift too.

"I have a gift for you, Eldon." Maud's voice was far too low for anyone to overhear but Celeste. Celeste smiled as Maud drew Eldon toward the hearth. In a moment, Eldon was grinning from ear to proverbial ear.

"Celeste?" Papa's touch on her elbow was light. "I should like to give you something too."

Her gift for him, a set of Dickens's novels, was wrapped and hidden upstairs in her armoire. "If you wait a moment, I will fetch your present—"

"This is not that sort of present." He took her to sit in the hard chairs against the wall. "This is one I should have given you long ago. The gift of my listening ear. You've voiced your protests, your dreams, your thoughts to me, but I never *listened* to them. I realized tonight, even before Jane was revealed, that Cheltham's break with his daughter caused unbearable pain. 'Tis not the same circumstance, of course, but I do not want you to loathe me, poppet, so I pulled Bennet aside and released him, as I release you. You do not need to marry, and when we return to London, I will make a donation to your meal house so you and the Brewers may continue through the New Year. But if you wish to marry Bennet, I will also make a donation for you to start a meal house in County Durham. I am certain there must be hungry children here too."

"Papa." No other words would form.

"You are my daughter. I will not lose you, Celeste."

She could do nothing but wrap her arms around him. "Thank you, Papa. I—"

"Celeste?" Bennet's gentle voice broke through the hall, hushing each conversation. "May I speak to you? In the Green Parlor?"

The Green Parlor, site of the traditional proposal. Celeste's heart lurched. She felt, rather than saw, every eye on her as she rose and walked toward him on shaking legs.

Bennet smiled and took her arm, linking it through his elbow.

"Where are they going?" Grandmama asked the room at large. Someone spoke quietly to her. "Oh yes, *there*. I know what's coming next."

Unlike Celeste. She hadn't an inkling what would happen in the next fifteen minutes.

Celeste's heart was thumping in irregular time when Bennet shut the Green Parlor door behind them. The room had been prepared for them, with a blazing fire in the hearth and a tray of beverages and sweets on the table by the sofa. Pine swags and red ribbons festooned the mantel and oh! Someone had moved the kissing bough from the foyer and hung it from the room's chandelier.

It was the perfect setting for a proposal and celebration, but here was where they would say their goodbyes.

"Bennet, I—"

"You were right," Bennet said at the same time, his tone not at all nervous like hers. "Go on."

She clenched her hands at her sides. "I am sorry I said what I did about your family and the necklace. I did not intend to pit your family against mine in a match of suspicious activities."

"But you were right." He smiled, as if amused. "Someone in my family did steal the Star of Wonder."

He teased, but it didn't put her at ease. "I regret that conversation."

"I do too, but not the part of it where you shared your suspicions with me. You were right to do so. Didn't we agree to find the Star of Wonder together?"

She nodded. "But I was unkind. I—what do you regret?"

"I regret growing defensive. I regret allowing my hurt to twist into anger when I spoke to you. And I regret saying our discussion was proof arranged marriages cannot work."

"It was a broad generalization, perhaps."

"No, Celeste. You see, I have come to realize that you and I are not our parents. We are friends. *Friends.* My parents were not well-suited, perhaps, but I do not think they tried to be friends, for their sake, or mine or Jane's. They resented one another, and the world knew it."

She thought back. "Perhaps my parents tried at one time, but not in my memory. They were polite to one another in the coldest manner possible. Even when she was dying, they did not seem to try."

"I would try, Celeste." He stood before her, so close she could see his pulse pounding in his neck, just above his starched white collar. "Rather, I would not need to try to care for you. I already do."

Her mouth went dry. "You do?"

He reached to touch the tendril of hair curling from her temple. "If we married, I would forever be your friend, make you feel supported and listened to, encourage your work at Lisson Grove, prioritize you and your needs and wants."

Her breath hitched. "What about your desire to wait to marry?"

"I fell in love with you, Celeste." His lips twitched. "When we met, we had no intention of ever being more than partners in the fight to change our fathers' minds. Then something changed. I have never met anyone who listens to me the way you do. Whom I want to listen to. Whom I never wish to part from. I don't know when it happened, but I desperately love you, Celeste."

"I love you too, Bennet. I do not know when it started. Cutting down the tree? Or at the telescope?"

He chuckled. "I always knew astronomy would pay off in the end." Then, as he took her hands in his warm ones, his expression grew serious. "After our decision not to marry, with all of your reasons against it, *could you* marry me?"

She couldn't resist a saucy smile. "Are you asking?"

His grin returned. "Before I do, you must know. Your father pulled me aside tonight, releasing us from his expectation. Then my Father did the same thing. While he was emphatic he didn't wish me to jilt you, he understood our desire not to wed and said he'd make things right with your father."

"My father said the same to me, so you are free."

"I do not wish to be. But recall my father's interest in your dowry. I don't want it, but it's part of our fathers' arrangement."

"That's their business. I am concerned with you and me."

"Me too. Once I am earl, it will mean time away from Lisson Grove for you, time away from the Royal Observatory for me, but I will not stand in the way of your work. We will adapt to our responsibilities, with God's help."

"The Brewers are more than capable of running the meal house in my absence, and I must trust them, and God, to continue the work. And Papa suggested I start a meal house in Durham. If I marry you, that is." Suddenly, she felt shy.

He released her hands and dropped to one knee, gazing up at her with love shining from his eyes. "This was not our plan, but I am delighted our plans failed. Will you marry me, Celeste? Live in a house full of telescopes and stars? And plans for children's meal houses? And love?"

"And love."

He smiled up at her.

"Yes, Bennet. Yes—"

He was standing, her face in his hands, before her next breath. Then she couldn't breathe at all, the way he was kissing her.

She was dazed and still breathless when he lifted his head sometime later. "We've made good use of the kissing bough."

She hadn't even realized they'd stood beneath it.

He stepped out of the circle of her arms. "One more formality."

Telling everyone? Oh—the necklace. He pulled it from his pocket and undid the clasp.

"Will you wear it?"

"With pride." She turned so he could fix it about her throat. It felt heavy, but a good weight. It felt. . .right.

God had sent a star to the magi to lead them to Jesus. God perhaps used this Star of Wonder to help Celeste see that she had not been open to His path for her, and in the process, led her to desire to trust Him more.

The clock on the mantel struck twelve. Bennet grinned. "Happy Christmas."

"Happy Christmas, my love."

Arm in arm, their smiles brighter than any diamond could ever shine, they left the parlor to share their joy with their loved ones.

**Susanne Dietze** began writing love stories in high school, casting her friends in the starring roles. Today, she's the award-winning author of a dozen new and upcoming historical romances who's seen her work on the ECPA and *Publisher's Weekly* Bestseller Lists for Inspirational Fiction. Married to a pastor and the mom of two, Susanne lives in California and enjoys fancy-schmancy tea parties, the beach, and curling up on the couch with a costume drama and a plate of nachos. You can visit her online at www.susannedietze.com and subscribe to her newsletters at http://eepurl.com/bieza5.

# The Holly and the Ivy

by Rita Gerlach

# Chapter 1

*"She hoped for a good man who would wed her at Christmastime—while the ivy and the holly hung in bowers over doors, and candles sparkled in window casements."*

*A Winter Day in 1900*

Lily Morningstar could not sleep. Eyes open, she placed her arms behind her head and sighed. The clock on the bedside table ticked away at three in the morning. Moonlight mingled with the last flurries of snow and floated through the window, bathing the room in translucent light. She stared at the ceiling in hopes the quivering shadows would cause her to drift off, but her excited mind would not settle.

Pushing back the covers, she swung her legs over the side of the bed and stood. Barefoot in her night shift, she hurried across the floor. The planks were cold, and she lifted her heels to tiptoe. She kept her journal in the sleeve of her valise, amongst snowy-white handkerchiefs and opaque stockings. Her heart leaped in her chest. She had to get the events of the night down in writing before they faded.

She took from a rosewood case the fountain pen she had bought in the Smithsonian gift shop and poised it over the page.

> *The moment I saw him, I had a knowing within me—he and I were to be together. I sat enraptured, listening to his discourse on the manuscripts he had discovered, studied, and preserved.*
>
> *I wore my hair up atop my head, tiny twists to frame my face. The tight lace collar surrounding my throat, the bone corset hugging my ribcage, all caught my breath. I sat by a drafty window. A tender flow of winter crept through it and caressed my face. I looked at the brochure an attendant had handed me at the door and pushed my coat from my shoulders.*
>
> *Dr. Stapleton concluded his lecture, followed by enthusiastic applause from the audience. I stood with the others. My head dizzied, my vision blurred, and all went dark. When I came to, I lifted my eyes to see him bending over me, his eyes riveted upon my face as if he were studying me as he would an illumination.*
>
> *To see him in the flesh proved his photo did not do him justice. Tall, robustly built, with hair the color of Christmas chestnuts, eyes warm as a hearth fire, he sent my heart to pacing. Shaky, I blamed the swoon.*

She lifted the pen and paused to ponder the gleam in his eyes. Her thoughts drifted deeper to the letters she kept in a stationery box under her bed at home. His handwriting was beautiful but in a manly kind of way.

He'd enticed her to reveal her true self, but she never did. She feared his rejection, believing she was in no way near to his class of person. Would he not view her as crass and unsophisticated?

> *His gaze drew me in when I saw him lower his lids and heard him whisper, "Thank God, you've come to." He possessed a type of chivalry any woman would appreciate. The words slipped from his lips like drops of honey. He meant them. Most men would have been irritated by my faint, their pride treaded upon by such an interruption. But not Andrew Stapleton. He was different.*

She placed the tip of the pen between her teeth. Eventually, he would find out she was a simple American girl without a dime. She could not help but write what she saw in his eyes.

> *He tried to convince Miss Twittle he should take me back to the hotel, chaperoned, of course, by her. She insisted it would be otherwise, and in some sense, I had to agree. My mother would be appalled I got into a gentleman's cab—a stranger no less. It would have been a lovely ride as it had begun to snow, so much so I was sorry to leave him. I could see in his eyes that same awe of the beauty that winter brought in a city of concrete and brick.*
>
> *Yet for all her objections, Miss Twittle conceded to Dr. Stapleton's kind offer, and we left for the hotel—after he rescued me from an icy puddle. The train home will seem slower than usual and the house quiet when I walk through the door. Mother, Papa, and the boys will be fast asleep. I'll tell Mother about it after breakfast. I'm curious about her reaction, as well as any advice she might give me.*
>
> *I hope Papa will not mind I've asked Dr. Stapleton to visit us Sunday afternoon provided the snow is not too deep for rail travel. Now I must close, to think about the events of the day, to sleep, and to dream of Christmas to come.*

In a room inside the Smithsonian Institute, Lily opened her eyes to a male voice. "Miss, how are you feeling? Better now?"

She blinked against the glare of the oil lamp on the table beside her and looked up at the most handsome brown eyes gazing at her. Startled, she scooted back.

"Dr. Stapleton."

"No need to be alarmed, Miss Morningstar. And please, call me Andrew."

"You know my name? Who told you?" *What a silly question. It had to be Miss Twittle or those gossipy girls.*

His brows lifted. "Everyone. You're a popular young lady."

Lily shook her head. "It has nothing to do with being popular. They're courteous, that's all." She put her hand to her forehead and tried to sit up. "I need to go."

He surprised her when he eased her back against the pillows on the settee. "Miss Twittle said you must wait."

"What room is this?"

"The anteroom."

"How did I get here? I remember feeling dizzy. . .and then I. . ."

"You fainted. I carried you in here."

She stared at him a moment. "Where is Miss Twittle?"

"She'll be back momentarily. There are ladies outside the door keeping an eye on us."

Lily looked toward the door. There they were, that group of giggles and frills she had been talked into accompanying. Four in all, they were younger than Lily, with enough age between them to distinguish her as the more mature. Their eyes were riveted upon her and Andrew. One smiled and waved.

"I hope they stay there," Lily said. "Let them in and they'll suffocate me. One bottle of smelling salts is enough, but four would be too much."

He stood, unlatched a window, and pushed it open. "Speaking of suffocating, you need fresh air. Let me know when it gets too cold."

Lily drew in a breath. The frosty air passed into her lungs and revived her more than smelling salts. Her corset forbade the air from going deeper, but she refused to entertain the idea of another faint. One was embarrassment enough.

His eyes shifted to the doorway. "Are those ladies your relations?"

Lily's eyes widened. "Thank goodness, no. They're a club. You know, a small-town ladies' club. They call it the Hopeful Homemakers Ladies' Society."

A sympathetic smile spread across his face. It had to be the word *hopeful* that caused it. When Lily first heard the name of the club, she'd found it witty. Each girl had a hope chest. Each swore they would marry before the age of eighteen. Lily was now twenty and two, and her dream was to be recognized as an exceptional female writer—married to a man who treated her as his equal and supported her talents.

Along with that dream, she hoped for a good man who would wed her at Christmastime—while the ivy and the holly hung in bowers over doors, and candles sparkled in window casements. The churchyard would be covered in snow, the stained-glass windows subdued by a powder-gray sky.

The door banged against the wall, and Miss Twittle blew into the room with a damp cloth in hand. "Stand aside, sir," she demanded.

"Beg your pardon," said Andrew. "Is there anything else I can do to help?"

Mimie Twittle threw one hand on her hip and pointed with the other. "You can close that window. You want Lily to catch pneumonia?"

"Certainly not." He pulled the sash down and turned the latch. Lily coughed. "I should send for a doctor." He charged to the door. The girls moved back.

"Stop," said Miss Twittle. "I know you were the speaker tonight and highly respected, but your attention to my charge is somewhat out of the ordinary."

He challenged her with a frown. "Madam, I feel some responsibility for the lady's welfare."

"Admirable, but surely you've seen this kind of thing before. She's not dying, for goodness' sake."

"No, but she might need a doctor."

"Doubtful. I'll handle this, if you don't mind."

Lily pressed her hands against her cheeks. Miss Twittle made matters worse by treating him so high-and-mightily. She clicked her tongue and put the wet cloth on Lily's forehead. "You poor, poor girl. So embarrassing."

"I'm perfectly all right. I'll never wear this torture device again," Lily whispered. She handed the cloth back.

"Corsets give you the petite shape you desire, and it is expected of you." Miss Twittle replied to Lily in the same low tone so as not to be heard.

"I don't care if corsets are in fashion—it's high time they weren't. *The Rational Dress Society* has been saying so since 1881."

"Don't read such falsehoods, Lily."

"If I had been of age, I would have joined in their protest against how these things can deform the body."

"Then why did you wear one?"

Lily inched closer. "I won't after tonight."

Miss Twittle straightened up. "Dr. Stapleton."

He walked over, having stayed at a distance.

"The next time you give a lecture, be sure they do not heat the room so high. I blame the temperature for this."

"I blame those blasted corsets you ladies wear." Had he heard their whispers?

Miss Twittle's mouth dropped open. "For shame!"

"Excuse me for mentioning it, but it's true," he said. "Still, I'll take your advice and think of the ladies' comfort the next time."

Miss Twittle's face flushed. Lily resisted the urge to giggle. "I agree with Dr. Stapleton, Miss Twittle."

"Such bold talk, the both of you," she replied.

"They are constricting. I wouldn't be shocked if my ribs are cracked." Lily handed Miss Twittle the empty glass. "May I have more water?"

Narrowing her eyes, Miss Twittle grabbed the glass. "I can if Dr. Stapleton can be trusted alone with you another five minutes."

"I'm sure he won't kidnap me and whisk me off to his hideaway, Miss Twittle. Besides, I know how to take care of myself, and the girls still linger in the doorway."

With a *harrumph*, Miss Twittle stood and stomped to the door. "I'll send his assistant in." Through the door she went, taking a gust of air with her. She moved the girls away, reproving them for gawking.

Andrew smirked. "She won't find him, and she'll be gone longer than five minutes. Does that bother you?"

Lily brought her hand to her throat, her lace collar coarse against her skin. "I've no reason to be. I'm sorry for all this. I've interrupted your evening terribly."

"Not terribly."

"You must forgive me if it did."

"It's happened before. I'm used to it."

"Are you?"

"I am, especially in summer. I was finished anyway, and people were on their way out."

Their eyes held for a moment. "I found your lecture interesting." She would have said more, but she had to be less coy, less talkative.

He gathered up some papers and shoved them into a briefcase. "Perhaps next time, I should forbid corsets—and hats should be set aside."

"You'd have a rebellion on your hands if you tried."

"Except from you, Miss Morningstar."

Oh, how his smile swept her away. He had the most handsome set of teeth, even and white, his lips tempting. Although he was a young man, his face had a few manly creases at the corners of his eyes. Lily found them distinguished. He wore his dark hair to the tips of his ears and along the edge of his collar.

She moved to the edge of the settee. "I removed mine. I mean my hat. . .I removed it."

"It's by the door when you want it."

A pause passed between them, and Lily felt compelled to change the subject. At ease with him, she wanted to hear from his own lips more than his letters had revealed. How, she did not know, but it might be her only chance, for there was no guarantee of seeing him again.

"I'm glad to have seen the manuscripts you brought. They're beautiful."

"Yes. . .beautiful." His eyes skimmed over her face. "You know—you have pretty eyes, Miss Morningstar. They remind me of Rossetti's painting *The Beloved, The Bride*."

Voicing his opinion of her eyes surprised her. Weren't Englishmen more reserved in their compliments to ladies? His letters to her were formal. His way of speaking in public too. Was he sincere? She never thought her eyes anything but ordinary.

"I've never seen a Rossetti painting. I doubt my eyes are anything like their subjects'."

"They are magnificent. I hope your husband or fiancé wouldn't mind me saying so."

"I'm unattached."

"I see." He gathered the last of his papers. "You're shocked I speak so freely."

"A little."

"I apologize, but I'm sincere in my compliments."

"Dear me," she breathed out. "You're quick to speak your mind. But I'm no different. My father tells me I'm too outspoken for a girl."

"Mine taught me to speak my mind. He was a vicar, and he gave me my love for *The Book of Kells*. It was only until recently I developed a fascination for American papers."

"And your mother loved being a minister's wife, didn't she?"

He gave her a curious look. "Yes. She's in heaven with my father."

"I'm sorry."

He made no reply. "What station were you born into?" she asked. "That is what the English call it, isn't it? You don't have to tell me if you don't want to. I'm just curious, and I'd say you were born into the upper class, your father being a minister and all."

"My father was also considered a gentleman."

"You must have grown up in a comfortable house with loving parents. That's all one really needs."

"All I'll say, Miss Morningstar, is I'm a simple Christian man who loves the written word."

"I love it too—in fact, I'm a writer." Had she given herself away, given him a hint as to her identity? She glanced at the floor. "What I mean is I enjoy reading and writing."

"You're not a novelist?"

She shook her head. "Nowhere near it."

He looked over at the door. The girls had slipped into the hallway and were complaining about the wait. "Your Miss Twittle is taking her time."

Lily shrugged. "I don't mind. I have enjoyed talking with you. I just wish you weren't leaving."

He gave her a curious look. "You know, the way you talk makes me think we've met before. Women are not so at ease with me."

"Oh, I'm terribly sorry. I say the wrong things sometimes. Mother says I'm overly curious and—"

Miss Twittle pushed her way into the room. "Your mother is right, Lily. I apologize for overhearing, but these are things a young woman should not be discussing with a stranger."

Lily shut her eyes tight.

"Here, take your water." Miss Twittle thrust the glass in front of Lily.

A gray head peeked around the doorjamb. "Time to lock up, if you folks don't mind."

Miss Twittle whisked her charges together. "Hurry, girls. Hats and coats. That includes you, Lily."

Lily stood and stepped toward the door. "I'm coming." She turned to Andrew. "Thanks for an eventful evening."

He gave her a warm smile. "It was a pleasure."

Lily's palms began to perspire and she grabbed her gloves. She moved to the door. A janitor pushed a dust mop across the floor and drew off his cap. Wispy gray hair fell forward over his forehead. " 'Night, miss. Be careful. It's snowing to beat the band out there."

She pulled down her hat, ready to meet the icy snowflakes. An arm reached around her, and Andrew's hand yanked at the door handle. "No need to worry about Miss Morningstar, Sam. I'll see to her safety."

Lily rummaged through her beaded bag and sighed.

"Is something wrong?" Andrew asked, pulling on his coat.

"I seem to have misplaced my room key."

"Do you have a way there?"

"I've my two feet if Miss Twittle can't find a cab."

"Walking is out of the question. The weather has turned."

"I walk all the time. It isn't far. I'm staying at a hotel. Someone is bound to be up. It is, after all, the Season, and hotel clerks are up much later than any other time of year."

They headed down the steps to the street. Miss Twittle ushered the girls to the curbside and spoke to the driver of a horse-drawn cab. The cabbie looked over at Andrew and pointed to him.

"As you see," Andrew said, "I have a driver. Why pay for a cab? Allow me to take you. We can all try to fit in."

"Miss Twittle would not approve."

"Miss Twittle must have a bit of upper-class snobbery in her."

"That's likely."

"I doubt you'll find a cab this time of night in this weather."

Lily buttoned her coat. "Then we'll walk."

He shook that lovely head of dark hair. One lock fell over his forehead as it caught snowflakes. He shoved it back. "You're made of tougher stuff, Miss Morningstar. The girls are complaining."

She headed for her party, Andrew keeping up with her. "I don't see any other cabs out on the street."

Hearing this, Miss Twittle lifted her chin and looked along the curb. "One will be coming along directly. I told the one who brought us to pick us up. He's late, but will be here."

"Then I'll wait until he does." Andrew gave her a slight bow, and Miss Twittle moved the girls away.

Lily yanked on her gloves and buttoned them at her wrists. "Thank you for waiting for us, and again for tolerating my faint." Her shoes sank into the snow as she headed on.

He stopped her. "I can't help but worry, Miss Morningstar. The weather is bad, and it's late. . . Ladies should not be out. . ."

Looking up at the sky, Lily smiled. Large snowflakes drifted and whirled, touched her face, and landed on her lashes. "It's snowing harder."

"Miss Morningstar," Miss Twittle shouted. "Come away. Your behavior is not to be seen."

Lily gave Andrew a sidelong glance then lifted her chin and looked at Miss Twittle. "No, Miss Twittle, I suppose it's not."

# Chapter 2

Out on the street, a shiny black cab drawn by a tall dabble-gray steed waited at the curbside. The horse bobbed its head and blew out its nostrils, sending a plume of fog into the chilly air. Lily looked up at the sky again. Snowflakes touched her face and made her smile.

She turned to Andrew. "You must be a wealthy man to afford such a roomy cab."

Andrew motioned to his driver to remain on his perch. There was no need to climb down when he could open the door himself. "The Institute provided my driver. Poor man had to wait all this time." He looked up at the smartly dressed coachman. "Sorry to have kept you waiting. I hope you aren't too frozen."

The coachman touched the brim of his high-top hat.

Andrew turned to Lily. "The offer stands, Miss Morningstar. For you and Miss Twittle."

Miss Twittle forged ahead with the girls, who continued to complain of the cold, the snow falling on their cheeks, and the late hour. Finally, a cab drew over to the curbside, pulled by an overweight horse.

Miss Twittle pushed the girls forward. "Come along, girls. Lily, do not dawdle."

"Can't fit you all in, madam," said the driver. "I've room for four."

"Four?" Miss Twittle huffed. "Ridiculous. We'll squeeze in."

"Four, ma'am. One will have to wait for another cab, or walk."

Miss Twittle threw up her arms and moved the girls toward the cab door. "You girls will have to go on without me. Looks like Lily and I are going in Dr. Stapleton's cab after all."

"No, Miss Twittle," cried one of the girls. "I'm scared to go without you."

"Dr. Stapleton can fit two of us in his cab," said Lily. "Lucy and I can go. With Dr. Stapleton with us she'll have no reason to fear a thing."

Miss Twittle narrowed her eyes. "Lucy, you say? The both of you with Dr. Stapleton? It would be improper. I'm coming with you, Lily, and the girls will follow."

The driver looked down, the crop in his hand, and snow on his hat and the shoulders of his coat. "The name of the hotel?"

Lily glanced up at him. "The Petersen Boardinghouse on Tenth Street."

Once Miss Twittle had gotten the girls situated, she took hold of Lily's hand to navigate the slippery walk. Dr. Stapleton also extended his hand to the older woman and she grasped it. Reaching the cab, he helped her inside. "I suppose having a gentleman with us is a rather good idea after all," she said.

Close to the step leading up to the cab, Lily's right foot slid across a patch of ice. As she fell, Andrew caught her around the waist and hauled her up against him.

He smiled, and she looked up at him. For a moment, their eyes locked. He kept her balanced and then slowly set her down. "That was close," he said.

"I didn't see it. Lord, I'm likely to have a real mishap before the night is over."

"Not with me around."

Miss Twittle frowned. "Dear me, Lily. I hope I can get you home in one piece. Do be careful where you're stepping."

Lily looked at Andrew. "Sorry. It was clumsy of me."

"Are you hurt?" he asked.

Lily drew in a breath. "I don't believe so. I feel so embarrassed. First a faint and then a spill."

"It could have been worse."

"You're right. Last winter, I fell skating and bruised my elbow something awful."

Slowly, he drew his arm away from her waist and whispered, "I haven't seen this shade of red on a lady's face in a long time."

The hansom cab drew away from the curb, followed in the rear by the other. The horse did well, stepping over the snow in the street. At least he didn't slip. The idea left Lily worried he might. Then what would they do?

A tinge of pain shot through her knee. It had always been a problem for her since she was a child and had fallen out of an oak tree in the yard. One wrong move and the thing would ache. Under her soaked stocking, it throbbed. Her shoe had gone into the water beneath the ice. It too was soaked through.

"Does it hurt much?" Miss Twittle couldn't seem to keep her hands still and kept adjusting Lily's scarf.

"I'm fine, Miss Twittle. Thank you for caring." Lily inched back in the seat.

Miss Twittle folded her arms. "If it weren't for your fainting and this blasted weather, we'd be at the hotel by now."

"Don't you love snow? It makes for a perfect Christmas."

"It makes for freezing temperatures, precarious outings, and flu."

Lily looked at Andrew. By the look in his eyes, she knew he was concerned for her. "Do you agree with her, Dr. Stapleton?"

"Please, call me Andrew."

Lily widened her eyes. "Really. . .Andrew?"

"It's what I prefer and, to answer your question, I agree with you both. It depends on the circumstances. Its beauty is enjoyable indoors near a fire or alongside a frozen pond. Yet on a city sidewalk, it is not without hazard—your fall, for example."

Lily felt her face get hot, but when he gave her a playful wink, she smiled. She tried to make the best of an awkward situation and laid a carriage blanket over her legs. With her shoe and stocking ruined from icy water, her skin began to sting.

"England was blanketed in snow when I left," said Andrew. "Have you ever seen ice floating in the North Atlantic?"

Lily adjusted the blanket and shivered. "I've seen photographs. I imagine it is beautiful, all white and blue in the moonlight."

Miss Twittle glowered and shifted in her seat.

"What about you, Miss Twittle?" Andrew asked, seated opposite the ladies.

Miss Twittle plopped her hands on her lap. She wore the thickest wool gloves Lily had ever seen. Not like her own feminine kid gloves lined with lamb's wool, closed with pearl buttons.

Miss Twittle pressed her lips and replied, "I'm no world traveler, as you should be able to tell. I wouldn't like the roll of the sea."

"No doubt about it," Andrew said. "It's a pretty rough crossing."

Miss Twittle turned to Lily. "You two should not be on a first-name basis, you know."

Lily opened her mouth to speak, but Andrew stopped her. "My apologies if that is not acceptable in America."

Miss Twittle pursed her lips. "Lily knows better. Don't you, Lily?"

"Well, yes, but if it is an English custom, I wouldn't dare do otherwise." Her answer caused the woman to raise her brows and Andrew to lift a corner of his mouth.

"You're full of surprises, Miss Morningstar," he said.

"Not really," she answered. "I'm actually pretty dull." She looked out the window. "Ah, the hotel can't be much farther."

Andrew looked out as well. "The Petersen. Your love of history must have drawn you to it."

She wouldn't dare tell him it was all she could afford, she and the other ladies. She looked out the window. "I avoid walking past the room where President Lincoln died. It makes me sad. I bet you're roomed at one of Washington's best."

"I'm staying at The Willard."

"Oh," she breathed. "The Willard is grand. I've never had the privilege. You see, this is my first time in Washington—overnight, I mean. Father brought me here once as a child to see the zoo and then to the Smithsonian." She sighed. "Dear me, there I go again, talking too much."

Miss Twittle snorted, and her eyes shot open. "I must have dozed off." Within seconds, she was snoring again and Lily laughed.

"She'll wake the whole town. Is that a dog howling?" Andrew said.

Lily flung her gloved hand over her mouth. "I do believe it is," she giggled.

As they rode down Wisconsin Avenue, Andrew leaned forward. "I'm curious why you came tonight. What interest do you have in old papers?"

"I write. I thought I could learn of something that could be developed into a romance."

"A romance?"

"Why, yes, especially at Christmastime, when men are apt to write a sonnet or two to their lady loves."

"You mean Valentine's Day."

"That too. Isn't it true, love letters and poems penned by famous Brits are in London's library?"

"Yes, but—"

"I should love to see those letters and poems. To think of seeing the actual hand they were written in." She looked at him. "Your profession must be rewarding."

He nodded, and Lily wondered if she were boring him. Their conversation ran in circles; she was repeating her thoughts. Maybe if she focused on his interests instead of hers, he'd admire her. She could fictionalize their meeting in her little column. Every woman in her small town would gobble up such a story. And perhaps some New York editor would read it and make her an offer to buy the piece. Her heart pumped with the thrill of it.

She looked out the window at the falling snow, the bright red ribbons hanging from lamp poles and streetlights. Wreaths were on the doors along with gold and silver ornaments. If only she could have a winter wedding, one at Christmastime, when the church would be decorated in holly and ivy, aglow with red and green candles.

"You're lost in thought, Miss Morningstar," Andrew said.

"I'm sorry. I was admiring the decorations. What did you say?"

"I replied to your question—about my profession, that yes, it is rewarding."

"Um, I must say I learned how important old documents are from your lecture, and how unfortunate it is that some people burn their papers before they die. My imagination runs wild when I think of what we've lost. I've often wondered what was in Jane Austen's papers. It's too bad her sister burned them after her passing."

"I suppose some people feel their diaries might cause a scandal. Or that the past should remain in the past."

Lily pondered his words. "You should know the answer to this, since you're an expert in these kinds of things. I'd like to understand why people are clandestine with romantic correspondences."

"Because they're private. You think they should not be?"

"Yes, of course, while a person is living, but afterwards perhaps not—as long as it doesn't cause a scandal, as you say."

He fixed his eyes on her more intently. "I'm curious. What caused you to have an interest in such things? It's unusual that a woman would speak so openly about love. Love is usually spoken of behind closed doors or in the shadows."

"I can't agree," she said. "It's openly spoken of in stories and poems."

"Well, yes, you're right about that. There's the Song of Solomon. It speaks of Christ and his bride, but clearly shows the love between a man and wife."

"Have you ever studied old manuscripts of the Bible?"

"I had opportunity to see the *Book of Kells* while in Dublin."

"There's a book in our library about the *Book of Kells*. You're fortunate to have seen it. Rarely will the world see such a masterpiece."

Miss Twittle leaned her head against the wall of the cab, and her lips flapped with an exhale. Lily said to Andrew, "She's positively worn out."

"Speak softly so as not to wake the poor woman."

A pause passed between them. Lily bit her lower lip. She couldn't hold back any longer. "I want to tell you about some letters I found."

His brows arched. "What kind of letters?"

"Love letters. I found them in a box in a secondhand shop. There was also a Christmas ornament painted with holly and ivy in the box. The shopkeeper let me have the whole lot for a dollar. I haven't the slightest idea who they belonged to." She narrowed her eyes. "I have an insatiable desire to find out."

Andrew looked intrigued. "There are no names with these letters?"

"Not a single one."

"An address?"

"There are no envelopes, but the script is masculine."

"He wished to remain anonymous in order—"

"To cause desire in the heart of the lady?"

"Or maybe he thought she would reject him outright if she knew who he was."

"Yes, that is clearly possible."

"Wouldn't unsigned letters speaking of love frighten you?"

"I'm not sure. It would depend on what is written." She looked at him with a plea. "Would you like to see them? You're an expert in manuscripts and might find them exceptionally interesting. You might even be able to tell me who they are from and who they were written to."

A moment's pause and Andrew narrowed his eyes. "It has dawned on me that you, Miss Morningstar, are a mystery as well."

Lily lowered her eyes. "You've figured me out, haven't you?"

"I have. Are you prepared to confess? I won't let you out until you do."

"I won't go until you tell me what you know."

He leaned forward. "Have you forgotten you wrote to me about this?" He moved closer. "We've been writing to each other for the last year."

"I didn't want to come right out and say."

"I wish you had told me from the start."

"I'm sorry."

"And you wrote to me anonymously. You baffled me from the start."

"If you recall, I signed with a sweeping L."

"For Lily. You wanted to remain a secret. For what reason?"

"It was a whim."

"There was no reason why you shouldn't have signed your name. I would have kept up our correspondence. There's nothing wrong in a man and woman writing to one another, is there?"

"I've been taught it is inappropriate, unless two people have. . .an understanding."

He smiled. "And when we met tonight, you aimed to continue this charade for how long?"

Her throat tightened. "I thought if you knew, you'd laugh at me."

"Why would I do that?"

"Because I'm a middle-class American girl of no importance."

A corner of his mouth lifted. "Not to me. Now that I know who you are, I feel as if we've known each other a long time. I always look forward to your letters. In fact, I've kept them all. They are interesting and intelligent."

"Finally, I did something right," Lily said. "I have a tendency to doubt my actions."

He tapped her gloved hand with his. She did not withdraw. "Are you always hard on yourself? Where's your faith, Miss Morningstar?"

"I have faith in God. How much faith, only He knows. A mustard seed is enough for Him. It's in myself I have little."

Miss Twittle shifted, and Andrew settled back. "I remember one letter in particular about the history of the Potomac and the settlements along it."

"I remember writing it. You enjoyed that one?"

"Very much. Coming to Washington gave me the opportunity to see it for myself, at least a portion of it."

She lifted her eyes. "I've kept your letters too."

They smiled at each other. Then Lily shivered.

"You're cold?"

"I'm wet."

"Give me your leg."

Surprised, she drew back.

"Come on, lift it over to me. You'll catch your death of cold."

Cautious, Lily did as he bade her. He held her ankle. "Does it hurt?"

"My ankle doesn't. My fall aggravated an old knee injury."

He looked at her shoe. "You'll have to put this by a fire. It's completely soaked."

Lily bit her lower lip as he slipped it off and set it beside him on the seat. Then he took off his gloves and rubbed her foot to warm it. "Is that better?"

"Dear me!" She jerked her leg away and pulled the carriage blanket tighter around herself.

"It was a deep puddle."

"Yes, a puddle, not a pool."

"If your stockings are soaked, you should take. . ."

She shook her head. "I will not."

"I'll look away. Do it before your keeper wakes."

He turned his head to the window, and Lily reached under the blanket. True, the stocking was soaked through. She could have wrung it out and had enough water to fill a tumbler. Though she shivered and her skin prickled with the cold, she could not do as he suggested. Instead, she curled into the warm wool and looked him straight in the eye.

"Dr. Stapleton?"

"Andrew, please."

"Andrew—promise you will not tell anyone you removed my shoe," she whispered.

# Chapter 3

Gaslights glowed on the first level of the Petersen Boardinghouse. Both cabs drew up in front, and the girls raced up the steps to get inside. Lily nudged Miss Twittle. She grunted and sat up.

"We're at the Petersen now," Lily told her.

Andrew got out first and extended his hand to the older lady. Lifting her chin, she took it and waited on the sidewalk for Lily. Someone had shoveled the snow off the red brick. Miss Twittle called out, "Miss Morningstar, please hurry. It's freezing out here."

Lily looked on the floor, on the seats, and then out at Andrew. "My shoe?" she whispered. Andrew turned to Lily's chaperone.

"Miss Twittle. Your charge has suffered a knee injury, and her shoe is soaking wet. I insisted she remove it, so don't be angry with her. Neither of us would want her to catch her death of cold, now would we?"

Miss Twittle's jaw dropped. "Of course not, but was that really necessary?"

"More than necessary."

Miss Twittle stepped away, and Andrew handed Lily the soaked shoe. Grimacing, she grabbed it and then, to her surprise, he threw his arm around her waist and lifted her out into his arms. He carried her up the stairs and through the door. The night clerked peered at them over his steel-rimmed glasses.

"The lady has taken a fall. Call for a doctor."

"We don't have a phone, sir, and no carrier this time of night."

Miss Twittle drew in a breath and weaved in and out around Lily and Andrew. "Dear me, this is awful. Mr. and Mrs. Morningstar will never trust me again. Poor Lily. I suppose you should bring her upstairs, Dr. Stapleton."

Andrew turned back to the clerk. "The lady has misplaced her key. Have you another?"

The man reached behind him, took a key off a hook, and handed it over.

Up the carpeted stairs he carried her while the girls looked on with wide eyes from the landing. Huddled together and speaking under their breath, they followed. It certainly was a sight to be seen, and a few guests looked out their doors when they heard the many pairs of feet shuffling up the staircase.

The desire to tighten her arms around Andrew's neck grew. Lily smelled the shaving cream he used and felt the stubble that had started to grow on his face.

Miss Twittle opened the door of Lily's room and waved him inside. Like a mother hen, she fluttered about the room, straightening pillows on the bed and grabbing a blanket to put over Lily.

As Andrew set Lily down, her bare foot peeked out from under her hem. She drew it back. "Don't worry. I've seen one before," Andrew said. "I'll call on you tomorrow to see how you are."

"We're leaving at first light," Miss Twittle said. "You don't need to."

"Then I'll call on you at home, Miss Morningstar. We have letters to discuss."

Lily could not take her eyes off him as he walked toward the door. To see him in the flesh, to hear his voice, to be close to him, sent her heart flying. More than anything, the way he carried her into the building and up the staircase made her wonder if she were falling in love. She wasn't at all like the googly-eyed girls lingering in the hallway. She knew how to behave without anyone knowing how fast her heart was beating.

"Wait." From her bag, she took out her calling card and handed it to him. "The address is on the back."

Smiling, he glanced at the back of the card. "Hmm. It's an address familiar to me."

"Yes, I know." She sat straight up. "I hope it isn't too far for you to travel from the city. It's a small town, but the train comes twice a day."

"It doesn't matter how far it is," he said, tucking the card into his breast pocket.

"If you can, come for Sunday evening dinner. We can continue our discussion, and I'll show you the letters."

His warm eyes focused on her. He leaned forward and said, "I'll see you Sunday, Miss Morningstar. Perhaps we can solve this mystery of yours together."

Lily paced the floor of her bedroom. Her sore knee bothered her and she bent forward. "Why did I have to be so clumsy?" she said to Titus, her calico, crouched at the foot of the bed. He narrowed his eyes and purred. Lily ran her hand over his ears. "You don't understand, do you? Still, you're a comfort to me. You haven't left my side since I got home."

A carriage rumbled by the house. Lily peered out the window to see if Andrew had arrived, but the rattling contraption drove on. Bits of snow lay scattered over the lawn. Most of it had melted, but the moonlight caused the remaining crusts to sparkle. The red brick walk coming up from the street could be seen against the starkness. There were no patches of ice. She smiled and turned away.

She opened the box on her dressing table. The letters were neatly drawn together by a faded red ribbon. The ornament looked new, the holly green as any evergreen bough she had seen. The ivy coiled delicately among ruby berries. "Who could have owned these?" she whispered. "I want to know, Lord, though I don't really know why it's so important to me. You've brought Andrew and me together through them. Maybe that is the reason?"

Outside in the hallway, a ruckus between her two younger brothers drew her away. Frustrated the little mischief-makers might ruin the evening, Lily opened the door and took them both by the ear. The pair squirmed and called out for their mother.

"Listen, you two. Behave. Stop this fighting or I'll tell Father."

"Wiley started it," Henry, the youngest, said.

Eight-year-old Wiley twisted away. He looked up at Lily and frowned.

"Is this true, Wiley?"

The fair-haired scamp glared and refused to answer.

"Well?"

"I guess."

"You'll both go to bed with no supper if you keep this up. Understand?"

Her mother, Edith Morningstar, appeared at the foot of the staircase. "What's going on, Lily? Are the boys misbehaving?"

Lily hurried to the steps. "Can't we have dinner without them just this one time, Mother?"

"You're afraid they'll embarrass you?"

"They'll do more than that. Look at them. They haven't even changed their clothes or washed their hands and faces. How on earth do they collect so much dirt in a day?"

"They're boys, Lily. Don't worry, I've arranged with Cook to have the boys eat their dinner early in the kitchen. They'll be upstairs when Dr. Stapleton arrives."

"I love my brothers, but you understand."

"I most certainly do." Her mother came up the steps, called the boys to her, and moved them down the hallway. "Wash your faces and hands, the both of you. And change your knickers. Grass stains on the knees, day after day. Then go down to the kitchen and have your supper."

Henry sidestepped Wiley. "Yes, Ma."

Wiley whined. "Do we have to eat in that ol' kitchen?"

"Do as you're told or no dessert."

Lily rushed back to her room as the boys scampered off. She glanced at her clock on the bedside table. He would arrive in less than fifteen minutes. That's all the time she had to finish dressing. "I don't know why I'm nervous, Mother."

"Come over here. You missed two buttons on the back of your dress." She turned Lily around to fix them. "No corset?"

"I'll never wear one again."

"Well, you have a pretty enough figure without one."

The boys marched out of their room. "We're clean, aren't we, Ma?" said Wiley.

She inspected their hands and faces. "Good enough. Go downstairs and eat."

Henry jutted out his chin. "Lily promised us a nickel if we do as we're told."

Lily narrowed her eyes. "I never said that."

After her mother scolded the boys, Lily turned them by the shoulders and sent them downstairs. "I'll have Papa give you each a dime," her mother called to them.

"Really, Mother. You shouldn't give in to them."

"I know, but just this time—for you, Lily."

"What has Mabel made for dinner?"

"A roast. I hope Dr. Stapleton likes crab soup. It's the first course."

"I don't remember Mabel ever making crab soup. Today is not the day to be trying something new."

"I've no idea what English gentlemen prefer for their evening meals. You don't think he'll have any objections, do you?"

Lily turned. "I don't think so. I read people in Britain prefer beef."

"I should have had Mabel make a leek soup."

"Mother, don't worry. He's a mind fixed on one thing—his work."

Her mother shrugged. "I've yet to meet him, but I doubt what you're saying is true, not with you sitting across the table from him. You look pretty, Lily."

"He'll probably want to scoot out of here as soon as he can."

"Are you ashamed of your family?"

"No, Mother. It's just that Dr. Stapleton is educated, and we're ordinary."

"Either you aren't listening or you're ignoring what I said." Her mother pinched Lily's cheek. "I'm sure you have sparked his interest, you and your ordinary ways."

"Me? I doubt it, at least not in the way you imply. He's been courteous, as any gentleman should be. But our mutual interest is what has attracted him. I'd never measure up to the elegance and charm of an English lady."

"You're too hard on yourself. You're the prettiest girl within miles. Besides, he'll find your little stock of letters interesting."

Lily picked a garment up off the floor and laid it over a chair. "They may be old, but they might not be of any importance. I probably shouldn't have written to him so often and made so much of them. I think the holly and the ivy ornament might be worth more than the letters."

"It's a miracle it has lasted this long," her mother said. "I know. We'll hang it on our tree." She checked her hair in Lily's mirror. "What was his reaction when you told him it was you who had written to him?"

"He was rather unaffected."

"You think?"

"I had expected shock."

"Then I was wrong."

"About what, Mother?"

"About how I warned you he would think you were forward and stop writing. Since he's continuing the acquaintance, I was mistaken."

Lily closed the clasp on her pearl bracelet. "It's turned out all right. He wouldn't have accepted my invitation to dinner if he felt differently."

Heavy shoes clumped up the stairs, and Bridget, their maid, appeared in the doorway. "The gentleman's cab has pulled up out front, Mrs. Morningstar, Miss Lily."

"He's early." Lily tucked a curl behind her ear, pinched her cheeks, and started down the staircase with her mother.

"One of us needs to check on dinner, especially the gravy."

"Yes, Mother."

"It's got to be right for your sake, Lily. Mabel isn't always on top of things, and her gravy the last few nights has been lumpy."

From what shadow Mabel had slinked out from was unclear. "There's nothin' wrong with my gravy, Mrs. Morningstar."

"I want to be sure everything is perfect, Mabel. You check it, Lily."

Lily's eyes went wide. "But I should greet Andrew at the door."

"As lady of the house, I will greet him. No, go on with Mabel and make sure everything is as it should be."

The doorbell buzzed. Lily's heart pounded. Reluctant to leave, she stepped through a side door that led downstairs to the kitchen.

# Chapter 4

"Something smells good." Lily grabbed a spoon and dipped it into a copper pot. She blew on a bit of crab soup and tasted it. "Too much salt," she said after a pause.

Mabel threw her hands on her hips. "It's just right, Miss Lily."

"Taste it, Mabel. You always use too much salt. You should let us salt our own food."

Henry pushed his soup bowl aside. Wiley looked up from his plate. "Lily's right," he said. "It tastes like seawater."

Henry giggled. "That's where crabs come from. It's seawater soup."

Mabel frowned and stamped her foot. "Oh, you can't insult me like that." Her hands flew to the back of her apron and she untied the strings.

Lily set the spoon down and gave Mabel an apologetic look. "I didn't mean it as an insult, Mabel. Let's try to fix it."

"I've had it up to here with everyone criticizing my cooking." With a grunt, Mabel tossed the apron onto the floor.

"I was only trying to be helpful. Remember, you told me that potatoes absorb salt? Wouldn't that help if we tried that?"

"Oh, so you're the expert now, are you? Well, you go ahead and do it yourself." With heavy shoes clunking across the parquet floor, Mabel reached for her hat and coat.

Alarmed, Lily hurried to the disgruntled cook. "Don't leave, please. Where are you going?"

"Home."

"But you can't. We have a guest for dinner."

"It's all made."

"What about the boys?"

"Those little hellions can finish feeding themselves." Mabel squashed her hat over the top of her bun. She moved close to Lily and poked her with her finger. "You'll have to serve the dinner yourself."

Dazed, Lily watched Mabel stomp out the back door. It slammed shut and she jerked. "Oh no. What am I going to do now?"

Lily stood in the foyer, smoothing down her dress. The sitting room door was open. Flames flickered in the hearth. Evergreen draped the marble mantelpiece. She hoped she could catch her mother's glance from where she saw her sitting by the fire. Lily could hear every word and hesitated to hurry into the room.

"What kind of name is Stapleton?" her mother asked. "And what kind of doctor are you?"

"My surname is English, ma'am. I'm a doctor of history."

"Have you enjoyed your stay in America?"

"I've only had opportunity to see a small part of your country. What I have seen, I've enjoyed."

"My side of the family, the Farlanes, have been here since the Revolution."

Lily's eyes widened and she bit her lower lip. *Oh no. She's about to go on and on about the Revolution and end up insulting Andrew.*

"Farlane—that's a name one doesn't hear too often. Are you related to the Farlanes of Pennsylvania?"

"Yes, just over the Maryland border on the way to Gettysburg. How did you know?"

"I've read some of Captain Farlane's papers."

"Really? I knew my uncle wrote something or another about the Civil War, but to know you have actually read something he wrote is surprising, and very gratifying, to say the least."

"Then my time spent reading through some of the Smithsonian's archives has been worth my time."

Lily sighed with relief.

"Uncle Christopher lost an arm at Gettysburg," her mother continued. "My aunt has his uniform hanging in an armoire in their bedroom upstairs. It's still dark blue, and the braiding is like spun gold. She has his pistol and saber too."

Suddenly, Andrew stood. "Miss Morningstar?" His eyes were fastened on her.

Lily took a step forward. "I'm sorry. I didn't mean to eavesdrop."

With a wave of her hand, Lily's mother motioned to her. "Lily, come inside and greet our guest. I explained to Dr. Stapleton that you were checking on dinner. Everything fine downstairs?"

Lily nodded.

"Your family has an interesting history," Andrew said to her.

Lily's mother poured coffee into Andrew's cup. "I was telling Dr. Stapleton about our Farlane relations."

"Mrs. Morningstar, is Captain Farlane still living?" Andrew asked.

"I'm afraid not. But my aunt is still with us, living in the same house they lived in when they were first married."

"She's a Civil War widow?"

"I suppose, in a sense, but they didn't marry until after the war. The way she tells it, theirs was a whirlwind romance. He swept her right off her feet, if you know the expression."

Lily moved farther into the room. "I need to speak to you, Mother. Please excuse us, Dr. Stapleton."

Graciously, her mother stood from her chintz chair and smiled at Andrew. "My husband should be arriving home any moment to keep you company." Then she stepped out of the room into the foyer.

"Close the door," Lily whispered.

"What on earth is wrong? You're as white as a sheet."

"Mabel left."

"What?"

"She put on her hat and coat and left."

"Oh dear. Why?"

Lily shrugged. "She said she wouldn't stay here to be insulted. I told her the crab soup was too salty and she should add potatoes to correct it. The boys made fun of it."

Wiley and Henry stepped out from behind Lily. "It was terrible, Ma. But we ate the roast beef," Wiley said.

They looked so innocent, even Lily felt bad for them. "Can we have dessert?" asked Henry. "You said we could if we behaved."

"No. Go to your room. You know better than to insult people. Oh, Lily, what are we going to do without Mabel?"

"I'll correct the soup, don't worry. The beef is cold by now. We could make sandwiches." She pinched her brows. "There's nothing else."

Her mother looked appalled. "Serve sandwiches to Dr. Stapleton?"

"I can do it, Mother, and I promise I'll do it properly."

"There are no mashed potatoes or green beans?"

Lily shook her head. "There's a nice loaf of bread."

"That's all? I'm at my wits' end, Lily."

"Don't be upset, Mother. You'll make things worse if you do."

"How can you be so calm?"

"What makes you think I am? I'm devastated. I might not ever see or hear from him again after this muck up."

"Dear me, Lily. What's he going to think of us leaving him alone in the sitting room while we're out whispering in the foyer? On top of that—sandwiches."

"I could make them open-faced."

"And risk him and your father spilling it on their clothes?"

"What else can we do? Besides, I've no doubt Andrew's manners would not allow it."

"I'll go back in and explain. You go on. Call Bridget and tell her to serve. She can't cook a whit, so that's out of the question. You're the next best thing, dear, even though you have such limited experience in the kitchen."

Lily drew up her shoulders. "With candlelight the food looks better." She turned to leave. "I hope you haven't overestimated me."

"That is to be seen, dear. Now don't forget, the soup is to go into the Spode tureen." Sighing deeply, Lily's mother craned her neck to look out the side window. "Where on earth is your father? He should've been home by now."

Lily stepped to the door leading to the kitchen. She stopped at the jingle of a harness and the bray of a dray horse. Her mother hurried to the front door and opened it. "It's Mr. Beale's wagon, and your father is with him."

Lily stood beside her mother and watched while her father and Mr. Beale, the town's woodsman, went to the back of the wagon and hauled out something enormous wrapped in a canvas sheet.

"We've plenty of firewood. What's your father up to?"

"It's obvious, Mother. Papa does this every year."

Her father barreled through the front door, dragging the wrapped bundle with him. The family spaniel came out of hiding, leaping and barking over the excited voices of Lily's brothers as they raced down the stairs. His hat sat askew on his head, and his cheeks puffed out. He grinned and tugged until the great width of an evergreen gave way through the door.

Lily's father stood erect and brushed off his coat. "Isn't it a beaut, Edith? Tallest tree on the lot."

"It's lovely, dear. You're late." Her mother looked somewhat dismayed.

Lily helped him with his coat. He took it from her hand and shook the snow off the shoulders.

"You're making a puddle in front of the door, Papa," Lily said. "Did you remember we are having a guest for dinner?"

"Ah, no. I don't believe I did. Sorry I'm late." He tossed his derby onto the hat rack. "I couldn't resist bringing this tree home. The minute I saw it I knew it was our Christmas tree. Paid a good price for it too." The boys circled around the tree in awe. "It's a big one, isn't it, boys?"

Lily tugged on his sleeve. "Papa. Mabel has left—"

"Go get the tree stand, boys."

Lily stomped her foot. "Papa!"

He looked at her. "What is it, Lily?"

"Our guest is in the sitting room by himself while we're out here."

"Well, call him out."

Lily huffed. No doubt with all this commotion, Andrew thought them low on the social scale, overly talkative, and a tad crazy, compared to his English friends. And they had left him alone. Add discourteous to the list and the chasm between their two worlds would widen.

She forced back tears, balled her fists, and shook her head. A pin came loose from her hair and dropped onto the hardwood floor. "Oh! Tonight is not at all what I had hoped for."

Turning on her heel, she headed back to the sitting room. She had to give Andrew a good reason why she had left him all alone.

Andrew sat in Mr. Morningstar's best lounge chair. The fire in the hearth quivered and heightened the color of his hair and the clothes he wore. The tips of his hair brushed along his collar without pomade and a stiff cut. She watched him turn the page with one finger. His eyes were transfixed. What had he taken from the bookshelf? A novel? A book of poems? She stepped forward. The hem of her skirt swept along the rug. He looked up and stood.

"Your parents have a fine library," he said. "This copy will be of some value someday." Carefully he closed the book and slipped it back into its place. Lily recognized the blue-jeweled cover and worn corners.

"My father's Civil War book. It's his favorite." She looked back toward the doorway. The boys were dragging the tree to the other side of the foyer, her mother scolding them for getting the branches too close to her favorite painting.

Andrew smiled. "Lots of Christmas cheer in your home today."

She stood in front of him. "I apologize. The evening has not gone as expected. Our cook went home, which means my mother and I are left with supper, and it won't be at all what I was hoping for. The boys are being rambunctious. My father comes home late dragging an evergreen into the house. My mother is—"

Andrew looked out into the foyer. "I should like to meet your father and brothers. Is it just the two boys or are there more?"

"Wiley and Henry are all Mother can handle. And you hear our spaniel out there." She pointed to the doorway. "Infernal creature doesn't give us a moment's peace."

"But you love them all just the same."

"Of course I do. I'm just—"

Andrew grabbed her hand and held it. "Lily, I'm not disappointed. In fact, I've enjoyed every moment I've been here. I cannot tell you how solitary my life is without the sound of children, without family and moments like this. You've nothing to apologize for or to worry about."

Her eyes filled. "I thought you'd be put off by us."

He laughed. "Put off? I'll eat bread and butter on a paper dish if it means staying with you."

Her heart leaped, and she lowered her head. "Do you mind a light supper?"

He touched her chin and raised it. "As long as it isn't blood pudding or kidney pie."

She scrunched her nose. "Ugh. Never."

His smile deepened. "Good."

"It won't be as fancy as what you get at The Willard."

"I'm bored with the food at The Willard. Can I help?"

"No, you're the guest. I hope you like roast beef sandwiches and crab soup. It hasn't quite caught on in America, but I adore French mayonnaise on sandwiches. We have apple pie for dessert."

"Well," he said, lifting her hand to his lips, "bring it on, Lily Morningstar, and save seconds for me."

He kissed the top of her hand, and a rush of pleasure raced over her. She slipped her hands over his lapels, eager to pull him close and kiss his cheek. Instead, she pulled at him with a light laugh and took him out into the foyer. Andrew shook Mr. Morningstar's hand and met the boys. Then, adding to Lily's growing fondness of him, Andrew assisted her father with the Christmas tree and set it into its wooden stand.

With her heart lightened, she left with her mother, determined she would prepare a huge platter of the most scrumptious sandwiches ever to be eaten on God's snowy earth—something even the chefs at The Willard would praise.

# Chapter 5

Lily's father sipped his soup, paused, and looked over at her mother. "Pass me the salt, dear. This soup is rather bland."

"It tastes fine to me, Albert." Her mother handed him the silver saltbox. "How about you, Dr. Stapleton? Is it bland?"

"Not at all, Mrs. Morningstar."

Lily smiled to see her mother's face beam. "We were afraid you wouldn't like it."

"Mother, we wouldn't have served it if that were true," Lily said.

Andrew fixed his eyes on her. "I hope one day I'll have a wife who knows how to cook food like this. Did you make it?"

Lily looked at him. He knew Mabel had, but oh, how sweet of him to suggest it had been her doing. "It's a wonder bachelors don't starve without wives to cook for them," she teased.

Her father cleared his throat.

Andrew gave her a challenging grin. "We get by. There are always restaurants."

"Yes, and cooks for hire."

"When I marry, if that is what my wife wants, she'll have any cook of her choice."

"Sounds expensive."

"One can always have a budget and stick to it."

"My father has one. Don't you, Papa?"

He looked up from his bowl. "I do, and that reminds me. With Christmas coming, you'll want to buy gifts. I can up your allowance a few dollars this month."

How embarrassing, to mention her allowance. She'd been writing for quite a while now and making some money of her own. "Papa, I don't need an allowance."

He pressed his brows together. "Why not?"

"I've been selling my articles to the newspaper."

He dipped into his soup. "Good for you, my girl. You see, Stapleton, my daughter is independent. She's talented too."

"Have you read any of my daughter's pieces, Dr. Stapleton?" Lily's mother's eyes glowed with pride over Lily's accomplishments as always when the subject came up among guests.

"I can't say I have." Andrew engaged Lily's eyes again. "But I'd like to."

Lily straightened in the chair, her back inches from the seat back as any lady would do. She pushed her spoon through to the other side of her bowl, and when Andrew sat there, still looking at her, she glanced at his empty bowl.

"More soup?" she asked, concerned he might still be hungry. He was, after all, a man of considerable stature. When she lifted the ladle, she bobbled it and dropped it back into the tureen. The broth splattered on the tablecloth. Lily grabbed her napkin and dabbed it.

"I'm sorry." Frantically, Lily blotted up the spill. "I hope I didn't get any on you."

"You didn't." He lifted the tureen and moved it to the side.

"Thank you. Do you still want some?"

"If there is any left."

"Enough for another bowl."

"I've never tasted soup this good in any restaurant."

Lily smiled at her mother. "See, Mother. It worked."

Her mother nodded, but Lily's father held his spoon in midair. "What worked, Lily?"

"Oh nothing, Papa. Have another sandwich." She held the tray out to him. "And you too, Andrew."

Lily's father had the bad habit of lighting up a cigar after dinner. She hated the smoke and hoped he would not partake of one this time, but he set his napkin down on the table and asked Andrew if he'd like to join him.

"None for me, thank you, sir," said Andrew. "I never took it up. I've something to show Lily, if I may."

Bridget removed the dishes and, once it was cleared, Andrew set a case on the table. He turned the key and lifted the treasured masterpieces from it. Lily's heart pounded with anticipation. Over the last year, she had devoted her reading to his papers on the various manuscripts he had discovered, which had only heightened her curiosity. With care, Andrew laid each page out on the table. Lily leaned down to see the beautiful handwriting. The loops and dashes were unlike any she had ever seen. Each line, each letter, was perfect in its execution, and not a single page was worn or faded after one hundred and twenty-plus years.

"These are the letters you spoke about?" Lily sighed. "The pages look as though they were written yesterday. There is barely a mark on them."

Andrew nodded. "Only a trained eye can see them."

"And you discovered these in an old church library in England? I wonder how they got there."

"No one knows."

Lily looked closer at the scripts. "Wouldn't you love to know? I know I would."

"There is no clear answer. If they had been in an estate library, it would have been easily solved. In a church, there is no telling. They are authentic. I'm donating them to the Smithsonian."

A sigh of approval went round the room. Lily's mother said, "That is generous indeed."

Thrilled to see Washington's and Lafayette's handwriting, Lily sat down. She drew in a breath, and Andrew looked at her, concerned.

"Are you feeling all right, Lily?"

She pushed back a loose lock of hair. "Yes, I'm fine. I'm overwhelmed. America will be grateful to have such a treasure."

Andrew placed the papers back in the box. "The Smithsonian will see that the letters are preserved for generations. Hopefully one day you'll take your children to see them."

"I hope the French do not raise a dispute. Lafayette is one of their greatest heroes."

Andrew stood closer to her, and she looked up. "And your letters?"

Bridget came into the room in her starched apron. "Your cab has returned, sir."

Andrew looked at his pocket watch. "You must forgive me. I promised a colleague I'd be back by ten." He put the case under his arm. "I'll miss my train if I don't leave soon."

Lily's father kept track of the comings and goings of the local railroad. He drew out his own watch and said, "The trains are always on time in our small town. I wish we had had more time for a man-to-man. Visit us again before you leave for home."

Lily narrowed her eyes. *What does he mean by a 'man-to-man'?*

Lily stood and followed Andrew to the door. With all the delays and endless disruptions, she hadn't had the chance to show him the letters and the ornament. Perhaps she'd never know the mystery behind them if he returned to England and never came back to America. And. . .was it just the letters that had her feeling so bereft? He was leaving. Yes, they could still write to each other, but now that they had met, she was afraid of how dull her life would be, not seeing him or talking to him. She thought she had fallen in love with him through their correspondence, but after being together, she realized it was now much deeper.

She shooed Bridget away and followed Andrew into the hallway to the door. She looked back and saw her mother pull her father into the sitting room, leaving them alone. Andrew shouldered his coat, and she handed him his hat. He stood close enough that his coat brushed against the lace of her bodice.

"I'm disappointed we didn't get the chance to talk about the letters, Andrew, but I'm glad you came."

"I have business to attend to over the next few days, but I'll come back." He slipped on his gloves. "Your father doesn't seem to mind my coming."

She gave him a weak smile. "I think my mother would like that too."

"What about you?"

She stared into his eyes. "I would be saddened if you didn't."

"I feel the same way. I want to see you again, Lily."

"I hoped you would."

He leaned down. "Don't you feel as if we've known each other for years?"

"Yes, years and years."

On the side table beside the door sat Lily's box of letters and the adored ornament. The gas lighting above shone over the glossy carved teak, and Lily rushed to pick it up.

"Take the letters with you. When you return you might have some answers for me. Mind the ornament. It's fragile."

"Don't you want it for the tree?"

She glanced back through the door at the huge evergreen. Then she shifted her gaze to Andrew. "I'll wait for you to bring it back. Let me show it to you."

Lily set the box down and opened the lid. The letters were set to one side and the ornament to the other. She lifted it out and held it up by the red ribbon attached to it. Frosted white glass glimmered in the gas lighting. Emerald ivy twisted through sprays of hunter green holly and blood-red berries.

"It's beautiful, isn't it?"

"Too delicate for me to carry. Keep it here, Lily."

She studied the glass treasure while it turned and caught the light. "You're right, Andrew. I don't want anything to happen to it." Reaching up to the hook at the base of the gaslight, she hung it. "It'll be safe here. If I put it on the tree, the boys are liable to break it." She stood back. "It must have meant something special to the owner." She turned to him. "Mother

131

thinks so too, but has no more clue than I do. Maybe I'll never know who the owner was."

Andrew took her hand and kissed the back of it. "We'll find out soon enough."

He drew her close, touched her chin, and raised it. "Lily." He placed a soft kiss on her lips. It lasted only a second, but enough to send Lily's heart soaring. He put on his hat and opened the front door. Cold swept into the foyer and Lily gripped her arms. Lantern lights moved over the sidewalk, and the bare trees bowed their branches.

The cabbie called to him. "I can't keep the man waiting any longer." He brought Lily's hand to his lips. "Good night, dear Lily."

He stepped through the door and headed out into the cold night. Lily stood on the front porch, crossed her arms, and watched him stride down the front walk. The cab lights spread over the glaze of snow along the street, over Andrew. He turned and tipped his hat to her—his smile warm even in the darkness.

# Chapter 6

The December 1900 calendar hung on the kitchen wall next to the pantry door. A snowy field, a frozen lake, frosted evergreens, and happy skaters cheered Lily. The couples in the picture held on to each other, one lady dressed in a green frock coat like the one she owned, her hat and muff made of snowy white fur. It had been ages since she last got out her skates. Could she persuade Andrew to venture onto the ice with her? He'd have her hold on to him, to keep her arm in his, to control her balance.

She picked up a pencil and crossed off the previous day. Christmas would come fast, and she had yet to wrap any of the gifts she had made. She turned to the mixing bowl and added cinnamon and ginger to the flour. The tin beside it was filled with cookie cutters of various shapes and sizes.

She was about to add the eggs and milk when the doorbell rang. Who could it be at ten in the morning? Her parents were downtown shopping, the boys at the schoolhouse.

Bridget's heels tapped across the parquet floor. The front door opened and there were muffled voices. One was a man's, and Lily's heart leapt, hoping Andrew had come to call.

Bridget peeked around the kitchen entry. "A man is here to see you, miss. Says his name is Bagen." She handed Lily the man's calling card.

Lily glanced at the austere beige paper and the stark black ink. "Hector Bagen. I don't know him. Did he say what he wants?"

"No, miss."

"I bet he's selling something."

"He says he ain't, miss. Just that it's important he speaks to you on a private matter."

Lily untied her apron and headed into the foyer. In front of the closed door stood a man dressed in fashionable attire from the top of his hat to the soles of his shoes. He drew off the hat, revealing gray hair slicked down with an abundance of pomade. The woody scent of aftershave overwhelmed her. A waxy handlebar mustache quivered over his upper lip. He wore wire-rimmed glasses with thick lenses, above them thick brows. He gave her a slight bow while turning his hat in his gloved hands.

"Miss Morningstar, I presume."

"Yes, do I know you?" Again, she looked at the card.

"We've never met. Still, may I have a moment of your time? It is of the utmost importance." The space between his teeth caused each *S* to whistle.

"I'm not interested if you are selling something."

"I'm not selling, Miss Morningstar. I'm buying."

Lily gave him a bewildered look. "The house is not for sale. If there is something else, you need to speak with my father."

Bagen looked up the staircase and then toward the sitting room door. "Is he at home?"

"He's out."

"It does not matter. It is you I need to speak to."

"I'm hesitant of strangers that come knocking on our door early in the morning. So I wish you would tell me straight out what you want."

Bagen's droopy eyes looked down the hallway through his spectacles. A brisk fire burned upon the hearth, and amber light flickered over the hardwood floor outside the door. "We can talk here in your foyer. But I would welcome the warmth of your fire."

Cautious to comply, Lily gestured toward the sitting room and, once inside, she sat down and bid the stranger to do the same. Bagen lowered into a chair opposite her and pulled off his gloves one finger at a time. That's when Lily saw his index finger was missing on the right hand.

"Ah, you noticed." He laid the gloves on his knee. "An injury I prefer not to discuss. It's too gruesome for a woman's sensibilities."

Her lips parted. "I would not dare ask. What is it you wish to tell me?"

"I'm here in the stead of a client."

"A client? I don't understand."

"I shall explain it as clearly as you, a young woman, can understand."

Lily frowned and raised her chin. "I'm not the dunce your prejudice implies."

"Forgive me, but the matter is business-like."

"You should read a few books on diplomacy, Mr. Bagen."

"A large word. From what I've heard, you're a short story writer for the local *Gazette*?"

A lump swelled in Lily's throat. Had she been stern with a man about to offer her a writing opportunity? She swallowed and offered him a brandy, which he declined.

*Dear me, I've insulted his faith.*

"I hope I haven't offended you, Mr. Bagen," she said. "My father keeps brandy on hand for guests. I can have Bridget bring you a hot drink. It is cold outside, and you must be chilled to the bone."

"True, Miss Morningstar. I've changed my mind. Please, a small glass, just a snort." She filled a small glass for him, and he took it and held it up. "To Queen Victoria."

"You're not English. Why do you toast the Queen?" Lily asked.

"I have always admired Queen Victoria. We should have a monarch like her. . .as a figurehead of tradition without governing. Still, our democracy is preferred over a monarchy." Bagen sipped the brandy and sighed. "This is good." He held out the glass for more. "How about topping it off?"

Frowning, Lily put the stopper in the decanter and set it back in its place. "I'm sorry, I cannot. My father only allows a small glass to guests," she said.

Bagen set the glass down. "Ah, I see. It is an added expense for middle-class folks."

Lily hoped to move the conversation on to writing. "Queen Victoria is a patron of the arts, particularly literature, is she not?"

"I suppose she is."

"Is that why you are here—to discuss literature?"

One side of Bagen's mouth curled mockingly. "Your tone has changed."

"Well. . .I was wondering if you were here to speak to me about my writing."

He laughed lightly. "Not at all, but I'm sure you're a fine writer and will find success one day. Money would help."

Lily tilted her head. "Are you offering me a job?"

"No, just money in exchange for something you have."

Stunned by the ardent look he gave her, Lily straightened her back. "You've been here long enough to get to the point, Mr. Bagen."

"If you will hear me out, Miss Morningstar, I have an offer you'd be foolish to refuse."

"I have nothing to sell, and I don't want your money. I think you should leave."

"And let you miss out on the chance to make a great deal of money?" He looked around the room and sniffed. Lily disliked what her eyes told her. Prejudice toward her womanhood was enough, but to look down his nose at her home irritated her.

He picked up his gloves in his mauled hand. "I've learned you have certain letters in your possession."

"How do you know? I haven't told anyone outside my family except for—"

"Dr. Stapleton."

Lily gripped the sides of the chair. "You know Andrew?"

"What does that matter? I'm interested in those letters. I'm prepared to pay a fair amount for them."

Lily frowned. "Why? What do they mean to you?"

"That is for me to know, Miss Morningstar. Can we discuss a price?"

"They are not for sale."

He huffed. "You wish to turn down cash for a stack of old letters?"

"Yes."

He narrowed his eyes. The fire in the fireplace flickered in his glasses. "Too bad. Dr. Stapleton will be disappointed."

If she were wearing a corset, she would have blamed it for the pain in her chest. Much the same, what he said caused her breath to catch. "He sent you? That cannot be true. He'd never do that."

"It's obvious you do not know him well."

"I know Andrew well enough to know he'd never deceive me."

Bagen grinned. "Can a woman ever be sure?"

"You should leave. I won't listen to another word."

"It would be wise to, Miss Morningstar. If I were to pay a good price, think of how much that money would help you and your family. The letters are of no great importance, merely curiosities. You wouldn't lose anything. You would gain."

Lily stared at him. With Christmas coming and Wiley's birthday the week after, some extra money would be a blessing. Still, the idea Bagen said that Andrew had sent him, that Andrew wanted the letters, troubled her to her core.

"Andrew should be the one to speak to me, not you. Go back and tell him."

Bagen twisted his mustache and stared at her. "Perhaps he thought you would grow emotional and cry. Men do not like it when women feign tears. He sent me so he wouldn't have to deal with your reaction."

Lily fisted her hands and stood. Her heart ached, and she pressed her lips together.

"Ah, I see tears in your eyes now, Miss Morningstar."

"I'm not crying."

"But you are. Let them be tears of happiness. Money is so needed these days."

Lily drew in a deep breath and rallied her composure. "The answer is no, Mr. Bagen."

"Shall I tell Dr. Stapleton you want the letters returned? I will offer to be his courier." There had to be some real significance why he pressed her, but she could not believe him. His shifty eyes said as much. Even though she might never know who wrote the letters and to whom, they were hers, and she would keep them. "No," Lily said, plain and simple yet with force.

"Unfortunate for you." Bagen shrugged and yanked on his gloves. "You may never see Dr. Stapleton after this. What if he leaves and takes the letters with him? Then what will you do? Weep? You're a foolish girl, Miss Morningstar."

"Bridget!" Lily wished she'd had Bridget there the whole time. A witness to the conversation would have been prudent. Did she even hear Lily call to her?

"I will raise the price." Bagen took a roll of bills from his pocket. "Fifty dollars to start. Another fifty later."

"You keep pressing me." Lily narrowed her eyes. "The letters must be important."

"Only Dr. Stapleton can answer that."

"Then I will speak to him."

"Miss Morningstar, don't be so sure he will want you to. Transactions such as these are usually done in this manner, through a second party."

"I'm not interested in conducting a *transaction* through you, sir."

"Not now, but I'll give you some time to think about it. I'll be back. . ."

"If you do not leave now, I'll send for an officer."

Bagen frowned. "An extreme reaction, Miss Morningstar. I cannot say I'm surprised."

Lily picked up his hat and thrust it at him. "Good day, Mr. Bagen."

Bagen grabbed the hat. Tilting back his head and lifting his chin, he slapped it over his greasy hair. Striding to the door, he spoke something under his breath and stormed out. When it closed, Lily peeked out from behind the window curtain beside it. She watched Bagen until he disappeared down the street. She touched the glass and the icy chill that blew against it caused her to shiver in the deepening silence.

It broke when Bridget plodded down the stairs. "You called for me, miss?"

"I did, but it's all right."

"That man, did he leave?"

Lily nodded. Lifting her skirts, she walked up the staircase to her room and plopped onto the window seat. Her spaniel, Misty, jumped up beside her and nudged her hand with her nose. Lily stroked the dog's ears.

She sat for a long time and pondered the matter. Snow fell over the trees and the icy pond beyond the church on the corner. She looked up through the frosty glass. Clouds had parted. The flurries were over. Stars would stand out that night, against a velvet sky. In a whisper, she asked God what she should do. Trust Andrew or doubt him? Should she believe he sent that squirrely little man with the slicked-back hair and roguish eyes to barter with her?

One thing she knew for certain. She had to get the letters back.

# Chapter 7

Lily kept Bagen's visit to herself. She made Bridget swear not to tell her parents. They'd worry, and they'd scold her for allowing a strange man into the house when they were not home. They had plenty on their minds with the holidays fast approaching, and she didn't want to ruin the most joyful time of the year for them.

By dinnertime, the family tumbled through the front door. Her mother carried an armload of packages. Papa too. He looked exhausted, huffing and puffing as he took the load upstairs. Lily's rascally brothers begged their mother to tell them what she had bought.

"Never mind, you scamps. If I find one package opened, and believe me I'll be able to tell, I'll give it all to the orphan children." Their eyes widened. Their mouths gaped.

"Actually, that's a good idea, Mother," said Lily.

Wiley sneered and Henry sulked up the staircase.

"Oh, Lily. Help me with these, will you?" Her mother tried her best to balance the wrapped presents. Lily took four from the top. "How has your day gone?"

"Never a dull moment, Mother."

"What does that mean? Is something wrong?"

"Nothing I cannot deal with."

"Ah, you're worried about supper. Where's Bridget?"

"In the kitchen. You really should raise her salary. Give her the same amount you gave Mabel."

"I plan to as part of a Christmas gift to her. Mrs. Merriwaite across the street gives a dollar in an envelope to her maid."

Lily balanced the packages in her arms. "Maybe that's all she can afford, being a widow and all. I was thinking we should send over a box of gingerbread to wish her a happy Christmas."

Her mother stepped ahead of Lily and started up the staircase. "What a nice idea."

Lily's smile quivered. "Mother, do you approve of Andrew?"

"He's given me no reason not to. Except. . .he is a Christian, isn't he?"

"Yes, Mother. He told me in his letters he is. The study of illumined scriptures drew him closer to Jesus, not merely from the beautiful drawings and bright colors but by the words themselves. His parents raised him in the love of God." She wondered if what he told her was true.

"I'm delighted to hear it, Lily. Your father likes him too. When is he going to visit again? It would be delightful if he would spend Christmas Eve with us."

They reached the upper floor and headed to her parents' bedroom. Lily wanted to tell her mother what had happened that morning. But she looked so gleeful as she set the boxes on the bed that Lily couldn't bring herself to ruin her mood.

"Oh, what is this? A postcard for me. Bridget can't seem to break the habit of putting mail on my dressing table instead of on the tray by the front door." Her mother handed it to Lily. "Here, I don't have my reading glasses."

Lily admired the embossed Christmas postcard framed in holly that read, *A Merry Christmas and Happy New Year*. A watercolor print on the front showed smiling children in a sled with a collie trotting alongside them. She turned the card over.

Lily smiled. "It's from Aunt Willamena."

"Read it to me, Lily. I'm exhausted."

" 'Dearest niece and family. Here's wishing you good health and happiness at Christmastime and throughout the New Year. Christmas in New York is intolerably lonely and it has been so long since we last were together, I've decided to impose upon you this season. I will arrive by train to spend Christmas with the entire clan. I shan't tell you the day of my arrival, for I wish to surprise you all! Yours devotedly, Aunt Willamena.' "

Lily's mother smacked her hands together and stood. "Oh, this is marvelous news!" She rushed out into the hallway and called for Bridget. Then she turned back into the room and began counting on her fingers. "The spare room has to be aired, fresh sheets, flowers, and. . . Lily, I'm so happy."

"We should put holly in her room, Mother. We won't find flowers this time of year."

"And evergreen to fill the room with a Christmasy scent."

"And cinnamon sticks on the mantel."

"Oh, I'll have to go out again and buy her a present."

"Why don't we make one?"

"Such as?"

"How about a crocheted shawl?"

"Perfect! I am fast at crocheting. I'll start right away and should be finished in just a couple of days."

"It's brave of Aunt Willamena to travel alone at her age. The last time we visited she had trouble getting in and out of a chair." Lily moved a box aside and sat on the edge of the bed. "I'm worried."

"Don't be. More than likely, she will be traveling with a companion, which brings up another thing. We should prepare for such a person, have a bed ready."

Lily took up her mother's hands and kissed her cheek. "I'm glad to see you so happy, Mother. I'll put the holly-and-ivy ornament in the window as a welcoming."

"Are you happy, Lily? You look troubled. Did something happen while we were out?"

"Nothing out of the ordinary," Lily said, not wanting to worry her mother.

At eight the next morning, her father left for the bank where he worked, her mother for the Ladies' Society at their church to finish the quilts they were making for the Christmas Bazaar. Wiley and Henry were at school and were to stay late to practice their parts for the Christmas pageant.

Lily finished wrapping their gifts in brown paper and tied each with bright red twine. Bridget came to the open door just as Lily hid them in the closet.

"We should bring the boxes of ornaments out of the attic soon," she said to Bridget. "It will be Christmas Eve before we know it. When are you leaving to see your family?"

"The train leaves tonight, miss. I hope you all can do without me while I'm away."

"You deserve the time off. I can't remember the last time you had any."

"I haven't since working for the family. I'm glad. I've missed my mother."

Lily lifted her watch and chain and looked at the time. "You better hurry. It's a long walk to the station." She picked up an envelope and handed it over. "Would you post this on your way there? It's important." She looked at the maid's young face. "Something wrong, Bridget?"

"Dr. Stapleton is downstairs." She handed the letter back. "Might as well give it to him in person, miss."

Lily picked up her shawl and swung it over her shoulders. When she reached the top of the staircase, he looked up at her. Color was in Andrew's cheeks, a light in his dark eyes. Under his arm—the box.

She sauntered down the steps, her hand running along the polished balustrade. She could not find the words to speak—not even a simple greeting. Her heart beat with a rise of emotions. The truth, even hurtful, had to come from his lips.

He brought the box out from under his arm and handed it to her. "As I promised, I've returned the letters."

"Are you disappointed to give them back?"

"Not at all."

"Were you hoping to sell them?"

"No, why would I?"

She looked him in the eyes. She craved to spit the words out that he was a fraud, a deceiver, but wisdom dictated her actions. She set the box on the side table and turned to him. How long could she continue to be cold toward him?

"Let me take you to lunch." Andrew touched her hand. "There's that place down the street near the railway station."

She stared at him a moment. His eyes remained fixed on hers. They were shining, warm, and she was about to give in.

"I'm. . .not dressed to go out."

"You look beautiful."

"There's no reason you should flatter me, Andrew. Others have tried and it got them nowhere."

"I mean what I say, Lily. You are beautiful. But you're rather quiet today. Something on your mind?"

Movement caused her to look up the staircase. She drew her hand away. "Bridget is leaving soon. You can't stay."

"All the more reason we should go to lunch. Come on. Where is your coat?"

He moved toward the door, and when she didn't move, he turned back.

"I'm not hungry. We can go into the sitting room and talk until she leaves."

She stepped away to the sitting room and he followed. The fire in the hearth had burned low, and Andrew set a log on the coals. He held his hands out to the heat. "Isn't your mother at home?"

"She's at the church."

"You haven't decorated the tree yet."

"Not until Christmas Eve."

"What's wrong, Lily? You look unhappy."

"You've known me for a short while and read me well." She faced him. "Do you know a man named Bagen?"

He frowned. "I met him briefly at the hotel. Why? Is he someone you know?"

"He spoke to me. . .here in this room." She kept her eyes on him to study his reaction. "He mentioned you."

"You need to be clear, Lily. Exactly what did Bagen want?"

Unable to engage his eyes a moment longer, Lily looked down at her folded hands. "You have no idea?"

"I'm completely in the dark."

"Are the letters valuable?"

"I don't believe they are."

"If I sold them, would the amount help my family?"

"I can't put a price on them."

"Bagen made an offer. He said—"

"You didn't agree to anything, I hope."

"Not to a man who speaks for someone else. He said you were his client."

"That's utterly ridiculous."

"Is it?"

"If you don't trust me, look in the box. They're all there."

Lily twisted a ribbon on her bodice. "If you've been deceiving me, tell me. Spare my feelings."

"You think I've been deceiving you?"

"I don't know what to believe, Andrew. Did you send him?"

"I give you my word, I sent no one."

"But you know of him and. . ."

"Lily, I've held nothing back."

"Nothing at all?"

"Nothing."

"Not even that you want to buy my letters?"

"If I wanted the letters, I would have asked you."

She sat down, and he took a chair opposite her. For a moment, they were silent. The scent of the spruce in the hallway filled the room. The Christmas cheer Andrew had mentioned the day he came for dinner had gone, the house silent except for the crackle of the fire.

Andrew stood and paced. "Haven't we known each other long enough for you to know me better?"

"It is easy to remain a mystery when writing letters, as those in that box prove."

"We have written for a year and known each other face-to-face. You trusted me enough to give me the letters. But it took a few minutes with that scoundrel for you to doubt me."

The worried look in his eyes caused her to distrust what she assumed. He never gave her cause to doubt him. Not once.

He set his mouth, glanced at the floor. "Two nights ago, I was having dinner with the superintendent of the museum. Bagen overheard our conversation and came over to the table. He asked to see the letters and asked questions. I was foolish and told him who I thought had written them. He told me he heard your name mentioned, and so I believe he put it together that you're the owner. The only reason I would assume he has asked to purchase them is because of who wrote them."

Lily's eyes widened. "Are you sure?"

"Without a doubt."

"But how?"

"I'll show you."

He brought the box over to her. She opened it and drew out one letter. "I've read all of these, but never could tell who wrote them. I still don't understand how you'd know."

"From other documents. The superintendent recognized the handwriting from other papers. Yesterday, I was at his office, and he showed me papers belonging to Major Robert James. The writing is an exact match."

"The letter writer," Lily sighed.

"And beneath the lining of the box, I found this." Andrew handed a card to Lily.

"To Major Robert James at Christmas." She looked at Andrew and let out a long breath. "The ornament. But it doesn't say who gave it to him except for a faded initial. It looks like either a *V* or a *W*."

"There is more. Read the letter you're holding."

" 'My Beloved, I won't survive this wound. Remember me each year you hang this on the tree. Remember the love I had for you and that I will await you when God calls you home to me. . .R.' " Lily set the letter back. "This sentiment makes my heart ache. The love they had seems so genuine."

"I agree."

"But you don't know who his beloved was?"

"That is the greatest mystery of all."

# Chapter 8

Later that day, Andrew took Lily for a walk in the park. The breeze blew gently through the trees as she gathered winter from the ground. She decorated the foyer table with pinecones and dried heads of thistle and clover, and laid the box in the center.

"What do you think, Andrew? Does it look right to be there?"

"You're asking the wrong person, Lily. I don't know anything about decorating. But I admit you have a woman's touch to such things."

"I'll put the box here each Christmas in honor of Major James and his beloved."

"Where's the ornament?" he asked, looking up at the gaslight.

"Upstairs in the front spare bedroom. My great-aunt is coming to stay with us for the holidays. We haven't seen her in years. She lives in New York in a big house—you know the kind, with dozens of rooms but no one to fill them."

"Sounds much like the house I grew up in."

"I remember you described it to me in one of your letters. You were lonely growing up, weren't you?"

"I'm lonely still." He brushed one of her curls back from her face.

"I have your letters in a cardboard box, but I shall buy a new one, like this one, only not carved. I'd like it to be smooth and polished, with brass hinges and a lock."

"My only regret is I did not write you love letters. So, here."

Lily gazed at the envelope in his hand.

"Read it later, when you are alone."

Her eyes glowed as her heart swelled. She clutched the letter against her lace bodice. "I don't know what to say."

"Maybe you will later. Maybe you'll tell me how poor a poet I am."

Her smile widened. She put the letter into her sleeve and turned to the table. She ran her finger over a cone. "Ouch!" She snatched her hand back and put her finger in her mouth.

Andrew took her hand. "You've nicked your finger." The warmth of his hand and the caress of his fingertips on her palm filled her with desire. He took out his handkerchief and wrapped it around the tiny wound.

She gazed at him, her lashes concealing the emotions racing through her. "Your handkerchief will be stained. I know how to fix it though. You soak it in lemon water, if you can find lemons this time of year. I'll make it good as new—that is, if you want it back."

He caressed her palm. "You keep it. I have others."

She nodded, and her gaze turned to the window. "Look, it's snowing again." Then her smile faded, and her eyes widened. "Oh no. Look who it is coming up the sidewalk."

Andrew looked out. "Bagen. Persistent but foolish."

Lily stepped away. "I won't answer the door."

A grin surfaced on Andrew's face, and he put his hands on Lily's shoulders. "No, let him in."

"Why?"

"It will give me the chance to confront him. I'll go into the sitting room and wait. Don't tell him I'm here."

Lily's eyes beamed. "Take the box with you. I don't want him to see it right off."

Bridget came down the staircase, suitcase in hand. Lily hurried to the bottom step. "Bridget, please don't leave yet."

"But the train. . ."

"You won't miss it. I promise this won't take long. Bagen has almost reached the door. Please stay."

Bridget nodded. "If it's that important, miss."

"It is. Listen outside the sitting room. I want you to back us up if anything happens."

Bridget widened her eyes and set her case down. "I hope you're not expecting any violence, miss."

"No, Bridget. Just an honest conversation with Mr. Bagen to put him in his place." She glanced back to the window. "There he is now."

Bagen knocked on the door. Bridget set her hand over the brass knob and looked at Lily. Then she pulled the door open as Lily hurried away to the sitting room and waited.

"If you have a bottle of smelling salts handy, you may want to get it," Andrew said, quietly shutting the door.

"I won't need them." Lily quickly took a seat.

Andrew smiled over at her. "I'm not thinking of you, my darling. I'm thinking of Bagen."

"You think he'll faint at the first sight of you?"

"Anything is possible."

She sat so still that Andrew touched her on the shoulder. "Are you all right, Lily? You're not afraid are you?"

"Not at all. I wish Bridget would hurry and bring him in."

Bridget spoke louder than usual, a warning she headed with Bagen to the sitting room. Andrew moved to the left side of the door, so as not to be seen by Bagen when it opened. Lily's eyes were riveted upon the glass doorknob. It turned, and the door opened. Bridget played her part well and dipped when she came through. "Mr. Bagen is here to see you, miss."

Lily stood. "Mr. Bagen, I did not expect you to return. It's a shame. You've wasted your time when you could have found something productive to do."

He swept off his hat and grinned. "No waste if I have one more chance to convince you to accept my offer."

"Your offer?" Her eyes shifted to Andrew and then back to Bagen. "I thought you said Dr. Stapleton made the offer. Where is he? Why hasn't he come?"

Bagen put his hand on his chest and bowed. "To the point, Miss Morningstar. The price has gone up—not much, but enough to make it worth your while."

She stepped forward and looked him in the face. "By how much?"

"Um, ten more dollars." His eyes left hers and fastened on the box. "Is that the box of letters?"

"It is. Would you like to inspect them before we negotiate your offer?"

Bagen rubbed his gloved hands together. "I'm thrilled. May I?"

"I suppose it wouldn't hurt. Tell me what you think of them, if you know who wrote them, and what makes them so interesting?"

Yanking off his gloves, Bagen opened the lid. "Ah. Here they are. Just as I had imagined." His hands trembled as he picked up one letter. "Just as I suspected. Civil War love letters. Oh, these are indeed interesting, Miss Morningstar."

"And you say Dr. Stapleton wants them."

"He will be as thrilled as I am. . .maybe even more." He rummaged through the stack. A look of concern surfaced on his face. "Where are the envelopes?"

"There aren't any," Lily said.

"What? Then they are worthless."

"Why?"

"No stamps? It's the stamps that are valuable, I mean important."

"Too bad," Lily said. "But don't be disappointed. How could old stamps mean anything?"

Bagen drew up his shoulders and tossed the letter back in the box. "A philatelist knows."

Andrew stepped out from behind the door. "He's a stamp collector, Lily, and a scoundrel at that."

His face white as a sheet, Bagen jumped back. "Stapleton. . .what are you doing here?"

"Finding out about you, you lying sack of. . ."

Lily slapped her hands over her ears. "Andrew!"

"Sorry," he said. He walked toward Bagen. Bagen kept stumbling back. "Lily, would you like to send for a constable? I'm sure they'd be interested in this fraud and his crimes."

Bagen threw up his hands. "Crime? I've done nothing wrong."

"You've done plenty wrong."

"Well, I used your name in an attempt to influence Miss Morningstar, I admit, but I meant no harm. I thought it would be more convincing that way."

"Well, you were wrong." Andrew grabbed Bagen by the lapels and met him nose-to-nose. "You defamed me to my future wife by telling her you were representing me. You're a liar and a cheat. I should take you outside and we could handle this as men. Then I'll drag your surly hide to the jailhouse."

Bagen took hold of Andrew's hands and tried to pull them away. "Please, don't. I made a mistake. It's Christmas."

Lily laid her hand on Andrew's arm. "Let him go, Andrew."

Andrew looked at Lily then back at Bagen. His brows furrowed, and he thrust out his hands to let him go. "Lucky for you, Bagen, my lady has a forgiving heart. I'll show you to the door."

Holding on to Bagen's coat collar, Andrew hauled him to the front door and set him out on the porch. Bagen straightened his coat and scurried down the sidewalk. "Don't ever let me see you near Lily again," Andrew told him.

"You won't," Bagen called back. "Let her keep those dusty old scraps."

Andrew turned and Bridget laughed. "Oh what a sight to be seen, sir. I'm surprised you didn't use your boot and kick him out."

As for Lily, she stood speechless, with the words *future wife* echoing in her heart.

# Chapter 9

"Who was that man coming out of the house?" Lily's father hung his hat on the hat rack.

"No one important, Papa."

Her mother pointed to the tattered brown case. "Why is there a suitcase in the foyer? You're not going anywhere, are you, Lily?"

Lily smiled. "Of course not, Mother. Bridget is leaving for home. Remember?"

"Oh, good. I do remember, now that you mention it."

They questioned the couple whether Bridget had been in the house with them. "We don't want the neighbors to start gossiping," her mother said.

"Too late," Lily said. "I'm sure some of them saw what happened here. You both will be glad to know that Dr. Stapleton—Andrew—protected me from a petty chiseler."

"A robber? A thief? Should we call the police?"

Lily explained and, once her parents knew their daughter was safe, they thanked her suitor and went on with the business of running their household.

"Boys, go upstairs and wash your hands and faces, and stop that running around," their mother said. "You're making Misty bark, and I have a headache coming on." She put her hand to her forehead. "Get me an aspirin, will you, Lily?"

Lily put her arm around her mother's shoulders. "You should lie down with a cold cloth, Mother."

Coat, hat, and gloves on, and a blue scarf wrapped around her neck, Bridget walked into the foyer and picked up her bag. "I've just enough time to make the train."

"Have a good time, Bridget."

"I will, ma'am. Merry Christmas to all."

"And to you and yours. Don't forget to come back."

Out the door went Bridget, head held high. Misty whined at the threshold and scratched the door. Andrew called her away and she bounded up to him. Lily drew her mother to the top of the staircase. She peered past the banister and listened to Andrew and her father talking.

"Come for the holidays have you, Stapleton?"

"If it is all right with you, sir."

"The more the merrier."

"I'm staying at the hotel down the street, next to the railway station."

"Edith," called Lily's father, "do you think we can break the rules and allow Stapleton to stay here with us?"

She turned. "I would say yes, but Aunt Willamena is coming, dear. She's staying in the spare bedroom."

"Edith, it's bound to snow, and you know how the streets are when it is snowing. I insist."

Andrew shifted his feet. "I don't want to be any trouble. I'll—"

Lily leaned over the railing. "Papa, Andrew could stay in the room above our garage."

"Capital idea. What say you, Stapleton?"

"Sounds perfect, sir." Lily caught his glance. "Thank you."

"We've a wood stove out there, enough to keep the room warm overnight."

"Sir, may I speak with you in private?"

"Why, of course. We can go into the sitting room."

Lily watched the pair step away. She and her mother looked at each other. "What do you suppose that's all about, Lily?"

"I've no idea." But she did. She remembered what he had said to Bagen. He used the words *future wife*. She didn't dare ask him about it for fear he'd think her too assertive. Were her hopes about to be fulfilled? She turned to her mother. "I need a moment, Mother."

"Where are you going? I need a cool cloth for my head."

"Don't worry. I'll get one."

Lily slipped quietly away to her room, shut the door, and sat on the edge of her bed. She took out Andrew's letter and opened it. She expected a lengthy missive. Instead, the few words said everything she needed to know.

> *Do you know that I love you? Do you know I adore you, worship you? I want to fill your lap with a dozen roses, kiss your lips, and make you mine forever. You are the reason I traveled so far, and you are the reason I will stay. Andrew*

If ever there were words that made Lily's heart race, it was these. At one time, she imagined he'd never say them, that she wasn't good enough or high enough for his liking. How wrong she had been. She tucked the letter in her bedside table, stood to catch her breath, and then left to tend to her mother's aching head.

In her parents' bedroom, her mother kicked off her shoes and let them fall onto the floor. Lily wrung out a washcloth in the washbowl and laid it over her mother's forehead. "Feel better?"

"Much better. You should go downstairs and. . ."

"Eavesdrop?"

"You need to be there when your father comes out of the room. Don't tell me you don't suspect Andrew is asking permission?"

"It crossed my mind."

"Go then. I'll lie here until the throbbing stops. As soon as you know what they've discussed, come back and tell me." A firm knock lay hard on the door downstairs. "What now? Whoever it is, tell them not to bang so hard. Some coins are in my purse in case it's the Salvation Army."

Lily headed back downstairs. Through the side windows she could see a man in a cap and double-breasted coat shifting on his feet. When she opened it, the baggage handler from the station gave her a toothy smile and tipped his hat.

"Good evenin', Miss Morningstar. I've brought your great-aunt up here. Our taxi driver went home sick with a sniffle. So I have brought her."

Thanking him, Lily rushed down the walk. There was Aunt Willamena, as regal as ever, sitting in the rear of the railroad taxi. A heavy blanket kept for cold weather engulfed her petite frame. A large-brimmed hat made her look even smaller. The baggage handler skipped past Lily and held his hand out to the great lady. The blanket slipped from her shoulders and she descended to the walk with as much grace as a young woman.

"Lily, you look younger than I had expected. You have good skin, dear."

"Aunt Willamena, welcome. I hope your journey wasn't difficult."

Cane in hand, Aunt Willamena strode up the sidewalk. "I enjoyed seeing the country-side and met interesting people in the Pullman. I'm early. You think your mother will mind?"

Lily put her arm through her great-aunt's. "Look and see. She is waiting for you at the door."

There were happy greetings and kissed cheeks, and headaches vanished the moment Aunt Willamena entered the house.

Lily could not wait to show her great-aunt the decorated spare room. She had placed evergreen over the mantel, sprays of boxwood and rosemary in a vase, and the holly-and-ivy ornament in the window. It slowly spun when they entered and caught the last rays of sunlight fading over the horizon. The red silk ribbon it hung from kept it centered between the mullions.

Aunt Willamena paused on the Turkish rug, her eyes fixed on the ornament. Lily noticed the expression of curiosity that sprang in her eyes. They narrowed as if to get a clearer vision. She stepped forward and stopped. She reached out her hand covered in a black lace glove and touched the ornament.

"It's lovely, isn't it, Aunt?" said Lily. "I found it in a secondhand store."

Aunt Willamena tilted her head. "A secondhand store?"

"I couldn't resist it. I think it was made in Germany. They make so many beautiful glass ornaments." Lily stood beside Aunt Willamena. "It's old, made sometime before the Civil War."

Aunt Willamena set her hand over her heart. "It is. . .familiar. What else do you know about it?"

"Nothing more, except it was in a box of old love letters. Andrew has solved the mystery behind them. Wait until you hear the whole story, Aunt. It is so romantic, and at the same time so sad. But you must be tired from your journey and want to rest."

Aunt Willamena turned. "I should like a cup of tea, Edith. But I wish to speak to Lily alone for a few moments, if you don't mind."

Lily's mother gladly obliged and left the room. Aunt Willamena sat down. "Come here, Lily. I am hale enough to hear the story. But first tell me about Andrew."

Lily started from the day she walked into the shop and found the box, how she paid a dollar to an indifferent clerk and took the box home. She read all the letters and was over-whelmed with curiosity about the persons they belonged to. She met Andrew after a year of correspondence, after a year of intimacy growing between them and then finally meeting.

Setting her cane to the side, Aunt Willamena smiled at Lily. "It is no coincidence the two of you met and that these letters came into your possession. Where are they?"

"Downstairs. Would you like to see them?"

"Take me to them, and ask Andrew to sit with me as I look them over." Gradually, the matron of the family stood. Lily helped her, and when they entered the sitting room, Andrew and her father stood. Her mother brought in a tea tray and set it on the table.

Lily fetched the box and brought it to Aunt Willamena. The elderly woman ran her hands over the lid. Her aged eyes filled, and she lifted it. Lily wondered what had caused this surge of emotion. Was Aunt Willamena reminded of her past, of the war that took the lives of so many boys she had known in her youth?

The lid now laid aside, Aunt Willamena looked at the letters, touched the faded red ribbon holding them together. Her eyes lifted to Lily's and tears ran down her face.

"Aunt," Lily said, alarmed. "What is it?"

"You know who wrote these?" she asked Andrew.

"Major Robert James, ma'am."

"Yes, Robert. And do you know to whom he wrote them?"

"That is something we have not discovered," he said.

Aunt Willamena gathered the bundle to her breast. "He truly loved me."

Lily widened her eyes.

"War separated us, along with his family. They thought I was not high enough for their son. We had planned to elope the week following his graduation from the academy. Then—Sumter happened. I promised I would wait for him. Here is the last message I received from him."

Her hand trembled. "He told me he was wounded and would not survive. I bought a ticket to travel to Alexandria to be with him. At the train station there was posted a list of casualties. His name was among them—that he had died and was buried in Arlington. I visited his grave only once and was never able to go there again. My heart was broken. Shortly afterward, I met your great-uncle. He was good to me, but our love was never as deep as what I shared with Robert."

"So, you are the major's beloved?" Lily lowered to her knees in front of her great-aunt.

"It was long ago."

"That may be, Aunt, but for some reason they have come back to you."

Lily looked over at her mother. Her eyes were misty. "We all have wondered how the letters ended up in a secondhand store."

"I put them away after I married. Somehow they were lost." Aunt Willamena gripped Lily's hands. "It is a miracle you found these—a real Christmas miracle."

# Chapter 10

Andrew, take my daughter into the other room."

Lily's mother looked confused. "What for?"

Aunt Willamena shook her head. "Edith, don't you know?"

The reason sprang into her face. "Oh, I do. Go to the kitchen, Lily, and bring back some cookies—you and Andrew, after you've had a discussion."

A soft fire flickered in the fireplace and spread over the hem of Lily's dress when she entered the kitchen. She reached for the tin of cookies. Andrew stood in the center of the room. "With all the activity, I haven't had the chance to tell you I've been offered a teaching position."

She set down a tray. "You're going back to England?"

"No, I'll be staying. I'll teach at Georgetown."

She smiled back at him. "That's marvelous."

He stayed her hands and got down on one knee. "I'm sure you didn't think this would happen in a kitchen."

"If you're about to say what I think you will say, no, but I don't care where you say it—as long as you do."

"Then here goes. I've loved you, Lily, from the first letter you sent, the way you shared your life with me, your intelligence and wit, your femininity, and your love for God. How can I live without you?"

She lowered her eyes. "I don't want you to, Andrew."

"Be my wife. Say yes."

He stood, held her in his arms. "Say yes, Lily."

She nestled against him. "Yes! I can't imagine life without you."

Andrew kissed her long and soft. She melted against him. "I'm so happy."

From his pocket he took a gold band with a blue sapphire. He slipped it on her finger. "Will this do?"

Lily held her hand toward the firelight. "It's beautiful." Then she looked into his eyes. "Can I be a Christmas bride?"

"I wouldn't want you any other way."

Before leaving to tell the family the joyful news, he pulled her once more into his arms and kissed her once—twice—three times.

# Epilogue

Christmas Day came as Lily had imagined. Snow fell and coated the trees and lawn as she stood beside Andrew in front of the local minister. When Andrew said, "I do," he leaned in close to her lips and added, "until the day I take my last breath."

Mother and Aunt Willamena wiped tears from their eyes, and when the last words were spoken that the couple were now husband and wife, and the kiss bestowed, the family feasted at a Christmas table full of joy and hope for the future.

Lily wondered how she could have ever doubted Andrew could love her. Just as the found letters belonging to Aunt Willamena were called a miracle, so had their union been one as well. God had brought Andrew across the ocean and Lily to the lecture room at the Smithsonian where they would meet and find each other. She met his eyes, and the warmth that glowed from them warmed her heart. He looked at her questioningly.

"What is it you're thinking, Lily?" he whispered, leaning close to her ear.

"I was thinking of when we first met," she quietly answered.

"And?"

"I was so attracted to you. However, I didn't think anything could come of it, me being a middle-class American girl, so different from English ladies."

He smiled. "And I thought the same, that you thought of me as a snobbish Englishman with no ambition to court you. We were both wrong, and now here we are husband and wife, in love and devoted to each other for the rest of our lives."

That evening, as the sun set behind pillars of winter clouds, Henry skipped through the front door. "Look what I found."

Lily looked at the mound of fur nestled in her brother's arms. Her mother bent forward to have a look. "What's that you've got there, Henry?"

"A kitten."

"Where did you find it?"

"In the alley."

"It's probably full of fleas."

Henry shook his head. "No it ain't."

Lily took the tiny ball of fluff from him and said, "It's so cute, Mother. Listen, he's purring."

"We've enough with the dog, and we already have a cat."

"He's starving, and it's cold outside." Lily held the kitten out to her. "Andrew and I will take it if you don't."

Wiley threw back his shoulders. "Cats catch mice, Mama. Henry and I can be sure this one does a proper job. All the other kids have more than one cat."

Aunt Willamena fluttered her hand. "Oh, for goodness' sake, Edith, let them have the little beast."

Everyone stared at the furry ball. It meowed, and Misty raced forward, her nails scraping the hardwood floor. She leapt at the kitten, barking wildly. The kitten hissed. The tiny tail fluffed. It hurdled out of Henry's arms, landed, and arched its back. It hissed and swatted at the maddened pup. It ran up the Christmas tree. Ornaments fell. Some broke on the floor, others rolled across to the rug. Misty jumped onto the trunk and the tree swayed. The kitten scrambled up to the star. The tree toppled. Everyone, except for Aunt Willamena, ran forward to catch it.

Laughing, Aunt Willamena slapped her hands on the arm of the chair. "I haven't had this much fun at Christmas in years," she shouted over the commotion.

And so—the Morningstars, Lily and Andrew, had a perfect Christmas, and Aunt Willamena found joy in knowing she had been deeply loved and not forgotten.

**Rita Gerlach** lives in central Maryland with her husband and two sons. She is a bestselling author of eight inspirational historical novels including the Daughters of the Potomac series of which *Romantic Times* Book Review Magazine said, "Creating characters with intense realism and compassion is one of Gerlach's gifts."

# Love Brick by Brick

## by Kathleen L. Maher

*God setteth the solitary in families: he bringeth out
those which are bound with chains.*
PSALM 68:6

# Chapter 1

D id I hear quite right? Did you actually say no tea is to be served?" Rufus Sedgwick III looked down his straight nose at her, setting SarahAnn Winnifred's teeth on edge.

She was not easily cowed by her patients or their interfering families, but this imperious Brit tangled the words in her throat. She planted her booted feet as a fire stoked in her cheeks.

Kindly Mrs. Sedgwick, her patient, spoke up before she could. "Never fear, Son. This lovely doctor is taking brilliant care of me."

SarahAnn released a pent-up breath, easing the tension with a laugh. "Oh, I'm no doctor yet, ma'am. I've one more year of training."

Her patient's son scoffed, and she wasn't sure if it was because of her statement or Dr. Gleason's dietary restrictions on tea and coffee. With his hands folded behind his tailored overcoat, the high collar of which framed a smooth-shaven face, Mr. Sedgwick proved every bit the lordly figure she envisioned the wealthy class in England. Her fondness for Dickens had filled her imagination with all sorts of characters, from Mr. Brownlow of Oliver Twist to David Copperfield himself. But this gentleman was too young, too vital, to be regarded with the platonic safety of a literary character. Her heart struck an inharmonious chord of fancy.

She tamped down the rebellious fluttering in her chest and raised her chin primly. "Rachel Gleason firmly believes stimulating beverages lend the patient artificial vigor and misrepresent the true health of the body. And as you know, sir, Mrs. Gleason is a bona fide physician, equal to her husband in every regard. You may trust that your mother's health is best served without teatime, however customary it may be to you."

Her moment of triumph crumbled at the tender deference the man paid to his mother. "I'm sorry you must be denied basic comforts, Mum." He stroked her age-spotted hand with the long, smooth fingers of an aristocrat.

Turning now to SarahAnn, his tone changed to rigid civility. "I'm astonished at the common frocks with which you have outfitted my mother, Miss Winnifred. Where, pray tell, are her mourning clothes?"

"Our regimen requires the least constrictive garments for our patients' digestion and circulatory processes. Tight clothing also impedes free movement and breathing."

"These shapeless cloaks are positively medieval. From the peasant class, at that."

SarahAnn hid her amusement, ducking behind her patient to retrieve a fallen menu. Reappearing, she spoke in her most ameliorating tone. "The healing arts sometimes require compromise, Mr. Sedgwick."

"My mother is the daughter of an earl. Surely you can appreciate the many compromises she has already made." He waved a hand at the sparse room with its iron-framed single bed, the utilitarian hearth, the gunmetal-gray wool blanket for which he had had to pay above the ten dollar per week cost of treatment, and the bare walls ornamented only by a window with a view of the grounds.

SarahAnn smoothed her jacket bodice over her skirt. "Hydropathy, despite what you must think, is not the uncouth invention of Americans. It was developed abroad. In Germany and England, as a matter of fact."

He tapped his toe on the floor and firmed the line of his mouth, but made no reply. She smiled and turned her attention to the patient once again. Mrs. Sedgwick's nutmeg eyes danced with merriment, and a droll curve of her lips betrayed a cheerful childlikeness cloaked beneath her quiet reserve as she appeared to watch them. Despite her son's airs, Mrs. Sedgwick was quickly becoming SarahAnn's favorite in residence.

"I'll see if I can procure you a cup of heated water, with toast and jam."

"Thank you, dear." The older lady patted SarahAnn's forearm, and warmth coursed through SarahAnn at the maternal touch. As a lump swelled in her throat at the unexpected affection, she couldn't put enough distance between herself and the threat to her professional mien at the suggestion of a mother's kindness.

The young lady—Miss Winnifred—turned abruptly and bustled away, her swaying cornflower skirts catching his eye. Rufus shook himself from the distraction and drew a chair to his mother's bedside. "I came as soon as I heard of your fainting spell. I thought you were regaining your strength."

"I am improving steadily," Mum insisted. "Miss Winnifred is a perfect delight, isn't she?"

He drew a breath and waited a beat before replying, a practice he employed to rein in his thoughts. "Perfect delight would be to have you settled in your home. I'm afraid there's been another delay."

"Don't distress yourself, Rufus. I'm in very capable hands. And despite the absence of teatime, I find it very agreeable here."

"You are positively spartan, Mum."

Her eyes sparkled under his teasing, as though he'd paid a compliment. She was a brave one, accepting these cataclysmic changes with the grace of a true noblewoman.

"Except, do you think your father will come this afternoon? I should very much like to see him."

"You remember, Mother, don't you? He's not coming. Not today or any other day." He winced at the familiar pain twisting inside him. She deserved so much better than life had given her. Than he had managed for her of late.

He sought to distract her. "I rode out to the building site earlier. The architect has had the foundation excavated, and there's enough loose native stone to build one of those charming slate walls so popular here. It's a pleasant piece of land. You shall have your orchards in due time."

Of course, fruit trees would take years to grow and bear. Years Mum may not have. But Rufus pushed past those darker stirrings and produced a specimen from his pocket he had saved for her. "I found this there." He set the chiseled, triangular stone in the palm of her outstretched hand.

"What is it, dear?"

"An arrowhead. The indigenous people—the Iroquois—fashioned them to hunt and to make war."

"Remarkable." She turned the piece in her pale fingers, admiring it with captivated wonder. "Perhaps it belonged to the very people who fought alongside your grandpapa at the Battle of Newtown."

He smiled, the first rays of joy reaching through since before they'd left Salisbury. "Yes, Grandfather Sedgwick patrolled these very hills and valleys during the Revolution." Surely his grandfather's service here for King and Country had left a proud legacy for them even his father's memory couldn't spoil.

Presently, the young medical student returned, bearing a tray. He stood.

"Your cup of heated mineral water, Mrs. Sedgwick." Miss Winnifred's gaze drifted from her ministrations with his mother to steal a furtive glance at him.

"Allow me." Rufus collected the tray from her. The china cup and saucer were of finer quality than he would have guessed. He nodded in gratitude, passing them to his mother's bedside stand.

"I appreciate your attentive care, Miss Winnifred. Mother only sings your praises."

"I'm delighted to see her improving. The afternoon remains warm enough for a stroll. Would you care to join us?"

"Doctor's orders?"

"Yes. Exercise is vital in recovering strength."

Once Mum finished sampling her refreshments, he offered his elbow. She grasped his arm and stood with steadier legs than when he'd visited last. He couldn't argue with the results, even if his protective instinct yearned to cosset her.

The aroma of savory cooking mingled with the scent of freshly scrubbed floors as they stepped from the room, strolled down the hallway, crossed the entry, and exited out onto the slate patio. Golden rays of sun penetrated the autumn canopy of elm, maple, and oak, igniting the air with the crisp, woodsy scent of the outdoors. The westerly view conveyed the busy town below with its railroads and canal. In between lay an open lawn grading at a gentle slope from the four-story building behind them. Patients seated on the three-hundred-foot veranda or on the balconies marking each floor were all given ample opportunity to enjoy the refreshing air.

"Where shall we go today, Mrs. Sedgwick?" A stray ray of sun lit Miss Winnifred's smile and caused him to notice the golden highlights in her wavy, chestnut hair.

Mum looked about the grounds, leaning on Rufus's arm for ballast.

The chatter of many species of birds competed with the gurgling brook to their right—the mineral spring that fed the resort's famed bath-works. A bridge spanned the shale glen not fifty yards from them.

"What lies over the gorge?" Rufus gazed to the northeast, toward the crest of the hill.

"Those trails lead to our orchards, a croquet course, gardens, and some rather spectacular views."

Rufus had to admit that the beauty of their new town made up for many misgivings he'd had crossing the ocean. "Perhaps we might see the groves and orchards, if you're feeling chipper, Mum. I should like to learn what grows best in this climate."

Their New York destination offered a slight improvement from the damp chill along the Avon River. If the elevation here hadn't halted his mother's decline, at least this individualized attention offered hope.

"Yes, Rufus, do let us view the fruit trees."

"Your mother tells me you are rebuilding your ancestral home here?"

A glimmer of some emotion lit Miss Winnifred's dark blue eyes with violet, reminding him of a storm over the English Channel.

"Quite right."

"Imagine. An English castle here in Elmira."

An amused grin sprang up at her naiveté. "It's hardly a proper manor, let alone a castle."

"My son, considerate to a fault, but given to extravagance, I'm afraid. When he suggested leaving Salisbury, I told him I could never leave my home. So, he imported it."

He patted his mother's hand resting on his elbow. It was a promise he intended to keep. His mother would have the home she had lived in and loved for six decades, and that of her ancestors centuries before, only on this side of the Atlantic. Far from the whispers and scandal which had driven them here. It was the least he could give her, after she'd had to leave so much behind.

They strolled in silence, broken only by the sound of Mum's breath, which became increasingly labored. Rufus slowed their pace to a halt. "I say, this is quite far enough."

Mum clutched his arm with a soft gasp. Rufus stooped to steady her, and Miss Winnifred swooped in the very moment Mum's knees buckled beneath her.

# Chapter 2

SarahAnn sprang to action, beckoning an orderly to bring a wheeling chair. Within a moment's time, she'd secured sweet Mrs. Sedgwick into its seat with the help of her son and the aide. She swallowed down the roaring of her own pulse in the rush of activity and bent to listen for her patient's breath sounds and heart rate by pressing her ear to the lady's chest.

"Where is Dr. Gleason? Go fetch him, man." Rufus Sedgwick dispatched the attendant toward the building. The aide's stocky legs pumped beneath his bleached cotton smock, scrambling up the path.

SarahAnn straightened to give Mr. Sedgwick assurance. "Your mother's heart is beating rapidly. It may be the exertion. You are welcome to wait in the parlor while the doctor examines her. I'll come and tell you when she can see you."

SarahAnn took the handles of the chair and steered Mrs. Sedgwick toward the house.

He dogged her every step. "I wish to speak to the doctor."

"I'll see what I can arrange."

His mother's voice barely lifted over the clatter of the wheeling chair, and her arm reached out for her son. "Have faith, Rufus. All shall be well."

Mr. Sedgwick preceded them to draw the door, and SarahAnn pushed her patient up the wooden ramp and into the building. Her last glimpse back showed him pacing the patio, hands behind his back, head down as though in prayer. Remorse pricked her innards for judging him as lordly. After all, the man clearly cared a great deal for the woman who'd raised him. She could appreciate such devotion, but only as one looking in on a warm domestic scene. Hers had been a view of family from the cold outer doors. The palpable affection between mother and son once again caught a lump in her throat. With squared shoulders, she forced personal feelings aside for practical concerns, patients who needed her, goals to achieve. There was no room for fanciful longings, even for a family who might have loved her.

Dr. Rachel Gleason rounded a corner, the attendant Mr. Sedgwick had sent flanking her, and both presently came to stand before SarahAnn and her charge. The doctor stooped, brushing back dark wisps escaping her hair net, and greeted Mrs. Sedgwick by name.

"Good afternoon, Beatrice. What is this I hear of another episode of syncope?" She placed a stethoscope on the patient's chest, and SarahAnn marveled at Dr. Rachel's skill. The woman put patients instantly at ease while taking information and vitals. SarahAnn determined that she would master her mentor's efficiency.

"Syncope. Isn't that a musical term? For being offbeat?" Mrs. Sedgwick's laughter at her own joke was weak and breathy. But her smile remained bright.

"It is a fancy word for fainting, Mrs. Sedgwick." SarahAnn answered so Dr. Rachel could focus, returning the lady's smile.

Dr. Rachel set aside her stethoscope. "The root of the word refers to omitting syllables from longer words, or literally, to cut short. Is that what your heart is doing, Mrs. Sedgwick? Abbreviating work it is supposed to do for you?"

"My, I never thought of it that way. Quite right, I suppose. What shall be done for it?"

"Treating low blood pressure involves increasing fluid intake. And no sudden changes in posture. Do not attempt to stand without assistance."

"Mr. Sedgwick is anxious for an update, doctor. Shall I bring him in?"

"Yes, SarahAnn."

Rufus's silent prayers drew to an abrupt close when Miss Winnifred crossed the front parlor. He rose from his upholstered chair by the unlit hearth and met her halfway. Her calm expression conferred confidence.

"The doctor will see you now. Thank you for your patience, Mr. Sedgwick." She turned and led the way back down the corridors to his mother's room.

Mum's pallid face arrested his entire focus once the door opened. Worry lines drew about her eyes, and he strode to her and took her hand.

The lady doctor addressed him. "Your mother has a condition called syncope. In common terms, fainting spells. We must determine what is causing this. Whether or not she has a heart condition, we are investigating. As a precaution to her risk of falling, we are enlisting some extra safety measures. She must not attempt to move about without assistance. She will have a bell to summon an aide at all times."

"Do you employ around-the-clock staff?"

"Our night staff is stretched throughout the building, but they will respond in turn. Your mother must wait until assistance comes."

Rufus ran a hand through his hair and expelled a breath. The idea of Mum alone and helpless in the dark suddenly overwhelmed his senses. "Is there no one who could be assigned to her? I'll gladly assume whatever the cost."

"We don't provide personal aides, Mr. Sedgwick."

Miss Winnifred extended a hand toward Dr. Gleason. "I could change my room to this wing. If I were closer, I would be sure to hear her right away."

"Miss Winnifred, you must protect your rest. I won't have you risk exhaustion."

Gratitude and admiration mingled inside Rufus for the young lady's consideration. Clearly, she went above and beyond the call of duty.

"Doctors are summoned for emergencies at every hour," Miss Winnifred replied. "It would be a vital part of my training."

The doctor folded her hands, locking gazes with a particularly determined expression, the very same which Rufus studied. He suspected he and the good doctor experienced differing responses to the young lady's deep blue eyes. He averted his admiring gaze before detection.

"Very well then, SarahAnn. You may move your belongings to the empty room next door." With that, Dr. Rachel Gleason departed and closed the door behind her.

Rufus turned to SarahAnn Winnifred. "Might I be of assistance to you, perhaps carrying boxes?"

"Very kind of you, Mr. Sedgwick. But we have porters for that." She stepped toward the door and he followed.

Did her cheeks blush just then? It was very becoming. And rare on such a self-assured lady of business. "Mr. Sedgwick is my father's name. Won't you call me Rufus? We're going to be seeing quite a bit of each other it seems, and I wouldn't think it inappropriate."

"Thank you. Unfortunately, I cannot while attending patients."

"Understood, Miss Winnifred." They paused outside Mum's door. "But if I should see you in town?" He gave her a smile that seemed to confuse her. Her big blue eyes widened, and blinked. He chuckled.

"I don't mean to confound you. But I should welcome the possibility of seeing you outside this infirmary."

"By chance or by design?"

"That's entirely up to you. . ."

She excused herself to tend another patient before he could qualify his intentions. Most likely a good thing. He stood and watched her full skirts sway down the hallway and marveled at the goodness and strength of this modern young lady, whom he had first misjudged. And whom he would very much like to get to know better.

# Chapter 3

After three years emancipated from the orphanage, SarahAnn feared the orphanage would never be fully removed from her. The children's names, faces, and stories had woven themselves into her heart like a rag-tag, patchwork quilt. She longed to mend every seam and tidy every stray thread, but time constraints and resources forbade the involvement these children deserved. Still, once a week she visited to render whatever aid she might. She came on Saturdays—the day most school children enjoyed a reprieve from their studies. These children, the poorest of the poor, lived among a hodgepodge of the mentally infirmed, the elderly, and the indigent in the county poorhouse. Today, she brought chicken broth to little brown-eyed Nellie, a tiny six-year-old with a perpetual cough. Also in SarahAnn's bag lay a folded crocheted wrap she'd completed this past week, hoping to save for Christmas. But as she thought of Nellie's warmth while the autumn nights lengthened and the cold pressed in, she knew she mustn't wait.

"Miss Sarah!" A gap-toothed grin spread wide when the girl caught sight of her entering the brick building. SarahAnn supposed her blue riding cloak gave her identity away immediately.

What the child's embrace lacked in strength, it more than made up for in length and fervency. SarahAnn's cheek heated against Nellie's fevered brow. She gently withdrew and cupped the flushed face in her palm. Eyes that shone with glassy brightness searched SarahAnn for the parcels she brought, and she didn't have the heart to withhold them a moment longer. "I brought a few things especially for you."

"Oh thank you, Miss Sarah!" Plunging into the black sealskin bag, she extracted the blue-and-white, scallop-edged blanket and pressed it to her chest. "Oh, Miss Sarah, blue is my favoritest color. Thank you!"

"You're welcome, Nellie. There's also a jar of soup. But first, let me look at you. How long have you had this fever?"

"The day after you came last, I woke up with red dots. And my throat is extra sore."

"May I have a look?"

The child obediently opened her mouth and SarahAnn observed the telltale white blisters on the child's throat. "Back to bed, my sweet. I'll feed you your broth there."

Nellie clutched her blue wrap, even though the temperature during the day in the closed building approached stifling.

"Might we have a window opened?"

When no one replied among the sparse staff, she strained against the sash and budged it a few inches herself. It was the best she could do. She would direct someone to close it again before the night chill encroached.

"Is your home a castle, Miss Sarah?"

"No, silly monkey. What gave you that idea?"

"You told me you live at the top of a hill where there's a hundred rooms."

Laughter spilled from her, and Nellie joined in, her congested giggles like a sparrow's trill.

"I do live in a large building, but it isn't a castle, it's a health resort. And it isn't my home. It's just where I live." A pang shot through her. Surely Nellie understood what that was like, that her present shelter would never be the same as having a home.

"When I grow up, I want to live in a castle. Do you think I could ask Santa Claus to bring me parents for Christmas? A king and a queen? I could be their princess!"

"Oh, sweet, silly monkey, Santa does not kidnap kings and queens, nor does he stuff them in his sack and force them down the chimney."

Nellie's laughter broke into a croupy cough, and for a moment, the fragile child struggled to draw breath. SarahAnn helped her to sit up, patting her back, worry piquing within her. If she were only married, she would adopt the child herself.

When at last the girl took a shuddering gasp, then two, and her coughing spasms subsided, SarahAnn let out her own pent-up breath. "There, now. No more talk for just now. Sip your broth and I will tell you a story. About a prince born a long time ago."

"A prince?" Nellie sat up and clapped.

SarahAnn nodded and settled the girl back on the old mattress. "Sometimes, princes and princesses are born in odd places. This prince had to pretend to be a commoner so that He could do the work He'd come to do."

"What work? What work, Miss Sarah?"

"He came to rescue His lost family."

The child's brown eyes grew into wide pools of wonder.

SarahAnn began, "Once upon a time, a star filled the night sky and led wise men on a journey from far away, because a baby had been born."

"Was it the prince?"

"Yes, now swallow your broth before you choke." SarahAnn wiped the girl's chin with her own handkerchief and resumed.

"His parents had been on a long journey also, to Bethlehem, their town of origin, because the government wanted to count all its people. The prince's mother had nowhere to have the baby, except a common stable."

Nellie sipped the broth directly from the jar and listened with rapt attention.

"Once the baby was born, His mother called him Jesus. Angels came down from heaven and told lowly shepherds about the prince who'd been born."

"Oh my. Did He have a crown?"

"No, but three wise men brought Him gifts of gold, frankincense, and myrrh."

"Did His father have a crown?"

"What if I told you the kind man who raised Him was not his real father? Jesus' real Father is God. Jesus is God's only begotten Son."

"Forgotten son?"

"Begotten. Meaning, His very flesh and blood."

"Is this a made-up story?"

"No, it is the real story of Christmas. Not the story by Clement C. Moore."

Nellie's left brow raised, and she scowled a bit, setting the jar onto the bedside table sans half its contents.

"What, you don't believe me?"

The child folded her arms.

"Do you know what Jesus' full name is?"

Nellie shrugged. "Jesus of Nazareth? I heard the cook say it when he dropped a platter of biscuits."

SarahAnn placed a hand over her mouth. "No, silly monkey. It is Christ. As in Christ-mas."

"Christmas?" The child's expression changed a bit, and a light sprang to her eyes that didn't owe itself to the fever. "It really is a true story?"

SarahAnn nodded. "Christmas is our celebration that the Christ child came into the world to save His family."

"Am I His family?"

SarahAnn hugged the frail child. "Yes, all that believe in Him get to be His children. And one day He will come again for us."

"Will He let us live in a castle?"

"Yes, Jesus promised to prepare a mansion with many rooms for each of us. In heaven."

"Do you think I could go there for Christmas?"

A pang lodged in SarahAnn's throat, silencing her. How this child had endured the many trials in her short life, she could only guess. She swallowed and dabbed at her eyes. "You needn't worry. The Lord knows when the time is right for each of us."

She caressed Nellie's fine brown hair until the child's sleepy eyes drew closed. Then SarahAnn sat there for some time praying in the quiet. "Lord, please allow Nellie to see Your goodness in the land of the living. Heal her body and answer the desires of her heart with a family that adores her. And I know Christmas is scarcely more than a month away, but please make it a grand one for her, and all these children. Amen."

As she stood to depart, her thoughts went unbidden to Rufus Sedgwick and the castle he was building. Rather, the manor house. She smiled at her own childlike imaginings, not unlike Nellie's. Perhaps a girl's wish remained alive in her own heart to live in a castle and be loved by a handsome prince.

She shook herself out of the daydream and redirected her thoughts. Mr. Sedgwick had mentioned that he might like to see her outside of her workplace. The swelling of hope in her chest threatened to stretch her stays. But as always, she deferred to a more sensible interpretation, forfeiting silly emotion. She wondered if he might be willing to accompany her here, to the orphanage, the following week. Surely with his considerable resources, much more might be done for these children than what she could accomplish alone. She decided then that she would extend an invitation to him for the following week.

Rufus stood at the rail station counter, his claims ticket in hand. The black-aproned clerk had already examined the document and handed it back, and now leafed through a file of requisitions, his frown deepening. "I'm sorry, sir. I have no records here for your shipment. You say it's coming in from New York Harbor?"

"That's where it was to reach port from Southampton. I was assured my cargo would arrive shortly after I did, and that was several weeks ago."

"Have you checked the telegraph office?"

"Yes."

"The canal office?"

*Not since yesterday. Could a day make that much difference?*

"Very well. I'll check again." He nodded thanks to the chap and returned to his parked buggy, now familiar enough with the city that he drove himself. He goaded the sturdy pony up Mill Street, which ran through the bustling downtown district. Then instead of continuing south toward the Rathbun Hotel where he had been staying, he reined left. East Hill rose to the horizon before him, and halfway there lay the canal. For a moment, he gave thought of how much more pleasant it would be to continue up to the Water Cure. To tease a smile from the overly serious Miss Winnifred sounded sporting. But he couldn't face his poor mother without some good news. He had hoped to have her house well underway before the fine autumn weather turned blustery.

Frustration threatened to spoil his good mood. How would he manage it all? To make it all come together in the right timing? The three years he'd been away, lending Christian aid to homesick soldiers and later to the starving people of Sevastopol in the Crimean War, he'd grown accustomed to shouldering big burdens and managing without the guidance of a father. But this undertaking loomed so large, so overwhelming. Starting over in a new country, caring for his infirmed mum, and keeping that stiff upper lip so she wouldn't worry—it would have been nice to have someone in his corner, working things out with him and for him. He hadn't felt this alone even when news of his father's disappearance had come.

A snippet of Scripture pulsed through his thoughts, as though his inner voice had spoken: "I will not leave you as orphans."

Yes, he had a heavenly Father who did indeed promise never to leave or forsake him, even if his earthly father had. A stirring of faith rose within him, and he dared to entertain what a miracle it would be if the house were completed for Christmas. After all, it might be Mum's last.

Despite his inner doubts, he voiced a prayer. "Lord, would you oversee my affairs and make the impossible possible? You can heal Mum's heart, both physically and emotionally." Yes, he believed the Lord could make her well again. Sustain her until her home was completed, and beyond.

The rented conveyance squeaked and rattled, seeming in need of a good oiling and tightening. "I really must purchase my own horses and carriage before long. It won't do to have Mum endure this jostling once she's well enough to leave the Gleasons' health resort."

He caught himself speaking his thoughts aloud and gave a chuckle. But what a pity that would be, to no longer have occasion to see the lovely doctor-in-training, a veritable American Florence Nightingale. He determined then to invite Miss Winnifred for dinner at the Rathbun, and then an evening at the local opera house. With any luck, he might even arrange it for the following Saturday.

Presently, he arrived at the business office for the Chemung Canal, a prosperous enterprise near Water Street. As he reined the little bay mare toward a hitching post, his view opened on a flurry of activity along the tow path.

Barges lined the bank and men came and went up the dock hoisting crates. Rufus's heart skipped a beat, and he leapt from the buggy. His stone! It had arrived, and a crew unloaded it before his eyes.

He jogged to the dock worker directing the disembarking and pumped his hand. "Jolly good day, sir. By the looks of things, my ship has come in."

"You Rufus Sedgwick?"

"I am. And this is my cargo."

"I have here thirty tons of stone, plus five more barges due to arrive with furnishings and miscellany."

Rufus perused the manifest. "Splendid, my good man. I'm eager to have this project underway before the snow flies."

The dock foreman led him up to the office and procured his paperwork, showing Rufus where to sign. As the ink dried, the man paused. "Do you have a builder?"

"I'm taking recommendations."

The man reached across his desk and handed him a business card. "Ward Farrar built the Female Seminary here. Huge undertaking. You might start with him."

"Thank you, sir." Rufus followed the man back out to the street. The protest of mules and the rattle of harnesses, the creaking of wood and the shouts of men filled the air. Dust rose from the tramping of many feet and the gust of a northeast wind.

"For local delivery, you'll want to see that man." The foreman signaled to a teamster strapping a load onto a flatbed wagon, and then he strode away to his next order of business. Rufus approached the wagon master.

The burly man turned from his work to regard Rufus as he approached. "Is that your stone, friend?"

"It is. I'm building on the bluff overlooking the river."

"Ho, so you're the English lord building the castle?"

Rufus shook his head with a grin. "I'm no lord. And our home is barely a cottage."

"You and your castle are the talk of the town." He reached out. "Name's Baxter."

"Sedgwick." Rufus clasped Mr. Baxter's hand. "I'd be greatly obliged if you'd give me a quote on delivery."

"I've already been commissioned. Your man said the price was right."

"You must have spoken with my agent then?" Rufus handed the man a card with his solicitor's information. "How soon might you begin?"

"Soon as I'm done with this load, I'll be back for yours."

Things were going well indeed. Rufus inwardly acknowledged the source of his good fortune and thanked the Lord. Now, as he climbed into the rented buggy, he focused on his next feat—to win Miss Winnifred's presence for a Saturday evening on the town. He would need more than a spot of charm to realize that ambition. He straightened his bow tie and told the pony to giddy up.

# Chapter 4

*The Water Cure*
*Several Days Later*

SarahAnn found herself smiling throughout the day, and her step held an extra spring as she dispatched her duties. She anticipated Mr. Sedgwick—Rufus—would arrive in the evening to see his mother, and though terribly unlike her, she found it difficult to keep her mind on her work. Never in her twenty-two years had she allowed a handsome face to so distract her. Of course, her patients' concerns remained paramount. If he decided to call before she'd made her rounds, he would just have to wait. A girlish giggle escaped her, imagining him pacing the parlor, looking at his pocket watch, anticipating her grand entrance. As long as she was dreaming, she imagined herself in a lovely tartan taffeta skirt with a matching red bodice and snow-white pelisse. What an extravagance it would be, to spend her entire savings on such attire.

She passed a reflective glass pane on her way to the ladies' bath and paused to smooth back a few tendrils that had escaped her tidy chignon. "Skilamalink!" She fussed a moment before surrendering to the inevitable—something about her appearance would always be awry.

The bathroom's one-hundred-foot expanse accommodated individual privacy for up to twenty bathers at a time. Presently, SarahAnn stepped down to assist, wrapping a towel around a woman's shoulders.

"Miss Penelope, would you be so kind as to help Mrs. Adelaide with her hair?"

The aide immediately set to work on wrapping the patient's cropped locks.

"Thank you. We must have these ladies dressed and ready for their afternoon nap."

The Doctors Gleason lectured on quality nutrition and a balance in exercise and rest, as well as the health benefits of daily taking the waters, both hygienically and nutritionally. SarahAnn could attest to patients' improvement time and again under their regimen, even challenging cases like Mrs. Sedgwick, who presently partook in the sparkling mineral water heated on wood-burning stoves, carried in by the bucket.

SarahAnn's heart filled with something beyond gratitude. What a privilege seeing vitality return to those she had grown to care about. She assisted Mrs. Sedgwick up from the bath onto a waiting bench and recounted how Rachel Gleason had taken her under her wing and brought her this far on her journey. If the good doctor had not recognized her potential. . . She almost shuddered to think what may have become of her. Now she would never have to worry about her future. And perhaps she could secure a better future for others caught in the grip of the county poorhouse too. Like her little Nellie.

A soberness came over her. As much as she'd enjoyed the notion of a handsome gentleman showing her interest, the truth was, much more important matters were at stake than nurturing starry-eyed wishes of marriage and adopting. Namely, securing a benefactor for all of the children.

She wrapped Mrs. Sedgwick in a warm robe. "You haven't had a single fainting spell in over a week. You look the picture of health."

"Thank you, my dear. I have been restored by a multitude of angels." She fluttered her eyelashes, making SarahAnn smile.

"In fact, I'm well enough that my son is taking me on a buggy ride to see the masonry work. You must join Rufus and me."

Why did SarahAnn's traitorous heart flutter at the mere mention of his name? "How wonderful to hear of the progress on your home."

Mrs. Sedgwick slipped her arm in SarahAnn's and conscripted her to escort her back to her room. SarahAnn found she had no defenses to the older lady's endearing ways and strolled in pace with her.

"Oh, how I adored buggy rides with Rufus's father. Mr. Sedgwick could set the trotters to their paces. Over hill and vale. It was lovely." Her melodic voice charmed SarahAnn in much the way Nellie's laughter did. Her soul drank in their contagious joy, musing how they both offered it extravagantly despite their difficulties. She wished she could be more like them, rather than veiling her emotions behind professionalism and duty.

"You are so young and lovely, SarahAnn. Surely even a doctor-in-training takes time for holiday."

"Are you referring to Christmas, Mrs. Sedgwick?"

A coy smile lit the elder lady's expression. "A merry heart doeth good like a medicine."

SarahAnn pressed her lips, consternation and amusement warring within her. She couldn't refute Scripture. "I keep Christmas in my own way."

"Of course you do, dear. But what about every other day? Each day should have ribbons and bells."

"And buggy rides, I suppose."

"Oh yes, especially rides in the open air, filled with laughter and singing. That is precisely the prescription for you."

SarahAnn's eyes grew misty, taken in by the spell of this delightful woman's words. Was such a life even possible for her?

Mrs. Sedgwick patted SarahAnn's hand. "I do so love to see you in that becoming blue riding cloak of yours. Will you wear it on our outing this evening?"

"But I didn't say I would—"

"We will expect you after dinner, dear. Oh, is this my room already? Splendid. I'd better take my rest so I'll be refreshed. Don't be late!"

Rufus gathered the flowers from the back of the carriage, careful to preserve the white asters and burgundy chrysanthemums from losing a single blossom. With the tickets he had purchased for Saturday night's opera securely in his waist jacket pocket, he rehearsed the words that he hoped would charm the lovely Miss Winnifred to join him. He stepped through the door of the health resort, a swirl of fallen leaves blustering in with him. The clerk at the desk gave him a deferential nod, and the crackling hearth enveloped him with warmth and welcome.

"Good evening, Mr. Nicholas. I trust the ladies are finished with dinner?"

"Indeed they are, Mr. Sedgwick. What's that you've got there?"

Rufus knew his schoolboy grin betrayed him. "Flowers for two special ladies."

Nicholas's bushy white brows rose to his missing hairline. "You'd better run a fever or practice a cough, Mr. Sedgwick. SarahAnn Winnifred only has eyes for sick folk."

Rufus chuckled. "If it comes to that, I'll take your advice. But then I don't know what I'd do with these opera tickets."

"I'll make a bet with you. If Miss Winnifred agrees to go with you, I'll drive you in the big coach myself. But if she declines, I'll solve your dilemma. Those tickets would be put to good use by the missus and me." He winked.

"You're a cheeky one, Nicholas. Agreed. You have yourself a wager."

He shed his overcoat as he made his way through the corridors leading to Mum's room. He would have to secure her an extra layer for their outing, as the weather had turned inclement. Early afternoon had been glorious, the sun bright on the bare tree branches, but it hadn't generated enough heat to overcome the brisk wind or the pelting sleet that began on his ascent up the hill. An extra woolen blanket ought to suffice in the snug conveyance.

He'd missed his daily visits with Mum for a few days, overseeing delivery and his new work force. But the courier he'd sent had assured him that his message had been delivered. The flowers beneath the fold of his overcoat were extra insurance that he'd receive the answer he hoped, from both ladies.

The evidence of the evening meal still hung enticing on the air. Roast with a savory gravy, he would guess by the aroma of celery, onions, and beef wafting from the dining room. Mum's appetite had remained healthy, and for that he was grateful. The spice of something else lingered as he neared Mum's room. It was a decidedly feminine fragrance, a patchouli that drew him to investigate.

And there, in the threshold of the room adjacent to Mum, stood a figure in a riding cloak the exact shade of the Union Jack's bold blue background. She stood with her back to him, securing the lock, but then she turned to face him, and a startled but becoming expression of pleasure adorned Miss Winnifred's face.

"Good evening, Mr. Sedgwick. I was just going to see your mother."

He straightened his posture, hoping his own smile did not appear too eager. "Indeed, it is a very good evening, Miss Winnifred. I . . ." He withdrew the two bouquets from beneath the overcoat folded on his arm. "I brought these for Mum, and whilst I was at it, took the liberty of getting double."

He presented one of the bundles to her, and she stood frozen for a moment, her eyes widening, reflecting the color of her lovely cloak.

"For you." He placed them in her hand.

She took them gingerly, still motionless otherwise.

He tilted his head to the side.

She finally looked up at him, her voice hushed as she said, "I've never received flowers before."

"A token of my appreciation for all you have done for my mother—for us both. Knowing you have been watching over her has alleviated my worries greatly."

A wavering smile lifted her serious expression. "I'll put them in water." She motioned to turn back to her room, and he grasped her forearm. "I'm sure they'll keep in my mother's room until later. We have plans, I believe?"

Her cheeks deepened in the most becoming blush. He firmed his hold on her arm and beckoned her to walk with him the few, slow strides to Mum's door. The scent of her patchouli wreathed about them, and he drew a deep inhale, allowing it to imbue him with hope.

"Sporting of you to agree to accompany Mum and me. The weather has turned, so I pray it won't be an ordeal for you."

"I'm no hothouse flower, Mr. Sedgwick. I'll keep as well as these hardy blossoms." She stopped and knocked at his mother's door and peered up at him with a hint of teasing.

He didn't mind if his admiration did show this time as he gave her a slight bow and drew the door open.

"Ah, my dear son has come to take his poor mother out," Mum said in a voice entirely too theatrical. "But mercy me, I am just not feeling up to an outing. My, how dashing you both look. Please, don't let my malaise spoil everyone's plans. Do go and enjoy the lovely crisp air together."

Rufus examined Mum, and aside from her ridiculously loose medieval peasant garb, there appeared nothing especially wrong with her. He smelled conspiracy, and he loved her for it. Though he would never let on.

"It would be terribly ungallant of me to leave you behind. Why don't we postpone until a later time?"

"I won't hear of it." Mum shook her head. "It would do my heart such good to see our Florence Nightingale relieved of duty for once."

Rufus stroked his shaven chin. She couldn't have known he thought of Miss Winnifred as the American Nightingale. Strange coincidence. "Very well," he replied, knowing he wouldn't win the debate even if he'd wanted to. "I suppose the sun will be setting before long. We'd better be off now if we're going."

"The flowers," SarahAnn reminded.

"Ah, yes. I brought you these, Mother. And would you be so kind as to look after Miss Winnifred's too, until we return?"

"Of course, dear." Mum gathered the colorful blooms and arranged them in her water pitcher, to Miss Winnifred's visible chagrin.

Before SarahAnn could protest Mum spoiling her mineral tonic, he spirited the lovely young lady out the door. He hoped to draw her away from the mundane concerns of patients and medicines long enough to pierce the shroud of mystery surrounding her. What manner of young lady chose to pore over medical books and attend the infirmed when she might have enjoyed social occasions and explored more leisurely pastimes? Only a most remarkable sort.

"I say, Miss Winnifred. I have a wager with your Mr. Nicholas at the desk that you might help me settle. I've put up two tickets to the opera on the gamble that you might consider plans with me this Saturday."

"Plans with you this Saturday? How serendipitous. That's the day I always help at the orphanage. I was hoping you might accompany me there."

Rufus's breath hitched. "The orphanage? But, what of the opera and dinner?"

The brightness in her eyes dimmed. "I'm sorry. That was presumptuous of me. Please, never mind."

He recovered a moment too late. She had already averted her gaze.

"What time do you have in mind for your visit? Perhaps we might do both?"

# Chapter 5

SarahAnn's pace had slowed to a halt, almost reaching Rufus Sedgwick's conveyance under the portico. She'd seen the way he flinched when she'd mentioned the orphanage. And she, an orphan. What had she been thinking? She regretted her careless words, regretted even agreeing to come out this cold evening. She had no place with this gentleman of pedigree.

"I've just remembered something I must do for a patient. Please accept my regrets."

She turned to flee back to the safety of her haven, her workplace, but she'd forgotten he still held her arm.

"Please, don't cancel. Perhaps I might be of assistance with whatever you must do, and then we might go?"

She faced him, her frustration mounting. Why must he be so unbearably chivalrous? She took a measured breath to uphold her composure, though panic clawed inside her. When he learned who she really was, he would recoil. She had yet to attain her degree, to be truly accomplished enough to even consider a social rank approaching his. She dared her gaze to meet his long enough to see a pained look on his face, which both puzzled and deepened her frustration.

"You are very kind, Mr. Sedgwick. But I am. . ." She couldn't finish the sentence. Her throat constricted with emotion.

"I had hoped you would call me Rufus now that we're technically outside your workplace."

His playful smile rallied her composure and she laughed. "Only if you promise to come and meet my friends at the orphanage Saturday." What? How did those words slip past?

"I would be delighted."

His earnest expression, with tilted head and lead-crystal eyes, stole away her resistance. She assented with a nod.

"Very well then. We shall visit these young people. Now say you will grace me with your presence for dinner and the theater?"

"But won't it seem incongruous?" She was allowing him to guide her up into the carriage, and the surrender was dizzying. His strong hands about her waist, his steady, assuring frame her ballast, she could almost resign herself to her deepest longings for such a caring presence in her life. Almost.

He didn't reply, but stepped briskly around the carriage and took the reins, drawing himself up to sit beside her. He gathered a woolen blanket from the dashboard and shook it open to cover them both. "Comfortable?"

She nodded, studying him with her medical student's eye for detail. He had donned a top hat with his overcoat, and the image of his dapper appearance lent to her general awe. How did such a privileged young man learn to be so attentive, so nurturing? Clearly by taking care of his mother. He would make someone a fine husband. She swallowed back misgivings again and smiled bravely. "Thank you."

The reins snapped and the sturdy Shire stepped forward. The motion rocked her—bold, confident, everything she was not.

"Incongruent, you ask? I am not sure I understand your question. Visiting friends and meeting new people is an experience not unlike partaking of the beauty of good food and skilled musicians. I find it awakens something of the divine."

"Divine? You don't find immersing yourself in others' privations, juxtaposed to partaking in luxuries somehow—"

"Disingenuous?" A knowing sparkle lit his crystal eyes.

"I wasn't accusing you," she quickly amended.

"No, of course not, no more than you are accusing yourself. I believe each experience serves to instruct. Is not the Lord ever-present, and yet unchanging, in His goodness?"

"I never thought of it that way." SarahAnn's ponderings turned to Nellie and their conversation last. How true, that Jesus had experienced both the splendors of heaven and the sufferings of earth, and no one could accuse Him of being disingenuous.

"Do you think these orphaned friends of yours would expect you to be any less than you are for their sakes?"

"Oh no, of course not."

"Nor, I am sure, would they want your pity."

"It's not pity that concerns me," SarahAnn quickly replied. But then she remembered her etiquette and settled the passion rising in her voice. "I just wish to share my good fortune."

He remained silent, reining the Shire through the falling sleet on the road. His lips were set in an inscrutable expression, and his gaze focused far ahead.

Pine trees swayed overhead, ice glittering on their boughs. A trio of deer crossed the road ahead of them, their tails raised in flashes of white before fading into the darkening woods. The world transformed under the first winter squall. Cardinals fluttered in the underbrush, their scarlet plumage a harbinger of Christmas to come. A hush enveloped them, and only the *clip-clop* of shod hooves on the road lifted over the swirling frost of their breath.

The waning light stretched over the treetops into a clearing, and beyond, the view opened to them of a waist-high wall of stone. Rufus slowed the Shire to a gentle walk as the sun set over the western hills across the valley, shedding a burnished glow over them.

SarahAnn sat forward on the upholstered seat and took in an expanse of cleared land set atop a slight bluff above the eastern bank of the Chemung River. The property reminded her of the Water Cure, and only a few miles away from it as the crow flies. Longer, of course, by winding road.

"It is as grand as any castle I can imagine, Mr. Sedgwick."

"Rufus. Remember our promise?"

His easy laughter invited her own. "Your mother will be delighted. Surely this view will console any longing for her former home."

"We wish to bring the best of what was, while embracing the hope of what will be." He removed his hat and gazed with her over the fields and silver strip of river below. "You spoke of good fortune, Miss Winnifred."

"SarahAnn."

He acknowledged the invitation with gratitude in the crinkles about his eyes. "SarahAnn."

His smile was genuine. He sighed. "Good fortune is tied to opportunity, and opportunity is a concept I have given much thought."

She folded her hands, both as a demure gesture of attentive listening and to warm them in the gale that swept up the hill.

"No one chooses the situation into which they are born. Granted, some have more natural privilege than others. But opportunity. . . I firmly believe opportunity is what one does with the world they are given."

The chill about her penetrated the illusion of warmth she'd fostered up until that moment, and she trembled. How easy for this man to say that privilege and opportunity were not one and the same. She lifted her chin and looked back to the road from which they had come.

She would rather not gaze upon the piles of hewn stone he had imported, symbols of his amassed wealth and imperviousness to the world and its elements. Hers was still very much a position of vulnerability. But even so, she would give her all to bring those less fortunate with her as she reached for any security this life might afford.

Rufus waved a hand. "Take that pile of stone. An apprenticeship in masonry might open the world to one man, but it might feel like prison to another. This is where opportunity must be tailored to gifting. An artist might use the same stone as a medium for sculpture. Same raw materials, different inclination—both, opportunity."

She unclenched her fingers from their tight fold. "So you believe each person is given a fair chance to become what they were created to be?"

"It is an idealistic view, I admit. But to me, it speaks of the nature of a loving Creator."

"I believe that our loving Creator must sometimes use his creation to open doors. And while some heed the call, others do not."

He gave a chuckle. "I see you are a philosopher of passion. No wonder my mother adores you."

Unexpected pleasure warmed her cheeks, and she rued blushing at his compliment. But she seemed a hostage to her own rebellious passions.

"I have an idea, if you would indulge me." He snapped the reins and urged the horse back toward the resort.

"When we go to meet these children, I want to give a listening ear for their gifts and callings. Then let us reconvene at dinner and discuss what we might do to make their Christmas merry and their New Year bright."

Her heart skipped a beat. "I'm delighted at your idea, Mr. Sedg—Rufus. Thank you."

He had replaced his top hat, and he peered down at her with a pride that surely originated from his station, or perhaps from some achievement known only to him. A notion troubled and delighted her: perhaps his regard had everything to do with her sitting by his side.

# Chapter 6

*The Water Cure*
*Saturday Afternoon*

Rufus checked his watch again, the gold still warm in his fingers from being pressed inside his waistcoat. One thirty-five. He tucked the piece back into its pocket and paced across the parlor of the health resort, once more approaching the desk. "Say, Nicholas, Miss Winnifred does know I'm here, doesn't she?"

"She said she'll be along soon." The older chap raised his bushy, white eyebrows. "But if she stands you up, I win the tickets fair and square."

Rufus grinned. "I haven't forgotten. But let's hope the afternoon doesn't go that badly."

"My missus says I never take her out. But I says to her, 'I prefer your singin' and cookin' to anyone else's.' So why doesn't she take that as a compliment?"

Rufus let out a chuckle, and Nicholas's laughter filled the room like the roar of blazing logs in the nearby fireplace.

Presently, a porter carried a basket on his arm into the parlor, accompanied by a familiar figure cloaked in a blue riding frock. Rufus collected the hamper from the man and bowed in greeting to the lovely young lady.

"So sorry to be late," SarahAnn said. "I was gathering a few things from the kitchen for the children."

"Never fear, Miss Winnifred. The children must have their goodies."

He withdrew a parcel from his long wool overcoat. "These were my favorite as a child."

She received the box, a bit larger than her palm, almost square. Inside lay a set of miniature wooden ninepins.

"Oh, they will love these!"

Her smile warmed him through. Mr. Nicholas held the door open for them, and the clerk's resigned nod and shrug seemed to concede that there would be no canceling of plans tonight. Miss Winnifred would be his lovely companion to enjoy for an evening out, and who knew what may come? The past with its troubles had been left behind, and he was ready to begin building a happier future.

For today he had rented a carriage with a driver so that he would be undistracted to enjoy Miss Winnifred—SarahAnn's—company.

A brisk wind blew up the hill, riffling her petticoats as he helped her up into the enclosed cab. He averted his gaze from the hint of her ankle boots peeking from beneath the lacy hem. Reminded of the cad his father had chosen to be, he frowned, and with great force of will, he remanded his anger to the farthest reaches of his thoughts. He chose to enjoy this day. His father's wanton spending on wine, women, and song had caused enough ruin. Rufus would not allow the thought of him to spoil this outing too.

SarahAnn removed the hood of her riding cloak, allowing a few curls to fall loose from her chignon. The lovely scent of her patchouli permeated the cozy interior, and he took the seat opposite her, basking in her nearness.

"Your mother has helped me prepare a bit of a surprise for you." She reached into her basket and retrieved a jar with dark amber-colored liquid, and the same teacup and saucer he had noticed on another occasion.

"Is that a spot of tea?"

"It is," she confessed. Her shy giggle delighted him. "I had to conceal it in the basket to keep it from detection."

He laughed as heartily as propriety allowed and removed his kid gloves. "Allow me, Miss Winnifred."

"SarahAnn," she reminded him with a flutter of her lovely lashes. "Thank you. I also have a small jar of cream and a bowl of sugar cubes, if you fancy."

"And will you partake?"

"I did pack another cup. . ."

"Delightful." Rufus relished the taste of genuine Twining's Earl Grey, guessing his mother had arranged his favorite.

"A small consolation of home, I hope. You must miss it very much."

"In some ways." He hoped his enjoyment wouldn't give quarter to that cloud always threatening to darken his thoughts. "Today, however, I much prefer the New York countryside and my present company." He was pleased to earn her lovely smile.

"Your mother has regaled me with stories of buggy rides along the Avon with your father. I daresay the charm she credits to him has been passed to his son."

The carriage hit a bump and the teacup tumbled out of his grip onto the floor between them. They both reached for it at the same time and bumped heads.

"Oh, gracious," SarahAnn sputtered, apprehending the saucer before it fell too.

"Terribly sorry," Rufus amended, holding his forehead with one hand and extending the other with an embroidered handkerchief. "Allow me." A few drops of tea had managed to splash her porcelain cheek, and he dabbed them away.

Her eyes met his, large, deepest blue, and winsome in their vulnerability. He found himself leaning in, drawn by an unexpectedly awakened impulse. An untoward man would steal a kiss at such a moment. But despite what she had innocently suggested, he was not possessed of his father's dubious charm. He placed the handkerchief in her hand and withdrew to a proper distance.

SarahAnn took the cue from his withdrawal and remanded her own posture to the back of her seat. She'd almost allowed a lapse of character. It appeared for a moment that he had intended to kiss her. Thank goodness, she had not acted the fool, since it was clear now he had never planned to do so.

"I'm afraid I've spoiled your surprise."

"Not at all. It was wonderful. Thank you."

The driver slowed the flashy pair of dapple-grays as they neared the county poorhouse. "It appears we've arrived." She slowed her rapid heartbeat with a few deep and even breaths.

Rufus turned toward the door and waited for the driver to draw it open. Then he alighted, waiting by the wheel to assist her, extending his hand.

She handed him her basket rather than her hand and helped herself down. There would be no more mistaking intentions. It almost seemed that the color had washed from his face at the mention of his parents' courtship, and she wouldn't presume to make reference to that happy station again. This was a business meeting, she reminded herself. For the sake of the children and not her own inconsequential longings. Her hope must never be placed in fallible relationships, but in the certainty of hard work and the fruit of her labors.

A warm, nutty aroma wafted on the air mingled with the pleasant smoke from a nearby campfire. A boy approached them as they stepped onto the walkway. "Care for roasted chestnuts, sir? A nickel for two bags, if you please."

SarahAnn smiled at young Chad, one of the more recent residents of the poorhouse. Despite losing the grandparents that raised them, he and his brothers showed admirable industry. "How clever of you boys. You've been working hard at collecting nuts and firewood all fall. Well done."

Rufus drew a coin from his pocket. "I'll just have the one and share it with Miss Winnifred. This is for you and your brothers."

"Thank you, sir!" Freckles on the boy's nose disappeared in crinkles of disbelief as he beheld the silver dollar.

"This is Mr. Sedgwick. He wishes to meet all my friends here."

"I'm Chad Squires, and that's my brother Billy." The boy pointed to the younger. "My older brother Charlie is selling down the block."

"A pleasure to meet you, Masters Squires. You've keen business minds."

Billy came alongside his brother, his head barely cresting Chad's shoulders, his unkempt hair trying hard to cover ears that stuck out a bit too much. SarahAnn's fingers itched to smooth one of his cowlicks.

"What does that mean?" Billy asked with a slight lisp.

"It means you're right smart lads." Rufus glanced at SarahAnn, the warmth in his eyes catching her off guard. "In England, we have the finest nutcrackers. Shaped like soldiers, they are, with their blue trousers and bright red coats—"

"Redcoats? We beat them lobsterbacks in the Revolution!"

Chad elbowed his brother. "Billy! Mind your manners."

"Well, that's what Grandpa used to say." Billy shrugged, his lips pouting.

Charlie came just then to see what the fuss was about. He stood a head taller than Chad, and the three of them together resembled stairsteps. "Don't mind our little brother, sir. He thinks he's a continental soldier."

"No offense taken. I had a grandfather who fought in the war."

Gasps of awe arose in trio. SarahAnn tucked her chin into her hood to hide her smile.

"I hate to disappoint you. I'm afraid he was a lobsterback." His crystalline gray eyes glimmered with mirth.

Billy extended his hand. "I reckon it's time to bury the hatchet."

Rufus shook on the peace offering. "Your accord is accepted."

"We don't have no fancy nutcrackers, but we got a stone that'll work for the ones what don't pop." Billy held up a river rock in his pudgy fist.

"Yes. Very resourceful."

The boy split open a chestnut on a nearby tree stump, steam rising with a vague sweetness as he presented it to them.

"Thank you." SarahAnn gave in to her temptation to smooth the boy's sandy hair. Rufus offered her a sample of the savory nutmeat.

"Mmm," she complimented. "Tastes like Christmas."

"Quite good, but for me, the taste of Christmas is plum pudding."

"I don't like Christmas no more," Billy said. "I asked Santa for lead soldiers last year, and I didn't get nothin'. And I was good as can be!"

"Well—" Rufus stooped to meet the boy at eye level. "I might know the reason. You see, Father Christmas was dreadfully busy last year, cheering the orphans of the Crimean War. I had it in strictest confidence that Santa was helping him gladden the hearts of children in England. But never fear, for Father Christmas is helping Santa Claus as a return favor this year."

"Really?" Billy's eyes widened, as did his brothers'.

And SarahAnn's. Her heart expanded with delight.

"Aren't they the same thing?" Chad asked, squinting in calculation.

"Oh no, my good lad. Next week when I return, I shall tell you all about Father Christmas and bring along some war relics of my grandfather to show you."

Rufus extended his arm again to SarahAnn, and her heart thrilled inside her as they strolled up to the door together. "You are a natural. If I didn't know better, I would think you were Father Christmas."

His mischievous grin stirred her, but she averted her gaze to his drawing the door open.

Two girls turned from their dusting and mopping to acknowledge their entrance. "Miss Sarah!"

One of them dropped her rag and ran to greet her. The other continued with her work, but smiled.

"Libby, I'd like you to meet Mr. Sedgwick. He is new to our town. I take care of his mother at the Water Cure."

The young lady curtsied in her calico cotton dress, a doll with a dirty pinafore. "How do you do?"

Rufus bowed deeply. "Good day, Miss Libby."

"And her shy friend is Miss Alice." SarahAnn beckoned the other girl.

She came, hesitation slowing her steps, her inquisitive expression rather owlish. She dropped a quick curtsy and scurried behind Libby.

"Enchanted." Rufus's gentle laughter earned him a peek from behind Libby's shoulder as Miss Alice's curiosity overcame her reserve.

"I imagine this would be a splendid room for a game of Ninepin. Once the chores are done, that is." He presented his box and set it down on a worn table.

SarahAnn remembered her basket. "Yes, and I've brought refreshment. Apple tarts and tea, if you girls would heat up the kettle."

"Polly put the kettle on, and we shall have our tea." Libby sang, sashaying to the hearth.

The shuffle of dragging footsteps and the thump of a crutch drew attention to the hallway.

Another figure appeared there, accompanied by an attendant. "Good day, Miss Sarah."

"Good to see you, Mr. Monroe. I declare, your posture has improved considerably."

"It's the liniment you gave me. Cuts the pain in half."

"Mr. Sedgwick, may I introduce Mr. Monroe? You'll never meet a more skilled carpenter."

"Until my accident, I was." He gave Rufus a half smile and a nod. "Fell from the scaffolding." He hung his head. "Haven't been able to work since."

"I'm sorry for your accident, Mr. Monroe, but meeting you is providence. You have just the skills I'm seeking. I'm in the process of building, and I'm looking to hire a consultant. I'll call on you next week."

The shadow hanging over the man's countenance lifted considerably. "Why, sure, Mr. Sedgwick. I'd be happy to help you if I can. Had to sell all my tools though to buy food."

"Tools can always be replaced, sir, but your skills, no one can take from you."

Her heart sang with Rufus's expression of charity. It seemed genuine, and not a show to please her. She prayed she was not merely hoping so.

The attendant who settled Mr. Monroe into a chair turned and placed a hand on her sleeve. "Forgive the interruption, ma'am, but there's an urgent matter. Was going to call on you, but since you're here. . ."

"Yes, what is it, Mr. Bernard?"

"Little Nellie. She's taken a bad turn."

# Chapter 7

Rufus was left standing in the parlor, holding the basket of apple tarts and tea. The sudden flight of Miss Winnifred was no surprise, given the apparent urgency, and her soon return was unlikely. He settled into a chair across from Mr. Monroe and held the basket out for him.

Monroe took one of the sweets inside. "Miss Sarah sets such store on that young'un. Sure by now, the girl'd be with the angels if it weren't for her."

"I see." Rufus thought again how Mum had called SarahAnn Florence Nightingale. The lady's famous ministrations during the Crimean War had nothing on SarahAnn's tireless efforts. He'd seen both ladies in action, and Miss Winnifred was cut from the same splinting cloth. Though he vowed after leaving home to serve at Sevastopol that he'd never interpose in matters away from his own hearth, he was already challenging that promise to himself. How could he not? The world and its needs continued to turn, no matter how affairs at home had unraveled in his absence.

Libby presently appeared with the kettle, holding it by its handle with a kitchen rag. Alice set out a chipped teapot and opened the lid for Libby to pour the hot water. The girls soon had a tea ball from Miss Winnifred's basket steeping, and the sweet blend of tea leaves and bergamot with lemon filled the air.

Monroe smiled as the girl handed a cup and saucer to both him and Rufus. "Miss Sarah never forgot where she came from. She may have risen above her humble beginnings, but she never forgot to help those she left behind here."

Rufus was just about to sip his tea, but stopped. "You mean, Miss Winnifred was an...?" He decided better than to finish his sentence. No wonder on their previous outing she'd voiced the soul-searching questions about privilege and opportunity. He felt like a first-rate cad. She had overcome adversity personally, and here he was, pontificating on it.

He pursed his lips and studied the spatterdashes on his polished leather shoes. What a fine fool he'd acted.

Miss Alice and Miss Libby sat on a shabby wooden bench, fluffing their skirts out like elegant ladies. They poured tea for one another and chattered in their best impersonations of his British pronunciations.

Drawn away from his folly and penitence, he raised his teacup. "I say, you hostesses are the bon ton."

The girls chortled and took mincing bites of their tarts.

The front door opened, and Mr. Nicholas, the front desk clerk at the health resort, entered. He took off his red tweed cap and held it to his chest. "Mr. Sedgwick, pardon my intruding on your outing, sir, but I've come to bring you some troubling news."

Rufus was on his feet. "Mum—is she...?"

"She's all right, sir. But someone has attempted to break into her room. Climbed the balcony and was caught entering through her window."

Rufus turned to Mr. Monroe, still sitting across from him. "Would you please give Miss Winnifred my regrets? My driver will bring her when she's ready to return."

With that, he swung his overcoat about his shoulders and followed Nicholas from the building.

"Has this blackguard been apprehended, Nicholas?"

"He has." The older man led to where he'd tied his work cart and pony, and gestured for Rufus to join him. "In fact, the man fell from the balcony and is being treated by Dr. Silas Gleason until the police arrive."

"What was the devil after, conducting such affairs in broad daylight?" He climbed onto the buckboard beside Nicholas.

"Your mother claims she knows him."

Rufus sat with an unceremonious thud that rocked the cart. "Knows him? How could that be? She's met no one here since we arrived in August, apart from the staff at the resort."

Nicholas snapped the reins and the workhorse moved up the road. "Claims he's your father, sir."

Incredulity rather than hatred filled Rufus, looking down on the man lying on the bed. In some ways, he preferred animosity to the pity which steeped in his turbulent thoughts like Twining's in steaming water. This was the face absent for over three years—older, somewhat thinner, but the one he remembered. Greying, thick hair combed back with a touch of pomade, and the same straight nose Rufus saw in the mirror when shaving every morning. Eyes closed in what Dr. Gleason assured him was a temporary blackout from his fall. The strong jawline, a bit bruised and showing a slight shadow of stubble. This was his father, in all his prodigal glory. But how had he come here? Why, was evident enough. No doubt, he'd come for their money. Must have burned through what he'd taken and was back for more.

"Did anyone check his pockets for purloined items?"

Dr. Silas Gleason raised astonished eyebrows to his silver hairline. "Then, you don't know this man? Your mother said—"

"No, Doctor. I'm afraid my mother may be suffering from a case of widow's wishing. My father is deceased."

"I will say that a man of his age shows great daring to have climbed that height. Had he been merely looking to burglarize, he might have chosen an easier entry point."

Rufus withheld comment. How long had the man been lurking about, studying their comings and goings, to learn where his mother slept? And had he been nosing around at the building site as well? Pity quickly flamed into his latent anger. "Is it a matter of public record who resides here? Perhaps this man heard that a daughter of the Earl of Havershire is in residence."

Dr. Gleason adjusted his spectacles. "We would never put our patients at risk, Mr. Sedgwick. And as you know, all valuables are locked away. Nothing like this has ever happened before."

"Please notify me when the constable arrives."

"Of course, I shall." The doctor's calm, steadying tone lent Rufus assurance.

"I should like to see Mum then. I imagine she is quite shaken."

Rufus covered the corridor in brisk strides, climbing the stairs up to her room two at a time. The pounding in his head reverberated like the siege guns of Sevastopol, and he wished only to outdistance the shame it summoned.

If only he hadn't gone to war. If only he'd learned that charity begins at home, where Mum needed him. Father would've never dared abandon her, let alone steal from her, with Rufus looking on. The coward had waited for Rufus to depart for the battlefield on his mercy mission to do his dastardly deeds.

Rufus didn't realize he'd fisted both hands until he had to unclench them to open Mum's door. It was partially ajar, and she sat in her highbacked chair, looking out on the view from three stories up. The town of Elmira glittered below them under a clear sky, bright despite the chill in the air. Far below, a locomotive's steam whistle rent the air while its smokestack percolated a dark plume, and Rufus wished he could so easily vent the turbulence within him.

Mum turned in her seat upon his entry. "You'll never guess who came to see me!" Her countenance practically glowed.

Rufus's stomach churned, while a servant turned down Mum's bedcovers. The handle of a bedwarmer in her hands, the woman moved the cast-iron box holding live coals in and out between the sheets, preparing for afternoon rest.

"Mother, you mustn't. . . Excuse me, madam, would you mind terribly if we had a moment of privacy?"

"Shall I help her into bed first, sir?"

"I'll assist my mother. Thank you for your kindness."

The servant bowed her head and departed.

"Mother, you mustn't place any confidence in that faithless wastrel."

"Do not speak of your father that way, Rufus."

Her uncharacteristically stern tone took him aback.

He paced the small room, praying silently for the right words to warn his mother that she needed protection from the man to whom she had pledged her vows. How could he reason with a heart impossibly committed to a man undeserving of fealty?

"He's the reason I had to force you to leave your home. He's the reason you're here, stuck in this provincial hotel for the infirm, when you might have enjoyed years more, watching your grandchildren born and raised in the place of your ancestry. He stole much more than your money, Mother. He stole our future."

Her eyes lost their sparkle, and she turned a weary gaze down at her hands. "I cannot believe what they've said of him. I refuse to believe it."

"I will not raise the specter of his behavior here, other than to say, you mustn't allow him a moment of your audience. He is a charmer, a liar, and the worst kind of villain to hurt you as he has."

"Oh, Rufus, you will see that the rumors about him are mistaken. I cannot convince you. I pray your own eyes will see the truth."

He ran a hand through his hair and willed the pulse to stop pounding at his temples. "I'm glad to see your vigor is intact despite the commotion. Allow me to help you to your bed, and I will join you for dinner later."

He stood by as she rose, her arm tucked in his, and then he nestled her into her warmed bedcovers. He placed a deferential kiss on her cheek and bid her sweet dreams.

He met a worker in the corridor who had come to tell him of the arrival of the police. The man led him to the conference room.

The uniformed officer motioned Rufus to a chair. "Do you mind if I ask you a few questions, Mr. Sedgwick?"

"I have a few questions for you as well. Carry on." Rufus sat and crossed a boot over his knee, settling in.

"The suspect has been identified as Rufus Sedgwick II. He had papers to that effect on his person. So naturally, I am curious. Why would your father make such an unconventional appearance, and why did you tell Dr. Gleason he was deceased?"

"Am I the one under suspicion?"

"Just answer the question, Sedgwick."

"The man is indeed my father. But I believed him dead. Perhaps wishful thinking. I hadn't seen him since before I left for the Crimean War three years ago. He abandoned my mother amid unseemly rumors that threatened to ruin our good name. He was seen in Exeter giving a young woman jewelry—my mother's emeralds. Mum's poor heart gave out, and I felt it my duty to remove her from the scandal and to seek a gentle cure for her ailing health."

"I see. But why here?"

"My grandfather served with distinction here during the Revolution. I thought it a place where the name Sedgwick mightn't carry disgrace."

The officer nodded, seeming satisfied that he was telling the truth. "So, this father whom you believed dead reappears now, here. Any theories as to why?"

"No doubt he's seeking to steal again."

"Since they're married, would it not be his money?"

Rufus rose, but as the officer touched his sidearm, he altered his course and paced to the side. "Because my mother was abandoned by my father and we believed him dead, British common law allows her to reassume property rights. Which she has done, and consequently, transferred her material wealth here. New York, if I am not mistaken, grants even married women the right to retain wealth as of the 1848 Property Act. I believe that explains more than sufficiently. If you have any further questions, I shall have to refer you to my solicitor."

The officer shook his head. "I hope that won't be necessary, Mr. Sedgwick. Unfortunately, I cannot charge your father for an alleged theft that occurred in Britain. And since none occurred here, my hands are tied." Then, turning to Gleason, he asked, "Do you wish to press charges for breaking and entering, Doctor?"

Dr. Gleason deferred to Rufus. "It's a most unusual case. Your mother hasn't been harmed, and nothing's been stolen. But it is unsettling. I need to assure my patients this will not happen again."

Rufus nodded his head. "Then I say, prosecute him to the fullest extent of the law."

"I have all I need," the constable replied. "Thank you for your time."

Rufus swept from the room like a November squall and almost collided with the jovial desk clerk.

Mr. Nicholas stepped aside, apologizing. "I beg your pardon, Mr. Sedgwick."

Rufus stopped. "No, it was my fault, Nicholas. Terribly sorry. And since I have you here, I might as well give you these. I won't be needing them."

He produced the tickets for the opera and handed them to the clerk. Before the man could refuse, Rufus turned on his heel and departed.

# Chapter 8

### The County Poorhouse

SarahAnn untied the borrowed apron, spattered with onion poultice and chicken broth, and placed it in the clothes hamper in the hallway outside of Nellie's room. By the slanting rays of the late afternoon sun, she guessed a few hours had passed. The child finally slept after a frightful coughing spell had left her exhausted. SarahAnn had done all she knew to do, and the rest was up to the Lord's mercy.

Entering the front room, she surmised what she had suspected long ago. Rufus was already gone. Mr. Monroe attempted to rise on feeble legs, and she waved. "No need to get up. I'm just going to have one of the Squires boys summon a livery to take me back to the Water Cure."

"You won't have to do that, Miss Sarah. Mr. Sedgwick left his driver here for you. He was called away suddenly."

"Oh?"

"Yes, ma'am. And I've been setting here, kicking myself for something I said to the feller. You've been nothing but kind to me, and it was because of my admiration for all you've done that I accidentally said something that wasn't mine to say."

"Whatever do you mean, Mr. Monroe?" She placed her palms at the small of her back and stretched, the ache traveling up her spine and into her neck. "I'm sure you would never do anything bad."

"Well, I surely didn't mean to, Miss Sarah, but I wasn't thinking. I told him how you always take such consideration for us here, and. . .and—"

"Yes? And what?"

"I said you never forgot where you come from." He hung his head. "I told him you were an orphan too."

Panic laced her stays even tighter, and her breath hitched. "Oh, Mr. Monroe."

"I know I had no business sayin' it. I don't know what come over me. I'm frightful sorry."

"And he left shortly after that?" Her voice was so weak she could hardly force sound. She would have told Rufus in her own time. But now? That stubborn hope in her heart was slow to die, the hope that whispered that she might find love with an honorable man like Rufus Sedgwick. The pain lancing through her middle was surely the death of that hope.

"Yes'm. As I recollect, he left shortly after that." Monroe nodded in a rather hang-dogged way.

Her eyes glazed over. Stepping blindly toward the glow of the door, she hastened to retreat. "Think nothing of it, Mr. Monroe. It's the truth, after all. I am an orphan, and I mustn't pretend to be anything else."

The driver saw her approach and scurried to open the door of the buggy. He tipped his hat and helped her inside. "Back to the Water Cure, ma'am?"

She nodded, numbness settling over her as she sank into the seat. Mr. Monroe's revelation had certainly settled the matter. Mr. Sedgwick knew her secret. Shame burned her insides, all the way up to the rims of her eyes. Mostly she chided herself for harboring the false hope of ever rising above her past. No amount of hard work or determination would turn her blood blue or forge a pedigree for herself. She drew in a deep breath and bolstered her resolve. Hard work may not change her humble station, but it would enable her to help others. And that was what she wanted more than anything, certainly more than the fickle attention of some high-toned Brit. She batted away a stray tear that had formed and determined to make this the best possible Christmas for the children and her patients, with or without anyone's help.

As the carriage arrived and turned a slow circle around the drive at the Water Cure, SarahAnn prepared to alight and to put on her brave mask of confidence for whomever she might meet inside. What she really wanted was a warm soak and a good book and early to bed. But, oh! The plans for dinner and the theater. She certainly would not hold the man to the pretense of the invitation. She pinched her cheeks, which she was certain held no color after a very draining afternoon, and stepped out. She would simply tell Mr. Nicholas to make excuses for her to Rufus—Mr. Sedgwick—saying she was under the weather.

As she approached the door, a policeman held it open for her, followed by another policeman who led a distinguished-looking older man from the building. "Thank you," she said, looking back at them with mild curiosity. She didn't recognize the man in custody as one of her patients, nor was he a regular visitor. But something about him was vaguely familiar. Putting her interfering thoughts aside, she continued into the quiet parlor. She'd returned at dinnertime. How fortunate. She would not likely run into anyone she didn't care to see.

Except there was still the matter of talking with the desk clerk. She lifted her chin and approached the desk. Mr. Nicholas appeared engrossed in a ledger and only looked up when she cleared her throat.

"Good afternoon, Mr. Nicholas."

"Yes, Miss Winnifred. A busy one, but good in its own way, I suppose."

"Would you be so kind as to tell Mr. Sedgwick I will not be attending tonight? Please let him know my regrets."

"Yes, ma'am. But—"

"Just tell him I am unwell." If the heartache constricting her middle and stealing her breath qualified as a malady, she spoke the truth.

"Shall I fetch Mrs. Gleason?"

"No, that won't be necessary. Perhaps you might have my dinner brought to my room though."

"Yes, Miss Winnifred. But I—"

"I hope it's not too late for you to enjoy the evening with your missus. You're a saint for all you do here and deserve an evening out."

"You weren't supposed to know about that, miss." His cheeks reddened, making him appear rather elfish, like Washington Irving's depiction of her childhood holiday favorite.

An idea sprang to her mind. "I'm organizing the orphans' Christmas this year. Perhaps you might do me a favor...?"

"Anything you need, Miss Winnifred. But I've been trying to tell you something."

"Oh yes, of course. What is it?"

The clerk looked about the room, as though to assure they were alone. He inclined his head, showing his balding pate with a white ring of hair surrounding. "Mr. Sedgwick has had to cancel for the night. I'm afraid he's had a rather bad shock today. He found out something that upset him a great deal. I'm sure he'll discuss it with you in his own timing. I hope you understand."

Darkness nipped at the edges of her sight, but she refused to give in to the strangling sense of mortification. Of course he'd had a bad shock. He'd learned the truth about her. Having no family was hardly an endorsement for an audience with the queen. She drew a steadying breath through her nose and expelled it through pursed lips, holding the edge of the desk.

"Tell Mr. Sedgwick he needn't bother explaining. I understand him quite well enough." She lifted her chin, turned, and fled before her tears spilled.

Mother refused to eat a morsel. Rufus had pleaded, cajoled, and almost threatened to get the doctor, but at last he was resigned that she deserved the dignity of choice in this. So many other choices had been taken from her. He sat beside her at the dining table, hoping to find something consoling to tell her. At last, he thought of the children. Mum always enjoyed the spritely ways of lads and lasses.

"I had a lovely time with Miss Winnifred today, meeting some very charming youngsters."

A smile lit her nutmeg eyes. "How lovely, dear. The little princes and princesses. What are their names?"

"I met Chad, Billy, and Charlie Squires. Three brothers. The youngest is an aspiring soldier. And the older two are young entrepreneurs."

She clapped her hands together. "I should like very much to meet them! Do let us have them to the house, Rufus. They must visit the Welsh ponies and pick their fill of apples."

He tilted his head at her. He was uncertain if she realized it might be a year before they rebuilt their stable and many years before the orchards were established. But that wasn't the first time she'd revealed a gaffe in her memory. He thought better than to correct her. The thought obviously gave her joy, and he would not spoil it.

"Yes, Mum. And there were two girls as well. Miss Libby and Miss Alice. Proper hostesses, they were."

"Ah, yes, a home isn't complete without lovely little girls spinning and playing the pianoforte and delighting their guests."

Rufus smiled, imagining the home she grew up in, with a brother and sisters and lively occasions. His upbringing had been less so, as an only child. It seemed her childhood years had returned to her more vividly these days than his. Uncle Edwin, the youngest and a bachelor, had been gone twenty-five years now. Rufus had fond memories of him. And Auntie Flora and Auntie Gertrude had also passed, but in more recent times. Spinsters both, they had lived with them his whole life.

"Your father should like to see your children, Rufus."

He shook out of his wandering thoughts, once again startled at her words.

"You mustn't hold grudges, dear. He came to return what he borrowed. Says he has the heirloom jewels in a safe place."

"You're tired, Mum. I should take my leave for the evening."

She looked at him with an urgency that sparked through him. "Listen to me, Rufus. He's come to make amends. You simply must arrange to meet with him."

After he had left the room, her strange words stayed with him. He would speak to the good doctor tomorrow about the new concerns over Mum's mental state. Exiting the building through a side door facing East Hill Road, he caught sight of the police wagon turning from the resort's drive and clattering down the hill. An ungentlemanly growl escaped him as he walked into the brisk winterlike air toward the front drive, where he found his carriage parked beneath the portico.

Miss Winnifred had returned from the orphanage safely then, albeit alone. The sudden realization of loss socked him in his gut. His father had ruined yet another good thing—the promise of what was to be a lovely evening with the woman who was quickly capturing his heart. The brave, selfless girl. Caring for the ones still caught in the grip of misfortune, after overcoming so much herself. A lady of such character was rare, even in the finest families of Britain. He gave way to a fond smile despite the pang swelling within him. The scent of spilt tea and her patchouli still hung in a fragrant wreath about the cab. He stepped back and closed the door instead of entering.

"Driver, begging your pardon, but I've one more thing I must do. Wait and I'll make it worth your while."

"Yes, sir."

He jogged to the front door of the parlor and swung it open, to see Miss Winnifred speaking to Mr. Nicholas. Ah, good. Just the two he hoped to see.

But what were they saying? Ho! Surely Nicholas wouldn't mention his father and the disgraceful events of the day?

Her posture visibly stiffened, standing at the desk, and her reply froze him in his tracks. "Tell Mr. Sedgwick he needn't bother explaining. I understand him quite well enough."

He watched her depart, the door to the doctors' offices shuddering in its frame in her haste. She might as well have struck him with it.

He stood there, quite immobilized, his hand over his waistcoat as though it might help him recover his breath. Only one thing could have caused that reaction. What she must think of him!

Mr. Nicholas turned sympathetic eyes to him and emerged from behind the counter. "I can't possibly accept these tickets, Mr. Sedgwick. I won't prosper at your misfortune. Our wager was all in good fun, but now, I don't feel very much like making merry with the missus. Thank you all the same."

Rufus stamped out the misery from his voice. "Nonsense, man. The carriage is waiting. Off you go."

"But. . ."

"I insist. Only, would you be so kind as to drop me off at the police station on your way? I have business to which I must attend."

# Chapter 9

*Chemung County Jail*

Iron gates groaned, swinging on their hinges, and Rufus winced at the strident sound as he passed through the front entry. Darkness had fallen, and the gaslight along the stone created flickering shadows. He expected to see the Artful Dodger or Fagin grimacing behind one of the corners as the guard led him deeper into the jail's interior. He would almost rather it had been a stranger he'd come to see.

The shuffling of feet behind a dark cell and the jangle of a key prickled an involuntary chill down Rufus's spine. This place was ill-fit for the lowliest vermin, let alone a human. Regret, and perhaps the smallest thread of sympathy, wove through him at the thought of his father languishing in such a place. If only there were some miraculous explanation for his behavior, as Mum believed. A flash of anger rushed in with the recollection of all the man had done to Mum and to him. Meeting clandestinely with women, offering them his mother's heirloom jewels. The man ought to thank Providence he had only been charged with the petty crime of loitering.

The guard held up a lantern, and its circle of light spilled halfway into the cell. Rufus could make out forms without features, but he could well sense his father even before he could see him. The signature oakmoss cologne and a hint of the rose boutonniere he wore in his lapel, as though he were a London dandy, turned even this musty cavern into an English garden. Rufus snorted.

"I knew you would come!" His father's irrepressible baritone sang from the shadows, and he strode with polished knee boots to the edge of the iron bars. "My son, let me look at you. My, how robust you've grown! Going to war has, I daresay, only improved your stature."

Rufus held his silence, and after a moment, his father's overly enthusiastic comments tempered as well.

"Yes, well, I suppose I owe you a good explanation for my absence. And I have one." The man tapped his breast pocket for a cigar case that wasn't there, and scowled slightly. "It was poor timing, I warrant. I should have consulted with you. But you didn't exactly tell me you were off to Crimea either, Son. You know I would have tried to talk you out of it."

"My charitable affairs are not at issue here. Your philandering and theft, Father. That is the matter at hand."

"I do say, is that what you thought?" His laughter broke apart on the brick and stone like shattered glass. "Hurting the woman whom I treasure?"

Rufus fisted a hand beside his overcoat and itched to strike a blow. The guard and iron bars spared him from dishonor.

Father's tone sobered and hushed considerably. "I can see why you must wonder now, reexamining the events. And I don't hold it against you, my boy. Your posture shows your honor, and your unwavering devotion to your mother is commendable, I must say."

"This was a mistake, coming here." Rufus took two strides toward the entrance. "Guard, you may take me back."

"Wait, Son. It's not in vain that you've come. I confess I am more old fool than romantic, but I thought to surprise your mother by climbing her balcony like I used to when we were courting."

Rufus paused but refused to turn.

"Did she not tell you of my letters?"

Swiveling, Rufus faced his father. "What letters?"

"The letters I sent to her, to both of you, from here in Elmira. You see, after I met the young lady at Exeter and learned her identity, I felt compelled to come. She claimed that your grandfather Sedgwick, when fleeing Sullivan's army after the Battle of Newtown, had escorted an Iroquois woman to safety in Niagara. The continental army was brutal on the indigenous people here. Razed their village and crops, forcing them to flee their ancestral homes."

Rufus snorted at the irony. His father went on.

"This young woman claimed my father and her mother had shared a common-law marriage. Though Grandmama had been dead over ten years by then, I still feared scandal if the news got out. The woman refused my bribe to keep her silent. So, I came here to investigate her claim."

The ground beneath Rufus's feet seemed to give way, and he grasped onto the solid bars beside him. "You've been in New York this whole time?"

"Not the whole time. But a good portion of it."

"And Mum—you've been corresponding with her all this while?"

"And visiting her. I'd been navigating her balcony quite well up until recently."

Rufus raked his fingers through his hair. "I'm flabbergasted. And Mother's jewels?"

"With your agent, for safekeeping."

"My agent?"

"Yes, my boy. Who do you think has been helping him look after your affairs, such as delivering your stone and arranging your workforce? You didn't suppose your agent had accomplished all of that alone, did you? Now, if you would sign my release papers, I would be delighted to introduce you to your cousin."

"Of all the outrages." Rufus's anger flared again. "I will do no such thing. You will serve your sentence until its completion."

"I see you don't believe me. Go and see if the gems are there. That will prove I am not the shameless lout you must think me."

"I will," Rufus replied. "And if there is no Indian maiden and no jewelry, then what?"

His father rose to his full height, clasped his hands behind his back, and looked at him squarely with the same grey-blue eyes as Rufus's own. "Then you shall boil me for Christmas pudding!" His laughter once again carried out too brightly on the dreary corridor.

Preposterous. "A good buggy whipping would suffice."

"Come, now. Your father is no blackguard."

Rufus took a deep breath and expelled it slowly. "The woman's address?"

"Yes, it is along the westernmost edge of town. Past Hendy farm, you'll find Fitch's boardinghouse. You must ask for Miss Emmaline."

*The County Poorhouse*

Days turned to weeks as SarahAnn fought the fever which raged through Nellie's fragile body. In between administering measured doses of the willow bark tea that Doctor Rachel Gleason had sent for the child, SarahAnn prayed. She prayed for the child and prayed for Mrs. Sedgwick, whom she'd left in the care of another of the good doctor's protégés. But mostly, she prayed about Rufus Sedgwick.

"Lord, I don't know why You've allowed me this glimpse at a future with him. But if it's not of You, please take this rogue desire from my heart." If the longing wouldn't die, she would prescribe her heart a starvation diet to cure it of a love that simply would never be.

She slipped out of the child's room to visit with the other residents. Christmas was now a little more than a week away, and plans had taken form in her mind. She and the children would make decorations for both their house and the Water Cure. SarahAnn had given Charlie Squires enough coins to purchase colored paper, thread, needles, popping corn, and a bushel of assorted fruit and cloves.

While she waited for the oldest brother to return, she gathered the others into the parlor.

"All right, children, form a circle. I want you to practice a few songs for the Christmas party."

"A party?" Stampeding feet and excited squeals filled the parlor. By the time they began the second verse of "Away in a Manger," order was restored and even the boys added their voices.

A knock on the front door interrupted their caroling. Chad sprang up to answer, and a courier stood, balancing a few packages.

"There a Mr. Monroe here?"

SarahAnn rose from her chair. "Yes, he lives here. Shall I bring him?"

"Just let him know he has an order. And who are the Masters Squires?"

"That's us!" Billy raced to Chad's side at the door. His eyes grew round as walnuts, and almost as dark, as pupils swallowed irises in sheer delight.

"This one's for you."

The courier glanced back at his rig parked at the street. "I've a few more, if you'll oblige me."

SarahAnn rose from the chair and strode to the doorway to watch. Many more bundles awaited.

The young courier allowed the Squires boys to assist, and after one more trip, the parlor table overflowed with bundles.

"What is all this?" SarahAnn asked.

"I have a note here," the deliveryman replied. "Says, 'From Saint Nick: do not open until December 24.'"

Excited chatter dissolved the orderly room into happy chaos.

A tug pulled at her sleeve. Alice peered up at her, spindly and timid like a fawn.

"What is it, sweetie?"

"I saw him."

"Who, child? Who did you see?"

"Father Christmas, I think. It didn't look like Santa Claus."

"Whatever do you mean?"

"A man, dressed like Mr. Sedgwick. Gray-haired and tall, not fat like Santa, but very merry."

"Where did you see him, and what was he doing?"

"He was talking to Charlie and Chad. Asking all about us here."

A slight chill tingled over her. "When was this?"

"The other day. He said he'd return."

SarahAnn took the girl's slim shoulders in her hands and looked into her eyes. "If he shows up again, be sure to tell one of the adults."

The description Alice gave matched the man led away from the Water Cure by the police. She needed to speak to Mr. Nicholas. He would surely be able to tell her who the man was.

Before the courier departed, he handed SarahAnn a lithographed card with a scene of a horse-drawn sleigh. She held it up to look for a signature. Instead, in the hand-printed text was a scripture: *Greet Rufus, chosen in the Lord, also his mother, who has been like a mother to me as well. Romans 16:13*

This could not have been the work of Rufus Sedgwick. As soon as Nellie was well enough, SarahAnn would return to the Water Cure and investigate her suspicions.

# Chapter 10

*Bluff Overlooking the Chemung River*

Rufus and his mother sat snuggly beneath a fur throw in his sleigh at the base of the road leading up to his property. Weeks had passed since SarahAnn had walked away from him and his tarnished family. He distracted himself by gazing on the completed façade of the Gothic-style home. Scaffolding and an innovative iron steam crane continued the work even into the snows of late December. The sight sent conflicting emotions through him. He'd almost expected it to look out of place, his ancestral home, here. But somehow, it did not.

"It's as though the land were carved to fit it," Mum remarked.

"Yes," he replied. If possible, it looked even more grand here than its original location on the Avon.

His mother's gains in health didn't escape his notice. Grudgingly, he had to admit her heart rallied as soon as his father had made his dramatic re-entry into their lives. But he avoided the man himself, now released from jail and assigned to serve the community, entirely too free to intrude on Rufus's carefully laid plans to forget the past. Nevertheless, the past had followed him here. No, it had led him here. Unwitting, he had followed it.

But for what?

"You should be proud of all you have managed, Son." Mum smiled.

True, he'd nearly attained what had looked impossible—rebuilding their lives brick by brick. And yet, he searched for a sense of accomplishment that would not come. His heart felt cold and barren, like the shell of the building itself. No light in the windows, no inhabitants, nor glow of a warm fire within. He felt empty inside, unfinished.

"Once the work is completed, perhaps. Christmas comes tomorrow. I had great hopes to move in by then."

"One never knows." Her nutmeg eyes hinted of secret-keeping. Heretofore, he'd thought her faculties weak or misguided. Perhaps she knew more than he.

"I saw Miss Winnifred yesterday."

"Oh?" He knew his voice betrayed the conflict which the name inspired within him.

"She looked well, except. . ."

He clamped his jaw. Mum was leading him, and he refused to take the bait.

"I often wonder why she looks so lonesome. As though she has no one in the whole world in which to confide."

"Apparently, she has Mr. Nicholas."

"What do you mean, dear?"

"Nothing."

Since hearing his father's story of Grandfather Sedgwick's Iroquois common-law wife and verifying that his account of the missing gemstones was true, he had been left feeling more unsettled than ever. As though he didn't know in whom or what to trust. Everything he'd doubted had proven upright, and nothing—and no one—he'd trusted seemed to hold weight. He thought he'd been making friends here, and the two he'd grown most fond of had only disillusioned him. Miss Winnifred had altogether disappeared, and if he passed Mr. Nicholas in the hall, he turned from the man's pitying glances.

"Won't you excuse me, Mum? I believe I will take a walk."

He climbed the rise toward the house, praying as he went. "What am I to believe, Lord? I thought it was You who led me here. Why, if not to find a new life?"

An evergreen hedgerow fringed the newly constructed garden wall, and in the midst of the low-growing vegetation emerged a song he knew in an instant. It was the trilling call of a nightingale. But how? They were not native to the Americas. Had one stowed away with the building material, crossing the ocean?

He paused and, there amid the branches, a reddish-brown form flitted, catching a stray highlight of sun. So much like the color of Miss Winnifred's hair. *The American Nightingale.*

Rufus stood transfixed. So lovely and yet, such a precarious existence, foraging for herself alone. He would gather her in his hands and rescue her, but the little bird was too proud. Or perhaps too timorous.

A red-coated cardinal swooped onto the branch next to the nightingale. Perhaps he had mistaken the duller red bird for a mate of his species. They bowed and curtsied to one another in what appeared to be a courtship ritual, and then they both flew away in unison.

Rufus's heart stuttered in his chest. How could he be certain of SarahAnn's true inclination unless he took a risk? He must go to her, speak to her. The worst she could do was rebuff him.

The pair of dapple-gray horses he'd recently purchased tossed their heads as he approached the sleigh, and the bells on their harness filled the air with a Christmas melody. He sprang into the driver's seat and Mum greeted him cheerfully.

"Your father is downtown serving today at the orphanage. Would you mind terribly if we brought him and the children up to the Water Cure? They're supposed to trim the Christmas tree today."

Rufus beamed at the fortuitous timing. The children. Of course. That would certainly get Miss Winnifred's attention. And perhaps Christmas Eve was as good a time as any to extend the forgiveness due his father. Perhaps the man had gone ahead of him and prepared more than just the material for building a house. Perhaps his father's path had led Rufus to secure a home and a family of his own.

He gave a shout and slapped the reins.

"Mr. Nicholas, might you have a moment?" SarahAnn approached the desk, pushing her crinolined skirts down to allow her to step closer.

"Of course, Miss Winnifred. Is this about the favor you mentioned a few weeks back?"

"Yes, and something else."

He stepped from around the counter, just as two young men entered the front door, hauling in a fresh-cut pine tree. "Excuse me one moment, Miss Winnifred. Gents, to the side of the hearth, if you please. Yes, perfect. Prince Albert couldn't have chosen better for the queen herself."

SarahAnn's ribs crimped her sore heart. Every British reference inevitably dragged her thoughts back to Rufus Sedgwick. Which only distracted her from her purpose.

"Mr. Nicholas, the night of the opera. . ."

"A little to the left, boys. Steady. All right! That'll do it."

She stepped aside with a slight sigh. The man's attention was impossible to hold. It seemed that the closer Christmas approached the busier he got.

"I'm sorry, miss. You were saying? The night of the opera?"

"Yes, that night, a man was taken away by the police. What can you tell me about him?"

He gave her a dubious glance and turned slightly away, toward the workers securing the tree. She stepped into his line of sight and folded her arms over her chest.

"Who was he?"

"Uh, well, Miss Winnifred." He removed his red cap and ran a hand over his glossy pate. "I hoped by now you'd a' heard for yourself."

"Heard what?"

He fidgeted with the herringboned wool in thick workman's fingers. " 'Twas Mr. Sedg-wick's father, miss. He should have told you. But I expect his shame kept him silent."

"Shame? Whatever for?"

"Then you don't know?"

"Mr. Nicholas, if you don't tell me this instant, I shall scream."

"Poor Rufus thought his father was a thief and had returned to disgrace him."

She pressed her hand over her middle, her jaw slacking a bit. "You mean, the shocking news he'd heard that day was that his estranged father had returned?"

So he wasn't put off to learn she was an orphan? A thrill of hope fluttered within her.

The clerk's head bobbed in a solemn nod, and the pencil he'd wedged behind his ear almost dislodged.

"Oh, Mr. Nicholas, thank you!" She reached out and embraced the clerk with a kiss, knocking the pencil from its perch and turning his cheeks crimson. "That's wonderful news!"

"It is?" The man stood there befuddled, scratching the back of his neck with the blunt end of the pencil.

"I must find Mr. Sedgwick at once."

He replaced his cap and shrugged. "Should be along soon. Took his mother for a ride in his new cutter."

She sped away to the cloak closet to retrieve her riding cloak. She had so many thoughts brimming within her, like what to say to him first? How sorry she was, or how delighted? By the time she returned to the parlor, the Christmas tree had been secured upright and was being fitted with a lovely garland of red velvet ribbon. Mr. Nicholas stood at the counter checking his lists, his cheeks still ruddy.

She approached him. "There's one more thing," she said. "The favor. The children at the orphanage have made decorations for the tree here, and—"

"Absolutely, Miss Winnifred. I've already arranged to have Mr. Sedgwick the elder bring them."

"How wonderful! Also, would you mind playing Santa Claus?"

A smile pushed his rosy cheeks back until they almost disappeared into his white whiskers. "I thought you'd never ask."

She nodded her thanks and flung her cloak around her shoulders then made her way toward the door.

# Chapter 11

Horses' harness bells rang as Rufus turned the pair on the snowy drive toward the front of the Water Cure. Behind his cutter, a many-seated market sledge followed, driven by his father. From that conveyance, the children's voices lifted sweet and clear on the frosty air, rounding out a chorus of "Jingle Bells." A porter approached with a lit lantern in hand, the late afternoon world of shadows growing darker under the snow clouds overhead.

The lantern man helped the children alight, while a pair of orderlies came to assist Mum in from the cold, Father attentive by her side. Rufus had no immediate occupation with the abundance of helpers, so he paused by the pair of dapple-grays. Fat clusters of snow drifted down from the heavens, piling cozily against backlit windowsills crackled with frost patterns. Rufus would have enjoyed the compelling sight so much more sharing it with a certain lovely young medical student. Where could a red-coated cardinal and a brave little nightingale find shelter from the storm? Surely their worlds were too disparate to make a suitable match together.

"Won't you come in for some warm, spiced cider, Mr. Sedgwick?"

He turned at the sound of the voice. And there she stood, her blue riding cloak silhouetted against the white background of snow on the lawn.

A deep breath filled his chest, taking in the essence of her patchouli and the milled spices of the drink in her hand. His frozen heart awakened with a rush. He stepped forward, and she took his elbow, smiling up at him sweetly.

He inclined his head to say the whispered words in her ear. "I'd be delighted, SarahAnn."

She closed her eyes, and a soft murmur responded to his nearness. But then she broke the trance and moved toward the door.

He escorted her inside, where Mum sat by the crackling hearth, her face aglow with a joy only love could inspire. Father stood by her side, gazing at her with a tenderness Rufus had never before recognized. He understood it now because he felt the same sentiment growing within the depths of him. Mum's delicate fingers lovingly caressed the emerald necklace that hadn't been there earlier. Father must have replaced it in a clandestine moment.

"Your mother looks positively radiant."

Rufus turned to SarahAnn. "I wish I had told you about my family before now."

SarahAnn shook her head. "No, I should have told you about mine. I'm ashamed you had to discover it by chance."

Candles created a soft ambience in the room, reflecting the luster in her eyes. Rufus couldn't deny the sincerity he read there. His hand sought hers. "You're a lady of uncommon character, Miss Winnifred. I've never met anyone I admire more."

Her throat moved as though she swallowed, and those expressive blue eyes of hers closed. He firmed his hold of her hand, and she squeezed his in return. When her lashes fluttered open, they were glistening with tears.

"You don't think less of me? That I've no family, no name. . ."

His heart twisted inside him. How could she not see how noble, how lovely, how worthy she was? "The only name I wish to confer on you is my own. If it wouldn't be considered a blight to you."

She bowed her head, and he lifted a gentle hand to push her hood back from her face, letting it fall to her shoulders. He cupped her chin and lifted her face to meet his gaze.

"Do you find me unsuitable because of my father's outrageous behavior?"

"Your family is delightful. I adore your mother. And it is obvious your father adores her as well. No, Rufus," she whispered. "You would come to regret marrying a woman with no mother or father at all."

"Miss Winnifred, my only regret at present is that I don't know who to ask for your hand."

The floor tilted as SarahAnn's world upended. And yet she stood on her own two feet, strong beside the man who had just declared his intention to marry her. How handsome he looked, with his gold jacquard waistcoat more festive than the ornaments bedecking the hall. She covered her mouth with her hand, and he removed it and brushed a kiss over her knuckles.

"Might you consider marriage in addition to your calling as a physician?"

She drew a bolstering breath until she recovered her voice. "The only man who might persuade me is standing before me."

Rufus's mother and father turned smiling faces to them. Their acceptance seeped into a chamber of SarahAnn's heart, stoking a cold, lonely space with the brightest and warmest of hopes—for family.

And another couple, standing a few paces away from Mr. and Mrs. Sedgwick, looked on as well. The doctors Gleason nodded at her and Rufus, and smiled. A twinkle illuminated Rachel Gleason's maternal eye.

"If you wish to ask anyone, I recommend Silas Gleason. Be quick though, before he's called away to tend one of his patients."

Rufus nodded and sought out the good doctor straight away.

SarahAnn gathered the children, who had been trimming the tree with their popcorn strings, dried fruit slices, pomanders, and candle lanterns. All had come—Chad, Charlie, Billy, Alice, Libby, and even little Nellie, pale and thin, but thoroughly happy.

"Why don't we sing the carols we've been practicing?"

She directed them to form a semicircle and took her place at the center. Gazing about the health resort's parlor where rows of chairs had been arranged for the patients, she felt surrounded by love. Each of these faces were as precious as any mother or father, sister or brother to her.

When she focused back on the children, she met six pairs of shining eyes eagerly awaiting her direction. She raised her hands, and they each drew a candle up to their face, holding them like perfect little watchmen. Then their voices broke the hush.

"Silent night. Holy night. All is calm, all is bright. . ."

An amber glow bathed each precious singer and onlooker and, one by one, the adults joined the chorus. Mrs. Sedgwick stood with Rufus, her arm resting in the crook of her son's.

"Sleep in heavenly peace, sleep in heavenly peace."

The song concluded, and the front door opened with a bluster of wind and snow. In walked Mr. Nicholas, dressed in a sporting red tweed waistcoat, black trousers, and white shirtsleeves. On his back, he carried a brimming sack of red burlap, the kind used for feed. He set it down at the base of the tree, and out tumbled a few boxes wrapped in brown paper and merry-colored ribbon.

SarahAnn recognized the parcels the courier left at the orphanage.

"Saint Nick!" she cried.

The children drew an audible gasp, but before they could fully react, in behind Mr. Nicholas strode the elder Mr. Sedgwick, striking a tall, elegant figure in a dark green overcoat with fur trim. He also carried a peddler's pack, out of which peeked a shiny-painted nutcracker, among other items.

Rufus laughed aloud. "Father Christmas!"

The children squealed with delight, and a happy pandemonium ensued.

SarahAnn took the opportunity to find Rufus in the crowd and stood at his side. "Did you arrange this?"

He shrugged, and the wonder in his grin made her heart flutter. "I have it in good confidence that Mr. and Mrs. Nicholas will be adopting the Squires boys."

"Oh, Rufus, how wonderful. And did you see? My little Nellie is well."

"Yes, our little Nellie," he repeated so low she almost didn't hear him.

"Do you mean. . . ?"

"Yes. And Libby and Alice too, if you're willing." He took her hand. "SarahAnn, I have one more surprise for you. Come and meet my father." He drew her to the center of the festivities. Children scurried away with gifts, clearing the way to Mr. Sedgwick as the couple approached.

Rufus's father turned to her and bowed. "Have you ever opened a Christmas cracker, my dear?" He placed a small, tube-shaped package in her hand, its twisted ends wrapped from gay paper.

"No, never."

"This one, I believe, is from my son."

He and Rufus exchanged identical winks and grins, and the warmth between them conferred an invitation to her. Anticipation sizzled in the air as palpably as the logs in the hearth. She took the cracker in her fingers and pulled the ends, opening the package with a startling pop. Out of the cylinder dropped a sapphire bracelet, a matching necklace, and a ring.

Rufus caught the gems before they tumbled to the floor, and lifted them to her. "Say you'll marry me?"

SarahAnn gasped and pressed her fingertips to her lips. "Yes."

Rufus clasped the beautiful pieces about her wrist, neck, and finally, her finger.

"Merry Christmas, my dear." Rufus whispered, sealing the moment in a tender kiss that promised much more to come.

Mr. Sedgwick enfolded both his son and her in an embrace. "Welcome to our family, SarahAnn."

**Kathleen L. Maher** is a twenty-first-century girl with an old soul. Her debut novella *Bachelor Buttons*, released in 2013 through Helping Hands Press, incorporates both her Irish heritage and love of Civil War history. She won the American Christian Fiction Writers' Genesis Contest for unpublished writers, historical category, in 2012. An avid history buff, Kathleen contributes to writing-themed blogs and writes book reviews. Kathleen and her husband share an old farmhouse in upstate New York with their family and a small zoo of rescued animals.

# A Christmas Promise

## by Gabrielle Meyer

# Dedication

To my grandparents,
The late Leo Gosiak
The late Patricia (Orton) Gosiak
The late Arthur VanRisseghem
and Charlotte (Ernst) VanRisseghem
So much of who I am is because of you,
whether you are here or at home with Christ

# Chapter 1

*Anglesey Abbey*
*Cambridgeshire, England*
*December 21, 1899*

Just five days. That's all Lady Ashleigh Arrington must endure before this horrid affair would be over. She stood in the echoing foyer, forcing herself to offer their first houseguest a warm smile and a curtsy. "Welcome to Anglesey Abbey, Lady Houghton." Ashleigh's voice didn't quiver as much as she had feared. "I hope you'll enjoy your stay."

"I doubt it." Lady Houghton's lips pinched in a distasteful expression as she clutched her small poodle in one hand and a cane in the other. "My rheumatism is acting up with this cold weather and the rich holiday food doesn't agree with my stomach. Rice and milk in the morning is all I can tolerate."

"Of course. I'll speak to our cook personally."

The older lady studied Ashleigh with a critical eye. "I do so hope you'll bring pride to your mother's memory this week. You have a lot to live up to, young lady."

Ashleigh didn't let her smile falter, though inside she cringed. This would be the first Christmas they would celebrate since her mother had passed, and it would be the most important. If Ashleigh didn't entertain her guests the way they were accustomed, the *London Examiner* would declare her a failure throughout England. More importantly, Anglesey Abbey would come to shame. She could not let that happen, for her father's sake.

"Lady Ashleigh will be a charming hostess." Father stood beside Ashleigh in a crisp black suit, his back straight and his confidence in Ashleigh evident for all to see. "She learned everything she knows from her mother."

Again, Ashleigh wanted to cringe. All around her, the large home spoke of elegance, refinement, and sophistication. None of which Ashleigh possessed, despite her mother's patient instructions. For generations, the mistresses of Anglesey Abbey had brought pride to the grand old manor house. Ashleigh suspected she would be the first in a long line to fail.

"Please allow Beatrice to show you to your room." Ashleigh nodded at one of the servants standing by to assist their guests.

At least a dozen maids and footmen stood at attention in a straight line along the edge of the echoing foyer. Their starched white aprons and tall collars gleamed within the dim interior.

"I hope you've given me one of the east-facing rooms," Lady Houghton said with a frown, as if Ashleigh had already disappointed her. "Your mother always gave me an east-facing room."

"Of course." Ashleigh hadn't planned to put Lady Houghton in an east-facing room, but if it made the lady happy, that's exactly what she would do. "Beatrice, please see that Lady Houghton is comfortable in the green room."

"Yes, my lady." Beatrice curtsied and indicated the stairs while two footmen followed with Lady Houghton's bags.

"Well done," Father whispered to Ashleigh as the elderly woman trailed Beatrice up the grand staircase. He gave her a reassuring smile, but it did little to alleviate her anxiety over the other fifteen houseguests they were expecting.

There would be days of extravagant meals, evening entertainments, sleigh rides, ice skating, and droning conversations. To top it all off, a ball was planned for Christmas Eve, the same ball her mother had hosted for twenty-five years, and her mother-in-law before her. The crowning glory of the evening would be the lighting of the Christmas tree, the most dreaded event in Ashleigh's week, because it held such bitter and distasteful memories.

"Ashleigh." Father leaned closer, as if he didn't want the others to hear what he had to say.

"Yes?"

"There's something I've been meaning to tell you for months now." His quiet voice held a hint of trepidation and urgency—a sound she did not like one bit.

"Months?" she whispered. "Why have you waited until this moment to say something?"

Lines of fatigue and grief had aged his distinguished features, and his brown hair was almost completely gray now. "I'm afraid I've run out of time."

"Run out of time?" She clutched his arm, fear filling her stomach at the ominous words. "What's wrong, Father?" *Was he ill?*

A carriage pulled up to the house bearing the Wessex coat of arms. The butler, Mr. Warren, stepped outside into the snow to greet their guests, leaving the large oak door open. Ashleigh caught a glimpse of a tall, handsome man in the carriage.

"Lord Wessex?" she asked quietly, relief making her want to sag. "Is that what you've been wanting to tell me? You invited the most eligible bachelor in London to our house party?" She almost laughed that he'd be so worried about such a thing. Cynthia, Ashleigh's friend and neighbor, would be overjoyed at the news.

Father shook his head. "That's not the surprise that will concern you the most. It's *why* I had to invite him that will upset you."

Two of the Arringtons' footmen met the carriage and opened the door for Eric Easton, the Earl of Wessex, to exit. Ashleigh didn't miss the excited twitter among the maids, nor did she miss the swagger to Eric's shoulders as he nodded a greeting to Mr. Warren and then helped his mother, Lady Wessex, alight from the carriage.

Just seeing the opinionated society matron again caused a shiver to run up Ashleigh's spine. Eric she could handle, but his mother? The pressure to impress the biggest gossip in England was more than Ashleigh feared she could bear.

"What could be more distressing than Lady Wessex?" Ashleigh asked under her breath. The woman held the power to elevate or destroy Ashleigh's reputation with a flick of her tongue.

Eric and his mother started the trek toward the front door slowly and with great aplomb, four of their personal servants close on their heels.

"The Americans will be joining us for Christmas," Father said just above a whisper.

"The Americans?" Ashleigh frowned, forgetting about Lady Wessex for a moment. "Which Americans?"

"The ones your mother was so fond of."

Ashleigh's eyes widened, and all her well-rehearsed manners escaped her as she gasped. "Not the Campbells."

"I'm afraid so." Father sighed.

Christopher Campbell would be in her home for Christmas? The very thought of it made Ashleigh want to disappear to her room for the remainder of the week. The last time she'd seen Christopher was eleven years ago, when she had been eight years old and his family had come to spend the holidays with them. Mrs. Campbell had been one of Mother's oldest and dearest friends, but she had married an American railroad executive and lived in St. Paul, Minnesota. The visit had not gone well—not at all. Christopher had been a horrid boy, just four years older than Ashleigh. He had played tricks on her, caused her to cry, and ultimately ruined Mother's entire Christmas Eve ball by setting the drapes on fire, though no one but Ashleigh knew he was to blame.

Instead, they had all blamed her.

"It's impossible," Ashleigh said with finality. "You must tell them there is no room at Anglesey Abbey."

Father quirked a brow. With over twenty-thousand square meters of living space, it would be impossible to say such a thing.

"I'm afraid it's too late." Father didn't like the Campbells any better than Ashleigh. He had never had anything good to say about the American family her mother loved so well. "They will be here any minute—and I suspect I know why."

"Why?"

Father spoke barely above a whisper as the Eastons drew closer to the house. "Christopher Campbell is coming to fulfill an agreement your mother made with his mother when you two were just children."

"What kind of an agreement?" Ashleigh whispered, not wanting their guests or staff to hear.

Father was very serious as he spoke. "It was your mother's wish, and Mrs. Campbell's wish, that you and Christopher marry—"

"Marry?" Ashleigh forgot herself for a moment and said the word much louder than she intended.

"Shh." Father's expression didn't change as he chastised her. "I suspect they're in need of money and they've come to make good on the agreement. But there is a way out," he said quickly. "The mothers agreed that if either of you were married or engaged to someone else by Christmas Eve 1899, you would not have to go through with their plans. But, if both of you were single. . ." He let the words trail away.

Ashleigh was single. Very much so. And that was exactly how she wished to stay. She enjoyed the freedom that came with being unencumbered. She had a comfortable home, a doting father, and more than enough money for the rest of her life. What more did she need?

"Lady Wessex and Lord Wessex." Father looked beyond Ashleigh, a smile plastered to his face. "How nice of you to join us at Anglesey Abbey for Christmas."

Ashleigh had almost forgotten that Lady Wessex was descending upon her house party. She forced herself to smile and turn to their guests, though she could hardly think straight enough to offer the necessary formalities.

Eric Easton was one of the most dashing and elegant men in all of England. He'd been eagerly sought after by dozens of young ladies for the past three years after he'd come into his inheritance and earned the title, Earl of Wessex. But he hadn't settled on a wife—yet. When he met Ashleigh's gaze, and offered a charming smile, her breath caught. Ever so gallantly, he took her hand to bow over it. "It is a pleasure to be in your company again, Lady Ashleigh. I am looking forward to spending as much time as possible by your side this week."

Father's eyes lit up at the statement, and Lady Wessex lifted a disdainful eyebrow.

Ashleigh nodded, hoping her cheeks weren't blooming with color. "Thank you for coming, Lord Wessex." She curtsied before Eric's mother. "It is a pleasure to have both of you in our home."

Lady Wessex watched Ashleigh closely. "The pleasure is mine, Lady Ashleigh."

"I imagine you'd like to rest before supper," Ashleigh said a bit too quickly. "Mary will take your things to your room."

Ashleigh summoned one of the maids, who blushed and stepped forward to assist Lady Wessex, while the footmen carried their luggage up the wide stairs.

Eric grinned at Ashleigh. "I look forward to seeing you again soon, Lady Ashleigh."

Her tongue felt tied in knots, so she simply nodded. Oh, how she'd fail miserably at flirting, if it came to that. She'd much rather be in her room drawing, or out of doors, or even in the stable with the horses—anywhere that didn't require her to interact with people and their expectations.

As soon as the Eastons were out of sight, Father clasped his hands together. "I think there is hope after all."

"Hope?" Ashleigh wanted to crumple onto the stairway.

"Hope that we can have you engaged by Christmas Eve so you don't have to marry that distasteful Campbell boy and move to America."

Ashleigh's mouth fell open again. *Move to America?* "What was Mother thinking? Why was I never told?"

Father patted her arm again, as if she were a small child needing comfort. "I suppose she and Mrs. Campbell thought they were doing the best thing for you and Christopher. Though I was against it from the first, I could never say no to her." He sighed. "Now that the time has come, I don't see how we can avoid the agreement—unless you're engaged by Christmas Eve."

It was the last thing she wanted, but it didn't look like she'd have a choice. She just hoped the ill-mannered American didn't ruin her Christmas—again.

Christopher Campbell had no wish to be in a frigid carriage, traipsing across the snow-covered English countryside. He'd much rather be in London trying to find investors for his railroad. "Will you finally tell me where we're going?" he asked his father, who sat across from him.

"Anglesey Abbey," Father said looking out the window, squinting at the passing village. "You remember the house."

How could he forget? It was the last place he wanted to spend the holidays. "Why couldn't we stay in London? The investment firm could come to a decision any day, and I want to be there when they vote."

"So you can be disappointed again?" Father finally met Christopher's eye. "No one will conduct business this close to Christmas. If they do, I told them where to send for you. But I doubt we'll need to worry about the investment firm. You'll have your money one way or another."

Christopher frowned. "What do you mean by that?"

"Nothing." Father waved his gloved hand in the air, as if to redirect Christopher's attention.

But Christopher sensed it wasn't nothing. "Why are we going to Anglesey Abbey, Father? After what happened the last time we were there, I didn't think you'd ever want to set foot in the Arringtons' home again."

Father was quiet for a moment. "That was eleven years ago. I doubt the Arringtons even remember. . ." His words died off, but Christopher knew nothing was forgotten.

How could anyone forget that awful Christmas Eve when Christopher had spoiled their party and almost burnt down their home? Mother had been mortified, and they had left the following morning, much sooner than planned, to return to St. Paul. But Mother had become sick on the voyage home and died before they'd reached Boston Harbor. Her death wasn't Christopher's fault, he knew that, but she had left her dearest friend in the world on bad terms and they hadn't mended their friendship before she died. The guilt had plagued Christopher his whole life.

"Why would they even invite us?" Christopher asked. The only time they'd heard from the Arringtons since that dreadful night was the announcement of Lady Pemberton's death two years ago.

Father didn't comment, but he tugged on his earlobe, a telltale sign that he was uncomfortable.

Christopher sat up straighter. "They *did* invite us, didn't they?"

"They are expecting us."

Dread mounted in Christopher's gut as he set aside a stack of papers he'd been reading and leaned forward, setting his elbows on his knees. "Did you invite yourself?"

Father settled back on his seat, his countenance aloof. "We have unfinished business, and it couldn't come at a better time."

"What sort of unfinished business?" Christopher had worked with his father in the railroad business for the past three years since graduating from Harvard. There was little business his father conducted that Christopher didn't know about.

"I suppose you'll learn about it sooner or later." The carriage jostled over the road as they passed the outskirts of the village.

Christopher waited, his patience already thin from their unsuccessful meetings in London. Like so many other American railroad men, they had come to England in search of investments. The Northern Union railroad was the missing link on their tracks from Chicago to Portland, Oregon, but they didn't have the capital to purchase the line. Despite Christopher's early hopes, their meetings had not gone as he had hoped. They had one final investment firm that would take the decision to its board any day. If they said no, Christopher's trip to London would be a complete waste of time and money.

"The last time we visited Anglesey Abbey, your mother and Lady Pemberton signed an agreement. We're simply returning to see that the terms of the agreement are fulfilled."

"What kind of an agreement?"

Father reached for his leather bag and pulled out an envelope. He handed it to Christopher. "See for yourself."

Christopher pulled out the single sheet of paper. As he scanned it, his frown deepened until he shook his head in disbelief and protest. "This can't be."

"Since you are not married or engaged, we are going to Anglesey Abbey to see if Lady Ashleigh is single as well. If she is, then you will work out the terms of your engagement and announce it on Christmas Eve." Father smiled, though it wasn't a look of joy that one would expect when speaking of his son's engagement—but one of triumph, as if besting a foe. "Once an engagement is announced in England, there is no backing out. Unless the person who forfeits the engagement wants their reputation to be forever tarnished."

"This isn't a legally binding contract," Christopher said, his pulse starting to slow. "Even if it was, there would be some way to get out of the agreement."

Father leaned forward. "You're right. It's not legally binding. But it was your mother's last wish that you and Lady Ashleigh marry." He stared at Christopher with the same look of disappointment he'd given him as they'd driven away from Anglesey Abbey the last time. "You wouldn't want to dishonor your mother's memory by saying no."

Guilt washed over Christopher. The least he could do was honor his mother's last wish—yet, he had no desire to marry. He spent almost all of his waking hours at his office. He had no time or space in his life for a wife, let alone Ashleigh Arrington! The girl had been a tattletale, getting him in trouble for things he hadn't even done wrong. He couldn't stand the sight of her when they'd visited Anglesey Abbey eleven years ago. How much worse she must be as a persnickety woman.

"I couldn't possibly get married. Especially to Ashleigh."

"Think long and hard about that decision." Father's voice was low and serious. "Ashleigh Arrington is the only child of Lord Pemberton, one of the wealthiest men in England. An alliance with him would ensure all the investment we would ever need for our railroads."

Christopher shook his head. "I wouldn't even think of marrying for financial gain." His parents had married for that very reason, and Christopher didn't have a single happy memory of his parents from childhood because of it. Theirs had been a strained relationship, with no love and little tolerance for one another. Nothing in life was worth that kind of trouble.

"It doesn't matter what you think," Father said, settling back into his bench seat. "The agreement was made by your mother and Lady Pemberton. Whether you want this to happen or not, it may be out of your hands. Lord Pemberton is honor bound to see it through."

Anglesey Abbey appeared in the distance, its towers, gothic architecture, and brownstone exterior jutting out from the rolling countryside.

Lady Ashleigh was probably awaiting his arrival eagerly. No doubt she was in need of a husband. What man in his right mind would marry that woman? A successful, unsuspecting American was probably just the person her father was hoping to come along and take her off his hands.

The carriage slowed and turned onto the gravel driveway leading to Anglesey Abbey. They drove through the gatehouse, which was open and welcoming, the gatekeeper waving at the driver as they passed by.

"I can't get married," Christopher said again, a hint of desperation in his voice. "We'll simply have to explain that the agreement is. . .is. . ."

"What?" Father shook his head. "A foolish decision made by two loving, devoted mothers?" He frowned. "You'd bring shame upon your mother, Lady Pemberton, and Lady Ashleigh if you tried to back out now."

The carriage rolled closer to Anglesey Abbey. The front door opened and a man stepped outside, his black suit in contrast to the snow-white landscape. He stood at attention, waiting for the carriage to come to a stop.

"I didn't think this trip to England could get any worse," Christopher said under his breath. Not only did he still need to secure investment for his railroad, but he'd have to find some way to get out of this ridiculous agreement.

"Remember this is the first Christmas they're celebrating since Lady Pemberton's death," Father said. "We don't want to add to their grief if we don't have to."

Christopher wanted to groan when the carriage finally stopped and the door was opened by the servant.

"Welcome to Anglesey Abbey," the servant said. "I'm Mr. Warren, the butler. If there is anything you need, please don't hesitate to ask."

Christopher steeled himself from the coming encounter with Lady Ashleigh, and remembered his manners. "Thank you."

He stepped out of the carriage, trying not to look too melancholy or frustrated. If the Arringtons hadn't invited them, how would they be received? What an awkward position Father had put them in.

Father exited the carriage. "Come, Christopher."

Gravel crunched under their feet as they walked toward the front door. An older gentleman and young lady stood just inside the foyer, though he couldn't make out any details. All he recalled about Ashleigh was her wiry blond hair, her sparkling brown eyes, and the spray of freckles across her stub of a nose. She had been whiny, obnoxious, and annoying.

Dread mixed with impatience and frustration. This was the last thing Christopher needed to deal with this week. Even though his father had instructed the investment firm to contact him when they planned to vote, he was still four hours away from London. Close, but not close enough.

"Here we go," Father said.

"Mr. Campbell, how nice of you to come." Lord Pemberton's voice was aristocratic and tight as he greeted Father. "I believe you remember my daughter, Lady Ashleigh."

"Lord Pemberton, Lady Ashleigh." When Father bowed, Christopher had his first full look at Ashleigh in eleven years—and he almost tripped over his own feet.

Gone was the gangly, awkward child. In her place stood a beautiful young woman.

"And you remember my son, Christopher?" Father asked.

"It's good to see you again, Christopher." Lord Pemberton nodded, though he didn't smile. "Ashleigh and I are very glad you've come."

Christopher met Ashleigh's brown-eyed gaze. He could hardly believe the woman before him was the same child who had caused so much grief last time he had visited. "Lady Ashleigh, it's a pleasure to see you again."

She stood tall and slender, her soft blond curls secure in a becoming hairstyle, her freckles a distant memory on her clear skin. The stub little nose was now an elegant complement to her lovely face.

"Mr. Campbell." She offered her hand and he bowed over it. "The pleasure is all mine."

She spoke the words so elegantly and deliberately, Christopher sensed they were not genuine. Was she happy to see him? Surely she recalled their last meeting with the same distaste as he. Thankfully he wasn't the same spoiled boy he'd been—but she wouldn't know that.

After the initial greeting, an uncomfortable silence filled the air as the four looked at one another. Christopher couldn't help but glance at her ring finger—and saw it was empty.

She slipped her hand into the folds of her becoming gown.

It didn't mean she wasn't engaged, or at least spoken for. But how would he find out?

"It's been so long since your last visit," Lord Pemberton said. "Much has changed these eleven years."

More than Christopher ever imagined.

"I'm sorry for your loss." Father sounded genuine. "Lady Pemberton will be missed."

"Thank you." Lord Pemberton's face was stoic as he spoke. He didn't offer any more or any less.

Again, silence descended.

"We hope you'll have a pleasant stay," Ashleigh finally said. "One of the footmen will show you to your rooms."

Christopher longed to speak to her about the agreement, yet he didn't think it was right to bring it up in front of the servants or so soon after their arrival. "I look forward to speaking to you later this evening, if I may."

She studied him with her dark eyes, distrust and apprehension wavering in their depths. "I will be very busy this evening, but perhaps we can arrange a few moments."

If that's all she'd give him, then it would be enough. It had to be enough. The sooner he could get out of the agreement, the better.

# Chapter 2

S hall we?" Father offered his arm to Ashleigh just outside the drawing room where all of their guests had gathered before dinner.

With a steadying breath and a quick nod, she took his offered arm and drew strength knowing she wasn't alone.

Father took a step and then paused. "Remember what you need to do tonight. The Campbells have come to arrange a marriage between you and Christopher, but we still have three days before they can make any demands."

What could they possibly demand? Ashleigh had read the copy of the document her mother and Mrs. Campbell had signed. It wasn't legal, simply a formality. The Campbells couldn't force her hand. But Ashleigh couldn't deny it was her mother's wish either. The last thing she wanted was to disappoint her mother, even if her mother was no longer with them.

"Eric Easton comes from a good family with a good title." Father squeezed her arm for reassurance. "He would be my choice."

Ashleigh hardly knew the man, but she would do her best to rectify that problem. "Let's go in."

Mr. Warren stood just outside the drawing room with the first footman nearby. They opened the gilded doors to allow Ashleigh and her father to enter.

The north drawing room was one of Ashleigh's favorites at Anglesey Abbey, especially now, decked out for the holidays. Large and airy, with cream-colored walls and gold trim, it bespoke of the rich heritage of the Arrington family and the women who had put their special touch in selecting the elegant furniture that graced the room.

Here and there, the guests had assembled in small groups. Women wore glittering jewelry, golden tiaras, and long white gloves. The men were resplendent in black evening coats and shiny black shoes. Laughter and conversation filled the room, but several people noticed their arrival and stopped to nod a greeting.

Ashleigh intended to meet Eric's gaze, but it was Christopher that caught her attention. He stood a head taller than all the other guests, his dark brown hair combed back into perfect submission, his intense blue eyes studying the room, the people, and then finally her. She was reminded again how much he had changed. If she were honest with herself, she had thought him a handsome boy when she'd met him before—but now, as a man, he was more than handsome. Dashing, strong, and confident were all words she'd use to describe him now. It would be impossible to miss him in a crowd.

"Lady Ashleigh." Eric approached and bowed before her.

Father stepped away and joined another conversation, leaving Ashleigh alone with Eric.

It was time to turn on the charm she didn't possess and try to attract the attention of a man she didn't want to marry. The very thought of it made her hands shake and her smile wobble. How did a person go about flirting? She'd watched countless women at countless balls and social gatherings, but she'd found their behavior to be ridiculous and embarrassing most of the time.

"Lord Wessex." She curtsied. "You look very handsome this evening." Her cheeks bloomed with heat, but she forced herself to hold his gaze.

He lifted a surprised brow. "Thank you. I was just this moment going to tell you how lovely you look."

Ashleigh glanced at her green gown, hoping all the tucks and pleats were in the right place.

Out of the corner of her eye, she caught sight of Cynthia, who hovered nearby. Was she waiting for an invitation to join them? "Cynthia!" Ashleigh was only too happy to have her friend close at hand.

Cynthia stepped away from the people she was speaking to, her cheeks pink and her green eyes glowing. She batted her long eyelashes in Eric's direction in an effortless gesture of appreciation.

"Good evening, Lord Wessex." She curtsied so elegantly, Ashleigh felt like a lumbering oaf in comparison.

"Lady Cynthia." Eric bowed, though his lips were tight, suggesting he wasn't happy she had joined them. "I was just telling Lady Ashleigh how lovely she looked this evening."

Christopher had not stopped watching Ashleigh since she'd entered the drawing room. She knew because she'd stolen several glances in his direction. She should be getting to know Eric better, but it was Christopher who had piqued her interest from the moment he'd arrived at Anglesey Abbey.

He started toward her group, his intent evident. He was coming to speak with her. Panic seized Ashleigh's stomach. Would he want to discuss the marriage agreement here, now? It wouldn't be the time or the place for such things, but Americans were so often vulgar and direct in their dealings. She couldn't be too sure.

"Would you excuse me?" Ashleigh said. "I need to see to one of my guests." If Christopher was determined to speak with her, she wanted as few ears to hear as possible.

Eric frowned, and his gaze traveled across the room to where Christopher was advancing. "Of course, though I do hope we'll get a chance to talk later."

Ashleigh nodded and moved away to meet Christopher in the center of the room. Her heart beat an unsteady rhythm and her palms were moist. What would she do if anyone discovered the real reason this man and his father were visiting? She must keep it a secret and hope he didn't make his intentions known. Once the rumors started, it would be impossible to attract another man's attention.

"Mr. Campbell," she said almost breathlessly. "I hope your room is to your liking."

"Anglesey Abbey is just as beautiful as the last time I was here. It hasn't changed a bit."

Memories of his last visit surfaced, and her anxiety was soon replaced with irritation. "The ballroom parlor is quite altered, actually. If you recall, we had a fire there the last time you visited. It required extensive renovations."

"How could I forget?" A shadow passed over his face as he frowned. "I never did get a chance to apologize for all of that. I'm sorry."

Ashleigh's mouth parted in surprise. It was the last thing she expected to hear. "Yes, well, nothing was broken that couldn't be mended." Except her mother's shame in Ashleigh. It was the last time she ever asked Ashleigh to put the star on the top of the tree, or perform any other social obligation that would require Ashleigh to be the center of attention. Mother didn't want Ashleigh to embarrass her ever again.

All formality slipped away and Christopher leaned closer to Ashleigh. "Is there somewhere we could speak privately? I know there is much to discuss, and I would like to get it over with as soon as possible."

Ashleigh's eyes widened as several people stopped to listen to their conversation. "I'm afraid that isn't possible right now. Dinner is about to be served."

"Then when? I would like to return to London, but it's my understanding that there is an agreement—"

"Please." Ashleigh shook her head and frowned, her body temperature rising. "Now is not the time."

Christopher straightened and nodded, frustration in the lines of his face and body. "Fine. But it must be soon. I'd like to take care of this situation sooner than later."

Sooner than later? Didn't she have until Christmas Eve?

Mr. Warren stepped into the room at that moment and clasped his hands. "Dinner is served."

Ashleigh was never so happy to hear those words in her life.

Father stepped forward and offered his arm to escort Lady Wessex into the dining room and Ashleigh joined Lord Majorly, the Count of Harmony Hall, who would escort her.

Eric offered his arm to Cynthia, who smiled up at the handsome young man in complete awe.

Ashleigh was no closer to securing Eric's proposal than she had been when she entered the room.

It would be a long night, especially if she had the conversation with Christopher to dread.

The candles danced and flickered, reflecting off the large windows in the north drawing room. Christopher sat in a corner of the room, on a surprisingly comfortable chair—the first one he'd found at Anglesey Abbey—and watched the young adults play Blindman's Bluff after supper. Besides himself and Ashleigh, there were six others in the room. Christopher had chosen not to participate, hoping to get time alone with Ashleigh. She, on the other hand, seemed content to avoid him. She stood in the opposite corner of the room, overseeing the game, though she didn't participate herself.

Laughter and conversation filled the room. Christopher was the only stranger among them, and the houseguests had tried to draw him out, but he had a different type of game to play tonight. One that was much more important and carried far heavier consequences.

His state of matrimony—or lack thereof.

Ashleigh glanced in his direction again, but this time Christopher had had enough. He left the comfort of his chair and walked along the outside of the room, narrowly missing the young lady who was blindfolded and feeling around the room, her fingers outstretched and wiggling for effect.

As he drew closer, Ashleigh's eyes grew wider. She started to move away from her place near the door, but he stepped in her way.

"How long must we play cat and mouse, Lady Ashleigh?" he asked quietly, for her ears alone.

Her large brown eyes blinked up at him in confusion. "Whatever do you mean, Mr. Campbell?"

"Each time I make an advance to speak to you, you either skitter away or distract me from my objective." He studied her, surprised again by how lovely she had become over the years. "I would like a private audience with you."

Her gaze circled the room. "It wouldn't be seemly to leave my guests or be alone with you."

"Then let's just step outside the drawing room and leave the door open." He wanted to return to London in the morning. They must talk now.

Her hand came up and rubbed the side of her face as she looked around the room in dismay.

She didn't act the way he'd imagined when his father told him about the agreement. Christopher had expected an overzealous woman, hanging on his arm, following his every footstep.

Ashleigh Arrington was anything but eager to be by his side—or any other man's in this room.

"I suppose we can't put it off forever." She nodded toward the door and led the way. "We will speak in the hall." She paused. "With the door open."

"Of course."

He followed her into the dimly lit hall. It ran the length of the main floor of Anglesey Abbey, with the large staircase at one end and the front doors at the other. The marble floors were polished and the high ceilings echoed with their footsteps. It wasn't the ideal place to have such an intimate conversation, but it would have to do.

Christopher squared his shoulders. He would have to tackle this problem just like he did all the other obstacles he came across in his business dealings. Straightforward, level-headed, and without emotions getting in his way.

Ashleigh turned and clasped her hands, but she didn't meet his gaze—neither did she speak.

Christopher opened his mouth to address the situation at hand, but didn't know quite where to begin. Straightforward was best. "I'm assuming you're aware of the agreement our mothers made when we were children?"

"Yes," she said quietly and still didn't meet his eyes.

"How long have you known?"

Her hands shook and she clenched them tighter. "I just learned of it moments before you arrived this afternoon."

Was that a quiver in her voice?

Christopher frowned. If she'd only just learned of the agreement, then perhaps she hadn't been eagerly anticipating his arrival. Maybe she was as bamboozled as him. "And you're not happy about the arrangement?"

She slowly tilted her chin up, her gaze vulnerable, yet confident. "I have no wish to marry anyone at this time."

He stared at her for a moment, relief flooding through him. "Neither do I."

Her brown eyes lit up with hope. "Truly?"

"I only just learned about it moments before we arrived." He almost laughed at the absurdity of the whole ordeal. He'd allowed himself to get worked up for nothing. "My father. . ." His words trailed away as he recalled the conversation he'd had with his father earlier.

"Your father?" she asked, her gaze eagerly searching his face.

Christopher shook his head. His father had reminded him that he owed it to his mother's memory to honor her last request. How could he not?

The sinking feeling returned. Even if Ashleigh wasn't agreeable to the arrangement, what did it matter? It was his mother's wish that they marry.

"My father told me that our mothers signed the agreement just a few days before we left Anglesey Abbey the last time." He hated the feeling of guilt that slayed him every time he thought about that last week before his mother died. He'd been such a disappointment to her.

Ashleigh nodded. "I believe my father mentioned that as well."

Christopher walked away, his footsteps echoing in the massive space. He ran his hand through his hair and rested it at the base of his neck. "She wanted this match more than anything."

There was a pause before Ashleigh spoke again. "What are you suggesting?"

He turned and couldn't miss her wide eyes. "I don't believe I could ignore this agreement in good conscience. Not when it came from my mother."

She lowered her lashes and let out a sigh. "Neither could I."

Her simple statement tugged at his heart.

There was something about this young woman that drew Christopher. As he'd watched her during supper, and then in the drawing room, she hadn't tried to stand out or be noticed, but neither had she shied away from attention. She had a humility about her that was very attractive.

"Where does that leave us?" he asked.

Ashleigh clasped and unclasped her hands and then looked toward the drawing room. Lord Wessex was blindfolded, chasing the young ladies.

"There is still time before the deadline," she said. "My father has made his hopes for my husband clear, so I will pursue those plans." She squared her shoulders. "If all goes as planned, I'll be engaged to someone else by Christmas Eve, and you and I will be free of the agreement."

Lord Wessex peeked out from beneath the blindfold as he cornered one lady after another. "Where has Lady Ashleigh run off to?" he asked.

Lady Cynthia pointed toward the hall, and Lord Wessex turned on his heel and started in their direction. "She cannot hide for long," he said.

Even in the faded light of the hall, Christopher saw the telltale shade of pink on Ashleigh's cheeks.

"Wessex?" he asked. "Has he proposed?"

"A lady doesn't speak of such things," Ashleigh said quietly.

"You and I can forgo such formalities, Ashleigh." He spoke her name with no nonsense. "We are in this thing together, for better or worse, until one of us gets engaged. We might as well work together."

Lord Wessex came to the door and lifted his head to peek out from beneath the blindfold again. When he saw Christopher, he took off the scarf and frowned. "Is everything all right, Lady Ashleigh?"

"Everything is fine, thank you." Her smile looked forced and uncomfortable. "We'll return to the drawing room shortly."

Lord Wessex sized Christopher up and down, the slightest scowl on his face, but he bowed to Ashleigh and returned to the drawing room without another word.

Ashleigh took a step toward Christopher, her face serious, her voice low. "I don't like this agreement any more than you, Christopher." She said his first name a bit awkwardly. "But it is none of your concern whom I plan to pursue." She swallowed and glanced at the door where Lord Wessex had stood a moment before. If she was this nervous and uncomfortable simply talking about pursuing the man, how would she actually accomplish her goal?

She offered a wobbly curtsy. "Now, if you'll excuse me." She walked away, her back straight and her shoulders stiff.

For all her elegance and grace, she didn't appear to know the fine art of flirtation. Lord Wessex, on the other hand, had practice beyond his years.

Christopher sighed. Just like all his other business dealings, he'd have to keep a close eye on this situation. If he didn't stay at Anglesey Abbey to ensure Ashleigh's success at securing a proposal from Lord Wessex, Christopher might be the one with a wife at the end of the week.

An unwelcome prospect, to be sure.

# Chapter 3

From a distance, Anglesey Abbey looked like a fairytale castle up on the hill, the setting sun casting shades of purple, pink, and orange across the vast winter sky. Ashleigh stretched out her hands toward the crackling bonfire near the edge of the frozen pond, warming her fingers and taking a moment to simply enjoy the scene before her.

It was the second day of the house party, and the younger guests had traversed the snow-packed road from the house down to the pond, ice skates slung over their shoulders. A roaring fire had already been laid by the servants, and the party had enjoyed hot cocoa before donning their skates to take to the ice. Eric and Cynthia glided along, their eyes glowing and their cheeks tinged with pink. Ashleigh had yet to put on her skates, preferring the quiet of the fire after the busy morning and afternoon of playing cards, visiting with the older guests, and overseeing breakfast and lunch.

Christopher sat on a bench near the edge of the pond and attached his blades onto the bottom of his shoes. He'd spent the day with everyone else, but hadn't tried speaking to her again. His father, on the other hand, had been by her side most of the morning, telling her all about life in Minnesota.

"Would you like to skate?" Christopher asked when he caught her watching him. He straightened and lifted her skates, which were lying on the bench near him. "I'd be happy to help you with your blades."

Cynthia laughed as she clung to Eric's arm, flailing about as if she didn't know how to skate, when Ashleigh knew full well that she was an excellent skater. Eric grinned down at Cynthia and then wrapped his arm around her waist to help her along.

If Ashleigh didn't do something soon, she'd lose her chance with Eric—and then who would be left? One of the other bachelors who was visiting? She quickly perused the options and shuddered. None of the other men appealed to her. Not in the least.

She could act like Cynthia, couldn't she? Feign weakness, ignorance, and inability. If it meant attracting Eric's attention, then she'd have no choice.

"I'd love to skate." Ashleigh left the fire and took a seat next to Christopher. "But I don't need any help putting them on, thank you."

He tightened the straps over his boots and nodded. "It's refreshing to have a woman who can take care of herself."

Ashleigh attached the blades to the bottom of her boots, tightening the straps for support. "Do you have much acquaintance with weak women?"

He laughed. "Ah, no. I don't have much acquaintance with women in general, but when I do, I find them to be tedious and needy."

She sat up straighter, irritation prickling her spine. "Not all women, surely."

Cynthia continued to giggle beside Eric, leaning into him for support, smiling up in adoration, her skates slipping out from beneath her from time to time.

Christopher looked away from Cynthia and stood, his left eyebrow quirked. "Not all women—but most." He extended his hand. "Shall we?"

Ashleigh lifted her chin and stood without his assistance. "I'm quite capable of standing on my own."

His eyes twinkled and his lips twitched. "Would you like me to escort you onto the ice? Or are you capable of that as well?"

She pinched her lips together and scowled, but it only increased his merriment.

He stepped aside and offered a slight bow. "Don't let me get in your way."

She started toward the frozen pond, her head high and her back straight. It took a bit of concentration to stay balanced on the blades, but she'd had enough practice over the years to manage without assistance.

Christopher walked close behind, but she didn't bother to speak to him as they followed the path the others had already broken in the snow.

Her clothing was stylish and warm, lined in brown fur and velvet, but it didn't stop the wind from nipping at her nose or ruffling her skirts. The crackle of the fire begged her to return, but she had a job to do, and she aimed to do it. Today. This very moment. She'd flirt with Eric, even if it was the last thing she did.

As she came to the banks of the pond, she estimated the drop from land to ice to be at least a foot. All the other women had accepted a helping hand down, but one look at the bemused expression on Christopher's face made her decide to do it herself.

She anchored her right foot into the packed snow, bent her knee, and put her left foot onto the ice.

"Oh, Ashleigh!" Cynthia waved from across the pond. "You're joining us!"

Eric glanced toward Ashleigh, so she waved her gloved hand and tried to flutter her eyelashes like so many other women she'd watched—and immediately lost her precarious balance on the ice.

Her left foot slipped out from beneath her, but her right foot was still anchored to the land.

A startled cry left her lips as she flailed her arms to regain her balance—but it was no use. She came down hard on her backside, while her right ankle twisted in protest.

Before Ashleigh could gather her senses, Christopher was by her side, concern wedged between his eyes. "My goodness, Ashleigh. Are you hurt?" He knelt in the snow beside her.

Pain radiated up her right leg, but she couldn't admit that she was hurt—especially when she'd been so stubborn and gotten herself into this mess.

"Ashleigh, darling!" Cynthia broke away from Eric's side and sped across the ice, coming to a magnificent halt within half a meter of Ashleigh. She knelt before her in a puddle of purple skirts, her green eyes filled with worry. "Did you hurt yourself?"

"Help me up, will you?" Ashleigh asked her friend.

Cynthia rose to lend a hand, but Christopher was already by her side. He reached beneath her arms and lifted her to her feet.

Embarrassment warmed Ashleigh's cheeks as she readjusted her skirts. "Thank you."

Eric and the others joined them on the edge of the pond, concern in their gazes.

She had to put most of her weight on her left foot, which was difficult in the skate. "I'm quite all right." She forced a smile. "Truly. Everyone, go back to your fun."

"Are you certain?" Cynthia asked.

"I'm fine." Her pride refused to share the truth. "Just a little bruised. I'll return to the house and wait for you to join me later."

"You can't return alone." Eric stepped forward. "I'd be happy to go with you."

"That won't be necessary." She didn't want the others to see her shame—especially Eric. If he walked her back, he'd know she was more injured than she let on. She tried to put weight on her injured ankle, but winced at the pain. She couldn't very well walk back on her own. "Mr. Campbell will accompany me to the house."

Christopher raised his eyebrows. "Wouldn't you rather go with Lord Wessex?"

"Who will help Lady Cynthia skate if Lord Wessex returns with me?" Ashleigh asked with forced laughter in her voice, desperate not to embarrass herself in front of Lord Wessex any further.

Christopher frowned, but bent over to unstrap his skates. "As you wish."

Eric shook his head. "I insist."

Cynthia wrapped her hands around Eric's arm once again and smiled up at him. "We'll join Ashleigh and Mr. Campbell a bit later, just as Ashleigh suggested." She skated backward, pulling Eric along with her, and for once, Ashleigh was thankful her friend was dominating Eric's time and attention.

The others moved away as well, leaving Ashleigh alone with Christopher once again.

"I thought you wanted Lord Wessex's attention," he said quietly. "Why didn't you take his offer?"

She lifted her chin and tried to put weight on her ankle to get to the bench. "I'd prefer he didn't see me embarrass myself."

Christopher's eyes wrinkled at the corners as he smiled. "But you don't mind if I do?"

"You've seen me at my worst already." Reminders of the last time he visited returned. She'd never been more embarrassed in her life than the night he set their Christmas tree and drapes on fire.

"Here." He bent down and put her right arm over his shoulder. "I'll help you back to the bench to take off your skates."

He was much taller than she was, so it was a bit awkward, but he helped her hobble to the bench. She tried hard not to limp, in case the others watched, but it was almost impossible.

She sat on the bench, and he knelt before her to loosen the straps.

After a moment, he chuckled. "I find it exceedingly ironic that you refused my help fastening your skates, but now you're forced to accept my help in taking them off."

Irritation stiffened her back, and she leaned over. "I am quite capable of taking off my own skates, Mr. Campbell."

He gently pushed her hands aside. "Don't be stubborn, Ashleigh." He looked up and met her gaze, his blue eyes quite serious—and altogether too handsome. "I want to help you."

Her cheeks warmed and she looked away.

When he was done, he offered his hand. "You've changed in so many ways, it's a bit refreshing to know you're still as stubborn as before."

She stood. "I prefer to think of myself as determined."

"Call it what you will," he said, a smile in his voice. "Are you able to walk on your own?"

Ashleigh put a bit of weight on the tender ankle and winced, but she nodded. "I believe I can."

"No, you can't." Without asking, Christopher swept her off her feet and held her in his arms. "You wear your emotions on your face, did you know that?"

She blinked several times before she had the wherewithal to protest. "Put me down, Mr. Campbell. I said I could walk."

"What you say"—he began to walk toward Anglesey Abbey—"and what your face tells me, are two different things." He met her gaze; his mouth quirked. "Your pride knows no bounds, Lady Ashleigh, but there's no need to pretend." He bent his head a little closer to hers in a conspiratorial way. "You don't need to impress me."

She crossed her arms and directed her gaze away from him, setting her mouth in a firm line. "I'm not trying to impress anyone."

"Really?" He continued to walk, following the path they'd taken to reach the pond. It was a dreadfully long road, uphill, but it didn't seem to affect him at all. "Isn't this whole party meant to impress these people?"

"I'm simply trying to create a pleasant experience for my friends."

"Is that what this is all about?" He shook his head. "You could have fooled me. I assumed you were trying to recreate the house parties your mother was so famous for. With her gone, I imagine there is a very heavy weight upon your shoulders."

Ashleigh's arms went limp. "Is it that obvious?"

His features softened, and he shook his head. "No. I just assumed."

She sighed and nibbled her bottom lip. If her ankle was hurt badly, it would be impossible to play hostess for the rest of the week. Everyone would have to go home.

How would she find a way to flirt with Eric then?

"You're doing a fine job, Ashleigh." He tightened his hold on her and smiled. "You've been impressing me from the moment I arrived."

Ashleigh warmed at his compliment.

"Especially when you fell so gracefully just now." He grinned. "It was quite impressive, if I must say so."

She narrowed her eyes again and lightly punched his shoulder, but couldn't stop from joining in his laughter.

The doctor had come and gone, but Ashleigh didn't like what he had to say, so she chose to ignore him.

"Why I even called for the doctor is a mystery," Father had said earlier when she'd met him in the hallway to go down to dinner. "Didn't he advise you to stay off your ankle for the remainder of the week?"

"Fiddlesticks." Her maid, Mary, had bound the ankle in a tight bandage, and Ashleigh had tried to overlook the discomfort as she walked beside her father. "It's simply a sprain. I've been icing it all afternoon. I'll be fine."

He had shaken his head, but didn't speak of it further.

Now, with supper behind them, they had all gone to the north parlor where they would pass the evening with songs, recitations, and games.

The room was warm, heated by the oversized fireplace and the dozens of candles in the wall sconces. Pine garland was draped across the fireplace mantel, and mistletoe hung over the entrance to the door. A footman stood at attention near the table where hot apple cider was being served, while Ashleigh's guests sat in small groups around the room.

"I've heard you're an accomplished violinist, Mr. Campbell," Cynthia said, clapping her hands in excitement. "Will you play for us?"

Christopher sat at a table in the corner of the room with his father and another older gentleman, a deck of cards in hand. He glanced up at the request. "Accomplished is too kind a word. Dabble is more appropriate."

A vague memory started to form in Ashleigh's mind. The last time he'd visited, she recalled walking into the music room on the third floor of Anglesey Abbey, drawn there by the most hauntingly beautiful sound she'd ever heard. Christopher had been standing near a window, an ebony violin in hand. He had been playing a song she'd never heard before. His face had been serene, almost peaceful, and she'd been surprised to find the annoying boy had a tender side after all. She hadn't moved a muscle, afraid he'd know she was standing there. Even then, as a boy of twelve, he'd played the violin better than anyone she'd ever heard.

"Do play for us, Mr. Campbell," Ashleigh said with a sudden longing to hear him again.

He studied her for a moment, a twinkle forming in his eyes. "Only if you'll sing for us."

Heat filled her cheeks as another memory surfaced. He'd come across her singing to one of her kittens in the barn on that long-ago visit and had teased her incessantly.

Did he intend to tease her again?

"If I recall," he said, rising to his feet, "you have a lovely voice."

"Oh, please do," Cynthia begged.

Others joined in, but it was Eric's encouragement that finally persuaded Ashleigh to agree. If she could make Eric happy, then it would be worth all the teasing she'd have to endure from Christopher.

"All right."

The group cheered and Eric smiled.

"I'll go and retrieve my violin." Christopher stopped by her side on his way out of the parlor and spoke quietly for her ears alone. "I've been waiting eleven years to hear you sing again."

She couldn't tell if he teased or if he was sincere. Before she could discern his meaning, he left the room.

Eric approached while the others spoke in excited tones around the candlelit room. The shadows played about the planes of Eric's face, accentuating his fine features. He was almost too pretty, truth be told, but it added to his magnetic charm. She was quite certain that every young lady in the room was smitten with the handsome earl. And she was running out of time. She must try flirting with him, and now would be the ideal moment.

"I've heard that you have a fine voice as well, Lord Wessex." She fluttered her eyelashes. "Will you sing for us this evening?"

"I might." He frowned and leaned forward. "Is there something in your eye, Lady Ashleigh?"

She stopped fluttering her eyes and opened them wide, shaking her head. "No." Embarrassment flooded her face with heat. "I simply . . ." What? Simply what?

"Yes?" he asked.

"I simply—nothing." She laughed, wanting to sound as lyrical as Cynthia, but it came out awkwardly. "Did you enjoy ice skating today?"

"Yes." His face smoothed, and he leaned closer, his voice deepening. "I've enjoyed everything about my activities at Anglesey Abbey—except for the times you haven't been with me."

She knew he was flirting—it was painfully obvious—but she didn't know how to respond. Oh! If only this came naturally to her. "Well, that's—wonderful," she said a bit too loudly. "I'm happy to hear it."

"Ashleigh." He paused. "I may call you Ashleigh?"

She swallowed. "Yes—yes, of course." Why did her pulse beat so strongly in her ears, and why did her voice quiver? No doubt her cheeks were pink.

"Then you must call me Eric."

She began to grow overly warm near the fireplace. Where was Christopher with that violin? "A–all right," she stammered, rubbing her sweating palms down her skirt.

"Ashleigh," he said again, taking a step closer to her, clearly wanting the others to be excluded from this conversation. "I've been meaning to speak to you privately since arriving."

He had?

"But every time I turn around, Mr. Campbell seems to have your undivided attention."

"Yes, well." She took a step back, but immediately wished she hadn't. She was supposed to give Eric the impression that she wanted his advances, didn't she? Without thinking, she stepped forward, her ankle protesting, to be even closer to Eric than she'd been before.

His frown returned and she wanted to crawl under the rug.

Now she stood too close to him. He must think her a complete ninny.

"I have been trying to devote my time to *all* my guests," she said.

"Yet, I haven't had nearly enough of your attention."

His words made the heat gather under her collar. "Lord Wessex."

"Eric," he said quietly, dramatically.

Cynthia watched them closely from the opposite side of the room, though the others pretended not to notice. Could they hear him?

What must they all think?

"Your words lead me to believe. . ." Ashleigh let her comment trail away because she didn't know how to finish the sentence. Was he interested in her? Was there hope that he might propose? How did she ask such a delicate question?

If only she could know for certain. She would be free of the marriage agreement with Christopher.

"Lead you to believe what?" Eric asked. "That I—"

"Why wait for my son to return?" Mr. Campbell stood to his feet and spoke in a loud voice. "Lady Ashleigh, will you sing for us now?"

Ashleigh wanted to cry out in relief, and sigh in frustration. What had Eric been about to say? She half hoped and half dreaded what it might be.

Eric was forced to move aside so Ashleigh could answer the older gentleman. It would be rude to deny his request, but she wanted to know what Eric was about to say.

"Wouldn't you rather I wait for Mr. Campbell to return with his violin?" she asked. "I'd sound much better accompanied by music."

"I'll accompany you on the pianoforte." Cynthia quickly took a seat at the large instrument. "What shall I play, Ashleigh? 'God Rest Ye, Merry Gentlemen'? 'Hark! The Harold Angels Sing'?"

The others waited in expectation.

"Excuse me, Lord Wessex." Ashleigh took a step around him, trying not to limp. "Whatever you prefer, Cynthia."

Cynthia offered a satisfied smile and began to play "Good King Wenceslas."

After a few popular carols, Christopher returned and Cynthia quietly left the pianoforte to take a spot near Eric on a sofa facing the fireplace.

Large snowflakes began to fall outside, brushing the oversized windows on their way to the ground. Inside, the fireplace crackled while Christopher took his violin out of its case.

The look of reverence on his face made Ashleigh recall the way he'd held and played the violin as a child. When he lifted it to his chin and laid the bow across the strings, he closed his eyes briefly and let out a sigh, though she didn't think he even realized it.

After a few notes and a little tuning, he lowered the instrument and smiled at Ashleigh. "What would you like to sing?"

She'd rather listen to him play, but he had asked her to sing, so she would. " 'Silent Night'?"

He nodded. "My favorite."

It was her favorite as well.

The violin came up again. He waited just a moment until she indicated that she was ready, then he began to play.

The sound was exquisite, just as she remembered. Beneath his expert hands, the song became at once joyful and melancholy, as if he poured his very soul into the music. She found her voice following the ebb and flow of the emotions, caught up in the moment.

*Silent night, holy night,*
*All is calm, all is bright. . .*

The others faded and it became just the two of them. She couldn't take her eyes off him as he played the familiar song in a way that was his very own.

When it came to an end, they stared at one another. The others remained quiet for a heartbeat, but then they began to applaud and call for an encore.

For once, Christopher didn't smile or tease as he watched her.

Something had happened while they sang. Something she couldn't define—or maybe she didn't want to.

Whatever it was, it both scared her and made her feel as if she could fly.

# Chapter 4

Long after everyone had gone to bed, Christopher stood in the north parlor watching the snowflakes dance against the windowpanes.

His violin had been returned to its case, the fireplace had been banked by a servant, and the candles had been extinguished. Still, he stood near the window, his mind too awake to find rest.

"I thought you might be here." Ashleigh's voice was quiet, almost reverent in the stillness of the late hour.

Christopher took a long breath before he turned to look at her.

She had taken his breath away more than once that evening. First, when she'd appeared in a stunning gown in the drawing room before dinner; second, when she'd mesmerized the entire room by singing "Silent Night"; and now, as she stood with the light of the hall sconces illuminating her in the doorway—under the mistletoe. She still wore the same gown, her curls were still piled atop her head, but now she was wrapped in a silver shawl, one that shimmered in the light of the candles.

"Shouldn't you be resting that ankle?" he asked, just as quietly.

She walked across the room, the slightest limp evident. Either she had not injured it as badly as he suspected, or she was a good actress, because he might not have noticed had he not been watching for it.

He suspected the latter.

"I couldn't sleep." She stopped before him and wrapped the shawl tighter around her shoulders.

"Too much on your mind?"

Her brown eyes were warm and inviting as she studied him. "Too much on my heart."

He wanted to ask her what she meant, but she turned her gaze to look out the window.

"I'm hopeless," she whispered, blowing her breath against the windowpane. A circle of fog formed on the glass, and she made a star with her finger in the fading frost.

"Hopeless?"

"At flirting."

He finally found something to smile about again. "I hadn't noticed."

She rolled her eyes and shook her head. "You're only being kind."

"When have you known me to be kind?" he teased.

She shrugged. "That's true." But the teasing gleam in her eye faded and her shoulders sagged. "I'll never secure Lord Wessex's proposal before Christmas Eve if I can't flirt with him."

The thought of her engagement to Wessex made Christopher feel angrier than it should. "Nonsense." He shook his head, trying to push aside his ridiculous reaction to her words. "Wessex is well aware of you—and it's not because you flirt."

"He is?" She looked up surprised. "How do you know?"

Christopher rubbed the back of his neck, irritation at her naïveté making him turn away from her to pace to the other window. "He watches your every move; he goes out of his way to assist you when necessary—and even when it's not. He barely tolerates the other men, and he doesn't look twice at the other women." Now that he was far enough away, he turned back to face her. "He'll make his intentions known sooner rather than later. Then you and I will be free of this agreement."

"Do you truly think so?" Her shoulders lifted and her eyes filled with hope.

He couldn't bear to see it. "I don't know why he wouldn't."

"Why do you sound angry? Do you think I'm not worthy of Lord Wessex?"

"Ashleigh." He took a step toward her again, wanting her to know the truth. "*He's* not worthy of *you*."

Silence filled the air as she studied him. "Do you jest?"

He shook his head, his face and voice as serious as they'd ever been. "I wish you could see yourself as the rest of us see you." He took another step toward her. "If you did, you would not settle for someone like Wessex. You deserve so much more."

A frown creased her delicate brow. "Lord Wessex is the most sought-after bachelor in England."

"Maybe you should look beyond England."

She didn't say anything for a moment, but then she whispered, "Where do you suggest I look?"

Everything in him wanted to suggest she look no farther than the man standing before her, but he had no right to make such a bold statement, nor did he truly believe he wanted her to. Nothing had changed since he'd left London two days ago. When he returned home, he'd be back at his demanding work, with no time for the finer things in life. . .namely a wife.

The conversation had become much too serious for him, and it was all his fault. "I hear Belgium is a good place to look for a husband."

Instead of smiling at his joke, she bristled at his words.

"Now, what's wrong with that?" he asked, trying to lighten the mood. "Don't you speak Dutch?"

She lifted her chin, just like he'd seen her do when she was a child. "You think it's funny that I'm trying to secure a husband?"

He'd embarrassed her, when all he'd meant to do was hide his own emotions. "That's not what I—"

"I don't think it's humorous at all." Her voice quivered, as if she might cry.

The very thought made Christopher panic. "It's not funny." He shook his head.

She took a step away from him, and he wanted to reach out to stop her before she left angry.

"Before you arrived, I had no intention to seek a husband."

"You blame me?" He pointed at his chest, indignation rising. "I had nothing to do with that agreement."

"No, you didn't, but if you hadn't come, it would have been forgotten and I would not be in this predicament."

"My father was the one who—"

"You're a grown man. You could have refused."

"Just like you're refusing?" He crossed his arms. "I thought we both agreed that we'd follow through with the stipulations of the agreement in honor of our mothers."

She rubbed her hands up and down her arms. "Yes, well, I'm having second thoughts. I don't believe I can go through with this after all. I have no hope with Lord Wessex, and I couldn't possibly marry you." She paused, her eyes softening with regret.

Her words stung more than they should, but he couldn't reveal as much to her.

"I'll do all in my power to see that Wessex has every opportunity to make his intentions known so you're not obligated to do something as horrible as marry me." He took a step back and bowed. "Good night, Lady Ashleigh."

With that, he left the drawing room.

Ashleigh stood by the cold window and watched Christopher leave. She wanted to call him back and explain that she hadn't meant to hurt his feelings. The more she had come to know him, the more she had found to admire. If he didn't live in America, she could almost see herself marrying a man like him—if she must.

When Christopher had hinted that she should look beyond England for a husband, she had half hoped he was referring to himself. But his joke about searching Belgium just confirmed that he was teasing her, and she had felt like a fool. He had made it clear that he wasn't interested in a wife, least of all her.

Yet, she couldn't deny that she had wanted him to be serious.

Suddenly, she felt far too tired to contemplate such things this evening. Her ankle was uncomfortable and she shouldn't be walking on it.

She left the drawing room and entered the large hall. The house was quiet and dark as she took her time going up the steps, her thoughts on Christopher. His bedroom door clicked shut to her left when she came to stand at the stop of the stairs.

Part of her wanted to go to him and explain that she hadn't meant to be rude, but it wouldn't be proper to go to his room.

A noise in one of the alcoves caused her to pause on her way to her bedroom. Feminine giggles were followed by a man's deep voice.

Was someone having a tête-à-tête? If she continued, the couple would see her and know that she had heard them. If she stayed, she took the risk of being an eavesdropper. It would be within her rights to confront these people, whoever they were, but did she want to? It would only embarrass everyone involved.

"Lord Wessex," the woman purred. "You are a rake!"

Ashleigh caught her breath. If she wasn't mistaken, it was the voice of one of the maids, Mary.

The woman left the alcove and entered the hall, adjusting her cap to sit properly on her brown curls. "The others will wonder why I'm not in my room," she said.

It was Mary!

"When will I see you again?" Eric left the alcove directly after her.

"We can meet here tomorrow evening when everyone is in bed." Mary's back was toward Ashleigh. She didn't see Ashleigh as she stood on tiptoe and received another passionate kiss from Eric before rushing down the hall toward the servants' stairs.

Ashleigh's cheeks burned as Eric watched the maid go. She would be forced to speak with Mary about the incident in the morning, but at the moment, she was more concerned about speaking to Eric.

He turned—and found Ashleigh staring. He didn't seem at all embarrassed to discover her standing there. "Ashleigh, what are you doing up so late?"

She wrapped her shawl around her shoulders by crossing her arms. "I should ask the same of you, Lord Wessex."

"I told you to call me Eric." He acted as if nothing untoward had just happened. "But what a happy coincidence this is. Now I can speak to you privately."

"Happy coincidence?" *Was the man mad?* "I just found you dallying with my maid, and you call it a happy coincidence?"

"That?" He waved down the hall with a shake of his head. "That didn't mean anything. Just a little bit of fun. Nothing serious."

Ashleigh's mouth parted. "A little bit of fun? Have you no morals, sir?"

"Morals?" His voice was serious. "I have the same morals as everyone else. I attend church, pay my tithes, and see to the needs of those beneath me."

"Those are not the morals I was referring to." She straightened her shoulders to reach her full height. "You are not married to that girl, nor do I suspect you intend to marry her."

He laughed. "Of course not. What does a midnight tryst have to do with marriage?"

Ashleigh moved back, hardly able to believe her ears. "I imagine it means a great deal to your future wife."

"Speaking of future wives." He came toward her, closing the distance between them, a charming smile on his face. "I've been meaning to speak to you about my intentions since I arrived."

"I no longer wish to know what those are." She began to move around him, but he put out his arm to stop her.

"I believe you do." He lowered his arm and studied her, much too close for her liking. "There are a hundred women who would marry me tomorrow, if I asked, but I've chosen you. I believe we would make a good match."

His statement would have been welcomed earlier, but now she wanted nothing to do with him. "You'd have more success if you asked one of the others."

"That's not possible."

"Why not?"

"Because you're the one I want."

His impertinence was beginning to annoy her. "Why?"

"You come from a good family, you'll have a substantial dowry, and you're beautiful." He touched her cheek with a feather-soft brush of his fingertips. "And you've played so hard to get among the ton, I decided I would be the one to win your hand."

His words and actions matched what she knew of him. He was a flirt, a tease, and a rake, just as Mary said—though Mary seemed enamored with that idea and Ashleigh detested it.

Eric bowed and took a step back. "But this is not how I intended to propose. You are a lady, and you should be courted and wooed."

"That won't be necessary."

He put his hand over his heart. "I insist. You'll see that I'm a good, honorable man, and I would make a superb husband."

"I—"

"Good night, Ashleigh." He walked away without waiting for her to respond.

He was the second man that evening who had left her feeling out of sorts, but for two very different reasons.

At least now she didn't need to worry about flirting with the arrogant Lord Wessex. As far as she was concerned, he was no longer a marriageable option.

But who would be? She couldn't imagine being married to any of the other men in her house party, and there wouldn't be time enough to find someone else.

That left her with two options. Either go through with the agreement and marry Christopher, or deny her mother's wishes and forget the whole thing.

Neither seemed like a good idea.

But there was a third option, one she hadn't thought of before.

Ashleigh smiled into the dark hallway.

She would need to speak to Christopher first thing in the morning.

## Chapter 5

The day before Christmas Eve was clear and bright. Ashleigh stood outside the library doors and braced herself to speak to Christopher. She had overheard her father telling Christopher about his immense collection of books, and Christopher had said he'd see for himself right after breakfast.

Truth be told, she'd rather spend all day in the library as well, but hosting a houseful of people did not lend itself to her quiet ways.

She opened the library door and found Christopher sitting in an oversized chair, near one of the large windows, a red-covered book in hand. It was well-worn, and when she drew closer, she knew why. It was Charles Dickens's, *A Christmas Carol*. One of her favorite stories. Her father had given her a beautiful fiftieth-anniversary edition a few years back, but she still cherished the original copy she'd grown up reading. The one Christopher held in his large hands.

He put his finger on a line in the book and looked up to see who had entered. When he saw it was her, he set it aside and stood. "Ashleigh."

The reminder of how he'd left the night before, when she had insulted him, was still fresh between them this morning. The last thing she wanted was to hurt him, yet what she had come to tell him would not sit well between them either.

"I thought you'd be entertaining Wessex this morning," he said with little emotion.

Ashleigh had been able to avoid Eric, but only because Cynthia was near his side, hanging on his every word. Ashleigh would have to work hard to evade him for the remainder of his stay.

"That's one of the reasons I came to speak to you today." She motioned for him to return to his seat, and she took the one opposite him.

"Wessex has proposed?" he asked once he was settled.

Ashleigh had been taught to sit tall in her chair, to keep her posture erect, but the chairs in the library were not meant for formality. Neither, did it seem, was her relationship with Christopher. She settled back in the chair and studied the man across from her. No longer did she think of him as the horrible, annoying boy he had been. The man before her was kind, sincere, intelligent—and utterly too handsome. She felt more comfortable with him than anyone she'd ever known, as if they'd been friends all their lives.

"I've decided I will not marry Wessex." Ashleigh tried to make her statement as light-hearted and confident as she could muster.

Christopher set his elbows on the armrests and frowned. "Who will you marry then?"

She crossed her arms and lifted her chin. "No one."

His frown disappeared, and he leaned forward. "What do you mean?"

"I'm not getting married. Not to Eric, not to you, not to anyone else."

"I don't understand."

It was her turn to lean forward. "Your mother is just as responsible for this mess as mine. Why should I be the one to marry a man I dislike, just so you can walk free?" She shook her head. "I refuse."

Christopher stood, his jaw clenched.

Ashleigh also stood. Though her head only came up to his shoulders, she tried to stare him down.

"I don't want to get married," he said. "I told you that the very first day I was here."

"I don't want to get married either!"

"Even if I did," he went on, "I don't know anyone in England, besides you. I wouldn't have enough time to return to America and convince one of my acquaintances to marry me."

"Surely, you could convince someone." Her admiration colored the conviction in her voice. "A woman would be foolish not to accept your proposal."

The moment the words slipped out, something shifted between them. It was evident in the way Christopher's shoulders relaxed and his face softened—and in the way her heart sped up and her mouth suddenly felt overly dry.

"What I mean," she said quickly, "is that you shouldn't have a problem finding a wife."

"By tomorrow?" He shook his head. "I'm not *that* desirable."

She wanted to disagree, but knew she'd only embarrass herself further. She said nothing, though she suspected the warmth in her cheeks revealed her thoughts.

"What happened with Wessex?" he asked.

"Wessex." She shuddered just saying his name and walked over to the fireplace where she placed another log on the dying fire.

"Did he do something?" Christopher's American accent grew thicker as his anger surfaced.

"I have discovered some things about his character that convinced me I could not marry him."

"You shouldn't rely on gossip."

"It wasn't gossip." She poked at the log with a poker and sent sparks dancing up the chimney. "I caught him in a compromising situation. When I confronted him, he acted as if nothing distasteful had happened. Then. . ." She paused, hating to recall how arrogant he was when he told her he planned to marry her. "He told me I would become his wife and wouldn't take no for an answer."

Christopher lifted his hand and rubbed the back of his neck. "I've never liked him."

"That leaves me with no other options." She motioned to him. "So that's where you come in."

He paced across the library, kneading the muscles in his neck. Finally, he came to stop before her. "This is ridiculous, Ashleigh. We'll have to call the whole thing off. If my mother were here, and she understood this situation, I know she'd agree."

Ashleigh nibbled her bottom lip. Would her mother agree to call it off too? She wanted to believe that Mother would be understanding—but she couldn't be sure. Obviously, the agreement meant a great deal to both women or they wouldn't have signed the documents.

But would they truly want Ashleigh and Christopher to get married, even if they didn't want to?

She couldn't imagine her mother wanting her to be unhappy.

But *would* she be unhappy married to Christopher?

"Maybe you're right," Ashleigh said slowly, watching his face to see how he felt about the possibility of being married to her.

"Then we agree?" There was so much hope in his voice. "We'll call off the agreement and be done with this nonsense?"

It was clear that he still wanted his freedom.

"Yes," she said.

He let out a relieved sigh and pulled her into his arms. "Thank you."

She froze in his unexpected embrace, her eyes wide.

He released her just as quickly. "I'm sorry." He laughed uncomfortably. "I'm just so relieved."

Ashleigh tried not to let his words sear her heart. Of course he'd be relieved not to have to marry her. He didn't love her, he didn't want a wife, and he definitely didn't want to marry an English woman who wasn't familiar with his American ways.

She clasped her hands and turned away from him to look at the fire. "I—I suppose you will leave now."

He was quiet for a moment and then kicked an ember back into the fire. "I have been eager to return to London. There is a firm who will vote on whether or not they will invest in my railroad, and I'd like to be there for the vote."

They watched the fire crack and pop for another moment as her pulse slowed to a steady beat.

"It's my last hope for purchasing a section of railroad that's vital to our business," he said after a while.

"What will you do if they won't invest?"

He put his hands in his pockets, his countenance heavy. "I'll have to forget about expanding our railroad. Someone else will pick up the Northern Union soon."

"You want this very much, don't you?"

He turned his gaze away from the fire, and she felt as if she was looking straight into his heart.

"More than anything. My father didn't have the time of day for me as a child. The first time I recall him meeting my eye was when we were driving away from Anglesey Abbey after I had started that fire." He lifted a heavy shoulder. "But it wasn't pride or acceptance in his gaze. He was ashamed of me. After my mother died, it only became worse. He didn't start to pay attention to me until I showed an aptitude for the railroad business."

"Is that why you've given your entire life to your work?"

"I suppose it sounds ridiculous, but I guess it's true."

"And that's why this acquisition is so important? Because you want to make your father proud?"

He slowly nodded. "I hadn't thought about my motivation so deeply before now, but you're probably right." He readjusted one of the logs with his foot. "Does that make me sound pathetic?"

She shook her head and put her hand on his arm. "It makes you sound like a loving son."

Christopher rested his hand on top of hers. It sent warmth up her arm and into her chest.

"It sounds as if that Christmas so long ago affected both of us profoundly, for different reasons," she said softly. "After that day, my mother never asked me to perform a social obligation again. I embarrassed her deeply and made her ashamed of me."

He turned to face her, but didn't let go of her hand. Instead, he held it tighter. "How could your mother possibly be ashamed of you? You're beautiful, intelligent, humble, and the kindest woman I've ever met."

The warmth in her chest grew, until it filled every part of her. "You're too generous with your compliments." She couldn't help but tease. "Just like an American."

"I think you like it," he said with laughter in his voice. "I think you'd like a lot about America."

She loved the feel of his hand holding hers and didn't want him to let go. But she knew if she didn't pull away now, she might lose her heart to this handsome, kind American, and that would never do. Especially because he didn't want a wife.

"I imagine we won't see each other again," she said quietly as she pulled away from his hold.

He clasped his hands behind his back. "If you ever come to Minnesota, I hope you'll stop in to see me."

She giggled, wanting to add levity to the moment. "I have never even considered visiting Minnesota, though your father speaks highly of it. I do admire Longfellow's 'Song of Hiawatha' and have always wanted to see Minnehaha Falls."

"You and everyone else who comes to Minneapolis." He smiled.

"You must agree to come and see me next time you're in London."

He nodded, but didn't say anything.

A week ago, she couldn't imagine inviting Christopher Campbell to be her guest—but now, she couldn't imagine waiting eleven more years to see him again. The very thought made her want to cry.

"Will you write?" he asked quietly.

She suddenly felt shy and couldn't meet his eyes. "Would you like me to?"

"Very much."

"Then I will."

He reached out and took her hand again. "Ashleigh—"

"Campbell." Eric stood in the open door, his jaw tight. "I've been looking all over for you two. I thought I might find you together."

Ashleigh took her hand out of Christopher's, her heart beating hard. "Eric."

He strode into the room, his gaze burning into Christopher. "You've been summoned to London."

"By whom?" Christopher asked.

"A representative just called from the investment firm of Thomas, Crenshaw & Hughes, I believe. I took the message and said I'd deliver it to you personally." Eric stopped beside Ashleigh, but addressed Christopher. "The representative said they will be voting tomorrow morning and would like to meet with you this evening to discuss a few more details."

Christopher met Ashleigh's gaze. "I must go immediately."

"Of course."

"If they vote early enough in the day, I will return before your ball tomorrow evening." He smiled, and the teasing gleam returned to his eye. "I know how much you want me to be at the tree lighting ceremony."

She had dreaded the ceremony every year since she was eight years old. Now, for the first time, she eagerly anticipated the event, knowing Christopher would be there with her. "More than you might know."

His smile faded and something far different shone from his face. Hope? Anticipation? Dare she think, affection? "Goodbye, Ashleigh."

"Goodbye, Christopher." She didn't want to be alone in the library with Eric, so she added, "I'll see you out."

He indicated for her to precede him out of the library and left her in the front hall while he went upstairs to pack a bag for the overnight jaunt to London.

"Now that Campbell is out of the way," Eric said beside Ashleigh, "maybe you'll pay more attention to me."

The very thought made her shiver.

The following afternoon, Ashleigh stood inside the ballroom with Mrs. Rodgers, her house-keeper, going over the final preparations for the ball that evening. All around, the servants were busy moving potted plants, hanging pine boughs, stringing ornaments, and replacing dozens of candles in the wall sconces.

"We will be expecting a hundred and fifty guests?" Mrs. Rodgers asked for the tenth time that morning.

"Yes," Ashleigh said patiently.

"And you are sure you want to serve the buffet at ten o'clock? Isn't it popular to serve a midnight buffet?"

"I would like everything to be exactly the same as when my mother hosted the ball."

"Of course," Mrs. Rodgers said, her voice dry. "Just like we've always done."

"There's no reason to change." Ashleigh clasped her hands and took a deep breath, just as her mother would have done when dealing with a difficult servant. "Is there anything else we need to discuss?"

Mrs. Rodgers bowed her graying head. "I believe we have everything under control."

"Then I will see to my other guests." Some of the women were napping in preparation for the late-night festivities, while the men were in the drawing room passing the time playing whist or chess. Though Ashleigh longed to join the ladies, there was far too much to do before the dressing gong would sound later in the day. She still needed to meet with the cook to finalize the menu and the butler to discuss a few issues that had arisen with one of the footmen.

The hall clock chimed three times when she left the ballroom. Almost of their own accord, her feet took her to the front windows where she looked out at the long, empty drive.

Longing filled her chest with an ache she'd never felt before.

Was Christopher on his way back to her? It was a four-hour ride from London. If the firm had met early in the morning, he might arrive at any moment. Joy filled her with excitement at the thought of seeing him again. Had he been granted the money? Would he ask her to dance? Her ankle still smarted, but she could endure almost any pain to dance in his arms. Would he be shocked to know she had placed him beside her at the table? It was a spot reserved for the most honored guest at the party. She could think of no one else who was as special as him.

She might not be able to stop him from returning to America, but she'd enjoy every moment she possibly could with him before he left.

"There you are." Eric strode toward Ashleigh from the drawing room doors. "I've been trying to find you alone since yesterday."

She had successfully avoided him since their unfortunate encounter in the hallway two nights before. Why had she allowed herself to be alone now?

"I hate to be rude, but I have many things to attend to this afternoon." She started to pass him, but he stepped into her way. "I beg your pardon," she said with frustration in her voice. "Please let me pass."

He put his hands on her upper arms and held her in place. "I will not be dismissed, Ashleigh."

"Unhand me, Lord Wessex."

"Not until you agree to stay here and listen to me."

Heat climbed up her neck and into her cheeks. If someone should happen upon them, they might think the worst, seeing her in his arms. "Fine."

"Good." He let her go. "I have something very important to discuss with you, and I cannot abide chasing after anyone."

*Except a lady's maid*, she thought ruefully.

"What do you need to discuss with me?" she asked, knowing full well she would not agree to any proposition he might make.

"I would like to announce our engagement this evening at the ball."

"Our engagement?" Her face contorted in disgust. "I have not agreed to marry you, nor will I."

"Is this about the American?"

"Christopher?"

"Do you fancy yourself in love with him?"

*Love?* The very thought made her heart quicken. Was she in love with Christopher? It seemed preposterous so soon after being reacquainted—yet, she couldn't deny her deep affection for him or the sadness she felt when thinking about him leaving without her.

"You are in love with him." Eric's voice filled with incredulity and accusation. "I had suspected, but now I'm certain."

She didn't bother denying or confirming his claim. "It's none of your business."

"I disagree." His eyes were hard. "I decided to make you my wife, so it is my business."

"I've tired of this conversation, Lord Wessex."

"Then I will get right to my point." He straightened his posture and looked down his nose at her. "We will announce our engagement this evening, or I will advise my board to vote down Mr. Campbell's request for the funds."

She frowned. "What are you talking about?"

"I am the principal financier for Thomas, Crenshaw & Hughes, the investment firm your American is asking to finance his railroad." His smile was triumphant. "Say the word, and I will tell my board to give him the money."

Sweat gathered on her palms, and her heart beat an unsteady rhythm. "If I marry you, you'll give him the money?"

"If you agree to marry me and announce it at the ball tonight, Campbell will get his money."

She put her hand to her throat, afraid to ask the next question. "And if I don't?"

"Then I will deny his request and see that your reputation is ruined as well."

Ashleigh didn't care about her own reputation as much as she cared about Christopher's dream. It would be within her power to grant him what he wanted: his railroad, and ultimately, his father's respect.

What did she have to lose? She didn't love Eric, but she imagined he would provide well for her, and she wouldn't be far from her father. If she had control over her own money, she would offer to give it to Christopher, but as it was, her father would never agree to finance something for the Campbells. His dislike of the elder Campbell was still strong, even more so with the boisterous man staying at Anglesey Abbey these past few days.

So that left her feelings for Christopher to consider. Perhaps she did love him, but he had made it clear that he didn't want a wife. She couldn't hold out hope that he might propose to her someday. He would return to America soon and would probably never reappear. Even if he did, it might be years from now, and whatever feelings he might have for her would be cold by then.

"What will it be, Ashleigh?"

"You promise to give Christopher the money he's asked for?"

He placed his hand over his heart. "On my honor."

"Then I agree," she said quietly.

A look of conquest swept over Eric's face. "You won't regret this, my dear. Despite what you may think, I will be a good husband. In time, you'll come to love me."

Tears stung the back of Ashleigh's eyes as she nodded, hoping he was right, but fearing that she had just sealed her own fate.

Once the engagement was announced at the ball, with over a hundred and fifty guests as witnesses, there would be no backing out of the agreement.

# Chapter 6

The sun had already set as Christopher paced in the hallway outside the boardroom where he awaited the vote. What was taking so long? One delay after the other had kept them from meeting until after five o'clock. Didn't these men want to be home with their families for Christmas Eve festivities? Even if they voted now, he wouldn't make it back to Anglesey Abbey until after nine, and then he'd need to dress. If he was lucky, he might be there in time for the lighting of the Christmas tree right before the buffet would be served.

He massaged the back of his neck as he walked the length of the hall, yet again. A carriage had been waiting for him for over two hours on the street outside. It would cost him a small fortune to pay the driver, but it would be worth it to see Ashleigh once again. He wanted to be there for the lighting of the tree, if for no other reason than to redeem his childhood mistakes.

The memory returned as if it were yesterday. As a child, Ashleigh had rescued many animals, but she had one cat in particular that she loved. It was a white, fluffy thing that her mother seemed to despise. Ashleigh carried it everywhere she went, so when it was time for the Christmas Eve ball, and it wasn't in her hands, Christopher had teased her about her cat not being invited to the party. She had stuck out her tongue and told him that the cat was in her room because it liked to climb trees and her mother was afraid it would get into the Christmas tree.

That gave Christopher an idea.

Just before it was time to light the candles on the tree, he had snuck up to her room and lured the cat into his arms with a piece of smoked salmon from the kitchen. And when Ashleigh climbed the ladder to put the star on the top of the tree, he let the cat go. He thought it would be funny to see the cat climb the tree, nothing more. He caught Ashleigh's eye the moment the cat leapt out of his arms, and she had scowled at him.

What happened next was branded into his memory for eternity. The cat made the tree start to wobble, which caused Ashleigh to lose her balance on the ladder. When the tree crashed to the ground, it looked as if it had been her fault.

The following hour was the most horrible one of his life. A nearby drape caught on fire, and the servant standing by with a wet sponge tried valiantly to put it out, but it was no use. Guests ran screaming from the room while the servants fought to get the fire under control.

The only people who saw what he had done were his parents. The very next day, they packed everything up and left for home, weeks earlier than planned. His mother had died on the way, leaving things unsettled with Ashleigh's mother.

It had been Christopher's fault, yet Ashleigh had taken the blame. She'd lived with the shame of it all these years. It was a wonder that she had welcomed him back to Anglesey Abbey—and that they had somehow found a friendship.

He paused as he looked out a window onto the bustling London street. A lamplighter walked on stilts, turning on the street lights as the evening sun faded. Snow had begun to fall, gathering quickly on the streets, the lamps, and the buildings.

Were he and Ashleigh friends or had they bypassed friendship all together? What he felt for her was more than friendly. Yesterday in the library, he had had the desire to bare his heart to her. He trusted her, admired her, and maybe, if he was honest with himself, he might even love her. The thought of putting an ocean between them and waiting for weeks on end to exchange letters was a gloomy one.

"Mr. Campbell?" The door creaked open and the mustached Mr. Thomas motioned him inside the room. "We've come to a decision."

Casting aside thoughts of Ashleigh for the moment, Christopher followed him into the boardroom and faced the nine men who had control over his future.

"All of us would like to get home to our families, so we won't waste any more time." Mr. Thomas was a surprisingly young man, and he seemed a bit perturbed at the moment. "We've agreed to invest in your railroad, though it wasn't a unanimous decision."

Christopher's mouth parted at the news.

"You may come back after Christmas to sign all the legal documents and collect your money." Mr. Thomas closed a folder and took his coat off the hook near the door. "I'm going home."

He left the room before Christopher could even thank him.

"If you'll excuse me," Christopher said to the other men around the table, "I'd like to thank all of you, starting with Mr. Thomas."

The others nodded as they stood to gather their things.

Christopher entered the hall again and sprinted to reach Mr. Thomas before he stepped outside.

"I'd like to thank you and wish you a Merry Christmas," he said.

"Don't thank me." Mr. Thomas put on his hat and tapped it firmly. "If I'd had my way, we wouldn't be giving you or any other American money to build your infrastructure."

Christopher wouldn't let Mr. Thomas's sour mood deter him or dampen his spirits. "Regardless, I'd still like to thank you."

"Thank Lord Wessex, if you must thank someone."

"Lord Wessex?"

Mr. Thomas gave Christopher a shrewd look. "He's the one who advised everyone else to vote in your favor. He is a principal financier, and they would not go against his wishes."

Christopher frowned in confusion. "Why would Wessex want to finance my railroad?"

The investor studied Christopher, as if trying to decide whether or not to divulge information. "Since I don't care for Wessex, I'll tell you what I heard, though I don't put much stock in rumors."

"What did you hear?"

"Apparently, he wants to marry Lady Ashleigh Arrington and this investment is somehow wrapped up in his personal problems." Mr. Thomas leaned forward as he pulled on his gloves. "She agreed to marry Wessex if he gave you the money. They'll announce their engagement this evening at Anglesey Abbey."

It felt as if a steel fist punched Christopher in the gut, and he could only stare at the other gentleman.

"I don't know how you're involved in the affair," Mr. Thomas said, "but I imagine you used the lady to your advantage. Congratulations." With that, he left the building.

Christopher stared after the man as the door slammed shut.

Ashleigh agreed to marry Wessex if he'd give Christopher the money? What kind of a man would ask her to do such a thing?

Anger burned in his gut as he pushed open the door and rushed into the street. Snow continued to fall, casting a thick blanket over the dirty city.

He couldn't let Ashleigh go through with it. There wasn't anything he wanted more than her happiness. Not a railroad, not his father's acceptance, and definitely not Lord Wessex's money. If he didn't get to Anglesey Abbey before the announcement was made, it would be too late. She'd be as good as married in the eyes of the peerage.

"Take me to Anglesey Abbey in Cambridgeshire, posthaste," he called out to the driver as he jumped into the carriage.

The next four hours would be the longest of his life. He had to get to Ashleigh before she made an announcement. Not only to stop her from agreeing to marry Wessex, but to tell her what he'd come to realize while he'd been away.

He loved her, and he wanted her to be his wife.

"Ashleigh?" Father spoke her name quietly, a question in his tone.

She turned away from the window where she had been watching the snow fall. The orchestra played a beautiful waltz in the ballroom, just down the hall. She should have been mingling with her guests, playing the part of the perfect hostess, but she didn't have the heart.

The ball gown she wore was the most beautiful dress she had ever owned. Dark green silk, just off the shoulders, with a slight train. She had hoped Christopher would return in time to see her in it—but now none of that mattered.

Father's eyes were sad as he smiled at her. "Are you ready?"

It was almost time to light the candles on the Christmas tree and make her announcement. Eric had hardly left her side all evening, until she insisted she needed a moment alone. But she hadn't been able to bring herself to return to the ballroom and into his keeping.

She let out a sigh and linked her arm through her father's. "I suppose I can't put it off forever."

"Why are you doing this?" He put his hand over hers. "Why are you marrying Wessex when you don't want to?"

She hadn't shared the truth with her father. Knowing him, he'd put a stop to such a thing—yet, he wouldn't give Christopher the money he needed either. Ashleigh couldn't allow that to happen.

"I need to marry someone. Eric is just as good as the next man." She tried to smile, to reassure him, but her lips quivered and tears threatened.

"If this is about that agreement with the Campbells—" His voice became angry. "I will insist we forget about the whole ordeal. If they want to take us to court over the thing, I'll—"

"It's not about the agreement." She shook her head sadly. "It's not that at all." If it was as simple as that, she might have a bit of hope.

"Then what is it?"

She squeezed his arm and lifted her head. "It's nothing, Father. Let's go light those candles."

"Only if you're sure."

Ashleigh nodded. "I'm sure."

He leaned over and kissed her cheek. "If you're happy, I'm happy."

Happiness was not an option for Ashleigh right now, but she would do all she could to make the most of this situation. She knew dozens of women who were married to men out of convenience. Love wasn't the rule; it was the exception in most marriages. Who was she to expect anything more?

Yet, she couldn't stop thinking about Christopher. If she'd been forced to marry him, she knew she would love him, even if he never returned the love. He was a good man, one she would be honored to marry.

"I'm proud of you, Ashleigh. You've done a beautiful job stepping in as mistress of Anglesey Abbey."

His words made her heart glow, despite the troubles she faced. "Would Mother be pleased?"

"More than I could say."

Ashleigh sighed and dropped her gaze, but her father lifted her chin with his finger. "What's wrong?"

"I just wish I could have pleased her while she was alive."

He shook his head. "You pleased your mother a great deal. She couldn't have been happier with you."

It seemed a preposterous thought. "Then why did she never ask me to put the star on the top of the tree after that horrible Christmas? Why did she not ask me to perform other social obligations?"

Father laid his hand on her cheek and looked deep into her eyes. "She knew how you detested being the center of attention, so she decided not to make you uncomfortable again. She admired your self-confidence and independence. Your mother accepted you as you were. It was her gift to you."

Memories flooded Ashleigh's mind of times when her mother had let her be, instead of demanding that she fulfill all the social obligations other young women performed. Not once had she thought it was because her mother understood her.

"Come," Father said. "And be the woman God made you to be." He led her out of the drawing room and into the hall. "And give Wessex a chance to prove himself. He might surprise you."

She nodded and smiled, just for him. "I will."

"That's a good girl." He rubbed the top of her hand as they walked down the hall toward the ballroom.

The Christmas tree was set up in the parlor off the ballroom, as always. The servants had spent all day decorating it with family ornaments, colorful beads, and shiny tinsel. Just before the doors would open, they would light each of the candles, then Father would wish everyone a Merry Christmas and announce the engagement.

There would be no turning back after that. The very thought made her stomach sour.

They entered the ballroom, and she greeted several guests as they walked to the parlor doors. By every account, the Christmas Eve party was a success. Everyone was laughing, dancing, and having a grand time. Candles dripped with wax, couples kissed beneath the mistletoe, and the smell of fresh pine garland filled her nose.

If only Christopher could be with her now to enjoy the festivities. His father stood on the opposite side of the room, laughing and making merry with the rest of the guests. Would Christopher be just as jolly this evening? By now, he would have learned about the investment. No doubt he was already making plans for his railroad. Just thinking about how happy he'd be took the edge off Ashleigh's melancholy.

"It's time." Father nodded to Mr. Warren, who signaled the orchestra to stop playing.

The dancers came to a halt, and Mr. Warren rang a bell to get their attention.

Eric and his mother joined Father and Ashleigh as they stood outside the doors to the adjoining drawing room.

"I hope you know what you're doing, Son," Eric's mother said under her breath.

Ashleigh pretended not to hear her and forced herself to smile at her guests.

"If you'll join us," Father addressed the crowd, "we'd like to usher in this blessed holiday with the lighting of our Christmas tree."

Two matching footmen opened the doors, allowing Ashleigh and her father to lead the way. Eric and his mother trailed close behind, followed by the rest of the guests.

Oohs and ahs filled the drawing room as people crowded in to see the magnificent tree. It stood fifteen feet tall and was aglow with candlelight.

*How like the Light of Christ*, Ashleigh thought. *He came into a dark world and shined bright for all to see.* If her own heart wasn't so heavy, she would enjoy reveling in the beauty of the moment.

At the top of the tree was a star, which had been placed there by a servant. Since that fateful Christmas, when Christopher had almost burned their house down, there was no special ceremony to put the star on top. It was done quietly and safely, away from the eyes of the guests.

Father squeezed her hand and stepped forward to address their guests.

"Thank you all for sharing this Christmas Eve with Ashleigh and me."

A commotion at the back of the crowded room drew Ashleigh's attention. People began to move to the side, some with frowns, and others with exclamations of surprise.

"We both feel Elizabeth's presence," Father continued. "It is a great comfort to know that so many of you carry her memory in your hearts, especially at this time of year."

Ashleigh tried to concentrate on what he was saying, knowing that the most important part of his address would come at the end, but there was someone pushing their way to the front of the room. She couldn't make out who it was, but they were not stopping. Was someone that desperate to see the tree up close?

"On behalf of our family." Father reached out and took Ashleigh's hand. "I want to wish you a merry Christmas."

The others wished her and Father a merry Christmas in return.

Suddenly, Christopher appeared on the edge of the crowd. He wore an afternoon suit and his hair was disheveled as he searched the front of the room with anxious eyes, until his gaze landed on Ashleigh.

Her heart leapt, and she almost took a step forward, but her father still held her hand.

"And speaking of family," Father continued, apparently unaware of Christopher's strange and sudden appearance, "I have a happy announcement to make."

Eric reached out and possessively took Ashleigh's other hand, his attention on Christopher.

The guests watched with open curiosity and avid interest. Cynthia, who had not been told about the engagement, blinked with surprise.

Christopher questioned Ashleigh with his eyes as he shook his head.

What was he doing? Ashleigh wanted to speak to him, but there was no way to step away from Eric now.

Father continued speaking. "It is with great pride that I—"

Christopher's eyes filled with panic, and he took a step forward.

Ashleigh opened her mouth to stop her father, but everything was happening so quickly.

"—would like to announce the engagement of—"

A scream filled the air as a flame licked up the Christmas tree.

Father's announcement was lost in the chaos that erupted as several servants rushed to the tree to put out the fire. More people screamed as guests began to run out of the drawing room and into the ballroom. Smoke stung Ashleigh's nose as she pulled her hands away from her father and Eric.

She lost sight of Christopher as people pushed and shoved.

"Ashleigh." Suddenly, he was beside her, his hand on her elbow. He led her out of the parlor and through a door that connected with the library.

She went willingly and gratefully, coughing from the smoke. A glance over her shoulder revealed that the servants had the fire under control, but she had no desire to stay in the parlor to deal with her panicked guests. She would leave that to her father and the servants.

When she and Christopher were safely inside the library, he closed the door, and without a word, pulled her into his arms.

"Am I too late?" he whispered into her hair.

"Too late?" She was breathless as she clung to him.

"Did you and Wessex make the announcement?" He pulled back and placed his thumbs on her cheeks, gently brushing away the tears that she didn't know she had shed.

"No."

Christopher leaned his forehead against hers, breathing just as hard as her. "Thank God."

"How did you know?"

"One of the investors told me." He shook his head and pulled back, confusion on his handsome face. "Ashleigh, why would you marry Wessex for my sake?"

More tears stung the back of her eyes and her lips trembled. "If I don't marry him, you won't get the money you need for your railroad."

"I don't want Wessex's money." Pain filled his voice. "Especially if it means you have to marry him. I would give up everything for your happiness, my love."

*My love?* She reveled in his declaration for a moment. "Do you truly mean that?"

In answer, he pulled her closer and lowered his lips to hers.

The sensation of his kiss was the most exquisite thing she'd ever experienced. His arms were strong, his lips tender, and his passion contagious. She wrapped her arms around him and tightened her hold, deepening the kiss.

After a moment, he broke away, a surprised laugh on his lips. "I had no idea how you felt."

She smiled, loving the way his blue eyes sparkled with joy. "I didn't know how you felt either."

He kissed her again, erasing every last shred of doubt she might have.

"I still don't know why you would make such a sacrifice for me." His thumb continued to caress her cheek, and she leaned into the touch.

"Because I love you," she said, watching the way her words changed the emotion on his face from happiness to wonder.

"I love you too, Lady Ashleigh." He shook his head. "I had no idea it could be possible in such a short time."

She could do nothing but smile.

He held her in his arms, and she was content to stay there all evening.

"I suppose we must face everyone sooner or later," he finally said.

She took a deep breath and nodded. "There's the matter of Wessex—and the fire—to deal with." She paused. "Did you start that fire?"

He shook his head and laughed. "No, but I would have if your maid hadn't set the candle to the tree first."

"My maid?" She searched her memory. Who was standing beside the tree when she'd come into the drawing room? Her eyes opened wide. "Mary?"

"I don't know her name."

It *was* Mary. Had she been jealous? Ashleigh beamed. Whatever her reason, Ashleigh was thankful for what she'd done.

"So." Christopher crossed his arms, a mock frown upon his handsome face. "Your maid may start the tree on fire, and you are overjoyed, but if I do, you hold it against me for eleven years?"

Ashleigh laughed and placed a kiss on his cheek. "Maybe we should have electricity installed and use electric lights next year."

Christopher's mood suddenly grew serious. "Where will we be next Christmas?"

The simple question begged another. "Where would you like to be next Christmas?"

"Wherever you are."

Ashleigh's smile began slowly, but it blossomed, until it radiated from her heart. "Say the words and I will follow you anywhere."

He wrapped her in his arms again and pulled her close. "Will you marry me and go home with me to St. Paul?"

She had never, in her wildest imaginings, thought she'd marry an American and make her home in Minnesota. But she realized something standing there with Christopher. She would never be at home, unless she was by his side. "I will."

# Chapter 7

The house was quiet as Ashleigh and Christopher met at the top of the stairs, just as the sun filled the hall with the first hint of sunshine. Christmas morning was clear, crisp, and filled with a hint of smoke.

"Good morning," Ashleigh whispered, feeling a little shy in his presence this morning.

"Good morning." He reached out and offered his hand, which she took without hesitation.

"Did you sleep?" she asked quietly.

"No. You?"

"Not a wink." She smiled, feeling refreshed, despite her lack of rest.

"Are you ready?" he asked.

In answer, she led the way down the steps. The previous evening, she had told Eric that she would not be marrying him after all. When he'd threatened to rescind his offer to finance Christopher's railroad, she had said it didn't matter. Christopher wouldn't accept his money. Eric had left the house with his mother before the party ended.

Who knew what Lady Wessex would say to the London papers about her party now?

Ashleigh no longer cared, because now it was time to face their fathers.

They held hands as they walked to the morning room. Her father always went to the morning room first thing each day. It was there that he read his Bible, drank his first cup of tea, and said his prayers. This morning would be a little different, since Christopher had asked his father to meet them there at sunrise as well.

"No matter what is said"—Christopher held her back for a moment—"know that I love you and I'll fight for you, if need be."

She placed her hand on his dear cheek and shook her head. "We can fight together." She started to open the door, but paused. "If it comes to that."

He grinned, but she saw the worry behind his eyes.

Truth be told, she didn't feel as confident as she'd like. If her father refused to let her marry Christopher, she could not dishonor him.

They entered the room, hand in hand, and found their fathers sitting at a table in the oriel window overlooking the gardens, now draped in a layer of fresh white snow.

Father's eyes immediately went to their clasped hands, and then he looked up in surprise.

Mr. Campbell was reading a newspaper, but he too showed surprise at their entrance.

"Ashleigh?" Father stood and waited for them to cross the room.

"I've come to share some news with you," she said with a trembling smile.

To his credit, Mr. Campbell didn't speak. Instead, he beamed.

"Lord Pemberton." Christopher addressed her father. "I would like to ask for your daughter's hand in marriage."

"I'm speechless." Father searched Ashleigh's face. "When did this happen?"

"I suppose it happened right away," she said. "But we weren't completely sure until last evening, during the fire."

"I love Ashleigh," Christopher said to her father. "And if you'll allow me, I'd like to marry her and take her to St. Paul."

"America?" Father didn't even look at Christopher. Instead, he continued to watch her. "Is this what you want?"

She held Christopher's hand in both of hers and nodded. "With all my heart."

For a moment, Father was quiet, but then he reached out his arms.

Ashleigh left Christopher's side and entered her father's warm embrace.

"Then I will give you my blessing," he said as he hugged her. "I told you that if you're happy, I'm happy, and I meant it."

Ashleigh hugged him tighter. "Thank you."

"Congratulations," Mr. Campbell said to Christopher as he extended his hand. "I'm very happy for you."

"Thank you, Father." Christopher shook his father's hand.

"Welcome to the family," Mr. Campbell said to Ashleigh. "I know my wife would be overjoyed if she were still with us."

"I'm sure both of our wives would be overjoyed," Father said with certainty. "It's what they wanted from early on."

Christopher reached out and captured Ashleigh's hand once again.

She returned to his side, not wanting to leave it again.

"I was made aware of the situation with Lord Wessex last night," Father said, his face serious. "And I'm disappointed that you didn't let me know what was happening, Ashleigh."

Shame warmed her cheeks, but she didn't respond.

"If you wanted to help Christopher finance his railroad, then you should have come to me."

Her mouth parted in surprise. "I didn't think you'd be interested."

"You never asked."

Ashleigh squeezed Christopher's hand.

"As a wedding gift to you both," Father said, putting his hand on Christopher's shoulder, "I would like to help. I have a few friends who have been interested in investing in American railroads, but have not had the ability to do it alone. I will gather them together and we will provide whatever you need."

"I would be honored to work with you, Lord Pemberton." Christopher reached out and shook Father's hand. "Thank you."

Father put his other hand on Ashleigh's shoulder and smiled at both of them. "Just take care of my daughter and we'll both be happy."

"It will be my greatest privilege," Christopher said.

"And I will do my best to take care of your son," Ashleigh said with a smile at Mr. Campbell.

Father stepped back and Christopher put his arm around Ashleigh's waist, smiling down at her. "I think we'll do a fine job taking care of each other."

Ashleigh returned his smile and marveled that she had fallen in love with Christopher Campbell.

The child she disliked most in the world had somehow become the man she adored more than any other. For the first time since his arrival, she was thankful their mothers had made that Christmas promise so long ago.

**Gabrielle Meyer** lives in central Minnesota on the banks of the Mississippi River with her husband and four young children. As an employee of the Minnesota Historical Society, she fell in love with the rich history of her state and enjoys writing fictional stories inspired by real people and events. Gabrielle can be found at www.gabriellemeyer.com where she writes about her passion for history, Minnesota, and her faith.

# The Sugarplum Ladies

by Carrie Fancett Pagels

## Dedication

To my aunt, Wilda Jane Roat Fancett
Always an encourager, always a gracious lady, always loved!

## Acknowledgments

Thank you, God, that you allow this cracked vessel to journey on and to write stories for Your glory. Thank you to my family members, who support my writing. I am extremely blessed to have my wonderful critique partner, Kathleen Maher, an amazing author and editor. Thank you to Becky Germany for the concept for this collection. Thank you to all the wonderful authors who contributed to *The Victorian Christmas Brides Collection*! And God bless my editor, Ellen Tarver, for her hard work on all the stories.

King's College Cambridge, 2008, Victorian-era carols on YouTube were the inspiration music for my story. Simply beautiful. Thank you to the friends who allowed me to borrow their names for this story—Carrie Booth Schmidt and Carrie Moore Gould's names came together for fictional Carrie Booth Moore's name (a character who will also appear in my novella "Love's Beacon" in *The Great Lakes Lighthouse Romance Collection* releasing November 2018), Tara Mulcahey, and my son's friend, Christian Zumbrun, and many more! Thank you to my Pagels' Pals members, especially the friends whose names are used as the Sugarplum Ladies in this novella: Kathleen, Nancy, Anne, Melissa, Tina, Deborah, and Lucy. Thank you to our Barbour collections readers too for visiting with us in the Victorian era!

# Prologue

Eugenie Mott yanked the velvet curtains closed to the September sun in the parlor. It was now or never. She paced back and forth over the tightly woven burgundy and gold wool carpet that covered the wide oak planks of the floor. She either must confide in her father or bend to his wishes. But how could she disappoint him?

Horace Ontevreden had become one of Father's closest companions only recently. How had he influenced her father so greatly in such a short time? Horace was over twenty years her senior.

From the beginning, both Eugenie and her housekeeper, Lorena, had judged the man to have hailed from the lower classes. Not that she was a snobbish person—not anymore. But if she were to influence Detroit's upper echelon of social circles, then Eugenie must have a husband of satisfactory character and possessing good manners. She wasn't sure Mr. Ontevreden was acquainted with either. But what did it matter? He was unlikely to allow Eugenie to engage in anything other than tasks which would support her role as wife of an importer of fine porcelain.

"Miss Mott?" Mary pushed a cart into the parlor. The scent of coffee and apple Danish permeated the close quarters. " 'Tis from your own batch of dough that you mixed up last evening."

"Oh." That meant the pastries were likely to be tough.

"You can dip them in the coffee, miss."

"What time does Mr. Ontevreden arrive?"

In the hallway, Father's tall clock chimed the hour.

"Any time now, miss."

"Is Father still in his library?"

"Yes, miss."

Which meant he was still working on an announcement that he intended to submit to the *Detroit Free Press*. Eugenie's heart clenched in her chest. Mr. Ontevreden had pressured Father to have the notice placed in the paper even before Eugenie had accepted his proposal.

"Should I pour for you, miss?"

"No." Regret would be the bitterest drink to swallow, if she went through with this. But with Father feeling so poorly of late, she wanted to bring him comfort. And Mr. Ontevreden was indeed a man capable of taking care of Eugenie.

Too bad Father couldn't see that Eugenie was capable of taking care of herself. Not only of herself, but of the ladies who attended her meetings at the public auditorium along the river. Ladies who had lost everything. But now, with her inheritance from her mother, Eugenie was free to explore ways of assisting the many Civil War widows and their children. Not that Father would approve of such a venture. Then again, perhaps he would.

"Mr. Ontevreden isn't such the bad-looking fellow, miss. I'll give him that." But Mr. Ontevreden was much closer to their aging Irish servant's age than he was to Eugenie's. "And he always attends services at your church."

"That's a good thing."

"Beggin' your pardon, Miss Mott, but have the two of you actually met with Reverend Hogarth yet?"

"No." Eugenie adjusted a satin bow on her new Worth gown. She did have a weakness for pretty clothing, but since working with her ladies, most impoverished, she'd taken to dressing in more drab clothing. She had to admit it was a delight to be attired in this beautiful cream-and-blue ensemble. Too bad her crinoline, a new purchase, dug into her waist.

Mary cast her a sideways glance. "One wouldn't know you were already thirty years of age, miss, not with that lovely skin of yours and your slender waist."

Had anyone else but her erstwhile parlor servant uttered such words, Eugenie would have been mortified. But she knew Mary intended no harm.

From outside the room, in the hallway, voices carried.

# Chapter 1

Eugenie Mott rang her mother's silver Austrian bell until Lorena slid the parlor's paneled mahogany pocket doors back. Mary must be feeling unwell again for her housekeeper to be answering. "Is the tea set up yet?" How strange to have tea set only for one, without Father.

"Yes, ma'am." Lorena glanced toward the fire. "Let me stoke the fire too, while I'm here."

Their—or rather, her housekeeper now, possessed a butter-soft Southern drawl that elicited feelings of warmth and yet also a concern for what she'd been through, growing up a slave on a Virginia plantation.

Lorena's dark uniform almost matched Eugenie's black bombazine mourning gown. How dismal for her to wear that same dark color day in, day out, all year. Was it wicked to be so relieved that she didn't have to marry Horace? Thank God they'd not had an opportunity to speak the night he was to have rendered his proposal.

As Lorena tended the fireplace, Eugenie surveyed the sumptuous room. Everything in this house was hers, from the wool rugs beneath her feet, to the silver candelabra, to the leather-bound books in the ornate case on the far wall. She had no one with whom to share these earthly goods, but she hoped that would be changing soon, as she desired to use some of her own furnishings to decorate the lodgings she planned to purchase for her ladies.

*Oh Father, why did you go now?* Was it so she wouldn't have to marry Horace? She exhaled a sigh of relief.

Lorena turned to face her. "You all right, ma'am?"

"Missing Father." But not Horace.

"We all are, miss." She bowed slightly. "I'll bring your tea right quick."

"Thank you."

As Lorena left, Mr. Morgan, the family's butler, entered. "Attorney Christian Zumbrun has sent the papers for you to sign."

"Thank you."

He handed her the creamy envelope and left. She went to the desk and opened the seal, then unfolded the letter and scanned for the conditions of the rental agreement. Although her mother had left her a monthly stipend, she'd not been able to afford a building rental for her ladies—until now.

From the hallway, the clatter of the doorknocker sounded. Not expecting anyone, she stood and took several steps toward the pocket doors to close them. When Eugenie spied Horace's shiny pate, she ducked back. What was he doing here, unannounced?

In mere moments, Morgan entered the room with Horace right at his heels. Eugenie felt her eyes widen. Horace hadn't sent a calling card nor had he waited to be announced. Instead, he pushed past her butler and opened his arms to her as if to embrace her. Eugenie took two steps back, positioning her mother's desk chair between herself and the man who was to have been her husband.

"Mr. Ontevreden, how surprising to see you."

His already pale face blanched further as he glanced between her and Morgan. "Eugenie. . ."

She cringed, wishing she'd not allowed him to use her Christian name. "What is it you wish?"

He rubbed his short silver beard. "Why, I've come to express my condolences, of course."

At the funeral service, he'd at least had the gentility to sit quietly, albeit in the row behind her, which would have held extended family members had she any who had come to sit there.

"Thank you." She should say something to him. Should at least let him know something. But no proper engagement had ever occurred. This didn't seem the time nor place.

He ran his tongue slowly over his lower lip, reminding her of a beggar about to snatch up a roll and devour it. "I wondered how I could be of comfort to you during this time."

Had they ever actually courted? Were her father's attempts at putting them together over and over again supposed to count as an official courtship? This "relationship" had been nothing like what she'd experienced with Pascal, before he'd been killed at Antietam. Tears welled up again.

"There, there, my dear." Horace pulled an embroidered handkerchief from his pocket and handed it to her. Was it her imagination, or was that one a woman would normally use? And the initial on it wasn't his.

"Thank you." She pressed the linen square to her nose and inhaled the distinct scent of rose, not a scent a gentleman would wear.

Lorena rolled in the tea cart. Her lips formed an *O*, for the tea was set only for one. "Excuse me, Miss Mott, but will Mr. Ontevreden be staying?"

"No," she blurted out. "I'll be taking tea alone."

"Yes, ma'am."

"No, Miss Mott is wrong." Horace's imperious tone caused Eugenie's spine to stiffen. "I will be staying."

Lorena, apparently cowed by the older man, backed from the room.

Morgan stepped forward. "The newspaper has arrived, Miss Mott."

"Thank you. I'll read it as soon as you can escort Mr. Ontevreden out, as he will *not* be staying."

The butler nodded toward the paper. "Your attorney sent a message that you may wish to take note of the society section."

Horace rocked forward and back, as self-satisfaction etched itself upon his aquiline features. "As your fiancé, I'll be staying so we can discuss our plans."

She glared at him. "You, sir, are not my fiancé." Eugenie grabbed the newspaper and opened it to the society section. At the top of the page, in large type-face font, was announced, "Miss Eugenie Mott to Marry Mr. Horace Ontevreden." The pages slipped from her hands to the floor, and Horace scooped them up.

"As you can see, indeed I am engaged to you."

*Windsor, Ontario*

How had Percy landed in such a backwater town? By being engaged in a profession, that was how. Seemed the Gladstone family had too many barristers in England. Percy's many social causes had caused his father no end of embarrassment, and he'd been shuttled off to Canada. Percy opened his office window's heavy blue brocade curtains and peered out. On the street below, carters carried goods to the market, with apples, potatoes, and cabbages piled high. Carriages rolled over the hard-packed earth. Lone riders hitched their horses to the posts by the boardwalk. Hard to believe that only a narrow body of water divided this tiny hamlet from both another country and a Michigan city teeming with people.

A heavy rhythmic rap at the door identified his secretary, who entered.

"Mr. Gladstone?" Antoine stood in the doorway, a stack of legal briefs in hand. "Miss Feuerstein is on your docket before you head off to court."

"Thank you." Why had he accepted the case with this young woman? He'd have to hire a detective to help him, and in this small town that wouldn't be easy.

It had started when Percy had been invited to dinner with a fellow barrister, and a single woman was seated beside him. Miss Feuerstein had confided that she might need legal help. An older businessman from nearby Detroit had been pursuing her, and she was considering accepting the Michigander's proposal.

Antoine remained in the doorway, rocking on his heels. "She's here now, sir."

"Bring her in."

Miss Feuerstein, a handsome brunette, was in her midthirties, if he guessed correctly. Bedecked in an attractive day suit, fashionable even by London standards, she entered the room and greeted him with a demure smile, eyes downcast.

"Welcome." He gestured toward one of his twin black Windsor chairs. "Please have a seat."

"Thank you for meeting with me."

Percy went behind the desk, always preferring to put a little distance between himself and a female client. Antoine left Percy's door open to the hallway, an unspoken understanding they had when a solitary woman was inside. His secretary nodded at him and departed down the long corridor.

Percy sat down and centered his notepad on his desk. "How may I help you?"

With hazel eyes and a heart-shaped face, this lovely woman should have been married long ago. Perhaps she had been. "I shared with you that I've been offered a proposal of marriage by a gentleman who seems to travel in high circles on the American side of the water. However, I'm finding that my American friends have been unable to learn much about him. So I fear I'm in a quandary."

"I see." Percy rested his elbows on his desk and steepled his fingers in front of him. "I'm afraid I'm not a detective, Miss Feuerstein."

"Can you at least offer me legal advice?"

"That I can do." He dipped his pen in the inkwell.

He listened for nearly an hour, taking copious notes, all the while tallying up the cost of taking this case. Detectives were scarce as hen's teeth in these parts, as his Southern cook, Sabina, liked to say. But he'd appreciate the extra income for Christmas gifts to his staff, both at home and at the office. He wanted to be a generous employer, not a tight-fisted Scrooge like in Dickens's long-titled novel, *A Christmas Carol, in Prose, Being a Ghost Story of Christmas. The author should shorten that title to something a little more catchy.*

Miss Feuerstein offered him a tight smile. "I guess that's all there is to it."

"I see."

Movement in the hallway caught Percy's eye. His secretary took the arm of a frail, white-haired woman whose shawl-covered, narrow shoulders were stooped with age. Antoine led her to a bench and approached Percy's still-open door. As he'd been instructed, his assistant was to interrupt him when precisely one hour had elapsed. But Percy had not yet decided if he'd take the case. "Miss Feuerstein, would you excuse me for one moment?"

He went to the hallway and closed his office door behind him as Antoine met him. "I don't remember having an actual next client," Percy said in a low voice.

Antoine smiled. "That, sir, is my mother. Or rather, the woman I call my mother."

"I'm sorry, either she is or isn't your mother, which is it?" His clerk was only in his twenties, and this woman looked to be well past seventy years.

"She's my *grandmére*. But she raised me."

"I see."

"She's asked if I might spend the holidays with her in Toronto."

Percy well knew that his secretary couldn't afford such a journey without a Christmas bonus. "Could we discuss this after court today?"

The younger man glanced down at his well-polished shoes. Antoine kept himself neat, never missed a day's work, and was loyal and trustworthy. He deserved both a rest and reward. Why should Percy put off till tomorrow what he could do today?

Bending toward him, Percy whispered, "My First Day gift to you shall be the fare to transport you home. And my Twelfth Day present, the funds to return."

His clerk raised his blue eyes to meet Percy's gaze, a grin splitting his narrow face. "Thank you, sir!"

"And there shall be an envelope with funds for you to purchase some trinkets and treats for you and your grandmother on the days in between, eh?"

"Oh, sir!" When Antoine moved forward as if to embrace him, Percy took a step backward.

He raised his hand. "You've well earned it."

"You are too kind. *Merci*."

And in need of more business. He returned to his office. "I'd be happy to assist you, Miss Feuerstein."

She rose with the dignity of any lady presented at court. "Thank you."

He escorted her to the door. When she departed, he closed his door and slumped down in the closest wing-back chair. Time to see his friend, Christian Zumbrun, for help.

The past twenty-four hours passed in a swirl, like the quick Lake Huron tempest that had kicked up and then calmed so that Percy could take the ferry across to Detroit. He hailed a taxi and soon found himself at Christian Zumbrun's legal office and greeted by his old friend.

Inside the gothic-style stone building, his friend's office reflected a life well-lived, even though it reeked of the thick cigars of which he was so fond.

Percy pointed to the shuttered windows behind Christian. "Open the blasted windows, man, and let some of that smoke out." He waved away the blue haze.

Christian smiled his lopsided grin and complied, twisting the metal handle and releasing the mullioned window outward. "Will that satisfy you?"

"Wait! That might summon the fire brigade volunteers. And with a city of this size, and enough buckets, your legal briefs might all be ruined when they come rushing to this office swinging water around!"

Swiveling to face him, Christian shook his head, but laughed. "What a lovely thing it must be to have no vices. How do you do it, Percy?"

"Very funny." He brushed at his pants' legs, which bore evidence of a previous encounter with his cat. "If my mother ever pays me a visit, I'll have her roll out her list of my shortcomings for you."

"No chance of that happening though, is there?" Christian coughed.

"My mother venturing to the wilds of Canada and out to the backwater of Windsor?" He gave a curt laugh. "About as much chance as me hosting you and your wild boys for Twelfth Night!"

The Zumbrun boys were probably no more rambunctious than others their age, but put them all together in one room, and *voila!*—a disaster was sure to happen. Would Percy ever be a father? He rubbed at his jawline, which could have used a sharper blade.

"Well, you're not here about that, are you?" Christian poured himself a short snifter of brandy. "Have some?"

"No, thanks. I'm here to get advice about a case and to ask which private detectives might be available."

"Hmm." He took a sip and replaced the stopper in the crystal brandy flask. "I can think of one or two."

"My client is considering a marriage proposal from an American."

"Someone from Detroit?"

"Yes." Percy eyed Christian's beautifully gilt-framed diploma from Harvard. Percy's own, from Oxford, had been framed by his first client in Windsor—a lumberjack falsely accused of theft. The man paid Percy's legal fees by carving a thick frame with bear, pine trees, deer, pinecones, maple leaves, and so on, indicative of life in Ontario. The woodsman had said, "Because now you're one of us, and I hope this will remind you."

Christian cleared his throat. "What do you know about this man?"

"He's reported to be a prominent member of Detroit society, but I've not heard of his name." Percy slouched into the nearby padded, leather-seated chair. "A Dutch name."

"That could be maybe a quarter of my fellow Michiganders."

# Chapter 2

*Detroit, Michigan*

Clutching the newspaper tightly under her arm, Eugenie mounted the steps into the dark-red brick building, careful to keep her skirts tugged aside to avoid tripping. How easy it must be to climb these infernal stairs in a pair of trousers. Alongside her, a dapper young gent attired in a burgundy tone-on-tone striped suit hurried up in a flash. She exhaled a long sigh. At least he'd waited at the top to hold the door for her. Slender, with a mop of golden-brown hair and possessed with an easy grin, the young man reminded her so much of Pascal that tears sprang to her eyes. "Thank you for holding the door."

"No trouble at all, ma'am." He nodded then headed off in the opposite direction from her attorney.

Eugenie followed the corridor, eyeing the narrow wooden benches that lined either side of the hall. On the left, a mother with two young children tried to keep them occupied by reading a storybook. On the opposite side, a silver-haired gentleman leaned on a narrow ebony cane propped between his open knees. The poor thing looked like he might keel over any moment.

She continued on toward Mr. Zumbrun's office and stopped at his assistant's desk in a cubby hole adjacent.

Mr. Logan looked up. "Good morning, Miss Mott. Mr. Zumbrun is expecting you." He rose and came from around the desk stacked high with files.

The door to the attorney's office opened and a tall man with thick, wavy, dark hair stood there, his hand on the doorknob, leaning in. His profile was very striking, and Eugenie, hesitating to follow the assistant, instead stood and watched. Attired in superfine wool expertly tailored to his athletic frame, this man had a presence. But she wasn't here to gawk at handsome men. She was here to speak with her attorney. The distress over Horace's publication of their false engagement must be addressed. Mr. Zumbrun simply had to sort this out.

His client seemed in no hurry to leave, however. The handsome man's laughter carried into the hall. Eugenie took several steps forward and discerned that he spoke with a British accent. Finally, he turned and grabbed his coat from the rack and laid it over his arm. He looked up at Eugenie and his light eyes widened. The stranger stood there for a moment, looking perplexed. She didn't recognize him. She'd have remembered. Would definitely have recalled those strong, handsome features.

Mr. Zumbrun tapped on his client's shoulder and finally the man moved out into the hallway as Mr. Logan moved past and announced Eugenie.

She should keep her eyes downcast. She should walk right past the stranger as she entered. She should...

"Good day, miss." This close, as he ambled past her, she could smell his piney scent mixed with cloves and something else—maybe bergamot.

Eugenie couldn't manage so much as a nod. She stared like a ninny before Mr. Logan gently took her arm and led her into the office.

"Excuse me for a moment." Mr. Zumbrun shoved a broad hand through his wavy golden hair and hurried out after the departing Englishman.

"Have a seat, Miss Mott." Mr. Logan gestured to one of a pair of heavy walnut chairs, their seats padded and upholstered in dark, masculine leather.

"Thank you."

In a moment, the attorney returned, followed by his previous client. "If it's all right with you, Miss Mott, I'd like Mr. Percival Gladstone, a barrister from Windsor, to also sit with us. He may have some insight."

How embarrassing it would be to recount her dilemma in front of this handsome stranger. But if he could help, why refuse?

When Eugenie nodded her consent, Mr. Zumbrun closed the paneled door and took his seat behind the desk.

Mr. Gladstone took a seat beside her. A smile tugged at his lips. He truly was the most attractive man she'd ever met.

If Percy had known Christian had such beautiful clients, he'd have come over to Michigan more frequently. This young woman smelled like delicate meadow wildflowers, which pleased him immensely, although he didn't know why.

"Are you paying attention, Percy?"

No, he was appreciating the lovely lady's creamy complexion. "Hmm? Yes, what was that?"

"I said, Miss Mott has a situation that we'll be addressing. I believe her faux fiancé and your client's want-to-be fiancé may be one and the same man."

Christian and Miss Mott proceeded to describe the man. When she procured a *carte de visite* from her reticule and handed it to him, Percy couldn't help chortling. "It's him."

Miss Mott's eyes widened at his outburst, and Percy struggled to put his best "barrister's face" back on.

She tipped her head at him, fixing him with her intense gaze. "Why so gleeful?"

It saved him money for the detective, for one thing. "Well, Miss Mott, you have solved my case."

"How is that?" Her tight voice held censure.

Christian cleared his throat. "Now Mr. Gladstone can let his client know that Horace was already engaged."

"What? He has proposed to another?"

Percy nodded gravely. "Indeed, to a young Canadian woman of some means."

"But, but. . .I am not engaged to this man. It is a farce. I never accepted."

"Good." Why had Percy so quickly said that? He needed to hold himself in check.

Both Christian and Miss Mott stared at him.

"How does that benefit you, if she's not engaged to him?" Christian sat straighter in his chair, his eyebrows drawing together.

Percy swiped his hand across his jawline. "Well, of course it is good she's not engaged to a charlatan who would propose to two beautiful young ladies."

"Two wealthy young ladies." Christian gave him a cautionary glance.

"That's what I said."

Miss Mott gently tapped his hand with her gloved one. "No, you said beautiful." She seemed to be stifling a laugh.

His cheeks heated. Time to leave. Miss Mott possessed a lovely and regal appearance—just the type of woman his mother always hoped he'd marry. He rose. "Since you hadn't given your consent, Miss Mott, then Mr. Ontevreden can't force the marriage."

She drew in a deep breath and exhaled it forcefully. "That's a relief."

"I wonder, though, if my client might yet foolishly have him as husband." Percy's gut clenched at the thought.

The dark-haired beauty squared her shoulders as she moved toward the edge of her chair. "As long as I am under no obligation to him, I'll be happy."

Christian offered her a Cheshire cat grin. "No consent, no engagement—despite this announcement in the paper. And I've asked Mr. Logan to check at the newspaper to see who posted the ad."

"I cannot believe Papa would have done so."

"Nor I." Christian frowned.

Time for Percy to go. "If you'll excuse me, I'll take my leave." He rose.

"Certainly. Sorry to keep you, Mr. Gladstone." She smiled up at him.

She'd remembered his name. A little thrill of victory coursed through him. "Miss Mott, a pleasure to make your acquaintance." He took her small hand and raised it to his lips. Was it his imagination, or did her fingers tremble?

The scent of Acorn Coffee filled the large hall, making Percy feel very out of place, yet this was where he was instructed to report. Everywhere Percy looked, golden oak seemed to cover every surface—from the floors, to the paneled walls, to the coffered ceiling overhead. At the far end sat a long table covered in pastries and carafes of the Acorn beverage and cream and sugar. A few cups and saucers remained. He'd only imbibed the liquid once—when calling on his lumberjack client in the logging camp outside of town.

Percy thumped his fingers against his hat. He had searched the entire building for his event—an attorney's international convocation—to no avail. The joint Canadian-American Legal Conference invitation had arrived from Christian two days earlier. Once again, he drew Christian's scrawled missive from his pocket. Gratiot Hall was indeed the correct place. Date was correct. He pulled his pocket watch out. Time was also correct. If he'd come all this way and the event had been canceled, then perhaps there would be time to call on Miss Mott. But he'd not managed a pretext under which he could approach her. Perhaps he'd share what his client had chosen to do and that would open the door to other conversation.

Huffing a sigh, he checked the chalkboard once more, knowing that the words wouldn't have changed in the few minutes since he'd first scanned them: CATERING LARGE OUTDOOR EVENTS—WOMEN'S SOCIETY OF DETROIT.

On a nearby table, he located a leaflet and opened it. At the top, Miss Eugenie Mott was listed as the founder of the society and one of today's presenters. He couldn't imagine such a refined young woman in a hot kitchen with an apron tied over one of her expensive Worth ensembles. Might be amusing to see what she had to say on the subject matter though.

He chose a lone seat far in the back of the auditorium. All other chairs were occupied by women and children. He did a quick headcount, estimating around fifty adults desiring to learn more about this venture. A buzz of excitement echoed through the chamber. The auditorium reminded him of how his father's Scottish hunting lodge was decorated with wood everywhere one looked. A pang of sorrow shot through him. He and Father had been close, hunting often and fishing in England and Scotland. Father had promised he'd come to Canada to visit, but he'd never come. *I miss him.* He missed his mother and brothers and sisters too, but he'd never harbored any illusions that they would ever cross the pond to visit him once he left.

The door behind him creaked, and when he spied the late arrival, a stoop-shouldered woman who shuffled slowly forward, he rose and went to her. "I have a chair I can move closer to the others if you wish, ma'am."

Rheumy eyes met his as a smile cracked her lined face. "Thank you, young man, but no need to move the seat—I should be able to hear fine."

"Yes, ma'am." He took her arm.

She leaned heavily upon him until he helped her into the chair.

At the front of the room, movement caught his eye as a slender, auburn-haired matron strode up the stairs and onto the platform and made an announcement about the privies. He stifled a laugh. But when Eugenie Mott, attired in a deep-plum day dress moved across the stage, he drew in a sharp breath. Even from this distance, her bearing and her handsome features made an impression.

Ahead of them, two ebony-haired women, dark woolen scarves tied loosely around their necks, pointed. "*Questa è lei—la nostra benefattrice.*"

Percy stiffened. What had they meant that Miss Mott was their benefactress? Or did they mean Mrs. Carrie Booth Moore who now joined them on the dais? He recognized her from the Detroit social pages. Mrs. Booth Moore was married to a well-known philanthropist. The three women appeared completely at ease in front of the crowd—which wasn't meant to include him.

Dutch, Irish, French, and Scandinavian accents mingled as women remarked upon the trio onstage. Detroit truly was a city of immigrants. Christian had, on more than one occasion, asked Percy to come and join him to translate conversations from German, French, and Italian clients. Having grown up with visitors from throughout Europe, and having been classically schooled, Percy had assumed all educated lawyers could translate documents and converse with their European-raised clients. But this catering group, save for a few, wore threadbare clothing, and their countenances bore evidence of hard living, unlike his family's visitors and unlike the well-attired society ladies before them on stage.

Percy's paltry contributions to church funds were nothing compared to teaching a skill which could bring a new life. *Lord, what can I do to ease suffering for these women? Show me.*

"Good morning, ladies! I'm Eugenie Mott, and I wish to welcome you back to our continued training in the manner in which we might establish ourselves as. . ."

Eugenie Mott's dark eyes met his, and the connection coursed through him, like a cup of warm treacle syrup.

"That is. . ." Miss Mott cleared her throat, her cheeks visibly pink even from this far back in the auditorium.

Over fifty women had arrived at this event, Eugenie's second meeting of the Civil War Widows Catering Association. Although not a widow herself, she intended to sponsor and train these women so they could support their families.

Mrs. Tara Mulcahey, a widow and a cook at the Empress Hotel, joined Eugenie at the steps that led up to the dais. "I'd better point out that the privies are out back for those who need them—quite a few have brought their children."

Eugenie nodded her agreement, and Tara mounted the stairsteps and then made her announcement. Several women conducted their young ones from the hall. How would they manage the children when the women were taking classes and learning how to cater events? Something would have to be done to keep them safe. Some of the children were in school, but the little ones needed supervision. She'd speak with Tara about it later.

"Please take a seat!" Tara brought the gavel down with a bang and Eugenie flinched.

When she joined the other women on stage, she took the gavel from Tara and placed it underneath the oak lectern and then made her introductory greeting.

Movement from the back of the auditorium caught her eye, causing her to stutter. A tall, dark-haired man in a navy tailcoat stood not far from the announcement board where "Civil War Widows Catering Convocation" was marked in chalk.

It was Mr. Gladstone. What was he doing there?

Eugenie moistened her lips. She had to proceed regardless of whether the most handsome man she'd ever met happened to be standing right there, looking at her.

"As you know, we have procured a lease for the Alcott building."

A resounding cheer went up. She laughed and pressed a hand to her chest. "The old factory is the perfect site for us to practice our skills."

"Amen!"

"Yes, ma'am!"

"And this afternoon, Mrs. Mulcahey will spell out our agenda for classes."

She turned to whisper to Tara, "Please proceed while I go speak with the gentleman in the back."

"Yes indeed."

As Eugenie departed the stage, many eyes followed her, but Tara quickly began to recount what the women would be doing the next week as they mastered cooking and catering skills. Moving as quickly as she could, Eugenie soon found herself breathless. Surely it was because her blasted corset was too tight and not because she was nearing the handsome Canadian attorney.

She tried to assume a politely interested expression and not stare at him with doe eyes. "Mr. Gladstone, what brings you to my assembly?"

He arched a dark eyebrow at her and leaned in. "This was supposed to be *my* event." He smelled of evergreens today, and cinnamon.

Heavens, she probably smelled strongly of the Acorn Coffee they'd brewed earlier as a demonstration in economy. "I don't think so—I've had it booked for several months now."

Chuckling, he reached into his pocket and drew out what she recognized as a Canadian telegram and handed it to her. "Read for yourself, Miss Mott."

Eugenie scanned the message. "This is an error."

"No, this, I believe, is Christian's, or rather Mr. Zumbrun's attempt at a joke on me."

"A joke?" She looked up into his smiling face. This close she could see the rim of navy in his gray-green eyes. Such beautiful eyes.

He leaned in. "Do you agree?" His warm breath fanned her cheek and she took a step back.

"I cannot say, sir." Weren't Englishmen supposed to be reserved? Mr. Gladstone was making her head swirl.

"If I were a betting man, I'd wager that's it." He crossed his arms over his broad chest. "Christian used to pull pranks on me when I first moved to Windsor, and now he's started it up again."

Were all attorneys so silly? Certainly not. And Mr. Zumbrun had always treated her and Father with the utmost decorum.

"Regardless, I have an auditorium of women to tend to." She spun on her heel and made her way across the long room and back up toward the dais, but paused at the bottom step.

She blinked a few times at the realization that she was mainly ornamental on that stage. Carrie would be speaking and then Tara again. All Eugenie had to do was offer a closing statement. Well, she'd make it a splendid speech. She sat on a bench at the bottom of the stage as the other women gave detailed instructions on catering etiquette and the preparation of the Acorn Coffee, artificial honey, and a substitute for cream. Eugenie made notes on a narrow tablet with a short pencil stub from the bottom of her reticule. When she finished, she'd joined her friends on the dais.

When she looked to the back of the auditorium, there stood Mr. Percival Gladstone, arms still crossed, leaning against the entryway, looking for all the world as though he intended to remain. When he grinned at her, Eugenie's heart did a little flip, and she averted her gaze, fumbling with her notes.

# Chapter 3

Miss Mott's passionate speech and her kindness toward the women reminded Percy of his mother's love for the villagers. Mother had always emphasized that as lady of the manor, she must reach out to others. A sudden pang of homesickness threatened to overwhelm him. He continued to lean against the oak-encased entryway as casually as he could, watching Miss Mott. She'd given him a pointed look several times in the midst of her closing speech, but he didn't leave.

When Miss Mott finished, to the ladies' applause, Percy went to the elderly woman he'd helped earlier and offered her assistance in rising.

"Thank you, young man. Your mother must be proud of the son she raised."

His cheeks heated. *Was the Marchioness of Kent proud of her now-Canadian barrister son?* "Thank you, madam."

The stranger smelled faintly of cloves and peppermint, reminding him of his childhood nanny. "Will you celebrate our Lord's birth with her this Christmas?"

What a strange way to put it. He stiffened. "I'm afraid not."

"But you'd like to?"

It was as though she'd read his mind. As an attorney, he often kept his face a blank slate. "I would, if only it could be possible."

She gave a low chuckle. "All things are possible. Especially at Christmastime."

Something about her words, and the way she said them, gave him pause. Someone called his name. Percy turned away as Eugenie Mott strode toward him, greeting several ladies as she moved, her cheeks flushed. He smiled in acknowledgment then looked back to see if the infirm woman, who'd struggled so hard to attend this meeting, required assistance. But she was gone. He turned and scanned the dozen or so women who were leaving. How had she departed so quickly?

"Mr. Gladstone?"

He swiveled around. "Yes?"

"You look as though you've seen a ghost."

He ran a hand through his hair. "Not quite. I was helping one of your attendees."

"I saw you. The last one in?"

"Yes."

"That was very kind." Miss Mott smiled up at him. "But I've never seen her before."

"She's not one of your ladies? Certainly acted like she was."

"No." Her dark eyebrows drew in and then quickly released. "Perhaps she simply wanted to come in from the street and the chill autumn air."

"No harm in that." Still, it was puzzling. But that wasn't why he'd tarried. "May I escort you home?"

"I'd planned on walking back. It's only a few blocks."

"It was threatening to rain again earlier. Why don't I hail us a cab?"

She nodded.

As they waited for the women to clear from the hall, he watched as the beautiful brunette greeted many of them by name as they departed. Most eyed him with curious gazes.

Before long, he'd procured a taxi and they were on their way to the Mott home. With the lovely woman seated close beside him, Percy had the sudden desire to cover her hand with his, but refrained. "I think it is admirable what you are trying to do for the Civil War widows."

"Thank you. I've felt a nudging in my spirit to do something ever since Pascal died."

"Who is Pascal?"

She averted her gaze. "He was a dear friend of mine. A childhood sweetheart. All of Detroit society presumed we'd marry when he returned from the war. But that never happened."

"I'm sorry."

The carriage rolled on. A gas lighter raised his light to a street-side lamp. Darkness came early as they eased toward winter and would soon be upon them this night.

"It was a hard blow." She ducked her chin, her hat's velvet ribbons dangling against her creamy neck. "I considered what might have happened if we'd married and had children. What would that have been like? I know it would have been so much harder."

Miss Mott didn't seem able to even use words that directly bespoke Pascal's death. Had she not recovered from the loss? "What made you consider accepting Ontevreden then?"

"That was my father's doing, and I like, or rather liked, to keep him happy." She wiped away a tear. "I think Father must have known he didn't have much time left—at least that's what his physician said. But his doctor didn't approve of Horace."

"Speaking of Mr. Ontevreden, I advised my client to end the courtship and she did."

"I haven't seen him nor heard anything of late about him." Eugenie nibbled her lower lip. "Horace wasn't supportive of my plans for the widows either. That was the thing I most regretted when I was considering marrying him to please my father."

"You really love this work, don't you?"

"I do. I love the idea of helping others help themselves. I've been involved in one way or another since Pascal died. So just past five years now."

The carriage rolled on over the macadam road, the horse's clip-clopping settling into a steady rhythm.

Miss Mott sighed. "About a third of my friends lost their sweethearts or husbands—if not through death, through severe injury or emotional distress that stole their loved ones away."

"A devastating toll. One many Canadians also shared, who'd decided to take up arms for the cause of freedom."

"Yes. So if I can do something to soften the blows they've taken, I shall." She was so earnest, it touched him.

Percy tapped his fingers on his knee. "Those who've escaped slavery, they too suffer even now as they seek work." His housekeeper, gardener, cook, and stable hands had all come north to freedom. They deserved a good Christmas. He'd make sure they all had time off this year. He'd manage to get by alone, bachelor that he was.

The carriage rolled to a stop.

Miss Mott pressed her hand atop his. "Please come in and have tea with me, Mr. Gladstone. I'd like to ask your advice about my plan to open some type of home where some of my ladies could live. There are a great many who sleep in the back rooms of shops or worse."

"It would be my pleasure." An inspiration hit him. "Say, this may be a schoolboy prank in return, but what if we call upon Attorney Zumbrun at home and tell him we received his invitation to tea?"

She laughed. "First let me apprise Lorena of where I'll be going. I don't want her and the staff to worry."

Might as well be bold. What could he lose? "Tell her I'll be taking you to dinner as well."

Her tinkling laughter delighted him. "I must have forgotten about that invitation you sent."

"Just so." He chuckled.

Percy assisted Miss Mott from the carriage. She hurried inside, her skirts swaying to and fro as she crossed the herringboned brick path to the imposing home. He scanned the gardens, going fallow and, to the left, the rosebushes bearing clusters of rosehips. On the right, a tall oak, maple, and birch clustered together near evergreen shrubs and a holly bush that would soon bear fruit. Christmas truly would be here before they knew it. The holly reminded him of the time when their estate gardener had allowed him to help with the Christmas greenery. Percy had spent the day, unbeknownst to his mother and father, cutting and wiring holly branches together. Cook had brought him every manner of beverage she was testing for the twelve days of celebration upcoming. Thankfully he'd sampled only small amounts of the eggnog, hot chocolate, spiced Russian tea, and heavily creamed coffee that Cook had brought him. If he'd overindulged, Percy would have been ill and Mother would have learned about his doings.

He instructed the cab driver where to take them. Soon, Miss Mott rejoined him and they made their way to the Zumbrun's three-story brownstone a quarter mile away. When Percy, with Eugenie Mott on his arm, knocked on the door, it was Christian himself who opened it. Behind him, three of his four sons were jumping on settees in the parlor, and his daughter was chasing their hound up the hallway stairs, his wife, Jenny, right behind her, calling, "Stop!"

Christian blinked at them several times before exhaling a loud puff of air, bowing dramatically and waving them inside. "Guess I shouldn't be too surprised, should I?"

"Of course not." Percy waved the telegram in front of him as they entered. "I got your invitation, after all."

"Papa!" One of the boys stopped bouncing and ran toward them. "It's my gadfather!"

"Godfather, not gadfather." Christian pulled Matthew up into his arms.

Percy closed the door behind him.

"But he says 'egad' when I show him my drawings. So he's my gadfather," the boy insisted.

"Mother told you to not say that word."

Christian set his son down again.

"He says it." The child jabbed a stubby finger at Percy's leg.

Percival's cheeks warmed. "I've been working on it, Matthew."

The boy raised his arms. "Touch the ceiling?"

"Of course." He picked up the child and raised him high overhead until little Matthew could touch the ceiling in the entryway.

The boy grinned and wrapped his arms around Percy's neck then planted a slobbery kiss on his cheek. "Got ya!"

"Indeed you have, young man." Percy lowered the imp to the floor then retrieved his handkerchief and wiped his face dry.

Christian cackled and mussed his son's tawny hair. "Good one, Mattie."

"Might even be a two-handkerchief one." Percy scowled at his friend. "You really shouldn't encourage him."

Miss Mott cocked her head at him. "Perhaps you shouldn't be so gullible. It appears young Master Zumbrun has your number, Mr. Gladstone."

Jenny descended the stairs, arms full of squirming beagle. "Good to see you, P.!"

"Now don't start that." The trio of boys now bouncing again happily in the parlor would begin their jokes if they heard their mother calling him "P." Percival held up his hands in surrender. "We're on our way to dinner, so no need to worry about us staying, Jenny."

The pretty matron joined them, passing the hound to Christian. Percy leaned in and kissed her cheek, catching the scent of talcum and lemons.

"I'm making lemon sponge cake."

One of his favorites. He chewed his lower lip. "We've got a cab waiting. Just wanted to say hello."

They made their farewells and were soon back in the snug carriage and on their way.

"They're so comfortable together." Miss Mott's voice held longing. "It reminds me of how my mother and father were."

"But without the many children."

"Yes, that was my mother's greatest sorrow—three little babes are buried in the church graveyard. I suppose I should put flowers on the graves, for Mother's sake, but. . ."

"I'm sorry."

"Don't get me wrong, my mother was a happy woman with a deep faith. But she'd have thrived having a household of children like the Zumbruns have."

"And you? Do you wish to have a house full of children?"

He heard her sharp intake of breath. What had made him ask such a deeply personal question?

"My dear Barrister Gladstone, was that the preliminary to a proposal of marriage, or are you simply interrogating me?"

They both broke into comfortable laughter. "I apologize. I'm so accustomed to asking questions. I fear you're the victim of that habit I've acquired."

"It's all right. Yes, I do suppose I'd like to have a house full of happy laughter echoing from children who are well-loved."

Well-loved. He'd been well-loved. He'd known it. But the requirements of his station in life had weighed his father down. And his mother as well. The two were often busy, but both had carved out time to spend with their children. Why, then, had Father not kept his promise to come see him?

She tapped his hand. "I give you leave to call me Eugenie."

He laughed. "And please call me Percy."

"Where are you taking me, Percy?" She leaned toward the window.

Ahead, on the right, sat the Waterview, a delightful inn where he stayed if he had prolonged business in Detroit. Anticipating possible business dining after the supposed "event," Percy had already procured a room. "The food here is excellent."

"Good friends of my family own this place." A frown skittered over Eugenie's brow. "Father brought me here once a month. He loved their roast beef."

"You must miss him."

"Dearly."

"I'm very sorry for your loss."

"Thank you. They say it gets easier with time, but I don't really believe that."

"I think grief changes over time. With God's help it becomes easier to bear, but that remnant is still there, like a shadow that pales but never completely disappears."

Over dinner, beneath the gaslight, Percy kept Eugenie talking about her childhood and shared about his, growing up in England.

"Are you truly the son of a duke?" Eugenie sipped her coffee.

"No, he's a marquess—which is below the rank of a duke." He was suddenly aware of the age and cut of his suit. His brother would be attired in the very latest fashion from London. "And I'm the fourth son, like little Matthew Zumbrun. I think that's why I've taken my godfather duties rather seriously."

"Do you have a deep faith?"

He eyed her over his uplifted cup of coffee. "I believe you have the makings of a barrister yourself, Miss Mott."

Her cup rattled as she abruptly set it in its saucer. "I'm sorry; excuse my forwardness."

He waved a hand as he set his own cup down gently. "Nothing to excuse you for. I was merely teasing, which I enjoy a great deal, I fear."

A low chuckle began before Eugenie gave a full-throated laugh, causing an elderly couple seated at a nearby table to glance in their direction. She raised her napkin to her rosebud mouth and patted it. "I believe you enjoy teasing almost as much as your godson does."

He leaned in on his elbows, a bad habit his nanny had failed to drill out of him, and steepled his fingers together before him. "Well, I'm not jesting about this—I've experienced a splendid time with you this evening, and I'd love to repeat dinner with you in Windsor sometime."

Her pretty face became somber. "I'm afraid I have far too many duties here between now and Christmas, with my ladies, to make any social appointments."

*Appointments?* He tried to hide his dismay. Perhaps all the conversation they'd had earlier in the dinner about her plans for housing had been like an appointment for her. He lifted a hand as casually as he could manage. "I've quite a few upcoming court cases I must prepare for as well. But should you require further assistance with your endeavor, please contact me." He retrieved a calling card from the sterling silver case his brother had gifted him with upon his graduation from Oxford.

She accepted the card, and her lips parted as though she were about to say something. She slipped the card into her bag.

"Well, then. Let's have the doorman call the cab for you, Miss Mott." Why had he thought that an American socialite would have any interest in him other than for business advice? Well, he wasn't going to simply lie down and roll over like the Zumbrun's hound had been trained to do. "But I insist on accompanying you home and making sure you're safely inside."

A smile tugged at the corner of her lips. "I don't suppose you come to Detroit often for business matters, do you, Mr. Gladstone?"

"I do now." He placed his hand atop hers and left it there. When she didn't pull away, his shoulders relaxed. "Would you object to me being your unofficial business advisor on the home purchase?"

Never mind that real estate purchases were well outside his purview normally.

"Are you donating your services, sir?"

"I am."

"Then on behalf of the board, I accept."

He pulled his appointment calendar from his inside coat pocket and his pencil. "How about we meet again in a few days?"

She nibbled her lower lip. "Can you join us at our new building, the Alcott, midday, during our break?"

"Splendid." For the first time in a long while, hopeful expectation rose in him like a flame sputtering to life in a trimmed-too-short candle.

# Chapter 4

R ain tip-tapped at Percy's mullioned window panes, as if demanding entrance to his cozy office. With coals burning in the grate, a hot mug of gunpowder tea with honey before him, and two inquiries already addressed, Percy wasn't about to be concerned with the pattering of raindrops. Surely it would cease before he joined Eugenie for the Scott's Theater production that evening. Twice more he'd gone to Detroit to visit with Miss Mott for "business" consultations—purely legal advice on her end, perhaps, but of a more romantic nature on his. Hopefully it wasn't his imagination that she was softening toward him.

A light knock on his office door brought him back to the reality of who he was—a small-time barrister in a tiny Canadian town with nothing to commend him as anything other than an advisor to the beautiful woman.

"Come in!"

"Cable for you, sir." Percy's assistant handed him the telegram. What an amazing invention—wiring messages across the ocean, something his uncle had been involved with on the English side of the ocean.

When Antoine left, Percy read the message.

*Maidstone, England*

*P, Arrive Windsor 23 December Love M*

"What?" He dropped the message onto his desk blotter. Hopefully his mother had also sent a letter outlining when and who all were arriving. He needed specifics—he was a man who required details, and well she knew it.

He'd only just that morning given his staff early Christmas bonuses and time off for the holidays. He couldn't rescind it. He wouldn't. But oh, this was joyous news too!

Percy got up and went to the door and called to Antoine, "I need some help."

"Yes, sir?"

"I need a list of all the servants in Windsor who might be available for Christmas work." His clerk's face pulled into a frown. "Are your servants not sufficient?"

"I told Venus, Sabina, and Lemrich that they have the entire holiday season off. They've been wanting to visit their relatives in Ohio." His houseman, Scipio, would remain.

"Are you not a bachelor?"

Percy braced himself against the door. "My mother sent me a rather cryptic message that I have company coming for Christmas."

Antoine's dark eyebrows raised into an inverted *V*. "You've put yourself into a *difficile désordre* then, I fear."

A difficult mess. "Why is that?"

"Because you can't simply go out and find *Noel* workers. It's not like right after the war. People have. . ." Croteau looked upward at the wood-paneled ceiling, one of his habits when

270

searching for the right words. "*Se sont établis.* They've become established already in a household, like your workers."

"Do you have any suggestions?"

"*Certainement.*" He gestured west. "Put them up in Hotel Cadotte on the river."

"In Detroit? I can't do that." He certainly couldn't afford it, not on his earnings. They'd likely stay several weeks after traveling so far. "And don't you mean *L'hotel Cadotte*?" He couldn't resist the tease.

"I sometimes forget my French, sir, with your insistence on English. *Merci*, for the reminder!"

Percy shrugged playfully. "No trouble at all."

Croteau rubbed his short goatee. "As far as the requests, I'll do my best, sir. But no *promesses.*"

"Thank you. Oh, and I'll need the best figgy pudding you can find."

"But with no actual figs, *oui*?" Antoine jested about this every year.

"*Non, monsieur.* No figs in my figgy pudding." Raisins were used, not figs. "And while you're out, please ask the *patisserie* to put up several Queen's cakes and fruitcakes for me for Christmas." The bakery's fruitcakes required weeks of soaking and preparation, so he'd best get on the list.

Panic threatened to rob his focus. He had to get his work accomplished so that he could spend time with his family when they arrived. And he needed to set up a hunting expedition for Father. And get reservations for musical entertainment for Mother.

His trip to Detroit might need to be sooner, rather than later, today.

Croteau cleared his throat. "Will that be all, sir?"

"Yes, for now. If I'm not here when you return, I'll have departed for Detroit."

"Again?" The way Antoine drew out the word suggested frustration.

Heat coursed up Percy's neck and settled in his cheeks. "I have a social engagement."

The younger man shrugged. "Even a lowly *légiste* such as I knows you haven't brought in your evening clothes for no reason." Antoine inclined his head toward the wooden hanging valet in the corner, upon which hung Percy's dinner attire.

"You're no lowly law clerk. You're talented, and I don't know what I'd do without you."

"*Merci.*"

Percy cleared his throat. "Not all of my activities in Detroit are personal. I also must take care of some business there."

"*Certainement.* I'll make sure everything is in order for tomorrow morning's case."

"Thank you. And while I'm in Detroit, I'll ask a friend. . ." Never mind that it was the woman who was far more than a friend. "If they know of any workers who might be available."

Antoine tapped the side of his head. "Good thinking, Monsieur Gladstone."

Especially if it meant he got to spend more time with Detroit's most beautiful lady. And if he encountered the elderly lady he'd assisted at Eugenie's seminar, he'd tell her that she was right. Anything was possible at Christmastime.

Eugenie smoothed her black satin skirt and examined her reflection in the looking glass. Perhaps satin was too gaudy for mourning. But Father would have approved. Would Percy?

She picked up her long jet and silver earrings from her cherry bureau that flanked the high-boy in her room. She screwed the back onto the first one and tugged. It was safely attached. Then she repeated the procedure with the other earring.

"Miss Mott?" Lorena's voice trembled. "Would you take a look at my dress?"

Standing in the doorway, attired in a new deep-green damask ensemble that enhanced her hazel eyes, her maid appeared younger than Eugenie had thought her to be. "You look lovely."

She cast her eyes downward. "Thank you, ma'am."

"Your sister and her family will be delighted to see you." At least Eugenie hoped so. The theatre troupe members had sent only a brief note back, acknowledging their receipt of her servant's note.

"I should have let Angelina know I was alive." Lorena nibbled on her lower lip. "I don't blame her if she's angry."

Before long, Eugenie's driver had transported them to the opera house. Lorena shared her concerns that with Angelina and her children apparently "passing" as white, perhaps the sisters' relationship should be kept secret. Angelina, whose father was white and only one-eighth of African descent, had been freed from slavery years before Lorena had escaped.

Eugenie and Lorena arrived at the theater just as a clock chimed the half hour. That gave them a half hour before the performance. They descended the staircase, the scent of warm ham wafting up.

"That do smell good." Lorena smiled as they joined the catering crew downstairs where the reception had been set up. "But my nerves too on edge to enjoy any of this food tonight."

"We'll have to trust in God. Surely your sister will be glad to see you alive." Their reunion was a tricky one for both. Eugenie prayed the sisters could work out their difficulties.

"I pray so." Lorena drew in a deep breath. "After the performance, I think I best go to the players' back rooms, Miss Mott, and see my sister."

"That might be best." Eugenie squeezed her servant's hand. "You'll have some privacy there." Unspoken, but implied, was that if Angelina and her family chose not to acknowledge Lorena as kin, then she'd not be joining in the reception.

Lorena departed. She'd be seated in the back section of the theatre, despite being a family member of the Scotts. It was a shame, but there was nothing Eugenie could do about the theater's policies.

Laughter from nearby brought Eugenie's attention back to her task at hand. The ladies had outdone themselves in transforming the utilitarian basement into a welcoming space for the reception. Linens leant by Carrie covered the four long tables. Tara had loaned three sets of china from her first two marriages and one from her mother. Silver shone in baskets lined with pale blue napkins. Crystal goblets and decanters occupied one of the tables featuring a massive silver-plated bowl retrieved from the Mott's attic—one Mother had never used.

Nearby, Tara placed sugar-glazed berries atop a five-layer cake. "It's all ready. Now, you go back upstairs and find that handsome attorney who was here looking for you."

"Mr. Zumbrun?" Eugenie feigned surprise. "Why, he's already married, Mrs. Mulcahey." Her friend laughed. "And well I know, as he's married to my cousin."

"So you must mean Mr. Gladstone has arrived."

Tara glanced past Eugenie.

"I have been seeking you out most desperately, Miss Mott." Percy's deep voice held a tease.

She swiveled to face him. "Most desperately?"

"Indeed." He pointed to the cake. "Mrs. Booth Moore informed me I'm not to touch the ladies' creation until later, but how might I offer my expert opinion if I'm not allowed a taste?"

Tara's throaty laugh started Eugenie giggling. Her friend moved beside her. "You'll just have to imagine, Mr. Gladstone."

Eugenie cocked her head at him and gazed up at his handsome face. "You've got some creativity in that lawyerly brain of yours, haven't you?"

His lips pulled in. "Creative ways to steal a bite, perhaps."

She and Tara both shook their heads, her friend's teal plume tickling Eugenie's nose.

Percy extended his arm. "Shall we go upstairs before I am tempted to put my plan into action?"

Tara's eyes widened. "You make the action sound positively sinful."

"Which it is." Eugenie wagged a finger at Percy and laughed. "Touch that cake before the party and you'll have all of us ladies to answer to, and don't forget it!"

"Yes, ma'am." He made a show of bowing and clicking his heels together before he offered his arm.

They went upstairs and found their seats in the front semi-circle.

"I think I've found another place for your ladies to cater." He shifted in the velvet-upholstered seat.

"You have? Where is it?" Some of the women suffered from a very real desperation, unlike Percy.

"My family is coming from England—" A crease formed on his forehead.

"How wonderful." Was it really? Would she be alone this year?

"And I could use some help." His lips twisted, as though discussing the need was distasteful.

"What about your staff? I thought you had several workers." Eugenie adjusted her skirt.

"I've given them leave to travel to visit with family in Ohio."

"I see. I take it that was before you'd heard from your parents."

"From my mother, actually, but yes, quite right." He angled his body toward her and leaned in.

"I can check with my ladies and see if some can help." There were some who'd welcome a change of pace from the squalid conditions they lived in. "Might they stay at your home?"

"Yes." He named the compensation, which was generous. "And I have two upstairs attic rooms they could share."

The theater manager stepped up onto the dais. "And now I present, The Scott Family Players performing *The Wiclow Wedding*."

The curtains parted, and soon Eugenie was swept up in the play, filled with dramatic turns and romance. But she never forgot who was seated beside her and the wonderful way he made her feel.

# Chapter 5

Sabina stood at the center of Percy's mahogany dining table, waving a wooden spoon in the air like a scepter. "I won't have anyone messing up my kitchen now, ya hear, Mr. Gladstone?"

"I hear you." Percy wiped at his mouth with his napkin. "And as I just explained, Miss Mott will assemble a group of ladies who will take over the household duties while you are out."

"Humph!" Sabina crossed her arms. "If I'd a knowed your Ma and Pa and kin were comin', I'd not have told my folk I'd be a-comin' to visit."

"It's all right." Percy set his napkin on the table and pushed aside his breakfast plate. "I'll instruct them that the kitchen must be returned to its original pristine condition before they leave."

"Prissy?" Her dark eyes widened. "My kitchen be so clean you coulda et your eggs off'n that floor in there."

"*Pristine.* It means 'immaculate.'"

When her face remained skeptical, he added, "Extremely clean to the point of perfection."

"'Zactly. My kitchen is in perfect condition, so don't let them ruin it."

"I won't."

Sabina took Percy's dirty utensils and placed them on the plate, and the napkin atop, and stomped off to the kitchen. Percy exhaled in exasperation. This was becoming far more difficult than he'd imagined. He was sorely tempted to threaten Sabina that he'd find an Irish girl to replace her—that's what Christian's wife did whenever their servants made demands. Although Percy would never do that to poor Sabina. She'd suffered enough in one lifetime. But he could have a little more backbone, as his mother always said about him. Strange how he could be so commanding and demanding in court, but when it came to the people he dealt with on a daily basis he was more kitten than tiger. Probably because of constantly placating his older brothers as he was growing up and looking for affection and approval wherever he could find it.

He ran his thumb over his lower lip, recalling how close he had come to kissing Eugenie good night after the cast party had ended.

His houseman, Scipio, who was in his twenties, shuffled into the room. His master in South Carolina had cut Scipio's ankles when he'd run away, leaving the young man with limited ability to walk. "Post arrived, sir."

"Thank you." He accepted the proffered missive, which Scipio had already slit open with the envelope knife. No fear of him reading Percy's message—all of his servants were receiving tutelage in reading and writing, but were yet working on basic skills.

Mother's even-handed script flowed across the paper. Percy inhaled a steadying breath as he read of all the people his mother intended to bring with her. Father wasn't mentioned, but the new Earl of Cheatham, Barden Granville IV, and his wife would be accompanying her.

He set the missive down, his knuckles rapping the tabletop. He liked Barden a great deal—had attended university with him, where Bard was great fun. But he'd never met his wife, whom his mother indicated was an American, named Caroline. Furthermore, Mother inquired if Caroline's sister Deanna, who lived on Mackinac Island in Michigan, might also be allowed to stay at the spacious home he'd described in his letters.

Yes, the six-bedroom home was spacious for a bachelor with a staff of three, but with so many visitors how could he accommodate them all? And it was quite unlike his mother to invite others into someone else's home. No mention at all of Father. He exhaled and frowned. Perhaps she'd simply not thought to say.

He read the letter carefully. His mother wrote that Barden's father and two older brothers had recently died. Lord Cheatham had succumbed to a heart ailment while his son and heir, Peter, contracted pneumonia and perished. The second Granville son had died from the London cholera epidemic. Percy exhaled a breath and dropped the letter to the table. *Oh my heavens.* His poor friend, Barden. That was too much, even for a clergyman like Bard, to contend with. Barden needed help, and Percy would do what he could to bring some comfort this Christmas. But Percy needed more assistance too, with a full house.

Seven years of Christmastide on his own. He covered the letter with his hand. He'd enjoy their presence to the fullest and not get bogged down in the "how" of everything. God would provide. Yes, he'd have to do his bit, but surely the Lord wouldn't send these riches of family and friends unless He had a plan. Barden had led Percy to the Lord while they were school chums. This was his chance to bless him in return and allow the new Lord and Lady Cheatham to lean on him if needed.

As Eugenie prepared to leave for the practice kitchens, she eyed the empty mail salver, the silver reflecting beneath the gaslight of the parlor. Father had disclosed that many of his friends disapproved of her social "do-gooding." Could that be the reason she'd received no Christmas invitations, or was it because she was in mourning?

*Christmas will be a lonely one.* Percy would be busy with his family. Last night when she thought he was going to kiss her, she'd almost raised up on her tiptoes to accept the press of his mouth on hers. Thank goodness she hadn't, or how embarrassed she'd be now.

She retrieved her velvet-trimmed coat and matching bonnet from the coatrack and headed to the front where the carriage awaited. After a short ride, her driver pulled up by the imposing old factory building. Ahead, a dozen of her ladies were entering the building. She could spy Carrie from afar, a brilliant red plume on her hat bobbing as she strode toward the entrance. If only she had Carrie's confidence. A little of her friend's self-assurance had waned when Carrie learned that her mother-in-law was coming to stay with them for the holidays. Carrie had let Eugenie know that she'd have to cut back on instruction time. Eugenie exhaled, her breath forming a billowing puff in the chill morning air. Winter was knocking at the door.

Once inside, Eugenie hung her coat beside those ranging from Tara's elegant fox-trimmed cape to a garment so thin that a white handkerchief could be seen through the threadbare front pocket. Eugenie sighed. They were giving these women real skills that could help them overcome their poverty.

Standing on an upside-down wood crate, Tara clapped her hands. "We're all working together today on traditional Christmas recipes, so gather round."

After the ladies had received instruction on preparing sugarplums, Carrie, Tara, and Eugenie sampled the shortbread cookies that had been baked and tinned the previous day.

Carrie quirked a dark eyebrow. "Delicious!"

Wiping a crumb from the edge of her mouth, Tara grinned. "Yes."

Eugenie savored the sweet, buttery taste. "Perfection."

Work continued, with a short break for lunch, followed by another lesson and demonstration.

"They're really mastering the skills, Eugenie." Carrie clasped her hands to her chest.

Tara rang the bell to announce day's end. As they began cleaning up, Eugenie grabbed the sturdy wood box and stepped up onto it. "I need to make an announcement. Actually, two." All eyes focused on Eugenie. "First we have secured a contract on a new building for those requiring housing!"

Some ladies gasped, a few began to cry, but most clapped loudly. When they quieted, Eugenie scanned the room. How many could help Percy? "Mr. Gladstone, the attorney who has been assisting us, at no cost may I add, is in need of household staff for Christmas. Might there be a few of you ladies who could help him out? There will be generous payment. Just remain behind for a few minutes and let me know. You're all dismissed for the day!"

How many would come forward? Asking someone to help out for a few days during such an important time of year might prove difficult. As the other ladies streamed out, only a handful remained behind. She quickly took a mental inventory of these ladies' strengths. Lucy, who was covering a tray of jam cookies, was becoming accomplished with pastries. Deborah set the prettiest tables. Anne worked magic on all manner of vegetables and fruits, Melissa could coax the toughest piece of meat into tender submission. Nancy's soups, consommés, and stews were unparalleled. Tina was happiest tidying up after everyone else. Kathleen preferred staffing the tea and coffee carts.

Kathleen finished cleaning up the Russian tea she'd practiced preparing and put her apron up. She joined Eugenie and Carrie. "I'll be alone this Christmas, so I'd be happy for work."

Melissa joined them. "Kathleen and I are sharing a room above the mercantile, and we've been told they'd don't plan to heat the building Christmas Eve and Christmas Day."

Shoulders raising and lowering with her sigh, Deborah stopped folding linens nearby. "My employer is doing the same, as the tobacconist will be closed then." Lucy joined the circle. "This will give us a chance to earn our keep." She eyed the other women. "We've been talking, and we won't take charity."

"We need our pride." Melissa pinched a torn piece of her skirt between her long fingers.

"Last week's catering event paid off my rent with enough left over to pay some toward renting my room at the new building." Deborah removed her apron.

Carrie's dark eyes shone with approval as she smiled at each lady in turn.

Anne covered the turnip casserole she'd practiced on and washed up before joining them. "My sons are both stationed at forts in Texas and won't be coming home. I'd be glad to help."

"How long does Mr. Gladstone need us?" Deborah exchanged a glance with Melissa. "We signed up for an extra cleaning job for after Christmas."

Eugenie tapped her toe. "A good question. I think he'd appreciate having help for about a week, when I imagine his household help will return."

"I can go a week." Lucy smiled. "I hope he's as generous as you say."

Eugenie told them the rate Percy had offered to pay her ladies. All were quiet for a moment, eyebrows raised. "His parents are the Marquess and Marchioness of Kent."

"Oh my." Kathleen's shoulders slumped. "I don't know if I'm up to cooking for the likes of that."

Eugenie leaned toward her. "I'd not have asked if Carrie, Tara, and I didn't think you were ready. Besides, Mr. Gladstone is a barrister in a small town. I imagine he's expecting a little more simple fare." But was he? Eugenie nibbled her lower lip.

Anne's fair eyebrows drew together in a straight line. "Will you be staying to help us?"

Maybe she should stay with the volunteers. "We'll have to work out all the details and I'll let you know."

On her carriage ride home, Eugenie berated herself for not getting more information from Percy. She'd see him soon for the opera on the Canadian side on Saturday. A touring company, with several members from eastern and northern Ontario, were bringing their production through before Christmas, enroute to visit family.

When she stepped into the house, the scent of roast beef enveloped her like a comforting hug. Would Percy's family enjoy roasts? Or would they prefer fancier fare like standing rib roast? Menus danced through her head as she considered several upcoming events the ladies were catering. A railroad executive had asked for a feast featuring only seafood, no meats, with a seven-course meal for fifty people at his estate outside of town, on the river. She removed her hat and set it on the wooden rack by the door.

Her butler, Mr. Morgan, came and took her coat. "Welcome home, miss."

"Thank you."

"You have a letter from Mrs. Swaine."

The Swaines owned substantial properties on Mackinac Island as well as a hotel in Detroit. It would be lovely to have Jacqueline Cadotte Swaine, one of her mother's closest friends, visit. Mrs. Swaine had lost two of her sons during the war. While it was rumored that her eldest son had fought for the South, no one spoke of it, especially now that Jacqueline's new son, little Robert Swaine, was toddling around. "Could you bring the missive to me in the parlor? And send Lorena with some tea."

"Certainly, miss."

Eugenie eyed the Morris chair that Father had brought back from England the previous Christmas. With darkly stained wood, including the spindles, and beautifully artful fabric for the heavily padded seat and back, it was a bit of an oddity in the parlor. Eugenie had originally protested the piece's placement there, but considering the comfort it gave with the ability to recline, surely this unusual style would someday catch on. Until then, she had to endure visitors' comments. But not tonight, and apparently not during the holidays. She pulled the ottoman close and sat down, removed her shoes, reclined slightly, and propped her feet up. Mother would have scolded, and Father would have rolled his eyes. Unexpected tears trickled down her cheeks. How she missed them. Her first Christmas all alone in this big house. Percy had his family coming, and her ladies would be there working while she was on this side of the water, alone. Yes, she was falling in love with him, and yes, he seemed to care for her too. But surely it was too soon for her to meet his family. Besides, she was in mourning for her father. But her Sugarplum Ladies needed her—didn't they?

She exhaled a huge sigh as Lorena entered the room with the tea cart and the letter. Eugenie inhaled the scent of orange, pekoe, and bergamot as her servant poured her tea. Lorena passed her the envelope and then placed the teacup and saucer on the cherry side table next to her. Mother's and Father's tintype image beamed up at her from a nearby silver frame on the table. Eugenie read the message. Jacqueline, her husband, and their two children would arrive soon and wished to visit. Eugenie was welcome to stay at the hotel with them over the holidays. Tears pricked her eyes again. It was good to be asked. Also, Jacqueline asked if Eugenie could refer her to an attorney who was known for his discretion. Oh my, this sounded serious. Mother would have wanted Eugenie to help. She pressed the missive to her chest.

Lorena shifted from side to side and tugged at her apron. "Miss Mott, I got a favor to ask."

Eugenie looked up.

Concern crinkled Lorena's brow. "It's just that, well, my family is going to be coming back to visit with me."

"The Scotts?"

"Yes, ma'am, and Mrs. Roat, she was like a second mother to my sister."

The two half-sisters had been separated when Mrs. Wilda Roat bought Angelina's freedom and taught her the trade of seamstress work. "That's a blessing."

"I was wonderin' if I might have a few days off from workin'."

"Of course! I'm excited that you got to reconnect with your family."

"I don't know 'zactly when they comin'. They lookin' for a place to stay."

And this place would be almost empty. She would not be like the uncharitable protagonist in Charles Dickens's recent story. "Lorena, why don't you ask them to stay here? The third floor has two smaller rooms for Julian and Charity, and I have two more rooms on the other end of the second floor that they're welcome to use."

Lorena's pretty features froze. "You mean that, ma'am?"

Eugenie sipped her tea and set the cup back on the saucer. "I think it would be delightful. And you can order all the garlands and what-nots that Mother used to have to make the place festive."

"Even with you in mourning, Miss Mott?" There was no censure in her servant's voice, just concern.

"Would not even the bereaved invite the Christ child in?"

"Yes'm, I'm guessin' they would."

"So shall we. Feel free to have Mr. Morgan help you bring out the decorations at the appropriate time. The Swaines are arriving from up North, and I may be at their hotel much of the time. Plan some dinners just for yourselves too, and I'll gladly pay the expenses."

Lorena reached into her apron for a handkerchief and blew her nose. "You too good to me, miss."

"Every good thing we have comes from God. I thank Him we can offer shelter to your family."

She sniffed. "Thank you. And if you don't mind me sayin', ma'am, I believe the good Lord may have brought Mr. Gladstone to you, for your good."

"I pray you're right."

"That old Mr. Horace was a bad man. I near 'bout wore my knees out tryin' to pray him outta your life."

# Chapter 6

Percy crossed out the previous day's date on the calendar atop his blotter. How could only one day spent without seeing Eugenie Mott seem more like a week?

A grim-faced Antoine rapped on the open door and strode to the desk. He passed his notepad to Percy. "I've procured a carriage driver, footman, lady's maid, chamber maid, handyman, and *un garçon* to run errands, but no cook nor kitchen servants."

"I don't need an errand boy." Percy exhaled a breath and set the notepad down on his desk, scanning the names, recognizing one in particular. "The lady's maid has served time for, ahem, soliciting, so she's out."

Antoine coughed, his cheeks red. "Sorry, sir."

"The chambermaid's name is also familiar for the same offense." He lifted his pen from the inkwell and crossed out the two names.

"Most of the extra service help in town, *les cuisiniers et leurs aides,* were already contracted from the previous year."

"I've asked Miss Mott if any of her ladies might do the duties." Hopefully Eugenie could supply the cooks and their helpers.

"It is so late to be inquiring, sir."

"Yes, well, this visit was rather unexpected."

"But a welcome one, *n'est ce pas?*"

"Yes, very welcome. I'll ask Miss Mott, when I take her to the opera, if she might have found some American women who can help."

"Speaking of which, you might wish to return home and *préparez-vous pour ce soir,* sir."

Percy pulled his watch from his vest and checked the time. Plenty of time to prepare for the evening.

Finally, he met Eugenie at the docks and accompanied her to their venue, instructing his driver to return for them in two hours. Eugenie, attired in a deep-charcoal wool cape with fur collar, looked stunning. She was far too beautiful and privileged for him. He glanced toward the cedar-sided building that resembled a massive cabin. Which might be what it was originally intended for—perhaps a building for trading furs. He exhaled slowly. What passed for a theater here in Windsor would be laughable on the American side, but it was all he had for entertainment.

Percy squared his shoulders and offered his arm to Eugenie. They followed a lumberjack dressed in ill-fitting clothing over the boardwalk and to the unvarnished pine entrance door. The big man held the door for them, and Eugenie didn't bat an eyelash as they entered. Lanterns hung overhead from the rafters and on the walls. At each end of the building, fireplaces provided the limited heat. Seating was on long wooden benches strategically placed in the cavernous room, facing the makeshift stage.

The theater building could have been one of Eugenie's father's hunting lodges, albeit without the antlers mounted on the walls. But it was warm. And Percy was with her, and that was what mattered. She'd not be a snob. But truly, fitted with this bustle, how would she manage two hours seated on a wooden plank?

"Let's find a seat." Percy pointed to the end of the back row, which was empty, and guided her along. In the front row, a mother ineffectively tried to corral a half-dozen young children. In the second row, a matron grabbed the pipe that her husband was trying to light and pointed to a placard on the wall which forbid such a practice.

Movement from behind and a familiar voice distracted Eugenie. She turned to face the door. Horace entered with a pretty young woman on his arm. Eugenie gasped. "What is Horace Ontevreden doing here?"

Percy narrowed his eyes. "That's him?"

"Yes. I can't stay here with Horace sitting over there." She recognized the woman he was with, but couldn't place her. And if Eugenie was overdressed in her mourning clothes, then this young woman was even more out of place. Dressed in a deep-rose satin skirt with a contrasting white-and-navy plaid blouse, a blue short-waisted jacket, and a small cap affixed at an angle to her piled-high red hair, the woman stood out like a lone cranberry fallen into a bowl of rice pudding.

"What would you like to do, Eugenie?"

And here she wasn't going to be a snob. She shook her head, not wanting to do anything that might cause trouble for Percy. He was, after all, a prominent member of this small community. "Can we please leave?"

"If you wish."

She felt dizzy and raised a hand to her brow.

Percy tucked her arm closer. "Let's go."

Horace and his lady friend hung their cloaks, and Percy guided her out the door.

But where would he take her?

He leaned in. "My home is but a block away. Can you walk it?"

She took in a fortifying breath. "Yes."

"I can show you my home, and that way you'll have a better idea of what to tell your ladies."

"A good idea. They may have a great many questions."

"My housekeeper can serve as chaperone if you wish." He quirked an eyebrow at her.

"Would she mind?"

"I don't believe so."

Outside, a gust of chill wind penetrated Eugenie's cloak, and she tugged the fur collar tighter around her neck. "Brr. . . I feel winter coming for certain."

Percy laughed. "And old Father Time isn't far behind Old Man Winter—with 1868 yet ahead of us in His capable hands. Well, not in Father Time's hands, but in the hands of God, who is Father of all."

Ahead of them, gas lights lit almost every room of an imposing three-story brick home. "Who lives there, Percy, and why is it all lit up?"

"That's mine." He tapped the brim of his hat. "I despise coming home to a dark house, so the staff keeps the house well lit until I return each night."

Her eyes widened. "I wasn't expecting so grand a home here."

She didn't have to say the unspoken—that he lived in a small backwater town in Ontario a fraction of the size of Detroit.

"I wanted a place where my. . ." He drew in a chill breath. "Where my family could come visit."

Straightening, Eugenie frowned. "But didn't you say this is the first time they've visited, and you've lived here—"

He raised his free hand. "Nigh on seven years now." With nary a visit from them.

"Oh." She frowned but didn't push the interrogation further.

He might as well push the margin. "I hope to fill all three stories with children someday too."

"Oh!" Eugenie's eyes widened in surprise, and then she suddenly cried out in pain and stumbled.

Percy caught her as she tripped over a fallen tree branch that was underfoot in the street. He held her elbows fast and looked down at her, her face so close he could simply lean in and kiss her perfect lips. But he was a gentleman. "Are you all right?"

"Yes." She pulled free but took his hand as she stepped tentatively on one foot and then the other. "Ouch!"

A gentleman did what was needed. Percy scooped her up into his arms. "You're not taking another step on that foot until we have it looked at."

"What?" But she kept her arm wrapped around his neck. "You should put me down."

"I fear I may have caused part of the problem."

"How?"

"Forgive me for speaking of indelicate matters, Miss Mott." She fit perfectly in his arms.

Eugenie leaned her head on his shoulder. "So, you are not the committed bachelor that some believe you to be?"

"Certainly not." Three more strides, and then he carried her up the four steps to the door. "Simply waiting for the right lady."

What would it be like to carry her into the house as his wife? He'd better put any such thoughts aside and be on his best behavior.

The front door opened, revealing his butler standing there, eyes wide. "Mr. Gladstone, what brings you back so soon? Is Miss Mott injured?"

"Yes, I fear she's injured her ankle."

Lemrich held the door for them and then closed it behind them.

"Please send Venus for the doctor."

"Yes, sir."

"I'll bring Miss Mott into the parlor, if you'll open that pocket door for me, please." Percy shifted her in his arms.

When his servant had opened the door, Percy carried her inside a cherry-paneled room with a rich burgundy, green, and gold wool carpet covering the floor. A fire burned in the hearth. Atop the mantel, tintype images in lacy silver frames formed a long row. Percy set her on one of the rococo chairs.

"Is this a John Henry Belter chair?" She ran her hand over the elaborate woodwork.

"Yes. My mother sent it with me from England."

"It's lovely." She winced as her foot began to throb.

"Let's put that foot up." He pulled a maroon ottoman closer and gently lifted her ankle. "I think I better remove your shoe."

Eugenie frowned. "I have a bad feeling this is going to hurt."

"Likely so, but I'll be careful." His cheeks turned a shade of rose. "I'll have to lift your skirts up a little too."

"It's all right."

A petite woman with skin the shade of strong tea strode into the room, hands on hips. "What's goin' on here, Master Percy?"

"Miss Mott has twisted her ankle, Sabina."

"I knows that, Lemrich done told me, but what you tryin' to do?"

"Get the boot off before her ankle swells further."

"Um, hum, I'm thinkin' I'll do that. Now you shoo out of here."

Percy departed.

"I'm Sabina—sort of cook and housekeeper rolled into one. But I'm thinkin' I'll be chaperone tonight."

Eugenie's cheeks heated. "I'm Eugenie Mott, from Detroit."

"I knows who you is. You the gal got Master Percy's head on backwards the past month or two."

Eugenie laughed, but it made her foot hurt more and she groaned.

The tiny woman bent over her, gently undid her boot, then pulled it off little by little. "It's done swolled up bad."

Eugenie leaned forward to look and became lightheaded when she saw how large her ankle had swollen. "Oh my. I need to get home."

"You ain't goin' nowhere tonight, Missy Mott. Not on my watch." Sabina brushed her hands against her plaid apron. "Now let me have Master Percy get me some snow to pack on there."

Percy's servant departed, and Eugenie sat there, tears pooling in her eyes. She needed to get back to Detroit. She had to think of her ladies. And she had company coming.

Soon Percy returned with a silver ice bucket. "Are you willing to try this?"

She shrugged, her coat suddenly snug around her shoulders.

Sabina joined them, a tray of what smelled like hot chocolate in her hands. She set it down on a nearby table. "Let's get you out of that coat, Miss Mott."

"But I must get home!" She struggled to cope with her pain and the situation she now faced.

"We'll see what the doctor says, Eugenie." Percy leaned close to her. "Let me and my staff take care of you."

What else could she do?

# Chapter 7

loves in your pickled tomatoes?" Eugenie watched as Sabina used a fish fork to painstakingly remove the nubby cloves from the mason jar of tomatoes she'd just poured into a blue-and-white china bowl.

"They give it flavor, but you don't want to be eatin' a passel of whole cloves."

"My physician says they can be dangerous if you swallow them."

"That's why I'm removin' them, miss." Sabina's eyebrows tugged together as she bent closer over the bowl. She forked a dark clove out of the bowl and transferred it to a saucer. "There."

Eugenie inhaled the pungent aroma. "Are you sure you got them all?"

"Only put in twelve. And I got 'em all. So that's the trick—ya'll use my canned tomatoes, ya'll need to pull the dozen cloves out of each jar."

"All right." Eugenie shifted her foot on the wooden stool it was propped up on and picked up her menu cards.

"You got easy victuals planned for Christmas Eve and Christmas Day." Sabina nodded in approval.

"And we have a subdued menu for the following five days." Eugenie tapped at her hastily written, recalled-from-memory receipts scattered on the large mahogany table that was beautifully inlaid with ebony. But how would she manage if her foot didn't heal?

"That make a week's worth of 'em. . ." Sabina seemed to be leaving something unsaid.

Eugenie eyed the menus that she'd scribbled out earlier that morning. "Should we prepare a few back-up menus in case we can't find what we need?"

"Mr. Percy's folks'll be here soon. In a few days." Sabina frowned at the calendar. "Maybe ask your ladies to cook ahead a few things and bring 'em on over."

"That's a good idea." She should see what Mrs. Roat was putting together for Lorena and the Scott family. Eugenie moistened her lips. "My own cook will be enjoying the Southern fare that she and her sister grew up with in Virginia."

"My sister and I be doin' the same thing when I get to Ohio." Sabina grinned. "Just a few more days and then it'll be chitterlings, greens, corn pone, mmmm."

"I was thinking more of fried chicken, mashed potatoes, and gravy and biscuits."

"That goes without sayin'—that's Master Gladstone's favorite meal."

"But won't his family want more traditional English fare?" At least they had a few more days to make quick adjustments.

Sabina went to the tall kitchen cabinet nearby and pulled out three stained cards. "His cook back home say his family love these." She handed them to Eugenie.

Eugenie scanned the paper. "Who doesn't love sugar cookies?"

Whistling, Percy strolled into the kitchen, hands tucked in his jacket pockets. "Sugar cookies?" He scanned the room.

"Not here!" Sabina placed her fists on her hips and cocked her head at him.

He puckered his lips in mock dismay. "And no Dutch apple pie?"

"A ham sandwich and tomato relish be enough for your lunch, Master Percy." Sabina clucked her tongue. "But them Sugarplum Ladies gonna spoil you while I'm gone."

Eugenie re-organized her receipts. "You said your mother eats like a bird, so I hope some good old American cooking might tempt her to eat."

"Father used to threaten Mother with a tray of seed to peck at if she kept eating like a bird."

"They got suet balls at the mercantile." Sabina quirked an eyebrow at her employer. "If'n you want Venus to run get you some before we go."

"I think not." Eugenie flinched as her foot spasmed.

In a flash, Percy's arms were around her, and he lifted her from the chair. "Off you go. The doctor said this foot should be kept high and not on a low stool like that one."

Eugenie clung to Percy's neck as he carried her out from the kitchen, into the hallway, and up the stairs to the entryway. "I'm going to put you to bed, right this instant." His voice rang loud in the stairwell.

"Shhh, people will hear you!"

He carried her out to the hall as Lemrich opened the door. A half-dozen guests stood staring at them while a gust of icy breeze carried through the hallway. Eugenie felt Percy's shoulders stiffen, and for a moment thought he'd lower her to stand, but he held her fast. "Welcome Mother and Father, Bard and wife! How lovely that you're early!"

Percy's parents and Eugenie stared gape-mouthed at one another.

Percy shifted her in his arms. "Let me get Eugenie situated, and I shall come back to greet you properly!"

He carried her down the hall, and she couldn't help but be keenly aware of the gazes that followed them. The tall, distinguished-looking man had to be Percy's father and the stately woman his mother. The younger couple with them looked exhausted, with dark rings under their eyes. Had the older couple been so demanding? Or was it simply the long journey?

"Oh, Percy, I should go home."

"Nonsense, you heard what Dr. Quinlain said."

Soon he had her settled in the four-poster bed, her foot propped up on a feather pillow. A gentle rap sounded on the door.

Mother hugged him and then moved gracefully to Eugenie's side and took her hand in hers. "I wondered when Percival would finally find himself a bride."

Stepping beside him, Father coughed, covering a laugh, and then embraced Percy. When had he grown so thin? Percy could feel his father's ribs even beneath his thick tweed jacket. "My boy, it is so good to see you again."

"I'm so glad you could cross the pond, sir."

"Of course I would. I'm just sorry it has taken so long."

Mother had settled down on the bed alongside Eugenie, as if they were long-separated friends. "You remind me of someone, my dear."

Father narrowed his eyes. "Indeed. Our Austrian friends' daughter."

"My mother was Austrian." Eugenie smiled up at Mother, but the pain lines around his beloved's eyes suggested she needed some rest.

Percy moved closer. "Do you need something for the pain?"

Eugenie dipped her chin.

Mother stood, and he gave her another quick embrace. She wasn't one for much affection, but she returned a heartfelt squeeze.

Turning to face Eugenie, Mother cocked her head, her silver and chestnut curls bobbing against her pale cheeks. "We'll leave you to rest, my dear."

Percy poured one of the powders into the glass on the bedside table and then poured water from the carafe into it. He stirred until it was dissolved. Then he assisted Eugenie to sit up, placing an extra pillow behind her back. He handed her the glass.

She drank a few sips. "You go, be with your guests."

"My holiday staff arrived this morning while you were in the kitchen. I don't want you alone in here. I'll be sending one of them to sit with you for a while."

"Percy?"

"Yes?"

"Will you be telling your mother that we are not to be wed?"

He'd not become a barrister nor crossed an ocean by being faint of heart. "No. I doubt that will be necessary."

Percy waited for the "tell," the sign that he'd scored a point in the court of love. His heart thumped in his chest, and his breathing slowed as he waited. When Eugenie laughed, despite her pain, and a smile bloomed on her beautiful face, he had his answer. He exhaled the breath he'd been holding and bent and kissed her hand.

Now, to find a ring to go on that fair hand.

That evening proved to be the best he'd ever spent with his family. The next morning his parents and his friends slept late. He'd carried Eugenie to the front parlor earlier. Now Percy paced the hall, checking how his new crew had done. Thank goodness Scipio hadn't wished to travel this Christmas and was helping organize the newcomers as the other servants prepared to depart. The paneling had been dusted and shone from the lemon oil that had been applied. The chandelier sparkled overhead. The brass doorknobs glowed, as did the coatrack, which awaited the arrival of Eugenie's Sugarplum Ladies. The overflow of coats could be taken to the hall closet, which normally held Percy's black overcoat and umbrella and boots. Why was he so anxious? Truth be told, he was more nervous about these ladies' opinions than that of his parents'. He inhaled the scent of the holly garland and pine that one of the temporary workers had festooned from the stair rail.

A scene from long ago ran through his mind. The servants had all been lined up in the grand hallway to receive their Christmas boxes. Percy had hidden on the landing, behind the stair rails, looking down. He'd refused to accompany his family in the ceremony. He'd claimed he had a stomachache, but the truth was that he'd been embarrassed by the way his father condescended to the servants, who all year long worked so hard to make their life lovely—and his bearable. His parents loved Percy, loved all of their children, and cared for their servants, but Mother and Father were a product of their own upbringing. He knew, even as a child, that he'd never as an adult live in such luxury. He'd had to look to their staff as he grew up to model for him what real work meant.

He went to check on Eugenie. His sweetheart sat in the parlor sipping her tea while reading a treatise on *The Canadian Federation—The Dominion of Canada*. Strange how natural it seemed to have her there. Stranger yet was her choice of reading material.

"Should I try to find you something a little less esoteric?"

"My father discussed all of these changes with me last July, when they were occurring." She closed the narrow tome but kept a finger at about the middle.

"I'm sure my own father would be glad to bore you with the details too, if you'd allow him." He laughed.

Light shuffling announced his houseman. "Sir?"

"Yes?"

"The carriage has returned with the American ladies."

Percy stepped forward and parted the parlor's Irish lace curtains. "I don't see them."

From where she was seated, Eugenie turned and craned her neck to look.

When Percy turned back around, Scipio's eyes were downcast, color high on his dark cheeks. "They've come around to the back, sir."

"What?" Of course, that was how it was done, but these were Miss Mott's ladies— would she be offended?

Scipio clasped his hands at his waist. "Sabina asked if you'd like to greet them or if she should acquaint them with the kitchen first before she leaves."

Eugenie's shoulders slumped. "Oh, I wish they'd come see me first!"

Percy bent and squeezed her hand. "I'll go down and send them up to you, Eugenie."

Someone banged the brass knocker on the front door and Percy flinched. Scipio moved to open it, and Percy followed him in the hallway to see who might be calling.

Rocking back and forth on his heels was a youth whose shaggy auburn hair, beneath his oversized wool cap, almost obscured his light eyes. He looked past the houseman at Percy.

"Got a message for ya, gov'nah." The boy's thick accent announced him as a recent British immigrant, likely from the East End. Was he one of the children who'd escaped to make his own way instead of being sent to a farm? The boy held out a grimy palm, his fingers and wrists covered with a makeshift moth-eaten mitten.

Percy plucked a coin from his vest pocket, stepped forward, and handed it to the urchin. "What is it?"

"Mrs. Jack-Will-Ine Swaine says send yer carriage to the station."

Percy felt his eyes widen. "Who?"

"Mrs. Jacqueline Swaine?" Eugenie's plaintive sigh carried into the hall. "Oh my! I was supposed to see her in Detroit."

"That's right, gov, her and a real pretty girl with her." The urchin scratched his cheek. "Sister of Lady Cheat-ham. Mrs. Swaine owns the Ca-dot ship what brought Miss Tumbles-town here."

"Ah yes, Lady Cheatham's sister was expected from Mackinac Island." Percy smiled at Eugenie. "And I take it you know Mrs. Swaine?"

"Yes, she was dear friends with my mother. She's from what some would consider Mackinac Island 'royalty.' She must have brought Deanna down from the island with her on her husband's steamship."

"Might not want to keep 'em waitin', gov." The child pushed a lock of greasy hair under his cap.

Patting his pocket for another pair of matching coins, Percy retrieved them. "Here. Take this. Run to the station and tell them we're coming. I'll send my carriage."

A wide grin revealed the lad didn't yet suffer from tooth rot. "Will do."

Sudden conviction got ahold of Percy's tongue. "Come back here after and knock on the back door. I'll tell the staff to give you lunch with the new workers."

The boy touched his cap brim. "Much appreciated."

Percy might regret his offer later, but compassion reined now. "Where are you staying?"

The youth shrugged. "Here and there."

"If you need a place to lay your head, we've a hay loft over in the carriage house. And I could use a reliable errand boy."

"Yes, sir!" With a curt nod, the boy ran off.

Good heavens, unexpected guests were calling, his family was here after seven years, and his sweetheart had an injured foot. This was not the way he'd hoped Christmas would go! But he'd seen many a trial become complex and convoluted, and he was by no means a man faint of heart.

Eugenie hated to leave Jacqueline on her own, but there had been work to do, something the busy matron understood well. And frankly, Jacqueline's private questions about wills and codicils and such left her feeling a bit rattled. Thankfully, Percy said he'd meet with Mrs. Swaine to discuss her concerns about her two remaining children. How awful it must be to lose even one child, much less two. No wonder she wished to ensure both of their futures. Now seated by the second stove, Eugenie smiled at each lady in her crew. "You have all worked hard today."

Her Sugarplum Ladies had managed to become acquainted with the stoves and their peculiar functions and the ovens, as well as where the bachelor kept his dishes, crystal, and silver stored. They'd prepared numerous side dishes as well as sauces and a pudding while ducks with apples roasted.

Outside, the breeze escalated, casting dead leaves against the windowpanes. But the warmth in the kitchen and the sweet scent of cloves and cinnamon surrounded Eugenie. What if there was a storm when her crew needed to bring more catered goods to the house? *Don't borrow trouble.*

Melissa, who'd become the leader of the group, clasped her hands at her waist. "This has been an excellent opportunity for us to practice catering private functions."

"Yes." Eugenie watched as Nancy stirred a pot of lentil soup, the scent of celery, onions, and beef broth tickling her senses. "A number of you may go on to work on your own one day." And she'd be so proud of them.

Kathleen and Anne beamed.

Pausing from cutting out Percy's requested sugar cookies, Lucy looked up from the table. "Thank you for taking us through some of Mr. Gladstone's favorite recipes today."

Sleet tapped at the row of kitchen windows, the gray skies outside promising a storm. "We should pray for Sabina, Lemrich, and Venus in their travels."

As the wind gusted, wet sleet and ice rattled the panes against the window frame. In the corner, the young messenger boy finished stuffing a roll into his mouth. He looked outside and shivered.

"We'll make a pallet on the floor for you to sleep on." Eugenie pointed to a warm corner of the room.

"No, miss, Master Gladstone said I could sleep in the barn loft."

Pretty blond Anne shook a wooden spoon at him. "Not tonight you won't."

Kathleen quickly made up a plate of food with a small amount from each of their dishes. "Come sit down and sample our meal for the night."

Eyes wide as saucers, the boy shook his shaggy head.

Lucy laughed softly. "The Sugarplum Ladies request your presence at our table." She patted the seat beside her.

Eugenie blinked back tears as the boy slowly rose and went to sit at the table. This was what Christmas was truly all about. *Loving others as Christ would love us.*

Deanna Tumbleston entered the kitchen, her curls bobbing around her pretty face. "Lord Percival has finished chatting with Mrs. Swaine. They've been in there ever so long! And he bids you to come say your goodbyes, as she wishes to depart for the last ferry before the storm comes in."

Lord Percival indeed. Eugenie almost snorted. But it was true. He could rightfully claim that title. If he wished. Which obviously he didn't. She smiled, her esteem for him rising even further. And how good of him to take time to advise her mother's friend.

Deanna came forward and squeezed Eugenie's arm. "Mrs. Swaine has been a good friend to me on the island, despite the difference in our ages. But I don't wish to keep her from her family, even though it was very kind of her to escort me here."

Eugenie gave the younger woman a quick hug. "Let me bid her adieu." *And pray that all travelers made it safely to their destinations.*

# Chapter 8

Attired in formal dinner wear, Percy tugged at his cravat as he strode down the hall in his snug-fitting gray-and-black plaid wool trousers. Caroline stood in the hallway outside Eugenie's room, tapping her toe. "Hurry up, Barden."

"Coming." Bard emerged from Eugenie's room carrying Percy's wide-eyed darling.

Despite his friend being a married man, jealousy coursed through Percy. "What are you doing?"

Deanna waved him back. "We're trying to get her to the table and seated."

Eugenie's cheeks reddened, and she ducked her head against Bard's pristine white collar, sending another surge of jealousy through Percy.

Barden lumbered like a woodsman carrying a load of logs. "Out of my way, old man!"

"Don't drop her!" Percy snapped, then instantly regretted it as he looked up to the stairway to see his mother's wide-eyed look of disapproval.

Father took Mother's arm and led her down.

Where was the temporary butler? Percy waved everyone on. "Let's move to the dining room."

Deanna slid into her chair. "These are so much more comfortable than those ship benches that were bolted down to the floor."

Barden installed Eugenie in her seat next to Percy as the rest of the guests took their places.

The hall clock chimed the hour and the first of the servants appeared. She dipped a curtsy. "Soda water is prepared, sir."

Father sent the girl a scathing look. "Lady Kent and I shall have claret with the meat course and white wine with the fish."

Eugenie cleared her throat. "There is no fish course."

Percy laid a gentle hand on her shoulder as he addressed his father. "Not tonight, sir." But he'd go over the next night's menu and feed Father a sardine if that's what it took to satisfy his demand for a fish course. Where did he think he was?

"We have a lovely trout almondine for tomorrow." Eugenie took a sip of soda water.

"Good." Was that Percy's imagination or did Father look a little embarrassed at his outburst? He kept his eyes averted as another servant filled his crystal goblet half-full with claret.

The servants continued to fill the goblets with soda water, wine, or apple cider.

"Shall we toast the queen?"

Mother raised her goblet. "To Victoria."

Hard to believe Mother's childhood friend was now queen of England. After they'd made their toasts, the Americans somewhat awkwardly, Percy rose. "I shall lead us in prayer."

Perhaps it was the flickering gaslights that caused the sheen he saw in Mother's and Father's eyes before both bowed their heads.

Eugenie tried to keep her head down, waiting for Percy's mother's first volley of criticism. When would the bombardment begin? Hadn't her sweetheart said she was very peculiar about what she ate? Seated beside Percy, attired in his finest, Eugenie regretted her mourning clothes. But she was keenly feeling the loss of her father. Across from them, Percy's father coughed. He had the look her own father had, before. . . *Pray dear God, not Percy's father too.*

Lady Caroline was the only one at the table with an appetite, it seemed. The servers had given her seconds on everything. Pausing between bites, the pretty woman beamed at Percy. "This is a beautiful home, Mr. Gladstone."

"Thank you. And please, call me Percy."

"And a lovely meal, Eugenie."

Eugenie flushed with pleasure. "Thank you, Lady Caroline."

The American woman waved her hand in protest. "No need to call me that. It feels quite odd. Just plain old Caroline is fine."

Barden's eyebrows drew together. "It's been a very strange journey for us. I don't wish to cast a pall over dinner by discussing it though."

Percy cast a sideways glance at Eugenie as he took a bite of the duck. He'd told her earlier that Barden had lost his father, his two brothers, and an infant nephew in a short time. He'd also had to return to England recently, even though he'd made a new home in Kansas with his wife. So many changes.

Pretty dark-haired Deanna gave her brother-in-law a saucy wink. "Barden's title doesn't give me much more respect at the fort—because most of the soldiers met Barden when he was washing up dishes and tossing slops at our inn back in Kansas."

Percy's parents' eyebrows rose at exactly the same moment, and Eugenie stifled the urge to laugh. Lady Kent set her fork down and placed her hands in her lap. Oh dear, there were several more courses to be served yet.

"Can you recommend any entertainments on the American side?" Lord Kent aimed his query at Eugenie.

She named the many festivities they could attend. Each guest expressed a desire in a different outing. This could get hectic traveling back and forth. "Of course, we can only engage in these pursuits if weather permits."

Percy gestured to the servants to remove the first set of dishes. "Remember, we'll have several beautiful church services to attend. Although the Anglican church is small, they boast a lovely choir. Granted, most of the singers are either lumberjacks, natives from the area, or newer residents who escaped from the South on the Underground Railroad."

Eugenie anticipated his parents' shocked expressions, but they were not forthcoming.

"Of course, dear." His mother waved a hand airily at him. "That goes without saying."

As the next course was served, Eugenie held her breath. She could picture her Sugarplum Ladies downstairs, awaiting the verdict on their creations. So far, everything had been sublime.

Conversation turned briefly to politics, music, theater, and a heated debate as to whether Dickens or Thackeray was the more literary writer. Much laughter and a few taunts between Barden and Percy, as well as Percy and his father, had Eugenie's sides in a stitch. By the time dessert was served, she knew the evening had been a success.

Lord Kent pushed away from the table. "I've not indulged in such fine fare in a long time."

Percy leaned in. "Well done, my dear."

Patting his lean midsection, Barden made a face of consternation. "If we keep this up, we'll be fatter than the stuffed goose by Twelfth Night."

*Twelfth Night?* Eugenie suddenly recollected that the British followed a different tradition than most Americans. She couldn't swallow. Maybe it was related to Church of England or Anglican traditions. She quickly searched her memory as to when Twelfth Night began. She bit down on a sugar cookie and chewed as she considered.

"Will you be staying through Epiphany then?" Caroline smiled warmly at Eugenie.

She began to choke on her cookie.

Percy patted her back. "Are you all right?"

Eugenie shook her head, covering her mouth with her napkin, coughing.

"Here, take a drink." Percy pushed her goblet toward her.

Eugenie sipped the soda water until the spell passed.

All eyes seemed fixed upon her.

Her nondenominational church did not celebrate Epiphany. "Uh, that's January fourth? Or fifth?"

"Epiphany is the sixth of January." Lady Kent cast a glance between Eugenie and Percy.

Her ladies had gotten the dinner just right. Too bad Eugenie hadn't done the same for her ladies' contract.

Now what was she to do?

It was Christmas Eve morning, and most of the guests had occupied themselves in the parlor. Her Sugarplum Ladies needed to know of her error. Eugenie had spent the morning having a fascinating discussion with Lord Kent. He was keenly interested in business. Since Eugenie had grown up discussing such things with her father, she'd enjoyed sharing her thoughts with him. And the man genuinely seemed appreciative. She still sorely missed her father, but Lord Kent's presence had brought her some comfort.

Percy emerged from his study. "Eugenie, how is your foot this morning?"

"Improved, but still sore." It was several shades of purple. "But I need to go down to the kitchen and speak to the ladies."

"Certainly." He bent toward her.

She wrapped her arms around Percy's neck as he lifted her from the settee, her heartbeat kicking up a notch. The curls around his collar tickled her hands, and she relished his warm breath against her cheek.

"I'll carry you downstairs just this once, and then you must allow your Sugarplum Ladies to work their magic." Although his voice was stern, she could feel his chest constricting as though he was holding back laughter.

"On my honor, sir, I shall endeavor to remain upstairs thereafter." *Today at least.*

Lord Cheatham laughed. "That's a good girl."

Lady Caroline took her sister's arm and pulled her up from the wing-back chair at the fire, where she was knitting a red-and-navy scarf. "Come on. Let's take a look outside."

"Oh no," Eugenie protested. "Please, Lady Caroline, rest." She'd learned Caroline was expecting her first child.

"She has no intention of resting. If you don't take her to the kitchen, I shall be forced to skate upon yon pond with her." Lord Cheatham pointed toward the wavy frosted window-panes. Across the field, a pond had already frozen over.

Deanna wagged a finger at her brother-in-law. "You'll be skating over there within the hour, so get your warm clothes on, Bard."

One of the servants carried in another armful of wood for the fire as Percy carried Eugenie out into the hall. She could get used to the wonderful feeling of having him so close.

"Your mother and I are going for a jaunt in the sleigh." Father crooked his finger for the servant to come over. "Fetch us our coats, boots, and hats, and have the carriage man hook up my boy's sleigh, would you?"

"Yes, sir."

Percy feigned a scowl at his father as he stopped by the stairs to the kitchen. "I see you feel quite at home here, Father."

"Keep those Sugarplum Ladies feeding him and I shan't be able to get him to return home, dear." Lady Kent rose up on tiptoes to kiss Percy's cheek.

*Oh my.* When should Eugenie tell Percy that her workers would be leaving in several days?

Something was awry with Eugenie besides her aching foot. But Percy knew better, as a barrister, when to push for information and when to wait. For now, he'd be patient.

He returned from downstairs to find several of his servants shoving a pine tree through his front door. "What's this?"

"Lord and Lady Kent requested it."

"In honor of the queen."

Barden looked up from sharpening his borrowed skates. "Queen Victoria does love her Christmas trees."

Percy watched, open-mouthed, as outside, snow floating around them, his mother and father waved from the sleigh. Percy's household had completely gone out of his control.

He'd arranged for an extra rented carriage to be sent from the livery for their travel to church that evening. The Christmas "crackers" had been delivered, with the one specified for Eugenie left empty for him to fill. Percy patted his pocket and grinned. Mother had gifted him with Grandmother's diamond ring, affirming his parents' approval of his and Eugenie's union.

A servant carried in the newspaper and presented it to Percy.

"Thank you."

He sat in the parlor as the others began setting up the tree. When they placed it directly in front of the window, blocking his light, he stood, retaking his ground in his own home. "Bring that to the dining room."

Soon they were gone, leaving the scent of pine, as well as a trail of needles. Percy sighed and opened the Detroit newspaper. Nothing much on the front page. But when he reached the social page, he stilled. Beside a picture of the happy couple was the headline: Horace Ontevreden to Wed Canadian Heiress. His jaw dropped.

"What's wrong?" Bard stood in the parlor entryway, dressed for a blizzard.

Percy shook his head and scanned the article before he began to laugh as he recognized the pseudonym that Miss Menter, the titian-haired street walker, had used. Would such a union be valid? And what would Mr. Ontevreden do when he learned the truth? Sometimes there was justice in the world. The man had been taken in by someone even more scheming than himself.

The Christmas Eve service and the dinner couldn't have gone any better. But only two of Eugenie's helpers could stay past Monday, the day before New Year's Eve. What would 1868 hold? She'd explained the kitchen situation to Percy, who'd seemed most distraught. He'd asked her to meet him in the parlor in a few minutes. With the crutches that the new errand boy, Harry, had found in the barn, she took her time and maneuvered down the hallway. Upstairs, soft conversations continued behind closed doors. A maid moved past her, head down. "Excuse me, milady."

Everyone in the house had become "milady" in the past few days. She'd even heard one of the servants whisper that there might be a new "Lady" in the house soon.

Eugenie paused, clutching her crutches, then took a tentative step on her ankle, which was less swollen and discolored, and only a little painful. The crutches were a blasted nuisance.

Footfalls carried from the parlor, and Percy stood there, hands on hips. Was he so terribly angry with her? He certainly could have been clearer in telling her what he'd wanted with her.

"Can you manage?"

"I think if I walk slowly I'll be better off than with these things." She leaned the crutches against the wall.

Thankfully, both feet felt steady beneath her. She smiled tentatively until she caught Percy's sharp gaze. Was he considering how she was out of his parents' and friends' aristocratic set? The daughter of a businessman. Some businesswoman she was—failing to learn the end date of an agreement.

He held his arm out for her. It was time to go home. But who would help Percy when the ladies left?

The parlor was fully lit, and the cherrywood card table had been opened, with two chairs seated adjacent one another. An inkstand and pen stood at the ready, with a sheet of creamy paper laid out that had a list numbered one through seven with brief notations made afterward. What was going on?

Percy pulled out a chair for her and helped her sit. She adjusted her skirts. "You look like you're about to write a legal brief."

"I am." A smile tugged at his perfect lips. "A contract, since we've gotten this agreement with your Sugarplum Ladies mixed up."

"I'm sorry, Percy—"

He raised his hand as he took his place and dipped the pen into the well.

Eugenie shook her head. "This is truly beyond the pale, to think you would draw up a contract now."

"Eugenie—"

She interrupted him this time. "No. I will not have my ladies losing out on anything you have promised them, not even if I have to stay and perform the duties myself."

Someone hiccupped nearby. "Good idea!" Lord Kent rose, hoisting an empty brandy carafe.

"Father!" Percy rose, but his father gestured for him to sit. "I didn't realize you were lurking there."

"If you don't marry her, you're a fool." He set the crystal container down and stumbled from the room, humming, "On Christmas Day in the Morning."

The color seemed to have drained from Percy's face. "Well, I guess you've discovered Father's little secret hobby too."

Eugenie bit her lip. It wasn't for her to judge.

"At least Father isn't dying, which is what I feared." He quirked an eyebrow at her.

"So his 'illness' is a little more complicated than you thought."

"Quite so." Percy gestured toward the document. "And this has nothing to do with household cooking. Caroline, Deanna, and even Barden have volunteered to help. They did, after all, run an inn in Kansas."

"Oh." She exhaled in relief. Someone had mentioned that to her in explaining how Barden and Caroline had met. "Then what is this about?"

She leaned forward and read the writing scrawled across the top.

*Wherein our petitioner's heart has been stolen by Eugenie Mott of Detroit, Michigan, it is deemed only proper and fitting that Miss Mott shall: 1) Surrender her heart in return, 2) Promise herself evermore to be known as the wife of the petitioner, Percival Gladstone.*

She stopped reading as tears blurred her vision.

Percy dropped down on one knee and took her hand in his. "If you'll agree to my terms, then you shall make the petitioner the happiest barrister in all of the Dominion."

"I will."

Percy slid the ring onto her finger then leaned in. He kissed her so thoroughly that dizziness threatened to overcome her. Thank goodness she was seated else she might have swooned.

Someone clapped in the hallway and then there was a distinct hiccup. As they broke the kiss, Lady and Lord Kent peeked in.

"Does Grandmother's ring fit, darling?"

"Perfectly." Percy raised Eugenie's arm up, the diamond flashing back light from the lamps.

"Wasn't going to ask this now..." Percy's father exchanged a telling look with his wife. "But might a wedding take place before we return home?"

"Yes." Eugenie and Percy's voices joined in agreement.

"You've just given us the best Christmas present." Percy's mother wiped tears from her eyes. "That of seeing our son happy, loved, and living a godly life."

Percy's father nodded in approval. "What every parent wishes for."

Surely that was what her father had wanted for Eugenie when he'd tried to marry her off to Horace. But God's ways really weren't man's ways. She'd never have envisioned the future that was before her now. But God had known all along. And she could trust His plans.

# Author's Notes

This is a fictional story. While there was a Marquessate of Kent, by the time of this story, 1867, there was no Marquess of Kent, as I've titled Percy's father. Similarly, fictional Barden Granville IV didn't inherit any real-life Earldom of Cheatham Hall—which is named for a military base near where I live.

The Historical Society of Michigan's magazine included a story about Detroit socialites who assisted Civil War widows in learning to make a living by catering. That article inspired this story. While I "borrowed" the Mott name, I have no indication that the Mott family was involved in this venture. Eugenie was named for and inspired by the beautiful Austrian princess Eugenie. I also had a great-aunt by the name of Eugenia.

The Detroit and Windsor areas did have a huge influx of both escaped slaves on the Underground Railroad and post-Civil War freed African-Americans. Unfortunately, many people had been separated from their family members, some to parts unknown. So both households in my story have African-American servants being reunited with family members.

Many of the unusual recipes or food preparation activities are from *Worbly's Magazine* of 1867. Thank you to the writers who have revived the *Worbly's Magazine* for modern readers.

Readers will recognize many characters from my other stories who make appearances here in this novella—some from *My Heart Belongs on Mackinac Island: Maude's Mooring*, some from *Seven Brides for Seven Mail-Order Husbands*, and some from my debut in Christian fiction *Return to Shirley Plantation*. Also, a number of new characters from this novella will appear in my novella, *"Love's Beacon,"* in Barbour's *The Great Lakes Lighthouse Brides Collection*, releasing November 2018.

ECPA bestselling author **Carrie Fancett Pagels**, Ph.D., is the award-winning author of fifteen Christian historical romances. Twenty-five years as a psychologist didn't "cure" her overactive imagination! A self-professed "history geek," she resides with her family in the Historic Triangle of Virginia but grew up as a "Yooper" in Michigan's Upper Peninsula. Carrie loves to read, bake, bead, and travel—but not all at the same time! You can connect with her at www.CarrieFancettPagels.com.

# Paper Snowflake Christmas

by Vanessa Riley

# Chapter 1

*Framlingham, England*
*December 20, 1837*

Having bartered with Providence one too many times, Ophelia Hanover knew she was on her own. It was up to her to keep Lord Litton from taking her son.

And there Litton was, standing at her door, shivering in the cold, knocking snowflakes from his hat brim.

"Took you long enough to answer." The earl stepped into her home.

Her heart stumbled and stopped. The only reason Litton would be at Norring Hall today would be to take custody of Joshua. *No. No. No.* To keep from falling apart, she gripped her elbows, holding tight to the soft Mechlin lace of her shawl. "You've come too soon. We agreed you'd come after Christmas. That's five days from now."

The earl marched past her in a coat covered with snow. He left her to voice her complaints to the paneling in the entry.

Though he carried himself with a slight limp, he barreled through the hall as if he foreclosed upon her modest estate, tracking slushy snow onto the burgundy carpet of her late husband's study. Something that would have wearied her poor departed Benjamin's nerves.

"Madame, I never agreed to delay my visit. My note said I would consider your request, but I fear the weather will degrade over the holiday. I had to come now."

Her breath caught at the finality of his words and stuck deeper in her throat. No more smiles sailing paper boats. No more wiping tears from a costly tumble. No more keeping Joshua safe.

Litton trudged past the grand pianoforte and plopped into Benjamin's chair, the snow surely ruining the velvet covering.

"You can't barge in here. You don't own Norring, or me, or my son."

He fussed with the buttons on his coat. "Didn't say I did."

Wet wool was not good for a man who had been ill. The snow matted on his collar would give him a chill. Wondering why she'd care about the man charged with taking her son, she pressed at her brow. "Lord Litton, let me dry your cloak by the fire."

He lifted his face and exposed a short scar on his temple. "No thank you. I don't intend to stay long. It's a four-hour ride back to London. Waiting will allow this weather to grow worse."

"Stay until the storm passes then enjoy the offerings of Framlingham. St. Michael's church is very fine. It's from the fifteenth century. The bells and the organ—"

"I didn't come for a tour, Mrs. Hanover. I'm here for my ward." Litton motioned to the chair opposite him. "Please, sit. There are documents you must sign."

The commanding tone in his voice made her drop into the chair. She sat almost breathless on the other side of the mahogany desk.

"Nice to see that you do listen, Mrs. Hanover. The last time we met, you were not to be reasoned with."

Every ungenerous thought crossed her mind. He'd caused all the problems between them, but she was in no position to stir more ill will. She watched how he curled his fingers—closed, open, closed, open. "Are you not fully recovered from your accident?"

He slammed his hand onto the desk then grimaced as if he'd shot himself in the foot. "If you're wishing I'd died in my horse racing folly, I can assure you I'm quite well."

How could he think her so cold? She tugged on the fringe of her shawl as if it were the only thing keeping her grounded. "I've prayed for your recovery, sir, and for your change of heart. My wishes for your health and my son's happiness are not opposing."

An I-don't-believe-you smile filled his face. "I sounded haughty, my dear widow." He loosened his scarf. "We can be civil. I owe that to Benjamin. He was my dearest friend for a long time. God rest my cousin's soul."

What of her suffering? "Nothing for me, your cousin's widow, mother to Joshua Hanover. Whom you've never seen, not even at his christening? Now you've come to steal him from me."

"Now you're being harsh."

Ophelia pinched her wrist and focused on the pain to keep from crying. "This is hard. It's too soon, my lord. I need these five days with my son."

He tossed his top hat onto the desk and raked ice crystals from his auburn hair. "It's hard for me to be here. And you know very well why I couldn't come while Benjamin was alive. You. You and a mistaken kiss beneath a Jamaican moonlit sky."

Ophelia dipped her head, wishing for a hole to open, to swallow him, maybe spit him across the sea. "You blame me for our past? I was a joke to you. You kissed me on a dare, like you'd done hundreds of others. Benjamin said so."

The earl sank back in the chair. "Not hundreds. Dozens, maybe. And you were never a joke."

Litton's indigo eyes that had seemed cold now held an uncomfortable warmth. "I wouldn't be here if Benjamin hadn't died and left detailed instructions as to how his son was to be educated."

"I'm sorry you two quarreled. Benjamin needed you, especially in his last days. The will was written when he wasn't in a stable mind-set, probably under the duress of his mother. She knew Benjamin was ill and manipulated him."

Folding his arms, Litton released a sigh that almost covered a moan. "I won't debate the will's origins. The papers are valid, the provisions explicit."

She pinched herself again. The light skin of her wrist now held a purple bruise, and the weight of unspent tears made her eyes sting. She was close to a crying jag.

"Your solicitors should've prepared you, ma'am. Don't look so weepy-eyed. I'm immune to such missish sentiment."

One raise of her gaze caught Lord Litton glaring at her. If his cheek bore the imprint of her palm, he'd look the same as seven years ago when she'd slapped him for his duplicity.

"Lord Litton, I know you think ill of me, but I planned a good holiday for Joshua. Norring was in mourning last year when his father passed. Stay for Christmas, and I promise to make Joshua's leaving less strained."

Shaking his head, he fingered a tattoo carved into the polished desk. "That's not a promise you can keep, Ophelia."

"It's Mrs. Hanover. My little boy just turned six. This is such a special time. He's growing—"

He nodded as if he listened, but she didn't sense he was. Just another weepy female to him. A sorry joke.

The earl whipped off his gloves, reached into his pouch, and tugged out papers. "Mrs. Hanover, I could have come two weeks ago and removed him the night of his birthday. I thought I could wait until the new year, but my plans have changed. I want the boy settled as soon as possible."

"I thought you came early because of the weather?"

"Yes, but I also wish to have my household in order. During my long convalescence, I've reconsidered my life and found it lacking." His face paled, jaw trembling as he straightened his posture.

The begrudged caregiver inside responded to his pain. "Let me dry your coat or get you a warmed towel for your back."

"A new delaying tactic? Feigned sympathy?" Taking a small breath, he stretched his arms. "I've drafted additional monies for your settlement. You do understand money? I believe that's been part of the contention between us."

Ophelia had paid most of her fortune to employ any legal trick to slow Litton down, hoping he'd bore of his role as guardian. But nothing had deterred him. Nothing ever had.

He pushed papers to her. "I'm not the villain. Read the new settlement. Reading is the only type of risk I remember you willing to take."

"I don't like your wagers or these English rules. In Jamaica, children aren't ripped from their mother."

"Tsk." He clicked his tongue. "Still too sentimental when it comes to me?" The earl yanked the papers away and made a show of unfolding them. "Your solicitor has reviewed this with mine. You have a more generous settlement. Sign it then give me Joshua. The boy and I will beat the winter storm back to London. You can begin your new life. Aunt says there are plenty of suitors to keep you company."

"Did she also say I have no interest? Tell her I will never marry again."

Lines pinched his forehead. "That sounds like a challenge, a sweet dare. Will the widow, or won't she?"

Why did she let him goad her into saying something he'd twist up? She lifted her palm and spread her fingers. "Stop. I'm not a joke. Will nothing change your mind?"

He tapped his temple, scar and all. "It's stone, ma'am."

"Given your accident, you should be open to change."

Watching the lift of his eyebrow, she tensed, awaiting the cutting remark he never uttered.

Frustrated, she moved from the desk and navigated between the wets spots he'd created. Opening the crimson curtains, she glanced out the window. Snow blanketed her garden of crisply cut boxwood shrubs. The fountain in the center dangled icicles like diamond earrings. The next wintery gust made them dance and sparkle. She didn't think she could love any place as much as tropical Saint Ann Parish. But after seven years in Framlingham, the cold still enchanted. Joshua loved Norring in winter. How could there be a Christmas without her son?

"Is the weather still holding or has the storm worsened?"

"It's snowing a little, Lord Litton."

The window fogged from her breath and reflected the earl checking his pocket watch, probably counting the seconds before he left with Joshua.

"Time's wasting, Mrs. Hanover. Or are you trying to keep me? That's a change."

His voice surrounded her like a soft, fuzzy scarf, one tied too tight, and it strangled. Why did he torment her, hinting at their past? Yet, could the past be a way to change his mind? "You still like dares, Lord Litton?"

"Yes."

"I dare you to stay at Norring and prove me a horrid influence."

"Why, Mrs. Hanover, you are bold." His chuckles started slow, dripping like an icicle, then sped to a dangerous flood.

His warm tone roped a memory trapped in her chest and yanked it free. She saw Litton laughing in a tree she'd teased him to climb, climbing high, bending boughs, dropping coconuts. His deep voice had teased questions of her goals, her duty to her father, and the mystery of love.

Ophelia put a hand to her bosom and shoved the memory into a vault and buried the key.

Her history with Litton was as much at fault of ruining Christmas as Benjamin's will. Her little boy couldn't leave. She prayed and purposed to work harder at building a truce with the earl. It was the only way to keep Joshua safe.

# Chapter 2

Geoffrey Landson, the Earl of Litton, stretched in his late cousin's chair and stared at the widow. Ophelia didn't seem anything like what his aunt said. Not mercenary or hunting for a new marriage. No, she was very much like the girl he'd known in Jamaica. Could it be she truly cared for the child?

He bristled at the notion of softening toward her and sank a little more into the chair's cushions. The four-hour carriage ride had worn on his back more than he wanted to show. "Will you stand at the window until Christmas or will you retrieve Joshua?"

"Reconsider leaving, my lord. It looks very cold in my park. I'd hate for your grooms to freeze waiting for you. Perhaps you should hurry to them and return for Joshua in the spring."

"You want to drag out the anticipation of seeing me again? Anticipation was catnip for you, as I recall." He chuckled and opened his coat more. "I wish this was easier."

"Easy?" She turned and faced him. "Do you want me to beg? I will. If you want another apology, I'll do that too. I'll take full blame for the past."

"That's a mighty change of heart. What will you say next?"

"You think me low, but I'm not the one ripping a boy from his home and taking him to be with strangers for Christmas."

He was being ungenerous, but who was to be believed, his loving aunt or the woman he'd ruined himself over? Geoffrey put his hands behind his head and gazed at the coffered ceilings. "You're searching for a villain, Mrs. Hanover. Sometimes there isn't one."

"There has to be one, Litton. Else, why would two good people keep hurting each other?"

He gaped at her logic, her self-control in the face of adversity, her shiny ebony hair bobbing at her neck. Against his will, he marveled at how her pale gold skin made an out-of-fashion bronze-colored gown seem beautiful and stylish. She could be eighteen again, not five and twenty.

Geoffrey tapped the settlement papers. "My aunt, the boy's—Joshua's—grandmother is anxious to have him about."

"Wilhelmina Hanover has the makings of a villain. She has never visited nor invited us to town. Neither of you responded to my correspondences when I asked for assistance with Benjamin. You could have urged him to take more care. You might've spared my son the loss of his father."

The unanswered letters at his London townhouse—no, he could not trust his mind, addled with laudanum and pain, to think of her. "You did write me, Oph—Mrs. Hanover, but I couldn't risk. . . You and I—"

Her eyes bloomed like a sunflower chasing the morn. "This isn't about Joshua at all. This is punishment for a girl who wouldn't elope with a boy who kissed her on a dare. One she watched sail away from Saint Ann Parish's port when he couldn't be honest."

Ophelia had watched him leave Jamaica? But hadn't she said she thought nothing of him? A smile found his lips. "You did say you'd beg. But now you're reinventing history?"

Hand on hip, she moved back to the desk. "It doesn't matter what you think of me. The only thing that matters is Joshua."

"I'll let nothing happen to him. I know Benjamin wanted his son integrated into society and to have the education he'd had."

"I want this too, when he's older and more prepared to hear the slurs people will throw at him, like 'half-breed.' They will come." She tugged on her shawl as if that would cover the ugly word used for mulatto people. "Do you know what it's like to protect him?"

There was a sense of pleading in her teak eyes that Geoffrey couldn't answer. Instead, he riffled through the desk, sorting through Benjamin's lighter, his crisp blue stationery, and a pair of sharp shears. "Ah, ink and a quill."

He slid the papers back to her. "You'll see the settlement has increased to five thousand pounds." His aunt had assured him that this amount would buy Ophelia's signature.

She picked up the pages and tossed them at him. "I won't sign. You're misguided to think any payment is enough for my son." She put her hand up as if to silence him. "You're wrong. The Earl of Litton is wrong."

"Still a spitfire, Oph. . .Mrs. Hanover. I love how you can stand there in want of more money and act the victim. I suppose my aunt underestimated your price."

Shoulders quivering, she closed her eyes and mumbled something that sounded like a prayer. *God, where are You? Why can't I feel You near?* She took a deep breath then caught his gaze. "Litton," she said in a voice fainter than before, "my dowry, which paid the taxes and the repairs on Norring Hall, was three times this amount. Why offer payment at all? To assuage your guilt?"

"This is somewhat a widow's pension. A little something to dangle for your next situation."

She tugged on her collar. "I told you I will never marry again. And I have nothing left to barter with. No more legal tactics. I'm begging you to let Joshua stay a little longer. A few more days. I've a special surprise for him. We could have an early Christmas. The decorations could be put out tonight. Norring will be dressed for a celebration. Then I'll drop him to you in the city. You can show me where he is to live."

Geoffrey leaned back in the chair again and drummed his fingers along the polished arms. "I want Joshua settled into my household before I announce my engagement."

Her mouth opened wide. The wobble in her fingers became more pronounced. "You're building a family and taking my son to complete it. You cruel, wicked man."

Tears gushed from her eyes. She backed away from the outstretched handkerchief he dug from his waistcoat. Her grief sounded authentic, but surely not. . . "Mrs. Hanover."

She waved him off but kept sobbing. Lonely, thick tears.

It grieved his soul. How was he to honor his renewed commitment to live right if he made a poor widow cry? What of his promise to be a new man, to be used of the Lord if only he could walk again?

It was an effort to rise, but Geoffrey couldn't let this continue. Maybe he was a villain. He pushed his stiff limbs until he was at her side and placed his hand on her shoulder. His fingers tangled in the softness of her hair. "Ophelia, I'm sorry."

The door to the study burst open. "Mrs. Hanover, what has that brute done to you?" The redheaded Mrs. Gilmore entered swinging a broom handle. "Get your good-for-nothing mitts off her."

He moved backward, trying hard not to make a jerking motion. "Nothing is amiss. Lay down your arms."

"No, dearest," Ophelia said as she clasped the end of the broom. "The earl has done nothing to me. He's merely intent on taking Joshua today."

Mrs. Gilmore lowered her sweeping weapon. "No. It's not Christmas yet. The decorating. The storm outside. No."

Ophelia pulled her housekeeper into an embrace. "We have no choice."

Geoffrey slunk back and sat atop the desk, slowing his motion to keep his spine from stiffening. The wrong lift, too sudden a move, could make his limbs lock up, and he'd drop everything as his arm lost its strength. A leftover punishment from his stupid dare with a duke. "If you need an hour or so, Mrs. Hanover, you may have that, but Joshua and I must leave before the snowstorm rages."

"You'd risk traveling in worsening conditions?" She wiped her face with her shawl. "Despite the ill will between us, Lord Litton, I mean this. You are welcome to stay. I couldn't bear you having another carriage accident. I surely do not want Joshua's safety at risk in any way."

The look in her wet irises—not quite loving, but far from hate or indifference—indicated a measure of concern. Her eyes raised too many questions, ones he'd thought he no longer cared to know. In Jamaica, had she loved him too? Why did she go through with marrying Benjamin? No, those questions need never be answered.

He tapped the desk. "Then we must leave now. Ready the boy. You can sign the papers when you come down."

"I won't sign your bribe." She lifted her chin and moved to the door of the study. "Mrs. Gilmore, get the earl some tea and sweet biscuits. Dessert will keep him company while I finish Joshua's packing."

Ophelia remembered his fondness for treats. What else had stayed on her mind?

Mrs. Gilmore frowned as she picked up the broom again. "As you wish."

The housekeeper left, and it seemed as if Ophelia wilted, her shoulders drooping.

"You look as if you are about to fall to pieces, Mrs. Hanover. Fighting is draining." He glanced at the fire, which spit out little heat. The coals were sparse. "I know the solicitor's fees have been heavy. Sign the settlement. I will not deprive you of income."

"Burn those papers, my lord. I'll do nothing to accept this separation as permanent. No offer will be a sop for your conscience."

Pulling to his feet, he followed her to the door then forced his weak arm to clasp her elbow. "I'm concerned about your welfare."

"No, Litton. I'll never be fooled so easily, not again. There aren't Jamaican moons in Framlingham."

He released her and watched her pick up her skirts and sail up the hall stairs. Pumping his hand, he worked the muscles that had stiffened in the cool air of the study. If he were still a man given to danger, he'd stay at Norring and determine the truth about the good widow's situation. Maybe when she came down, he'd find a way to resolve their tension. But if not, he'd still live up to his promises and honor his cousin's will.

# Chapter 3

Outside of her son's room, Ophelia brushed tears from her eyes. She'd been preparing Joshua to leave Norring but never thought it would be before Christmas. Litton had his revenge. This was the second time he'd broken her heart.

She inhaled deeply the cooked fat scent of the cheaper tallow candles of the upper hall. Bright white expensive beeswax ones should have been lit for Joshua to make his last day feel a little like Christmas. If only she'd known.

With dried eyes, she focused on the paintings of brave Hanover men framed in gilded boxes lining the walls. Her Joshua would be one of those men, brave and strong. That is, if he didn't carry in his body his father's illness.

She pushed her son's door open and found him playing with his blocks. "What is it you're making today? A castle like the Norman one in the center of town?"

The boy's curly sable locks bounced as he nodded. His tongue tipped out to the corner of his mouth as he concentrated on balancing one blond block upon another. "Almost done, Mama."

The high windows of Framlingham Castle would hang wreaths Christmas day. St. Michaels would too. Her son would miss it all. "Joshua, your cousin, the Earl of Litton, has come."

The boy did not look up.

She cleared her throat. "The earl is the man your papa wanted you to live with."

"No!" Joshua shrieked and fell onto the floor, pounding his little fists. "Why? Why. . .do I have to. . .Mama?" His voice had become choppy with long breathy sobs, the kind that cut her insides up.

"I. . .don't. . .want. . .to go. Don't. . .make. . .me."

She sank down upon the emerald-colored rug and scooped up her son. "You're not a baby. You're a big boy, and big boys do what they must, not what they wish."

He kicked at his castle, knocking blocks everywhere. "This is Papa's fault for dying."

"No, dearest. He'd be with us if he could." Ophelia said the words, but even she wasn't convinced. The man had grown more restless, riding his horses at night at top speeds, leaving for days without sending word. "Let's hope he's found peace."

Joshua jumped up, bunching up his blue pinafore in his hand. The garb's pleats matched those of her gown. That was wrong. It was more than time to breech Joshua, to give him the ceremony of transitioning from a babe's robe to pantaloons like a man. She'd planned to do it at Christmas, but Litton would have to. She'd miss it and so much more of Joshua's life.

The remaining pieces of her insides shredded. The peace in her heart couldn't help but leak out, pooling in her eyes. "I said I wasn't going to weep. I'm not doing a good job at being strong."

"Mama's the strongest."

She wasn't, but she'd pretend for Joshua. She hugged him deeply to her bosom. "Know that I don't want this. The Court of Chancery, all these English men, tell me I have no choice. The whole country is being run by a girl not yet twenty. Soldiers obey Queen Victoria, but the law says I can't raise you." She put her palms to Joshua's face, squishing his chubby cheeks. "Listen to Lord Litton. Show him the wonderful boy that makes me so proud."

"Yes, Mama." He brushed at his chin, wiping the droplets streaming down.

With a kiss to his brow, Ophelia stood and pulled the shiny brass handle on the trunk, opening the roomy brown box she'd already half-filled with clothes and toys. "Put your blocks in here. I'll take down your mobile."

She moved to his big pine bed and spun the mobile she'd created from papier-mâché stars of gold and silver. "I'll get my scissors from the study to cut this free."

"No, Mama. Don't take it down. That would mean I'm not coming back."

She twirled the mobile again, and it made a sweeping revolution. "It will be here waiting for you. This separation can't be forever."

He tossed a block into the trunk. The lid slammed shut, barely missing his fingers.

"Joshua!" She covered her mouth and went to him. "You have to take care. You could hurt yourself. You could bleed." She put a hand to her mouth to stop any more fears from being said aloud.

"I don't want to go, Mama. Who will take care of you?"

With care, she reopened the trunk and stared at the toys and clothes, the precious treasures that spoke of a young boy growing and learning. "God will keep me. And He'll keep you. You have to go live with Lord Litton. You will get to know your grandmother. They are. . .good. . ." She made a loud swallow. "Good people."

"Are you dying like Papa? Is that why you are sending me away?"

"No, dearest. I'm quite healthy, but sending you away is breaking me."

He threw his arms about her neck. "I knew you were hurt."

"I'm praying for a miracle. I'll get another solicitor. I'll find the money to fight for you. Know when you're away, you're never far from my heart. Let no one tell you I don't love you or that I've forgotten you. Those are lies."

The boy shrieked again, and now they both were sobbing.

She patted his head, mussing up his hair something awful. "You're brave, Joshua Hanover. I need you to be even braver. It takes courage to be good when everything is wrong."

"Mrs. Gilmore said we should run."

"We aren't criminals. We are Hanovers, and you have my people's, my mama's blood too. That means we are stronger than most."

Forcing a smile, Ophelia stood and took Joshua's hand. "Let's go meet the earl."

When she opened the door, Lord Litton stood there, mouth open. "Downstairs wasn't an act. You really do love the boy."

Releasing Joshua's fingers, she swung her arm and came very close to swatting Litton. "You're spying? Did someone dare you to seek out my weak moments?"

The earl rubbed his neck. "I heard the boy's screams. I came to make sure all was well."

"You thought I hurt him?" She lowered her tone, but Joshua wasn't deaf. "Your opinion of me is low, sir. Very low."

"No, Ophelia." The earl's face held a sheepish grin. "I don't move quickly anymore, for anyone. I merely wanted to be of aid. In the new year, my household will be set. You'll visit."

She turned to her son. "Joshua, this is Lord Litton. You will meet with him formally downstairs. Go to my room. There's a box under my bed; please bring it."

The boy wiped his eyes and shot from the room as if he'd been propelled by a flintlock.

Ophelia tugged on the earl's onyx greatcoat, moving him into her son's room, then closed the door. "I don't know what lies your aunt has told you, but she doesn't want to see my face at her celebrations. Though she'll see it, and my late husband's, every time she looks at Joshua."

Litton clasped her hand. "I'd never tire of your face. I'm serious. You will visit."

"Your bride won't want me to." Ophelia stepped over an errant block and teetered into the closet. She pulled out a folded pinafore, but balled it up. Once breeched, Joshua wouldn't need it. "Your countess will not want me or any woman of my situation underfoot."

"It will be my choice."

He surely didn't understand how marriage worked and what was necessary to keep peace. "If you say so." She turned too quickly and tripped over a block. The earl caught her before she smashed headlong into the trunk.

"I said I don't move so quickly for just anyone." He winced as he towed her upright. "I haven't picked my bride yet. But I've narrowed the selection to two suitable candidates."

Ophelia clung to his lapels to keep from floating off like a hot air balloon, one heated with fear for Joshua. "Your choice is a marriage of convenience? Oh, Geoffrey, don't marry unless you are sure."

Those indigo eyes of his perked up, and his signature grin returned. "You said my given name, like an old friend. Nice to know you care for my domestic happiness."

She pushed from his arms and tried to fan the heat rising in her cheeks. "Joshua's happiness is my only concern. Do you know how horrible it would be for him to be caught in the tensions of a new marriage, particularly one not formed of love?"

"Did you mean caught *again*?"

She opened her mouth then shut it. Sounds of her marriage—uneven laughter, unexpected words, unhinged door slams—returned. A union that should have been everything eroded when sickness took control. "You have time, Lord Litton. You've the luxury to find love. Deep, unwavering love."

The earl grinned more. "You are concerned about me."

Ophelia wanted to correct him, but Joshua returned carrying a box almost twice his size. He bounced like a happy puppy. "Mama, what is it?"

"Something very special. You and the earl will open it in London."

The disappointment in her wee boy's face made her head hurt. She pivoted, closed the trunk, and set the box atop it. "Go down to Papa's study; get your father's blue stationery. You will use it to write me."

The boy wiped his cheek with his sleeve and headed for the hall. "I thought you'd make paper boats out of it."

"Not without you. And, Joshua, don't touch the scissors or the sharp letter opener."

His big brown eyes went wide. "I'll be careful."

When the boy slipped from view, she retrieved the box and handed it to Litton. "Before the new year, get your aunt and fiancé and make a big celebration of this."

He put his hand on the lid and pried it up. "The boy's first skeleton suit. The smart cut of the coat will make Joshua look very well. He'll be the envy of other six year olds."

A smile lifted Ophelia's lips as she imagined how happy her son would be. "I sewed them, for he's my priority. Have his celebration before you marry."

"I'm sure my new bride will dote upon him."

Headache pounding, she folded her arms beneath her creamy shawl. "How do you know? You haven't selected her. I'll fret every day, wondering if she's mean to him. Joshua's quiet. He may not tell you how much something hurts."

"He's like his mother then. Does the boy hold grudges too?"

"Take the trunk—"

"Ophelia, I'd never have fully believed how difficult this was upon you without seeing for myself. My aunt hasn't been kind."

"Your aunt thinks I'm cold, but she knows the fears of a mother. She, of all people, knew Benjamin's condition. She could have warned me of how his sickness would take a toll on his mind."

"The bleeding? The uncontrollable bleeding? I thought he grew out of it."

"Never, and he became more and more reckless." She put a hand to her hip. "Complaining to you about risk is nonsensical. You like dares, and the more dangerous, the better."

He leaned against the wall with a grimace forming on his countenance. "Yes, but my racing accident gave me a great deal of time to think. I'm more careful now."

She didn't believe him, and a thousand more fears ran through her mind. "Take this trunk downstairs."

The earl's mouth flattened to a line as he turned to the door. "I'll send my steward up for it." He grasped his arm as he headed into the hall. "My strength isn't quite what it was."

If they were still friends, she'd inquire more about his health. Instead, she'd remember him as she knelt in prayer. "Make sure Joshua doesn't have scissors."

He nodded, and Ophelia closed the door. Sliding down it, she melted in a puddle of fear, fear for her boy. Joshua would be the ward of a man who could be careless and a bride who could be heartless. And a poor marriage would make Geoffrey suffer too. *Another miracle, Lord, just one more, not for myself but for Geoffrey and Joshua.* They needed to grow close, to listen and care for each other. This was her new prayer.

But God was silent in her heart.

Rubbing her temples, she purposed to figure out how to make this closeness occur.

Geoffrey dragged down the stairs as Joshua climbed them. In the middle, they met. "Joshua Hanover, I am pleased to meet you. I'm your cousin, Geoffrey Landson, the Earl of Litton."

The boy, who bore more of a swarthy tan coloring, darker than Ophelia, stared in Geoffrey's direction with large hazel eyes.

"So, you want me to live with you?"

"Yes, Joshua."

The boy nodded. "May I go to my mama, sir?"

"Yes."

Joshua continued up the stairs, his little legs wobbling in the drape of the pinafore.

This wasn't going to be easy. Though Ophelia hadn't poisoned her son against the family, he seemed to have his mind made up. Geoffrey was on the side of villainy, probably next to Napoleon. No, this wasn't going to be easy at all.

Stretching, Geoffrey slipped into the study and remembered how anxious Ophelia sounded. Everything felt wrong. Lord, am I doing Your will? Is my life available to You?

The door to the study pushed open with a bang.

Mrs. Gilmore carried a teacup and a plate of chocolate-dipped biscuits. She stomped past him and set the tray down on the desk with a thunk. "Tea, your lordship."

"No hemlock, ma'am?"

The housekeeper folded her burly arms. "That would be too good for you."

"I don't know what Mrs. Hanover has said, but I am executing the will of my cousin."

"She hasn't mentioned you, but I hear her cries. How could you think of taking a boy from his mother?" The woman dished a biscuit onto a fine china plate and shoved it at him. "Here. I think you should choke on it. Making Mrs. Hanover give up her boy is bad, but before Christmas is horrible. She should've run." She put her hand to her mouth. "I shouldn't have said that."

"I suspected as much. That is one of the reasons I've come early. Tell me, Mrs. Gilmore, why is Hanover's will so specific? I am to take to custody of the boy at age six and ensure he is educated at London's St. Mary's church until age thirteen. Then off to Eton. Why would my cousin be so exact in this matter unless he had doubts of Mrs. Hanover's care? Was Mrs. Hanover a faithful wife? My aunt says there have been suitors even before her time of mourning was done."

The woman fumbled with her apron. "Mrs. Hanover was a saint of a wife and a good mother. She can't help if fortune hunters come for her. She'd raise the young master to be a fine man if given the chance. You'd see for yourself, if you weren't so set against her."

The woman didn't curtsy as she backed out of the room, slamming the door.

As much as Geoffrey wanted to be on the road to outrun the storm, a feeling of injustice settled on him, constricting like a tight bandage. He was so sure of his plans. His aunt was explicit in the neglect she felt the boy had endured. The nature of the will seemed to cement Geoffrey's actions. Could he have let his history with Ophelia blind him to the truth?

A vision of her unopened letters stacked on the mantel of his London townhouse returned, amplifying his guilt. Believing the letters were personal, a temptation to their brief past, he'd left them unanswered. He should have read them. Perhaps he'd think differently about Ophelia. Perhaps he'd not have been so ready to believe the worst.

The door to the study opened. Ophelia entered, clutching the box in one hand and Joshua's hand in the other. "The trunk upstairs is ready for your steward. Joshua says you met on the stairs."

"Yes, we'll become more familiar with each other on our long carriage ride."

"Joshua, go see if Mrs. Gilmore has a final treat for you."

The boy didn't hesitate. He ran.

Geoffrey sat on his cousin's desk, scooped up a biscuit and munched it whole, then wiped his mouth clean. "Seems I've judged you more harshly than you deserve."

She stepped to him with reddened eyes. "Are you still taking my Joshua to a strange place and marrying a woman who could be careless with his life?"

"Yes, but I'm not a villain either. Can we agree upon this? I will take care of Joshua."

She poked him in the lapel. "I'm not bereft of hope for my son. I should be, for all the unanswered prayers I offered for Benjamin or the ones for you when I received word of your accident. At least those were heard. You're walking."

Geoffrey caught her fingers and clasped her hand to his chest. "Ophelia, I'll let nothing happen to him. You have my word."

She looked up with such hurt in her eyes that his chest stung. "Yes, but what is that worth, Lord Litton? You're the man who crashed his gig on a dare. The man who'd kiss a girl on a dare."

She pulled free and moved to the door. "Let me help Joshua with his gloves. Excuse me."

He watched her drift away, her chin lifted with a dignity that didn't equate to the treachery his aunt painted. He'd let his own disappointments and the legal wrangling color his opinion. Perhaps he should have tried harder to visit sooner to determine the truth.

What's done was done. He tied on his scarf, scooped up his hat, and went to the hall.

Ophelia sat on the stairs with Joshua.

The little boy shook his fist in Geoffrey's direction. "Mama, how will you put up the fir decorations? I'm big enough to go get them from the woods. That was Papa's job, and now there's no man to do it."

Her lips held a small smile, but it was false. Her teak eyes held no light, just sadness. He remembered how clear and joy-filled they'd once been, offering hints of blue and gold. That was how he'd known her behind her mask at the masquerade ball seven years ago. How he knew her joy when they kissed.

"Joshua, don't fret about me. Draw a picture in your heart of how Norring will look for Christmas. The fir branches and white candles on all the mantels. Cinnamon will scent the halls. It will be like it was before your papa's. . . Wish for it to be beautiful."

"It won't be." The boy wrapped his arms about her neck. "We won't be together. Papa would be so sad for us."

Mrs. Gilmore had returned with a handkerchief affixed to her face.

Stomach twisting, Geoffrey walked to the entry door. "We should be going. I'll send a note when we arrive in London. Perhaps we can arrange a visit in the spring. You can see how well-adjusted Joshua is."

She nodded, picked the boy up, and walked him over to Geoffrey, placing the teary-eyed child into his good arm. "You make sure he has the ceremony we talked about and a good Christmas walk. He loves church bells."

The doors to Norring opened. His steward, Smithers, entered along with a very blue footman. Before they could get the doors shut, a pile of snow blew into the hall.

"Lord Litton," Smithers said. "The River Orr has frozen the bridge to Norring. It's completely iced over. No footing for the horses. The clouds are low and thick. We'll have no visibility on the road. We're not going to be able to leave."

The relief steaming in Geoffrey's chest surprised him. The revelations of the past hour—Ophelia's concerns, the possibility of Joshua being stricken with the blood sickness his cousin bore—had shaken his resolve. "I'll endanger no one, even if it means delaying my plans. If that is well with you, madame. Mrs. Hanover, may I and my servants stay?"

"Of course, Lord Litton. I would suffer no one in this storm." Her voice was almost gleeful. "Norring is small, but there is plenty of room here."

He returned the child to Ophelia's arms.

Her face lit with such relief. She rocked Joshua, hugging him as if he'd been rescued from the grim reaper.

Wanting to see for himself how bad the conditions, Geoffrey slapped his beaver-trimmed hat tighter onto his skull, went to the entry door, and cracked it open. Ice pelted his face, wiggling its way between the folds of his scarf. "We probably won't be leaving in the morning either."

Resigned, he closed the door. "The storm I tried to beat has beaten me, Mrs. Hanover. No one is leaving Norring for at least two days."

He turned and saw the boy smiling. "You were right, Mama. God does answer prayer."

"Sometimes, baby. Your prayers must be in His ears each night. Mrs. Gilmore, take my son, settle him in my room, and prepare his for Lord Litton. His people can find rooms in the upper levels, the servants' quarters."

"With those big ears of his, the earl should be grabbed by them and turned out into the snow, Mrs. Hanover." The housekeeper's whisper was loud.

Smithers spun and looked at Geoffrey, but he could do nothing but wait on his hostess.

Ophelia shook her head. "I'll hear no more of it. These are our guests and there is room. Joshua, go with Mrs. Gilmore."

"Yes, Mama." Joshua grabbed Mrs. Gilmore's hand and bounced up the stairs.

Geoffrey took off his gloves as Ophelia directed Smithers and the groom to follow the housekeeper.

Soon all was quiet in the hall, leaving Geoffrey alone with the unusual Mrs. Hanover.

Ophelia was all smiles, maybe the first he'd seen since he arrived.

The tightness in his chest started again, but he had to make sure she understood that a delay was not a change of plans. "Mrs. Hanover, as soon as the roads are good enough for travel, I will leave with Joshua. We won't be here for Christmas."

"I know, but I have another day or two with my boy. You'll never know what that means.

I'll go see to dinner."

She left as he struggled to pull off his wet coat. Staying in Framlingham wasn't his plan, but learning the truth about Mrs. Hanover and the goings-on of Norring Hall might aid in coming to an understanding in rearing Joshua. That had to be for everyone's good. If they were lucky, he and Ophelia could find a way to forgive one another for a dare taken at a masquerade ball under a Jamaican moon.

# Chapter 5

Ophelia crept to the door of her bedchamber in rhythm to Joshua's snores. The little boy slept snuggled in blankets beneath the sheer drapes of her canopy bed. If she had time, she'd make a mobile of green wreaths and holly berries to enchant him when he awoke.

With a full heart, she moved into the hall of portraits and closed the door. She lifted her palms, thumbs touching, to make a frame. Could she decorate up here too, so that Joshua woke up to a beautiful Christmas-like morn?

"Planning to paint the walls, Mrs. Hanover? Burn the portraits of my ancestors?"

Litton's voice.

Hand on hip, she turned. "I'm wondering if I have enough garlands and ribbons to deck the sconces. This is Joshua's last Christmas here. I want it to be as special as his father had it."

"The storm can't go on for five days. We will be gone before Christmas Eve."

"It may take time for the roads to thaw and clear." She rushed to him and clasped his arm. "Oh please, Litton. Don't rush back. I know you are set in your ways, but it is no loss to be cautious."

He glanced down at her, but she saw no hope. His eyes were too filled with pity.

She instantly released his stylish chestnut-colored tailcoat and stepped away. "Sorry, my lord." She went to Joshua's door. "Now that you've finished your meal, you'll stay in my son's room. I had Mrs. Gilmore place one of Benjamin's robes and sleep shirts inside."

He folded his thick arms. "Tell me why my cousin's will takes the boy away from you at such a young age. Was your marriage a happy one?"

She didn't want Litton's pity or his prying. "If I knew how my husband's mind worked, would it change anything? I think not. As long as you are here, Lord Litton, you're a welcome guest. Tomorrow, assist me with Joshua's breeching ceremony. That way I can send my baby boy away with you as a young man."

Before he could ask another thing or look at her as if his stare could bore into her mind, she hurried to the stairs.

"Ophelia. Mrs. Hanover."

She stopped halfway down. "Yes, Lord Litton."

"Thank you for your hospitality. I will show you the same courtesy when you visit the boy in London."

"The boy is Joshua. While you are trapped by the storm, get to know him. He's a remarkable child."

"I will. There are many things to discover or rediscover about Norring."

Unsure if that was a threat or a tease, she kept moving. Head high, she headed to the study.

Mrs. Gilmore was inside, opening boxes taken from the attic. "Mrs. Hanover, I knew you would want the decorations. I have the corn cooking in the kettle so that it bursts big and white. And the wassail is steeping with heavenly cinnamon."

Wassail, the way Mrs. Gilmore cooked it, tasted like tea made with sweet cloves and cinnamon. It made a perfume for the nose and a savory treat for the tongue.

Ophelia felt her lips curl from a small smile to a grand one. "You know my thoughts well." She picked up the wire sphere that Benjamin had fashioned and twirled it. "We won't have mistletoe or evergreen, not until the snowing stops. What can we use to trim this decoration? I want this room, the whole house, to feel like Christmas."

Mrs. Gilmore laughed. "Oh, I don't know. I have rosemary drying in the kitchen."

"As long as you have enough for the goose in the larder, I'll take it."

"Nothing comes before the meal, Mrs. Hanover, although I wish the earl would choke on his portion."

"No. No. No. Lord Litton is our guest. Perhaps if he sees how loving this home is, he will change his mind and not take Joshua as those papers demand."

The Scottish woman had put on a red tartan skirt, as she did for the twelve days of Christmas, but her countenance seemed distant, beleaguered. "I know the master wasn't well, but I still wonder why he was so cruel to you."

"I'll use ribbon, Mrs. Gilmore. And maybe I have some gold paper to make flowers. That and the rosemary will make these spheres look well, even without mistletoe or evergreen fir branches. And candles. Lots of candles."

Her friend nodded.

Ophelia grimaced at her own unwillingness to say what had hurt her, just as Litton said. Putting down the sphere, a symbol of when things were good between herself and Benjamin, she glanced at her earnest housekeeper. "I don't know why Mr. Hanover did so. I want to blame the illness, but what if he hated me? What if it was his way to punish me for not loving him enough or holding on too tightly?"

Mrs. Gilmore was at her side. "You don't have to be so brave all the time. I was here, ma'am. I saw the illness cloud the master's judgment. I saw the rages. I nursed your bruises."

Ophelia turned and clasped her friend's hand. "No one needs to know how far his mind had deteriorated. We'll keep it our secret."

"Yes, ma'am, but the earl. If he knew, that might change his opinion."

"He'll only think it a lie. That I'm willing to make Benjamin into a monster to keep Joshua. I'm just the foreigner his cousin married."

Mrs. Gilmore shook her head. "You're no liar. I saw the suffering." She patted Ophelia's hand. "I have a basket of silk ribbon upstairs. I'll go get it."

The crackle of the fire nestled in Ophelia's ears. The house was quiet save this sound. The scent of cinnamon filled the air, and the desire to make decorations with her family filled her heart. She thought of her father, her sisters, and cool nights on their sugar plantation in Saint Ann Parish. Then her new English family, Joshua and Mrs. Gilmore. God still gave Ophelia joy in the midst of her sorrow.

Mrs. Gilmore returned with her darning basket and had even retrieved gold paper from Ophelia's room. "Joshua is snoring hard. And so is the earl. I passed his bedchamber to see if he was skulking about."

"Good. I think we can have the place transformed before either awakens." After retrieving her razor-sharp scissors from Benjamin's desk, Ophelia trimmed gold stars and circles to be pressed into flowers from the paper. After minutes of careful concentration, she looked up and caught Mrs. Gilmore's look.

The woman's scarlet curls fluttered beneath her mobcap as a huge brooding frown filled her face.

"Go ahead, Mrs. Gilmore. Ask your question."

"It's not a very English thing to do, ma'am, to surrender." She went to the corner, sat at the gleaming rosewood pianoforte, and plunked the ivory keys. "Not very English at all."

"I've only lived here seven years. I suppose I am still foreign. One could say my mother's people were used to being conquered, with their enslavement from the Gold Coast. But I would say she learned to adapt to horrid circumstances. Then somehow, she and the evangelism of George Liele conquered my father's heart. She gained her freedom, and later they married."

"Maybe you should conquer Lord Litton's heart."

"What?"

"Did you see the relief in his face when he saw he couldn't leave with Joshua? And do you know he's been asking if you're courting anyone? I think he likes you."

Blinking like an incredulous fool, Ophelia put down her scissors. "He doesn't like me at all."

"I think he does, Mrs. Hanover."

Geoffrey liking her was worse than pity. Ophelia shook her head, gathered her folded stars, and placed them on the mantel. "This would look so much better with branches of dark green fir trees. Twists of holly." She leaned against the warmed wood trim of the mantel. "It does not matter, Mrs. Gilmore. I don't like him. How could I when he's determined to take Joshua?"

"Perhaps. Perhaps not, Mrs. Hanover."

"Nonsense." She tweaked the position of a star and imagined placing apples and fruit around the arrangement to dress the mantel. Yet, if it were true, if Litton did care for her, could that make him more reasonable, more apt to change his mind?

"Mrs. Hanover, look. The window glass is completely frosted over."

Ophelia glanced at the housekeeper pulling open the curtains.

"The snow is higher, ma'am. We may have guests all the way to Christmas."

Ophelia hummed "O Holy Night" as she arranged her paper flowers. "Even when I thought I'd begged too much, God has given me a Christmastime miracle."

Done with the mantel, Ophelia grabbed Mrs. Gilmore by the arms and spun in the reel she'd learned for the ball her father threw. What a confusing, crazy time, with pretty gowns of light silk, cap sleeves, and silver satin gloves. And two men of the Hanover family, one a landowner, the other a sailor, Benjamin Hanover and Geoffrey Landson, come to visit.

With one, her father had negotiated a marriage contract. With the other, a flirt who did things on a dare, he hunted. If Papa had known of Benjamin's difficulties and chosen the sailor, would Ophelia's life be different? Would her son have a father to guide him? With Geoffrey's risk-taking, Ophelia could still be alone. "Mrs. Gilmore, please bring me a mug of wassail and check to see if the corn has cooled. No burnt fingers making the garlands."

"Yes, ma'am."

Dusting her hands of gold bits, Ophelia went to the door. "I'm going up to the attic for more decorations. But the John Canoe boat is here atop the shelf."

"The Jamaican decorations too? Lord Litton might think them wild."

"I'm in my own home, Mrs. Gilmore. I won't hide who I am. This might be Joshua's last Christmas at Norring. I will let him see my colorful heritage blended with English Hanover traditions."

"You sure?"

"I'm not sure about anything except I have two more days. That's more time than I had this morning."

She swept past Mrs. Gilmore but stopped on the other side of the door. The scents of cinnamon and popped corn wafted through the hall.

Ophelia resolved to be brave and not think of how crushed she'd be when Litton finally left with Joshua. Two days wasn't enough time. Starting for the stairs, she purposed to make the most of them. But was there still a way to convince Litton to leave without Joshua?

Yes. Yes, she'd figure it out. And do so without the method Mrs. Gilmore suggested. No *conquering* the man. Or his heart.

# Chapter 6

I ce pelting the window roused Geoffrey from a deep sleep. He rolled over, but the chilly air made his shoulder stiffen. No more sleep would be had tonight. Tapping the mobile above his head, he stared at the stars like a witless twit.

His plans were rubbish. From the sound of the storm, he'd be lucky to leave with Joshua in two days. Two days in a house with a woman he'd avoided for seven years. It was easy to think ill of her after the way things ended between them. And with his aunt's complaints and the harsh terms of the will—all these things reinforced every negative opinion he had of the former Ophelia Rutherford.

Now it all seemed wrong.

Having grown closer to the Lord, Geoffrey could be honest, more honest with himself. The woman he saw today wasn't the same girl he knew in Jamaica. The spitfire was now cautious, more measured in her words, and more anchored in her faith. Had she changed enough that they could be civil, nay, even friendly?

The door to the bedchamber opened.

At first, he looked for Smithers, but no one with height, a man's height, entered. Geoffrey rubbed his eyes and concentrated on a lump that moved along the floor. Reaching to the table, he lit a candle. Avoiding igniting the mobile, he hoisted the light high. "What are you doing, Joshua?"

The boy stood. He wore a big frown. "You like my bed?"

"Yes." Geoffrey tapped the papier-mâché mobile, swirling it. "It's quite a view."

"I like it too. I suppose a big boy shouldn't like stars. It's silly."

Geoffrey sat up, easing his head around the mobile. "I don't know. I'm a big boy, and I like them." He held out his hand. "Come on up here. Get to know your cousin."

Sable locks scattered; the boy didn't move.

"Let's pretend it's a boat. Did your mother tell you I was once in the navy?"

The boy hesitated, but then came closer. "Mama makes pretty paper ones. We sail them in the fountain and in the big river next to Norring, the River Orr."

"Paper boats?"

"Yes. She has a big one of purple and gold, but she won't sail it."

Ophelia? A paper boat maker? "Sounds fun. I miss piloting a ship through the ocean. Has your mother mentioned running awa—going on a boat?"

"No." The boy's pout grew bigger. "Mama won't leave Norring, except to visit when I live with you."

An honest answer about what appeared to be an honest woman. Geoffrey sighed and tapped the mobile, sending it spinning, whirling round and round. "I have a room picked out for you in London. Maybe we'll decorate it with boats."

"I like boats," the child said again. Now only inches from the bed, he fingered the blanket in a manner that suggested ownership, and Geoffrey felt bad all over again.

"Thank you for the use of your room, Joshua. Perhaps we could ask your mother to send this mobile with us."

"No, it stays. So she'll know I'll come back." The boy clasped the oak bedpost within his tiny palms. "Why is this your first time? And you come to take me away?"

Geoffrey swallowed the guilt. "I've been busy, then I was recovering from a terrible accident. But I'm here now, and I'm doing what your father would want."

"Well, Papa made Mama cry sometimes. I didn't think he could keep doing that now that he's gone." Pulling up the long hem on his pinafore, Joshua climbed onto the bed. "But Papa wouldn't want her alone. He was sorry when he made her cry." He drummed on his chest. "I should stay aaa–and protect her."

Ophelia had suffered because of his cousin. If Geoffrey had been available, been willing to give his time, could he have helped? And what new sorrows required protection? "What makes her fearful? Have there been a lot of visitors?"

"No. Just sololi. . .solicito. . . legal people."

That would be his legal people and the ones Ophelia hired to challenge the will. Geoffrey scrubbed his chin and wondered for a moment how he'd have a morning shave. More borrowed items from his late cousin?

Well, at one point he had wanted everything Benjamin claimed—including Ophelia.

"No one else visited? Doesn't sound like she needs protecting. Perhaps all the suitors your Grandmother says come to see her—"

The boy looked at Geoffrey as if a horn had sprouted from his head. "Suitors? To marry my mama? No, no, no. I'm big enough now to get the evergreen branches for her Christmas decorations. It was Papa's job. But I can do it."

"I'm sure you can. Your mother is a young woman, a beautiful one. She should remarry." Perhaps that was why Benjamin's will was so drastic, to ease the path for Ophelia to wed again. That was the only thing that made sense.

"Why marry and make her sad again? No. Just the two of us, forever. And Mrs. Gilmore sailing paper boats."

"Though paper boats sound more fun, you may change your mind when you are older and settled." Geoffrey was settled, sort of.

"No fun. Mrs. Gilmore says you haven't married."

"Mrs. Gilmore seems to do a lot of talking."

"She does to Mama when she thinks I'm not in earshot."

"Did your father tell you where he wanted you to go to school?"

"No. He wasn't much around." The boy tugged on Geoffrey's nightshirt. "You ask many questions. May I ask one?"

The serious pout on the lad's face looked like Ophelia's when she studied the settlement papers. That made Geoffrey smile inside. "Yes, Joshua. Ask your question."

"Why do some think mama isn't good? She takes excellent care of me. She visits the sick in the village. What else does she have to do to be good?"

A sigh filled Geoffrey's lungs. There was no answer. "It's easy for people to make assumptions about things they don't know about. Your mother is a private person, and those she's turned to haven't been available to help. I'm guilty of that."

Joshua's arms lifted as he yawned and nodded. "Avail–available to do right."

The beginnings of a soul of great understanding was there. Another point attributing to Ophelia's care.

"You should go to bed, Joshua."

"Because we leave early?"

"No, I suspect the weather will keep us here for a while longer."

The boy launched himself back to the floor. "If we give my mother a good Christmas, I promise to go with you and be good without another tear. I'll be a big boy."

He couldn't promise the boy that. Christmas was five more days away. "We'll see. But I suspect you'd be a good boy anyway. You have to barter with more, something unexpected."

The boy yawned. "More adult tricks."

It was, as were the consequences. "You sleep well, Joshua. Your mother has something special planned tomorrow here at Norring."

" 'Night, Lord Litton." The boy pattered out of the room.

Geoffrey tried to lay back but bopped his head on the mobile. The sound of the pelting ice from the storm had grown louder, but not enough to smother his conscience. He should find Ophelia and apologize for thinking ill of her. But how, given their history and the haggling over the will?

Perhaps the talkative housekeeper could give him insight.

He ducked as he lifted from the bed and tied on the robe. He moved to the halls, intent upon finding her.

Wandering the upper hall, he couldn't tell where Mrs. Gilmore's quarters might be. Looking in servants' rooms near the attic revealed his sleeping staff.

Yawning, he gave up. He'd trust that an opportunity would present itself. Easing down the stairs to return to bed, he met the housekeeper on the landing. "Ah, just the lady I wish to see."

Carrying a basket filled with colorful ribbon remnants, she slid the handle up her forearm. "Is your room not comfortable? I hear the snow could be refreshing."

Though the woman might be serious, he chuckled. "You've worked for the Hanover family for a long time, even with my aunt and my mother. You know we're not cruel people."

The woman's stance softened. "Your mother, God rest her soul, was the gentlest of women. Christmastime was her favorite season."

"You remember?"

The housekeeper's manner eased more, with a hint of smile appearing. "My mistress would give Mrs. Landson a good run. Never saw two so inclined to gold paper and ribbons."

Would his mother like Ophelia?

Well, they both held tightly to their children. If not for his uncle's intervention, Geoffrey would have followed the church as opposed to his true passion for sailing. He fumbled with the sash to his claret-colored robe. "Perhaps Mrs. Hanover is too much like my mother. Perhaps that explains the dictates of my cousin's will."

A frown overtook her rosy features. "Many missed Mrs. Landson's practical nature and prejudged her for being German. Hanover roots are very German, very like our new queen's. Many, including your aunt, looked upon your mother with disdain. It's no wonder she treats Mrs. Hanover so miserably. I just never thought you, Geoffrey Landson, would erect such troubles."

"You speak of the widow's goodness. Tell me why my cousin would deprive her of their son. Was their marriage a happy one? Did Ophelia do something to offend him?"

"Nothing that I know of."

"Was she pining for another? Did Mr. Hanover suspect she loved another or failed to love him? Theirs was a marriage of convenience."

Mrs. Gilmore's face riddled with lines. Her sherry eyes held a horrible squint. "Maybe she loved Mr. Hanover too much. The more she tried to help him, the more distant and erratic the man became. The night he died was horrible."

Too much? That wasn't exactly what Geoffrey, or his ego, wanted to hear. He tied a bigger knot in his sash. "Then maybe my cousin was prescient, knowing his life would be short, and didn't want her to remain alone or have his son caught in a mother's tight apron strings. You remember my own mother's struggles."

"It's a mother's duty to be cautious. If the master had listened, my mistress's heart wouldn't be breaking. She wouldn't be downstairs working her fingers to the bone to give her son a last celebration before you rip him from Norring."

The woman began to stomp past him, but he stepped in her path. "I promise to make things as easy as possible. I'll also make sure that you and Mrs. Hanover visit often. I don't want this to be cruel."

"You're taking her son. How could it not be? She's used up most of her meager savings fighting for him."

"I'll send my carriage for her. She won't be troubled by this. I'm trying to be a better person, and that begins by living up to my responsibilities. The Court of Chancery makes Joshua Hanover my responsibility. His father's will dictates where he should live and go to school."

The woman nodded. "Don't you have the power to leave the boy here and tear up those papers? No one has come to check up on him. You could let that continue."

Geoffrey did have that power, but it wasn't his cousin's wish. Constantly coming to Norring wasn't advisable either, not with his mind softening toward the widow. "I'm bound by the will."

The woman shrugged, and her basket shook colored scraps like colorful snowflakes.

He bent and gathered a few pieces for her. "Tomorrow will be a breeching ceremony for Joshua. May I count on you to help? Mrs. Hanover may not know all the traditions."

"Anything for Mrs. Hanover and Joshua." She continued up the stairs, but stopped at the top, casting him a long, sad look. "Though she hides behind a smile and will pray for you faster than St. Peter, Mrs. Hanover hasn't been happy for a while. Goodnight, Lord Litton."

Selfless widow or unhappy wife? What was Ophelia? Now he had to find her. He couldn't rest until she told him the truth.

# Chapter 7

Sparrow-like humming filled the air of the lower level, haunting and lonely. Yet yummy cinnamon stroked Geoffrey's nostrils. The contrast between sorrow and sweetness struck his curiosity as much as his fancy. He had no choice but to give chase down the paneled hall to the study. The door was open wide and inside was Ophelia.

Her back was to him as she arranged paper flowers on the mantel. She turned, caught him gaping, and dropped a big ball wrapped in red ribbon. "You startled me, sir."

He scanned left then right, peering at the transformation of the study. The formal room where they discussed wills and ultimatums was now a winter wonderland. Paper stars hung on white garland that looped about the mantel and spiraled the brass sconces in the corners of the room. Tiny white candles lit the pianoforte and the bookshelves. "Seems you've made some headway. Father Christmas would be proud. You've enough candles to light his path or burn down Norring."

"There are never enough candles, Litton. And nothing looks as splendid as white bees-wax. If they were set in greenery, this would be perfect."

"I think it fine, Mrs. Hanover. And it's snowing too much to retrieve any. Not quite worth the risk when there's little to improve upon."

"Good to hear you say that about risk and my decorations, but I do wish I had a few limbs." She picked up her ribbon orb. "Benjamin taught me how Hanovers celebrate. He used to make a show of collecting the evergreen fir from the wilderness and dressing the mantels and windows."

Watching her long fingers wrapping more shiny ribbon on her sphere, Geoffrey eased deeper into the room. "When did my cousin stop?"

As if her concentration had broken, she set the decoration aside. "A while ago." She sank again upon the floor and tucked her ankles under her green gown, the fetching thing with capped sleeves she'd worn to dinner. She was barefoot, and her toes wiggled to the mysterious tune she hummed. "Was there something you need? Is your back hurting?"

"How did you know about my accident?"

"Your aunt. I wrote for assistance in finding Benjamin. She said he was busy helping you and explained the circumstances."

"My cousin didn't come to my aid."

The dance her fingers had begun, the parsing of fluffy white corn onto her needle between dark orangey-rust-colored berries, stopped. "I assumed he hadn't. His mother tried to hide his absence. No one knew where he'd gone."

"He died in an accident. What is the whole truth?"

Her eyes closed for a moment. "After being gone for weeks, Benjamin returned to

Norring. He was agitated. That night, he found that I'd accidentally left bits of paper on his desk. The litter upset him. He grew angry and he—"

Her eyes shut again. The lack of words, the lifting of her hands as if to block a punch said so much.

It grieved Geoffrey's soul.

"He left, sorry for what he'd done. He rode his horse into a tree. The gash to his forehead wouldn't stop bleeding."

The anguish in her voice ripped at his gut. "I'm sorry. I regret not being available to help."

She nodded with a quivering, untrusting smile and threaded more garland. "It doesn't matter. I hope he's no longer chasing rest. I hope his nerves are finally soothed."

With great care, Geoffrey eased down beside her, and the smell of cinnamon which led him to her seemed stronger. A copper mug of dark tea sat near. He picked it up and tasted the heady spice along with cloves. "Wassail?"

"You could've asked for some. I would gladly get you your own cup."

"At least I know this one is not poisoned."

"I would never—"

"I know, Ophelia." He took another swig of the warm yuletide punch. "Is there something I could help with?"

She looked down. Her concentration returned to the garland. "No, I am just about done. You could tell me about your suitable candidates."

If he hadn't tasted the wassail, he'd wonder if Ophelia drank courage. "I beg your pardon?"

"The ladies vying to be the new Lady Litton. When you take Joshua to town, this woman should be like a mother to him. I would like to know more of her. Maybe I could help you narrow the selection."

Ophelia was daft to think he'd talk of his choices with her, but it was bold and daring to ask. "What type of help, Mrs. Hanover? You mean to find fault in each candidate."

"Geoffrey, I want you to be happy. I'd never begrudge you."

There was a sweetness in Ophelia's voice that spoke of sincerity. And the use of his given name, as if they were friends, felt authentic, maybe even warming, but that was probably the steam of the wassail, the sugar coursing through him with each sip. "Well, there is an heiress my aunt introduced."

"She's helpful like that."

Ophelia's tone held a little bite, and that pleased him. He pulled the bowl of popped corn kernels closer and tossed a few of the crunchy treats into his mouth. "Her father's in shipping. The other candidate is the daughter of an earl. Kindhearted, but likes the drafty theatre a little too much for my tastes and my back."

"Joshua could help you. He's a pretty good discerner of character."

"Let me know what he says of me. We just had our first man-to-man conversation."

Her eyes lit. The bits of gold and blue in the sea of teak reflected the roaring fire. "About what? You didn't tell him of the ceremony?"

"No. We talked about you."

The concern in her eyes was palpable. And that humored his spirits even more.

"What did Joshua say?"

"Oh, that you'll need to visit quite often. The boy will fret over your welfare if you don't."

She popped up from the floor. "He wouldn't have to fret if you weren't taking him away from Norring."

"Let's not argue, Ophelia. I'd rather sit here helping you string corn and. . . What's in this other bowl?"

"Dried gooseberries. They are like raisins." She climbed on a ladder and began to hang her garland about the gold stars she'd placed on the high shelf of the bookcase. "They are tart and sweet."

"I know." He popped a few of the berries into his mouth, enjoying the tang on his tongue. "My mother was known to make a nice pie with this fruit. She'd also string popcorn and nuts about a fir tree. And put candles on it too."

"Your parents dragged a tree indoors? A whole tree?"

"That is what my mother said they did in her home country. She was from Saxe-Coburg. A little German duchy of little consequence."

"Like Jamaica is of no consequence." She stretched to reach the highest shelf. "But a notable dowry makes a difference. Why else would your father or anyone in the Hanover line import a bride?"

"Father married for love. And he stood by her when others in the family tried to make her ways seem quaint."

A smile graced Ophelia's features before she turned back to the tall bookcase. "I hear love can make one do strange things, but I never thought that included indoor trees. Could you hand me the stars? I think the shelf could use more."

Holding his breath, he stood; his back twinging from the motion. After a stretch, he scooped a basket of folded paper trinkets.

When she took the basket, she rocked a little too much and clutched the ladder. "I'm glad your parents found love and your father stood up for her." Balancing herself, she added more stars. "What do you think?"

He scanned Ophelia's tall frame, admiring the way the lace of her gown hung on her curves. "Beautiful."

"Now to get the John Canoe." She tossed her head back and lifted on her tiptoes. "It's on the top of the bookcase."

Though Geoffrey was tall, lifting a box above his head that looked weighty enough for two hands wasn't advised. Hurting his back could mean a longer stay at Norring. And, the way he kept glancing at the humming Ophelia, that wasn't advisable either. "Do be careful."

"Always."

He moved closer to see her expression. "Always careful, Mrs. Hanover?"

Her fingers stilled on the box she tugged. "Benjamin's death made me more cautious. Joshua only has me now."

"He has me too. I should have answered your letters."

"It no longer matters." Her voice had a breathy tone. "I was desperate, but Benjamin made his choices."

She reached a little too far this time. Box in hand, she fell.

Geoffrey caught her and pulled her to his chest, but his left side gave way. Like the hail pelting against the window, they crashed to the floor.

The breath went out of him as every muscle on that side ached anew, but he'd protected

Ophelia, cradling her against his chest. Wheezing, he brushed the silky onyx hair from her neck. "You made me move fast again."

She scrambled off Geoffrey then hovered over him, her eyes wide like saucers. "I hurt you?"

Ophelia looked scared and unsure. The scowl she'd had for most of his visit had fully lifted. The woman was more beautiful than when he last laid eyes or hands upon her under that Jamaican moon.

"Geoffrey, say something."

"Just. Don't move. This will pass."

She clasped his lapel. "There must be something. A mustard plaster, a hot towel."

He took her hand and kissed it. "Just hum or call me Geoffrey again."

"What? Did you hit your head too?"

Her fingers went to his hair, massaging and parting locks.

"I dare you to stop and hum, to not fret for a moment."

"No more dares. We—"

"If I had told you what started out as a dare between cousins changed to something more, would you have believed me?"

Her pale gold cheeks bore the hint of a red glow. "Do not say more on that. It's the past."

She was right, and he needed to accept that. "Show me a peek at the box you retrieved making us fall."

A lift of the lid exposed a boat made of eggplant-purple and scarlet paper. "It's not a whole tree, Geoffrey, but it is something from my family's traditions."

"It's a very fine sailing vessel. Is this one you and Joshua float?"

"No, it's a John Canoe decoration and shouldn't be sailed. It's something my family celebrated at Christmas to honor the defeat of the Germans. John Canoe freed a part of Jamaica."

"Jamaicans conquering Germans. Hmm. Well, I'm glad I'm English. Don't like to think about being defeated, even by a beautiful Jamaican."

"No conquering you, my lord."

"Time is conquering me. This injury is my own fault, a dare in Hyde Park over a fiver. You were right about not taking all dares." He took a deep, soul-cleansing breath. "My back is feeling better."

Ophelia put down the boat. "May I help you sit?"

With a nod, he consented. With her offering a slow tug, he sat up, leaning upon her, savoring the soft feel of her palms and the spot betwixt her neck and her shoulder where she cradled his head.

The crackle of the hearth.

The thump of her rising pulse. All too comfortable, too dangerous, if he wanted the slushy ice wrapping about his heart to stop melting.

Gingerly, reluctantly, he stood. "Ophelia, can we talk about what happened between us? Maybe the anger and mistrust is—"

"Warranted? I'm sorry for injuring you." She retrieved the paper boat and put it on the mantel. "Joshua will love this."

To think of their past with charity was a challenge only he'd take. He should accept this.

"Yes, Mrs. Hanover." Geoffrey plodded to the door, taking short steps, his spine jarring more and more. It could lock up. That was dangerous, more so here at Norring. Seven years had passed, and he still liked Ophelia too much. "Good night, Mrs. Hanover."

As if she'd been kissed, her pale gold cheeks had darkened to rust. "Dream well, Lord Litton."

Up the stairs and back into bed, Geoffrey hoped his back pain would ease, hoped the weather cleared before his list of suitable marital candidates grew by one, the addition of his cousin's widow.

# Chapter 8

In the kitchen's larder, Ophelia washed her hands in the bucket of cold water. "It was nice of the earl's steward to retrieve more coal from the stables and firewood from our park."

Mrs. Gilmore clicked her tongue. "They should've picked up the fir branches Joshua's been squawking about. And we've run low heating all of Norring for our guests. You know they could leave tomorrow, three days shy of Christmas, and you spent the whole time nursing Litton."

It was nice having a patient who listened. The earl did as he was told, smelly mustard plaster and all. She dried her hands, flicking droplets about her clean kitchen. Something Joshua would do. "He fell in the study helping me. And I was able to witness him and Joshua talking and laughing. It was worth it to see them grow closer."

Mrs. Gilmore helped Ophelia turn her pudding out. The dense, sticky cake slid out, perfect—smooth sides, evenly brown. Hours of fretting, unwarranted.

"I told you it would be fine, Mrs. Hanover."

Following her housekeeper to the dining room, Ophelia paused and reveled in the sight.

The sconces held fine beeswax candles, the ones she'd saved for Christmas. Ribbons of gold and silver draped the sides. Her table showcased white garland surrounding the half-empty Wedgewood platters of goose and roasted potatoes.

A lump caught in her throat as Litton tapped Joshua then pushed back from the chair and stood. Her son did the same, like a little man, though his eyes barely cleared the table's top. He sat again when the earl retook his seat.

"We do this when ladies enter," Litton said.

Joshua beamed in his grey pinafore. For a moment, she saw wisdom in Benjamin's will, but only for a moment. She'd never cede custody of her son.

"Oh, Mama's plum pudding. So yummy." The boy wiggled.

"Litton, my son's sweet tooth is as big as a man's."

Mrs. Gilmore set the pudding onto the table. "We usually save plum pudding for Christmas Day, but since we...well. . . . I'm glad Mrs. Hanover made it to serve today."

"You made it?" Litton stretched and wafted his hand as if to draw the smell of sweet allspice and cloves from the dense cake to him. "I didn't know you cooked."

Ophelia took her seat opposite Joshua on the other side of the earl. "I'm a holiday cook. The Christmas plum pudding is very similar to a fruitcake we make back home. 'Twas my papa's favorite."

His gaze tangled with hers. "I look forward to a slice after Joshua's ceremony."

She'd wanted to stretch things out longer, with them all getting along. "Now, Litton?"

"The weather has cleared. I feel fit, and Joshua and I will leave at first light."

She nodded and kept her chin from drooping. "I will go get—"

"No, Mrs. Hanover. I took the liberty of working a truce with Mrs. Gilmore. I want this to be one thing you didn't do. No more fretful lines to your brow."

"Smithers," the earl said, looking at the man gobbling down a forkful of sliced goose. "Could you get the screen? Mrs. Gilmore, will you get the gift?"

Portly Smithers wiped his mouth of crumbs as he stood and extended an arm to the housekeeper. "Shall we, Mrs. Gilmore, maker of the juiciest bird?"

The woman's schoolgirl giggles did nothing to soothe Ophelia's unease. She tapped her fingers as she stared at her baby, her growing young man, and kept all the love in her heart from spilling out of her eyes. "Joshua, this is your special day."

The boy dimpled. "It's not my birthday, and Christmas is still three days away."

Before standing, Litton patted her nervous, tapping hand. "Joshua, this is a very old tradition. When a parent or guardian feels that a boy has matured, he is now ready to be a young man. It is time to be breeched."

Her son's angelic face twisted, and his lips pouted something awful. "Sounds painful, sir, and Mama's the one to decide. She knows me. You don't, sir."

Litton's smile waned. And something, perhaps a sense of true regret, lowered his gaze to his cleaned dinner plate.

"Joshua," Ophelia said, "your cousin can tell you're a very mature, very smart boy. You're ready."

The earl, whose hand had remained on hers, gave her a tweak. "Thank you. I've been known to make snap judgments. Most of them are spot-on."

Her son smiled, exposing the front tooth he thought was loose.

Smithers returned with the dressing screen, a dark-stained wood frame with panels of block-printed flowers on muslin fabric.

Litton towed Ophelia to stand, seeming to offer her his strength. "Set that up in the corner."

Mrs. Gilmore handed her the white box with the silky red bow. Ophelia moved from the earl and approached Joshua. "You're not Mama's baby anymore." She handed him the present and fingered the collar of his pinafore before unpinning it. "Go behind the screen. Change into what some call a skeleton suit, the breeches and waistcoat of a man. You'll be dressed like the earl."

Eyes dancing, Joshua took the box and lugged it behind the screen.

The bow vaulted over the side followed by tissue paper that fell like snow. Soon, he stepped out. New boots, a damask silk waistcoat of indigo blue, a tailcoat of dark chocolate, and tan breeches made her little boy look so well.

The earl knelt beside him and buttoned up the man-like vest then tied the snow-white cravat to perfection. "Now you look the part of a brave young man. Go to everyone. See if they have something for you." He reached in his pocket and drew out a guinea.

Ophelia closed her eyes. She'd forgotten this part of the ceremony. Though she'd borne the cost of the clothes, she couldn't compete with Litton's deep pockets.

As if he could read her mind, the tall man frowned for a second. "This gift is from your mother and me. It serves as a token of our unity on your education and welfare."

Joshua hugged the earl's knees, and Ophelia mouthed "thank you" to Litton.

Her little man ran to her next. She stooped and let him toss his arms tight about her neck. "I am so proud to be your mother."

"Mama, I can be the man of the house. I'm even big now, big enough to get the greenery for the decorations."

She didn't have the heart to correct him. He wouldn't be at Norring for Christmas. There were papers on his father's desk that said otherwise.

Hoping for that next miracle, she watched Litton put coins in Mrs. Gilmore and Smithers' palms. "Joshua, go see if the rest of our party has something for you."

"This is enough. Seeing Mama smile. Now I am big like the earl. This is enough."

Ophelia's lips trembled, but she said what she must. "You're big enough to do what is prescribed, whether rituals or legal papers. So, go and show Mrs. Gilmore and Mr. Smithers, my best little man."

Joshua gave her neck another little squeeze before he marched with a wobble over to Mrs. Gilmore.

In her heart, Ophelia thanked the Lord. This moment didn't have to be. It was a gift, with a bright ribbon to keep her heart together.

Not knowing what to do with her hands, she leaned over to slice the pudding.

"Joshua seems happy." The earl's voice was low in her ears.

Caught in her thoughts, she hadn't noticed that he'd moved beside her with his plate outstretched. "I never miss dessert, Mrs. Hanover."

She couldn't look up at the grin she imagined flowing from his face, not without tears. "You won't miss any desserts with Joshua's sweet tooth. You're taking custody of him tomorrow." She covered her mouth. "I don't wish to ruin this." Handing him the biggest slice of the pudding, she sucked in a breath of the strong cloves. "Excuse me, there's a sauce. Mrs. Gilmore, go into the study and play the pianoforte. Everyone can enjoy the decorations and the pudding as if it were Christmas. Joshua, I put out the boat."

"You hadn't let me see it yet." He jumped up and down then stopped as he thought the action wasn't mature. "I'll make sure Mrs. Gilmore gets there safely." He held his hand out to the housekeeper.

"La-dee-da, Mr. Hanover." She bent and took his arm. "I do need the escort. Wait until you see your Mama's decorations."

Wanting to smile, but knowing it was a losing battle, Ophelia ducked through the servants' door and dashed to the kitchen, almost in a full run. Sinking onto the kitchen bench, she folded her arms and put her head down then released every bitter tear she'd held in her soul. She needed her whole body cleansed of sorrow or she'd never survive watching Litton leave with her son.

# Chapter 9

**W**ith plate in hand, Geoffrey had followed Ophelia to the kitchen. Wondering how she could make the wonderfully creamy pudding better, he found himself eager. Yet, catching her crying made something in his chest tighten then break.

He put the dessert plate carrying his second slice onto the wooden table. When he put a hand to Ophelia's cheek, she startled and bolted upright.

"Lord Litton, please go rejoin everyone in the study." She brushed at her eyes. "I'm well. Go."

"The young man is taking care of things in the study. I dare to think I'm needed here. And I hadn't thanked you properly for caring for me. You could have left me ailing in bed. You'd have your Christmas."

"That would be wrong." She brushed at her face and moved toward the hearth. "You have a sweet tooth, my lord. The warmed vanilla sauce will go very well atop the pudding."

Tugging on a blousy gray apron that tied about the waist, she covered the pale-yellow gown and the thick gold ribbon circling her bodice. Her dress, with its straight skirt, was a decade out of fashion but complemented her well. Neither the heiress nor the fashionable earl's daughter would wear such. But neither would be in the kitchen making a sauce either.

"If you insist on staying," she said with a voice that still held tears, "could you hand me the cloves? I think they are on the shelf in the larder."

Assuming she meant the room to the side with supplies and food stuff, he went inside and found a jar of what looked like cloves. He lifted the lid and sniffed the scent that reminded him of Christmas and his own happy childhood celebrations. He closed it quickly before he became sentimental and carried it to Ophelia.

She tossed the cloves along with fragrant bark of cinnamon into a stone bowl and ground them with a marble pestle. "You don't have to watch. I'm in control of myself."

"Maybe I like watching your trim forearms working so hard." He clutched her hand. "Or maybe I want to be here this time when you break."

She jammed the pestle into the mortar. "The will you're administering is breaking me. What do you want, Litton?"

"I want to know why you chose Benjamin over me. It wasn't my ego alone that suspected you were partial to me. My heart had convinced me I wasn't the only one to find love."

"Love? My father had completed a marriage contract with the Hanovers. I couldn't go against him."

"Did you want to, Ophelia? Your family had the money, my ascension to my uncle's earldom wasn't assured, and my cousins' side of the family needed your dowry. You had the power. You could have voided the contract, just as you want me now to void my cousin's will."

"Papa was dying. He wanted none of his daughters to stay in Jamaica, knowing he couldn't protect us. A mulatto without a protector—our freedom could be taken. He wanted us married, settled, safe. He died a few months after I wed. I don't know what happened to my sisters, if they made it out or became enslaved."

"If you thought I could protect you, would you have chosen me? Did you love me?"

"Does it matter? You left. Benjamin said I was a joke to you. The contract was my only option."

"Things started as a joke. I'd finished a difficult tour in the Royal Navy. Benjamin wanted me to go with him to Saint Anne Parish, Jamaica, to visit a family friend, Mr. Rutherford. Benjamin knew I liked challenges and dared me to prove you, our host's daughter, silly. For a guinea, I pursued you. For three days, I went after you, being the best version of a romantic buffoon, quoting you Shakespeare, climbing trees to get you a coconut."

"You were relentless, Geoffrey."

The music from the pianoforte crept into the room and the urge to twirl her about the kitchen pressed his heart. He sat on the table and pried her fingers from pulverizing the poor cloves. "Ophelia, I was wrong to chase you, but believe me when I say the bet meant nothing, not after the first day. You were the dare, the unforgettable woman, the challenge I always wanted."

Her pulse raced at his touch, and his surely gave chase. "I think I loved you when I kissed you."

"Geoffrey, had you known of the marriage contract, would you have done so?"

"No, but then I'd have a greater torture of never knowing the joy of kissing you."

She pulled free and scooped up the ground spices. "This will just need to be warmed through. Then your plum pudding will have an extra treat."

He couldn't help himself. He followed behind her and put a hand on her shoulder. Pulling her from the hearth, he spun her, his fingers fumbling in the billowing apron until he found her.

"Geoffrey, what are you doing?"

"Dancing a waltz with the prettiest woman in Norring, in Framlingham for that matter."

They twirled to the tune "Deck the Halls." Ophelia hooked her spoon behind his neck and they circled the kitchen.

For a moment, they were at her father's estate. As she had seven years ago, she bloomed in his embrace. Like a blue Mahoe flower, her cheeks were a pale primrose then turned a deeper red the longer she stayed in his arms. Would this feeling blossom into love before the pianoforte stopped?

He leaned down, enraptured with the rhythm of her breathing, the press of her lips.

She pushed free. "No, Geoffrey, you're leaving with my son in the morning. You can't take my heart again too."

"Too? You did feel as I did under that Jamaican moon. You loved me. You should have sent for me."

"You haven't answered a single letter this past year. Why should I have gone against my father for someone who kissed on a dare and left without fighting for me? I was worth more than that, Geoffrey."

"My pursuit began as a dare, but I dared to love you. I couldn't respond to your letters. I knew they'd lead me here, wondering about us."

"This is ancient history." She turned from him, captured his plate, and drizzled a healthy portion of her sauce into the nooks and crannies of his pudding. "I can't be vulnerable or foolish. You have all the power now. I won't disgrace myself or dishonor my husband's memory, making eyes at his cousin, not knowing if this is just another test to see how low I will go to keep my son. I can't be burned by your fire again."

She returned to her sauce and poured the fragrant cream into a cup that looked like a gravy boat.

Desperate to convince her, he freed her of the pot and set it on the table. With both hands, he framed her face. Vanilla clung to her, and he imagined her lips tasting sweeter than the dessert. "I am different. I've changed."

Her breath came in sputters. Her gaze locked upon his. "Lord Litton, what is it I'm to do about that?"

Couldn't she see a man drowning, wanting to know if they finally had a chance? "A kiss. I think a kiss would convince you that we have found each other again."

"Just a kiss? That is your offer?" With arms folded about her apron, she pedaled away. "I refuse. I don't take dares anymore."

How could she not understand? He took a step closer, crossing the line of dance partner to unrequited suitor. "It's not a dare, Ophelia. It's a gesture to prove we can trust each other."

"Why should I trust you now? Your deceit crushed me. It made us enemies."

"My heart has changed. Being trampled by a horse because of my recklessness changed me. Wrestling with death, praying to walk again, made me desperate to be a new man, to no longer squander favor. It's why I came here, to be responsible for my ward. It's why I'm settling down. It's why I stand before you bared of jokes or guile, clothed in truth. I loved you then. I could love you again, if you allow me."

He put his palms on her shoulders. Their gazes blended, the distance between began to thaw, melting away.

Then a vessel steamed and whistled.

Blinking, she turned and went to the hearth.

"This teakettle will become silent when the flame is gone. I won't become a woman made to fret over dares or reckless behavior, not again." She leveled her shoulders. "Let's stay as friends, Geoffrey. A multitude of candidates vying to be Lady Landson would settle for a kiss. Not me."

He let her walk past him this time, for what could he say? He must seem the bounder, but he wouldn't take the biggest risk in his life, not without knowing her heart awaited his. The dare to love her was too great, and he wouldn't take it unless he was sure. He'd become cautious, and he couldn't risk hurting Ophelia and Joshua. Picking up his dessert, he spooned a hearty dip of pudding and cream onto his tongue, wondering, *Lord, is this where You've led me?*

Geoffrey purposed to leave in the morning, trusting that he'd know without a doubt if sweet Ophelia was his path to love.

# Chapter 10

Ophelia didn't want to rise from her bed.

But she had to. Joshua would leave with Geoffrey this morning. She threw off her thick wool blanket and put on a brave face. She'd had a great deal of practice pretending, sitting in the study listening to Mrs. Gilmore play "Joy to the World," while her heart had none.

Geoffrey had pulled a chair next to hers, sitting so close she could smell vanilla on his breath, the scent of cloves on his hands. Torture.

She sank back onto her pillow, thankful that she'd made it up to her bedchamber with Joshua in her arms without the earl asking again for a kiss.

Wanting to trust him, she might've weakened under a Framlingham moon. *Where are You, Lord, when I am weak?*

"Joshua, time to get up."

The little fellow didn't stir.

She hated to make him rise, not after he muttered in his sleep, "Big boys don't cry."

Big girls did.

She had wept through the night, a silent whimper. Maybe she should have kissed Geoffrey and gained Christmas. But how could she trust him? If he wouldn't stay because it was the right thing to do, without a kiss, there was no reason for either of them to trust one another.

"Joshua, let's get you a hot breakfast. The earl will want to leave soon. Joshua?"

With a yawn, she sat up and pulled on her warm pink robe. "Joshua, big boys don't lie about. Joshua?"

She pulled at the bedclothes but didn't find him. Ophelia sprang off the mattress and scanned her room. No Joshua.

Stooping, she looked under her high bed. No son.

His nightshirt was on the floor, his new boots and breeches gone.

Anger filled her belly, hot like vomit. How dare the earl take Joshua, slipping away without a goodbye because she rejected him?

She marched out into the hall. "Mrs. Gilmore, Mrs. Gilmore!"

The door to Joshua's room opened. The earl came out, his hair parted and wild. "What is the matter, woman? Why are you waking the house?"

"Because you... left... You left with Joshua."

He tied the sash on his robe. "As you can see, I haven't. What has you flustered?"

Her sharp anger turned to cold, sticky fear. "Joshua's gone." A shake took possession of her limbs.

Geoffrey grabbed her and held her until she stilled. "Listen to me. I'll find him. When last did you see him?"

"Bedtime." Her head felt light. "He kept saying big boys don't cry."

"Anything else?"

"Oh, he talked about fir limbs." She ran to the window and looked out at frozen Norring and the icy River Orr that bordered the property. "No. No. He's out in the cold."

Geoffrey took the sobbing woman from the window and pulled her to his chest, comforting her with all his strength. "I'll find him."

He moved fast, risking his limbs locking up, but he had to find Joshua. Yanking breeches over his nightshirt and wrapping on his coat and scarf, he readied. Passing Ophelia on the stairs, he kissed her brow. "Wake up Smithers and my groom. Search the house in case he's hiding in Norring."

"I know he's out in the cold like his Papa. I should come."

He put on his hat. "I can't fret about you too. Prepare a way to warm him up to stave off exposure. Trust me, Ophelia. Be ready for us."

She nodded, but fear clouded her eyes. It mirrored his own.

Out the door, he dashed through the portico and slid over the icy bridge that crossed the River Orr. The haunting water had frozen, but it held no sign of Joshua.

The wind swirled the snow, erasing any hope of seeing small footsteps. The boy could have run to the left or right. Geoffrey cupped his hand over his eyes, looking up to the silver blue sky.

*Lord, I am available to You. Use me. Lead me.*

He'd spent his convalescence trying to figure out how to have his life mirror righteousness—settling down, fulfilling his role as guardian. Yet he hadn't fully committed.

In the kitchen, he'd tempted Ophelia with nothing but a kiss, not marriage or a compromise on Joshua's rearing. It was a time for full commitment. *Lord, I'm available to You.*

"My hands of suspect strength, my limped walk struggling to stay aright, my whole heart. Lord, all is available to you."

Trudging deeper, he aimed for a line of evergreen fir trees. His breath steamed in the air. How long could a small boy survive the cold?

Joshua wouldn't have run if Geoffrey weren't taking him to London. If Joshua had hurt himself and had the same blood illness as Benjamin. . .

Fear, cold, chest-pounding fear, seized him. "Lord, I'll leave him in Ophelia's care. Let him be well. I'll give up everything for her."

A fork in the path spoke of decision. Left would take him around the Orr again where Joshua and Ophelia sailed boats, to the right was more wilderness. He cupped his eyes and saw bits of greenery sticking out of the white landscape.

Geoffrey ran to the greenery. "Joshua! Joshua!"

A weak moan caught his ear.

He stilled. "Joshua, call out. It's your big cousin."

"Big boy."

Scanning high and low, he spotted the child high in a tree. "Come down, Joshua. Let me get you back to the house."

"Scared. Not a big boy."

"Yes, you are, but even men get scared. I'm terrified."

Hatless, hands shaking, Joshua clung to the tree, teeth chattering. "Mama mad."

"Mothers always fret. It becomes their profession."

Edging closer, Geoffrey wondered how much longer the boy could hold on.

"F–fir branch."

"I'll get her a whole tree, Joshua. Come down."

The child's hands were blue. Exposure would do him in.

"Jump to me. I'll catch you."

Opening his arms wide, Geoffrey hoped his limbs would stay strong, lest they both tumble and get stuck in the snow. "Now, Joshua. Now."

The boy pushed and launched, then hung in the air. It seemed like a lifetime passed before he hit Geoffrey's chest. The child's weight smacked him in the ribs, and they tumbled backward. Freezing snow swallowed them. The boy wasn't hurt. A praise left Geoffrey till he tried to stand and couldn't.

"I hurt you. Mama said. . .take care. . .you."

"Your mother said that?"

"In prayers. Last n–night, every n–night. More when she heard. . .you sick."

He bundled Joshua deeper into his coat and found the strength to push from the ground. Geoffrey's full heart raced. He had to get Joshua back to Norring. He knew the right path, the one leading to the woman he loved.

Pacing in the hall, checking the windows every minute, Ophelia prayed. Her little boy couldn't be lost, and brave Geoffrey—he couldn't be hurt either. *Lord, let my family, the Hanover family, the family You've given me, be whole for one more minute.*

Mrs. Gilmore's hair held curl papers as she hugged a cup of hot tea. "Litton will find Joshua. You'll see."

"My son kept talking about fir trees. If I hadn't made a fuss about decorating, this wouldn't have happened."

"Mrs. Hanover, boys want adventure. You can't hold on so tight."

"Did I hold too tight to Mr. Hanover?"

The housekeeper clicked her tongue. "A scratch could kill him, but he liked risks. His fate wasn't your fault. Sometimes, you let go and grow your faith."

The doors rattled open.

Ophelia held her breath as Geoffrey, supported by Smithers, entered.

A moment of joy at seeing the earl's face disappeared. Joshua wasn't with him.

Another half-answered prayer? She sank to her knees, the fear of death squeezing air from her chest. Then, Geoffrey unbuttoned his coat and drew out Joshua.

The vise on her lungs released, and she repented of her doubts.

Geoffrey staggered toward her as Smithers took his wet coat. "Ophelia, blankets. He has my warmth but needs more."

She jumped up, towed them into the study, and seated her loves in front of the fireplace. "Mrs. Gilmore, help me cover them."

The women draped them with nearly every blanket in Norring. With her arms out-stretched, Ophelia held Joshua and Geoffrey tighter than she could imagine. "Smithers? Can you retrieve more wood from the kitchen?"

"No, Mama. Hot enough."

The complaint brought a smile that lifted her lips. "Joshua—"

"Sorry, Mama. I wanted the limbs, wanted to be big."

"Big boys makes mistakes, Ophelia." Geoffrey said. "Big ones."

Her gaze entwined with his. "Big girls too."

"Mr. Smithers," Mrs. Gilmore said, "could you help me in the kitchen? There's some conquering I need help with."

The steward waggled his busy brows but followed.

Ophelia pried off Joshua's boots and counted each healthy pink digit. "Lord Litton, you'll never know how grateful I am. You saved my son. He'll do very well with your guidance in London."

"Mama, you so angry you want me to go? I'm sorry. Sorry."

"Never, sweetness. But you're alive and well because the earl found you. I know I can trust him with your safety. He'll teach you to be a fine man, like him."

"Ophelia, we can't leave today. Christmas is in two days. We can leave after the holiday. I'd like to spend Christmas, maybe more. . .with you."

She wasn't sure what he implied, but she had to be as selfless as possible. She left the pile of blankets and went to Benjamin's desk, took out the ink and blotter, and signed the papers. "I have to do what is right."

Geoffrey turned his face toward the roaring flames of the fireplace. "Is that what you want, Ophelia?"

"I've held on too tightly to the past, even to old misunderstandings. This is right. Take the John Canoe. That way I'll be with you two in spirit." Retrieving a towel, she sat beside them and dried Joshua's locks then Geoffrey's. The scent of winter, of fresh snow, mingled with the salt stinging her eyes. God granted this final miracle, and she had to do what was best for everyone, no matter how much her heart broke into bits.

# Chapter 11

Christmas morning arrived and found Ophelia nestled in blankets. The same place she'd crawled since waving at Litton's departing carriage. Two days in bed, lying about as she'd warned her son not to, seemed appropriate. A sop for her suffering soul.

At least her smile the day they left was true. Geoffrey had proven to be a caring influence. Her new prayer was again for a miracle, that the earl would find a bride who'd love Joshua as her own.

A quick knock led to the door of her chambers being thrust open. Mrs. Gilmore barged inside. "Up with you, lazybones."

Ophelia drew the covers over her head. "Must I? Can't I sleep through Christmas?"

"No. The sun is up. It's not too chilly outside. You should go for a walk through Framlingham."

A groan ushered from Ophelia's mouth before she could stop it. "Why, when the blankets are warm?"

"Get up, enjoy the evergreen wreaths and white candles in the windows of Framlingham. That was your tradition."

Her and Joshua's tradition. How could she get up in a house devoid of a child's laughter?

"Come on, Mrs. Hanover."

"A walk? Fine."

Mrs. Gilmore went to the closet and found Ophelia's warmest walking dress, a deep indigo wool with onyx-trim braiding and military-like fobs down the front. "Perhaps a good walk could convince you to go to town. London's only four hours away."

"Unannounced? The earl might have his aunt to his townhouse or his new fianceé." She shook her head. "Not without a proper invitation."

"Seems to me he was inviting you, but you surrendered. Again, not a very English thing to do."

Ophelia yanked off the covers. "A walk before breakfast. Is that English enough?"

Mrs. Gilmore chuckled. "Being spirited becomes you."

Ophelia hated being goaded into action, but she dressed and was soon outside.

The crisp air greeted her as she crossed underneath the high crimson bricks of the portico. Dripping icicles dressed the way. Even the River Orr had begun to stir.

More ice jewels hung from her fountain and, like the river, held patches of slushy water. Joshua would ask to make boats. He'd even want the John Canoe sailing. Perhaps she'd return to Norring and make a few.

Guilt seized her.

"No boats will sail without you, Son!" She shouted it again and hoped Joshua could hear her in London.

As self-pity filled her heart anew, she lifted her head and let the fresh air kiss her cheeks. Joshua was safe. Geoffrey would protect him and be the father figure the boy deserved.

Walking another mile or two, she came to the high brick walls of St. Michael's Church. The fir-lined windows with bright white candles were so beautiful. The bell tolled, the vibration trembling her through her cloak. God had not abandoned her. Where there was beauty and a breath in her lungs, also lived hope. Perhaps she would go to town tomorrow and visit with Joshua and Litton, even smile at the future Lady Litton. She wanted Geoffrey happy, even if her heart ached for him.

Resigned, she headed back to Norring. Thick smoke billowed from the chimney. Imagining the warmth of the hearth fire, she moved faster.

Her gaze fell upon a paper boat moving in the river. Could it be a survivor from last autumn? Closer to the portico, she saw bits of red and purple bobbing in the fountain's slushy water. The John Canoe? Something was amiss.

Running into Norring, she found paper snowflakes littering the entry. "Mrs. Gilmore?"

Picking up one with diamond and star shapes cut out, she saw that the paper revealed legal words like custody and settlement. "Mrs. Gilmore?"

The paper snowflakes led to the study. Confusion mixed with fear in the pit of her stomach. She opened the door.

All the images hit her at once. Joshua sitting close to the fire folding paper boats with Mrs. Gilmore. A huge fir tree at the side of the pianoforte wrapped with some of her white garland. A cup and a saucer with pudding crumbs near the sleeve of Geoffrey's buff-brown tailcoat. He reclined in Benjamin's chair, cutting more snowflakes.

Breathing heavily, she sank to her knees and scooped up her boy.

"Merry Christmas, Mama." He kissed her cheek. "Don't be mad."

"Why? Why would I? Not with such a Christmas surprise." With her chin atop her son's head, she smiled her thanks to Geoffrey.

"Lord Litton dared me. He said the John Canoe couldn't float. He was right." Joshua handed her bits of soggy purple paper.

Giggling and squeezing Joshua, she breathed easier. "It doesn't matter. Nothing matters today."

Geoffrey rose and came to her side. "Mr. Hanover, why don't you go with Mrs. Gilmore for more plum pudding?"

"There's a little left that Lord Litton didn't eat." The housekeeper winked and took the boy's extended arm, leaving Ophelia alone with the earl.

Geoffrey held out his hand to her. His indigo eyes blazed with reflections of the flames. Never in all the back and forth of their legal ramblings did she fear Geoffrey, but now she did.

"My lord, if you've come to ask me to keep Joshua during your wedding trip, it will be no trouble."

"Arise, Mrs. Hanover. I dare you."

"I can hear you fine from my present position."

"It seems a reckless man cut up my cousin's will. The part that forced Joshua Hanover to be taken from his mother's custody is no more."

She wanted to jump up and down, even shout to the heavens.

This time she offered no resistance when he extended his hand and pulled her to her feet. "My lord, how can I thank you?"

Geoffrey held her, enfolded her within arms that bespoke safety and strength. "Don't thank me, Ophelia. Love me. Dare to say yes to our future. I love you. God's created no more suitable bride than one who has my heart."

"You've made me dizzy and weak. You've returned my son. How can I refuse?"

"Only accept my dare if you can live with the consequences, a lifetime of loving me. I have loved you, Ophelia, since that first kiss. I don't want gratitude. I want your heart."

She did love him. "I didn't know I could possess so many miracles. My son is home, and you stand here telling me you love me. The love of my young heart has returned."

She kissed him when he dipped his head toward her. The world spun as if they waltzed under a Jamaican moon, but they stood still, shadowed in Norring's candlelight. Her arms encircled his neck, and she savored the rush of his pulse against her wrist. His love washed over her like waves thawing the River Orr. "Geoffrey, you've been in my heart, my prayers, always."

He smoothed his palms along her arms, but her trembles weren't from the cold or the shock of Geoffrey at Norring. They were from knowing he truly loved her.

"Marry me, Ophelia. Dare to love me too."

"Yes, I love you, Geoffrey."

A second brush of his lips sent her head spinning. His deeper kiss tasted of wassail and plum pudding and forever. The best Christmas miracle.

"I should dip on one knee, Ophelia, but I'm still finding my strength."

"You've found strength. Here in my heart with a God who has kept us."

"A good place for hope to live. I must marry you. Becoming Joshua's stepfather is my only claim to him. I've cut snowflakes of the guardianship papers."

"You took a mighty risk, sir."

He slipped her head to his shoulder. "Ophelia, some risks, like a lifetime with you, are worth it."

# Epilogue

In the fifteenth-century church of St. Michaels, Geoffrey's heart filled with pride as the Thamar organ, with its metal pipes the size of Joshua, belted music from above. The gentle notes the vicar's wife played mirrored the solemn vows Geoffrey repeated to Ophelia of forsaking all others, the joy of the mystical union, and the sobriety of the holy estate of matrimony. He purposed in his heart to be like the sacrificial lamb blessing his Christmas bride.

"Those whom God hath joined together," the vicar said, "let no man put asunder. Forasmuch as Geoffrey William Landson and Ophelia Rutherford Hanover have consented together in holy wedlock."

Ophelia looked up with such beautiful clear eyes of teak. Though her bronze gown was the best that could be managed the day after Christmas, he thought her the most beautiful girl in the world.

The vicar placed her hand in Geoffrey's. "By giving and receiving of the ring and by joining of hands, I pronounce that they be man and wife together, in the name of the Father, and of the Son, and of the Holy Ghost. Amen."

Their small wedding party of Mrs. Gilmore, Joshua, and Smithers repeated, "Amen."

Coveting Ophelia's fingers, Geoffrey led her to the wooden pew where Joshua clapped. Beside him, the housekeeper swiped at tears. A surprising shift in five days when the spry woman wanted him to perish in the snow. Must be another of those Christmas miracles Ophelia gushed about. He ducked his head to his bride, very near the lips he wanted to savor. "I hope you don't mind a small wedding, Lady Litton."

"It must have cost a small fortune to get a special license so quickly."

"Just collected on a dare."

She swatted his fine white damask waistcoat. "Geoffrey."

"Old habits, my dear. I'm mostly reformed. You'll have to work on me."

Smiling, she pushed her veil made of sheer netting with silver paper stars along the trim to her ear. "I suppose your aunt won't mind missing the occasion."

"She will have to become more acquainted. Though I've grown to love Norring, I'll not hide you or Joshua away."

Ophelia's cheeks brightened. "Everyone who is important to me is here."

"There could be more. I have my solicitor looking for marriage licenses of your sisters."

Her eyes grew large. "You've given me so much, even more hope."

"Only the beginning." Clasping her palm, he kissed her satin glove then headed to his steward and the vicar to sign papers. He stuffed the completed documents into his coat, purposing to protect them from Ophelia's sharp shears.

After offering the vicar a nice fee, he returned to Ophelia. "Shall we?"

Claiming her with his right hand, he bent to pick up Joshua and managed to raise him a few inches, but the weakness in Geoffrey's left returned. As if she knew, Ophelia fluttered to his other side and wove her fingers about his struggling arm, hiding the union in the lace of her gown.

With his strong arm free, he picked up Joshua. Geoffrey's heart melted for Ophelia again. She was his strength and at his side as God intended, the perfect suitable wife for the Earl of Litton. "Let's go see about a wedding breakfast. I know Mrs. Gilmore must've created a wonder."

Carrying the giggling boy out of the church, he lifted him into their awaiting carriage, then assisted Ophelia. Leaning back in the seat, he covered them both from the pelting of paper snowflakes Smithers and Mrs. Gilmore threw. "Joshua, you don't mind that I've married your mother?"

"Look at her smiles." The boy caught a paper snowflake. "This marriage won't make Mama sad. And I have my favorite people together. What could be better?"

Geoffrey hugged the boy more tightly to his chest and tugged Ophelia to his shoulder. "I have my favorite people too. It's the best dare I ever took."

**Vanessa Riley** is captivated by the Regency era, drawing the award-winning author to create stories of diverse souls who were integral in erecting this society: serving in her wars, adding to her arts, loving and dying for her causes. Riley is a multi-published author of Christian historical romance. She lives in Atlanta with her military hubby and a precious pony-loving child.

# Father Christmas

by Lorna Seilstad

*A soft answer turneth away wrath:*
*but grievous words stir up anger.*
PROVERBS 15:1

# Chapter 1

Blackpool, England
1880

**D**rip. *Drip. Drip. Drip.* The droplets fell from the ceiling into the tin pot in perfect four-four time. Despite the incessant pinging, Beatrix Kent almost smiled. God's gift of music was everywhere. She needed to focus on His providence and fight the desperation pooling in her stomach. Sure, things like leaks were the incidents her beloved Jonathon always handled, but he was gone, and rain during a Blackpool winter was a certainty. She could manage this little trickle. She was an intelligent, accomplished, capable young widow who could handle anything.

Well, almost anything.

Without so much as a rap or a ringing of the bell, the front door flew open and Fern Kent, mother-in-law to be revered—or rather feared—blew into the house.

"Beatrix!" Fern screeched. "Where are you? Do you know it's pouring outside?"

Beatrix stepped through the parlor doors into the vestibule and took her mother-in-law's damp wraps. She hung them on the mirrored hall tree then obediently kissed Fern's cheek. "Why did you come out in this weather?"

"I come every day for afternoon tea, don't I?" Fern made her way into the parlor and took her customary position beside the low table, already set with a tea tray complete with scones and tea cakes. She motioned for Beatrix to sit down. "I'm chilled to the bone. Don't make me wait to pour."

Beatrix took a deep breath. Even in her own home, she wasn't allowed to be hostess when Fern Kent was around. And though she preferred two lumps of sugar, she'd only have one in her cup. Fern thought two was extravagant.

Fern set the teapot down and picked up the thin china cup sporting pink roses and a gilded handle. She took a sip, cocked her head, and scowled. "What is that noise?"

Beatrix motioned toward the leak in the ceiling in the back parlor. "I sent Thea back home to see if Geoffrey Black's boys would come make a repair."

"Hmph."

Fern clearly didn't approve, but Beatrix wasn't sure what had irritated the older woman—the leak, the sending of the housemaid, or contacting the Blacks—but she had no desire to ask her mother-in-law for her opinion. She would get regular doses of that without bidding.

"Those Blacks are shysters. Jonathon would never approve of them working on his house."

Beatrix pressed a hand to the knot in her stomach. At least the mention of his name no longer stirred sorrow in her heart, but she felt a pinch thinking of how his will had given her much more than was usually left to a wife, a final reminder of his love and devotion. As long as she didn't remarry, at least this home would remain hers. "It's my house now, and I have to manage it as best I can."

"As I told you before, I think Jonathon would have wanted Thomas to help you with such matters. I'll speak with him tonight at dinner, and—"

"Thank you, again." Beatrix set down her cup. "But I need to tend to my own affairs. As much as I loved Jonathon, he's no longer here, and I have to be able to move on."

"Move on?" Fern's eyes grew wide, and she pressed her hand to her chest. "As in remarry?"

"No, Mum." Using the term of endearment she saved for rare occasions, Beatrix selected a scone from the tray. "I have no desire to do that."

Fern dabbed at her eyes with a napkin. "Good, because you'll never find another man as wonderful as my Jonathon."

Beatrix sighed. For once, she had to agree with her mother-in-law.

Fern cleared her throat and nodded toward the door.

Broomstick-thin Thea, damp hair secured in a bun, smoothed her apron. "I apologize for my appearance, miss, but I wanted you to know the Blacks will be here within the hour."

"Thank you, Thea. I do hope they arrive soon since Clara Sherman is expected for her lesson shortly."

Thea bobbed. "I will let you know as soon as they arrive, miss."

Fern scowled. "With such an emaciated housemaid and cook, no wonder you've lost so much weight. Don't you know you can't trust a skinny cook?"

"Thea isn't emaciated, and you've never complained about her scones and cakes." Beatrix broke off the corner of her perfectly shaped scone. "She's tall and thin, and does an excellent job both taking care of the house and taking care of me."

"If you'd let Thomas and I help, you could have a whole staff."

"I only need one person, and that person is Thea." Beatrix dabbed her lips and set her napkin beside her plate. "I hate to cut our tea short, but I do need to prepare for Clara's lesson."

The older woman rose to her feet. "I'll leave then. I can tell when I'm not wanted."

Beatrix led the way to the hallway and draped Fern's cape over her shoulders. "You are always welcome here. I simply have to take care of my students. Without students, I have no income."

"Again, if you'd let us help—"

"I know, and I am truly thankful for your generous offer. However, I feel I need to do this on my own. Please try to understand." She pulled the door open and a gust of damp air drifted inside. The rain, however, had come to a stop, and a willful sun peeked out from behind gray clouds. At the end of the walk sat Fern's carriage and driver.

"What I understand is you are remarkably stubborn, and my Jonathon would not like it. He would not like you teaching music any more than he liked you performing in public, which you went ahead and did." She drew her cape closer. "Good day, Beatrix. See you tomorrow."

As soon as her mother-in-law was seated in the carriage, Beatrix closed the heavy door and leaned her cheek against the cool wood.

Was Fern right? Was she being stubborn? She barely had enough income to support this home and her needs, and the Kents had offered her a generous allowance.

No, the allowance would come with invisible strings attached. Strings that would allow Fern, the puppet master, to pull her daughter-in-law in any direction she chose.

Beatrix made her way back into the front parlor and pulled out the Christmas piece she wanted her pupil to begin work on.

"Miss, the Black brothers are here. Do you want me to show them in here to take a look?"

"Yes, please do." She scowled. "And I suppose they'll need to get onto the roof as well. We do have a ladder, don't we?"

"In the shed. I'll show 'em." Thea left and returned with two young men in their twenties. Each held a cap in his hands, one black and one brown.

Beatrix stepped forward. "Thank you for coming, gentlemen. As you can see, I have a leak that needs to be attended to."

The two men eyed the round spot on the wallpapered ceiling, and then their gaze swept over the contents of the parlor.

"We'll take a look, ma'am, and get started right away." The man holding the black cap, whom she guessed to be the older brother, gave a firm nod.

Beatrix cleared her throat. "Excuse me, but if you don't mind, I'd like for you to give me an estimated cost for the repairs prior to your beginning the work."

Brown Cap, the younger of the two, crossed his arms over his chest and frowned. "On paper?"

"A verbal estimate will suffice." Beatrix stepped back, giving the Blacks access to the leak. "Once you've finished your examination, let Thea know and we'll meet to discuss your estimate."

"All right." Black Cap slid a glance toward his brother. "But if you want us to fix this right, the price could be steep."

*Steep.* The word kept returning to her thoughts long after the Blacks left the room to climb on the roof.

⚘

Hugh Sherman squeezed the small mitten-clad hand nestled in his much larger hand and smiled down at his daughter. "Are you ready to see Miss Beatrix today?"

"Miss Beatwith lets me call her Miss Bea since I can't say her name good." His six-year-old daughter stuck her tongue into the gap left by the missing front teeth.

"Well. You can't say her name *well*." Hugh chuckled. "And those teeth will be back in no time, Clara May. Did you practice every day like Miss Bea told you to?"

She nodded vigorously, but he already knew the answer to his question. Clara loved Miss Bea, and since she'd begun lessons a few months ago, she'd blossomed under the music teacher's tutelage. Without a mum, Clara needed a woman's touch in her life, and Miss Bea's warm, encouraging ways had brought out more than simple melodies in his sweet-natured Clara.

They made their way up the walk to Widow Beatrix Kent's fine Stick–Eastlake-style home. As an architect, he immediately identified the Gothic Revival and Queen Anne elements in the wood-framed house. Naturally, Clara never tired of admiring the gingerbread woodwork complete with a white-trimmed wraparound porch. From her first day of classes, he'd had to drag his daughter off the porch swing nearly every week. He, however, questioned the use of so much wood on a house in a coastal city like Blackpool. He feared upkeep would be a full-time job.

As they neared the music teacher's walk, he noticed the door was open and two men stood outside speaking with Miss Bea at the top of the porch steps. One man was broad shouldered, and the other looked as if a good gust could carry him away. Besides a burgundy woolen cape, Miss Bea wore a dove-gray skirt, a symbol of her continued mourning. He understood mourning, but he'd lost Evie when Clara was only two years old. He'd not asked, but given Miss Bea usually wore a gray skirt rather than a harsh black dress, he imagined she was in half-mourning and her husband had been gone for nearly two years.

"That much? Are you certain?" The widow seemed to pale at the sum the beefy young man with a thick country accent gave her.

"You can trust us, ma'am." He rubbed his chin. "We'll not charge you a pound more than we have to, and you'll see nary a drop of water from that leaky roof."

Hugh stiffened at the sum they quoted her. For a leaky roof? He glanced up at the house and took note of its resilient slate tiles. Most likely, one had slipped and was letting rainwater run along the joists. Unless they were planning to put on an entirely new side, these men were trying to hoodwink Miss Beatrix.

And what were they doing at her front door? Members of the working class knew better. Their business was to be conducted at the back door only. He should know.

"What's wrong, Papa? Why are we stopping?" Ever the worrier, Clara looked up at him with a scowl on her young face.

He forced the tight muscles of his jaw to relax and squatted down to his daughter's level. "Miss Beatrix has visitors. You wait here while I go speak with them."

It was none of his business, but no one was going to take advantage of a widow while he was standing only a few feet away.

# Chapter 2

"M r. Sherman, is it time for Clara's lesson already?" Beatrix watched the man take a few long strides toward the porch and stop at the foot of the stairs.

"No, we're a bit early. I apologize, ma'am, but I overheard something about roofing issues. If I may, I'd like to take a look at the situation. I'm quite sure I could repair it for a lower cost than these fine men have proposed."

"Thank you, Mr. Sherman, but I couldn't impose on you."

The tall, skinny man hit his brown cap on the porch railing and chuckled. "And what would a gentleman like you know about climbing in rafters and putting on roofs?"

"Actually, seeing that I'm an architect, I've often spent my days in rafters, and before I took my Voluntary Examination, I spent most of my hours building with my own two hands. However, if I can't do the work personally, which I'm fairly certain I can, I will find *reputable* men to complete it."

Beatrix didn't miss the narrowing of Black Cap's eyes. Mr. Sherman then directed his attention to her. "It would be no imposition, ma'am. Any repair costs could be taken out in lessons for Clara. A fair trade of services. Do you believe that arrangement would suffice?"

Unless she accepted her in-laws' assistance, she didn't have the funds for extravagant repairs. Still, this offer seemed almost too good to be true, and she didn't want to take advantage of Mr. Sherman's kindness. "Are you certain it wouldn't be an imposition?"

"None at all. I can check the situation out while Clara is having her lesson."

"In that case—" The young widow's lips bowed, and she turned toward the two young men. "Gentlemen, it appears I am no longer in need of your assistance. Thank you for coming."

"We came all this way for nothing?" The skinny one's face reddened.

She paused to consider her options. They had, after all, come at her request. "Go around back to the kitchen and see Thea before you go. Tell her I said to provide you tea and to send you each home with a loaf of fresh bread and some of her black currant jam. Thank you both for coming." She motioned Clara forward. "Now, if you'll excuse me, I have a lesson to give."

"Don't call us if you need help in the future," Brown Cap mumbled as he descended the stairs.

Mr. Sherman stepped in front of him. "I do believe you forgot to thank the lady for her hospitality."

Oh dear. Didn't Mr. Sherman understand these men hadn't taken kindly to the interruption of their business deal? "It's fine, Mr. Sherman."

He didn't move. "Gentlemen?"

Black Cap nudged his brother. "Tell her thanks."

"Why me?"

" 'Cause I said to."

With a huff, he muttered, "Thank you, ma'am."

Mr. Sherman stepped aside and let the men pass then he looked up at her. "I hope I didn't overstep, but I couldn't let them take advantage of you. The sum they quoted you seems outlandish."

Beatrix's cheeks warmed. "I appreciate you stepping in, but honestly, I can secure some other workers to fix the leak. I don't want to put you out." She wasn't sure who those workers could possibly be, but surely she could find someone.

"I wouldn't have said I'd make the repairs if I didn't want to do the work." Mr. Sherman met her gaze with warm eyes, but when he spoke, his words were firm. "I don't say anything I don't mean."

She hated feeling indebted to Clara's father, but she did need his assistance. With this roof issue, she was literally in over her head. Besides, his services in exchange for Clara's lessons seemed a suitable business arrangement—and one she could afford. Although as much as she enjoyed Clara, it hardly seemed fair.

Beatrix held her hand out to Clara. "Shall we get you out of this chilly weather and inside so I can show your father where the water is dripping?"

Inside, Beatrix helped Clara remove her cloak and mittens before leading Mr. Sherman through the archway dividing the front and back parlors. She rarely had the doors swung open during lessons. He examined the circular stain on the ceiling. Wallpaper now hung from it like a schoolgirl's hair ribbons. After removing his suit coat and tossing it on a straight-backed chair, he tugged on his waistcoat and excused himself to locate the source of the leak.

Clara squeezed Beatrix's hand and looked up at her with Dresden-blue eyes. "Don't worry. My daddy can fix anything."

"I certainly hope so." Beatrix smiled down at the darling little girl. "But right now, I can't wait to hear your scales." As her student began playing, Beatrix said a quick prayer, asking the Lord to help Mr. Sherman find the answer he sought.

The clock struck the hour and Beatrix placed a hand on Clara's shoulder. "I think our time is up."

The little girl turned, her lower lip quivering.

Beatrix knelt before her. "Sweetheart, what's the matter?"

"You said if I tried hard next time you'd play your harp for me."

"Oh yes, I recall that, sweetheart." Beatrix stood. How could she have forgotten Clara's need for affirmation? "I'm sorry I forgot. What would you like to hear?"

Clara gave her a toothless grin. "Fairy music."

# Chapter 3

Hugh followed the sound of music down the stairs and through the hallway. He'd found the source of the leak, and now he paused in the doorway to watch Miss Bea's fingers cascade over the strings of the ornate, gilded harp. Young Clara watched, mesmerized by her teacher's movements and the dancing trills coming from the instrument. The harp seemed to have a life of its own, a history of sorts, full of sadness, joy, and hope all at once. He'd never heard anything so beautiful.

His gaze traveled from the musician's hands to her face, hidden behind the strings. Peace and joy now replaced her earlier pensive expression. Since she had no sheet music in front of her, he guessed she'd committed every note to memory. Her face was alight with scenes only she seemed to see, and he could no more pull his gaze away than stop his beating heart.

When Miss Beatrix at last lowered her hands, Clara applauded. Hugh joined Clara's applause from his place in the doorway.

Miss Beatrix's eyes widened. "Mr. Sherman, I didn't see you there."

"I didn't want to disturb you."

Clara scurried over and tugged him into the room. "It was fairy music."

"Ah, that would explain the spell it cast on me." He smiled at the teacher, and for a brief second she allowed her lips to lift as well. "You are amazingly talented, Mrs. Kent. Shouldn't you be performing—"

"What did you discover about the leak?"

That was odd. Her words tumbled out, stopping him midsentence. Clearly, she did not want to discuss her harp playing further. But why? While he was no expert, any musician of her notable accomplishment should be on a stage playing for royals, not in a parlor entertaining a six-year-old.

She heaved the instrument back in place and stood. "I certainly hope the repairs won't be too difficult."

Hugh snagged his coat from the chair and shoved his arms into the sleeves. "I found a few tiles that have come loose on the roof. There are some rotted boards which need to be replaced as well. I'll pick up a few supplies and return tomorrow after work to make the repairs. I'll have to bring Clara along. Is that a problem?"

"Not in the least." She smiled at the little girl. "After you practice your Christmas piece, would you like to help me make some gingerbread biscuits?"

"Gingerbread men and women and boys and girls?" Clara bounced on her toes.

"I even have a tin biscuit cutter of Father Christmas." She winked at Clara and helped her fasten her cloak over her shoulders. She turned to Hugh. "I'm planning to take a basket of treats to the ragged school on Friday afternoon, so Clara and I will have a grand time tomorrow making biscuits."

He didn't much care for the idea of the lady going into that part of town alone, but he didn't voice his concerns. He knew all too well that the ragged schools, named after the ragged clothes the poor children wore, were charity organizations designed to feed and educate the poor children, and they could use all the help they could get.

He glanced down at his daughter and her wide, gap-toothed smile. He'd not seen her this happy in quite some time. Not wanting the magic of the afternoon to slip from her grasp, he stepped into the entryway and laid his hand on the door's latch. "Did you hear that?" He motioned to the door. "Clara, put your ear on the door and listen." His daughter complied.

Miss Bea's brows furled. "What is it? What do you hear?"

He grinned and winked at her. "Fairies."

Clara beamed. "I hear them, Papa. They're singing, but if you open the door they'll run away."

"We'll have to take our chances, Clara May." He opened the door and turned back to Miss Bea.

"Fairies?"

"You must have enchanted them with your music." He bowed. "As you have enchanted Clara and me."

Beatrix arranged tea cakes on a flowered plate. The clock gonged, and she looked toward the door. Where was her mother-in-law? Promptness was sacred to Fern Kent, and tardiness akin to breaking one of the Ten Commandments.

No use wasting the time. She crossed the room to her harp and tuned the large instrument. Mr. Sherman's words from yesterday lingered in her thoughts: "*As you have enchanted Clara and me.*" What did he mean by that? It seemed a bit too familiar, but he had seemed especially moved by the music, and such reactions were not unheard of.

The front door swung wide and Fern marched in with two men in tow bearing boughs of greenery and holly. Pine scent filled the entryway and front parlor.

"Set them over there." Fern pointed to a library table. The two men did as told then held out their palms. Her mother-in-law pressed a coin into each man's hand, and they departed as quickly as they'd come.

Beatrix fingered a sprig of holly. "What are these for?"

"Your home—or rather, Jonathon's home."

"Thank you, but it's only Thea and I here, and I'm not feeling terribly festive."

"Of course you aren't, but you must keep up appearances. *Cassell's* says every proper lady should endeavor to make her home festive for the Christmas season just as the queen herself does." Fern settled in the chair in front of the tea set and began to pour. "Please, do sit down. You know how I dislike waiting."

Beatrix took her seat while her mother-in-law poured. She lifted her cup to her lips and sipped the now tepid tea in need of more sugar. Should she offer to pay for the unsolicited greenery? If so, how? She released a sigh as unnoticeably as she could. Even when she refused the Kents' help, they found a way to make her indebted to them. She had enough students now to make ends meet, but not for extravagant extras like pine garlands.

Fern withdrew a card from her handbag. "This is for you."

Beatrix accepted the card and read the invitation. She examined the reverse and found it addressed to her. Why would the Spencers invite her to a Christmas dinner party?

"I had to pull strings to get you invited, so I hope you won't embarrass me by sending your regrets." Fern took one of the tea cakes and nibbled on it.

Nerves taut, Beatrix reread the card. "But I don't even know the Spencers."

"Jonathon did. We expected him to marry their Olivia, but alas, that was not to be." She added more tea to her cup.

"I'm still in half-mourning." Surely, even Fern couldn't deny that.

"You can wear your purple gown. It's dated, but will do." She set down her cup with a clink. "It's only a dinner party, so no one will think twice about your attendance."

Beatrix's chest tightened each time Fern spoke. Why couldn't she simply tell the woman *no*? "I'm not sure—"

"Nonsense. You need students, and this party may open doors to some wealthy parents who need to hire a music teacher for their daughters' training. That would certainly be a step up from your current clientele. Even I understand an upper-class young lady cannot expect to marry without accomplishments. And as much as I hate to admit it, you do have admirable—if not prideful—accomplishments. Thomas and I will call for you on the designated date, and we'll all arrive together." Fern patted her lips with her napkin then stood. "Do try to get Thea to freshen that purple gown with a bit of lace, and I expect those garlands up before Saturday."

Beatrix rose to her feet as well. "We don't have tea together on the weekends."

"Perhaps I'll stop by to check on your progress." Fern let Beatrix slip her cloak over her shoulders. She leaned forward so Beatrix could kiss her cheek. "Well?"

Beatrix raised her eyebrows.

"Aren't you going to thank me?"

Beatrix clenched her teeth. *Patience. Patience. Patience.* "Thank you, ma'am, for the greenery boughs."

"And?" Fern adjusted her hat.

Like a chastened schoolgirl, Beatrix stiffened under Fern's gaze. "Thank you for garnering an invitation to the Spencers' for me."

"You're welcome, Beatrix. I hope you realize how fortunate you are. Not all in-laws would continue to foster a relationship with their former daughter-in-law under the circumstances."

Another jab. Tears filled Beatrix's eyes. Would Fern never tire of reminding Beatrix of her role in Jonathon's death?

Beatrix swallowed hard. "I'm blessed, I know." The words sounded flat to Beatrix, but Fern didn't seem to notice.

Not that Fern noticed anything other than what made her look good in front of her peers.

As soon as the door closed, Beatrix sat down at the piano and poured her anguish, frustration, and anger into the music she played.

At the end of the piece, she lifted her hands, out of breath and emotionally spent. The piano had been a good choice.

It was hard to sound angry on a harp.

Determination pulsed in her veins. Why did she let Fern control her choices? Why did she allow the woman to heap more guilt on her? Didn't she carry enough of that on her own? All her life she'd wanted to make her own choices and stand on her own. Now was her chance.

She had to stop allowing Fern to be her puppet master. Fern pulled all the strings, and like a marionette in the children's theatre productions, Beatrix danced. If she didn't need additional students, then she'd send her regrets to the Spencers after all. However, Fern was correct. This dinner party was a way to secure connections to additional, possibly wealthier, pupils.

But this was the last time.

Steeling her shoulders, she made a vow to herself. After this dinner party, she'd refuse to be summoned by Mr. and Mrs. Thomas Kent ever again.

She pushed to her feet. Now, it was time to begin making garlands to hang over her doors.

Beatrix mounted the step stool, balancing a prickly pine garland in her hands. It had taken hours to make the pine ropes, but soon she'd have the creations mounted in case her mother-in-law decided to make an early visit.

She fought the cloud hanging over her. Christmas shouldn't feel like such a burden. It should be a joyous time. But without a family to share the occasion with, it simply wasn't the same.

"Miss, I told you that I'd climb up there this time." Thea held up the other end of the evergreen rope. "It isn't right for a fine lady like you to be climbing up and down."

"Nonsense." Beatrix hooked one end on the nail she'd put in the woodwork only minutes ago. She'd already draped the doorway leading into the dining room and the doorway that led from the entryway to the parlor. Now, they only had to secure the second side of this garland over the arch which divided the front and back parlor. "If we keep working, we'll get these hung before Mr. Sherman and Clara arrive."

The brass knocker on the door sounded and Thea shrugged. "Too late. Shall I answer the door?"

Beatrix climbed down from the step stool and repositioned it on the other side of the doorway. "Yes, go on while I fasten this one in place."

Even though she hated to admit it, the Christmas decorations did seem to warm her home. As soon as she'd first decorated the banister, the hallway began to feel festive, and she hoped it would inspire her pupils to work hard on their Christmas pieces.

From her rather precarious perch on the step stool, Beatrix could hear Thea directing Mr. Sherman and Clara into the parlor. She needed to hurry. She tacked the garland in place, but the center slipped from its nail. Reaching as far as she could, she snagged the errant swag and lifted it over the nail. The step stool shifted beneath her. Her breath caught. She reached for the doorframe but only brushed the wood as she fell.

Strong hands encapsulated her waist and steadied her. She looked down to find Mr. Sherman holding her, and her cheeks burned. He lifted her from the step stool and set her feet on the floor. "That was close. Are you all right?"

She nodded and drew in a deep breath. Odd. He didn't scold her for attempting the task like Jonathon would have. Mr. Sherman simply shoved the step stool over a foot, climbed up, and hooked the center of the garland. Once his feet were back on the floor, he looked up at the festive decoration. "Very pretty. Did you do all this by yourself today?"

"Thea and I worked together. My mother-in-law thought the house needed some Christmas decorations."

"And you? Has it helped your Christmas spirit?" His gaze seemed to cut through her façade.

"I guess I still need a bit of yuletide cheer." She smiled, and for the first time noticed he'd come in work clothes. It made perfect sense, but in the months since she'd been teaching Clara, she'd never seen him in anything but professional attire. With his dark hair tucked inside a winter cap and his neck wrapped in a woolen scarf, he had a more roguish appearance, and he seemed as comfortable in well-worn trousers and a heavy work jacket as he had in his suit the day before.

"What do you think, Clara May? Shall we carol for Mrs. Kent?" He took Clara's hands and swung them. "Deck the hall with boughs of holly." Unabashed, his baritone voice rang out.

Clara giggled and joined him. "Fa, la, la, la, la, la, la, la, la!"

He motioned with his head, inviting Beatrix to sing out as well. It was impetuous and silly, but she couldn't help herself. His enthusiasm was infectious. She lifted her voice to match his. " 'Tis the season to be jolly."

When the last "fa, la, la" came to a close, laughter bubbled up in each of them.

"Oh, that was delightful." Mr. Sherman cupped his daughter's face. "Lovely singing from lovely ladies. I am a blessed man."

Heat again crept up Beatrix's neck. His words, she knew, were directed more toward Clara than her, but strangely, they had touched her. He met her gaze with coal-colored eyes, and she quickly turned away.

An awkward silence cloaked the room.

Mr. Sherman cleared his throat. "I think it's time for me to get to work and let you ladies begin your biscuits. Please, do save me one, Clara."

Clara moved next to Beatrix. "Is that okay, Miss Bea?"

"Of course."

"Then, I'll save you a lady biscuit—one as pretty as Miss Bea."

He chuckled. "In that case, I'll be a lucky man indeed."

"Miss Bea, I already practiced my scales."

Beatrix cast a glance to Mr. Sherman to confirm Clara's words. "Well done. I'm proud of you."

They watched Mr. Sherman leave then went into the kitchen where Thea was setting out the tin biscuit cutters. Beatrix picked up the carefully shaped lady cutter with her narrow waist and bell-shaped skirt. *A lucky man indeed?* Was Mr. Sherman simply saying something sweet to his daughter or did his words carry a subtle innuendo?

She needed to be careful. As a widower, he might be lonely. He appeared to be both handsome and kind, but she couldn't return any affections. At the same time, she didn't want to hurt him any more than life already had. Besides, love only came once in a lifetime, and she'd had hers.

"Here ya go." Thea held out an apron to Clara. "Put this on so you don't get flour on that pretty dress."

Beatrix assisted the little girl and tied a big white bow at the back. Clara spun to model the fit, her blond curls bobbing. "Is it okay?"

Again, the need for approval she'd noticed earlier appeared. Clara needed to find confidence. She could help with that.

How strange that one minute she was trying to find her own courage and the next she was prepared to help a child find hers. Maybe she and Clara could find some together. She showed Clara how to roll out a piece of dough and cut through it with the tin cutters. The little girl delighted in each creation and soon Beatrix felt joy pulsing through her.

Mr. Sherman's words about the lady gingerbread biscuit came back to her, and she realized she'd read too much into them. He was simply doing his best to bring happiness to his daughter's motherless world. Clara could certainly assist him in that endeavor, especially at Christmas.

Hugh pried the old clay tile off the roof using more force than necessary. Frustration burned inside him. Foolhardy. Insensitive. Boorish. He could call his actions nothing less.

Why had those words come out of his mouth? Yes, Beatrix Kent was indeed a pretty lady—molasses-colored hair, warm hazel eyes the size of a sixpence, and long, graceful fingers. When he'd caught her about the waist, he'd been surprised at the surge of heat that shot through him. It wasn't as if he'd not stepped out with another woman since Evie's death, but this was the first time he'd felt moved by another woman's nearness. Surely it was just the mixture of Christmas spirit and the kindness she'd shown Clara. Good heavens, Miss Beatrix was an accomplished lady, and she still wore mourning clothes.

He jammed a pry bar beneath another tile and pressed downward. A pleasing pop sounded and the tile gave way. At this rate, he'd be done in no time. Leaning back, he drew in a long breath. He'd better slow down or Clara wouldn't get her biscuits finished.

And he'd not get his pretty lady biscuit.

*No. No. No.* He tossed the damaged tile off the edge of the roof. He needed to focus on his work and stop thinking about Beatrix Kent. Even if he did have feelings for her, which he did not, she'd married into the fine Kent family. If she knew the truth about his upbringing, she'd never give him a second look.

Wanting Clara to have as much biscuit-making time as possible, he finished his task and returned the tools to the shed before going back into the house. Once inside, he followed the voices he heard into the kitchen. He found Clara busy pressing tin biscuit cutters into a slab of rolled gingerbread under Miss Beatrix's watchful eye. Thea then carefully eased them onto a baking sheet.

"Look, Papa!" Clara held up a baked gingerbread star. He noticed a hole in the top. "Miss Bea said I can hang it on our Christmas tree."

"We haven't gotten one yet. Why don't you hang it on hers?"

"I'm not having a tree this year." Miss Beatrix snitched a piece of gingerbread and popped it between her lips. "Since it's only Thea and I, it hardly seems necessary."

Clara's worried brows scrunched. "But where will Father Christmas put your toys?"

Miss Beatrix smiled. "I'm sure he'll think of something."

Hugh turned toward a basket heaped with biscuits of all shapes. "Now, that's a lot of biscuits."

"I'm taking them to the ragged school on Chapel Street tomorrow afternoon." She laid a hand on Clara's shoulder.

"What's a raggedy school?" Lines creased Clara's brow.

"A ragged school." Beatrix added more biscuits to the basket. "It's a school for poor children, so this will be a special treat for the boys and girls there."

"We're being kind, right? 'Cause they don't have as many nice things as we do—like biscuits—so we're giving them ours?"

"You mean we're giving them Mrs. Kent's, but it's still a kind thing to do." Apparently, Miss Bea had used the opportunity to teach his daughter something. Hugh grinned and dusted the flour off Clara's nose. He met Miss Beatrix's gaze. "The leak is fixed. I'll take care of the wallpaper after Clara's next lesson."

"I'm sure I can handle that."

He chuckled. "I've seen how you manage a step stool. I'd hate to think of you on a ladder. It's time for us to depart, Clara." He tickled her as he tugged on her apron strings and she burst into giggles.

He passed the apron to Miss Beatrix and nudged his daughter's shoulder.

Clara smiled up at her teacher. "Thank you, Miss Bea."

"You're very welcome, Clara." She glanced to Thea. "Since you're up to your elbows in flour, I'll see them out."

At the front door, she passed them their wraps and knelt in front of Clara to secure the girl's cape. "Now, remember what I told you. Father Christmas is watching to see how kind you can be to others."

"Then maybe he'll bring me a doll like he did you when you were my age?"

Miss Bea grinned and cocked her head toward her father. "Maybe—if you're extra kind."

They said goodbye, and he shook his head as they began their short trek home. A doll? What did he know about buying a doll? Building a theater, a mansion, or even a dollhouse he could handle, but finding an appropriate doll for Clara was beyond his skill set.

He was going to need help, and he knew just the person to ask.

# Chapter 4

Beatrix tucked the basket of biscuits in the crook of her arm and pulled the door shut behind her. The temperature had dipped overnight and hadn't warmed much by noon. She was glad she'd worn her burgundy woolen cape. It wasn't mourners' gray or even dark blue, but she didn't think anyone at the ragged school would notice.

She started down the lane and crossed over to the next street. A hansom cab stopped in front of her, and when the passenger turned, she drew in a quick breath.

"Good afternoon, Mrs. Kent." Hugh Sherman smiled at her. "Are those the biscuits for the ragged school? I'm headed in that same direction on some business. May I give you a ride?"

"I'll be fine."

"I'm sure you would be, but it's rather cold." He climbed out of the cab and waited for her to accept his offer.

She glanced at the cab driver, perched high on his sprung seat. He seemed annoyed at the interruption of stopping. Perhaps she should acquiesce before they made a scene. "Very well."

Once she was seated beside him in the carriage and the driver moved his lever to close the wooden doors, her thoughts began to tumble. What if someone saw them together? What if accepting a ride from Hugh indicated to him she'd accept his advances?

*Don't be silly. You're merely sharing a cab.*

Mr. Sherman tapped the roof to tell the driver she was settled, and the steady *clip-clop* of the horse's hooves on the cobblestone street began. He shifted in his seat to turn toward her. "Clara hasn't stopped talking about yesterday. I don't know if I thanked you."

"I should thank you. It rained during the night, but my parlor remained completely dry."

"Good. You have a fine home."

She adjusted the basket on her lap and caught a whiff of gingerbread. "I'm more attached to it than I probably should be."

"Oh?"

"My memories are there."

Silence sat between them until the hansom cab veered to the right toward the wharf. The street narrowed and the cobblestone streets gave way to mud. Small shops lined the way. Beatrix pressed her kerchief to her nose to block the offending odors.

"You do know the 1870 Education Act ensured all children had a right to a secular school placement, so some say the Chapel Street Ragged School is unnecessary."

She raised an eyebrow. "Look around. Does it look like these children have a fine secular school?"

"No, but at least they're being educated."

"How can they ever improve themselves if they start so far behind?"

"Education is a tool. Those who choose will use it to build."

"And what would you possibly know about that?" Her eyes burned with unshed tears. Didn't he understand? Jonathon hadn't either. There was nothing fair or proper in this area, and these children deserved more than gingerbread biscuits. Unfortunately, that was all she had to offer. If she had the kind of money Mr. Sherman did, she'd buy new slates or clean clothes for the children.

Or oranges.

Wouldn't that be a grand Christmas treat?

He signaled the driver to stop the carriage in front of the school and helped her down, but instead of returning to the carriage, he withdrew a large crate from the space near his feet and instructed the driver to wait for them.

Beatrix stared at him. "Where are you going? I thought you had business?"

"I do."

Then without another word, he followed her inside.

Unwilling to interrupt the morning lessons, Beatrix paused in the doorway and surveyed the windowless classroom. She'd been there before, but every time her heart sank at the conditions she found—over sixty students, many filthy and in threadbare clothes, sat at desks, sharing slates.

"Ah look, children, we have visitors." The headmaster, a middle-aged man with rounded spectacles, motioned Beatrix and Mr. Sherman forward. "What do we say to welcome our guests?"

"Good morning, Mrs. Kent," the children sang in chorus. "Good morning, Mr. Sherman."

She whirled toward him, eyes wide. "You've come before?"

His eyes twinkled and he quirked a grin. "We have Christmas treats for the children, Mr. Winchester. Do you want us to pass them out now or would you like to save them for the end of the day?"

The headmaster rubbed his chin. "Well, I don't think they'll learn another thing until they find out what you brought." He stepped toward the long front bench. "I'll release you row by row, children. Mind your manners and be sure to thank Mrs. Kent and Mr. Sherman."

Beatrix set her basket on the desk while Mr. Sherman pulled the teacher's chair out from behind the desk and set his crate on it. The children fell into a perfectly straight line. Beatrix pulled back the towel protecting the cookies and placed one in the dingy hand of a little girl about Clara's age. A broad smile bloomed on the child's face, and she thanked Beatrix profusely. The girl proceeded to Mr. Sherman. He tugged off the burlap covering the crates contents and Beatrix gasped.

Oranges.

Beautiful orbs of fruit. In order to have a whole crate of oranges today, he would have had to order it weeks ago. Her heart leapt with joy for the children. He spoke to each of the children, wishing them a "Happy Christmas," and before they left, he persuaded the headmaster to let them all sing a few carols.

Her previously unkind thoughts battered her conscience. She should not be so quick to judge. It had been unfair and unkind. As they departed, her heart warmed toward the man who obviously had a soft spot for children in need.

Mr. Sherman insisted on taking her back home.

"Your business?"

"Was to deliver the oranges." He helped her into the carriage before taking his place beside her. The driver closed the doors, and the horse trotted off. "Every child deserves something special this time of year—like your biscuits. Clara will be excited when I tell her about how happy they made the children. I only wish she could have been here."

"You'd bring Clara down here?"

"It would be good for her to see that children are children, no matter how clean they are or how well dressed. I want her to respect all persons, regardless of class."

"I find that admirable, Mr. Sherman."

She found herself looking at the man anew. He was a devoted father, but there seemed to be more behind his actions. Was he a man of faith? A part of her wanted to ask, but it would be intrusive. They were merely acquaintances, not even friends. Or had they crossed that line?

"Mrs. Kent, will you please call me by my Christian name of Hugh? After what we've shared today, it simply seems too stuffy for friends. I don't, however, expect you to allow me the use of your Christian name."

She bit her lips, her stomach twisting. She didn't want to open this door, but she also didn't want to close it either. Something about Hugh Sherman intrigued her, and she did need friends. But letting him call her by her given name? Fern certainly wouldn't approve.

"Beatrix." There she'd said it. "But please refer to me by name only when no one is around."

"I think Clara already knows your name." He chuckled. "And speaking of Clara, she has not stopped talking about receiving a doll for Christmas. I believe she said you got a doll from Father Christmas when you were her age. She said you were living in France?"

"I was, and yes, I did get my treasured playmate for my sixth Christmas, but I apologize if I overstepped in sharing my story. I didn't mean to encourage her."

"I'm glad you did, but I may need your help."

"Mine? How?"

"I know nothing about purchasing a doll. Since you got me into this situation, would you be so kind as to help me out of it? All I'm asking for is one afternoon of toy shopping."

She could understand the widower's position. To him, buying a doll probably left him feeling as out of sorts as fixing a leak had to her. And what would one afternoon in public places hurt? Even widows weren't expected to stay indoors all the time.

She fidgeted with the ties of her purse. "I'm sure we can think of something that will work for both of us."

"Thank you. And I mean that most sincerely."

They arrived at her home, and he climbed down to help her alight. A stout woman marched toward them from the front porch. Beatrix recognized Fern immediately. She swayed.

Hugh steadied her. "Are you all right?"

"Yes, but please go." She stepped away from him. "Quickly."

Beatrix steeled herself for what was to come and said a prayer asking for wisdom to handle this situation. She watched Hugh's hansom cab drive away as she waited for her mother-in-law's ire to descend. She prayed she could get the woman to hold her tongue until they were out of earshot of the neighbors.

Fern stopped in front of her. "And who exactly was that?"

*You're not a puppet*, Beatrix reminded herself. *Please, Lord, let me be brave.*

"Can we speak inside?" Ignoring the churning fear inside her, Beatrix left no room for her mother-in-law to disagree and headed toward the house.

Fern stomped up the stairs behind her. This was not going to go easy.

Beatrix opened the door, removed her own cloak, took Fern's, and called for Thea to bring tea.

She took a seat in her customary place in the parlor, and Fern did likewise, seemingly on the edge of an angry outburst.

Thea brought the tray, and Fern reached for the teapot, but Beatrix beat her to the handle. "I'll pour. It is my house, after all, and I'm sure you're chilled to the bone since you were sitting on the porch waiting for me."

"Well, you certainly aren't. Riding in a hansom cab with a complete stranger. Beatrix, how could you?"

*"A soft answer turneth away wrath."* Beatrix mentally repeated the scripture over and over, until it became a gentle melody and her spirit settled.

"He's not a stranger. His name is Hugh Sherman. He's a widower, and I teach his daughter, Clara. We are merely acquaintances, and he offered me the hansom cab ride since we were both headed in the same direction."

"And where exactly was that?"

Beatrix's calm flickered. She'd stepped into this part. "The Church Street Ragged School."

"You went there? You know Jonathon hated you going down there to help those miscreants. He'd be appalled."

"They are children, not miscreants. I took them gingerbread biscuits, and Mr. Sherman surprised them with oranges." She sipped her tea, which, for the first time in years, was perfectly sweetened with two lumps of sugar. "Every child deserves a happy Christmas."

"And what about me? Don't I deserve a happy Christmas rather than hearing about my son's wife canoodling with another man? Wearing a red cape, no less? Have you no respect for Jonathon?"

Beatrix set her cup down so hard tea splashed out. "I was not canoodling." She didn't raise her voice, but she also couldn't keep the frustration from lacing the words. "And it was *I* who lost *my* husband. It's been two years, and the *burgundy* cape is the warmest I own. Jonathon is not here to approve or disapprove of my choices. I miss him, as I'm sure you do, but as I told you before, I'm doing my best to move on."

"Without him." Fern's watery eyes flashed.

Beatrix nodded. "What other choice do I have?"

Fern quieted and took a sip from her cup. After a long moment, she eyed Beatrix over the brim. "Well, my dear, remember, if you do have designs on another man, be it this Mr. Sherman or someone else, it would be wise for you to recall what the barrister explained as the conditions of my Jonathon's will. If you remarry, this house and its contents revert to Thomas and me."

An imaginary rope tightened around Beatrix's midsection. For the first time, what had seemed like such a gift from Jonathon now felt like a noose. If she was to ever love again, she'd have to forfeit this home and all the memories it contained.

"Good. I see you understand." Fern stood, setting her napkin on her chair. "You've always been too headstrong. I cautioned Jonathon before the two of you wed. Your parents were artists, free thinkers, and I doubt there were many restraints in place in your home. However, Jonathon, being several years older than you, was certain his strong hand would bring you under control. But he was wrong. You didn't heed his wishes, and if you had, my son would still be alive. You could have at least given us a grandchild."

Unable to keep them at bay, tears trickled from Beatrix's eyes. Even now, not being able to give Jonathon a child was one of her greatest regrets. What Fern did not realize was that their long-trusted family physician had confided that a riding injury in Jonathon's youth had most likely led to his inability to father a child. Unwilling to lay that kind of shame on her husband, she'd accepted all of Fern's unkind remarks for an empty womb.

Everything in her wanted to spew the words of truth at her former mother-in-law, but God's words returned to her. "*A soft answer turneth away wrath: but grievous words stir up anger.*" She dabbed her eyes. Her words would indeed be grievous, but didn't Fern deserve to be hurt like she'd just hurt her?

In truth, perhaps she might, but extending grace was not giving one what they deserved. It was unmerited favor. Could she give Fern any less than Christ had given her?

Beatrix could not add to Fern's grief. She was Jonathon's mother and, as such, Beatrix had promised herself to be as respectful as possible. Still, it was time for a change. She could no longer let Fern verbally pummel her on her visits. It was simply too painful to endure over and over.

Beatrix stood. "I think it's time for teatime to be over."

"I suppose it is." Fern carefully folded her napkin and set it aside. She rose slowly and shook out the layers of her bustled, taffeta day dress. "Until tomorrow then."

"No, it's time for you to move on as well." Beatrix clasped her hands at her waist. "On many occasions you've mentioned how our teas have kept you from your friends. Our standing daily tea is no longer necessary. I'm busy with my pupils, so I'll send you an invitation—when I'm ready."

Momentary surprise on Fern's face was instantly replaced with her seasoned authoritative mask. "Very well. I shall enjoy being freed from this obligation."

Beatrix followed her to the front door, but no solicitous words came to mind. Maybe silence was the softest answer of all.

"Do try to look presentable next week at the Spencers', Beatrix. Like it or not, what you do reflects on Thomas and me."

Without a word, Beatrix shut the door.

# Chapter 5

"You played beautifully today, Clara." Beatrix jotted a note in her journal. "I think you're well on your way to performing your Christmas piece perfectly. You'll be a star at our recital."

"I have to play in front of people?" Worry creased Clara's brow.

"Yes, but you'll do fine. Playing in front of people is part of mastering an instrument."

Clara's face scrunched, a question forming. "How many pupils do you have?"

Beatrix glanced at the parlor's mantel clock when it struck the hour. Why wasn't Hugh here to collect Clara? They'd already gone overtime. It wasn't a problem because Clara was her last student on Wednesday, but it was a bit off-putting for him to be inconsiderate.

"Are you counting?" Clara asked.

"No, I was wool-gathering. I have twenty-two altogether, but I may get some additional students soon."

"Are they all learning Christmas pieces? Does anyone play the harp like you? Are there any other girls my age?"

"My, aren't you full of questions?" Beatrix jumped when the brass knocker sounded on the front door. "But I think your father must be here, so I'm afraid your questions will have to wait."

Beatrix opened the oak door to find an enormous fir tree filling the doorframe. Hugh tipped it to the side to reveal his rosy-cheeked face. "Special delivery for Mrs. Kent."

"But I don't need a tree."

He nudged her aside and carried it across the threshold. "Everyone needs a Christmas tree. After all, where will Father Christmas put your presents if you don't have one, right, Clara?"

Clara drew her hands together and bounced up and down. Another man followed Hugh in bearing a crock of stones.

"Where do you want it?" Hugh motioned toward the bay window.

Beatrix raised her eyebrows. "I didn't say I did."

"Don't be a spoilsport." He turned to Clara. "Even Queen Victoria has a tree. What do you think, Clara? Here? Or by the staircase?"

"By the window!" The little girl danced around in a circle.

Beatrix softened. She didn't want to damper Clara's joy—or Hugh's. "That's a good choice."

The delivery man seemed relieved. He set the heavy crock in place with an *umph*. Hugh set the tree in the crock and dropped a coin in the delivery man's open palm. "Thank you, James. Now, Clara, go ask Thea for some pitchers of water. We need to give this thirsty tree a drink."

Clara giggled and skipped off.

He turned to Beatrix. "So, what do you think?"

"It's huge." She drew in a deep breath, and the pine scent tickled her nose. "And beautiful. You shouldn't have."

"I was cutting a tree down for Clara and me, and this one was next to it. It was meant to be."

Thea carried in two large ewers. Hugh took them and filled the crock.

Clara stared up at the tree and made a face. "It needs to be dressed. It's naked."

Beatrix stifled a laugh. "Would you like to help me dress it?"

"Oh yes, Miss Bea!"

"Thea." Beatrix turned to her maid. "Can you set three places for dinner?"

Hugh started to protest, but Beatrix held up her hand. "You brought that monster in here, so the least you can do is stay and make paper fans to trim it."

"Me?" He placed his hand on his chest.

"You design buildings. I believe paper-folding is well within your abilities." Beatrix pointed to the dining room. "I'll meet you in there in a few minutes. I have a few supplies to gather."

"And I'll start making popcorn to string," Thea offered.

"Popcorn, I can handle." Hugh took Clara's hand. "One to string. One to eat."

Beatrix called from the other room. "Don't let him eat any, Clara. The popcorn is for the tree."

If she was going to have a tree, it was going to be breathtaking, for Clara's sake. After locating the box of Christmas candles she and Jonathon had used, she rummaged through its contents. If she recalled, there were still pieces of colored paper to use in making decorations. Once located, she went to the hall closet and tucked a few secret items in with the rest.

She couldn't wait to see Clara's face light up when she saw this tree come to life.

Hugh lifted the box from Beatrix's arms and set it on the built-in buffet. The table, a rich walnut, had been hastily set for three, and Thea was busy filling glasses with water. He took in the fine china set, possibly a wedding gift, artistically arranged behind the glass doors above the buffet. Turning, he noted a dark still-life painting of two hunting dogs standing guard over a large dead hare. The painting hardly matched the rest of the room in style, and it certainly didn't seem like something Beatrix would choose. A protective twinge pinched inside him. Would her husband insist on making her dine under the auspices of this painting?

Beatrix moved to stand beside him. "It's by a French painter named Gustave Courbet, and I dislike it as much today as the day Jonathon brought it home."

Hugh kept his eyes on the painting. "Then why don't you take it down?"

"I guess it reminds me of him."

"I'm sure there are other things in this house which would serve that purpose with much fonder memories."

Clara tugged on Hugh's hand. "Papa, it's scary."

Beatrix stared at the painting for a long time. Finally, she drew in a deep breath. "Today, I've decided there are some things which have to change in my life if I'm to be happy, and I might as well start with this." She moved toward the painting, grasped the edges of the gilded frame, and started to lift it.

Hugh came up behind her and placed his hands above hers on the frame. "Allow me."

She slid out from beneath his outstretched arms. He lifted the frame from its peg and set it on the floor, facing the wall.

"I think the food will taste better than usual tonight." Beatrix wiped her hands together then motioned toward the table. "Shall we?"

As soon as they'd consumed the light supper, Thea cleared the table and spread a protective bedsheet over it. After Hugh brought over the box of Christmas items, Beatrix displayed the paper trimmings she'd made in the past. Clara immediately found an angel with a sparkling halo and declared it beautiful.

Hugh picked up the intricately cut paper man and woman posed dancing together. "You and Jonathon?"

"No, he didn't care for dancing, but my mother and father did." Beatrix called Clara to her side and showed the girl how to fold a paper fan.

As soon as Thea arrived with a bowl of fluffy popcorn, she directed Hugh to start making the garland. "And don't eat all the popcorn."

Moments later, Thea scurried back in with another bowl. "This one is for eating, Mr. Sherman."

"Thank you, Thea. Do you want to stay and help?"

She glanced from Hugh to her mistress, so Beatrix hastened to tell her they'd love to have her join them.

"Thank you all the same, miss. I've dishes to do and some handwork to finish on a gift I'm making. You three enjoy yourselves."

And they did. They laughed, ate popcorn, and made decoration after decoration. They took turns hanging the strings of popcorn and tucking their paper creations on the tree's stout boughs. Clara advanced from Fan Maker to Paper Rosette Queen, but at last, she began to nod off and Beatrix suggested Hugh let her nap on the settee. Once she was nestled in the blanket he'd found, he added a log to the fireplace and the room warmed considerably.

Beatrix met him in the parlor. "Ready to make magic?" she whispered.

"Excuse me?"

She held up a jar of liquid gum and a jar of Epsom salts. "We're going to make it sparkle with hoarfrost."

"Truly? Beatrix, you continue to surprise me."

She warmed at the sound of her name on his lips. He took charge of dipping wool in the gum and touching the branches wherever the frost might form, while Beatrice expertly sprinkled the coarse salt on each spot. She tucked in the few blown-glass ornaments she owned, one a Christmas gift from Jonathon. Hugh asked her about her parents.

"My father played the violin and my mother, the harp. They performed together throughout Europe."

"So you learned the harp from her?"

"Yes, and she left me her harp when she died." Beatrix gazed at the instrument. "I can still see and hear her playing when I close my eyes. It's my most prized possession."

"How long has your mother been gone?"

"Seven years. I was eighteen. I played with my father until—" She stopped herself.

"Until you met Jonathon?"

"Yes." She relaxed. They were friends. They could talk about their spouses. "How did you meet your wife? What was her name?"

"Evie. We met at a party." Hugh excused himself and returned with the box of candles. "The final touch."

They clipped the lights to the branches and, finally, Hugh took a taper and lit each candle.

"Shall we wake Clara now?" Beatrix adjusted a tilting candle.

"Not quite yet." He brought two chairs over so they could sit in front of the tree. "Let's have it all to ourselves for a minute or two."

Beatrix settled beside him and arranged her mauve skirt. The tree cast a magical glow on the room, but the intimacy of sitting side by side in the quiet suddenly replaced the comfortable comradery she'd felt all evening. She swallowed hard. "You mentioned your wife, Evie. Tell me about her."

He leaned forward and propped his elbows on his knees. "We married young, so we had a lot of growing up to do. Evie was a good mum, and I tried to be a good husband."

Beatrix picked at a loose thread on her skirt. "How did she die?"

"Pneumonia." He sat up straight and sighed. "Clara was only two."

She did a quick mental calculation. He had to be only a couple of years older than her, and his Evie had been gone four years. She shivered despite the warmth coming from the fireplace. "Does it get easier? Living without them?"

He reached over and squeezed her hand. "The unbearably hard times come further and further apart, but I doubt they ever go away." His touch was gone seconds later. He stood and snagged a blanket from a chair. He draped it over her shoulders. "And you? How did you meet Jonathon?"

She pulled the blanket closer. "My father and I performed at a party he attended."

"Ah, so your playing captured him."

"Not at all. He wasn't particularly fond of the harp, but he said he enjoyed seeing me behind it. I was quite enamored by his attentions, even though he was ten years my senior. We courted for only a few months before he asked my father for my hand. After the wedding, my father returned to performing without me."

"And where is your father currently?" Hugh returned to his chair.

"At Drumlanrig Castle, staying with the Duke and Duchess of Buccleuch."

Hugh raised his eyebrows.

"I'm sure you already know nobility of all nations are great patrons of the arts. Some patronage the arts for good reason, but others use it to endorse their political ambitions, social positions, and prestige. Sometimes they've even used the arts to rid themselves of ill-gotten gains."

"And this marquis?"

She shrugged. "He is treating my father well, and my father is playing the best concert halls. That's all I know. I'd love to see him for Christmas, but he probably won't visit until spring."

They heard stirring on the settee, and Clara's head appeared over the back. She yawned, and her eyes grew as large as the walnuts on the tree. "It's soooo pretty."

Clara was correct. The tree glistened and sparkled like a star in the sky.

"It sure is." Hugh scooped his daughter up so she could get a better view. "I guess I should get you bundled up and taken home to sleep in your own bed." He set her down. "Go find your cloak."

Still sleepy, she zigzagged into the hallway.

Hugh picked up the empty candle crate. "Thank you for tonight, Beatrix."

"Shouldn't I be thanking you?" She smiled up at him. "I needed a friend today, more than you know."

"Anytime." He brushed some salt from her hair. Their gazes met, and like the pretend frost on the tree, froze in place. He cleared his throat. "Have you considered helping me in my Father Christmas quest? All I need is one afternoon."

She shouldn't. She could feel the tug of her heart, desperate for companionship. Besides, someone might see them and say something to Fern. But she was so tired of Fern's intrusion, what would it hurt? She simply had to remember they were friends, and she deserved to have friends. The problem, she feared, was enjoying Hugh's company a great deal more than she should.

Her nerves tingled and her stomach knotted. She wanted to be brave, to take control of her own life, and to make her own decisions. If she turned him down for doll shopping, what kind of coward was she?

Pulling the blanket tighter around her shoulders, she nodded. "Saturday afternoon I'm free."

"Perfect. I'll get my maid, Molly, to keep an eye on Clara, and I'll pick you up at one."

"No, I'll meet you at Pickwick's at one thirty. It will be easier."

"Whatever you like."

"Papa, I can't reach it." Clara's voice had a whiny edge. The child needed sleep. Hugh must have heard the same thing, for he hurried to help his daughter and left with a quick goodbye.

Once they'd departed, Beatrix stood in front of her tall Christmas tree. Claiming it was woman's work, Jonathon had never helped her decorate one, but they'd always shared a special kiss on the first night they put it up.

There'd be no kisses tonight.

She began to douse the candles. The glitter faded and the familiar darkness of night surrounded her. Grief swooped in. Would the crushing sadness of night ever go away?

# Chapter 6

Hugh paced in front of Pickwick Toy Emporium on Market Street. He paused to check his pocket watch. Beatrix had said one thirty, he was certain, but she was now ten minutes late. Perhaps she'd changed her mind.

A hansom cab swayed down the street and stopped in front of him. Beatrix smiled at him, and he stepped forward to assist her out of the cab.

She accepted the hand he offered. "I apologize for my tardiness. It was harder to find a cab than I expected."

"No worries." He waved toward the door. "I'm simply glad you agreed to help me. Shall we start with tea? There's a nice tearoom next door."

"That sounds divine, but we should probably get started. I'm not sure how long it will take for us to find Clara the perfect companion."

"Is there a list of requirements for said companion?" He led her toward Pickwick's.

"Not a particular list, but yes, there are requirements, in my opinion." They stepped inside the three-story toy store and she gasped. "Heavens, I had no idea it was so large."

A clerk asked if he could help them, and Hugh told him they were there to find a doll. The young man directed them upstairs. "The 'Doll's Life' display takes up the entire third floor, sir."

With Christmas less than two weeks away, shoppers filled the toy emporium. Hugh grasped Beatrix's elbow to usher her through the crush. The stairs opened to a huge room where dolls of all sizes had been poised in rocking chairs, having tea at tiny tables, and arranged in all sorts of other positions. Hugh couldn't begin to count the number of dolls, but their collective staring eyes were enough to give him gooseflesh.

"Why do you look terrified?" Beatrix chuckled. "Don't worry. I'll protect you from them."

"Can I simply repeat, 'I am so glad you are here'?"

"Follow me." Her teasing grin tickled him to no end.

He fell in step behind her as she made her way to the viewing line. Many mothers had brought their daughters to view the display. They oohed and aahed at every stop.

"What are we looking for?" Hugh stopped in front of a huge doll, nearly as tall as Clara.

"First, I think she should be able to carry the doll." Beatrix looked up at him and smiled.

"I agree."

"And second, Clara is young. She doesn't need a doll dressed as a lady. She needs a child or baby doll."

He shook his head. "I had no idea." They moved on to a stop where a doll was displayed playing a miniature violin. "She might like that."

"It's a possibility, but I prefer Kestner dolls to Simon Halbig dolls, although both have lovely artistry."

"You have to be jesting."

She shook her head. "Dolls are serious business."

"And you can tell the difference?"

"Can't you?" She glanced up at him. "Look at their eyebrows. The Kestner's eyebrows are much fuller."

"Certainly, I can see that." Sarcasm laced his tone. He cocked his head to the side, enjoying this. "And what was this doll of yours like? The one you told Clara about?"

"My Angel was unmarked, possibly a French Jumeau bébé but I don't think she was as pretty as these dolls. She had a very long face, but I loved her all the same. She had a whole trousseau of clothes too."

"And that was a good thing?"

"Yes." She endured his teasing. "What good is a doll if you don't have costumes for it?"

He rubbed the back of his neck. "I see this costing me more than I expected."

They wandered from display to display. At each, Beatrix would study the specimens offered and give reasons why the doll wouldn't do. Some were narrow faced, others had permanent expressions she feared Clara would tire of, some too small, and some too large.

"What about this one? It looks soft." He pointed to an India-rubber doll.

"It would be perfect if you want to make her sick. I read an article only the other day which talked about how that 'harmless' doll has made a number of children sick."

"Again, have I told you how glad I am you're here?"

She turned toward him and laughed. "Ah, there. Look."

He spun and followed her to a display of two dolls. The standing doll had brown hair and brown eyes, but the one sitting in a wicker chair had blond curls and blue eyes like his own Clara. This baby doll wore a bonnet with a huge, starched ruffle surrounding her face. Her equally starched pink dress would be sure to please. He leaned close and noticed her mouth was parted slightly.

"Are those teeth?"

Beatrix's smile widened. "Yes, they are. And can you see her hands. She has a composition body with jointed limbs."

"Are you speaking the King's English?"

"Her arms, legs, and even hands move." She laid her hand on Hugh's arm. "Clara would love her."

He covered her hand with his own. "I couldn't agree more." After signaling a clerk, the doll was removed from the display and carefully wrapped in a box.

Beatrix glanced back over her shoulder, frowned, and sighed.

Hugh stopped short. "What's wrong? Did we forget something?"

"No, I sort of feel sorry for the sister doll who is all alone now."

"This doll will be fine. Clara only needs one doll." He walked toward the area the clerk had said contained additional costumes.

"But—" She gave him a wistful look.

He left Pickwick's Toy Emporium with two dolls, four doll costumes, and a beautiful woman who already seemed much more than a friend. Before he took her home, he wanted her to know she was capturing his heart. But he had to be patient. He wasn't sure why he believed it so, but in his opinion, Beatrix had experienced enough of others pressuring her to do their bidding. He prayed God would show him a way to get her to trust him.

When they stepped outside, he smiled as sunshine greeted them despite the cold wind swaying the bare branches overhead. Even though their shopping might be concluded, the afternoon was far from over.

When Hugh suggested they take the dolls to his house and then continue to enjoy the remainder of the afternoon, Beatrix agreed. She was reticent for their time together to end so quickly.

"We could go to Dr. Crocker's Aquarium if you'd like," he offered.

She agreed most readily, and he hailed a hansom cab. Once they were settled and on their way, Beatrix asked him to tell her about the architecture of the buildings they passed. He seemed more than willing to oblige. He pointed out buildings sporting the flattened, cusped arches and lighter trims of the Jacobethan style and explained the Italian influence on the Renaissance Revival buildings.

She marveled at the expanse of his knowledge. The cab driver turned, and in a few minutes they were out of the city's buildings and among the familiar houses. She had no idea where he lived, but knew it was within walking distance of her own home.

They neared a truly unique expansive home with strong clean lines and a graceful elegance. "And this one?"

He grinned. "Is mine."

Before he got out, he explained he'd designed his house based on emerging new ideas that went against excessive ornamentation. "This is part of a new concept where the craftsman is the artist."

She waited in the hansom cab while he took the dolls indoors to hide as it would be improper for the two of them to be alone together. However, she had to admit she ached to see the inside of the home he'd shared with Evie.

He climbed back in. "Are you up for a drive on the promenade? It's a little chilly to walk."

"That would be delightful. I love the ocean view no matter what the season." After he gave the driver directions, she asked, "Hugh, did Evie like the house?"

He explained she'd never lived in it, and for some reason that thought made Beatrix both incredibly sad and relieved.

"I built most of it by hand after she died. Clara and I moved in about a year and half ago."

"You built it by hand?"

"I did. Naturally, I had workers, but I was both craftsman and designer. Every nail was set with love. Kept me sane after she died." He studied her. "Are you disappointed in me? Please, don't think of it as lowering myself to the working class. Think of it as using my hammer as an instrument, like your harp."

"Do you think I would look down on you for working with your hands? If so, you couldn't be further from the truth. This is a work of art."

It was the moment he'd been looking for—the opportunity to share his secret with her, so she'd know all of her secrets were safe with him.

He clenched and unclenched his fists. Their relationship was so fresh and tenuous. What if his past made a difference to her?

Beatrix pressed her gloved hand to his arm. "You've grown quiet. What's wrong?"

"You need to know something about me. I spent more years working with my hands than I ever did as an architect."

"You clearly enjoy woodworking as a hobby."

"No, I was a carpenter as was my father before me. You wondered why I visited the ragged school and why I believed some would use what they learned to build things? It's because I attended the Charter Street Ragged School in Lytham."

"You grew up destitute."

He nodded. "We were poor, but we were happy, and the people at the ragged school gave me more than a good meal every day. Those teachers brought the desire to learn alive inside of me and opened a new world to me outside of my present circumstances."

"But how did you become an architect?"

"I met Evie while working on her parents' estate in Lytham. We fell in love, and her father, a good man, decided it was easier to help me become educated than to deal with a disgruntled daughter. After he found out the plans we were using on his house had been designed by me, he made the proper introductions to further my career." He exhaled a long, slow breath. "I understand if this ends our friendship."

# Chapter 7

**B**eatrix fell back against the seat. *End their friendship? How shallow did he think she was? But what would the Kents say if they learned of this turn of events?* She could only imagine Fern's reaction to learning Hugh had attended a ragged school.

She turned to him and took in the sharp lines of his face. Like the buildings they'd discussed, each line showed his character, and what she'd learned far outweighed any pedigree. "Hugh Sherman, I've spent time with nobility and royalty, but I admire you more than the lot. I know the work it takes, the time spent studying, and the hours of practice needed to master something. You've worked hard and educated yourself, and you obviously love what you do." She gave a decisive nod. "So, unless you are hiding something more insidious than this, our friendship stands."

"I see." He tapped the top of the cab. "In that case, let me show you where I've been working the last two years."

After instructions from Hugh, the driver turned onto Church Street and in minutes he stopped. Beatrix stared out the window. "The Winter Gardens?"

The cab driver opened the doors, and Hugh came around to assist Beatrix. "Do you recall hearing about the design competition that was held for the building about five years ago? My friend and partner Thomas Mitchell won, so we've been working here ever since."

"I've never been inside."

"What?"

"A proper widow doesn't go to amusements." The words came out flat.

"Then you are in for a treat." He offered her his arm, and she slipped her hand in the crook of his elbow. "Just follow me."

Right now, she'd follow him anywhere.

Inside the rotunda, Hugh paid the two-shilling entrance fee and they passed through turnstiles. He led her toward what he said was the Floral Hall. Beatrix gasped when she stepped inside. Never had she seen such splendor. Exotic palms, tree ferns, and showy flowering plants filled the enormous hall. A curved glass roof, nearly three stories above their heads, bathed the hall with natural light. It was supported by decorated steel girders, and the tiling on the floor boasted shades of cream and rose pink.

"It was created so we'd have a place to promenade in the winter, you know." They took their time, talking as they went. "This is the Grand Promenade."

Beatrix had to stop and study each of the nine relief panels of the "singing choir" on the walls.

"This has to be as close to heaven on earth as possible," she breathed. "Wait. Do I hear music?"

He nodded. "In the Fernery to the north."

It wasn't far, so they made their way there. They found empty seats in the back and sat down to listen to the talented cellist entertain the crowd. Applause erupted at the end of the piece, and the cellist bowed and packed up his instrument.

A man approached her. "Aren't you Miss Aberdeen, the harpist?"

"I was. I'm Mrs. Kent now."

Hugh stepped forward to make proper introductions. "Mrs. Kent, this is Archer Prescott, the general manager of the Winter Gardens."

"Oh yes. Pardon me, Mr. Sherman." Mr. Prescott pulled out a card and passed it to Beatrix. "This is a most fortuitous turn of events. I heard you play in Paris, and I've never forgotten the experience. We are in great need of someone of your caliber to perform the Tuesday prior to Christmas."

Beatrix handed the card back to him. "I'm sorry. I only teach now."

"All the better. Perhaps your pupils would play. I think they'd find it a great honor, don't you?"

"They would."

Hugh gave her a broad, hopeful smile. "I know Clara would be thrilled. And you'd have over a week to prepare them."

Mr. Prescott nodded. "Of course, there is no entrance fee for performers and their families, and you could finish out the recital with a piece or two of your own. You'll be paid, of course. Handsomely. A harp seems especially perfect to celebrate our Savior's birth, don't you think?"

"I haven't played in public for years, Mr. Prescott."

Hugh shook his head. "But you can certainly still play. I heard you only a couple of weeks ago."

Her palms turned damp and her heart raced. Oh dear, how was she going to get out of this without telling Hugh about Jonathon's death?

But she did need the money, and it was only one song. Could she do that? For Clara?

She forced a feeble smile. "All right, Mr. Prescott, you have a recital booked."

Hugh found a bench in the grotto of the Floral Hall. "Why don't you rest here while I secure us some refreshments?"

Beatrix agreed, and he left to find something he hoped would bring a smile to her troubled face. Despite the pleasant afternoon they'd spent together, the mood had altered after Archer Prescott had approached Beatrix. Yet, instead of sharing what was troubling her, Beatrix had grown quiet. It hadn't been uncomfortable, but he could sense her unease as they wandered the Ambulatory and then watched ice skaters glide across the indoor rink. Did he dare press for her thoughts?

When he returned, he came up behind the bench, bent over her shoulder, and carefully produced a rich treat sure to please.

"Hot chocolate!" Beatrix accepted the cup and smelled its contents. "Heavenly. I haven't had this in years."

"Now, that's a shame." Hugh sat down beside her and sipped at his beverage. "Anything this good should be enjoyed regularly." He paused. "Like the songs you play on your harp."

"Hugh." Her tone suggested he should abandon this topic.

"I know. You don't play in public any more. What I want to know is, why?"

"Not right now." She sighed. "It's simply too painful, and I've had the most delightful day. I don't want to bring up any unpleasant topics that might ruin it."

"Later then." He smiled and squeezed her free hand. "When you're ready."

"Thank you."

"I do have one more question." He laughed when she lifted a skeptical eyebrow. "I have been asked to an upcoming Christmas dinner party, and I was wondering if you'd accompany me."

"When is it?"

"I apologize for the short notice, but it's this coming Monday."

Her eyes narrowed. "And who is hosting the party?"

"Daniel and Violet Spencer. Daniel has been my business partner's friend most of his life, and I met them both a couple of years ago. They're fine people."

"I'm sure they are." She attempted to force a smile. "Actually, I'm already a guest."

"Perfect. We can go together."

"I'm afraid I can't do that. I'm attending with Thomas and Fern Kent, my in-laws." She emptied her cup. "But be assured, I would much rather be by your side." She paused and sucked in a breath. "Hugh, with the Kents there, I need you to know I will not be able to acknowledge our acquaintance. I'm a widow, and my mother-in-law would find our friendship inappropriate."

"I understand." He tried to offer her a reassuring smile. "As long as you remember one thing, Beatrix. Whether we arrive together or separately, whether we are seated next to one another or apart, or whether we are dancing alone or together, know I will be with you in my heart."

# Chapter 8

Beatrix sat still as Thea draped a string of pearls around her neck. She pressed a hand to her décolletage. Was this dress truly appropriate for a widow? Butterflies fluttered in her stomach when she thought of Hugh and what he would think when he saw her.

"It's perfect," Thea assured her as she jabbed yet another pin into the mass of curls piled on top of Beatrix's head. "And that satin trim you had me add is lovely."

Beatrix stood and smoothed her hands along the velvet bodice. "Thank you for completing it, Thea. I don't know what I'd do without you, and I probably don't tell you often enough."

"I can't think of anyone I'd rather serve, miss. You look beautiful tonight. There's a sparkle in your eyes that's been missing." The brass knocker on the front door sounded and Thea gave an awkward curtsy. "I'll tell them you're on your way down."

Beatrix gathered her sable-trimmed, seal plush jacket from the hanger. A gift from Jonathon on their first Christmas together, the tight-fitting jacket would be something with which even Fern could find no fault.

To her surprise, Thomas Kent himself waited at the foot of the stairs rather than a footman. Beatrix's heart lurched. He looked so much like an older version of Jonathon with his sharp features, dark eyes, and narrow Patrician nose.

"Good evening, Beatrix." He surveyed her attire and apparently found her suitably dressed. "I wanted to speak to you about tonight. Fern has been out of sorts since you turned her out the other day, and I want to make sure you will be civil tonight."

A red hot poker of anger knifed through her. He expected *her* to be civil? What about his overbearing wife?

She pressed her lips together to keep from blurting out her thoughts and prayed for control over her tongue. When she felt peace wash over her, she answered him. "Sir, I did not turn her out. I merely set her free from the obligation she felt to have tea with me each day, and of course, I'll be civil. Have you ever known me to be anything to the contrary?"

"No, I suppose not." He reached for the door. "As long as I have your word you'll not upset her. You know how she hates for you to draw attention to yourself."

"I cannot control how Mum feels, but I will endeavor to remain as quiet as a mouse." If there was to be a center of attention, Fern wanted to be it. It would not be difficult to let her have that place, but when Fern learned Hugh and Beatrix had become friends, she would most likely become undone.

"Very well. Shall we?"

Despite the sable collar around her neck, Beatrix felt chilled to the bone by the time they reached the Spencers'. The ride had been filled with icy silence, but when she stepped into the Spencers' large vestibule, she immediately felt the warmth of Hugh's gaze. After the butler took her jacket, she turned to be welcomed by the hosts. She glanced over Violet's shoulder to see Hugh speaking with a friend while surreptitiously watching her. While his friend was in full dramatic story-telling form, Hugh sent her a look which gave her goose bumps.

"And this is our daughter, Olivia, and her husband, Edward." Violet Spencer indicated a striking lady in an ivory gown on her right. So this was the woman Fern had wanted Jonathon to marry. They'd have made a handsome pair, but she hardly seemed Jonathon's type.

After pleasantries were exchanged and all the guests had arrived, the hostess informed the gentlemen which lady they were expected to escort to dinner. To Beatrix's secret delight, Mrs. Spencer had paired her to Hugh, and as social hierarchy dictated, they were at the end of the procession.

He extended his arm when it was their turn to enter the dining room. "You look stunning, Beatrix."

"Shhh." She cast a glance at Fern. "Someone might hear you."

He chuckled then added in a hushed tone, "You are asking a great deal of me tonight to pretend I don't know you when I'd much rather claim your hand for every dance."

"We're not dancing tonight," she whispered.

"I will be in my mind."

Heat crept up her neck and into her cheeks. Oh dear, ignoring the roguishly handsome man on her arm was nearly impossible. She needed to keep her distance, but what was she to do when Hugh made her feel at home in a room full of strangers?

Hugh followed the other men from the library into the parlor for the entertainment. While he'd turned down the after-dinner cigars, several had accepted their host's offer, and a heady mixture of cherry wood and toasted almond smoke hung on the men's clothes.

He found Beatrix seated on a settee beside the elderly woman she'd come with. He guessed the woman to be her former mother-in-law.

The hostess clapped her hands together. "For our after-dinner entertainment, my Olivia has agreed to sing. Mrs. Kent, we all know of your musical accomplishments. Will you accompany her?"

Beatrix turned to Fern. The older woman, clearly not happy, huffed and agreed.

It seemed to him Olivia Spencer's singing paled to Beatrix's playing, but when the song ended, the gathering praised the lady's aria.

Beatrix rose from the piano to return to her seat, but Olivia caught her hand. "I heard you're a harpist. Please, won't you do us the honor of a song? I promise our harp won't take long to tune, and it has a lovely sound."

Immediately, Beatrix's gaze shot to Fern. The older woman's eyes darkened.

"I–I'm sorry," Beatrix stammered. "I'm in mourning and no longer play in public."

Olivia smiled. "But this is an intimate group. Surely, it would do no harm."

"You heard her. She's in mourning." Thomas Kent stepped forward. "Come, Beatrix, it's time for us to leave."

Worry etched Beatrix's fine features as she made her apologies and followed her in-laws out of the room. The Kents offered no apologies, but having thanked their host and hostess, made a hasty retreat from the house.

Hugh ached to go after Beatrix. Why were the Kents unhappy with her? What would possibly make them willing to slight their host by leaving so abruptly? Was it simply to secret Beatrix away and waste her talents? He wished he could discover the truth.

# Chapter 9

The moment she sat down in the carriage, Beatrix steeled herself for what was to come, but the same frigid silence that had ridden with them to the Spencers' descended like a thick fog on the ride home.

As they approached her house, she released the breath she'd been holding. Perhaps she would escape this night without a dressing down. Maybe the Kents could see that she'd not requested the undue attention nor had she accepted the invitation to play.

The carriage stopped and Thomas stepped out, but Fern held up her hand when Beatrix began to exit. "Wait. I need to speak to you."

Beatrix sat on the edge of her seat.

"You and that man behaved scandalously." Fern turned to her, fists clenched and eyes flashing. "How did you do it? Arrange a clandestine meeting at this dinner party?"

"Excuse me?"

"He's the same man who brought you home the other day, is he not?"

"He is, but he was an invited guest just as I was. We planned nothing."

"I saw the way you looked at one another." Fern clutched her handbag. "Do you not have the decency to keep up mourning appearances? Have you forgotten my Jonathon so soon?" She fished a lace handkerchief from her bag and dabbed her eyes. "You are playing a dangerous game, Beatrix. I tried to give you counsel, but as usual, you have ignored it, so I'm going to make myself perfectly clear." She sat ramrod straight. "When you married, everything you owned became Jonathon's property. That is the law, and while Jonathon was generous in his will to provide for you if he were to pass, he stated everything was to go to us if you were to remarry. Unlike our son, Thomas and I do not have a desire to be so generous."

"What do you mean?"

"You need to be fully aware that if you remarry, you will not only lose this house, but you will also forfeit its contents, including your mother's precious harp. Good night, Beatrix."

Her harp? Beatrix staggered up the walk and into the house. Without removing her jacket, she walked to the harp and ran her hand along its neck and down its pillar. She could still picture her mother playing at the best concert halls with her father standing on stage beside her. She could hear her mother's words of instruction and feel her gentle touch as she taught her the first scales. And while the music her mother produced had nurtured Beatrix's muse and coaxed a love of music to life, it was her gentle spirit that had molded Beatrix the most.

Tears slid down her cheeks. This instrument was as much a part of herself as her arm or leg. No, it was more like a part of her soul. It bore the weight of her sorrows and carried the heights of her dreams. It had been her strongest enemy and her greatest friend.

How could she possibly ever let it go?

Hugh peeked in Clara's bedroom, expecting to find his daughter sound asleep.

Clara opened her eyes. "Papa?"

He crossed the room and sat down on her bed. "You should be asleep."

She rubbed sleepy eyes with her fists. "Was Miss Bea pretty?"

"Yes. Truly lovely."

"What color was her dress?"

"A dark purple velvet with creamy satin trim."

"Ummm." Her eyelids drooped and her long lashes fanned across her cheeks. "I like Miss Bea."

"I do too, princess." He kissed her forehead and waited until her breathing became even. "I like Miss Bea more and more every day, Clara May. More than I probably should."

Haunted by how Beatrix had appeared when she left with the Kents, Hugh went down to his study and attempted to concentrate on a book. After reading the same page for the third time, he finally slammed the book down on the table and stood.

Wednesday, he'd speak with her after Clara's lesson, and he'd get answers to all of his questions. Why wouldn't she play in public? Why did her former in-laws take her away so quickly? And most of all, why did she seem so afraid of them? If she were in some kind of trouble, he'd somehow make it right.

Beatrix was kind, talented, and just a bit impetuous—a perfect combination. He'd not been looking for love, but it had apparently found him anyway. And Clara had even loved Beatrix first. He'd declare his feelings had moved beyond friendship, but if she needed time, he could wait.

Everything in him wanted to go over there tonight and find out the truth, but he couldn't ruin Beatrix's reputation or leave Clara unattended. Instead, he would do something even more important.

He sat down at his desk and penned a letter. He'd post it in the morning and pray it got there on time.

Hugh stood at the end of Beatrix's walk with his newest creation in his hands. Since sleep had eluded him last night, he'd gone to his workshop and crafted the cradle for Clara's doll. He hoped Beatrix could help him find suitable bedding for it.

He knocked and waited. At last Thea opened the door. She said she wasn't sure Mrs. Kent was receiving visitors, especially so early in the morning after the late night she'd had, but she would check.

A few minutes later, Beatrix, pale and puffy-eyed, greeted him.

"Good morning, Mr. Sherman, how can I help you?"

He stepped back. Why was she being so formal?

"Beatrix, are you all right?" He set the cradle down and reached for her hand. "Are you ill?"

She pulled away, pain in her eyes. "I can't do this."

"Do what?"

"Be your—friend."

"Why?" His chest heaved. "Beatrix, what's going on? I thought we were growing closer. I saw it in your eyes. Tell me what's wrong. Is it the Kents? I saw what happened, and you don't need to be frightened of them. You can talk to me about anything. Surely you know that."

Her eyes pooled with tears. "I. . .I can't."

When she turned to leave, he blocked her path. "I told you about my past, and I deserve to know yours."

"And if I tell you, you'll go?" She lowered her gaze to the floor. "Are you certain you want to know? You'll only grow to hate me."

He cupped her cheek, lifting her face to look in her eyes. "Never."

Her lip trembled. "I killed Jonathon."

# Chapter 10

Hugh drew Beatrix into the parlor and onto the settee. "Go on."

"When we married, the Kents no longer wanted me to perform. They said since my accomplishments had garnered me the best catch of the season, I no longer needed to flout my musical skills, and Jonathon didn't want to be married to a lady in such a questionable profession. He wanted me to put my artisan past behind me."

"But you're a brilliant performer."

"Thank you, but please, let me finish." She wrung her hands. "During our engagement, I agreed, but after we were wed, I found I missed performing in front of an audience. Jonathon and his mother insisted I missed the applause."

"Did you?"

"Some, but mostly I missed the euphoria I felt when performing and the faces of those whom the music touched, like Clara when she listens to the fairy music. I feel like I'm giving people a gift through my music." She drew in a deep breath. "But I knew Jonathon didn't want me to perform. I did so anyway, and it killed him."

"Pardon me, but unless you shot an arrow through those harp strings, there's a big piece of this puzzle missing." He walked to the fireplace and added a log. He stirred the dying embers until they burned orange. "He didn't want you to perform, but you did anyway. Often?"

"No, only rarely." She moved to sit by her harp. She laid her hand on it, as if to summon strength to finish her story. "The night he died, I was asked to perform at a charity concert as the featured guest. It was a charity for the ragged school. I hadn't told him about the concert until that day. He was furious, but didn't forbid my participation. To do so would have reflected badly on him and his family." She paused and swiped a finger under her eye. "He came to the concert, which was an overwhelming success, but left before the last song. He was killed in a carriage accident while I was enjoying the thrill of a standing ovation."

Hugh crossed the room, took her hands, and lifted them until she stood in front of him. "He was killed; you didn't kill him. He could have died in a carriage accident going to the barber just as easily as he did returning from that concert."

"But if I'd obeyed him. If I'd not craved the applause. If—"

"I know all about the crushing 'what ifs' of grief, but those thoughts are not from the Lord. He tells us there is a time for everything, and Evie and Jonathon's time to die was not in our hands." Using the pad of his thumb, he swiped a tear that slid down her cheek. "Play again at the Winter Gardens. Let me be by your side. Let them hear your music again, Beatrix." He paused. "But know this. If you never play another note, I would still love you."

Beatrix's heart shattered like a broken windowpane. He loved her.

He was asking so little, yet offering so much. She ached to lean into his chest and feel his strong arms around her. This man understood her. He saw her flaws and loved her anyway, but loving him would cost her far more than loving Jonathon ever had. Jonathon had only asked her to give up performing in concert. Hugh didn't realize loving him would cost her music itself.

She glanced around the room. This house. Her harp. Her memories. She couldn't let them all go. They were all she had to hold on to.

"Hugh, I'm sorry. I can't."

"Not now?"

"Not ever."

# Chapter 11

The cradle forgotten, Hugh bounded down Beatrix's steps. A weight settled on his chest. How had he been so wrong about her? Maybe he wasn't good enough after all.

"Mr. Sherman!" Thea called behind him.

He turned to see Beatrix's maid carrying the cradle down the stairs. He returned to retrieve it.

Thea leaned close. "If she loves you, she loses her harp."

"What?"

"The Kents. She told me they'll take it from her. It was her mother's." Thea's teeth chattered, and she rubbed her arms. "I thought you should know." She bobbed and hurried back into the warmth of the house.

His anger flared. *Good heavens, how cruel could a person be?* He had half a mind to find Thomas Kent and have a word with the man, but he had a feeling it was Mrs. Kent who was behind this situation.

He marched down the sidewalk, cradle in his arms, trying to stem the surge of emotions coursing through him. It was unfair at every turn. Even Clara was hurt by this. She loved Beatrix, and this would keep their relationship from moving forward.

So many things in life he could take a hammer to and fix, but there was nothing he could do to fix this. Wait. Maybe he could. Beatrix may not be able to love him right now, but he could make sure she would play at that Winter Garden's concert.

God had given her a talent, and Hugh loved her enough to make sure the world heard her music.

Beatrix listened to the steady rhythm of Clara's arrangement of "Silent Night." This time, Clara didn't miss a note and her timing had improved.

"That's wonderful, Clara. Your piece is perfect." Beatrix gave Clara a hug. "Do you know what you're going to wear for the recital?"

"Molly says my royal-blue dress, but I told her it was itchy. I want to wear my burgundy one. It matches your cape."

"I'm sure you'll be pretty in either." Beatrix noticed one of Clara's formerly missing front teeth was now peeking through.

"Papa says you're going to play your harp."

Beatrix stomach twisted. "Sweetheart, I don't know about that."

"I do. Papa said so."

Oh, to have the faith of a child. Beatrix wished her trust of her heavenly Father would mirror that of Clara's trust in her earthly father.

Thea came to the door and said Molly had come to collect Clara. Beatrix felt a fresh gush of sadness at not seeing Hugh. As much as it hurt, she'd made her choice. Music, her father always said, owned a musician. Did her harp own her?

She tapped Clara's sheet music on the piano and aligned the pieces. "Keep practicing, and I'll see you at the recital in either your blue or your burgundy dress."

Clara hugged her and skipped away. The house suddenly felt empty again.

Beatrix sat down at her harp and drew it against her, but no song came. Did she love this piece of wood, metal, and wire more than she loved a human being? A man who'd opened his heart to her?

The answer frightened her.

Beatrix made her way to her writing desk and sat down. She pulled out a sheet of stationery and wrote an invitation. Following the recital, she and her mother-in-law needed to have tea.

Hugh waited for the signal from Thea indicating Beatrix had left her home for the Winter Garden recital. He'd asked for Thea's help, and she said she'd be happy to light a candle in the window when it was safe for him to come to the house.

He and his cohort had to work quickly. He drove the rented wagon up to the front of the house and hopped out. Inside, with the help of his partner, he carried the harp out of the house and leaned it against the blanket-covered board they'd propped against the back of the wagon. They then lifted the board bearing the harp and carefully placed it in the back of the wagon. They padded it well with blankets and secured it with ropes.

Despite his desire to hurry to the Winter Gardens, Hugh forced himself to take it slow. It wouldn't do to get there and have the harp unable to be played.

Once at the Winter Gardens, he and his companion brought the harp inside, but kept it out of view. Being an architect had its advantages. He knew the perfect place to hide it in the Fernery.

Hugh took his seat several rows behind the pupils. Beatrix was busy lining up the young men and ladies in the front row. They'd go from youngest to oldest, and he guessed their pieces increased in difficulty. The crowd began to thicken, and the seats filled. He wiped his damp palms on his pants. He wasn't sure if he was more nervous about Clara's first recital or his plan to get Beatrix to play. Would this open the door for the two of them again? He prayed it would, but if it didn't, it was still the right thing to do. Music was part of her soul. Even if he couldn't have her, the world should have her music. "Silent Night" had never sounded so angelic and yet so plunky. His six-year-old's music had a charm all of its own, and he applauded more loudly than anyone. The pupils around eleven or twelve years of age performed well with only a few missed notes or forgotten measures. The older students wooed the crowd with melodious runs and joyful rhythms.

When the last student was done, Alfred Prescott approached the staging area, and Hugh took the opportunity to slip out.

"And now, ladies and gentleman, you are in for a treat." Mr. Prescott's voice boomed. "May I present the renowned Mrs. Jonathon Kent, concert harpist. Mrs. Kent?"

From his place off stage, Hugh could see Beatrix turn snow white. She froze in place. Mr. Prescott had told him Beatrix did not plan to perform, but Hugh had insisted she would.

Mr. Prescott glanced back at Hugh with a desperate expression on his face.

Hugh didn't make eye contact with Beatrix as he carried out her harp and positioned it up front. He set a chair in place and stepped in front of her. "Hugh," she whispered. "I can't."

"Yes, you can. You won't be alone."

Beatrix followed the direction of Hugh's gaze and gasped. A man approached from the back of the chairs carrying a violin.

"Father?" She could hardly believe her eyes. She blinked. "How?"

"Later."

Her father walked up, held out a hand to his daughter, and drew her to her feet. "Let's play our favorite for old time's sake. Bach's 'Jesu, Joy of Man's Desiring.'" He kissed her cheek. "Play for the Lord and no one else."

"An audience of One."

He released her hand so she could take her place. She sat down and glanced at Hugh, who beamed at her, and then at Clara, who had her hands clutched to her chest. Joy surged through her like she'd never known.

She began to pluck the strings, bringing the song to life. She may never play in front of another audience again, but this time she'd play for those she loved—Hugh Sherman and his daughter Clara.

When the piece was over, the crowd begged for more until she and her father were obliged to give not one encore, but two. Hugh stood beside her as those in attendance came to congratulate Beatrix on both her performance and that of her students. Several asked if they might contact her regarding lessons for their children.

At last, she was left alone with her father, Hugh, and Clara. Beatrix snaked her arm through her father's. "Why are you here?"

"I heard you were having some trouble." He glanced at Hugh. "So I came."

"But what about the Duke?"

"He understands the importance of family."

Happiness filled her from head to toe. "I'm sorry to trouble you."

"No, sweetheart, it is I who should be sorry. I've stayed away far too long." He glanced at Hugh. "Is there somewhere we can all go to have tea?"

*Tea!* Beatrix's pulse raced. "What time is it?"

Hugh pulled out his watch. "Nearly four. Beatrix, what's wrong? You look faint."

"I need to get home to meet Mrs. Kent." She hiked up her skirt. "So please bring my harp home."

"Miss Bea?" Clara grabbed a fist full of skirt. "Can I come with you?"

Beatrix stopped and turned toward Hugh. He shrugged.

Beatrix took Clara's hand and gave it a squeeze. "Very well, but we must hurry."

# Chapter 12

A steady, cold rain fell on the streets of Blackpool, and Beatrix climbed out of the hansom cab trying to recall the last day of sunshine they'd had. Did the endless dreary days affect Fern as much as they did her? How could anyone possibly tell? Fern's sour disposition remained unchanged no matter what the circumstances.

And she hated to be kept waiting.

With Clara's mitten-clad hand clasped in her own, Beatrix quickened her steps on the slippery walk and rushed inside. Thea met them at the front door and helped them remove their wraps.

"The elder Mrs. Kent is in the parlor." Thea hung up Beatrix's cloak. "Shall I take Miss Clara into the kitchen for some biscuits?"

"And hot chocolate. She deserves it. She played beautifully." Beatrix stepped in front of the mirror to re-pin her hat. "How long has Mrs. Kent been waiting?"

"Only about fifteen minutes, but she does seem miffed. I'll fetch the tea tray right away. I finished a fresh batch of clotted cream earlier to go with the cinnamon scones that are ready to come out of the oven."

"Perfect. Thank you, Thea." Beatrix smoothed her mussed hair, said a silent prayer, and entered the parlor.

"It's about time you made an appearance." Fern kept her gloved hands clasped in her lap. "Whoever heard of someone inviting a guest to tea and then not being home when the guest arrived?"

Beatrix sat down at the low tea table. "I apologize. Something came up."

Thea brought the tea tray. Steam rose from the fresh cinnamon scones and the scent made Beatrix's mouth water, but her stomach knotted when she thought of the imminent conversation.

"Miss, please ring for me if you need anything. Since I'm working upstairs, I may not hear you call. I'll take Miss Clara up with me when I go." Thea bobbed a clumsy curtsy and hurried from the room.

"She's an awkward little bird, isn't she? And who is this Miss Clara?" Fern looked at the teapot but made no move to pour.

At least Fern now understood Beatrix expected to pour the tea in her own home. Beatrix would take her moments of victory where she could get them. She filled the china cups and passed a cup and saucer to Fern. She waited while Fern placed a scone on her plate along with a small dollop of clotted cream and a spoonful of Thea's black currant jam. Beatrix too made a plate, but doubted she'd be able to eat a bite. *Please Lord, help me find the words.*

"I invited you here because I have something to ask you."

"Beatrix, if you want us to reconsider our decision concerning the house and your precious harp, you shouldn't waste your breath." She glanced across the room and cut her gaze back to Beatrix. "Where is the harp? Have you hidden it? Because if you have, Thomas and I will not hesitate to contact our solicitor."

"I wanted to tell you I've decided to pursue a relationship with Hugh Sherman. I don't know where it will lead, but I care enough about him to risk my home and my harp."

"So where is it?"

This was not going the direction she wanted it to. "The harp will be back here soon."

"Back?"

Beatrix kept her voice steady. "I performed at the Winter Gardens earlier today with my students for a Christmas recital."

"I knew you would go back to performing eventually." Fern's cup trembled on the saucer. "It's your vanity. You crave the applause. You loved it more than you did my son."

Fern's words knifed through Beatrix, tearing open a wound which had only begun to heal when she'd performed with her father. She had invited Fern because she wanted to ask forgiveness for the resentment she'd allowed to take root in her heart toward her mother-in-law, but somehow this conversation had gone completely awry.

"You're wrong. I didn't love my harp more than Jonathon, and I don't love it more than Hugh Sherman." Beatrix pressed on before Fern could offer a retort. "You've made that accusation so often I almost believed it. I was ready to give it all up because I thought my passion for music was wrong, but I now I realize it was God who put a love for music inside me, and if I play for Him, how can that be wrong? Jonathon shouldn't have asked me to give it up and neither should you."

"But it killed him."

Thea stepped in the doorway, her face a mask of worry. "Miss, I apologize for the interruption, but may I speak with you? Alone."

Fern scowled. "How cheeky. You should set that girl straight."

Beatrix ignored Fern's comment and met Thea in the hall. "What is it, Thea?"

"Miss Clara found this in Mr. Kent's coat, the one he wore the night he was killed."

Beatrix recalled asking Thea to pack up Jonathon's belongings explaining, as she had to Fern, that it was time to move on. She took the note Thea held out and read it. Once. Twice. Three times.

Knees nearly buckling, Beatrix sank down on the bench of the hall tree.

"Are you all right, miss?"

She nodded.

"I'll fetch you a glass of water, all the same."

Beatrix stared at the note, feeling as if someone had cinched her corset until her ribs were about to splinter. How could this be? All this time, how could Fern condemn her?

Fern rounded the corner. "It's in very poor form to neglect one's guests. Beatrix, are you ill? You're as white as a handkerchief."

Beatrix stared ahead. "You."

"What is it, Beatrix? Don't mumble."

"Jonathon left my concert that night because of you." Beatrix pushed to her feet and turned to her mother-in-law. "You sent him a message telling him to hurry home because you felt poorly. Was that true, were you really ill, or were your trying to stop him from supporting me?"

Fern swayed, and Beatrix stood and caught her arm. She ushered the woman into the parlor, lowered her onto the settee, and called for Thea to bring the water. However, it was Clara who carried in the glass rather than Thea.

"Here you are, ma'am." Clara took Fern's hand and wrapped it around the glass. The glass tipped and some spilled on the rug before Clara was able to steady Fern's hand. "That's all right, ma'am. We all make mistakes. Papa says to give grace to yourself and others."

Beatrix's mouth grew dry. Grace. Unmerited favor. After all this time, after what Fern had kept secret, and after the threat of losing her beloved harp, could Beatrix offer Fern Kent grace? Clara climbed up on the settee next to Fern and took the elderly woman's hand. "Sometimes my tummy feels better when I talk. I asked Father Christmas to bring me a doll like Miss Bea's. What do you want Father Christmas to bring you?"

Fern glanced down at Clara then lifted watery eyes toward Beatrix. "Forgiveness."

# Chapter 13

**H**ugh sent Clara into the kitchen to help Beatrix and Thea while he slipped the gifts he'd brought beneath Beatrix's Christmas tree. Beatrix's father helped, and they had the presents tucked away in no time.

He'd worried about how he'd handle Christmas morning with Clara, but to his surprise, last night Clara told him she hoped Father Christmas would bring her present to Miss Bea's house because she didn't want her teacher to be alone on Christmas Day. He didn't tell his daughter, but he had no intention of leaving Beatrix alone on Christmas or any other holiday if Beatrix agreed.

The last couple of days had been a blur. He and Beatrix had grown closer than ever, and Beatrix and her former mother-in-law had spent a tearful hour talking only yesterday. Beatrix admitted to him that her burden of guilt had eased considerably, and she prayed Fern's had as well. She'd told him of her determination to remain part of the Kents' life and he'd agreed. She'd even invited her former in-laws to join them for Christmas dinner.

He jingled a set of sleigh bells he'd brought along. "Clara! Hurry! Did you hear the bells? Father Christmas was here and he left. You just missed him."

She raced into the room with Beatrix following close behind. When Clara's gaze landed on the cradle, her eyes grew as round as plums. She rushed to the cradle and lifted out the bisque doll with its face framed in lacy ruffles. "She's soooo pretty. Look Miss Bea! Look, her eyes open and close." She tipped the doll back and forth to demonstrate.

Beatrix took the offered baby and pretended to rock her. "She's a very lucky doll to have a mum like you."

"Speaking of mums, I think this gift is for you." Hugh held out a package wrapped in brown paper to Beatrix.

Excitement buzzed inside Beatrix. She glanced at her father, then Hugh, before tearing off the ribbon and paper. She withdrew the second doll he'd purchased that day. "Clara's new mum will need a doll so they can have tea parties, don't you think?"

Now Beatrix's eyes were as big as plums. "New mum?"

He knelt in front of her on one knee and fished a garnet ring from his pocket. He held it up for her to see. "I've already spoken with your father, but he said only you could make this decision. Beatrix, I don't have fortunes or titles to give you, but what I have is yours—my good, my bad, my home, my daughter, my love, and my heart. Will you do me the honor of being my wife?"

Clara bounced up and down. "And be my mum?"

"Oh yes. A thousand times, yes."

He slipped the ring on her finger, stood, and placed a tender, chaste kiss on her lips. His heart swelled, and he hoped to wear out the mistletoe before the day was through.

The knocker clanked as they were preparing Christmas dinner. Beatrix left the task of answering the door to Thea while she entered the dining room to remove the two extra plates she'd set in hopes of the Kents accepting her invitation. It had been too much to hope for. Although she'd told Fern she'd forgiven her and reminded the older lady of what Hugh had said—that they had no control over the times and seasons of their lives or of those they loved, Fern was reticent to let her guilt and anger go. They'd been companions far too long. And while Fern hadn't actually apologized, she'd reluctantly admitted that her solicitor had informed her that since 1860, any article Beatrix brought into the marriage remained hers under the law. She admitted she still wouldn't have taken Beatrix's harp away. To do so would have been cruel, and she did care about her daughter-in-law. It was the only affirmation Beatrix had had in years, but it was a start. When she asked them to come to Christmas dinner, Fern had neither accepted nor refused.

But on this Christmas morning, she'd sincerely hoped they would come. She didn't want the Kents to be alone. Loneliness only further sowed seeds of bitterness.

"Beatrix." She turned to see Fern in the doorway. "Am I still welcome?"

Beatrix crossed the room and took her former mother-in-law's hands in her own. "Always."

Fern immediately spotted the garnet, and her lips pressed hard to a thin line, then the corners curved upward. "You are engaged?"

"Yes. Hugh—and Clara—asked me this morning."

Fern stepped back and drew in a deep breath. "I am trying to be truly happy for you. I believe Jonathon would approve of Mr. Sherman, and you'll make a good mum."

Clara skipped into the room with her new doll in hand. She held her up toward Fern. "Father Christmas brought me a doll and a new mum. Isn't that wonderful?"

Fern smiled down at the girl. "It is."

Clara grinned at her. "Does that make you my grandmother? I suppose I need one of those as well."

"I'm not really—" Fern started to explain.

"Yes, Clara. Meet your Grandmother Kent."

Fern's eyes widened. Beatrix wasn't certain, but she thought she saw tears in Fern's eyes as Clara pulled her new "grandmother" away to go look at her doll and cradle.

After a day of dining, playing games, and laughing together, Hugh and Beatrix found themselves finally alone in front of the sparkling Christmas tree with its flickering candles. Hugh drew her close, lifted her hand, and kissed it. "There's one tradition we've not yet completed this Christmas."

"Oh?"

"Kissing under the mistletoe."

"I'm afraid there's none in my house."

He cocked his head to the side. "Don't you see it? The fairies brought it while you were playing your harp."

"Is that so? And where is this mistletoe only you can see?"

"Above your head, everywhere you go."

"Isn't that convenient?"

"I think so." He cupped her face and traced his thumb over her lips. "Happy Christmas to the future Mrs. Sherman."

Then he captured her lips with his own, kissing her until her joy reached a crescendo.

When the kiss ended, she laid her head on Hugh's chest and soaked in the heat of his embrace. This man and his daughter had pulled on her heartstrings, and now, as a family, they'd compose a Christmas carol all their own.

**Lorna Seilstad** brings history back to life using a generous dash of humor. She is a Carol Award finalist and the author of the Lake Manawa Summers series and the Gregory Sisters series. When she isn't eating chocolate, she's teaches women's Bible classes and is a 4-H leader in her home state of Iowa. She and her husband have three children. Learn more about Lorna at www.lornaseilstad.com.

# A Perfect Christmas

by Erica Vetsch

# Chapter 1

*London, England*
*November 7, 1887*

T oday of all days, everything must be perfect."
Melisande Verity adjusted the hand-dipped truffles on the display stand, making sure each confection was a precise distance from its neighbor. She swept up the tissue and cardboard of the delivery carton, stowing it beneath the counter and surveying her little corner of the Garamond Department Store kingdom.

Glass cases gleamed, dainty sweets lined up like little chocolate soldiers on pristine white china trays, and silver serving tongs sat at the ready. Divinity, petit fours, toffees, caramels, each came under her critical eye. Satisfied, Melisande checked that her apron was snowy and starched, and that the bow had just the right amount of perkiness at the small of her back. Everything was as tidy and appealing as she knew how to make it, and she hoped her hard work would translate into brisk sales.

This morning marked the beginning of the holiday commission pay scale, and each department head would receive a portion of the revenue his or her section earned between now and Christmas. If things went well, the extra income would add a bit of a cushion to her savings. Perhaps someday soon, she would have enough money to fulfill her promise to her mother and finally send her younger sister, Vonnetta, to music school. She'd had to give up her vocal training when they had been forced to move to the city and get jobs to support themselves. But if things worked out like Melisande hoped today—faint hope though it was—perhaps she would have a considerable bump in her finances. . .if only Mr. Garamond would choose her.

Around her, other Garamond's employees prepared for the opening bell. Melisande considered that she had the best view in the store, based as she was in the center of the three-story-tall atrium. From her vantage point facing the front doors, she could see to her right where the women's millinery, accessories, perfumes, and jewelry sections led on to the clothing department where London's well-to-do women could buy bespoke clothing.

To her left, men's haberdashery, accessories, and tailoring took up much less room than their female counterpart and shared space with a barbershop, shoeshine rack, and newsstand. The tobacconist had his own enclosed space and humidor to keep the odor of tobacco from infusing the other inventory.

For three years now, since she was sixteen and new to London, Garamond's had been Melisande's domain, five and a half days every week. Though she'd started in the gift-wrapping department, she'd quickly moved up to counter service and now to a department head. Granted, the chocolates and confections department was the smallest in the store—she had only one employee to supervise, and that only one evening a week—but still, it was hers.

On the floors above, railed iron balconies looked down on the atrium bathed in light from the stained-glass skylight far overhead. Floor two was filled with household items, furniture, china and silverware, and sporting goods. The third floor held offices and meeting spaces, most notably, the offices of Mr. Hamish Garamond, the owner, and his grandson, Gray, fresh from receiving an advanced degree at Oxford.

Just the thought of Gray Garamond made Melisande's heart thump a little faster and her face flush. Which was silly, since he didn't even know her name. Sure, he'd worked summers in the store during his holidays from university, but never in any department where they might've crossed paths. She'd do better to concentrate on someone in her own social sphere, though none of the clerks and shopworkers she associated with made her feel the way Gray Garamond did.

*And don't forget to call him* Mr. *Gray when or if you speak to him.* As was the custom, the employees referred to Hamish as Mr. Garamond and to his grandson as Mr. Gray, though in her head. . .or was it her heart?. . .she thought of him as just Gray.

The brass clock over the front door chimed nine a.m., and Bramwell, the elderly doorman, unlocked the brass-and-glass doors. Bramwell had been the doorman at Garamond's for so long that Melisande smothered a smile, wondering if the front doors would even open for anyone else.

Fat, white flakes fell on the street and sidewalk, the first snowfall of the year, and Melisande could believe that Christmas was only a few weeks away.

And today Mr. Garamond would choose who would be designing the store's Christmas window displays this year.

Melisande pressed her hand against her middle to still the butterflies bombarding her there. For a month now she'd waffled between anticipation and dread, hoping she would be chosen, but wishing she'd never entered. What made her think she could compete with others—all of whom were men more than twice her age with much more experience than she possessed?

Customers began to enter, shaking snowflakes from their sleeves, stopping just inside the doors to breathe deeply of the warm air redolent with the smells of perfume, polish, and prosperity.

Making sure she had a welcoming smile on her face, she nodded to each patron as they passed her station. "Good morning."

Responses varied. Some returned her smile, others gave a brisk nod, others ignored her altogether. One of the office runners brought down a handful of order slips, and Melisande set to work filling boxes of chocolates to be delivered or picked up later that day, trying not to watch the clock or glance too often toward the third-floor landing to see if Mr. Garamond was coming down to make his announcement.

"Concentrate, or not only will you not be selected, you'll be sent back to gift-wrapping," she scolded herself after having to refer to an order slip three times within the space of a minute.

"Talking to yourself again?"

Melisande looked up from fitting tissue over an array of bon bons.

Vonnetta grinned. "People are going to think you're ready for Bedlam if you don't watch out." She held a swatch book to her chest with crossed arms, humming softly— she was always humming when she wasn't singing. Her toe tapped softly to the rhythm of the song in her head.

"What are you doing here?" Vonnetta worked as a seamstress in the couture department and didn't have floor privileges. She was expected to stay behind the scenes, not wander the store.

"Mrs. O'Hair sent me to the furniture department to match some fabric. One of the customers bought a settee here last year that was upholstered in red brocade, and she wanted us to make her a Christmas dress in the same shade." Vonnetta flipped through the swatch book until she found a deep-red velvet. "It's going to be beautiful when it's finished."

"I'm sure it is, but you shouldn't be here." Melisande looked over Vonnetta's shoulder. Neville Strand, the menswear department head, stood beside a rack of bowlers and top hats, his narrow moustache twitching and his gimlet eyes piercing. Mr. Strand seemed to dislike everyone, but for some reason she'd never learned, and was afraid to ask about, he'd always seemed to have a particular dislike of her. "I'll see you in the lunchroom at noon." She inclined her head to where Mr. Strand stood, and Vonnetta took the hint, bobbing a curtsy and hurrying away to her post.

"I say." A lazy voice caught Melisande's attention. "I could use a bit of advice."

She turned to a dapper, bored-looking young man leaning on the glass display case. He tugged his gloves off one slow finger at a time. When she moved to stand before him, he opened his eyes wider, but his expression gleamed with mocking. "Well, aren't you a delectable bit of goods?"

She forced herself to remain calm. *Perfection, politeness, and poise.* The three *musts* for a Garamond employee.

"How may I help you?" Folding her hands at her waist, she waited, looking him right in the eye. She'd found that maintaining eye contact and not appearing flustered often brought an insolent young man up and reminded him of his manners.

This one appeared not to care, looking her over from her upswept brown hair to as far down her person as he could see behind the counter. "I'm here to find something sweet. You'd fill the bill nicely."

"Sir, did you want something from the display case? Perhaps for a special occasion?" She stepped a few inches to the side and slipped the toe of her shoe beneath the counter, ready to press the button concealed there that would bring a male member of the staff discreetly to her station if she should need help—something Mr. Garamond had installed recently, but she'd never needed to use.

"You're not going to play, are you? Has no one taught you the game of harmless flirting?" He tut-tutted, drawing his gloves through his fist with a sigh. "Fine, though you would've made more money if you'd have played along. I need a box of chocolates. What do you recommend?"

"Are you looking for a gift or are these for yourself?"

"A gift." He tucked his gloves into his topcoat pocket. "For a young lady."

Her lips tightened, and he laughed. "I want something that says, 'I'm interested' but not something that says 'I'll be around to talk to your father about my intentions.'"

"Might I suggest a selection of nougats?" Something with about as much substance as this dandy had himself? "They're handmade here in our own kitchens." She opened the case and removed a tray. Placing one on a paper doily, she offered it to him to sample.

He took it, chewing slowly before swallowing. "Very nice." Again he appraised her like a hawk examined a mouse. "I'll take some. Can you wrap them in a nice box?"

"Of course, sir. We have a special price on three-pound boxes at the moment." She removed a pink-and-gold Garamond's box from beneath the cabinet and showed it to him.

"Hmm, I was going to plump for a one-pound box, but. . .for you, I'll take the bigger one. Delivery?"

"Yes, sir." Handing him two cards, she instructed him to fill out the address information on one. "The other is if you should choose to write a personal note to tuck into the box."

He made his purchase and sauntered away as Melisande placed his money in her cash drawer and recorded the transaction in her ledger.

"You handled that very nicely."

She looked up into the faded blue eyes of Mr. Hamish Garamond himself. The elderly man leaned on his cane, his white hair thinning over his scalp and his dress impeccable as always.

"Thank you, sir." She bobbed a quick curtsy, her heart hammering.

"Grandfather, are you sure about this?" Gray Garamond stood behind his grandfather. "There's a lot at stake. It isn't too late to change your mind."

Melisande's heart quit hammering and stumbled to a momentary halt. Trying not to stare, she took in as much as she could without being too obvious about it. She hadn't seen him for several months, but if anything, he was more handsome than she remembered. Light brown hair; bright, blue eyes; crisp, snowy linen and black broadcloth perfectly cut to flatter his tall frame. Gray Garamond was much more vivid than his name would suggest.

"Of course I'm sure, my boy." Mr. Garamond held a sheaf of papers and waved them toward the cases and displays around Melisande. "All of this is her work. Everything is precise and neat and appealing, so we know she can design. You should've seen the chocolate counter before she took over. There's no comparison. She'll be perfect."

Neville Strand stepped over. "Mr. Garamond? You're looking well." Mr. Strand always had a half-obsequious, half-defiant manner toward their boss that made Melisande wary.

"Ah, Neville, I'm glad you're here." The store owner set the papers on the counter. "I was just about to tell Miss Verity here that I was greatly impressed with her vision for this year's Christmas window displays. While yours were very good too, and you've done some stellar work in the past, I've decided to go in a different direction and hand the reins over to Miss Verity for this year. Congratulations, my dear."

She had to force her open mouth to close. He was choosing her? It was more than she'd dared to hope. . .no, that wasn't true. She'd hoped hard and secretly for weeks. He had chosen her. Over Neville, who had been the Christmas display window dresser at Garamond's for the past three years.

"Miss Verity?" Neville's voice went high, and both customers and coworkers turned to look. "But, she's. . .she's. . .practically a child. And she's a. . ." He lowered his voice to a whisper, flicking a glance her way. "Melisande is a. . .a. . .female. A female with no experience."

Her cheeks went hot, and she gripped her hands at her waist. It would be a huge honor to be given the job, but it *was* highly unusual for a *woman*—she wasn't a *child*, no matter what Neville Strand said!—to have such responsibility. Would Mr. Garamond change his mind?

"He makes some good points." Gray put his hands into his pockets. "I did mention her youth and inexperience."

Melisande tried not to wince. Gray wasn't that much older than she, but no one second-guessed his role as the new assistant manager of the entire store.

"I thought her sketches were charming." Mr. Garamond's voice was strong, despite the frailty of his frame, and Melisande was reminded that he had been at the helm of Garamond's for more than forty years. His word was law. "Now, my dear, come to my office for a lunch meeting so we can discuss your plans in more detail." He consulted the clock over the main entrance. "Bring your entire portfolio. In half an hour, say?"

She had to work some moisture into her mouth, nodding. "Yes, sir. Thank you, sir."

Neville's mouth pinched like he'd just sipped pure vinegar, and Gray sighed, placing his hand under his grandfather's arm.

"I don't need mollycoddling, boy." The tone was gently chiding and indulgent. "I'm not on my last legs just yet."

Neville spun on his heel and marched away, head high, eyes hot.

Melisande pressed her fingers together under her chin, her whole being humming.

She'd won the job.

Several shopworkers eyed her from their positions behind the counters in menswear, and across the atrium, the girls at the perfume counter whispered behind their hands, skeptical and sidelong glances coming her way. The news would be all over the store in a matter of a few minutes.

And it seemed only Mr. Garamond had any confidence in her.

She raised her chin, drawing up her dignity. She'd just have to prove them all wrong.

If she could create the perfect Christmas display for Garamond's, she just might create the perfect Christmas for Vonnetta. . .and herself.

Gray dropped into the chair behind his desk and propped his chin on his fist. Grandfather had done it. Against Gray's advice and hopes, he'd appointed a complete novice—and a woman at that—to be the designer for this year's Victoria's Prize Window Display Contest.

He lifted the contest brochure from his desk. A Currier & Ives print adorned the front, a holly, sleigh, snow scene. Idyllic. Inside, the rules of the contest were laid out, as well as a sketch of the Victoria Prize medal and plaque to be displayed in the winning store. How long had his grandfather wanted to win? And how many times had their rival store, Clarke and Harris, beaten them? Every single year since the inception of the award. It was almost as if Clarke and Harris had built their store with the contest in mind, with their perfectly placed, perfectly sized front windows. Last year's display had taken Gray's breath away. The elaborate "Christmas at a Country Manor" scenes had been designed to perfection. In contrast, Garamond's windows were smaller, and they weren't symmetrical, with two on each side of the door, and one around the corner where most people missed seeing it. And as if that wasn't enough of a handicap. . .

How did Grandfather expect someone with no experience to create and execute designs worthy of winning the most prestigious commercial prize in the city? All Gray's grand plans of jumping right into the management of the store and delivering a historic victory for his grandfather straight away had been dashed like a dropped teacup.

"You don't approve." Grandfather entered Gray's office and eased himself down into one of the tufted leather chairs in front of the desk. He stacked his hands on his gold-topped cane. Those hands that had taught Gray how to tie his shoes, how to properly fold cravats for a display, how to dress and conduct himself as a gentleman, were now creped and age-spotted. Grandfather moved so slowly these days, pushing on when he should take time to rest. Nothing anyone said seemed to convince Hamish Garamond that he was no longer a spry youngster.

Fear gripped Gray's windpipe and skittered across his chest. He couldn't imagine life without his grandfather. His stand-in father, really, since Gray's own parents had died in a carriage accident before he could remember them. Grandfather was the only parent Gray had ever known.

"Let's just say choosing Miss Verity doesn't exactly dovetail with my plans." Gray put his hand on the drawings and charts he'd been working on for months. They had been part of his senior projects at Oxford, and he had hoped to translate them from paper to reality at Garamond's as soon as possible. . .plans to downsize the workforce; recreate, reprioritize, and remodel; boost sales, improve layouts. . .the lists were endless. . .and none of them involved working with Miss Verity and subsequently losing the Victoria Prize.

"You have always loved your plans and projects, haven't you? But things don't always work out according to well-planned designs. There are many things that are outside your control, and when surprises happen are you going to fold and fuss, or are you going to forge ahead and deal with what life throws at you?" Grandfather leaned back in the chair, letting his cane rest against his thigh. "You can't change everything in a day. People, both customers and employees, need time to adjust. If you make too many changes too soon, folks won't know what to think. What's on your agenda now?"

*Besides changing your mind about the choice of window-dresser for the contest?* Gray sorted through the pages until he found the one he wanted to implement first. "I think we should consider adding a high-end grocery department to the store. Especially for the holidays. Hampers of fine cheeses, pâtés, crackers, canned meats, quail eggs, and the like. Non-perishables. They would make great gifts for Christmas shoppers. I've already sourced the wicker hampers, the excelsior, and the foodstuffs. I think we could put a twenty-five per-cent markup on them. If they sold well, we could continue to stock them, perhaps chang-ing them seasonally. . .you know, picnic hampers in the spring and summer, wild game hampers in the fall. Great possibilities." He passed along the costing charts and profit estimates, the floor space, storage required, as well as the number of employees needed for the expansion.

Grandfather took them, pursing his lips as he scanned the documents. "You've done a lot of work. Very thorough." He paused at the store layout plan and frowned. "You propose to put the new department near the west entrance?"

"Yes, because that's where most of the domestics running errands for their employers enter, and they are the most likely to be sent to Garamond's for such a purchase."

"But your plan would require the couture dressmakers to give up nearly half their space."

"I wanted to talk to you about that too. We could save a lot of money by culling that department entirely. If we moved more toward pre-made garments rather than bespoke dressmaking, our profits would soar." He shuffled through his papers once more. "By far our greatest outlay is payroll. If we streamline some of these departments, we can save a lot of overhead."

Grandfather frowned, rotating his cane handle in slow circles. "At the expense of a lot of jobs. Some of these employees have been with us for decades. And what about the loyal customers? We've been creating the wardrobes of some of our buyers for years. Would you disenfranchise them for the sake of a few more pounds? Being a businessman isn't just about increasing revenue. It's about the relationships you form with your employees and your customers over time."

Gray shrugged. "But if you don't turn a profit, you can't stay in business. And not all the workers in the dressmaking department would be let go. While you might lose a handful of clothing customers, you'd gain even more who would buy the less expensive options. Consider what it would do for our bottom line." He tapped his papers into a neat pile and set them to the left of the blotter before lacing his fingers together and resting his forearms on his desk. "Increasing profits is the primary function of a business, isn't it? Which brings us back to Miss Verity and the window displays. Winning the Victoria Prize would garner us a lot of free advertising, but I can't see how you hope to win with her at the helm."

Leaning forward, Grandfather placed the grocery plans on the edge of the desk. "Perhaps winning isn't my objective this year."

Gray's eyebrows rose. "What other reason could there be to enter? The window contest is ridiculously expensive: the entry fee, the overtime pay, the supplies. If you don't come out on top, it's just a waste of money."

For a moment, Grandfather's faded blue eyes clouded. "Perhaps the reason is to give joy to those who will come by to see the beautiful displays. Far more people view the tableaux than ever come into the store to buy anything. It's sort of a Christmas gift to the city. Winning would be wonderful, but bringing happiness during the season is better."

"And you think Miss Verity is the one for the job? Neville was less than pleased not to have been chosen." Gray had worked under Neville Strand in the menswear department two summers ago, and the man was. . .difficult, at the best of times.

"Wait until you see her proposal. It's charming. She's caught the spirit of the holidays, with whimsy, heart, and not a little creativity. I think it will really please the public. And, the additional income we'll pay her won't go amiss. I have a feeling she's had a rough go of things, and I like the idea of helping her out some."

"I wanted to look over her designs before you made your choice, but you've kept them under wraps." Gray tried to keep his frustration out of his voice. Grandfather hadn't allowed him any say in the selection, and it grated. He was the new assistant manager of the store, after all. "All I can say is, she should have some help and some oversight. It's too big a project for her to do alone." Gray glanced at the clock. Their lunch meeting would begin soon. He would look over her plans then and judge for himself how big a disaster this might be.

"I was hoping you'd say that." Grandfather grinned. "I have a few suggestions of folks to put at her disposal, but I want you to supervise the proceedings this year, work closely with her throughout the process."

"But, what about. . . ?" Gray waved to the stacks of his plans and proposals for changes to the store.

"You don't have to tackle it all in a day. Anyway. . ." He bent a smile Gray's way. "I'm not expecting you to run the entire store by yourself. I'm still here and kicking."

Gray nodded and levered himself up. "I suppose we might as well get this lunch meeting out of the way." *Better to see for myself whether Miss Verity's designs are workable while there's still time to find someone else for the job.*

# Chapter 2

**M**elisande felt Neville Strand's disapproving stare on her back as she left the chocolates cases in the care of one of the girls from the perfume counter and gripped the banister. Her shoes sounded loud on the marble steps, and the brass handrail chilled her fingers. Halfway up, she remembered she was still wearing her apron and yanked at the bow, tugging it off and hurrying back to lay it on a shelf out of sight.

Mr. Garamond had chosen her designs, but she felt as if this meeting was the final part of the process of truly being selected, the final audition. She had to present herself and her plans well, or the opportunity might still be taken away from her. And Gray's expression had been skeptical to say the least. Had he been up here campaigning against her for the last little while?

By the time she reached the top floor, her breath was coming quickly, and she paused at the outer door to the office suites to settle herself. "Lord, help me. Help me not to hold this opportunity too tightly. Help me be articulate, to show them my vision."

Mr. Whytcher, secretary to Mr. Garamond, rose from his desk when she opened the door to the owners' offices.

"Ah, Miss Verity, right on time. Your meeting is in the conference room. Lunch will arrive in a few minutes." He smiled at her, and the knot in her stomach eased a fraction. Though Mr. Whytcher had an exalted position among the staff, he had always been friendly and kind, a good reflection of his employer. "This way."

He opened a door to a room she had never been in before. A long table surrounded by leather chairs, high windows, a soaring ceiling, and more wood paneling and plasterwork than in the entire boardinghouse where she and her sister lived.

At the far end of the table, both Mr. Garamond and Gray rose. Mr. Garamond came toward her, holding out his hand. "Miss Verity. Come, sit down. I can't tell you how excited I am about your designs." He held out a chair for her, seating her at his right hand, across the table from Gray.

Looking into Gray's intelligent blue eyes, her middle suddenly felt as if a half-dozen squirrels from Hyde Park were chasing one another around in there.

"Now. . ." Mr. Garamond rubbed his hands together. "Let's go over these plans. I haven't shared them with Gray here, so it will all be fresh and new to him. I want to see his reaction, and perhaps we can gauge the reaction the public will have too."

Melisande reminded herself she was a grown woman, a valued employee, and not thickheaded. It was time to put her best foot forward.

She untied the strings on her portfolio and drew a rectangular packet out, unwrapping the tissue that protected one of her dearest possessions. She set it on the table and spread out the more-detailed drawings she'd created since turning in her application, laying them on the table so that they were right-side up for Gray. Then she picked up the treasure. "I am hoping to create five scenes inspired by Dickens's *A Christmas Carol*. The story was my mother's favorite, and she read it to us every year during the holidays. This was her copy, and it was very dear to her." *And now to me.* Melisande caressed the battered copy of the story. Her mother had found it in a secondhand store years before, and she'd treasured every yellowed, foxed, well-thumbed page. Some of the leaves had come out, and Mother had carefully glued them back in, and while the book wouldn't win any prizes for beauty, it was beyond price to Melisande.

She held her breath while Gray picked up the first design, the one where Jacob Marley brought his warning to Ebenezer Scrooge. Mr. Garamond picked up the second sketch—Scrooge and the Ghost of Christmas Past observing a younger version of Scrooge dancing and enjoying himself.

"I chose what I hoped were memorable scenes from the book that would need little explanation, but if you think there are better ones, I'd certainly be open to that." She pressed her hands together in her lap.

Gray picked up another sketch. His face gave nothing away. Did he like them? Was he bored?

Mr. Garamond wasn't as reticent. "I love every one of them. And I think they'll catch the eye of every person who passes by. Five scenes, five wonderful displays."

Pursing his lips, Gray leafed through the pages. "These are certainly ambitious. Are you sure you can complete them in time?"

"I'll do my best. I've tried to plan well." She drew several more pages from her portfolio. "Here are the lists of supplies, as well as lists of the store's wares that we can display in each of the scenes. Aside from the construction materials, all the furnishings and décor will come from and be available to purchase at Garamond's."

"That is imminently sensible," Mr. Garamond said. "Don't you think so, Gray?"

"Hmm." He took the lists, scanning them.

The door opened, and Neville Strand burst in, closely followed by Mr. Whytcher. "Neville, please wait. I'm sorry, sir." The secretary directed this last bit to Mr. Garamond, who sat back in his chair, tenting his fingers, his brows raised.

"Was there something you needed, Neville?"

"Sir, how can you select her over me? Haven't I given you good designs over the past several years?" He stood rigid, his face red. "Did you even look at my plans?" Neville thrust a handful of papers before Mr. Garamond and Gray.

Heat rushed to Melisande's cheeks. She didn't know where to look and found her gaze locking with Gray's. His eyes held hers for a moment before he picked up Neville's wrinkled designs and glanced over them.

"Please, Neville, calm yourself," Mr. Garamond soothed. "You have given us many wonderful displays through the years, and you've been a good and loyal employee. None of that has changed. I assure you, I value your contributions, both to the contest and to the store. I'm sure we can reach an understanding."

Neville took in a deep breath, the flush of anger receding as he groped for a chair. "I knew you'd see reason, sir."

Melisande's heart fell. They were going to take the job away from her.

Mr. Garamond motioned for Mr. Whytcher to go, but the secretary lingered for a moment. "Sir, luncheon for three has arrived."

"Keep it under the cloches for now. We'll eat in a bit." Mr. Garamond waved Mr. Whytcher away with a kind smile.

"Very well, sir." The secretary cast a sympathetic glance at Melisande, who made sure her chin was parallel to the floor and her expression calm.

Though she had to blink hard for a moment and take a few breaths. She would not cry.

"Now, Neville, I have looked over your designs, and they are quite good."

Neville smiled, drawing out his handkerchief to mop his face. "I worked very hard on them, sir."

"However," Mr. Garamond continued, "as good as they are, I've chosen Miss Verity's designs. She might be young, but she brings a fresh eye and new enthusiasm to the project. Her theme is delightful, and she's managed to capture the spirit I'm looking for." He smiled at Melisande as her heart rushed with hope.

"I would have to agree." Gray laid the pages out before him, hers and Neville's, his voice reluctantly admiring. "Her designs are clearly superior. Though I have my doubts about her ability to conquer such an ambitious scheme in the allotted time."

Melisande pressed her lips together. She would prove herself, if only they would give her a chance.

"What are her designs? How can they be better than mine? After all, I propose to tell the story of the Nativity." Neville fisted his hands on the table, the color rushing back into his cheeks.

"Dickens's *A Christmas Carol* told in five scenes." Mr. Garamond held up the first design.

Neville's eyes widened, and his gritted teeth showed. "But, sir, that's. . .that's a ghost story."

Mr. Garamond lowered the page. "Neville, *A Christmas Carol* is a story of redemption. It's a work of fiction that employs the device of memories in the form of benevolent spirits— ghosts if you will—to bring a wayward man back to the path of righteousness. I appreciate your point of view, but I've made up my mind."

Stillness went through Neville, and he flattened his palms on the table. "Very well. I have no choice but to tender my resignation."

"Now Neville, there's no need for that." Mr. Garamond shook his head, seeming to sink a bit farther into his chair, his brow furrowing. His hand went to his chest for a moment.

Melisande froze. Neville Strand was as much a part of the fabric of Garamond's as Bramwell at the front door or Mr. Hamish himself. Surely he couldn't be so offended by her selection as to quit his job?

Gray leaned forward, shooting a concerned glance at his grandfather. "Mr. Strand, consider what you're saying. I can understand that you're chagrined at not winning the appointment, but to threaten to quit? This management doesn't respond well to emotional blackmail. I would suggest that you at least sleep on a decision like this, knowing that Miss Verity continues to be our choice for the contest entry and that you have a very nice place here at Garamond's for which you have worked hard. If, by tomorrow, you still feel the same, then we will accept your resignation. But until then, I would suggest you take your drawings and go back to your department and get to work." He butted the pages together and pushed them down the table, his tone brooking no argument.

Neville scowled at Melisande, snatched up his papers, and stalked out of the room.

Melisande sat back, her spine turning to water. Had Gray just confirmed her as the project head?

Mr. Garamond's hand trembled as he touched his chest again, and Gray was out of his chair in a trice. "Are you all right? Do you need a doctor?" The concern in his voice startled Melisande. He was normally quite crisp and decisive, but here he was, kneeling beside his grandfather, his eyes filled with worry.

"Of course I don't need a doctor. I just need some lunch." Mr. Garamond put a bit of verve into his tone. "Stop babying me." He brushed Gray's hand aside. "You handled Neville pretty well. A bit more abruptly than I would've, but you gave him a way to get off the cliff he'd climbed up."

"I'm still not totally convinced he's wrong about the contest and your choice of a designer, but he was out of bounds threatening to quit that way." Gray shot Melisande a doubtful look. "Let's get this lunch meeting over with. I have a lot to accomplish today."

As if he'd been listening at the door, Mr. Whytcher appeared, pushing a cart laden with covered plates.

Drawing a deep breath, Melisande picked up her precious copy of *A Christmas Carol* and returned it to her portfolio, careful to wrap it in the tissue once more. She felt as lightheaded as if she'd just danced an hour-long reel, her emotions all over the place.

But the most important thing was that she still had the job. She just had to prove to all of them—Neville, Mr. Garamond, and especially Gray—that she was up to the task.

Hours later, Melisande met Vonnetta in the employee cloakroom for the walk to their boardinghouse. Her mind was full of plans and ideas and opposing feelings. Excitement at winning the job, embarrassment at Neville's assessment of her unsuitability, fondness for Mr. Garamond for championing her cause. . .and uncertainty about working so closely with Gray Garamond over the coming few weeks.

And the realization of just how far a gap existed between herself and the heir to the Garamond fortune. It wasn't just the money or social standing. Ever since meeting Gray Garamond, she'd spun girlish fantasies about what he was like and what it might be like to be special to him. Having spent more than two hours with him today, she couldn't help feeling a bit. . .confused? Unlike his grandfather, all of Gray's focus seemed to be on profit, on winning the competition, on how Garamond's could benefit from the holiday season. Was he really like that down deep, or did a better man, less obsessed with success—a man more like dear Hamish Garamond—hide under the executive, workplace surface?

Vonnetta grabbed Melisande's elbow. "It's all over the store. You really got the job? And you had lunch with Mr. Garamond and Mr. Gray? Tell me everything. What did you eat? Is the third floor as amazing as they say? Did Mr. Strand really break into the meeting? Tell me." She shook Melisande's arm.

"You haven't stopped talking long enough for me to tell you anything." Melisande tugged gently free from her sister's grasp, keenly aware of the other employees around her. "We'll discuss it later."

Wrapping her scarf around her throat, tugging on her mittens, and gathering her portfolio and handbag, Melisande lagged, letting the room clear a bit. Vonnetta crossed her arms, tapping her foot as always, a bundle of energy just waiting to burst. "Is the song in your head staccato?" Melisande asked.

"It's a *rondo*," Vonnetta shot back.

The moment they were outside, bracing against a stiff breeze, Vonnetta linked their arms and demanded, "Tell me."

"I got the job."

"And I'm proud of you, but what about the third floor?"

Melisande halted at the curb to let a carriage go by. An urchin with a broom raced into the crosswalk and began sweeping furiously, his face almost obscured by his large, cloth cap. But when he glanced up at them, assessing their ordinary coats and shoes, he shrugged, propped the broom on his shoulder, and sauntered back to wait for a more lucrative opportunity for a tip.

"The third floor was beautiful. High ceilings, polished paneling, and a conference table long enough to host a State dinner at Buckingham. I felt small and insignificant when I walked in." She told Vonnetta almost everything she could remember, keeping her feelings about Gray to herself. She shouldn't be so hard on him. After all, they were at a business meeting, so his taking that business seriously shouldn't be considered a flaw, should it? And yet, the disquiet in her heart continued.

Vonnetta's questions lasted the entire walk home, by which time Melisande was thoroughly chilled. Their boardinghouse, uninviting on even the sunniest of summer days, squatted under the gray clouds that scudded by overhead. Vonnetta tugged on the handle of the creosote-coated oak door, the hinges protesting and the heavy wood dragging in the groove on the floor. The smell of damp wool and cooked cabbage greeted them. The girls mounted the steps to their third-floor back bedroom.

Melisande opened the drawer in the little table under the window and placed her portfolio inside, patting it to make sure the copy of *A Christmas Carol* was still safe. Turning, she bumped into Vonnetta.

"I declare, this room is so small, we have to go outside to change our minds," Vonnetta muttered as she checked her reflection in the mirror. "Remember our room at the farm? We had the whole second floor just for us."

For a time, Melisande had been reluctant to recall those memories, the ones where Mother and Dad were still alive, when they lived on their small farm, before the barn fire that had taken their father and the illness that had taken their mother and the debts had taken their home. . .those happy memories had felt like they belonged to someone else, a different Melisande, not the one who counted pennies, who took her responsibilities as the elder sibling seriously. . .who clung to the promise she had made to her dying mother to see that Vonnetta had the music education she longed for. But now she held the good memories close, bringing them out often, reminding Vonnetta and herself of their many blessings.

The sisters squeezed into their places at the dining room table, sliding down the bench that had been pushed tight against the wall to accommodate everyone. The house was crammed with boarders, every room occupied. Their landlady plunked dishes onto the table—cabbage, bread, and mutton. Cheap, filling, but unappetizing. Melisande couldn't help but think of the perfectly-cooked roast, the tender asparagus, and the waxy white potatoes she'd dined on at luncheon in the executive suite. Still, this was more than adequate. She would be thankful for both meals, since there were plenty in the city tonight who had neither.

When she and Vonnetta had eaten and climbed the stairs to their room once more, Vonnetta softly singing scales as they readied themselves for bed, Melisande told her sister the one piece of news she had been holding back.

"Mr. Garamond said I would need a team to help me with the window project."

"That's reasonable." Vonnetta brushed her long hair, holding her head sideways to allow the beautiful golden waves to fall over her shoulder.

"I asked him if you could be part of that team."

The brush clattered to the floor. "You what?" Vonnetta pounced on her, pushing her back on the bed, shaking her shoulders. "Oh, you beauty!" She stilled. "Wait. What did he say?"

"He said yes, now get off me!" Melisande pushed Vonnetta and sat up, righting her nightcap with a laugh. "But promise me you'll pay attention and do as I say. There will be a lot of costumes to prepare, and your sewing skills will come in handy if you can keep your mind on business."

"I will!" Vonnetta twirled on her bare feet, her faded calico nightgown belling out.

"And...you can't hum and sing while we're working, unless we're alone." While Melisande was used to it and understood the musical passion that drove her little sister, most people did not and found the habit irritating.

Vonnetta huffed, crossing her arms. "I *can* control it, you know."

"Good, because the other members of the team are Jimmy Cane, the delivery boy, Mr. Gray himself, who will be overseeing everything. . ." *Because he doesn't think I can do it by myself.* "And Neville Strand." Just saying his name filled Melisande with apprehension.

"Mr. Strand? Oh, Mellie, why?" Her sister plopped down onto the bed and reached blindly for the hairbrush at her feet.

That had been her reaction too when Mr. Garamond had suggested Neville. *Why?*

"He gets things done, and he has a good eye for detail." She dredged up a positive attitude. "And, I think Mr. Garamond is trying to mollify Mr. Strand for not being in charge." She also sensed she would have a difficult time reminding Mr. Strand that he *wasn't* in charge.

"And Mr. Gray will be supervising? He's so handsome." Vonnetta sighed, fluttering her eyelids comically. "All the girls in the sewing room are keen on him. And there you'll be, working with him every day. . .and I will be too." She straightened. "Won't that be a feather in my cap? The girls will be so jealous." She gave a smug smile.

"You're a silly goose. Mr. Gray won't even take notice of you unless you aren't doing your job. Now go to sleep, or we'll both be wooly-headed tomorrow."

She waited until Vonnetta slid under the coverlet and then blew out the small oil lamp. As Melisande drifted off to sleep, she reminded herself that what went for Vonnetta went for her too. Gray wouldn't take any notice of her unless she failed. She would do her job, she would do it well, and she would stop hoping for anything more than approval where Gray Garamond was concerned.

# Chapter 3

Gray leaned against the bank of pillows, tilting one of the papers in his lap toward the light. His mind, as it so often did, refused to allow him to sleep. There were just too many things to think about, too many problems at the store to solve. This particular problem, though, didn't have an easy solution, because it involved people and not strategies.

Specifically, it involved Grandfather. How could he change his grandfather's mind about bringing in pre-made garments? Sure, it would shake things up for a while, but. . . he consulted a ledger sheet. . .the profit potential was enormous. At least he had wrung tacit permission to deploy the gourmet food basket venture. But only for the holidays. And only in the space he could find without cutting into the fitting and sewing rooms.

The clock in the hall chimed twice. Gray grimaced. He really should try to sleep. But as he reached for the gaslight key on the sconce by the bed, the drawings for the window contest caught his attention.

Sliding the top page toward himself, he studied it. Miss Verity had skill, he'd give her that. If the actual displays looked anything like the drawings, they might have a real shot at the Victoria Prize this year—if she could pull this look off. A big "if."

He let the paper fall to his lap and closed his eyes, resting his head against the pillows. Miss Verity. Melisande. Her image clarified in his mind. Very pretty, intelligent eyes, with a clear affection for his grandfather. She did nothing to draw attention to herself or flatter Gray. Not like some of the shop girls who all but flaunted themselves around him, the grandson and heir.

A grimace twisted his lips. Several invitations had arrived this past week, some for himself, some for his grandfather, some for both. Invitations to dinner parties, dances, soirees, concerts, and the like. Nothing unusual there, but the invitation to the Drapers' Ball stood out because it said "and Partner," meaning he would have to find someone to take to the affair.

But who?

It wasn't that he didn't enjoy female company, but he'd been so busy, so focused on finishing his degree, on making a place for himself at the store, that he hadn't spent much time thinking about courting, settling down, and the like. There was time for that later. After all, he was only twenty-five and fresh out of graduate school.

He'd cast about for a suitable partner for the Drapers' Ball in the coming days. After all, the party wasn't for several weeks.

A firm knock on the door startled him. "Who is it?"

"Sir, it's your grandfather. Please come."

Gray's feet were already swinging over the side of the bed, and he was reaching for his dressing gown as he recognized the voice of the butler. Yanking the door open, he met Camden, who had been in his grandfather's employ since before Gray was born. The gaslights in the hallway hadn't been lit, but Camden held a lamp in his trembling hands.

"What's happened?" Gray shoved his arms through the sleeves of his dressing gown and tied the belt with quick jerks.

"Mr. Garamond has taken ill, sir. I've sent for the doctor. Mrs. Mouton is with him now."

Gray started down the hall toward his grandfather's suite, his heart racing. The door stood ajar, and he hurried into the room.

Mrs. Mouton, the housekeeper, still in her nightclothes and frilly cap, bent over the bed. Gray went to her side.

"Grandfather?" He reached for the age-spotted hand on the covers.

His grandfather's eyes opened, two dark holes in his pale face. His lips wobbled, but no sound came out. Gray squeezed his hand gently. There was no squeeze in response. Gray's heart sank. Something was seriously amiss.

"Can you talk to me? Are you in pain?" he asked.

Again the lips trembled...or rather one side of his mouth trembled. The other remained motionless.

Mrs. Mouton drew Gray back to stand near the windows. "I fear it's apoplexy. Peters heard a noise." She motioned to the connecting door to Grandfather's dressing room, where his valet slept. "When he came to check, he found Mr. Garamond on the floor."

"Where's Peters now?"

"He helped me get the master back into bed, but he's so shaken, I sent him to the kitchen to make some tea. He wasn't much good in here, wringing his hands and leaking tears." She sniffed, crossing her arms, clearly disgusted with the valet's frailty in the face of a crisis. To his knowledge, Mrs. Mouton had never met a crisis she couldn't whip into a corner without much effort.

"Has Grandfather spoken at all?" Gray stuffed his hands into his dressing gown pockets.

"Nary a word. He can't seem to use his left side, and he can't speak."

Gray's windpipe constricted, and his heart sounded loud in his ears. "Very well. Go supervise Peters in the kitchen. Don't rouse the rest of the staff, but those who are awake should dress. Make coffee for me, if you would. Camden, stay with Grandfather while I dress."

"Right, sir."

He went to his room where Reeves, his own valet, had already laid out clothes for him. The man was invaluable, one of many priceless employees in the Garamond household. Just as at the store, his grandfather had a knack of assembling a very loyal, industrious staff.

"Is it bad, sir?" Reeves asked.

Gray shook his head. "We'll wait to see what the doctor says." His fingers fumbled on his buttons. He didn't want to say what he was thinking, that it looked bad, that Grandfather might not make it through this.

Footsteps clattered up the main stairs. Gray went into the hall and met the doctor coming toward him.

At least he assumed it was the doctor, since he carried a black bag, but the man was so. . .young. Gray glanced over the doctor's shoulder at the footman who had been sent to fetch medical help.

"Where's my patient?" The young man removed his top hat, handing it to the footman without a glance.

"I'm sorry, but are you my father's regular physician? What happened to Dr. White?"

"He's retired. I'm Dr. Coker, and I have taken over his practice. I assure you I am a fully-qualified physician with a degree from the University of Edinburgh, a fellowship at St. Bart's, and a full client list. Your grandfather has been my patient for a year now."

Heat flushed Gray's face at being so transparent, but it was his grandfather's health at risk.

"This way." He led the doctor into the master suite. Reeves and Camden were there, turning up the gaslights, stirring the fire. Someone had pulled a table over beside the bed and laid it with fresh towels and a basin of clean water. Efficient.

The doctor shucked his coat and rolled up his sleeves. "Mr. Garamond, it's Dr. Coker. I'm going to examine you. You don't have to do anything. Just relax."

His voice even soothed Gray a bit. Until the doctor turned to him. "I'm going to ask you all to leave the room. I'll come to you as soon as I know anything."

Gray wanted to protest, but the look in the doctor's eyes told him it would do no good. He went into the hallway with the rest of the staff.

Camden's bushy eyebrows bunched over his crooked nose. "I wish it was Dr. White. This young jackanapes is barely out of school."

"But Mr. Garamond likes Dr. Coker," Reeves was quick to put in. "He says he's got smart new ideas."

Gray didn't much fancy cooling his heels in the hall. His chest felt hollow, as if a giant hand had scooped it out, and yet, it felt heavy too. Surely there was something he should be doing. But what? Helplessness swamped him, and he jammed his fingers through his hair.

The door opened, and Dr. Coker came out, wiping his hands on a towel. "You are Gray Garamond? Hamish's grandson?"

"Yes. How is he?"

"He's sleeping now. Is there somewhere we can talk?"

"Just tell me." The doctor's tone unsettled Gray.

"Very well. Your grandfather has suffered a stroke. He is paralyzed on his left side, and he's suffered aphasia of speech. He cannot speak, but he can blink yes or no to questions asked, which is a good sign."

Couldn't speak. Paralyzed. Stroke. The words hit like blows.

"What is his prognosis?" he managed to ask.

The doctor pursed his lips, his eyes narrowing for a moment. "It's hard to say. Each patient responds differently, and the causes of stroke vary. He might have thrown a blood clot, or he might have a slow cranial bleed from an aneurysm. He indicates that he has a headache at the moment, but that isn't unusual. The next few days are vital. I'll leave instructions for you." He began rolling down his sleeves. "I must tell you, most stroke victims don't survive very long after such a major event, and if they do, they are rarely the same. At least some of the paralysis is likely permanent. Hard to say on the speech.

He might recover some ability there, but he won't be up to returning to his work soon, or possibly ever. For someone so vitally involved in his career, this is going to be difficult. Keep his stress to a minimum, give him the pills I prescribe, and don't push him to do more than he can."

Don't survive long. Can't return to work. Permanent paralysis. Again, Gray could only focus on occasional words and phrases.

The clock behind him rang out, and he glanced at the face. Three thirty. In the space of ninety minutes, the world had changed drastically.

Two hours later, Gray greeted the night watchman at Garamond's as he let himself in the side door. He gave no reason for his early-morning arrival. He would address the staff later. For now, he just felt compelled to come to the store.

"Sir, I should tell you—" the watchman began.

"Not now." He wanted to be alone. Tugging his gloves off, he stuffed them into the pocket of his greatcoat, brushing a few snowflakes off his shoulders. Once inside the brass-and-glass doors, he breathed deeply, the first deep breath he'd taken since racing down the hall to his grandfather's room.

It didn't help. He still felt starved of oxygen. What if Grandfather didn't recover? Gray would be alone in the world. He had no uncles or aunts or cousins. His parents were gone. He only had Grandfather.

His footsteps echoed on the marble floor as he walked down the aisle between the display cases. When he reached the center of the store, he found himself beside the chocolate counter. He paused. In the faint glow of the street lamps outside, he studied the displays. He'd never really taken the time to observe the chocolate counter before. It seemed like such a small cog in the great machine of Garamond's, a rather insignificant niche in the grand scheme of things.

And yet…everything in the glass counter was perfect. Exquisitely tied tartan bows decorated the corners of a plate of shortbread cookies. Gold ribbons curled around petit fours and caramels. Boxes artfully arranged stood ready to be filled.

He looked high above to the stained-glass skylight, a beautiful extravagance his grandfather had insisted upon when building the new store as a gift to his grandmother. Wrought iron railings, marble staircase, gaslight chandeliers, walnut woodwork, brass fittings, everything of the highest quality, just like the wares they sold.

Gray swallowed as the weight of responsibility wrapped around his shoulders. He'd been born to this, had always aspired to this, leading the company, but now that those aspirations were reality, doubt as to his ability crept into his mind.

By the time he reached his office, he wondered why he had come in so early when there was no comfort to be found here either.

He frowned. Light glowed from beneath one of the office doors across the hall from his and his grandfather's office suite. *Wasn't that the room assigned to Miss Verity for the window project? Who would be in there at this hour?* He strode over, annoyed at the intrusion when he wanted to be alone.

He yanked on the knob and stuck his head in. Miss Verity jumped, dropping a pair of scissors onto the carpet. Her hand shot to her throat.

"Oh, Mr. Gray, you startled me." With shaking fingers, she smoothed her hair and stooped to pick up the scissors and set them on the bench.

"What are you doing here at this hour?" His voice was harsher than he intended, and she flinched.

"I...I couldn't sleep. I wanted to get started on the display for the first window while the vision was fresh in my mind." She motioned to the work space.

"What is all this?"

She laced her fingers, pointing with her index fingers. "I laid out the dimensions of the window here on the floor with seam tape, so I could get a feel for the area I need to fill. This mannequin represents Scrooge." She touched the nightshirt-and-dressing-gowned figure. "And this mannequin will be Mr. Marley." The other figure was only draped in a sheet and looked a bit like the apparition it was to portray.

"The clothing is from the menswear department, the finest silk dressing gown I could find. I'll need slippers and a nightcap from haberdashery, but I thought I would have Mr. Strand choose those, as well as some of the masculine accoutrements to furnish the room. The pipe stand, the paintings, and the like."

Gray ran his hand over an ormolu clock. "This is from Garamond's too?"

"Oh yes. I intend to use only things that can be purchased in our store for the furnishings and decorations."

He glanced at the lists and drawings hung on the wall over the workbench, and at her. Gaslight picked out the highlights in her dark hair and put a luminous circle of gold in each of her dark eyes. A flush rode her cheeks, and she bit her lower lip. He was reminded again of how pretty she was...and petite. Her head just came to his shoulder.

She asked, "Do you always come to work so early?"

Which brought his thoughts back to where they should be. "No. I usually come to work with my grandfather at seven thirty. But. . ." He shifted his weight. "Grandfather won't be coming to work today...or for the foreseeable future. He's taken ill."

Compassion and worry flooded her face, and she brought her fingers up to her lips. "Oh no. Poor Mr. Garamond. Is there anything I can do?"

Her immediate response underscored just how much the staff cared for Grandfather. If he had been at the helm of Garamond's for many years, would his employees feel the same way about him?

"There's nothing to do at the moment but wait. The doctor says he's had a stroke and the next few days are critical. I'm hoping he will make a complete recovery, but if what the doctor says is true, it will take a miracle."

Her eyes glistened, but she raised her chin. "Then we'll just have to pray for a miracle. After all, we're coming into the season when we celebrate miracles."

Looking at the window display sketches, the bits of décor and clothing, it all seemed so empty and silly. Why pursue a prize when his grandfather was probably dying? He should call off the entire thing now, save the store the money and expense, and focus on his grandfather and taking charge of the store.

"Miracles. Those are things that happen to other people in other places and other times...or in books and fairytales like that one." He motioned to the battered copy of *A Christmas Carol* lying on the bench. "Most of us just keep putting one foot in front of the other, taking whatever life throws at us."

She said nothing, but he could tell she disagreed. Well, fine, but she wasn't going to change his mind with her starry-eyed outlook. She might believe in miracles, but in his experience, they were few and far between, and none had come his way in a long time, if ever.

# Chapter 4

At Whytcher's suggestion, Gray moved into his grandfather's office, though it felt all wrong. Mr. Whytcher had gone pale at the news of Hamish's stroke, but then he'd nodded and asked what he could do to help.

The staff meeting first thing had been. . .awful. Some of the women had cried, men had frowned, and silence had reigned. Doubtful looks cast his way had done nothing to bolster his confidence.

"Sir. . ."Whytcher spoke around the edge of the door. "There seems to be a bit of an issue in the couture department."

"What is it this time?" Gray felt as if all morning he'd been running here and there putting out fires. How did his Grandfather do it? How did he get any office work done if he had to leave it so often?

"A customer has requested to speak with management."

"Can't Mrs. O'Hair help her? She's the department head." Gray pinched the bridge of his nose. He needed to finish this order for the gourmet foods and submit it today or the inventory wouldn't arrive in time to take advantage of the holiday shopping market.

"The customer has asked for you, sir."

Gray screwed the cap onto his ink pen and tossed it onto the blotter, pushing himself up. "Go ahead and order my lunch. I'll eat at my desk when I get back."

"Yes, Mr. Garamond."

Both men paused. It was the first time someone had addressed him as Mr. Garamond, the head of the store.

Whytcher looked stricken.

"It's all right." Gray waved his hand. "I miss having him here too."

Gray elected to use the lift rather than the stairs. He'd trotted up and down the flights enough for one morning. As he stepped into the brass cage for the trip down, Miss Verity hurried by, her head down. "Hold the door," he told the elevator operator.

"Miss Verity, if you're going down, you may join me." He stood in the doorway, arm held toward the interior of the car.

"Thank you, sir." She held a clipboard across her chest, and a furrow sat between her brows.

"Good morning. I hope your day is going better than mine." He shoved his hands into his pockets. The dial over the door arced to the left at floor two and then floor one. The operator faced the doors, his hand on the lever. Another expense Gray planned to cut. He could operate the elevator himself. It was a waste to pay a man to pull a lever a couple times a day.

"This morning has left me wondering how Monday-ish one Tuesday can be, sir," Melisande answered his inquiry.

A chuckle forced its way out of Gray's throat. "That's an excellent way to describe it."

The elevator man wound back the doors. "First floor, sir."

They exited, and Miss Verity glanced up at Gray. "Has it been difficult, stepping into your grandfather's place?"

"Not the strategy aspect of management. I'm working on plans to streamline our workforce, reduce costs, and update our methods. It's the personnel side of things where I get bogged down. I had no idea how much time Grandfather spent smoothing things over and placating different personalities. At least if I can put my plans into action, I won't have as many employees to deal with and our customer base will change its expectations that Garamond's will cater to their every whim. I think a more 'take-it-or-leave-it' approach to our inventory and customer service will improve our bottom line."

She paused, waiting until a pair of young, female shoppers went by. "You're planning on firing employees and doing away with Garamond's customer service?" She wore the same expression his grandfather had.

"It's just smart business. Payroll can be a huge black maw, gobbling up profits. There are more employees than necessary on the payroll right now." He gestured toward the front door. "Like Bramwell. We don't really need a doorman. I plan to install revolving doors at the main entrance. They'll be more efficient, and no one needs to stand there and open them. The same with the couture department, the cobbler shop, and even the operator for the executive elevator. I can slash payroll by as much as thirty percent and not lose much in the way of meeting customer needs. In some cases, I can even offer pay raises to remaining employees and still come out ahead on profit margin."

"But. . .what about the people you let go? What about their loyalty to the store, their long years of service?" A dart appeared between her brows, uncertainty clouding her eyes.

Gray shrugged. "They would be given a nice severance amount and a good reference." Then it dawned upon him what she must be thinking. "You needn't worry about your position. The chocolate counter turns a tidy profit with minimal overhead. You practically run the place by yourself."

She pressed her lips together, and if he didn't miss his guess, she seemed more disappointed than fearful. They reached the women's clothing department, and he expected to part from Miss Verity at that moment, but it seemed they were headed to the same place.

"I've got to consult with Mrs. O'Hair about the gowns for the second window." She checked her clipboard, a frown still marring her features. When they entered the modeling room of the couture department, a stern-looking woman stood before the triple mirror, clearly unhappy.

On her knees beside the woman, a girl with honey-colored hair fussed with the woman's train, her lips clamped tightly on half a dozen pins and her eyes glistening with tears.

"I told you, no amount of pinning will do. It has to be taken apart and re-sewn, you silly girl." The woman wearing the gown pinched her lips together, eyes hot. "And I don't want you to do it. You'll just ruin it again. I don't know what Garamond's is coming to, hiring someone so unfit for her job as you."

Melisande stiffened at his side, her arms tightening on the clipboard. Mrs. O'Hair, the head of the couture department fluttered nearby, her hands flapping, shooting him an appeal without words.

"Excuse me," Gray stepped forward. "Perhaps I can assist you?"

The woman whirled on the stand. "I very much doubt it. I'm waiting for Mr. Garamond. I ordered this dress weeks ago, and it still isn't finished. And look at it. If I wanted a gown my mother would wear, I'd take something from her closet. The train is all wrong, and the décolletage is so. . .matronly." She appeared at a loss for words, but that quickly passed. "I never thought I would live to see the day when Garamond's standards would slip so far. I haven't been best pleased with the last two dresses I purchased here. If things don't change, I'm taking my business to Clarke & Harris."

Gray was tempted to tell her to go right ahead. He couldn't see anything wrong with the dress except the woman wearing it. The shop girl fussing with the hem of the gown sniffed.

"Miss. . . ?" he asked.

"Verity, sir."

He glanced at Melisande, who had her bottom lip tucked in, her eyes full of worry. She was related to this girl? They bore little similarity to one another on first glance, but as he looked closer, there was a resemblance in the brow and chin.

"Miss Verity." He helped the girl to her feet. "Would you be so kind as to fetch a tray of refreshments for our client here?" It was the first thing he thought of to get her out of the room. She obviously needed some time to settle herself without the virago on the perch berating her.

"Yes, sir. Thank you, sir." She hurried out of the room.

"Now, Miss. . . ?" He turned to the customer.

"It's *Mrs.* Mrs. Stanford Blythe-Sommers." Her chin went up, and she looked down her narrow nose at him as if he should know very well who she was. "Now, where is Mr. Garamond? I don't want to talk to an underling."

Gray fisted his hands, his temper going from a simmer to a boil. The nerve of the woman. Before he could speak, Melisande entered the conversation.

"Mrs. Blythe-Sommers." She smiled. "I'm sure we can alter the gown to your satisfaction. It is Garamond's policy that if the customer isn't pleased, she's under no obligation to purchase a garment. I assure you, Garamond's has the finest modistes in the city." She stooped and picked up the train, gathering it at one point and tucking it up to fall in a small poof. "Perhaps if we tucked it up here." She tilted her head slightly. "Yes, that accentuates your small waist better, don't you think?"

Gray couldn't see that it did any such thing, but the change in expression on Mrs. Blythe-Sommers' face said she believed it.

Melisande stepped back, tapping her lips with her finger, eyes narrowed as she studied the front of the gown. "I'd have to say, the bodice looks about right to me. Because you've chosen such a bold color, it wouldn't do to have the neckline too revealing. That pushes the dress into. . .well, a direction that is beneath your station." She smiled conspiratorially. "I believe the burgundy color is enough to attract attention without making it *unwanted* attention, don't you agree? A woman of your breeding and presence doesn't need to use cheap tricks to garner appreciation, does she?"

As Gray watched, Melisande coaxed responses from the woman, soothing her ruffled feathers, and in the end, sold her the gown with a few minor alterations and earning some begrudging praise in the bargain. Gray began to feel very unnecessary, but he couldn't seem to make himself leave, so impressed was he by Melisande's tact and salesmanship.

The younger Miss Verity arrived with a tea tray. "Ah, thank you." Melisande said. "Would you be so kind as to pour for Mrs. Blythe-Sommers. And a cup for Mr. Garamond."

"Mr. Garamond?" Mrs. Blythe-Sommers stepped off the platform.

"Oh yes, I'm sorry. I failed to introduce you. This is Mr. Gray Garamond. He's Mr. Hamish Garamond's grandson." Melisande handed Gray a cup of tea.

The customer had the grace to blush then simpered in a way that made it hard for him to swallow his tea. Melisande conversed quietly with her sister and Mrs. O'Hair about the alterations to the gown, and by the time they had finished their tea, Mrs. Blythe-Sommers had also decided to purchase a hat, gloves, and a wrap to coordinate with the new dress.

When the room was clear of all but Gray and Melisande, she sighed, tucking a tendril of hair behind her ear. "I didn't get a chance to speak with Mrs. O'Hair about the gowns for the window." She checked the timepiece on her lapel. "And now it's lunchtime."

Gray shook his head. Almost an hour to satisfy one persnickety customer. Not only that, but it had taken up the time of himself and three employees. "This is just one of the reasons I want to discontinue bespoke clothing and go to off-the-rack. If a customer doesn't like what's in stock, they can shop somewhere else."

Melisande paused in filling the tea tray with empty cups. "Not do custom dressmaking? What about all the seamstresses and designers and fabric buyers? What would happen to them?"

She sounded like Grandfather. Sometimes sacrifices had to be made in the name of progress. "We'd try to find places for most of them. Others would move to other stores or dressmakers."

"I see." Disapproval colored her slow words.

"Things can't stay the same forever. You have to move with the times." He supposed she was worried about her sister's position. That was natural, but business was business. "If you don't, you get left behind. It's a businessman's duty to be successful and turn a profit for the good of the company."

Her eyes clouded, and she shook her head. "That sounds a bit like something Ebenezer Scrooge would say." She gathered her clipboard and swept out, leaving him puzzled and not a little dissatisfied.

Neville Strand was going to be the death of her. Or at least the death of her vision for this project.

"Who moved the buffet table to this wall?" Melisande stood in the second of the five windows, hands on hips. The panes were covered in butcher paper to keep passersby from seeing in, which was just as well, since the tableau was in chaos.

"Mr. Strand tol' me to." Jimmy Cane shoved his forelock back defiantly. "He made me move it right after you left." He pointed to the brace of silver candelabras she'd brought for the refreshment table for the portrayal of Mr. Fezziwig's Christmas Party. "I wish you'd make up your minds. You tell me one thing, he says another, and I'm always in trouble." He jammed his hands into his pockets, chin set mulishly.

Vonnetta climbed through the small opening to the display area, her arms full of dresses. A flush rode her cheeks, curly blond ringlets framed her face, and she hummed a few bars of an aria. "Here they are. Mrs. O'Hair wasn't best pleased that you're taking some of her display dresses, but she let them go."

Melisande smoothed a strand of hair up off the back of her neck while consulting her clipboard. That was another frustration. Getting the department heads to take her seriously when she requested items for the displays. They almost acted as if she was stealing from them. Was this more of Neville's handiwork, spreading discontent and distrust through the departments?

"Very well. Jimmy, here's a list of what I need from housewares. Don't try to carry the chandelier yourself, have one of the workers bring it. And be careful with the glass on those wall sconces. We don't want any more accidents." She raised her eyebrows, assessing him. He'd broken a platter this morning, sending china shards to every corner of the workroom.

"Yes, miss." His voice was barely a grumble as he ducked though the small door.

"Vonnetta, take the sheets off those mannequins and let's get them dressed." For propriety's sake, Melisande had kept them covered until they could be properly clothed. Neville was supposed to be bringing the clothing for the male mannequins, and he would see to dressing them. Yet another thing they had tussled over. He didn't feel it proper for young ladies to dress male mannequins, though they were just wire and canvas forms with no detail other than articulated joints for posing. "Oh, wait. First, help me move this buffet table back to the other side of the space." Neville would pucker, but he'd have to accustom himself to the idea that she meant what she said when she directed a layout.

The buffet table was substantial, but they got it situated. Now, to set out the dishes she'd chosen from the china Garamond's had to offer. Bone white with a plain, gold rim, it was simple and elegant, and it would match anyone's décor.

"Use the lavender dress for Belle, will you?" Melisande pointed to the shrouded mannequin seated along the right-hand wall. A young Scrooge would sit beside her, holding a ring. She knew it wasn't straight out of the book, but she had always imagined that Ebenezer had proposed to Belle at Mr. Fezziwig's Christmas party. And it made for a nice, romantic detail that she hoped shoppers would like. Who didn't like an engagement? Which reminded her, she would need to get a ring from the jewelry department. Something not too valuable, since Scrooge was still poor at that point in the story. . .and she didn't want to encourage a window smasher to break the glass to snatch the ring. But it should be something pretty. Perhaps a little silver circlet with a pearl?

So many details. And she was determined to get them all right.

"Miss Verity?"

One of the shop men poked his head through the doorway. "There's a delivery man here who says you are the only one who can sign off on his invoice."

Puffing out a breath, she stopped setting the table and left the window space. "Where is he?"

"Loading dock. He's got a lot of boxes. Fussy with them. Won't leave them." They wound their way around the tall, velvet-curtained screens that had been erected around the construction area to block it off from the retail floor.

At the loading dock, she took one look at the invoice and exhaled. Whew, this was a major chunk of her budget and the cause of some of her stress. "I'm so happy to see you." She shook the delivery man's hand, much to his surprise. "Twenty boxes? That's wonderful."

"If you say so." He scratched the side of his head under his hat. "If you'll sign, I can get on my way." He held out a slip of paper.

Melisande shook her head. "I'll have to check the boxes against the invoice, just to make sure everything's here."

"Lady, I have six more deliveries to make," he protested. "Just sign."

"Not without checking." She was spending a considerable amount of Garamond's money and a large slice of her budget for the project. Taking the time up front to make sure the order was correct would be easier than trying to rectify it later.

All the while, the delivery man tapped his foot and huffed.

"It looks like everything is here."

"I told you it was. Don't know why I'm dealing with you anyway. Usually just have one of the shop boys sign. But no, you had to put in special orders that only you could take delivery." He snatched the paper out of her hand, stuffing it into his pocket and wheeling his cart away.

"Well done."

She whirled, clutching her clipboard to her chest. Gray Garamond stood in the storage area doorway, impeccably dressed as always. The stockroom boys all snapped up straight.

"Thank you?" She wasn't sure to what he referred.

"Never let an impatient delivery man keep you from doing due diligence." He walked over, surveying the stack of boxes. "The details are important. What is all this stuff?"

She swallowed. "It's the wax food and decorations for the displays. For windows two and three especially."

"I see."

"Was there something you needed from me?" The table setting in window two was calling her name, begging to be finished so she could cross something off her list, and now that the replica food had arrived, she was itching to see how it looked on the table.

He slipped his watch out of his vest pocket, light winking off the chain and fob. "Weren't we supposed to have a progress meeting at two?"

Melisande gasped. "Oh no. I'm so sorry." She'd forgotten clean about it.

"The others are waiting in the conference room." He held out his hand toward the door for her to go ahead of him.

Why had he come himself rather than send someone for her? It wasn't a very. . . head-of-the-store thing to do. She winced at forgetting the meeting. It had been preying on her mind all day, and yet, she'd been so excited about the arrival of some of the props, she'd lost track of the time. That didn't speak very well for her management skills, did it?

When they entered the conference room, Vonnetta sat across the glossy table from Neville, who raised a rather supercilious eyebrow, his mouth a thin line. Vonnetta's brow bore furrows, and her eyes were wide with questions. Jimmy slouched in his chair, but as soon as Gray entered, he shoved himself upright, cap twisting in his hands.

"Now that we're all here, we can get on with our business. Miss Verity?" He politely held out a chair for her, but his words were crisp, as if he and everyone else were aware that she had wasted his time.

"We could've started the meeting early while you sent someone for her. I would have been happy to fill you in on the progress. . .or lack of it." Neville straightened his tie.

"I needed to stretch my legs. Proceed, Miss Verity."

After she gave her report, she remembered to compliment the work of her team. "Jimmy's been very helpful with running errands. Vonnetta's done a wonderful job with the costumes for the women in the displays, and I've placed Mr. Strand"—she never called him Neville to his face—"in charge of the suits and haberdashery of the male figures. He's got a detailed list, and I'm sure he'll begin work on them soon."

She tried to keep the frustration out of her voice. A good team leader took care of her own problems without whining to the boss. If she worked hard enough at it, she would find a way to get Neville to play on her team.

*Please, Lord, help me find a way.*

"Very well." Gray laid his index finger along his lips for a moment, studying the timeline in his hand, looking up to consider first Melisande and then Neville. "You're a bit behind this schedule. I'll expect you to be up to date by the next meeting, one week from today." He set down the paper. "If not, I'll have to make some changes to the team."

Melisande's heart sank. He hadn't been in favor of her in the first place. If she couldn't get Neville sorted out and get the project back on the rails, Gray would remove her as lead, probably putting Neville into the spot he coveted.

It wasn't fair, when he was the one causing most of her difficulties.

"Miss Verity, if you would remain behind for a moment?"

"Mr. Gray—I mean, Mr. Garamond—I can explain about the schedule—"

He held up his hand, stopping the flow of words. When everyone was gone, he said, "Miss Verity, as you know, my grandfather is ailing."

"Yes. I wanted to ask after him, but I didn't want to intrude. Is he recovering?" She missed him at the store, his genial smile, friendly eyes, his kind words scattered around like gold dust, making everyone feel better and work harder. She wouldn't have had any problem coming to him for advice about Neville.

"He is, some. That's what I wanted to talk to you about. He's fretting over the window project, and he insists that I bring you to the house to see him. Would you come and allay his fears? I'm afraid his worrying is setting back his progress." Gray rose and went to the window. He put his hands into his trouser pockets and stared out at the London skyline.

"Of course." Poor Mr. Garamond. "If I can help in any way."

"Just come talk to him, show him a few of the sketches, bring him up to date. For some reason, he doesn't believe me when I say things are progressing. I'm trying to keep him from worrying about the store so he can get better, but it's like he doesn't trust me to take care of things." He smoothed his hair back, his shoulders coming down as if a heavy weight pressed upon them.

Her heart constricted. He must be under so much pressure, running the store alone, concerned about his grandfather, wanting to win the Victoria Prize, full of new ideas and notions for changes to the store, but meeting resistance and reluctance—some of it warranted, some of it not—at every turn.

Gray shook his head, as if coming out of a reverie, and turned to her. "Would you be available this evening? I'd like to set his mind to rest as soon as possible."

Logistics stayed her tongue for a moment. If she went right after work, Vonnetta would have to walk home alone. No, that wouldn't do. Vonnetta would have to catch an omnibus, though Melisande hated to spend the fare. Still, it couldn't be helped. And Melisande would need to take a cab to the Garamond house. She wasn't even sure where it was, but it certainly wouldn't be anywhere near the neighborhood she lived in. And then she would have to get home in time for supper or she would miss out. Mrs. Swale served one meal a day, and if you weren't there, that was too bad.

But it was for Mr. Garamond. She'd suffer more than a missed meal for him.

"I would be glad to come after work this evening."

"Thank you. Meet me at the west door at closing time."

"Meet you?" Her voice went high.

"Of course. My carriage picks me up there." He sent her a puzzled glance. "I don't expect you to ferry yourself there and back when I have a perfectly good conveyance at hand."

A frisson went up her spine and tingled over her scalp and down to her fingertips. She'd never even dreamed of riding in a carriage with Gray Garamond.

At six o'clock exactly, Melisande stood at the west entrance to the store, hat on, coat buttoned, pulling on her gloves. Vonnetta had gaped when told she would need to make her way home alone after work.

"You're going to their house? You must tell me every detail. I declare, this window-dressing lark has opened quite a few doors for you, hasn't it?" She'd grabbed Melisande's hands and swung her around the workroom.

"Stop it. This 'window-dressing lark' is hopefully going to open doors for you, not me. Stop gadding about and finish styling those wigs. If we don't catch up, I'll be removed from the position, and it will take forever to save enough for music school." Melisande gave her sister a little push back toward the workbench.

Several times during the afternoon, she had to remind herself to focus on her task. Her thoughts wanted to stray toward that carriage ride and what the Garamond house might be like.

And now the time had come. Employees streamed by her in ones and twos, pulling on their wraps, ducking their chins against the blowing snow, tromping home to their families and their supper.

Vonnetta, holding up her hand to remind Melisande that she'd tucked her coin for the omnibus into the palm of her glove, grinned as she went through the doorway.

"Ready?" Gray appeared, Mr. Whytcher behind him, holding Gray's top hat and overcoat.

The carriage drew up to the curb. Gray shrugged into his coat, nodded to his secretary, and took Melisande's elbow. Her throat tightened, and her breath hitched.

"Careful, it's slippery out." Gray motioned for the driver to stay where he was, opening the carriage door himself and handing her up inside.

She sank onto the velvet seat, noting the heated stone at her feet. The carriage lurched as Gray climbed in, bouncy on its soft springs. He sat across from her, and Mr. Whytcher gave him a leather briefcase. Melisande held her own portfolio in her lap, grateful to have something to occupy her hands.

The carriage started. "Is it a long ride for you each evening?" she asked, by way of finding out where they were going.

"Not too bad." He closed his eyes, and she was able to study him in the light of the lamp in the wall bracket. His silk top hat reflected that light, but his woolen coat seemed to absorb any illumination. Light brown hair just touched his ears and the collar of his coat, longer than she remembered him wearing it before. Perhaps he hadn't had time to get it cut.

His blue eyes opened, and she looked away, embarrassed to be caught staring.

"I'm sorry. I'm not being a very engaging traveling partner, am I?"

She looked out the window at the streetlamps going by, the lighted windows, other carriages. "You must have a lot on your mind."

"It's been a fairly trying day. I've been interviewing department heads all day, going over their profit/loss statements for the year, trying to organize them into a pecking order for what I can consolidate, what I should keep as it is, and what I can remove altogether."

She gripped her portfolio, pressing it into her thighs. "Are you still intending to change so much at the store? Do the managers know their jobs and their workers' jobs are on the chopping block?"

"You make it sound so brutal, as if I was the only person ever to lay anyone off work. I have a responsibility to run a tight ship, to increase profits, to keep Garamond's on the leading edge of retail in London. Garamond's is majority-owned by my grandfather, but we also have shareholders to whom we answer. If they don't receive dividends on a regular basis, they'll pull their money out of the company." He spoke to her as if she were a child.

She said nothing. The way he spoke, Garamond employees weren't people, they were notations in a ledger. She could appreciate that he wanted to be successful in business, but that didn't just mean making the most money. Success couldn't be measured in pounds and shillings. Mr. Hamish understood that. Why couldn't Gray?

Gray glanced out the window. "Our house is on Portland Place, south of Park Crescent. We'll be there in about ten minutes or so, traffic willing."

The Marylebone area. She'd never been in that part of London before. It was well out of her social sphere.

They pulled up before a red-brick Georgian home, a chandelier just visible through the fanlight over the door. Gray helped her down, and they walked up the stairs. Melisande was very aware that if she hadn't been with him, she would have needed to use the lower floor servant's entrance.

An elderly man opened the door just as they arrived on the top step. "Good evening, sir."

"How is he, Camden?" Gray tugged off his gloves, one finger at a time, placing them into his hat and handing them and his coat over.

"Much the same, sir. Dr. Coker has been and gone. He left a note for you."

"Very well. Send up a tea tray, will you?"

The butler remained standing in the same spot as Gray went to the sweeping staircase. Melisande stood still too, not knowing what to do. Gray stopped, turned, and raised his eyebrows at her.

"Your coat, miss?" the butler murmured, and Melisande blushed, feeling the heat swirl into her cheeks as she thumbed the buttons on her brown coat.

"Come, Miss Verity."

Halfway up the staircase, Gray took her portfolio. "My manners are slipping dreadfully. This way." At the top of the steps, he turned to the right. A woman in a rustling, black silk dress emerged from the doorway at the end of the hall.

"Mrs. Mouton. How is he?"

"Awake. Fretting. He's so restless." Her light blue eyes held worry, worry that Melisande was well-familiar with, seeing it in the eyes of her coworkers every time the subject of Mr. Garamond came up. His household employees were no different in their regard for him than his store employees, it seemed.

"Thank you for looking after him." Gray pushed open the door. "We'll visit for a bit, but we'll try not to tire him out."

The drapes were pulled against the night, and a fire blazed in the grate. Someone had placed Christmas greenery along the marble mantel, festooned with pinecones and red berries. Nestled in and among the boughs were cards and greetings.

A massive tester-bed stood on the far wall, hung with deep-blue bed curtains. Mr. Garamond looked small and pale in his nightshirt and robe, covered to the waist by the duvet.

Gray bent over his grandfather. "I've brought someone to see you."

Melisande braced herself, schooled her features, and stepped forward. It was so hard to see Mr. Garamond, who was so vital and charming, laid low like this.

He seemed sunken, his breathing shallow, his skin tissue thin—almost a stranger. But then she looked into his eyes. There he was, the sparkle, the interest, the kindness she knew. She knew in that moment that she couldn't discourage him by asking about the proposed changes at Garamond's. She should only share happy things that would comfort and cheer him. If she could hasten his recovery in any way, perhaps he could be the voice of reason where Gray's plans were concerned.

Gently, she took his right hand as it lay flat on the sheet and gave it a tiny squeeze. "It's so good to see you, sir. You've been missed at the shop."

His left eyelid and the left side of his mouth drooped a bit, but the right quirked up, and he returned the pressure of her fingers. A small sound came from his throat, but she couldn't make out what he was saying."

"Now, Grandfather, don't try to talk just yet. Save your strength. I brought Miss Verity so she could show you all her progress on the window project herself. You lie back, and she'll do the rest."

Melisande took the initiative, hiking her skirt a bit and taking a seat on the edge of the feather bed. Gray handed her the portfolio, and she opened it across her lap. Page by page, she detailed what she had done, what she envisioned, and how she planned to accomplish it.

"And just today, the biggest outside piece of the project arrived. I ordered all the wax food props for these two displays. The roast goose looks so realistic. I don't know that it could be better if we had a real goose fresh from the oven. It was quite expensive, but I think it will be worth it." She shuffled the pages. "I've finished painting the backdrop of Mr. Fezziwig's warehouse where the party will take place, and the carpenters have almost finished the Cratchit dining room in window three. So there's just the cemetery trees and the final street front scene to build. I have a surprise for that last scene that I'm so excited about, I can hardly bear it." She held up her finger as if he had uttered a question. "No, I'm not telling you or your grandson just yet. I want you to be surprised too." She lowered her designs back to her lap, growing serious. "I'm praying that you will be well enough to come to the unveiling, even if for just a short while."

And she hoped it would please both of them, whether they won or not.

Mr. Garamond stirred. He raised his right hand a bit and pointed to the mantel. Gray was out of his chair in a trice, heading over there. "You want something from here?"

The frail man nodded slowly. One by one, Gray touched each card, brows raised, until when he landed on one near the middle of the row, Mr. Garamond grunted.

Gray picked up the card and frowned. "The invitation to the Drapers' Ball?"

Mr. Garamond flicked his wrist, and Gray brought the card to him and placed it in his hand. Though he trembled, Mr. Garamond pointed the card at Gray and then at Melisande.

Melisande eased off the bed, so Gray could take her place. Mr. Garamond repeated the motion with the card.

With great effort, he inhaled and spoke. "Take her. Thanks. . .for. . .hard. . .work."

Heat rushed through Melisande. Was he really suggesting Gray take her to the Drapers' Ball? She'd heard stories about the event, but it was exclusive to wealthy merchants and their invited guests. That couldn't be what Mr. Garamond meant. . .and yet, it was.

"Oh, Mr. Garamond, that's a lovely gesture, but I couldn't attend, really."

He shook his head, his strongest movement yet; his eyes clouded, color coming into his cheeks. His chest rose and fell rapidly, and he stirred. "Least. . .we. . .can. . .do. Take. . .her."

When it became clear he wouldn't be satisfied with anything less, Gray looked at Melisande and shrugged. "Would you do me the honor?"

Mortified, she nodded, more embarrassed than she could remember ever being. Then another thought struck her. What on earth would she wear to such a function? She had no fancy clothing. In fact, her work clothes were the best she had, but she couldn't show up at the Drapers' Ball in black poplin and white apron.

They took their leave of Mr. Garamond, whose eyes were closing as he relaxed into his pillow, and once they stood in the hall, Melisande put her hand on Gray's arm—something she never would've dared to do at the store. "That was very kind of you to make him feel better, but you don't have to take me to the ball. You can make my excuses to your grandfather later."

Gray's brows rose, and he tucked his hands into his trouser pockets, leaning his shoulder against the brocade wallpaper. "Are you saying you wouldn't like to go with me?"

Flustered, she clutched her portfolio in front of her. "Of course not. . .I mean. . .You don't have to. . ."

"Miss Verity—Melisande—I want nothing more than to set my grandfather's mind at ease about anything I can. If it would give him pleasure, I will do it." He paused. "And, it would give me pleasure too."

"I would do anything for your grandfather, but, sir—"

"Outside the store, perhaps you could call me Gray. And don't get into a fuss. It's the least I can do for all you've done for the store and my grandfather. I watched him while you were speaking in there, and it's the most alert he's been since the stroke. An evening out is small potatoes in comparison."

He overrode any other protests she might have made by taking her hand and squeezing it. "I really would like to take you to the party. Will you come with me?"

Looking into his deep blue eyes, she found herself nodding.

# Chapter 5

Gray surprised himself with how quickly he grew accustomed to the idea of partnering Miss Verity to the pinnacle event in the drapers' social calendar. He was also surprised at how often he found his thoughts straying in her direction. Not just as an employee, but as a person. . .as a woman. . .

"Sir?" Mr. Whytcher entered his office. "Miss Verity is here to see you." Gray started, chagrined to be caught daydreaming. "Show her in." He stood, smoothed his hair, and straightened his tie.

She came in, a troubled light in her eyes. No clipboard. Odd. "Mr. Garamond, there's a bit of a problem." She glanced at the door, left open by Mr. Whytcher as per company policy when two people of opposite gender were in a room alone together. "The night of the Drapers' Ball." Her voice lowered, since it wasn't public news that they would be attending the event together.

"Yes?" Surely she wasn't backing out now, not after giving her word. Not after he'd become rather attached to the notion of taking her. His muscles tightened, his regret bigger than he would've anticipated.

"We were just informed today that the Employees' Christmas Party has been scheduled, and it's the same evening as the Drapers' Ball. My sister has been engaged to sing at the Garamond party, and I can't miss it." She twisted her fingers together, looking up at him with sorrow.

Gray relaxed and chuckled. "Is that all? I thought it was something serious." He took her elbow and led her to one of the chairs in front of his desk, taking the other for himself. "Miss Verity, I'm the one who scheduled the employee party, remember? The Drapers' Ball doesn't begin until ten o'clock. The employee party will be winding up by that time. I had planned to make an appearance at the party early in the evening and attend the ball afterwards."

"Oh." Her hands dropped to her lap. "That's all right then."

"Your sister is singing that night? Is she good?"

"Yes. She's gifted. It was my mother's dying wish that I somehow find a way to get Vonnetta the training she wants so badly." She bit her bottom lip for an instant. "That's one of the reasons I submitted a proposal for the window project. The extra pay will go a long way toward tuition."

"What about your father? Isn't Vonnetta's education his responsibility?" Gray frowned.

"It would be, but he passed away before my mother. It's just the two of us now."

It seemed too large a burden for one young lady.

"What about your own ambitions?"

"I have none other than to see Vonnetta launched in operatic circles. She has the talent and the desire, and between the two of us, hopefully someday, the funds, to reach her potential."

Gray wondered at the truth of her statement that she had no dreams for herself. Anyone with the ability to draw and paint and design such as she had, the ability to transform a space into something beautiful and full of story, shouldn't have her talent seconded to anyone else's, not even a younger sister.

"The evening of the parties I will pick you up and bring you to dinner at my home, then we can attend the employees' party before heading to the ball."

Her eyes went round, and her lips parted. "Oh, I don't think that's a good idea. I mean, appearing together at the store party. What will people think?"

"That we have nothing to hide?" He frowned. "We're not doing anything clandestine by my partnering you to social functions. I would rather everything be out in the open rather than invite speculation when word gets out that I took you to the Drapers' Ball."

She fidgeted with her fingers. "I suppose you're right." There was clearly something else bothering her.

"I'm beginning to think you regret accepting my invitation." Which was a bit of a blow to his pride.

Shaking her head, she glanced up at him, giving him the full impact of her beautiful eyes. "It isn't that. It's just that I feel you were coerced into it, wanting to please your grandfather."

At first he had been, but no longer. "Put that notion out of your mind. I am my own man. However. . ." He wondered how she would respond to this. "Speaking of my grandfather, he gave me a note for you. Actually, he had his housekeeper write it, but the words and intentions are his." He drew the envelope out of his breast pocket. "He let me read it, and I completely approve. I want no argument from you about it." Placing the letter in her hands, he drew her to her feet. "It's settled. We'll go to both parties."

He had to admit, it was nice to be able to assert himself a little, to fluster her a bit, since recently, being in her presence flustered him. "Now, back to work. The contest will be here before you know it."

As they reached the door, Neville Strand's voice came from the outer office. "I must see Mr. Gray. That woman is ruining everything. I won't be a party to this disaster." Something thumped, and Gray envisioned the haberdashery manager pounding his fist on the secretary's desk.

A sigh worked its way up his chest. Handling people wasn't his strong suit. His grandfather had the knack, but then again, it was his grandfather who insisted that putting Neville on the window-dressing team was a good idea.

Melisande's cheeks flushed, and she had her eyes closed, as if praying for patience. Well, he'd run out of patience. Enough was enough.

"Mr. Strand." Gray made his voice quite loud. "Come in here."

The thin salesman marched through the door, stopping abruptly when he spied Miss Verity. His lips pinched, and he rallied. "Sir, you must come down and put things right. This woman. . ." He waved at Melisande as if she were a street urchin caught pilfering inventory. "She's crossed the line."

"I wasn't aware there was a line. What is the problem, Mr. Strand?" Gray moved a step closer to Melisande.

Neville's face reddened, his eyes snapping, "This woman has mesmerized you. You're letting her do anything she wants, and it's going to cost you not only the contest, but customers and Garamond's good name."

Melisande gasped. "Mr. Strand."

Gray's temper rose. "Mr. Strand, I resent the implication that Miss Verity has had any undue influence over me. Now, explain yourself."

Neville sputtered. "Do you have any idea what she's done with window number four? She's put the Ghost of Christmas Future in the scene. It's indecent. I warned you about using that secular story as the inspiration for this year's display. I warned you about the ghosts, but you wouldn't listen. I'm supposed to be a part of this team, but every time I suggest something she refuses to budge. Every time I change something, she changes it back. I won't be challenged like this. She's a woman and should know her place." He scowled at Melisande, who blinked at the venom in his tone. "Either that woman goes, or I do."

"Very well. Inform the accounting department on your way out and pick up your pay packet." Gray pointed at the door. "Thank you for your service here at Garamond's."

For a long moment, silence reigned. The blood drained from Neville's face, leaving it blotchy and slack. Then he pulled himself up to his full height. "Fine." He shot another scowl at Melisande and turned on his heel.

Mr. Whytcher, sidestepping quickly in the doorway to avoid Neville, bore a startled look. Melisande looked dismayed, twisting her fingers at her waist, and Gray simmered, near the boiling point. When she opened her mouth, he put up his hand.

"Don't. Both of you, just get back to work." He was too angry to want to talk, but when Melisande flinched, he regretted his sharp tone. Before he could apologize, they disappeared and Gray stalked to the window, his gut still burning. That arrogant man.

Yet, Gray was ashamed too. His grandfather would be upset when he found out Gray had fired Mr. Strand—well, hadn't fired him exactly, but let him quit in the heat of the moment. Grandfather would've handled it differently. Would've taken the time to talk to Strand, get him to see reason, or at least to part on friendly terms if they couldn't agree.

Gray had been raised better than to give in to his temper. . .but when Strand had denigrated Melisande's designs, management, and gender, Gray had seen red.

Or, was it the fact that Strand had come uncomfortably close to the truth that bothered Gray the most? That perhaps his growing regard. . .admiration. . .feelings for Miss Verity were blinding him to his mission and plans for the store.

Melisande was so flustered by the encounter in Gray's office, she forgot about Mr. Garamond's letter until she was alone in the fourth window space. Tears burned her eyes, heat burned her cheeks, and shame burned her middle.

She studied the scene she was creating. Silver birch logs had been erected to create a contrast with the black painted walls, fake, fluffy "snow" covered the floor, and in the center, a headstone—made of plaster, but painted to look like granite—bore the name Ebenezer Scrooge.

The mannequin of Scrooge himself crouched on the snow before the headstone in his dressing gown, his face in his hands. And at the very edge of the display, the hem of a black drape showed, with one, long, slender hand pointing to the grave.

The Ghost of Christmas Future.

Which had been the final straw in Neville's estimation.

She tried to be objective. Was it controversial? Was it wrong?

Mr. Garamond had liked her displays, had given his approval well before his illness.

"Lord, how can I know? Everything seemed so clear to me when I drew up the designs. I had such peace. But now, with so much pressure, with differing opinions, with Neville's animosity, I'm doubting myself." And not just about her designs and choices for the window displays either, but about her heart's judgment too. "Lord, I don't know what to do. What's right? How are You going to work through these circumstances? How are You going to show me the way?"

Melisande had seen how kind Gray was to his grandfather, how concerned he was, revealing a softer side of his nature. And Gray had defended her to Neville and refused to take the other man's part and make her a scapegoat. And yet, he seemed not to understand how his single-mindedness about his plans to "modernize" Garamond's would harm long-time employees. Which was the real Gray?

Gray Garamond was management, wealthy, sophisticated, while she was a simple country girl forced to come to the city to find work, living on a meager salary, saving all she could in order to afford to give her sister the future of which she dreamed.

The chasm between herself and Gray seemed too broad to ever cross.

And yet, Gray was taking her to the Drapers' Ball, even seemed eager to do so.

Which brought her to another problem. What was she going to wear? She had nothing suitable for such an event. If she purchased something truly appropriate for the occasion, it would cost her a year's savings. It would cost well more than she was earning in extra payment for the window designs. . .and would take every bit of her portion of the winner's purse if she was so blessed to bring home the Victoria Prize.

No, she couldn't do that. Vonnetta would never get to go to school at that rate.

But how could she refuse when Mr. Hamish was so set on her attending? When she'd already agreed to go?

Which reminded her of the letter Gray had handed her. She pulled it from her apron pocket, slitting the envelope with a hairpin, seating herself on a birch log stump at the edge of the display to read the single sheet.

The note was in a tight, neat hand, but the signature was a scrawl. He'd dictated a letter to her and signed it himself.

> *Dear Miss Verity,*
>
> *Thank you for the window displays. They are beautiful. Don't change anything.*
>
> *Thank you for attending the party with Gray. I want you to show him the joy of Christmas. He needs to see people are our business.*
>
> *Please choose a dress from Garamond's for the party. A gift from me. Mrs. O'Hair has instructions.*
>
> *Don't argue. If you can share Christmas joy with Gray, I will be in your debt.*
>
> > *Hamish Garamond.*
>
> *P.S. Miss Verity, this is Mrs. Mouton, Mr. Garamond's housekeeper. He's dictating this letter to me and it has taken him several tries, he's so weak and tired, the dear man. He's very concerned that you will let yourself be swayed to change your*

*window designs to suit other people, especially Mr. Strand. That man's been around to the house twice to complain about you. The first time I let him in, but the next time he showed up Camden and I sent him away with a flea in his ear. Upsetting poor Mr. Garamond when he's been laid so low. Your visit chirked him right up though. He kept your drawings, and he looks at them every day. I'm only hoping he'll continue to regain his strength. He's that pleased with the idea of kitting you out for that fancy party. I hope you'll pick out a real bobby-dazzler of a dress. Mr. Garamond will enjoy seeing you in it. And Mr. Garamond is right. Mr. Gray needs someone to show him the joy of Christmas. Mr. Gray is so worried about his grandfather and the store and all, he's forgotten some of the things he's been taught about people. Maybe you can remind him.*

*Mrs. Mouton*
*Housekeeper*
*Garamond House*

Melisande read the note twice, but both times her eyes blurred with tears. A dress from Garamond's? Such a generous man. How could she ever repay him?

And wasn't Mrs. Mouton a sweetie? How awful for her that Neville had shown up there hoping to cause trouble. What was wrong with that man?

Using the hem of her apron, she dried her lashes. Though she might not win the Victoria Prize for Garamond's, she could put forth her best effort in the attempt. She would stay true to her vision for the displays, and she would put her heart into every aspect.

"Thank You, Lord, for showing me the way in this, at least."

As to how to show Gray the joy of the season. . .where could she start? Would he listen to her?

Vonnetta stuck her head through the little doorway into the display area. "There you are." She clambered into the space, carefully stepping on the fake snow. "Guess what?" Gripping Melisande's shoulders, she gave her a little shake. "It came! It came!" She dug into her pocket and pulled out a yellow slip of paper. "My acceptance to the Academy."

Melisande's heart lurched. "What?"

"I applied. You know, just to see if I could get in, if there was any chance we could afford it, even one term. And I did it." Her sister clutched the paper to her breast. "Last month, I asked Mrs. O'Hair for a half day off, and I went to the auditions at the music school. I didn't want to tell you because you'd say I was putting the cart before the horse, but I had to go, had to try. And it worked. They gave me very high marks, and they say I can start in the new term. In three weeks, if we can swing the tuition."

"But, Vonnetta—"

Her sister squared her shoulders. "Don't. I have faith. You're going to win the Victoria Prize, and then we'll have enough for at least this term. I just know it."

Which was more than Melisande knew. If she didn't win, Vonnetta would be crushed. Would the music academy defer her enrollment? Or would they feel Vonnetta had been wasting their time, auditioning for a position when she didn't have the means to attend?

"What's that?" Vonnetta pointed to the paper in Melisande's hand. "More window ideas?"

"Um, no. Actually, it's from Mr. Garamond. Mr. Hamish, that is. He's instructed me to choose a gown from the store. . .as a thank-you."

Vonnetta's squeal could be heard clear up in the baby furnishings department, Melisande was sure. Once her sister had calmed down, she took a couple of deep breaths, eyes shining, gripping Melisande's upper arms.

"You have to come to the dressmaking department right now. There's a dress there that would be perfect for you. I thought it at the time, though I never imagined you'd get to own it." She was already tugging Melisande to the door. "Hurry. It's so beautiful it will sell the minute we get it on a mannequin."

The night of the Drapers' Ball, Melisande mounted the front steps of Garamond House, her fingers tucked into Gray's elbow. All the work of preparing the window displays was finished. She could think of nothing else to improve her designs and execution. Now it was up to the judges. Hopefully she had done justice to both the story her mother had loved so much and to Mr. Garamond's faith in her. Tomorrow would be the big reveal.

And she hoped she could bring joy and cheer to all the shoppers who stopped to look at them.

Camden opened the front door as they arrived on the top step, allowing light to spill over them and warmth to rush out. "Good evening, sir. Miss."

"Camden? Did he manage it?" Gray asked as he unbuttoned his woolen topcoat.

"And very pleased with himself." The butler took his coat, hat, and gloves.

Gray turned and helped Melisande with her cloak, a black velvet creation that covered her from head to hem. As she slipped it from her shoulders, Gray sucked in a breath.

Melisande smoothed her skirts and rested her hands on the deeply pointed polonaise, trying to still the quiver in her middle. Would he approve of her choice of gown? Had her hairstyle—primped and prepared by Vonnetta, even as Melisande had styled her sister's hair for the Garamond party tonight—survived the hood of her cloak?

Gray's brows rose. "Very nice. You are a credit to Garamond's couture department."

His voice was deeper than normal, and surprise rested in his eyes, as if he were seeing her for the first time.

"Fine feathers make fine birds, I suspect." She blushed under his scrutiny.

"I suspect otherwise. Come." He took her elbow. "Grandfather is waiting."

He led her down the hall to a beautiful dining room. At the head of the table, in a high-backed invalid chair, sat Mr. Garamond.

"Oh, sir," Melisande hurried to the old man. "It's wonderful to see you like this." Though the left side of his face still drooped, he was sitting upright, his skin had some color, and his eyes sparkled. She knelt beside his chair and took his right hand.

"Good. . .to. . .see. . .you." The words were slow but distinct. "Let. . .me. . .see. . .your. . . dress."

She stood and moved back a few paces, giving a slow twirl. "Do you like it?" The peacock-blue satin gleamed in the gaslight, and the golden lace trim twinkled. She'd fallen in love with the dress the moment Vonnetta had brought it out of the workroom. Even Mrs. O'Hair, who was known to have a critical eye, and occasionally critical tongue, said she couldn't believe how well it looked on her.

"Beautiful. . .perfect. . .so. . .pleased."

Melisande couldn't remember later what they had eaten for dinner, just that it was more sumptuous and plentiful than anything she'd had before. And Gray was charming, completely at ease in his own home, and obviously happy at the progress his grandfather was making in his recovery.

Mr. Garamond did not dine, but a look from Gray kept Melisande from inquiring. It was probably not easy for him to eat at the moment, and doing so in front of others might embarrass him. So she said nothing, keeping up a stream of conversation about the store and the employees and her work on the window displays.

By the time they were ready to depart for the Garamond employee party, Mr. Garamond's strength had begun to flag. Melisande knelt by his chair once more, taking his hand between hers. "Thank you so much for all you've done for me. I'll never forget your kindness." She kissed his wrinkled cheek, and the tears that sprang into his eyes were mirrored in her own.

"Thank. . .you. . .my. . .dear. Blessings. . ." He squeezed her fingers lightly, and she felt as if a benediction has fallen upon her shoulders.

Gray helped Melisande into her cloak, fastening the frog closure at her throat. "Thank you for caring so much for my grandfather. The moment he heard you would be coming for dinner, he was determined to get out of bed and join us. It's been his motivating force all week."

"He's very easy to like, because he cares for so many. It's his strongest attribute, the way he cares for others. That's what makes him a great leader." She hoped Gray understood that.

Their arrival at Garamond's caused a bit of a stir, but no one seemed to think it unusual that they were together. Some of the single girls whispered and tittered, but for the most part, her fellow employees seemed happy for her, as if accompanying Mr. Gray to a party was merely a reward for all her hard work on the window project. Everyone had heard about Neville's implosion and resignation, and for the most part, it seemed that the sympathy was on Melisande's side.

The cafeteria had been decorated for the occasion with swags of greenery and ribbon. A long table of festive foods ran along the wall, but the rest of the tables had been removed to clear space for dancing.

The workers provided the music. Bramwell, the doorman, played the violin, and Mr. Ford, the tobacconist, played the pianoforte. Mrs. MacGuire, who ran the cafeteria, had brought her flute, and the three of them combined to fill the room with song.

"I had no idea anyone on the staff played." Gray surveyed the room. "Who is that?" He indicated the top couple in the reel being performed.

"That's Mr. Milner, from accounting, and his wife. They've been married for more than forty years." The white-haired couple swung in a circle, as sprightly as the younger folks around them, beaming at one another.

"And that's Jane Parker. She works in the perfume department. Her husband was injured in the coal mines in Newcastle, and she brought him down here to London so she could find a job." Melisande indicated the pretty young woman whom she saw every day across the atrium. She sat beside a pale young man in an invalid chair, holding his hand.

As they made their way through the crowd of revelers, Melisande made a point of introducing him, telling him their stories—the janitor who supported his elderly parents, the gift-wrap girl who had half a dozen siblings at home and took her pay packet to her mother every week to help out. The husband who had taken in his wife's orphaned nephews.

Their jobs at Garamond's were all that kept many from being destitute. And not just them, but the people who counted on them. Mr. Garamond would have known all of this, since he made a point of finding out people's backgrounds and situations. Because employees were more than company assets to Mr. Garamond.

Gray drank a cup of punch, sampled a bit of fruitcake that Mrs. O'Hair had brought, and shook hands with nearly everyone. But he was reserved, unlike he had been over dinner, almost as if he wore a different persona now that he was at the store.

Was that it? Did he feel he had to be the "boss," even at a social event?

Yet everyone was pleased he had come, proud to introduce him to their spouses or guests, thanking him for the party and the Christmas bonuses.

"I have friends who work at other stores, and none of their bosses add on a bonus like Garamond's, sir." The stockroom worker gave his wife a squeeze. "It means me and the missus can put money down on a little house of our own. Don't know of another stockman that could afford to do that, and it's all due to you and your grandfather's generosity."

The thanks were repeated by nearly everyone as Gray and Melisande made their way around the room. Nearly everyone had a story about how the extra holiday money would make a difference in their lives.

When it came time for Vonnetta to sing, chairs were moved into place and everyone found their seats. Gray was given a place of honor on the front row, and Melisande sat beside him.

Vonnetta went to stand beside the pianoforte, smiling at Mr. Ford, whose fingers rippled over the keys. Melisande took a long, slow breath, knowing what was coming, and rather than watch Vonnetta, she glanced up at Gray.

The opening strains of a Verdi aria filled the air, Vonnetta's voice caressing some notes, conquering others, lost in the beauty of the story and the melody.

Gray paid rapt attention. His fingers fisted on his thighs, and he leaned forward. Melisande's heart swelled. He could see it too. That Vonnetta was doing what she had been born to do.

When the aria finished, the room burst into applause. Gray was the first to stand, clapping, and others followed suit. Vonnetta beamed and curtsied. Melisande was so proud, she had to wipe away tears.

Her little sister sang three more songs, receiving applause, and then invited everyone to sing carols and partake of more food before the final dances began. Gray touched Melisande's arm and bent down. "We need to go."

"Of course. Let me say my goodbyes." She slipped through the group around the piano and squeezed Vonnetta's shoulder. "You were wonderful," she whispered under the sound of the carolers.

"Thank you!" Vonnetta gave her a hug. "Now, go enjoy yourself at the ball and remember everything so you can tell me about it when you get home."

Once more in the carriage, Melisande clenched her fingers tight in her long, gold satin gloves. "I'm so nervous. I've never been to a function like the Drapers' Ball. I hope I don't. . ."

"Don't what?"

She swallowed. "I hope I don't embarrass you."

"You won't. You look beautiful tonight."

A thrill zinged through her, but. . .did he only think she would not embarrass him because she looked nice? Is that all the partygoers tonight would be concerned about, how people looked?

"Your sister is extremely talented. I've been to some of the best opera performances in London, and I've never heard better. You're right that she needs the opportunity to train professionally. She'd be a sensation."

"If I had the money in hand, she'd enroll for the next term. In fact, she already applied and was accepted, unbeknownst to me. There's a spot waiting for her if we can assure them we can pay the tuition."

The carriage pulled to a halt in front of the Langham Hotel. "The ball is being held in the Palm Court." Gray waited for a footman to open the carriage door.

The Palm Court at the Langham. . . . Melisande hoped she didn't gape like a gauche child. Only London's highest society frequented the Palm Court.

Inside, warmth and light and noise greeted them. The party appeared to be in full swing. An orchestra played at the far end of the room, and waiters circulated with canapés, caviar, and champagne. All around her, women in fashionable dresses, glittering jewels, and wafting ostrich-feather hair adornments floated by in the arms of their dancing partners.

It was all a long way from the cafeteria at Garamond's, a country reel, and Mrs. O'Hair's fruitcake. Melisande felt as out of place as a brussels sprout in a box of bon bons.

Gray took her hand and tucked it into his elbow, skirting the dance floor and greeting people he knew. He introduced her as Miss Verity, saying nothing about her being his employee.

Women looked her over from head to toe, taking in the beautiful dress and gloves, plainly curious. The farther they got into the room, the more speculative looks and whispers were directed Melisande's way. She tried to write it off as natural inquisitiveness at a newcomer, but she grew more uncomfortable by the minute. While Gray was engaged speaking to a male colleague, the man's wife raised her eyebrow and looked at Melisande through her lorgnette. "Do I know your parents?" She soaked her voice with ennui.

"That's very unlikely."

"Your dress is lovely, dear, but. . ." She lowered her head as if to impart a secret, but failed to lower her voice to match it, making sure those around her heard. "You look positively bare with no jewels. Not even a simple string of pearls? If my maid let me out of the house like that, I'd release her without a character." The woman fluttered her fan and rolled her eyes. The group of women nearby tittered and giggled, nodding behind their fans as they whispered to one another.

Heat swirled into Melisande's cheeks. She hadn't forgotten jewelry. She didn't own any.

Gray reached over and clasped her hand, drawing her to his side. "It's my preference, actually. Melisande needs no adornment to be the most beautiful woman in any room." He tucked his arm around her waist, his fingers warm on her hip. "I find that quite often, copious jewels are really just trying to mask a lack of substance. Don't you feel the same?"

Without waiting for a reply, he swirled Melisande out onto the dance floor, joining the waltz. Melisande followed his lead, wanting to laugh, but feeling ashamed just the same. Every woman in the room wore diamonds, pearls, sapphires, rubies, or emeralds. Even the youngest had at least a cameo threaded on a velvet ribbon around her neck.

Gray danced flawlessly. He murmured into her ear. "Don't let Mrs. Clarke bother you.

She's known as a bit of a virago. Her husband owns half of Clarke and Harris, your main rivals for the Victoria Prize. It won't do her any harm to have a setback in the criticism department."

But Melisande hardly cared anymore. She was in Gray's arms, gliding over the floor to exquisite music. And he had called her beautiful.

By the supper break, she had been introduced to so many people, she couldn't possibly keep them straight.

Every conversation centered around commerce, which she supposed was to be expected, but the level of cattiness and competition surprised her. It was as if all these department store owners and drapers couldn't put aside their struggle for pounds and shillings to enjoy one another's company or the Christmas season.

Though Melisande would have much to tell Vonnetta about the Drapers' Ball, part of her wished they had been able to stay at the Garamond's party. The glitter of society was intriguing, but it didn't feel genuine and comfortable at all.

Gray watched Melisande from across the Palm Court. She wore a pensive expression as she listened to a gray-haired old man with an impressive set of side whiskers talk. . .and talk. . . and talk.

If his words were anything like what Gray had been hearing tonight, she must be bored to the point of stupor.

"Your loss was my gain. Never thought you'd part with someone like Neville Strand, but when he walked through the doors looking for a job, I snapped him up." Bart Huron, who owned a store on Saville Row, rocked on his toes, fingers stuck into his waistcoat pockets. "He's already made a difference. Plenty of Garamond's customers have followed him over to my shop. He's here somewhere tonight, you know. My guest." He chuckled, showing a lot of teeth, reminding Gray of a predator.

So, Strand had found another job. That was good. Maybe he'd be happier at Huron's. He certainly hadn't been happy at Garamond's. Hopefully they wouldn't cross paths in the crush here tonight.

Huron launched into another story about how his store was the best in London, his customers laying out lavish amounts for his menswear simply because it came from his shop. Gray let his mind drift.

The differences between the employee party at Garamond's, humble as it was, and this soiree were striking. Not one time during the Drapers' Ball had he heard anyone say they were grateful for what they had or how business had gone over the past year. Information was shared grudgingly, unless it was to gloat. Women flaunted their jewels; men boasted of their profits. The food was rich and expensive, and Gray felt. . .sad.

There was no joy here. A brittle façade perhaps, a veneer of happiness put on because it was expected, but not the exuberance and open friendliness of the party at the store. These men spoke of their employees as either lazy or a drain on profits, something to be cut or maneuvered or exploited.

As if each of them didn't have a story, a life outside of retail sales.

Guilt pricked Gray's heart.

He was one of these people. Focused on profits, he'd been making plans to ax a fifth of his workforce, streamline, and cut and impersonalize Garamond's in order to increase revenue. And until tonight's party, he hadn't been able to put a name to more than half a dozen faces at Garamond's.

Until Melisande had introduced him to them, one by one.

Over the past few weeks, Melisande had opened his eyes to many things. . .not the least of which was her own sweet character.

Their eyes met across the room. She was genuine; she understood happiness.

He felt better when he was with her. He excused himself from the banal conversation of his peers.

She nodded to her companion and started his way, her skirts swishing as she wove around the tables, the gold lace catching the light, but no match for the glow of her eyes. Even without jewelry, she outshone every woman in the place.

Before he could reach her, a gentleman stepped in front of her, stopping her with both his body and his words. The man's narrow shoulders, the thinning grey hair, and the look of dismayed recognition in Melisande's eyes told him that Neville Strand had found her.

Gray quickened his pace, and when he arrived, he caught the last of Strand's words.

". . .no better than you should be, feathering your nest like a kept woman. No wonder you got the window commission. Favors returned, I assume? It's the talk of the party that you're his mistress now."

The color drained from Melisande's face, and Gray's hands fisted. He spun Neville around, and at the last minute had the good sense not to punch him in his supercilious face. Strand recoiled, and Gray realized they were attracting an audience. Without a word, he nudged Strand out of the way and took Melisande's hand, linking it through his elbow and leading her away from the confrontation before he forgot himself and thrashed an old man.

"Are you having a good time?" he asked, wry sarcasm filling his tone.

"Yes, thank you." Her voice sounded thin and strained, her face still white.

"Me neither." He took a calming breath. "Let's get out of here."

Once in the carriage, Melisande, still visibly shaken by her encounter, huddled under her velvet cloak. Her hands were hidden, or he would've reached for one, just to comfort her. What did a man say in these circumstances? She hadn't deserved a word of that attack, nor of the suppositions and whispered gossip of the people at the ball.

"I'm sorry, Melisande. I hope your evening wasn't spoiled." And yet, how could it not be? "Let's forget the Drapers' Ball and remember the party at Garamond's instead. Remember your sister's performance and the friendliness and. . .the joy, I guess."

She nodded, but she kept her face turned away from him.

When they pulled up in front of her plain boardinghouse, he was struck again by how simply she lived, by the gulf between them. And yet, he wanted to bridge that span as effectively as the new Tower Bridge across the Thames.

They had worked closely for the past several weeks, and he didn't want that to end. She had shown patience and kindness, even when he had been as opposed to her selection as Neville Strand had been. The hours she had put in, the way she sacrificed for her sister, the way she treated people—everything added up to someone appealing, something that reached inside him to places he didn't even know were neglected.

And on top of it, she was stunningly beautiful. Not that he'd been bright enough to notice at first. It wasn't just the gown she wore tonight, though he had to admit the moment she'd taken off her cloak in his foyer, he'd felt as if he'd been punched in the gut. She was every bit as lovely in her black dress and white apron behind the chocolate counter at the store or sitting on a crate in the workroom going over one of the lists on her clipboard.

Because her beauty began on the inside and shone outward.

He felt her staring across the carriage at him in the dark and realized they'd been sitting there in silence for some moments.

"I'm sorry." He leaned forward and opened the door, exiting and reaching up for her. Instead of taking her offered hand, he spanned her waist and lifted her down. When her feet touched the cobbles, she stood only a few inches away.

Moonlight caressed her face as his fingers longed to do, and star-shine glowed in her eyes.

"Thank you for a lovely evening." She rested her hands on his forearms, her lips parted.

Dizziness drifted through his head, his heart pounded so hard. Without stopping to wonder if it was a good idea, afraid he would talk himself out of it, he leaned down and kissed her.

Her lips were warm and full and tasted of the fruit punch served at the ball. Her skin smelled of lemon verbena, and somehow, his arms had gone around her waist, bringing her to him.

She fit perfectly into his embrace.

In that moment, he knew he wanted her to fit perfectly into his life.

Just as he would've deepened the kiss, she withdrew, her eyes wide, biting her bottom lip.

She looked stricken, aghast, as if she'd somehow transgressed. "Good night." And like a flash, she was up the steps and closing the boardinghouse door, leaving him on the street, arms empty.

# Chapter 6

Melisande took a firm hold of her thoughts and emotions. Today was too important to let her mind be clouded by the cacophony of feelings that had been crashing through her all night.

He had kissed her. And she'd let him. More than let him, had responded, kissing him back, entwining her arms around his neck for a moment, fitting herself into his embrace as if she had every right to be there.

How would she face him again?

Because everything had changed.

She had fallen headlong in love with him. Not the girlish infatuation she'd felt when she first met him three years ago, but a mature, grown-woman love inspired by the real him. The brilliant thinker, the loving grandson, her protector and defender.

It was all she could do to tell Vonnetta, who had waited up for her, enough about the Drapers' Ball to make it sound like a nice time without revealing how out of her depth she'd felt. Of Neville Strand she said nothing, but slipping out of the beautiful satin gown and into her night clothes, Melisande felt as if she had taken off a false persona and donned her real self.

As morning light crept around the shutter, she knew she had to forget last night and remember her place. She was an employee. After today, she would be back behind her chocolates counter, filling boxes and arranging confections.

Hours later, she stood on the street in front of Garamond's among the crowd of onlookers, her heart pounding in her throat. The culmination of all her hard work was finally here.

Of Gray she had seen nothing, which made her uneasy. Where was he? The moment of the reveal was nearly here, and he hadn't come into the store. Was his grandfather worse? She could think of nothing else that would've kept him away.

The judges for the Victoria Prize stood near the first window, waiting, and more and more people gathered on the sidewalks as they realized something was about to happen. Vonnetta stood at Melisande's elbow, gripping her hands together under her chin.

"Three! Two! One!" Bramwell shouted. At "one" the drapes covering the display windows were raised, revealing the vignettes behind the glass.

A gasp went up from the crowd, followed by a swell of applause.

There was Jacob Marley, towering over a cowering Ebenezer, delivering his warning.

And the party at Mr. Fezziwig's, with its laden table and merry dancers, with young Ebenezer proposing to sweet Belle.

On the opposite side of Garamond's front door, in the next window, the Cratchit family sat around their Christmas table, portrayed at the moment when Tiny Tim pronounced his "God bless us, every one!" benediction.

Melisande's eyes traveled to the fourth window, the cemetery, the snow, the bare birch trees, and the gravestone.

As one, the crowd moved around the corner to the last window, her *pièce de résistance*.

Ebenezer, his face beaming with kindness and joy, stood in front of a store. Tiny Tim, sans his leg brace, rode on his shoulder, pink-cheeked and smiling.

At the front of each window, she'd placed a copy of Dickens's *A Christmas Carol*, open to the passage portrayed in the display. The final window held her mother's copy.

More applause filled the frosty air, and several of her friends came up and shook her hand. They drew her to the front of the store again as the judges began inspecting the windows, whispering and making notations. Garamond's was the last one to be judged today. They would know soon what the results were.

Then the crowd parted.

Gray was coming toward her, and he was pushing an invalid chair. At the sight of Mr. Garamond, bundled up, but here, Melisande forgot to be awkward and shy seeing Gray for the first time since their kiss. She rushed to Mr. Garamond's side.

"You came." She ignored everyone around her, giving him a gentle hug, tears in her eyes. His hand trembled as he took hers. "Had. . .to. Wouldn't. . .miss. . .this."

"May I show you?" Glancing up at Gray, she indicated the first window. He looked deeply into her eyes and nodded, his face giving nothing away as he pushed his grandfather's chair close to the glass.

Slowly, she pointed out details, such as the wisp of steam she'd created out of fine thread to come up from Scrooge's bowl of soup, and the coin purse peeking out of his dressing gown pocket. It was the same at each window, some treasure she'd taken great joy in designing.

But when they rounded the corner to the last window, Melisande held her breath. This was the surprise she'd been holding back. Behind Scrooge and Tim, she had recreated the front of Garamond's Department Store, its windows lit and filled with Christmas wares and greenery. And at the front door, Mr. Garamond, leaning on his gold-topped cane, his smile welcoming a patron.

At the joy on Mr. Garamond's face as he recognized the figure, she decided she didn't care about the results of the contest. She didn't even care if no one else liked the displays. She had her reward for all her hard work.

"My dear." He held her hand. "Perfection."

A lump in her throat stopped anything Melisande might say, so she gave his fingers a squeeze and nodded.

Bramwell came over, and Gray spoke in low tones to the elderly man.

"Yes, of course." He put his hand on the back of Mr. Garamond's chair. "Sir, you let me know where you'd like to go, and I'll assist you."

Gray turned to Melisande and took her hand. "We need to talk." He led her through the crowd, acknowledging greetings with a wave, but stopping for no one. Melisande tripped along in his wake, her heart thudding in her ears.

Once inside the store, he headed up the marble stairs, through housewares and furniture, up the next flight, not releasing her gloved hand and not stopping until he had reached the conference room.

"At last." He let go of her and turned to lean against the table. "I've been trying all day to get here, and it was one thing after another. Grandfather was determined to come today.

Nothing would stop him, but it's a slow process for him to do anything at the moment." He crossed his arms.

Melisande pressed her lips together, touched that Mr. Garamond had come, but bewildered as to why Gray had brought her here. Shouldn't they be downstairs?

"Forgive me for taking you away from the accolades that should be yours, but I wanted to thank you privately for the amazing gift you've given me."

She inhaled. "You're welcome, but the window displays were my pleasure to work on. I am the one who should be thanking you."

With a grin, he took her hand, pulling her glove off one finger at a time. "The windows? Yes, those are nice too. But I wanted to thank you for something else. I want to thank you for reminding me about what is important, not just at Christmas but every day of the year. I've learned more about the people of Garamond's, and about myself, from you than I ever would've on my own. I learned that business isn't about money. . .or at least not just about money. It's about the people who work for you and with you, and about the people you serve."

His hand clasped hers, and his thumb made small circles in her palm. "Melisande, I am so tired, I hardly know what I'm saying. I didn't sleep a wink last night for thinking about it all. Actually, it was my Christmas gift to you that finally got my thoughts out of a jumble." He laughed. "No, that's not true. It was the Christmas gift that I had intended to give you, but that I now know is all wrong."

"You're not making any sense. Are you all right?"

"I am making a hash of this, aren't I?" He pulled out a chair, and to her amazement, he drew her down into his lap, coat and all. "Melisande, when I bought your Christmas gift a couple weeks ago, I thought it was the perfect present. But that was before you changed my thinking. You see, I went to my favorite bookseller and bought a brand-new, leather-bound, gilt-edged copy of *A Christmas Carol*, figuring you could get rid of that tatty old copy you've been carrying around here for the last month."

Her breath hitched.

"I know. I was a fool. Because it wasn't the story, it was the memories. The fact that your mother had loved and owned that book, that she'd read it to you and shared that love with you, that made the old copy priceless. You wouldn't trade that old book for an entire library of new ones. And I realized that the book was just a small illustration of how you've changed my thinking the past few weeks. You've shown me the people of Garamond's. Told me their stories. Showed me their true value."

She couldn't believe he was saying this. Happiness broke over her. When she made to stand, his arm tightened around her waist.

"Oh no you don't. I'm not finished yet." He leaned forward until his forehead was touching hers. "Melisande, I can't explain it, so I'm not even going to try. I need you. I never want to let you go because I want you to keep teaching me about the important things in life. You make me want to be a better man, and I don't want to lose that. The simple truth is, I love you." He hitched up and dug in his coat pocket. "I know I said you don't need jewels to be beautiful, and I hold to that, but I'm hoping you might make an exception." He held a small velvet box, and with a deft flick, he opened it.

A lovely diamond ring in a bed of satin. . .with the gold-embossed name Garamond's in the lid.

Her hand went to her mouth, and she looked up into his eyes.

"I'm serious. Marry me, Melisande."

His lips found hers, his arm tightening around her waist, the ring dropping to his lap as his fingers came up to touch her cheek.

She found herself clutching his lapels to keep from spinning right off into space. He loved her.

Mr. Garamond found them there, Melisande still in Gray's lap, whispering, wondering at their newfound joy. Bramwell pushed the invalid chair into the conference room, a twinkle in his eye as he closed the door behind him as he left.

"You. . .have. . .good. . .news. . .for. . .me?" Mr. Garamond asked.

"Yep." Gray nuzzled her nose with his before setting her on her feet and getting to his own. "I've brought you a new granddaughter for your Christmas present." He tucked Melisande into his side as she held out her hand to show Mr. Garamond the diamond.

Mr. Garamond smiled as broadly as he could, his eyes bright. "Brought. . .a. . .present. . . too." He indicated the parcel in his lap.

Gray left Melisande to lift the parcel, sliding a piece of wood out of the paper wrappings.

"You did it." He turned to show it to her. "You won the Victoria Prize!"

Grabbing her in a hug, he spun her around. "I can only think of one thing to say. God bless us, every one!"

**Erica Vetsch** is a transplanted Kansan now residing in Minnesota. She loves books and history, and is blessed to be able to combine the two by writing historical romances. Whenever she's not following flights of fancy in her fictional world, she's the company bookkeeper for the family lumber business, mother of two, an avid museum patron, and wife to a man who is her total opposite and soul mate. Erica loves to hear from readers. You can sign up for her quarterly newsletter at www.ericavetsch.com. And you can email her at ericavetsch@gmail.com or contact her on her author Facebook page.

# Brand–New Christmas Romance Collections from Barbour. . .

## Christmas Stitches: An Historical Romance Collection

Return to Christmases of yesteryear with three seamstresses who use their talents to succeed in the late 1800s— Hannah to land a dream job, Rachel to find her purpose, and Penelope to help others. But can love also be stitched into the fabric of their lives?

Paperback / 978-1-68322-715-1 / $14.99

## Old West Christmas Brides

It's hard for a woman to make a decent living in the Wild West of the late 1800s, and as the Christmas season approaches, prospects for a happy celebration seem dim. From the Dakota Badlands across the desolate Nebraska prairie and up to the rugged Colorado Mountains, six women are praying for a Christmas miracle.

Paperback / 978-1-68322-716-8 / $9.99

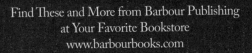